THE CHRISTOPHER WREN SERIES

BOOKS 4-6 BOX SET

MIKE GRIST

SHOTGUN
BOOKS

SHOTGUN BOOKS

www.shotgunbooks.com

ISBN - 9781739849603

CONTENTS

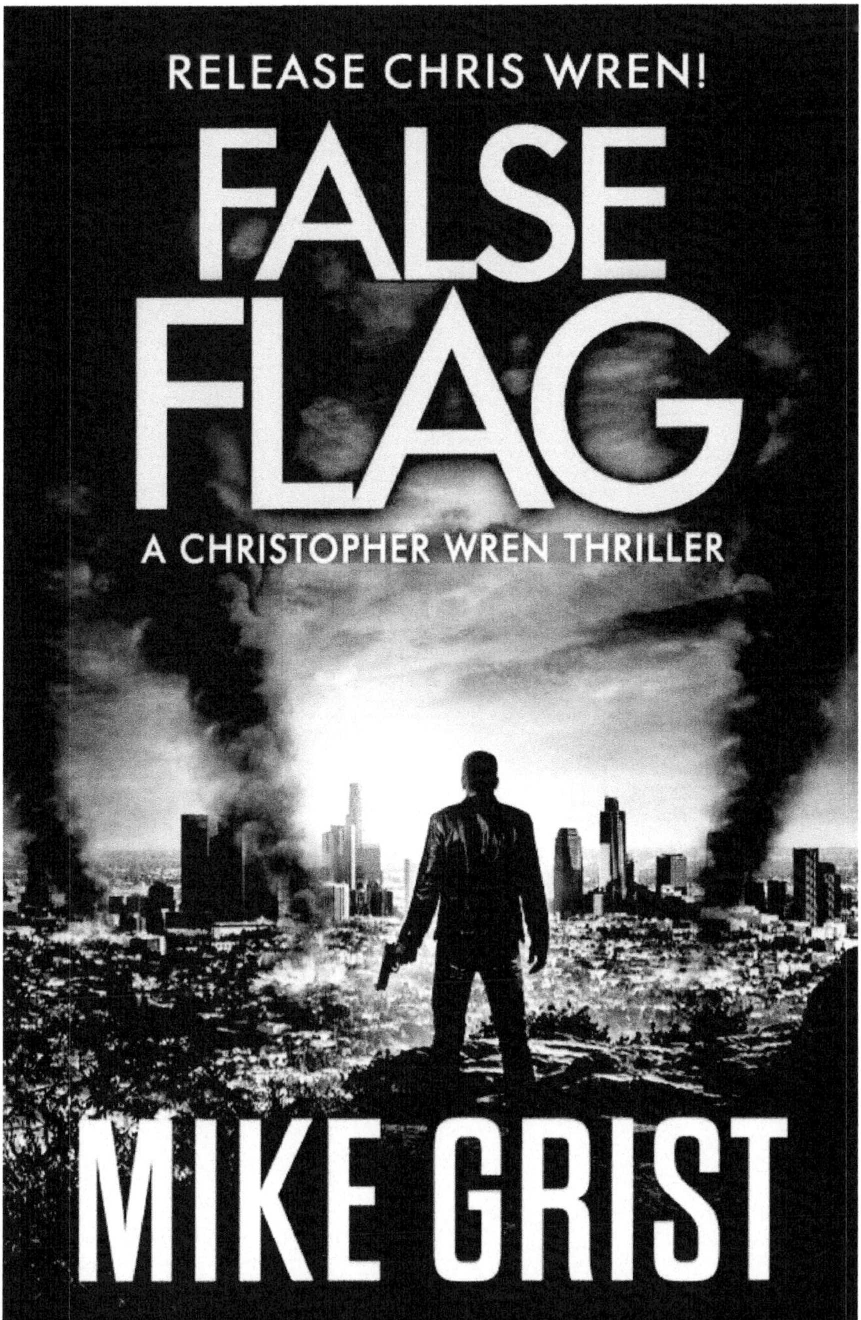
RELEASE CHRIS WREN!
FALSE FLAG
A CHRISTOPHER WREN THRILLER
MIKE GRIST

1

BLACK SITE

Christopher Wren liked his cell well enough.

It was small. Bed, sink, toilet. A CIA black site off the coast somewhere, probably, not bound by US law. No window, but he didn't need one. Enough room to exercise, when he wasn't too weary from the interrogations. Putting him through his paces; the old field guide, not the new one, all the 'enhanced interrogation' they could manage and twice on Sunday.

Waterboarding. Extreme stress positions. Deprivation of food, water, sleep, bodily autonomy. Beatings. Humiliation. Sometimes, questions.

It was awful. All-consuming. The best thing about it was it gave him no time to think.

Today it was the cold. He sat on the bed, naked and wet on the bare metal frame, and shivered. Sometimes the door opened, someone came in and tossed a bucket of icy water on him. A reminder. They were doing him a favor, really. Holding back the fear. He counted three months since his ex-lieutenant CIA Agent Sally Rogers had put a black bag on his head outside his wife's duplex in Frederica, Delaware.

Since he'd seen some shadowy figure raising a hatchet over his wife's silhouette in the duplex window.

He'd shouted in the van until they sedated him. Only as he'd plummeted down into the morphine dark, had Rogers leaned in and whispered through the bag, close enough that none of her team would hear.

"Your family are fine, Christopher. I swear it. I don't know what you saw, but it wasn't what you think."

Those words had haunted him ever since.

His family were fine.

It wasn't what he thought.

It was better not to have to endlessly think about what those words really meant. Taking them apart into their tiniest fractions and rebuilding them, every second of every minute since, deconstructing the tiniest hints in Rogers' inflection, parsing the instants as the hatchet came down. Trying to comprehend what it meant, what he could possibly do, on and on and on...

Torture next to that was a mercy.

The door slammed open. Wren looked up, expecting another bucket. It came, drenching him. Good. Core temperature had to be below ninety degrees now. A dangerous line to walk; much lower and his extremities would start to rot alive. Frostbite was a real possibility.

The door slammed closed. There'd be more questions soon. The questions were always the same, trying to break open his Foundation. The names of his members. The keys to his darknet. Everybody broke in time, of course. Wren was curious how long it would take for him. They'd be better off just leaving him alone in the dark with his own fears; he'd be begging to be let out within a week.

The door opened. He looked up. This time no bucket came.

Instead someone was standing in the entrance, looking down at him. A blur at the moment, his eyes too frigid to work properly. It took long seconds of blinking.

"Christopher," the figure said.

Wren smiled through the shudders. It was genuine. He was glad to see him.

"H-Humphreys."

Humphreys just stood there. Director of the CIA. A big kahuna. Cabinet seat next to the President. Nice of him to make the time. He wore a new black suit, had a tightly trimmed black moustache and short dark hair in a crew cut, hands relaxed at his side; no gun at his hip, no shoulder holster. The Director didn't need a sidearm. That was just another sign of his power.

Once Wren might have gone for him in a bid to break out, but not now. Couldn't even if he wanted to. His legs would give out after the first step. Muscles palsied by the cold. Give him half an hour and some ketamine, he'd be game to give it a shot.

"I asked them to stop the torture," Humphreys said.

Wren almost laughed, but his lungs didn't want to cooperate. Filling with fluid; early-onset pneumonia, probably. You had to love Humphreys. 'Asked', like the Director didn't control everything.

"Th-thanks."

"They didn't listen."

It was hilarious. Wren let his head drop. It hurt too much to hold it up, to meet Humphreys' eyes. No shame in that. Correction; plenty of shame in that, but shame was par for the course these days. The only way to endure was to embrace it; to self-brainwash fast, before your old ideas of reality made your spirit crack, like freezing water poured into a too-hot glass.

"We need to talk."

Wren grunted. Probably this wasn't even Humphreys. The number of times he'd hallucinated in here? If anything, that was the real threat. They'd tried him on various truth serums, some kind of lab-grade LSD. In his lucid dreams he'd spoken to Tandrews, to the Apex, to Adolf Hitler on one hand and Abraham Lincoln on the other, and his interrogators had written it all down, searching for meaning in the Rorschach test of his mind.

He didn't think he'd given up a single Foundation member, but there was no real way to know. Maybe they had them all already, locked up in parallel cells to either side. He laughed at the notion. Couldn't help it. Alli in a cell? Hellion in a cell? Forget it.

"S-So talk," he stuttered.

"It's about your Foundation."

Of course it was. He looked up. Humphreys' expression hadn't changed. Ah, Humphreys. Once he'd looked at Wren with respect, maybe a hint of fear. A legendary ex-DELTA cult breaker, the first Agent Without Protocol in sixty years, but no longer. Humphreys' face was totally blank.

It was good to see through to the truth, sometimes. Nobody stayed on a pedestal. The sooner you fell off, the better for all involved.

"They've c-come for me," Wren hazarded a guess, stumbling over his consonants. "R-rescue attempt."

Humphreys just stared at him. Disapproving, cold, beyond intense. "Worse."

He laughed. "You're on board. You're running th-things now."

"Last guess."

"The Apex b-became President. First executive order: b-burn yourself alive."

"Closer." Humphreys took a step in. "Your cult's gone mad, Christopher. It has to be stopped."

That woke Wren up. A dump of adrenaline helped with focus. It would last for a few minutes only, but for that time the shuddering receded. His vision sharpened; he looked into Humphreys' eyes and thought he was telling the truth.

"What have they done?"

"They're trying to start a war."

A second adrenaline dump brought Wren up like a shot of methylphenidate. The last of the shivering paled away and he straightened. Humphreys wasn't here to gloat. Humphreys was here for something else.

"What w-war?"

"Easier to show than tell," Humphreys said, and four soldiers stamped in. Not Wren's torturers, not even CIA. A new team, a new uniform. Marines, by the cut. Humphreys' old gig, before he became Director of Operations Coordination. Wren scanned them; side-holsters, tactical weaponry. "Get up," the Director said, and strode out.

The Marines picked Wren up and dragged him along behind. They weren't gentle.

2

SHOW NOT TELL

The Marines carried Wren out of his cell, feet trailing uselessly along the concrete floor. The walls were raw cement here, his home for the past three months. Left along the corridor led to the interrogation room, right to the way out.

They went left.

The interrogation room had a table and two chairs, with metal eyelets on the table and the floor. Wren blinked against the harsh white light. In the last few months they'd bombarded him with endless questions, trying to worm their way into his head.

No dice. Wren knew all the tricks. He'd written half of them himself.

Humphreys took his seat. There was a laptop waiting on the table. The Marines seated Wren, cuffed him at the wrists to the desk eyelet, at the ankles to the floor eyelet, then stepped back. Restrained like cannon fodder.

Humphreys sat down, his face a slab of blank white alabaster. A perfect poker expression, giving nothing away. That was new.

"I can tell you're pleased to see me," Wren said.

Humphreys ignored him, opened the laptop, spun it around so Wren could see and hit play.

It was news footage playing in split screen. All the major news networks in their own quarter, CNN, CBS, FOX, NBC, all showing the same thing. Street protests. Signs. People marching, chanting, with banners scrolling along the bottom announcing their demands. The shots looked like different cities, different days even, judging by the weather, the timestamps, the headlines.

It took Wren a second to process what he was seeing. The messages on their signboards.

DUMP THE DEEP STATE

FREE THE FOUNDATION

RELEASE CHRISTOPHER WREN

He looked up at Humphreys. Speechless for a moment. "Release Christopher Wren?"

Humphreys gaze drilled right back into him. "You've gained fans."

Wren snorted. "Bullshit. You deepfaked these."

"To what end would I deepfake this, Christopher? Don't play games. This 'movement' is spreading across the country like a cancer. These people think you're a hero, thanks to your speech bringing down the Reparations." A hint of revulsion cracked briefly through Humphreys' stony exterior. "Video of your 'amnesty' announcement has been seen over a billion times. You've conned the whole country, Wren. Now they think we're the enemy, because we're holding you. It doesn't matter that you're an avowed murderer. They just love you more."

Wren didn't need to think about that. "So let me go."

"Well, precisely," Humphreys said, and clicked three times on the laptop, starting up another video feed. "Watch this one."

Wren leaned in. The feed showed a dark room with three shadowy figures seated in the middle. It was a cheap and grainy visual shot at an odd slant; a low-spec camera performing poorly in the low light cast from a single swaying bulb. Dusty air, a hint of cement walls in the backdrop, no natural light. No date stamp, GPS, nothing. Some kind of prison.

"What am I looking at?" Wren asked, squinting.

"It's not a deepfake either," Humphreys pre-empted. His eyes shone now, watching Wren closely like he was waiting for a tell. "These people have been taken. The video is authentic."

The light brightened, and Wren felt the change like an electric shock down his spine as the prisoners were illuminated. He knew all three of these people. On the right was Steven Gruber, an NSA agent and member of the Foundation's Board, in the middle was Jay Durant, a trucker in the Foundation, and on the left was Sally Rogers, Wren's lieutenant at the CIA.

All were naked, shiny with sweat, with their hands bound behind their backs. Two members of the Foundation and the woman who'd put him away.

"We just received this an hour ago," Humphreys said. "I commandeered a Chinook to come see you. All the protests, that low-level BS in the streets, I thought it would blow over until I saw this."

Wren stared at the three seated figures, mesmerized by the swaying light. Ball gags in their mouths. Rogers sat upright, seemingly unbroken, blond hair pasted to her cheeks, powerful shoulders tensed. Heavy-set Jay slumped against his bindings like a beaten man. Gruber gulped at the air, mid-twenties and junkie-thin, eyes darting side-to-side like a lizard, until a figure entered the side of the shot; a towering, broad silhouette in some kind of military uniform. Jay didn't move. Rogers' eyes widened. Gruber began to hyperventilate.

The huge figure moved across the front of the camera, like he didn't know it was there. Footage taken illicitly, Wren guessed. The guy had ramrod posture, a confident gait, an assured manner. Left he went, then right, hypnotically. Instilling terror. Only Jay didn't react, he was too bowed already. With each step Gruber paled further.

"What is this?" Wren demanded, looking up at Humphreys. "What's going on?"

Humphreys met his angry glare with the same cold expression. "You tell me, Christopher. We already know these are members of your cult." He tapped the screen twice. "Jay Durant, 3-year coin; Steven Gruber, 2-year coin. We've had them and others under surveillance for months. As for Rogers," he tapped the screen a third time, "the public don't know she brought you in. To them, she's become a poster girl for your cult."

Wren stared. It was a lot to take in, and that pissed him off. "Poster girl? But you know she's not, so why have you renditioned her?"

Humphreys' steely gaze sharpened. "This wasn't us, Christopher."

Wren had no words for that. Not a CIA rendition? He looked back at the screen. All the tell-tale signs were there. "So, who-"

Humphreys just tapped the screen.

Now the big silhouette was holding a cigarette lighter. A small yellow flame burned in the dark, and Wren's vision instantly tunneled around it, abruptly picking out details like a drowning man grasping for firm ground. Gruber's eyes flaring, pupils dilating wide into the whites. Rogers gasping. Their skin shining, too slick to be sweat.

"This wasn't us," Humphreys repeated sharply. "It was you."

The figure threw the lighter. It hit Jay's chest, bounced into his lap and he went up in flames like a flashbang grenade. Napalm, painted on his skin.

Sudden phosphorous-white light temporarily blinded the low-grade camera. There was muffled screaming. Jay thrashed, fiery limbs flailing.

The video ended.

3

FALSE FLAG

A cold bomb dropped in Wren's belly. He felt instantly sick. The shaking came right back, bulling through the adrenaline so hard his cuffs rattled on the table.

Jay had a family; a wife, two kids. He'd made big strides in the coin system, turned his life around, become a man Wren was proud of, a man to make his family proud, and now...

It was hard to breathe. Three months in the black site had been heaven next to this.

"I know you're behind it," Humphreys said, cold eyes drilling into him. "The man with the lighter is yours. The ones burning are yours. It's all your setup, your people willing to die for the 'cause'. Now you're going to tell me how to stop it."

Wren blinked. Stop it? Behind it? That didn't make sense at all. His voice came out rusty and thick. "What are you talking about?"

Humphreys was unrelenting. "You're an expert in mind control. The best I know. You made your cult love you so much they did this."

Wren just stared. After-images of Jay going up in flames flashed across the Director's pale face. He swallowed hard. "You think I ordered my own Foundation to burn themselves alive? Why?"

Humphreys' expression didn't budge. "You're the only one who benefits. Ever since we locked you away, your 'Foundation's' been driving this victimhood narrative." He tapped the laptop precisely. "Release Christopher Wren. Down with the Deep State. They make you the hero, make us the villain. Now this execution is custom-built to make us look like monsters, and your people like innocent victims."

Wren flailed. He spun back through the video in his head: the concrete walls, the uniform, the military bearing. It looked like footage from past atrocities; Abu Ghraib or Guantanamo Bay. Like what the US government had been doing to Wren for three months, except here was Humphreys saying he hadn't done it.

"You think I've framed you," Wren said. "Set up a false flag attack."

"Exactly right," Humphreys said, his tone utterly flat. "We haven't touched your cult. We weren't going to until this, but the people on the streets don't know that, and to them this video is proof we're killing off the Foundation. They're taking it as a declaration of war."

Wren just stared. War. "What possible benefit do I gain from that?"

Humphreys just stared. Wren had never seen him like this before. The rage absolutely contained. Presenting nothing but a sheer rock face. "You build a groundswell. Turn the people against us. Force us to let you go."

Wren blinked. It was convoluted, but made some kind of sense. Except he hadn't done it.

"Just think for a second, Humphreys," he tried, seeking out the cracks in the Director's rocky façade. "How could I arrange something like this? It's a conspiracy theory at best. Am I such an expert on mind control that I could set up a false flag attack from prison?"

Humphreys was ready. "You set it up in advance. Left instructions in the event we locked you up. Your get out of jail free card."

Wren's eyes widened. There was no give there at all. Humphreys really believed he was responsible. "Instructions to do what," he blurted, "cosplay as CIA, find some craphole black site-looking bunker and run through an actual execution of my own people? Film it on some crappy burner phone then release the video so that the general public will, what, start riots trying to set me free?" He took a breath. "That's an insane conspiracy theory, Humphreys. Open your eyes! You really think I ordered my own people to burn themselves alive?"

Humphreys met the accusation hard. "Why not? You've done it before."

Wren flinched. Of course, Humphreys was partly right. On the last day of his father's cult he'd burned one thousand people to death. He'd only been twelve years old at the time, but he'd done it, painting the napalm onto their bodies one-by-one, lighting every match. He'd confessed to it in the Reparations videos, so everyone in the country knew.

"I was just a kid then. I didn't-"

"But you did," Humphreys spat, and now there was fire in his eyes. Anger building for years, nursed like magma at the center of this cold stone mask. "You are completely capable of this. You are responsible for what you've done and who you are. So take ownership of it."

Wren didn't know what to say. Humphreys had never liked him. They'd both known it. They'd exchanged their share of harsh words, but this was something more. This was a bridge forever burned, a refusal to acknowledge Wren as even human.

Humphreys' watch vibrated. He looked at it then flicked the notification away. "The riots have already begun. Crowds just broke a cordon in LA, flipped a police car, and it's still broad daylight. In your name. You still want to say it's a conspiracy theory? News stations are picking up the video and we can't slow them down at all, thanks to blowback from your assaults on the First Amendment. The social media companies are black boxes to us now. People are going to die if you don't tell me how to stop this."

"Jay already died," Wren countered, his mind racing on adrenaline fumes. If it wasn't him and it wasn't the CIA, then that left only one likely perpetrator. A genius manipulator, capable of coming up with a convoluted plot like this. The man truly behind the Pyramid burnings, twenty-five years ago.

"This has to be my father, Humphreys," Wren rushed on. "Apex of the Pyramid. He drove the Saints, the Blue Fairy, even the Reparations, and now he's driving this. He's framing us both, making us fight each other. You need to be hunting him!"

Humphreys listened in silence, the fire fading so his face became a crag of alabaster again; unmoving, unfeeling, cold. "Your lies don't work on me anymore, Christopher. You're a proven liar. Manipulator. Cultist. You want to talk about past attacks? It's always been you! You are a delusional sociopath, and I've been your patsy for years." His knuckles whitened. "But not anymore. You're nothing to me now. Not an agent, not a sympathy case, barely an entry in the record book."

Wren felt himself slipping. The rock face had no finger-holds, toe-holds, nothing. It was getting hard to breathe. If his father had really done this, it meant everything was coming to an end. Wren wouldn't be able to save the Foundation, or his family, or his country. The Apex would swallow them all.

All he had left were Hail Marys.

"At least get me to LA," he sped on, sucking in a fast breath. "Put me in an ankle monitor, whatever it takes, but get me in front of all the news channels walking with my hands out, peaceful, free. Take away his leverage. Give the people what they want and the riots will end."

Humphreys didn't bat an eye. His watch vibrated in the silence but he didn't look. If anything his gaze grew colder still. "You're saying you want footage of you out calming the five thousand, your arms wide, spreading peace through the masses?"

Wren saw it too late. A perfect trap.

"America's second coming." Humphreys went on, his voice choked up with rage. "A messiah for the new millennium. We could never lock you up again. You'd be above the law for life."

"That's not what I want," Wren tried to backpedal, "I'm saying-"

"I know exactly what you're saying." Humphreys stood. "I was a fool to think I could reason with you. I won't be your fool anymore." He snapped the laptop closed and started away.

Wren sucked in another sharp gulp of air. No purchase on the rock, only freefall into the dark. "At least look for my father," he said swiftly. "You think he'll stop at killing the Foundation and starting some riots in the street? Look at what he did to the Pyramid, Humphreys! He's a psychopath addicted to death; he won't be happy until there's a body count like you can't imagine, rivers of blood to drown us all."

Humphreys turned, and the ice in his eyes said it all. "The people don't love you that much, Christopher." He paused a moment, weighing one final blow. "And frankly, I don't care if your whole cult kill themselves. We'd all be better off."

Humphreys turned. Wren sagged. First Jay, then Rogers, then Gruber, then more. It wouldn't end, and he saw it all stretching ahead like a vision of hell. His father ascendant as America burned. The chaos of the Pyramid revisited upon the world.

There was just one Hail Mary left, the most dangerous yet. He took three more fast gulps of air, rocked back as far as he could in the chair, then slammed his face forward onto the metal table.

There was a crunch of bone and cartilage as his nose crumpled; blood burst down his throat and out over his shackled wrists. The shock trumped the pain, but he was already coming back up before either could bed in. For a second he saw the surprise in Humphreys' eyes, then he took another fast gulp of air and went in for the double.

His face slammed into metal and darkness snatched him down.

4

PIT

When Wren was only nine years old, the Apex had buried himself alive.

Out into the wild deserts of Arizona he'd gone, leading the Pyramid in a long, solemn procession. Wren, then known only as 'Pequeño 3', a half-caste child with wide eyes and a mop of unruly black hair, had run along at his father's side.

It wasn't their first procession into the wilderness, headed for new wonders. Excitement mingled with terror in Wren's young mind; another spike in the rollercoaster of his everyday life. What treasures was the great man about to unearth. What tortures.

The Apex stopped every few minutes, pausing to suck in lungfuls of air, survey the sight lines, toe the hard crust of sand. Each time his cult hushed and waited with bated breath. Soaking it all in. Guessing silently what today's lesson would be.

At last the Apex settled on a space a mile from the town. He marked a circle in the sand with his heel, eight feet in diameter, and ordered his cult to dig. It took a day, as his people dug by hand. They foraged for stones to bank up the walls as the pit sank down into the desert, mixing up mortar with their precious supplies of water. They placed and mortared the stones in one after another. Ten feet deep, eight feet wide, a dry well in the earth.

By nightfall the hole was complete. Nobody knew what its purpose was, until the Apex was lowered in alone. At ten feet deep, the walls were too high to climb out. The muddy mortar had set smooth and hard. In a midnight ceremony, he ordered them to pull three supply sleds over his head and seal him in with sand.

The Pyramid obeyed.

Young Christopher Wren stood at the side of the hole and tried to be brave as his father disappeared from sight. The man whose whims he'd lived by for every moment of his life now steadily disappeared from sight. Standing there at the bottom of the pit, arms spread and eyes shining, he looked like a miracle. Like the Earth turned at his hand.

Under flickering torchlight, the Pyramid wailed as they swept two feet of sand over the sleds. Mourning their leader already, for surely he was going to die. The walls were too sheer to climb. There were no gaps for air to trickle down.

For three days the Pyramid waited in the desert. Their scant supplies of food and water ran out, but no one complained. They were silent and watchful. Few slept, none spoke. With the Apex gone there was nothing to say. Wren hardly left the side of the pit, now a faint mound. He didn't eat a thing, barely drank a drop, rarely slept. If the Apex was suffering, so would he suffer. None were so devoted as little Pequeño 3.

Through those three days and three nights he came to think of the pit as an extension of the Apex's body. At night the sand swelled as he exhaled. Through the day it sank as he drew in deep, nourishing breaths. The sky swirled in time with his pulse, the clouds shifted as his slow eyes blinked, the wind blew as he licked dry lips.

He would survive. Wren knew it. Though only nine years old, he'd learned much from his father's experiments already, searching for the limits of the body and the mind. If you believed otherwise, why should pain be feared? If you had faith enough, what need was there for food, water, air? With sufficient strength of spirit, what need did you have of your eyes, your ears, your arms and your legs?

So Christopher Wren dreamed of the Apex in the darkness below, lying still as a corpse. His heart stopped because he willed it. His lungs fell silent because it was his desire. Proving to his people what wonders could be done.

Three days and three nights passed. The silences above ground grew longer and starker. A thousand people could not shift their eyes from the faint mound, beneath which lay their master, too afraid to blink lest they miss something.

At midnight, they finally dug up the pit. Eyes were wide with fear. What would they find? They raked their fingers bloody on the sand, scooping it hungrily, desperately. With grunts they dredged the supply sleds out, showering dust to the pit floor below.

Women wailed. Men cried out.

By torchlight, flickering as if afire, the Apex stood exactly as he'd stood before, arms spread and eyes shining with some inner light.

The Pyramid dropped to their knees and sang his praises. People entered hysterical fits, moved by the strength of his faith. Their Apex was alive. Their Apex was reborn.

It was only to little Pequeño 3 in the early hours of the morning, after the Pyramid had gone back to the façades of their fake town, that the Apex revealed the truth. In the perfect smooth wall of the pit, the Apex opened a gap. The mud mortar crumbled with ease, stones spilled out, and beyond lay a tunnel built with sturdy wooden boards, barely two feet below the surface of the sand. The Apex led and Pequeño 3 followed, crawling along together. The tunnel continued a hundred feet to an opening in the desert.

Standing on the surface in the moonlight, the Apex explained with a kind of furious glee. He'd crawled out as soon as they'd put the sleds above him. All eyes had been on the pit, so no one had seen him walk away. For three days he'd lived in the fake town alone. Enjoying the silence. Under cover of darkness as the third night drew in, with all eyes on the pit, he'd crawled back underground and re-mortared the wall behind him.

Pequeño 3 had only stared. The Apex's grin was infectious. Sharing the lie with his favored son. He'd sent his cult to dig the tunnel months earlier. Blindfolded, they'd carved what they believed was a channel for water. If anything, it was all a test of his Pyramid's devotion. Not one of them had left his side.

Wren remembered few details of the Apex; not his face, rarely the exact words he'd said, but he remembered the thing the Apex said to him then perfectly, as the smile fell swiftly from his face.

"But you know what's real, don't you, Pequeño 3?"

The smile came back just as swiftly as it had left.

But you know what's real.

For months after that, little Pequeño 3's dreams had been haunted by images of the Apex alone at the base of his pit, as cold and unmoving as a hibernating cicada. He always woke sweating and afraid, as if he'd somehow failed. He couldn't forget the tunnel and the Apex's grin, but next to the three days he'd spent standing watch over the pit, feeling the earth breathe in and out with the Apex's dying gasps, that memory felt false. It felt cheap, nasty and unreal.

So he hollowed it out. Like the Apex tearing down the crumbling mortar, he erased the truth day by day from the inside out. He worked hard to believe the lie, until finally he made the false memory real.

Lying in the dark of his own shallow pit in the sand, after long months of practice, he effectively halted his pulse, stopped the flow of breath from his body, and entered a kind of hibernation. For three minutes he appeared dead to the outside world. It was called aortal flutter.

5

AORTAL FLUTTER

Wren's body flopped, head bouncing off the metal, shoulders rolling sideways, his center of gravity tilting him off the chair to fall taut on his outstretched arms, still cuffed to the the table.

On some level he could still sense the world; dim sounds, sensations, images through his glassy eyes. He'd worked to maintain some level of consciousness while entering the state of 'aortal flutter'. Hyperventilating the lungs, but only so far; inducing hyperarousal, the fight or flight response, through acute trauma, but only to a certain extent.

The right combination of stress and hyperventilation sent the body into a compensatory panic: pulse rising to catastrophic heights of three or four hundred beats per minute; breathing cut right back to an undetectable wisp; all motor and neural capacity lost.

To the outside world he'd appear dead. The chambers of the heart beat so fast and shallow that the aortal valve didn't fully close, gushing blood in an even stream that made a pulse indistinguishable. The fraction of air passing through his windpipe would only be detectable with a mirror held close to his mouth.

Dead to the world.

The risks were very real. If the state went on too long the heart could be irreparably damaged. Brain death could occur without ever waking up. Hallucinations, confusion, memory loss were common. A mad magician's trick, too dangerous for laboratory study. In all the world, there was likely no person as adept as Wren.

Seconds passed, minutes, and he was deep underwater throughout. They moved his body; first to sitting upright in the chair, checking his pulse, listening for his breath, but feeling nothing. Right there, they had a choice.

Let him die or revive him.

The next thing Wren knew, he was laid out flat. Wrists and ankles uncuffed. Someone was pumping his chest. Dangerous for a heart that was wide open. Breathing air into his overloaded lungs. More dangerous still. Wren felt a warm breeze on the bare soles of his feet; the door to the cell was open. Someone bringing a crash kit. He saw the Apex's face in the darkness; a blur, as ever. His father.

Time for the grand reveal, arms spread at the bottom of the pit.

He loaded the motions up in his brain before he moved. His reactions would be shot for an hour, longer maybe. The vascular hangover would last for days. Punch. Grab. Aim. Shoot. It had to happen smoothly, as there'd be no way to course-correct as he went.

His chest compressed again. Someone breathed in his mouth. He used the moment to bite down. There was a shriek, and his eyes flashed open; it looked like the world was filmed with candlewax. One of the Marines, barely the pink smudge of a face, was recoiling. Wren chased him with a jerky sit-up, his whole toned core driving the sweet spot of his forehead hard into the guy's jaw. Crunk, and the guy sagged.

For a second Wren reeled. Dizzy, fuzzy. Two more Marines in the room, barely blue smudges on gray, one caught burrowing through a bright yellow plastic box. The crash kit. Humphreys a white face at the door. Shouting.

Wren's pre-loaded program rolled on. He grabbed the unconscious Marine and pulled him in like a shield, snatching at his tactical side-arm. It took three pulls, then the gun was in Wren's palm. Ten seconds, all in. Black metal before his eyes, a Glock M007, index finger pushing in the trigger bar, then the gun was barking in his hand.

One shot, two, three, cacophonous sound roaring in the contained space. Recoil sent his wrist every which way. Random.

Wren rose, on his knees. The Marine-smudges had their guns up now. Wren held his gun to the head of the one that was his shield, and breathed.

His pulse slammed in his head. Dropping from its frantic pace, valves closing and opening, blood tearing around his body. The chance of permanent damage every time. He blinked; the waxy film came off his eyes, sound rushed in, and he held the Marine in front of him. Almost fell, but the man's body kept him steady.

"Shoot him!" Humphreys was shouting, words in an endless stream, but the Marines didn't shoot. Three of them now, but none of them could shoot, not with their colleague between them and Wren. Training dictated otherwise. Give them ten more seconds and they'd figure it out; leave the room, lock the door and take control.

Wren couldn't give them the ten seconds.

He shot Humphreys.

Little time to aim. No way to stabilize his shaking arm as blood stormed through it. Spray and pray.

He hit the wall, the corridor, a Marine in the thigh then Humphreys in the arm. A crunch as the guy's femur blew apart; he shrieked and dropped. Humphreys spun in his tracks, clutching his bicep. The second Marine assessed quickly, saw Wren's gun trained on Humphreys, and went to his fallen colleague. Greatest threat to life, and all that. Admirable. The others held fast, weapons pointed at Wren.

Wren let the unconscious Marine go and rose slowly, his legs just taking his weight, his gun shaking on Humphreys. Director of the CIA, right-hand man to the President, big kahuna at any table. Absolutely livid.

Humphreys looked to the Marines either side, figuring it out. "I won't be your hostage," he hissed through gritted teeth, with blood leaking through his clamped fingers.

There was no need to argue. Wren strode the gap between them in a second, snatched Humphrey's injured arm and twisted it behind his back, wrist up between his shoulder blades. Instant pain. Instant compliance. Humphreys cried out and hopped up onto his toes.

"Resist if you want," Wren slurred, barely comprehensible, but the first thought Humphreys had to be thinking. "I'll dislocate your shoulder and use the other arm. Resist some more, you'll never swing a golf club again. Now march."

Humphreys grimaced, cursed, and marched.

Out into the corridor, Wren's mind worked feverishly. Two more Marines out here with their guns drawn, but they wouldn't fire either. Not with the CIA Director at stake, Wren's gun pressed to his head. Humphreys shouted something but Wren ignored it, running calculations.

Fresh adrenaline would last maybe three minutes. His legs might last five, his heart ten before he crashed. He hoped the black site wasn't big, and the Chinook wasn't far. That was all he could think. Beyond that, God knew what. Riots. Revolution. His father. His bare feet slapped noisily on the concrete floor, matched by the desperate clatter of Humphreys' heels.

6

CHINOOK

Humphreys wailed. Wren didn't listen; his legs were already giving out. Together they staggered along three tunnels of lichen-smeared greenish cement, two flights of murky concrete stairs, faces looming from open doorways and an alarm caterwauling. At last there was a heavy metal door, a crash as he shoved through, then a sudden burst of light.

Wren was blinded and squeezed Humphreys' arm tighter, tottering into the full bright of day. There was fine gravel underfoot, jet fuel exhaust in the air and the sun on his skin.

Three months underground with no sights, no smells, nothing real except what they'd given him, left him feeling like a shuddering cicada reborn naked into the world.

The thunder of the Chinook came to him like a manic pulse; the downdraft stinging his bare calves with blown sand. He forced his eyes wide open and saw the dual-rotor helicopter squatted like some massive beast in the midst of a strange, pitted landscape. Orange clay stretching into a distant heat haze, punctuated by strange berms in the earth like prehistoric burial mounds. His flagging mind ticked over. Blue sky, a few clouds striated like torn muscle fibers, and now this.

Missile silos? Fallout bunkers? Wren dragged Humphreys with him. The man was barely conscious now, faint with blood loss. That made two of them. Far off stick figures ran out from one of the berms; red clay sloping walls, a metal blast door. Who knew what lay within?

Voices on tinny loudspeakers ordered him to stop, barely audible over the thunder of the Chinook's blades. Both sweat-soaked, pale and flagging. Wren charged at the massive creature: twin rotors, an olive-green shell big enough to swallow a squad thirty Marines strong. The side bay door hung open like a toothless mouth.

In seconds they came under the furious downdraft.

"Get in," mumbled Wren, and hoisted Humphreys bodily into the Chinook's steel belly, rolling in after. Cold metal on bare flesh. He caught a flash of the CIA Director's face; pale as alabaster, but disbelieving. A new relationship, now. Their phone calls would never be the same again.

Wren stood and weaved; there was webbing on the walls, low benches, equipment crates bolted down. A cornucopia of medicines, MREs, weaponry, gear, clothing kept in ergonomic cabins.

Humphreys went where he was pushed; up to the cockpit where the pilot was staring back.

"Get out," Wren said, and levelled the Glock.

A Marine pilot. He unstrapped the helmet calmly like he was untying his shoelaces, opened the door, shot Wren a disapproving glance then hopped out. Good training. Marines weren't hostage negotiators, and knew it.

Wren shoved Humphreys into the co-pilot's seat and strapped him in. People were closing in now, the loudspeaker voices growing louder. Wren fell into the pilot's seat, took the cyclic, pushed the throttle and the bird launched like a wobbling rocket. The roar of the rotors became a tornado.

Away.

He fought for control as the berms and silos fell behind. The voices and people and torture. The breeze felt good. He surged to one hundred feet then hit the automatic pilot, set the course to the flat orange line of the horizon and staggered into the back.

Moments passed him by like postcards in a zoetrope as he sucked down a strip of combat sharpeners, some methamphetamine mix that bought him a few more minutes; enough to strap Humphreys' wound tight, to tug on some black tactical kit and boots, to stuff a rucksack with MREs, water, meds, assorted gear. In the front Humphreys lolled unconscious.

There wasn't long. With Humphreys aboard they wouldn't shoot him down, but they would track the Chinook. Soon a jet would overpass, assume remote control of the helo and divert it. His window would be minutes only. He throttled the speed, down to twenty miles an hour, then leaned into Humphreys.

The man was barely conscious. Wren pushed his face right up to the whites of his eyes. "Go after my father," he hissed, then staggered away.

In the back he yanked a rappel line clear of its rotary dispenser spool. Hooked the end on to his belt harness. Below lay endless scrub, desert, red loam and clay. No more berms. Barely any cover. Heat haze, false oases, sharp spines of rock. The sun was high. Zero cover. His eyes blurred on the orange spread.

He jumped.

The rappel line caught. He paid it out fast, spiraling and falling. Nobody knew where; no way to know. His heart beat artificially fast, the meth hit taking it to the limit. Wired and flying. The Chinook soared, the dusty landscape seared up, then he hit.

At the last moment he cut the rappel line, and the impact came; his body tumbled like a skipped pebble, bouncing and rolling in the dust until he finally slammed to a stop curled against a spiny gray bush. He barely felt the pain. No time left for pain now, anyway. He dropped his cheek to the hot earth with the darkness surging, as the Chinook thundered away into the distance.

7

DESERT

Wren woke to the worst headache he'd ever experienced, hammering from his temples to the back of his head like hydrostatic shock, each beat of his pulse a bullet.

He curled his body tighter. Every muscle cried out in pain. These were his various tortures coming home to roost; the freezing, the adrenaline hangover, the comedown from prolonged aortal flutter.

Stupid. He groaned and opened his eyes on stars. How long had he been out? A slim crescent moon cast little light over the barren landscape. The pole star was high; early hours, at least past four in the morning, given it was summer. Dark, but now there were flashes of light spiking in the distance.

Searchlights.

He dry-swallowed, blinked raspy eyes, listened. Through the roar in his head there were distant rotor blades; as if the Chinook had never left the skies, as if Humphreys was up there still, circling...

Helicopters. Drones.

That meant thermal imaging.

He grunted and curled his body tighter. From a distance his heat profile, obscured by the spiny brush and huddled tight, could pass for anything. A sleeping coyote. A warren of meerkats. But the moment he moved, extended an arm or a leg, they'd have him.

He took stock.

Alone in the middle of nowhere, likely south of the border, absolutely decrepit and drained, with God-knew how many CIA squads out looking for him, unable to move. No darknet, no Foundation, no GPS to localize his coordinates, and no place to hide. As for Humphreys, he had infrared eyes in the sky and a clear line from the Chinook's navigation computer to follow. Now they'd be working their way back along that line, looking for the spot he jumped.

Judging from the sound, it was a thorough search. Fifty agents? Multiple support vehicles. Humphreys himself in attendance, arm bandaged up tight.

And assets? With minimal movements, he rummaged through the backpack, found a bottle of water and drained it. There was also a flashlight, some MREs, a compass, a mylar blanket, a tool kit, a lighter, and a holster for the Glock with several spare magazines. He'd have trouble aiming, though, given his condition.

Not great. The choices before him were abysmal. This was going to be touch and go.

Choice one was to run, but that was a non-starter. With thermal imaging they'd have him the instant he moved, and even if they somehow missed his infrared signature, they'd find his trail in the sand. He ran a hand over the gritty surface dust, still lukewarm from the day's sun. No way to hide footsteps in this. They'd drag him down like dogs on a wounded deer.

Choice two was go to them. He envisaged the search pattern they'd be running, likely one broad search cordon, support vehicles in back. If he could somehow bypass the infrared, maybe he could sneak through the search cordon, try to pass as CIA on the other side, commandeer a vehicle and flee. But the chances of pulling that off and getting away clean were infinitesimal.

It left choice three. His fried mind raced. Some combination of the two. They had him on the Chinook's straight line; if he could get off that line and out into the open, without a clear trail or infrared signal to follow, they'd never find him. Drone coverage was useless when the area multiplied to many square miles. He just needed an escape vector that obscured both his physical trail and his heat signature.

The thunder of helicopter blades rolled closer. Minutes only, and his mind sped ahead. Back in his days undercover with Taliban groups in the Loe Nekan mountain range, Afghanistan, the jihadis had used multiple tricks to evade Predator drones tracking them via infrared: started fires, sheltered underground, hidden beneath thick goatskin blankets; anything to mask the heat of their bodies. In high summer even large rocks would work, holding enough of the sun's warmth to obscure a human's infrared signature and render American overwatch blind.

A rudimentary plan began to take shape in his head.

Carefully he got his knees under him, hunched over the backpack. From within he took one of the two spare magazines, field-stripped the bullets onto the back of the mylar blanket, then used twin pliers from the tool kit to prize the first bullet apart. In the darkness he operated largely by feel and sound, feeling it as the bullet casing 'pulled', listening as the black grains spattered down on the sleek mylar. He moved to the next as the searchlights splashed closer. Within minutes he'd pulled seven and had a small mound of black grains gathered in a crease of the fabric.

He took a deep breath. Everything that followed would have to be fast and precise. A blessed rush of adrenaline pushed the headache back and gave him room to breathe. Now he caught voices carrying through the still night air; clipped and professional, sharing constant status updates. Maybe five hundred yards away.

He pulled the backpack on, tipped the black powder grains into a natural crook of the spiny brush tree's roots, nudged the heap to spread out a simple 'fuse' one grain thick, then unfurled the mylar blanket. A thin and staticky silver material designed to trap heat, it spread out with a crinkly whispering that sounded like an engine roaring to his sensitized ears. He pulled it over his head, back and arms like a cloak of invisibility; instant cover from infrared overwatch, as long as he kept his core, his hands and his head largely hidden from above.

Slowly he shuffled backward two feet, waiting for a cry to go up, but none came. The blanket was working. He shielded his face with his elbow, held the lighter to the end of the black powder trail then pulled the metal dial across the flint.

It sparked. The black powder caught, ignited with a puff of smoke and ran up the makeshift fuse in a split second, giving a little explosive puff when it hit the pile, sending flames searing up the spiny brush tree's dry side.

Instant conflagration.

The tree caught and spewed out heat and light. Wren lurched to his feet, ducked low and sprinted parallel to the search cordon, getting off line. Ten steps, twenty, until he almost ran into a large rock jutting up through the sand. He dropped at once, hands to the rock's surface and feeling the captured heat emanating outward. An infrared island, offering additional cover.

Had they seen his transition? It was hard to say. He looked back.

They definitely saw the burning bush. It was an inferno now, burning like Jay, sudden heat flaring like a crocus through the cold air. Any stray heat leaked from the mylar should have been a ghost trapped in that explosion.

The helicopters were already thundering closer, their floodlights illuminating the night. Maybe ten seconds had passed. Shouts grew louder, feet were already stamping across the few hundred yards between here and there; call it two football fields, twenty seconds each at a dead sprint, longer over unknown terrain. That gave him less than a minute.

He pushed off the rock and ran right at the lights, mylar snugged tight. In ten seconds he was well beyond the bush's halo of firelight and charging headlong at the search cordon, twenty seconds and shouts tore toward him, twenty-five and he slid into the heat shield around another large rock like a runner into home base, pulling away the mylar blanket just in time for a streak of flashlight to track wildly down his side.

His dark outfit in the darkness offered nothing to fix on, with no reflective splash off the silvery blanket, and the figure ran on. Wren felt the stampede passing him by; outstripping their slower support vehicles in the race to catch Christopher Wren, driven by their own endocrine systems pumping out adrenaline. He heard the bark of a rifle report, chased by others. Even better; in the chaos of the chase, confusion was his friend.

He'd made his own gap; lodged now in a dark gulley between the bristling lights of the front cordon and the floods of the trundling support vehicles, maybe a hundred yards wide. He set off at a terrifying blind sprint into the dark, running perpendicular across their angle of approach, head low, risking a broken ankle off uneven ground and rocks with every step, putting his faith in his sense of the land and reactions until-

He hit an obstruction full on in the belly and staggered off line, spinning back to see what he'd hit.

A guy in the dark, rifle barrel extended, night vision goggles strapped to his head. For a moment only Wren stared and the guy stared back. Night vision gave tremendous clarity, but the peripheral vision was useless; he hadn't seen Wren coming. Now he did, already swinging his rifle barrel back around. There was no time for Wren to draw his gun, instead he spun the dial on the lighter just as the rifle fired and a bullet zinged by his shoulder.

The figure screamed as the lighter's flame flooded his retinas, scrabbled to get a hand up in front of the lenses, and into that gap Wren plunged. A shoulder in the guy's gut, hoisting him bodily off his feet and down into the scrub. Wren muscled his way on top, put a knee on the rifle stock, punched the guy three times hard in the chin, then yanked off his goggles.

Panting while the guy groaned, Wren took a second to reorient himself. Humphreys had really prepared; adding a second search cordon to patrol in the darkness. It was hardly standard operating procedure.

No time to waste. Now the helicopters were spiraling wider around the burning bush, looking to pick up his trail. He retrieved his mylar, wrapped it around his shoulders, snugged the tight goggles over his head and instantly saw everything. The dark gully lit up bright.

He ran into the light.

8

GULLY

There were two more figures in the gully but Wren bypassed them easily, in stealth-mode now, covered by the shouts and gunfire rattling off to the left. Seconds were counting down; as the agent he'd punched recovered, signaled on his radio, and they all figured it out. Wren just had to stay ahead of that bleeding edge.

He burst through the cordon with no fanfare. The inner core of vehicles and lights were all in back to the right, the choppers and flashlights strobed in back to the left.

Wren broke right.

Heat would be escaping around the edges of his mylar blanket by now. Nothing he could do about that but pray; that the analysts at their screens weren't inclined to buy a flicker of heat-spill as a person in flight. Tunnel vision ought to have their eyes trained on the immediate few hundred yards around the burning bush.

Every yard he gained now bought him time, out of the lens before they clicked the focus wider. He ran on for a minute or two, avoiding obstructions easily with the goggles, then stopped by a big rock parallel to the core convoy, slipped the night visions off and unwrapped the mylar, letting some of the heat escape while he had cover. Steam poured off him.

The core was five vehicles strong: three troop carriers, a big-wheel Humvee and a long support truck on caterpillar tracks. Where the hell did they get that? Flown in during the night, he guessed. Figures stood on the roof training floodlights ahead. They had no idea he was already flanking them.

He turned to the burning bush; its light carried through all the dark brush and cacti, and the two helicopters hovered over it like flies on carrion. Pretty soon they'd figure out his play.

He flung the mylar around his shoulders again, pulled the goggles back on, took a breath and ran into darkness. Two more minutes and he rounded the rear of the support vehicles. No foot patrols back here. He swung in tight to their trail; every wheel track and footstep frozen like a river leading back across the desert, caught in the silvery goggles' display.

They'd be coming for him soon. He turned to face the receding convoy and ran full tilt backwards along their trail, mylar blanket whipping around his face. Invisible, and if not invisible then barely a glitch of stray heat in the algorithms. Facing forward, his boot marks would be near-impossible to distinguish from the fifty pairs of boots and tire tracks that had come this way already; a trick he'd learned from his adoptive father Tandrews, in the forests of Maine some twenty years ago. Enter a river, you were covered. As long as your exit point was disguised, your trail was gone.

He ran backward hard, until his hamstrings burned and his knees felt they might jolt out of lock, until the helicopters were circling back with their floodlights spinning like disco balls. They knew they'd lost him, but they didn't know just how bad.

As they zoomed back toward him, he sidestepped fast to the 'river's' edge and leaped onto a long spine of rock. Five steps on he jumped to another rock, then another, then dropped back to the sand some twenty further feet away, obliterating his trail. He was a ghost.

One helicopter roared near as he ran full tilt into the wilderness, floodlights sweeping like Vegas skybeams. Humphreys' voice came over loudspeaker.

"I'll lock them all up, Christopher! Every last member of your damn cult. They'll never see the light of day again."

Wren ran on, hunkered low. Humphreys had already said all that. There was no new threat here. If it wasn't Humphreys taking out the Foundation, it would be his father. The crosshairs were on them all now, and imprisonment was better than burning alive any day of the week. The helo sped past his exit point on the trail and carried on.

Wren ran. The darkness unfolded for him, a sole meteor in the wilderness. Stars blazed overhead, painfully bright through the night vision goggles. The sound and light of the search teams diminished the further he went, boots stamping down, doing his best to ignore the myriad pains in his thighs, gut, head. Adrenaline fading, replaced by lactic acid.

Still he ran. At some point he shrugged off the mylar blanket, crunched it into the suit's belly flap and kept on at an even long-distance pace, putting miles between him and the convoy. Thirty minutes. An hour. Slow thoughts turned through his battered mind.

He saw flashes of Jay burning again. Of Humphreys making threats. Most of all, he thought about his father. Apex of the Pyramid. Out there somewhere, bringing ruin down upon America. Forcing people to turn against each other. The same old box of tricks, now amplified big enough for a whole country to swallow.

The moon and stars tracked across the sky. Call it eight miles. If they couldn't find his tracks, there was no way they'd find him now. The wind would help disperse whatever trail he'd left. Animals passing by.

He dropped to his side beside a boulder and gasped for air. He managed to pluck another water bottle from the bag, drank half of it in one go, then lay there panting until exhaustion claimed him.

9

CIVILIZATION

Wren groaned awake with the sun on his face. The heat was blistering and his lips felt scabbed over from exposure. His mouth was dry, his eyeballs were gritty in their sockets and his whole body felt pummeled.

But better.

He rolled up, blinking hard. A family of small brown roadrunners froze some fifty yards off, alarmed by the sudden movement, then darted swiftly away. Orange scrub sand stretched as far as Wren could see, broken by clumps of juicy-looking prickly pear cacti. There was no sound but the odd rustlings of animals and the whispering of a nearby ocotillo's hydra-like flower heads in the hot wind. The sky was swimming-pool blue and devoid of jet contrails, with the sun high overhead.

Early summer south of the border, in the desert drawing close to the twentieth parallel, about as wild as the surface of the moon.

He rose to his feet. His heart hammered, his breath rasped noisily, and he reached up to his face, remembering the slam into the desk. There were no loose teeth, but his nose was broken. He took a breath, took a grip, and gave it a twist.

Cartilage clicked and gristled. The blue sky grayed out for a second, blood trickled down his upper lip, then he could breathe.

A day and a night since Jay had burned.

He sifted through the rucksack, came up with a bottle of flavored water and two MREs. He drank half the bottle and slugged the first MRE down in moments. The hit of the sugar was immediate; his senses sharpened, his head cleared.

Time to go.

He dropped the MRE tray and looked around, taking in the flora, the heat, the sand, the smells. It felt like the Sonoran Desert. Not hot enough for the Mojave, with too much wildlife, which meant a straight shot up to Arizona, if he could trek a thousand miles through scrub. Aim to stumble upon a road or a settlement before then, get a vehicle, hit the border before nightfall, and the next body burned.

The clock was ticking.

He took a deep, hot breath. It was good to be out in the desert. It was where he'd been born, darting through the sands of Arizona spearing tarantulas, bark scorpions and ridgenose rattlers before he'd even learned to read, hunting and eating cactus wrens, packrats and jackrabbits like they were candy dropped from the sky. To some the desert was a place to go die, but to Wren it was just one big banquet table stretching out to the horizon.

No time like the present. He took a deep, hot breath, pulled the rucksack on and set off at a loping jog for civilization.

Three hours on and maybe twenty miles covered, Wren hit upon a trail. The sun had swung halfway toward its zenith overhead, his pack was one more bottle and an MRE lighter, and his muscles felt like they were singing, as the hangover of aortal flutter cleared out.

The trail ran roughly east-west, marked out in tire tracks. One pick-up, he figured, a desert hermit. The arrow treads headed west, so Wren started west

An hour or so along there was a shift in the air; a kind of intense brightness, as if an array of search beams had been turned up to the sky. He sped up, guessing what it was before he saw the first glint of light off silver atop a long, low wall of dark pipe scaffolds.

A solar array.

They'd been springing up in the Sonoran and Mojave deserts for twenty years now, fueled by government subsidies and the push toward renewable energy. Wren knew about them from his undercover work with the Qotl cartel; gangsters trying to shake down construction work for protection money.

The big companies usually paid. It was easier than rebuilding whatever the cartel pulled down, and less damaging for their reputation than images of butchered employees spread across the web. On one occasion, though, they'd gone to the US government, and they'd dispatched Christopher Wren.

He'd been tasked to deal with early sabotage of the Don Jose array. That had ended with a fresh deal being cut, two Qotl cartel members dead in the brush and a certain measure of peace in the desert.

He ran on toward the emerging wall of scaffolding, until he folded neatly into a narrow access alley between the array's giant black panels like a pinball in a slot. With his head and shoulders just bobbing above the angled plates, it felt like he was running through a choppy dark sea. The giant five-by-three panels stretched away in a massive oblong to the west, perfectly aligned to the track of the sun.

Up ahead lay the control hub; a two-story structure with large wraparound windows like an air traffic control tower. Wren reached the edge of the solar scaffolds and strode out without pause, gun drawn. A gravel parking lot, a transformer array buzzing behind a fence to his right, a blacktop road running off to the left, and two pick-ups clustered into the tower's scant shade. Through the second-floor window Wren saw one guy's eyes widen on him.

A man in dusty black tactical gear emerges from the array, gun drawn, what was the guy supposed to think? One hand already on the phone to the Federales. Wren levelled the Glock and the guy froze. A mop of black hair and an open mouth, staring out.

Cartel business, he'd be thinking. No two ways about it. Survivor of a hit, maybe. Nothing the police were going to do to help him. Nothing the government were going to do, either.

Wren shoved his way into the lobby. No security in the desert. A locked door blocked the stairs, card swipe in a plastic frame, and Wren kicked it through. Up the stairs, he came face-to-face with two guys in the control room; the one with wide-eyes, still staring, and another holding an antique Mossberg 500 shotgun, 1965 if it was a day, wooden stock with filigree, 12 gauge, 410 bore, enough whammy to blow a manhole-sized tunnel through Wren's chest, if the range was right.

Wren stopped in the doorway and smiled, let the Glock drop at his side, looked at Wide-eyes and spoke in fluent Spanish.

"¿Soy Qotl cartel. Hiciste la llamada?" I'm Qotl cartel. Did you make the call?

The shotgun guy answered, shaven-head but with a bald pattern growing through dark on his scalp like a monk's hair line. "¿Qué llamada?" What call?

Wren didn't look at him. He only looked at Wide-eyes. Coffee stain on his rumpled white shirt, mid-thirties, maybe a doctorate in electrochemistry, cursing every day of this cattle prod gig out in the middle of nowhere.

"Federales," Wren prompted.

"No lo hice," the guy managed. No I didn't.

Wren grunted. Shotgun wanted to say something, but Wren acted like he wasn't even there. He put the Glock down on a filing cabinet and surveyed the control room, eyes skipping over the weapon pointed his way like it was of no more interest than a ripe banana. That was how you showed power.

Several workstations, signs of hotdesking, a used coffee mug declaring 'Una mala madre-', 'One bad mother-'. Nothing he could use. He looked sharply back at Wide-eyes, who flinched as if struck.

"¿Tienes ropa de repuesto?" Do you have spare clothes.

Shotgun took a step closer, maybe thinking to make his play. Wren took one step in too, away from the gun on the cabinet, still ignoring him. No threat. No fear. All his focus on Wide-eyes.

"¿Qué?" the guy asked.

"Necesito ropa de repuesto. ¿Tienes?" I need spare clothes. Do you have some?

Wide-eyes stared then nodded hard. "Sí."

"A ver." Show me.

Wide-eyes looked over at Shotgun. Wren didn't. The guy with the shotgun only had the authority Wren afforded him, and he afforded none. The man to listen to was Wren.

"Ahora," Wren said, and put a little sting into it. Now. Enough to get Wide-eyes moving. Shotgun tracked him, but that didn't matter. The time to shoot had been the moment he walked in.

Wren followed Wide-eyes as he bustled over to a locker. Ask just right, and he'd get clothes, a phone, a car, and these two would never tell a soul. Write it up as theft; company insurance out here, in bandit country, would cover it. You didn't cross the cartel, not if you wanted to live, and what else could Wren be, if he wasn't the cartel?

Twenty minutes later Wren climbed into one of the dusty pick-ups in the lot with both his Glock and the Mossberg, wearing tight borrowed jeans and a check cotton shirt, swigging Coke from a liter bottle.

The desert always provided.

10

DARKNET

Sitting in the driver's seat with the engine running and the AC on, Wren booted Wide-eyes' iPhone and flashed a glance up through the windshield as it downloaded an anonymizing VPN. Both guys were peeking out of the window above, waiting for him to roll out.

They'd have to wait a little longer.

The app chimed and booted; Wren typed in the link to his Foundation darknet immediately and saw-

Nothing. He hit reload but it didn't help. He tried a random news site, it loaded, then he hit the back button but still no Foundation site.

His mouth went dry. There was no site there. It didn't even return a 404 Missing Link page, just blank white. He'd half-anticipated this, but it still stung to have it happen. There were redundancies, though, baked in by his uber-hackers Hellion and B4cksl4cker; back-up sites on their secret 'weathernet' which afforded them constant oversight of the whole Internet. Now he had to hope one of them was still live.

He typed in the first backup, and got nothing. The second and third both went the same way. He tried a few back channel links, direct routes into the deeper layers of his darknet, but they all returned the same.

It was worse than he'd thought.

His thumbs flew over the keys as he dredged up more links from memory, and every one hit a blank. The erasure was total. It left him utterly blind to the activities of his Foundation. Had the 'Deep State' already grabbed all his members? Had the Pyramid?

His heart pounded. He took a long pull on the Coke, calculating possibilities. He loaded up three different news sites and left an identical message on comment boards that were several years old: a secret trigger code and his new phone number.

Hellion, B4cksl4cker and anyone else in the Foundation core was free, they'd have an instant Internet alert set for the code and would call him as soon as it chimed.

He sat still, waiting for the phone to ring. Sweat beaded down his cheeks; the hot gust from the vents didn't help. Still no call. He checked the dashboard clock, 11:17 in Mexico made it 18:17 Central European Time. B4cksl4cker would just be getting started for the day. He wiped his forehead. Minutes stretched on.

Still nothing.

Bad.

He scrolled to the front page of a news site. It seemed the riots in LA had tamped down with the dawn, which was something at least. The same story was echoed across New York, Cincinnati, St. Louis, Berkeley, and other cities. Live casualty counts splashed in red banners: five dead in LA, thirteen hospitalized, including both protesters and cops; three dead in New York, seven in Cincinnati and more across the country.

At least there'd been no fresh burnings. Steven Gruber and Sally Rogers should be OK for now.

Still nothing from B4cksl4cker or Hellion.

Wren paged through headlines. The riots led every story, some critical and some in broad support. 'Deep State Brutality' was a popular logline. His name was mentioned everywhere: 'Where is Christopher Wren?'; 'Release Christopher Wren!'; 'Who is Christopher Wren?'

One name kept popping up, 'David Keller'. Apparently he'd been dropping hints about running for the November presidential election as an Independent. A successful CEO and millionaire, now he was out at every protest stoking the crowd to fight for Wren's release.

There was one thing he could do about that right now. He opened the phone's camera app and swiped to record video, turned the lens on himself, then began to speak.

"My name is Christopher Wren. I'm the leader of the Foundation, ex-agent of the CIA, and I am no one's prisoner. I am not being held in a black site, I am not being tortured, and I do not need your help to be released."

He took a breath. Thinking through what kind of message he wanted to send.

"Yesterday my Foundation member, Jay Durant, was murdered, but it was not at the hands of some imagined 'Deep State'. Jay was murdered by my father, Apex of the Pyramid, the suicide cult I survived twenty-five years ago." He fixed the lens with a glare. "The rioting yesterday is his end goal. I believe he wants more of it, in every city across the country, because he likes to see people die. Do not do his work for him. Do not be a vector for this disease. I am a free man. You are a free people. Trust that I will hunt my father down, and step back from the streets. Go back to your lives."

He stopped talking, ended the recording then uploaded the two-minute clip to several social media sites. For long moments he watched the video post, barely breathing, as it was watched, upvoted, and commented upon.

'Who is this guy? Is he for real?'

'He looks like Christopher Wren, but something about the audio is off.'

'The audio is way off, and look at the setting!! It's totally fake, green screen like a B-movie. This whole thing is more propaganda."

'Vote it down, sheeple! It's clickbait. Do your research!'

Within minutes, downvotes throttled the video. Accordingly the apps responded by making it invisible.

Wren just stared. He could make another video, but it wouldn't help now. The people didn't want to be calm. They didn't want to go back to their homes and wait to be saved from some shadowy manipulator. They were angry and they wanted blood, and nothing Wren could say was going to stop that now.

Still nothing from his hackers. At least the AC was pumping cold air at last. Wren started the engine and revved the pick-up out of the sandy lot, dialing another number from memory.

11

ROOTS

The phone rang and Wren tore down the buckled desert road flanked by solar mirrors, envisaging the landline ringing in the study of a timber-frame house far away, hand-built by Wren and the old man himself. Backwoods of Maine, a place to go when you needed a little 'me' time.

Tandrews had said as much early on, back when the young Christopher Wren had no sense of the cultural zeitgeist. What was 'me' time to a child fresh out of the Pyramid, still scarred by the burning of a thousand people alive?

The phone rang, an old rotary model, Wren remembered, trilling through the study and into the den, where he knew his once adoptive-father James Tandrews was most likely sitting, sipping a whiskey in the late afternoon, maybe listening to jazz, looking out through the glass into the dark of the forest.

The phone clicked twice; no doubt they'd bugged Tandrews' phone and were listening to every word, but Wren didn't care. He needed to think, and that meant bouncing ideas off a sounding board, and what better board than his 'other' father?

"Hello?"

It was the voice of an older man; still strong, just beginning the slow glide toward his seventies. Wren would recognize it anywhere.

"James," he said. Using Tandrews' last name didn't seem to hit the spot now.

It only took a second. "Christopher?"

Wren's throat seized up. Grit rattled in the wheel wells as he sped on. Grit seemed to get in his eyes even though the windows were closed.

"They told me you were dead," Tandrews said.

"I'm not dead."

Another pause. "Then they lied."

"Humphreys?"

"Him, or one of them," Tandrews said, like it didn't matter. "Christopher, is it really you?"

Wren rubbed his eyes. After three months of torture and twenty-four hours of being chased, the old man's voice came like a balm on his soul. Kindness always broke you hardest after cruelty.

"It's me. I know they're listening in. Don't get yourself arrested."

"Don't worry about me, Christopher," Tandrews said. "They don't know what I'm capable of. What you're capable of."

Wren couldn't say anything to that. He cornered hard out of the solar array and shot into open scrub desert like a rocket reaching escape velocity, heading north and swallowing hard. There were whole acres of regret assigned to Tandrews in his mind. The last time they'd spoken, the old man had urged him to make peace with his children. Well, he'd tried.

"You escaped," Tandrews said, putting the pieces together from the silence. "They were holding you."

"That's about it," Wren managed. "Mexico somewhere, a black site. I'm on the run right now."

Tandrews didn't reply immediately. Wren imagined him lifting his old bones up, stepping up to the glass to stare piercingly into the dark backwoods. They could've been father and son, if Wren hadn't been so broken. It hurt every time he thought of it.

"You saw the burning video?" Wren asked.

"I saw it. They're saying-"

"They're my people. The one who died, he had a family. The woman was my lieutenant at the CIA. The other's NSA, covert for me; he's a good man."

"I imagine you must be grieving for him."

Wren felt his eyes prick sharply. "It's my father," he said, bulling through. "The Apex. That rat bastard's doing this, framing me as a hero, framing the

CIA and the rest as lawless to get the people riled up. I know Humphreys isn't behind it, though. He's not smart enough."

A pause. "Yes. I have met him."

Wren snorted. "I had him. I let him go."

"You did the right thing, Christopher. It wasn't Humphreys. He's only a pawn."

Wren blinked. "So you agree? That this is my father?"

"I'm certain," Tandrews said swiftly. "This is undoubtedly your father's work. You know I have studied men like him all my professional life. I have studied him in particular for thirty years now, long before I ever met you in the desert. I know his mind as much as any person can. I knew this was him from the moment the protests began."

Wren wiped his eyes. It was getting hard to drive for all the grit. Talking to Tandrews felt like tapping into a deep, cool well of strength.

"He is a master gamesman," Tandrews went on. "There are second and third-order effects of this latest onslaught he'll have planned out decades in advance. On some level, I've been expecting this ever since I found you in his fake town, without him."

Wren could only listen rapt as the pick-up charged roughly over the sand.

"He left so many signs, Christopher. The arrogance of his youth. Did you know he's a younger man than I? Perhaps twenty-nine back at the fake town; younger than you are now. I saw him once, or thought that I did. I think of that night often. Huckstering on a street corner in some off-Vegas town, performing card tricks for gullible tourists. We exchanged a glance. This was back when the Pyramid were actively recruiting, charming people on the streets and drawing them in. I thought to myself in that moment, this man's a killer. But I didn't act. I thought there'd be time to surveil him. He must have seen something in me too, because within an hour he was gone. We rushed out to their camp; all scrubbed and empty. My one chance."

Wren didn't know what to say.

"That's my guilt. I never told you this, but I've carried it. You have the spark I don't have, the ability to make snap judgments and act on them without hesitation. There's a ruthlessness there, an absolute obedience to the truth. How it ever endured in the smoke and mirrors he made of those people's minds, I'll never know. But I have been grateful for it."

Wren frowned. Grateful? He pulled north onto sandy blacktop and revved the pick-up to eighty.

"Watching you all these years has been a source of the greatest pride to me," Tandrews went on. "Even as a child you were as true as a compass, Christopher. When I doubted, you set me straight. Your obedience to absolutes hasn't made you many friends, I know that, but it is your greatest strength. The ability to see things as they really are and respond accordingly, immediately. I believe it is the reason you will defeat your father." He paused briefly, taking a wheezy breath. "He has no sense of what's real, Christopher. Only of what he wishes to make real. It explains all his bizarre experimentation; his tanks, his pits, the efforts to substitute his willpower for the thinking minds of others." Another pause. "Perhaps he is a psychopath, as the pop psychologists all said; I don't know if he was born or made that way, or burned any sense of empathy out with his own hand, but he cannot accept a shared worldview not authored by him. I think it pains him every day, to not be seen as the sole creator of people's experience. He could never tolerate the kind of leader relationships you constantly build, where all are free to challenge you at will."

Wren blinked. "You're talking about the Foundation?"

"I am," Tandrews allowed, "but not only them. Every person you meet, Christopher. Americans are afraid, and you and I know how frightened people lash out. It doesn't make them evil. It only means they need help. We have to help them see what's real, so their better angels can come to the fore."

Wren sucked in a breath. "But I've lost my Foundation. There's no darknet. I can't reach any of my teams."

"So make new teams," Tandrews answered, like it was nothing at all. "The people are crying out for a leader. Fight for them. Meet your father's poison with the truth. Inoculate, immunize, protect. It's what you do."

Wren ran a hand down his face. What he did. What did he do? Send out mass text messages. Smash vehicles into buildings. Kill people. He'd become so beaten down with slaughtering the Pinocchios that he'd lost sight of what it was all for. Now Tandrews was talking about something much bigger.

"I don't know how to do that."

Tandrews laughed. "Of course you do. You learned at the knee of the best. Your father is a genius, Christopher, but here's a secret I'll only share with you. You are smarter than him."

Wren squeezed the wheel tight.

"You are stronger. You are better. It's probably the reason he spared you, after you burned the Pyramid down together. He saw it and curiosity stayed his hand. He wanted to see what you became. Now he's made you central to all his plans, by branding you a hero. Use that fascination against him."

"I already tried. I made a video. It got crushed by downvotes."

"If only one video could hold back the flood..." Tandrews said in a tone of mock sadness. "You're not asking for permission here, Christopher. You take what you want from this man. He'll never listen to reason. You beat him until he's dead, then you salt the earth above his grave. The truth doesn't need to negotiate for terms."

Wren sucked in a breath.

It helped. Already his mind felt clearer. The truth. Reality. Tandrews hadn't suggested any strategy, hadn't laid out next steps or some grand plan to bring things to a head, but already Wren felt those things happening in the back of his mind. Gears turning, reality bending. Permission being granted.

"Thank you, James."

"Always, Christopher. You know I'm here for you. If I can help in any way, let me know."

Wren smiled. "They're probably going to arrest you now."

Tandrews laughed. "I have a few tricks of my own. But yes, I expect so. Humphreys will be in here, stamping and pouting."

Wren laughed too. "He does a mean pout."

"Put on a good show, Christopher. The world will be watching."

The world will be watching. He was counting on it.

He killed the call. All that lay ahead was desert, but Wren saw the true scale of this thing spreading into the distance. America. His father's plans. Three hundred twenty million people, and beyond that? Seven billion on the planet.

The Greatest Show on Earth.

12

BORDER

It was an hour's ride on barely visible dirt tracks through El Destierro, 'The Abandoned' desert, before Wren rolled into a dust-scoured shanty town three miles south of Puerto de Libertad, north-west Mexico. A kid stood by the road at a cardboard shack hawking watermelon slices on ice. A wrecker's lot lay across the gravel road; acres of rusting Fords, GMs, Chryslers. An old woman knelt by a roadside shrine sprucing up flowers.

Wren stopped the pick-up, opened the window and took a deep breath. His heart fluttered threateningly. It had never been this loose before. Shouldn't have drunk all that Coke. He closed his eyes and settled in to wait, until-

Hands dragged him out of the truck, yanking him awake. He let them frog march him a blurry three yards into a waiting sedan, which rapidly pulled away.

"My man, Christopher Wren," said Hector Gutierrez.

Wren blinked. Skinny, wiry Hector was sitting in the passenger seat looking back. Qotl cartel, making a show of force. There was one big guy either side of Wren on the back seat, one big guy at the wheel.

"You're famous now, cuz," Hector said, grinning wide to show his diamond inlays. "Everybody wants a piece of the great Christopher Wren. Honey, where you been all my life?"

Wren snorted. Hector was a Qotl coyote; born and raised in Baja California. Riffing a style of Beach Boys meets Biggie, he'd found a natural home pitching the wonders of the United States to all points south. Part snake-oil salesman, part desert guide, he sold a package of goods to souls broken by gang warfare in cities all the way down to the Guatemala border.

Once upon a time he'd been Wren's way into the Qotl cartel. Now he was the only guy left Wren could call in a pinch.

"You're too much of an uptown girl for me, Hector," Wren said, which cracked the skinny guy up.

"You hear this cabrón?" Hector slapped the driver's thick arm. The man didn't budge. "CNN got his ugly mug on the side of a barn, farmer's bragging he's some messiah, and this is how he talk?"

Wren had seen that in the news feeds; his face graffitied onto a barn wall in New Hampshire, with the now-standard message, RELEASE CHRISTOPHER WREN. It galled all the more now that he had *actually been released.*

"I'm no messiah."

"That's right, homes, you're just some sweet baby doll in the back of my truck, never been kissed."

Wren frowned. That wasn't quite how he saw it. "I'm hardly a blushing bride."

Hector cracked up, slapped the driver some more. "This guy, man. How you like to be renditioned, Mexico-style?"

Wren just gave him a look. "Three points I could've kneecapped you, Hector. These guys either side of me are dead in two point five seconds if I want." Wren made a show of looking. "Throat. Throat. God gave me two elbows for a reason. Headbutt in your face, take the driver's eyes, now I'm really feeling like a messiah."

Hector didn't stop laughing. "Oh, me. Christopher Wren. Release Christopher Wren!" He trumpeted this a few times. It seemed to bring him no end of joy. The two guys either side of Wren edged a little away.

It went like that for three hours on the ride north-west to the border town of Mexicali, passing through desert and little scrub towns, skirting the Gulf and watching the arid desert shift as the sun rolled overhead. Hector teased Wren, or tried to, invariably mocking anything he said using a fake bass voice, spinning tall stories about the work Wren had done taking out rival coyotes with extreme prejudice. Really putting to the test Tandrews' theory that Wren allowed people to challenge his authority.

Wren ignored him as best he could, setting up gigs via his stolen iPhone on various mercenary darknet sites, requesting intel hacks on FBI, CIA, NSA,

DHS databases. He needed to get up to speed on the hunt for Gruber and Rogers ASAP.

Within an hour, after thousands of dollars spent in untraceable blockchain coins to blackhat hackers in cells spread around the world, all his hacks came back empty. Wren stared at the screen while Gutierrez rabbited on about how haunting Wren's eyes were, maybe he was part Chupacabra.

Results would be better if Hellion and B4cksl4cker were running the search, but maybe not by much. It seemed there was hardly anything in the 'Deep State' record about how Gruber, Durant and Rogers had been taken, they'd just disappeared.

He brought up what meagre pickings his mercenaries had scoured off traffic cams and prized out of intelligence silos: CCTV footage showed Gruber leaving his office in East Hollywood three days earlier just after noon, getting on the #175 bus along Santa Monica Boulevard, then simply vanishing.

There was no explanation. Between stops, with no chance for Gruber to get off, he was just gone. Wren played the videos back and forth. One second he was sitting there at the window, the next second he wasn't. Sally Rogers and Jay Durant were even worse; complete black boxes. They'd gone home three nights back, Rogers to her apartment in New York, Jay to his home in Nevada, and never emerged. Sally hadn't turned up for work the next day. Jay never came down to breakfast with his family.

There was nothing to go on at all. So what did that leave?

Wren's thumbs flew over the phone screen. There was no way he could go investigate directly. Humphreys would be watching the bus route, all the drivers, Gruber's work, his apartment, but Wren had contacts still. People in the 'Deep State' who might still take his call.

He found the number for Robin MacAuley on a private repository site. She was a hotshot pattern analyst he'd requisitioned for his Agent Without Portfolio team under Rogers. They'd worked together for three months to bring down the Blue Fairy, and he'd seen something of the devil in her. Deeply loyal to Rogers, she might be amenable to bending a few rules if it meant getting her old boss back.

He prepped an anonymizing VPN that would bounce any tracking three times around the world, then made the call.

13

MACAULEY

The cell rang three times and picked up.

"MacAuley."

Business-like. Purposeful. Probably right in the middle of the Christopher Wren manhunt.

"Don't hang up," he said.

A beat passed.

"You're shitting me," she said. It was the first time he'd heard her curse. Back in their Pinocchio-hunting days she'd been a formal paragon of by-the-book behavior.

"You know who this is?"

"This is a joke, is what it is. I'm hanging up."

"Sally Rogers," Wren said quickly. "Your boss. My lieutenant. We both want her back."

Another beat passed. Figuring out how she wanted to handle this. "So give her back, you psychopath."

Psychopath? Still, a little heat was good. Better than hanging up. "Whatever you think I did, they'd want you to stay on the line. Initiate tracking, record this call, all that."

A second passed, but no longer. She'd always been quick. Doubtless she'd already rigged the record function, was now setting up tracking. "It's really you? I'm actually speaking with Christopher Wren?"

He smiled. For the benefit of the tape. "As I live and breathe. Now, there's something I was hoping to talk about."

"Of course," MacAuley said. "You want to play catch up, talk about old times, I've got all day."

"The topic's Rogers. Are you on the hunt for her?"

The by-the-book response came immediately. "I can neither confirm or deny any active -"

"I'm thinking yes," he interrupted quickly, "because everybody is. Did you know Director Humphreys came down to Mexico to see me? Haul me out of my black site cell for a chinwag, seems he thought I could help him out?"

Silence for a second. Thinking what to say that wouldn't get her fired. "That's above my pay grade," she settled on.

That was fine. He hadn't really expected her to talk; she'd be ending her career on a dime if she did. It was enough that she listened.

"So let me talk you through what I'm seeing. Your job is to keep me on the line, right? So don't react in any way."

"I won't."

"Perfect, don't." He pressed the phone tight to his ear, listening for her breathing, any gasps, any fluctuations. Play it right and he could get a read. "What I'm seeing is nothing. I've hired some brilliant hackers to dig into the Federal record, and they say you're blind. No trails whatsoever leading away from Rogers' apartment or Durant's house, and just the bus for Gruber. Am I on track so far?"

Her breathing quickened slightly. Just barely audible. Wren pumped the volume to max and ground the phone against his ear.

"So Gruber, he gets on a bus," he went on. "East Hollywood, the 175, and he disappears. Real magic trick, what's going on with that? My question is, is that you, wiping the footage? Swapping in deepfakes to turn anyone else off the scent?"

Silence. Not breathing. Then a breath. She'd held back for a second

"Not you," Wren said, tasting the words. Thinking through the possibilities. "So that's my father's doing, too. He's got himself a deepfake crew, running simultaneous alterations, good enough to fool the best you've got." Listening, but she gave nothing. "Good enough to hack traffic cams, municipal CCTV, also social media posts, videos, satellite footage, then cover the hack in ways you can't track back."

Her breath was quickening. "You're guessing," she said, and he almost thought she did it on purpose. Giving him a tell to read. It just confirmed everything he'd suspected.

"You really haven't got a clue, have you? How it was done. Who took them. You're genuinely blind."

Faster breathing still. A dead giveaway. It explained why Humphreys had come out to see him; clutching at straws, with rioters piling up in the streets and no way to dig themselves out. Now add Christopher Wren to the mix, on the loose and stirring up trouble?

"Tell Humphreys I'm going to fix this for him," he said firmly. "And when that's done, I'll come around for another little chat."

He hung up. Breathing a little heavily himself, now.

Hector turned around and started giving a slow golf clap. "Very impressive, hermano. The great detective at work!"

"Thank you," Wren said, which somewhat took the wind out of Hector's sails, then bent over his phone, mind racing.

Humphreys must have tried every trick in the investigative book to get a lead. There was no way he'd have come to see Wren until he'd exhausted every other possibility. So Wren needed a trick that wasn't in any book. Maybe something so far off-book that only a madman would attempt it.

A slow smile spread across his face. That was pretty much the government line on him these days, anyway. MacAuley had just called him a psychopath, so why not play the part? Tandrews had set him on this course, after all.

Greatest Show on Earth.

His thumbs danced over the phone. Firing up fresh gigs. Making new hires. Setting a new plan in motion.

"Hey, Christopher."

Wren looked up from the screen, finishing up his final orders. They were pulling in next to a ramshackle one-story shop on a dusty street. He oriented himself quickly; they'd arrived. The west side of Mexicali, some four hundred yards away from the new US border wall, beyond which lay the little American burg of Calexico.

"So what I get for all this?" Hector asked. "Coins?" He stared earnestly at Wren for a long moment, then cracked up laughing the loudest yet.

"Yeah," said Wren, and held out a hand. "Gun."

"Oh man, the stories I'll tell," Hector cheered, tears coming from his eyes now. "The infamous Christopher Wren, in my car! Yeah, give him his gun."

One of the big guys gingerly handed Wren the Glock. Wren checked the breech, magazine well, magazine then tucked it in his waistband and got out.

He didn't mention the Mossberg shotgun and neither did Hector, but that was fine. He wouldn't need a shotgun where he was going.

"We'll see you real soon, cuz!" Hector called, leaning out the window as the sedan drove off. "Love you."

Wren watched him go. What a clown.

A wizened old guy was standing in the doorway of the shop, looked like a dye works. Wren looked around. A sun-bleached blacktop street set in the tight suburban gridwork of Mexicali; telephone lines running overhead, freshly planted cypress lining a dentist's clinic, chunky palm trees and low buildings stretching on and on. You could almost be in the States.

"Por aquí," the old guy said. This way. Wearing cracked glasses and a long stiff apron that seemed more purple dye stain than original fabric. Wren followed him into the shop, barely two rooms big with ceramic dye vats on one side, bolts of cloth on the other, through to an outhouse door in back.

The old guy heaved and lifted a filthy toilet off the ground; unplumbed. A round metal platform lay underneath, polished like the top plate of a scale. A single piston industrial elevator. Maybe three feet in diameter. Just one of thousands of such rabbit holes under the border.

He stepped onto the platform and the old guy pushed the button to send him down. Twenty feet he descended, featureless dirt walls banked with steel brace rings passing up to either side. At the bottom he ducked and crawled off the plate. The tunnel ahead was tight; no more than compacted sand held in place with more braces. Sufficient unto the day. He lay down on a waiting trolley and the circuit kicked in, the rope attached to the trolley pulled tight and dragged him into motion. Six hundred yards to get under the wall, out of one country and into another.

Let Hector laugh as much as he wanted. With his head down and the anger just beginning to surge in Wren's heart, he felt like a bullet on an unstoppable trajectory. His father was going to pay for all the people he'd killed.

14

GREATEST SHOW ON EARTH

Wren emerged off the borehole elevator into a filthy bathroom stall in a two-pump gas station on the fringe of Calexico. An old leathery-skinned Mexican woman watched him from the station's counter, chewing tobacco. There were a few sun-worn buildings nearby, adobe and white plaster gleaming in the late afternoon sun, and blacktop roads running in a mostly bare grid. Nobody in sight. He blinked against the brightness.

The old lady pointed. Under the station's sagging canopy sat a ridiculous powder-blue two-seat micro car, barely more than eight feet long. The keys were in the front wheel well. Wren scarcely fit behind the wheel even with the seat racked all the way back. Hector's idea of a joke. There was an earpiece, a bodycam, a wallet with five hundred dollars cash and a hot pink Google Pixel smartphone in the glove compartment, wrapped in a simple note that spelled it all out.

THIS IS IT

Pretty much what he'd asked for. Wren looked up at the old lady. She just stared right back, a thousand yard gaze of her own. So this really was it. No more cartel help. No Foundation. He was truly on his own, with only mercenaries to come at his call.

He stripped the battery from the iPhone, broke the handset, dumped both pieces by the side of the road then booted the Pixel. Curved screen. No buttons. Likely it was filled with all kinds of spyware, but Wren had a bypass for that, downloading a pirated Operating System over-install.

He checked in on the darknet gigs he'd ordered then set off. Out of Calexico onto I-8 heading west, he revved the little car up to its top speed of ninety miles an hour. It felt like overloading a souped-up golf cart; the chassis shook, the engine throbbed and the windows rattled in their frames.

Two hours to LA, arrival time around 4 p.m. He tuned the radio and listened to news of the protests growing in numbers. David Keller again; holding a rally in New York, whipping the people up against the 'Deep State'. Every time he mentioned Wren's name or his Foundation there was a cheer that came like a gut punch. Pundits suggested this rabble-rouser might actually have a chance in the presidential election. Five months out, there was no time to get on the ballot on any State, but as a write-in candidate?

Wren raced in the passing lane up the coast. With every blink he saw Jay burning again, until the suburbs of Los Angeles bloomed around him like bacteria. Desert sand and bare ocean gave way to impersonal strip malls, massive parking lots, windowless fulfilment centers and cement-lined flood control channels. An orange/gray exhaust haze hung over the metropolis like a poison fog, smearing out the horizon.

He tore up through Mission Viejo then Lake Forest on the five. In Irvine protesters were hanging out in brightly colored clots at intersections, yelling his own name back at him like hippies sixty years out of date. Black-clad Anti-Ca protesters wearing skull and bones handkerchief masks clustered side-by-side with groups of sun-weathered homeless. Wren pulled over and asked one such group for a mask and ball cap, ten bucks.

He got one of each, cinched the mask around his face like an Old West pistoleer, tugged the cap down low over his eyes and drove on. Good enough to obscure his face from traffic cam overwatch.

The air felt febrile entering Santa Ana, like the poison was deep in the bloodstream here. He saw it in burned-out storefronts tarped over with plastic, in handmade posters trumpeting his name plastered across the busted windshields of cars, in arguments firing up at crosswalks over nothing and sirens wailing out only a few blocks over. The stink of ash was in the hot afternoon air, and people were gathering on corners everywhere, holding signboards and wearing masks.

Wren felt a greasy, ugly tension building just beneath the surface. The last year of attacks weighed down the air with a thickening sense of dread, as people waited for the night, and the next burning video, and the violence to come.

Steven Gruber's place was a third-floor apartment on Baird Avenue, Reseda, twenty miles northwest of downtown. It was getting on for 6 as Wren passed into Van Nuys, rolling up Amigo Avenue one street west of Baird. He pulled into a parking lot beneath an elevated apartment block. Security cameras caught his license and signs warned RESIDENTS ONLY, but the most they'd do was issue him a fine. He rolled to the back of the dark lot, parked up and sat for a second feeling the anticipation swell up from his gut.

The Greatest Show on Earth. It all came down to this.

Through the windshield he surveyed the back corner of Gruber's building. Orange terracotta and brick, it had no real security other than the CIA agents likely staking it out. He figured they'd be parked on Baird across the way, maybe an agent in the room, a camera in the corridor. He brought up the building plans on his phone; Gruber's apartment, 306, was right in the middle.

He slipped the cartel earpiece in then tapped out a message on the ops task app and sent it to his mercenary team.

IN POSITION?

Multiple responses chimed in on the earpiece. Wren's heart hammered in his chest. Curtain's up. He got out of the vehicle, pulled his cap down firm and sent the order to activate mercenary one.

Somewhere in the shadowy lot there was a sound, and Wren focused on it; a woman emerged from the dark by the side of a tricked-out motorbike, carrying a sleek black suitcase.

"It is you," she said in a faint Israeli accent.

Wren said nothing. She was tall and willowy in black leathers, wearing a motorbike helmet. Rigged with all kinds of voice controls, he figured. Top of the deck when it came to tech, she went by Alighieri on the darknet gig boards. Two thousand dollars an hour for various hacker services. Ex-Mossad, he guessed, looking to cash in.

"You are Christopher Wren," she went on. "Infamous wrangler of the hacker collective H4cksl4cker, and a man much in demand. My rate just went up."

So she recognized him. He pulled the mask and the cap off and let them drop. He wouldn't need them now anyway.

"We had a deal."

"Forget that deal," she said. "The new rate is ten thousand an hour. Decide."

It was extortion. Wren didn't care. You couldn't buy loyalty. He had funds enough for this. "Put it on my tab. Now, how's the lighting in here?"

She started over to him at once, hips rolling sinuously, the suitcase swaying by her thigh. Wren saw strong cheekbones through the visor, wide almond eyes, over six feet tall.

"For ten thousand an hour, I brought my own lighting array." She lifted the case, popped the clasps and held it up flat, then opened the lid and gave the command. "Rise."

A light buzzing came from the case, two-toned, and within seconds twin micro-drones rose into the air. Four rotors each on four molded radial arms, central housings no larger than a kitten, hovering in the air in front of Alighieri's face. She closed the case and let it drop back by her side, while the drones remained hanging in the air. "Lights," she said.

The smaller drone flashed to light; a triple array of high-powered beams, one for full flood, two for fill.

"Camera?" Wren asked drily.

"Action," said the woman.

The drones moved in concert, covering the short distance to Wren in a second and swirling around him as Alighieri slid a tablet from the case and took control.

"Ready to go live," she said. "On your word."

Wren grunted. He'd prepped a single live video stream with a request written in a banner over the top, soon to be broadcast out through his Megaphone app across all the video streaming apps. Time to capture some eyeballs.

"Go live," he said.

The camera drone blinked red, and Wren let it survey him for a few seconds, the lights playing across his face. The more light, the more motion, the less chance they could explain this away as a deepfake.

"My name is Christopher Wren," he growled in his gravelly bass, "and I'm looking for my people."

That was enough. No need for a long speech this time. Actions spoke louder than words. He turned, and the drones swerved through the air as if on a gimbal, tracking him as he vaulted over the low wall out of the parking lot and started toward Gruber's building at a run. At the same time, Alighieri would be activating his second mercenary, a man on a pizza delivery moped waiting at the bottom of Baird Avenue.

Wren reached the building and jumped to grab the first balcony, pulling himself up. The drones rose with him smoothly, capturing the action. The sun beat down. The pizza guy should be at the building's entrance by then, even as the third mercenary should be pulling up Baird in a stolen vehicle. Wren had requested the theft of a sports car, but it was a lottery what model he'd get.

He hauled himself up to the third-floor balcony, Gruber's apartment, careful not to silhouette himself through the sliding glass door. Pressed against the wall, he listened carefully. Pizza guy had to be heading up the stairs now. Seconds ticked by.

"He's in the corridor," came Alighieri's clipped accent in his ear. "Five seconds."

Wren braced. Twenty feet away through rebar and plasterboard, the pizza delivery guy would be reaching for the doorbell. A second later, he heard the chime faintly through the wall. He risked a glance through the sliding glass and saw the man waiting for him inside. He was bulky with protective Kevlar beneath a suit jacket, the clear profile of a pistol in a shoulder holster. Easily as big as Wren, maybe bigger. Heading over to the door now.

"Music," Wren said.

"Of course," answered Alighieri.

From out front his third mercenary turned the stolen vehicle's high-powered speakers on, churning out raucous death metal at full volume. Enough noise to drown out a gunfight.

"FBI stakeout have activated," Alighieri said. "Two black suits getting out of gray sedan, they look angry. I'm calling in the police. Time to go."

Wren hit the sliding door with the Glock's grip. The glass crashed through, barely audible over the music, though the agent heard it and spun. Wren already had the Glock trained on his face. The guy's eyes went wide; trying to figure out just what was going on. Pizza. Music. Now Christopher Wren?

Wren slipped one hand through the broken glass, popped the lock and worked the sliding door. At the same moment the guy moved fast like a QB, getting off-line behind the kitchen partition. No doubt radioing through to his team, but they wouldn't hear him now, not with the death metal booming out.

Ten thousand dollars an hour and then some, just to buy Wren three darknet mercenaries and five minutes uninterrupted in Steven Gruber's apartment. The drones followed him in. Let the show commence.

15

BIG GUY

Wren scanned the apartment in a second: dust marks on the desk where Gruber's computer had been, pin marks on the walls where notices had been untacked, the bed stripped back, the wardrobes hanging open. The Deep State had tossed the place thoroughly and snatched up any evidence of Gruber's disappearance, but that was fine. Wren hadn't come here for evidence.

The drones buzzed at his side; the noise louder in the contained environment.

"Where is Steven Gruber?" he shouted at the wall where the agent had taken cover. The agent answered by putting a gun around the corner and firing.

Wren was already in motion, getting offline so the bullets crashed through the sliding door. Mid-stride he snatched the lighting drone out of the air like he was plucking an apple and hurled it in an angled curveball. It flew through the air, rotors revving manically as the internal gyroscope struggled to equalize, cornering perfectly around the wall until it hit-

The agent let out a yelp; struck by the blades, maybe blinded by the sudden light, then Wren was on him too, slamming a knee up into his groin while isolating his right arm, forcing the gun away. Three bullets discharged into the wall in a half-circle; parabellum rounds from a Taurus G2S subcompact. The guy was huge, strong, but in the throes of shock he wasn't thinking tactically, too focused on the gun.

Wren got his left hand on the guy's wrist, right hand on the barrel and pushed the safety in before the guy could bring it back to bear. The hammer clicked uselessly on the safety, and Wren gave him no more time, driving ahead like a linebacker. His shoulder slammed into the guy's gut and drove their combined mass of some four hundred fifty pounds into and through the thin plasterboard wall to Gruber's bathroom. Wren caught a glimpse of tasteful raw rock paneling, a rainforest shower, then the big guy was back on the beat and dropping a brutal elbow into Wren's shoulder blade.

Wren roared, pulled back in a spray of choking white plaster dust and sent a big right cross that glanced off the guy's temple.

Hand-to-hand fighting trumped a firefight for drama any day, and drama was what Wren wanted now, yanking eyeballs to his video livestream. The big guy didn't know about that though, and from his lodged position in the wall clicked the safety and tried to bring the pistol back into play again. Wren stepped inside his outstretched arm, grabbed his elbow and wrist while ducking his own shoulder into the guy's armpit, then with a gargantuan roar and squat hoisted him bodily into a massive judo throw.

The guy scooped out of the wall like a roll of vanilla ice cream, sailed overhead with his feet scuffing a line down the plasterboard, then pounded down to the sleek gray carpet. Wren held his forearm in isolation, spotted the drones watching him tight, then performed an almighty grunt as he yanked the gun away.

Good so far.

"Delivery boy's out of the building," came Alighieri's disinterested voice in his ear. "Your stakeout agents are focused on the music; the driver's refusing to cooperate. I see police three minutes out."

Three minutes. Wren mimed an incapacitating elbow lock long enough for the big agent to recover sufficiently to throw a punch into Wren's chin. Wren slipped it but oversold his reaction; tumbling five big steps across the apartment, judging it just right so that he came down hard on his back across a classy glass coffee table, anticipating a big dramatic smash.

The glass didn't shatter. It just hurt like hell.

The agent didn't come for him either, or go for the stripped gun. Instead he went for the door.

Wren cursed and surged up. A more dedicated controller like Hellion would be stepping in right then, using her lighting drone to block and confound the guy, but Alighieri's allegiance was clearly to her gear. The guy had the door open by the time Wren put a jump knee into his back, flat across the spine; impressive to see but no more damaging then a firm shove. The guy bounced into the open door then stumbled comically back into Wren, who pulled him down into a tumbling ball.

"View count rising," Alighieri said dispassionately.

Not quite the greatest show on Earth, Wren thought absently as he tumbled. More amateur wrestling, but people loved wrestling. Wren himself was a huge fan.

"Who took Steven Gruber?" he roared above the death metal blare, as he tussled with the big guy on the ground. The agent tried to throw elbows and gouge Wren's face, but Wren rolled the blows and controlled the guy's grasping fingers. The drones circled above them, filming two men sweating and tussling.

Not too much of this, Wren figured; shapeless clinching on the ground didn't make for good television. Time for a power move. Wren prompted a surge and steered the fight up to their feet. The guy was strong, with some grounding in ju-jitsu he was just beginning to utilize, but Wren had been born redirecting force, and it was an easy thing to control the flow of the battle. He ducked his head to the left, which drew the guy into another ill-advised elbow, committing his weight onto the front foot. It gave Wren the opportunity he needed.

He punched both his thighs into an upward drive even as he scooped his right arm between the guy's legs, his left arm trailing across the guy's right shoulder, and lifted. The guy gave a squeak, flailed madly as Wren hoisted him bodily, rotated him, then body-slammed him squarely on his back onto the hardwood floor with a resounding thud.

"And they say wrestling's fake," Alighieri said sarcastically.

Wren stood panting, soaking in the moment, the hero or the heel, surveying his fallen opponent. The guy curled up instinctively, more shocked by the slam than anything. It was a lot of punishment, though no lasting damage. It was what people wanted to see.

"Tell me everything you know about Steven Gruber," Wren boomed in a fake deep voice. "Who took him, where he was last seen?"

The guy stared up numbly. Maybe he was beginning to grasp that Wren was performing. He'd know that Wren could have killed him three times over by now, but hadn't. He saw the drones circling and had to put the pieces together.

"What are you-" he began, but Wren descended and threw three massive blows at his head which, to the audience watching, would look tumultuous, but which Wren actually pulled, faking the noise of the impact with his foot stamped on the floor.

The guy stared. Barely believing he was still conscious after that.

"I-" he managed.

"Tell me who took him!" Wren bellowed. The drone zoomed in close, rotors spinning barely inches from the faces of the two heaving, sweating men. Wren so intense. The guy frowning in confusion, not sure what on Earth he'd fallen into.

"I, I mean..."

It didn't matter. Wren didn't care what he said; that wasn't why he'd come. What would a guy left to guard an apartment know that Humphreys himself hadn't? Nothing. But somebody out there knew, somebody had seen who'd taken Steven Gruber, and Wren just had to reach that one person and win them to his side.

Greatest Show on Earth.

"You better tell me what I want to know," he roared, gave the guy a look as if to say 'sell this', then hit him with a massive backhand. It didn't connect. The guy rolled with it well, though. Maybe some amateur dramatics in his past. The drone reeled to keep track of the action. Wren dragged the agent up, trapped him into a headlock, then pulled off a crunching DDT headslam into the floor, cushioning the guy from the worst of the blow. Getting ridiculous now, maybe. They both shouted and tumbled. Breathless. Faking was harder than he'd expected.

"Tell me!" Wren hollered. The guy just stared.

"Police are in position," Alighieri said in his ear, bored-sounding. "View count spiking. Ready for phase two."

Wren let go of the big agent. He just sagged and stared.

"Saved by the bell," Wren rumbled, then scrambled for a closing one liner as he stood over him. "Tell your mother I said hello." It was the first thing that came to mind, and only baffled the guy further. It wasn't Wren's best work. Still, he knew he'd cut a powerful figure as he strode toward the door.

16

GTA

Down through the building followed by the drones, Alighieri's voice came in Wren's ear.

"You have several thousand watching your stream now."

Several thousand wouldn't cut it. Passing the first floor landing he growled back at her. "Any comments on the request?"

He'd written it and she'd overlaid it atop every instance of his video:

DID YOU WITNESS THE KIDNAPPING OF STEVEN GRUBER, SALLY ROGERS OR JAY DURANT? DID YOU SEE THEM BEFORE THEY WERE TAKEN? WHERE? WHEN? BY WHOM?

"Nothing meaningful yet," she answered. "Just compliments on your bodyslam and requests for a piledriver."

Trolls. Wren grunted and pushed out through the building's front door. Late afternoon light washed over him; Baird Avenue looked much as before, though there was now one patrol car pulled up beside a Porsche; source of the banging death metal. Wren's eyes widened; a two-seater Porsche 718 Boxster, mid-engined, sleek, silver, gorgeous. He'd spent another ten grand on the theft, and the guy had really delivered.

Now he was sitting in the driver's seat while two cops were squaring up to two FBI agents, flashing badges and making demands, while the music continued to pump out.

"Get him out of there," Wren said as he took the steps down to street level in large bounds.

"He's moving," Alighieri came back.

The guy in the Porsche abruptly hopped over to the passenger side, opened the door and ran off. The cops and the agents watched after him in confusion, and Wren strode right into that. The drones buzzed at his shoulder and drew the attention of the nearest cop, whose eyes widened. His jaw dropped and he tapped the roof of the patrol car to get his colleague's attention, temporarily struck dumb. Within two seconds they were all looking.

Christopher Wren, the man all the protesters were talking about, in LA in broad daylight. The FBI agents raised their weapons first, barked some nonsense about stopping, but Wren was already right between them, at the Porsche's door. Move fast and you could bull right through confusion.

He slipped in, slammed the door and revved the engine. They pointed their weapons awkwardly through the window at his face, but Wren figured they wouldn't shoot. No crime, as of yet. He didn't hang around to find out, though, slamming the stick into reverse and punching the gas.

The Porsche burst away like a bottle rocket. The cops fired but it was too late. The FBI were already getting in their vehicles. The death metal pounded like a grand mal seizure in Wren's ears as he accelerated away backward.

Stage two.

"Do you have me?" Wren shouted.

"I have the dashcam," came Alighieri in his ear, clear and sharp over the screaming music. "Just syncing now."

Wren hit the end of Baird where it butted onto Rayen Street and pulled a hard handbrake turn, burning rubber across the two-lane so the car rocked to a halt facing east. Wren wound the windows down and looked left; there were seconds only until the pursuit was on him.

"Where is it?" he barked, scanning the skies over Gruber's apartment.

"Any second," Alighieri said, and Wren cursed under his breath. Hellion would have had it mounted and ready to roll. His foot twitched over the gas pedal, then-

There it was; a much larger version of the micro-drones, shooting up over Gruber's building and coming straight for him; a DJI Inspire 2, the fastest commercial camera drone money could buy.

"Got it," he said and slammed the gas; the Porsche blurted onto Rayen and accelerated with phenomenal speed, hitting sixty within seconds and forcing Wren into another big handbrake turn south onto Reseda Boulevard. A quick glance in the rear view mirror showed the Inspire tracking him easily, hovering just above the FBI sedan.

"You have twenty-seven minutes flight time on the battery," came Alighieri's voice.

"Are you on these intersections?" Wren barked back, swerving madly around slower-moving vehicles. Already he'd torn through a red light at the four-way with Gresham Street and was closing rapidly on Parthenia Street, also showing red.

"One second," said Alighieri.

Wren didn't have a second; he flew onto the intersection blind at sixty, scanning to left and right. A semi thundered in and missed him by inches.

"Alighieri!" he shouted. "If I die you don't get your bonus."

She said nothing, leaving Wren to accelerate and lane-jump toward the Chase Street intersection on his own.

"Done," she came back, and the red light ahead flipped to green seconds before Wren shot through. "Police frequencies are scrambling all cars your way. There's a call for road blocks on major lanes ten blocks out."

"And the request, do we have witnesses?"

She was silent for a second, and Wren inched the Porsche up to seventy. People flew by either side; mouths wide, fingers barely raising in time to point his way. Another intersection blew by green, seven more until he hit anything like a road block.

"Alighieri."

"It's a lot of data," she answered, sounding flustered. "Comments are coming in too fast. I can shunt them to a sub-team. It'll cost you another ten an hour."

Wren laughed. A great time to tell him that, in the middle of the chase. "Do it. Get me that data."

"Working."

Wren buzzed another intersection, too fast to pick out any details now. At least it was green, at least there was no one on the crosswalk. Blue lights flashed everywhere now as the LAPD swarmed; side streets, in back, firing up ahead.

Another intersection blew by, then a squad car shot out of a side street ahead and swung out wide to part-block Reseda. Wren swung the wheel, worked the handbrake and fishtailed a lane to the left, shearing off the squad car's front fender in a spray of sparks. The drone buzzed along in back, capturing everything.

Wren corrected and accelerated, taking the Porsche closer to eighty as Reseda emptied out ahead. Now he could see the road block going up; four intersections south, call it a mile, looked like three squad cars pulling end to end across the street. He could probably blow right through the middle, but that wasn't the plan.

"Anything yet?"

"Yes," Alighieri answered after a delay. "Feed up to fifty thousand viewers, most streaming apps are carrying you on the front page. You're getting comments, lots of garbage, we're working on relevance."

Wren grunted. Fifty thousand was just the beginning; he hadn't expected anything else. Full saturation would require an OJ Simpson-level event, squad cars trailing him for over an hour, but bigger than OJ's slow roll.

Another intersection blew by. He swung hard around a guy on a lowrider.

"Is network news covering this?"

No answer. Two intersections left.

"Alighieri."

"You just went up on CNN. Fox have you on the banner. Sounds like they're redirecting a pool traffic helicopter your way."

That was better.

"Send the drone ahead and shoot me tight from in front for this," he directed over the thump of the music. "Transition in five, four-"

The cops were standing in front of their barricade now, weapons up. The drone hammered overhead as Wren reached Sherman Way and yanked a huge handbrake turn across the whole intersection, scorching burned rubber trails in an arc that bounced him off the south-west curb even as bullets starred then shattered the windshield.

Wren bobbed back up and raced west, the drone hovering just ahead and pointing back at his face, taking in the contrail of pursuit vehicles. Wren saw them in his rearview: the FBI sedan, the original squad car plus some others he'd picked up along the way.

"Reaching a hundred thousand on the stream," Alighieri said. "Network's picking you up, interrupting regularly scheduled programming. That's a lot. My price just went up twenty thousand."

It was ridiculous. "Fine," Wren said. "Hang the drone back after this. Anything on the comments yet?"

"Nothing statistically viable," said Alighieri, "except several reports he's been seen in East Hollywood. Looks like he was last spotted there on the afternoon of the fifteenth."

"I know that already! Get me something new. Where did he go?"

"Working."

Two hundred yards ahead the road opened up to left and right. At one-fifty the thumping blades of a helicopter sounded over the death metal, at one hundred the officers fired and at fifty Wren wrenched the Porsche left, swept across oncoming traffic, tore through a chicken wire fence and down a brief grass embankment then hit air.

The Porsche flew for a second, two, as it fell fifteen feet into the Aliso Canyon Wash; a concrete-lined flood control channel with a trickle of water running down the center. The Porsche tipped front-heavy, Wren braced then took the impact.

The fender struck sparks then shattered, the license plate spat out its screws and flipped away like a spent shell casing, the chassis barked and bounced as it took the full momentum of the car, followed by the bodywork grinding on concrete like balsa on an industrial lathe. The front tires hit next and jammed into the top of their wheel wells, mangling the hydropneumatic suspension with a vicious double screech, and the Porsche skidded for a half second on its nose before the rear end slammed to earth like a jackhammer, bursting the back rear tires and shattering the axle.

Wren's head lashed forward and was punched back by the airbag even as he pulled left, forcing the jammed front wheels to pop out of their wells just enough to turn a dead-slam against the wash's solid wall into a brutal graze. The right headlamp and indicator blew out on concrete, the side mirror spun off like a tossed coin and the glossy silver bodywork scratched down to the bone in a flurry of sparks.

Wren kicked the gas and forced the battered vehicle on, shooting out from beneath the hovering Inspire 2. He was woozy from the impact but watched in the rearview as the pursuit vehicles variously stopped on Sherman, overshot or risked the leap to the floor of the wash.

The FBI sedan made the jump and hit the concrete wall flush, dead-ending their momentum with an engine block forced up through the hood. A patrol car made the leap and would have landed it clean, if the sedan hadn't already tangled up the narrow landing strip. Instead it tumbled and rear-ended the sedan with a tremendous metal bark.

No others jumped after that. Immediate pursuit ended.

Wren turned his eyes to the front and pushed the Porsche ahead on all-wheel drive, dragging sparks from the busted back axle as it accelerated along the concrete channel like a Tomahawk missile up a launching tube.

17

ALIGHIERI

In thirty seconds the Porsche hydroplaned across a broad skin of water then burst onto the grand sweep of the Los Angeles River: a concrete canyon splitting LA in two, easily as wide as a four-lane highway with a deep water trench down the center. Either side lay sloping banks of yellowed grass leading up to green backyards.

Wren pulled east and pushed the gas all the way down. The Inspire 2 strained to catch up with him in back, accompanied now by a small blue weather helicopter, beating low. More eyeballs meant more heat. He imagined this pursuit running fast up the chain of command, fresh roadblocks being authorized, the Deep State wading in and riot police being called, while on the news excited anchors puzzled over what in hell was happening.

OJ Simpson's slow haul in the white Bronco had hit 95 million viewers at its peak. Wren needed to go bigger; big enough to pull in just one person who'd seen Gruber snatched on the fifteenth from East Hollywood. The biggest call for witness testimony in history.

"Alighieri, how many now?"

Nothing came back on the earpiece. He edged the Porsche down from its clattering breakneck pace, sixty from eighty. Bare bones white cement bridges flew by overhead, people staring down.

"Halt the vehicle immediately!"

A police helicopter hailed him on loudspeaker from above. Wren ignored it. He flipped the radio and found Freebird by Lynryd Skynyrd, just starting to rock out as it headed for the guitar solo. The sound washed over him and out like flames trailing a comet. The police helicopter dropped in front of him, flying backward so close he could see the pilot's eyes. In his rearview a stream of blue light vehicles poured down the embankment.

"Alighieri," he said, but still she didn't reply. He spun, but the Inspire was gone now too. That was a bad sign; without analysts riding herd on his comment feed, this whole show could be for nothing.

"Another ten an hour," he shouted. "Twenty, Alighieri! Do this or I'm coming after you."

Nothing came back but wind through the blasted windshield, Skynyrd's wailing guitar, the chop of the helicopter and the chorus cry of sirens. He brought up his phone and scanned the comment feed. Best guess, a few hundred thousand were watching online, with a lot more on cable and network news. The comments thread was a firehose, too fast for him to read.

Still, nothing he could do about it except hope Alighieri would come back soon. For now he needed to focus ahead, already drawing in on the Sepulveda Basin Park, three miles of green on all sides that would force him down a narrow channel ending in the Sepulveda Dam. The Porsche wasn't going to make it, but he could do something about that.

He tapped the app to activate his fourth contractor directly, now waiting in the parking lot of Pedlow Field Skate Park to the left. There was no time to watch for a confirmation; he shot under the narrow bridge for White Oak Avenue, hauled left and sent the Porsche up the river's inclined bank.

The front tires creaked on impact then strained as they took the full weight of the car, with the back wheels dragging lamely in back. By the top of the bank his momentum stalled out and the transmission finally snapped with a back-breaking crack, leaving him rocking at a dead stop. He kicked open the door and strode out just as the Porsche began to roll back down. Now there were five helicopters circling overhead, and a tide of emergency vehicles sweeping in some thirty seconds behind.

He ran. Into the skate park's long, crowded parking lot he sprinted; farmer's market to the left, Army National Guard base to the right, and the skate park dead ahead; grey peaks and troughs in cement like a convoluted swimming pool, filled with young people pulling off ollies and rail grinds. Wren ran along the edge tracked by a sky full of helicopters, and was greeted by stunned expressions and rowdy catcalls as the skaters stopped, recognized him and held up their phones.

"We're with you, brother!" one of them shouted.

"Release Christopher Wren!" another cried redundantly.

"Stick it to the Deep State!"

Ahead he picked out a fresh inflow of unmarked vehicles into the lot; intelligence agencies, Wren figured, on standby waiting for a moment like this. Between them and the charge chasing him in back, there was just about no way through. Except-

His stage three transport was parked right where he'd ordered; a twelve-foot tall, twelve-foot wide hot blue roll cage atop bulbous 66-inch tires, five tons if it weighed a dime, pushing a supercharged fuel injected big block American V8 engine, with two tall flag poles off the roof trailing picnic blanket-sized Old Glory flags.

A monster truck. Far from street legal. An expensive, off-book 'birthday rental' from a rally at the Staples Center; getting it in position had taken a double-wide trailer truck. Another fifteen grand right there. Now Wren's contractor, a custodian with access to the Monster Truck lot, saw him and the helicopters coming and clearly had second thoughts, hitting the gas just as Wren sprinted up, forcing him to leap like a hobo hopping a freight train.

Wren banged off the passenger side and barely grabbed one of the roll cage's bars, then righted himself, forced open the door and stared at the guy inside.

"Get out," Wren said. "Sell it and you'll keep your cash." The guy grimaced, clearly regretting his life choices, then made a show of throwing up his hands, kicked open the door and tumbled out as the huge truck kept rolling.

Wren swung into the driver's seat and hit the gas. Two of the unmarked vehicles were coming right for him then, agents holding pistols out the windows, and Wren steered right at them. They fired and bullets pinged off the truck's undercarriage and massive axles. Too late they realized what was going to happen.

The truck's huge wheels ate up the first car's hood like it was made of grits, crumpling the A and B columns under its tank-like weight and forcing the agents inside to hunch down in their seats like anchovies in a crushed can, then he was over and rolling onto the next.

"Crush the Deep State, man!" came the cry from the skate park.

The second vehicle fed under the huge truck's wheels like a giant corn dog, doors cracking outward like deep-fried batter, agents firing pointlessly into his hand cut half-ton rubber treads as their windshield shattered and their roof caved in. Wren's truck bounced down on deep coilover shocks then sped across the lot at thirty miles an hour rising to forty, and met the tide of squad cars just as they breasted the top of the river's bank. He had just enough time to strap in his flight-style safety harness before he hit them square on.

The left wheel sprang off a squad car's hood, the right wheel caught a roof coming up and bounced, then the rear wheels clipped and sent the truck into a forward spin even as it launched into the air. For a second Wren flew, ten feet above the cavalry charging in below, ten plus vehicles strong, then the dive steepened, twenty feet now to the inclined bank with him rolling headfirst into a somersault. The front wheels barely touched down on the third rank of roofs before the truck overbalanced and sped into a cannonball roll.

Wren lolled like a ragdoll as the truck tumbled taillights over bumper down the slope, crushing cars beneath it like matchboxes until it hit the channel floor and found its fat, sticky tires once more.

Wren hit the gas and sped away, leaving a trail of wreckage in his wake.

18

HELLO, CHRISTOPHER

Wren tore into the Sepulveda Rec Area with the oversized flags streaming from the truck's twin poles, maxing out the engine at sixty miles per hour, ball fields to the left and Encino Village to the right, two miles and two minutes until the dam and still no clue where he was going. Helicopters buzzed everywhere like summer flies now, but he didn't anticipate any more barricades until Burbank Avenue and the other side of the dam.

"Alighieri," he shouted, even as he clicked frantically through screens on his phone, "do you read me?"

He brought up his master video feed; with the Inspire 2 drone gone, it had been set to auto-grab pertinent footage from news sites, and it was doing that with gusto. Four split screens showed the 'chase' from both above and behind as he raced down the tree-lined concrete channel.

"Alighieri!"

He slammed the wheel and cursed. He'd considered multiple points of failure but not her. The Foundation had spoiled him, having Hellion and B4cksl4cker always there in his ear, pulling magic strings in the background.

A minute thirty, the dam, and then what? Without someone corralling the thousands of comments his escapades were generating, sorting the trolls from the wackos from the truly deluded, his 'Greatest Show on Earth' strategy was leading him nowhere; at worst seven feet under, at best irreparably damaging the 'Christopher Wren' brand.

A minute twenty, seconds ticking down relentlessly. Beyond the dam they'd have him. You couldn't outrun the cops forever.

"Alighieri, give me something now!"

Still nothing. Wind whistled in his ears, the chop of the helicopters hunting him down. He veered round a bend in the pinball launcher and saw the dam up ahead.

"Alighieri!"

"Hello, Christopher."

Wren blinked. The crisp voice in his ear was not Alighieri. He held a finger to his earpiece and craned to hear. Had he detected a Russian accent?

"Christopher, yes, I see you can hear me. Wave for the cameras."

His jaw dropped slack. Could it be? "Hellion?"

"Yes, it is I, your best friend."

Wren tried to frame words but they wouldn't come.

"While it is a special pleasure to see you struck dumb," Hellion went on swiftly and sternly, accompanied by the familiar sound of keys clacking in the background, "it seems you have gotten yourself into quite a pickle. That naughty bitch Alighieri has made off with your money, and now what are you to do? A lucky thing your hacker friends are here to save the day."

Wren tried to force his mind to catch up. "But, how are you-"

"Christopher," came B4cksl4cker's rich Armenian baritone, "perhaps there are more important matters at hand, yes? For now, let us say we have just become aware of your newly-freed status. You are seeking a trail for Steven Gruber, is that correct?"

Wren just stared ahead. Hacker gods descending from above, stealing access to his earpiece and riding shotgun in his head? He wasn't sure they were even real; wasn't strange voices in your head just how madmen thought the lizard people spoke to them?

"Gruber or the others," he managed to say. "I haven't got anything."

"So you are canvassing the country in a clown car," B4cksl4cker said. "Very innovative. I am working on your comments now, Christopher. We will find something."

The relief that brought was unexpected, to have his hackers back on the case. They said kindness was always the thing to break you after any ordeal. He wasn't through this ordeal yet, though.

"Good," he managed, then shot beneath the Burbank Boulevard bridge and onto a broad and shallow concrete floodplain. The art deco Sepulveda Dam stood barely two hundred yards ahead. The concrete flood plain rose sharply to meet it in a steep ramp, interspersed with six sleek cement columns holding up the narrow bridge.

Barely twenty seconds until he hit.

"I have banished thief bitch's toy drone," Hellion said. "Say hello to your new fleet, Christopher."

Abruptly the air ahead swam with drones, all shapes and sizes buzzing up from beyond the dam like a firework display. Fifteen seconds, and Wren just stared. Greatest Show on Earth. She'd seen what he was trying to do and slotted right in. Alighieri would never have come up with that. Where had she even gotten them all?

"You should see your face," B4cksl4cker said with great amusement, then there were just five seconds and Wren braced.

The monster truck hit the dam's forty-five degree ramp at sixty and bounced hard on its tight front suspension, only stopped from hurtling into a backflip by the propulsive force of the big rear wheels driving it on. Wren was crushed into the seat under sudden intense g-force, the roll-cage cab sprang tall as the truck breasted the dam's shallow peak in milliseconds, then he was launched into the air with his flagpoles streaming.

He flew.

Wheels roaring. Wind rushing. The truck soared like an artillery shell, the sharp upward ascent of a projectile before air resistance and gravity had their way, climbing still, all his forward momentum jolted into this massive upward trajectory.

Drones captured it all. The whole of LA spread before him; flat, gray, limitless. Another barricade was going up ahead, a couple of SWAT vans and a commandeered news truck underneath a slip road for the 405 Freeway, building a tall wall of metal topped by concrete that the truck couldn't bust through. He saw rifles aimed his way, radios raised, blue lights flashing, but they all looked like toy soldiers in some extravagant child's playset.

Three seconds of flight, four, and he felt the precision stamp of bullets smacking their tiny heads against his plate steel underbelly, trying to drill their way through. It was glorious.

Then his stomach sank as the monster truck began to fall. Two long seconds, maybe thirty feet, but the truck was perfectly balanced for jumps and didn't nose down like the Porsche; rather it landed rear wheels first with a cushioned thump, the front wheels swiftly followed and bit easily, sending up sprays of gravel like a bull pawing the arena's sand.

"Beautiful landing," B4cksl4cker said.

"Save the commentary," Wren shouted as the truck tore into incoming fire. "Cover me."

"Covering," Hellion answered, and her mismatched array of drones flung themselves forward like a volley of arrows, moving in perfect unison. Within seconds they formed into a triple-layered shield flying just ahead of him, effectively intercepting almost all of the incoming fire.

Ten seconds until he hit the barricade. Stray bullets worked their way through the buzzing cloud and pinged off his roll cage

"Clear the way, please," he shouted. "Nicely."

Half the drones shot ahead like a spear strike and instantly swarmed the barricade line. Wren had seen Hellion run this play before, battering drone housings and blades against the bodies of the Pinocchios in Idaho, killing a handful and injuring dozens. Wren could only hope she'd interpret 'nicely' to mean non-lethal.

The truck charged into the chaos of the drone storm as her keystrokes clattered like a manic drum solo, putting her four hundred actions-per-minute skills to good use and single-handedly pacifying the SWAT line. Wren braked hard and the big wheels screeched away his momentum, leaving him to thump broadside into twin vans. Wren was already releasing the safety harness and climbing up through the roll-cage.

"Hurry, Christopher," came Hellion's voice. "The storm's dying."

He stood atop the cage and jumped, caught his fingertips around the lip of the slip road's low wall then hauled himself up.

Abruptly he was standing in a whole different world. LA traffic lay before him, vehicles bumper to bumper in the evening rush hour. The roar of the drones and the shouts and the crash of gunfire seemed very far away. He turned and jogged along the row of vehicles.

"Tell me you have a destination."

"In theory," B4cksl4cker answered. "Perhaps. Head east."

Wren grunted, then found what he was looking for, another theft he'd requested and paid richly for, a superbike. He wasn't disappointed to see a sleek black Suzuki Hayabusa on its kickstand at the side, all molded chrome frame and fiberglass fairings, a truly beautiful piece of machinery capable of outlandish speeds.

A skinny guy stood there, looking terrified. Wren strode up, took the keys off him and hopped on. The helmet fit neatly, the engine fired up with a beautiful rush, and he roared away down the line of traffic.

19

MUCH TO SAY

Wren flew east on the 405 alongside six gridlocked lanes at a hundred and climbing, tracked by a single paramilitary drone.

"Talk to me," he said.

"There is much to say," B4cksl4cker answered. "First, you are ten minutes from your target at current speeds."

"I'm accelerating."

"Then perhaps eight minutes. Time enough. Christopher, we have been searching for you ever since Agent Rogers renditioned you from Great Kills. That event has since had unforeseen ramifications."

Wren blitzed over Mulholland Drive and into the Topanga foothills at one hundred and twenty, buffeted by the wind and trailing a chorus of car horns. "What ramifications?"

"A crackdown on the Foundation. They came for us on every vector, Christopher, online and off; hunting the darknet, your known associates, your most visible members."

"Like Gruber?"

B4ckls4cker's voice took on a chiding tone. "They have been watching Steven Gruber since he drove to the NameCheck campus in a yellow Prius during the Reparations. Likewise Jay, Teddy and Cheryl and many others. Your government turned passive surveillance into a coordinated effort to break us. As such, we have had to take unusual precautions."

Wren wasn't sure he liked the sound of that.

"Firstly, darknet site is not down, but cloaked," B4cksl4cker went on before he could ask. "You of course know about our second skin on the Internet, taken from Lance Gebhart? It has given us ability to 'float' an Internet domain, just as he floated Pleasure Island. The Foundation site is currently floating in cloud, rendering us invisible, unless we want to be seen."

"But I tried-"

B4cksl4cker pressed on. "We saw your efforts to reach us from Puerto de Libertad in Mexico nine hours ago. There have been hundred such attempts each minute, every minute for past two months. Trying to hack us, Christopher. We could not allow any of them through."

Wren sucked in a breath. It was a lot to take in, but really, he'd known it already. Humphreys had hinted at the level of anti-Foundation feeling in the intelligence community. "So you didn't see my first video either?"

"It caught our attention," B4cksl4cker said. "But there have been similar deepfake attempts before. Only this grand 'show' is proof. As soon as we were sure, we kicked out Alighieri and took command."

"Her operation was slack, Christopher," Hellion chimed in angrily, and Wren couldn't help but smile grimly. "Neither of you should have attempted 'God mode' without capable operator."

He grunted. That was fair criticism. This was 'God mode' and then some.

"Seven minutes left," B4cksl4cker went on. "Now, you know that Gruber, Durant and Rogers went missing three days ago, on the fifteenth. Yes? We began searching for them immediately, but hit only brick walls. Hard locks went up around CIA, NSA other agencies, as if they knew we had backdoor. Air gaps, Christopher, requiring physical intercept to breach data moat. We were in process of phishing agents for access when this death video came into new app ecosystem."

"The video of Jay burning."

"Exactly. We doubled our search, but we are limited, Christopher. If I tell you extent Hellion and I have gone to for safety, I would have to kill you."

Wren snorted.

"There is nothing out there," Hellion said. "Nothing on kidnaps. Data record is wiped clean in real time. Rogers, Gruber, they have become ghosts. CCTV, dashcam footage, social media posts with them in background; they are X-ed out completely, as if they never were. Perfect deepfakes, leaving nothing for us to find."

Wren was topping one hundred forty. The sky was clear of helicopters now. Move fast enough and nobody could keep up. Scrub desert hills raced by on either side. "Alighieri said as much."

"On this she was right. It seems you have stumbled upon only possible method of tracking these people down: the human record."

Wren considered taking issue with her use of the word 'stumbled upon', but decided not to. "Now we're getting up to date. So you have a lead for me. Where am I going?"

"Wilshire Federal Building," B4cksl4cker said. "Hellion is preparing your way. Two-tail analysis of over hundred thousand comments on your video indicates this was last place Steven Gruber was seen. As you may know, Wilshire houses LA field office of FBI. Yesterday's riots began here. Perhaps you have seen news reports covering crowds gathering outside? Your country has split around you and Foundation, Christopher. Coming riots will be worse, expected as soon as second video comes. LA has 9 p.m. curfew, but crowd shows no signs of thinning. Three-block radius is locked down, many troops wait in surrounding buildings, ready to stamp down any violence."

"You're saying it's a death trap."

"It certainly could be," Hellion joined in. "I am taking measures to prepare, but they take time. This is our only lead. You won't have long before FBI find you, Christopher. There are three people in that crowd who claim to have seen Steven Gruber passing through. One gave deep level of detail. We have exact GPS coordinates of his phone, and I will direct you, but you must get out when I say."

Wren saw it now, up ahead. The Wilshire Federal Building, a thick white block stippled with dark windows rising seventeen stories high, like some grand mausoleum at the head of the long LA National Cemetery, off to Wren's left.

"Or not," he said, thinking through the possibilities.

"Or not?"

Events unspooled in his head, a chess game played many times per second across three dimensions. "If the heat's in the crowd, maybe I can bring them down."

B4cksl4cker laughed. "Have you ever seen crowd in this riot, Christopher? These are not people interested in listening."

"So I'll use a big voice. If it comes to that. For now, what's my extraction?"

"This is next on to-do list," Hellion said, and her casual tone almost made him laugh.

"Well, as long as it's on the list."

"Yes, it is high priority for me," she said sincerely.

Wren gave up on sarcasm and bore down. The long braille-like lines of the Cemetery's graves were running toward their end. Thirty seconds and he'd almost be in the Federal Building's lobby. The number of chess moves filled up his mind. "And my target?"

"I'm sending witness coordinates to your phone," Hellion said. "No photo yet. I will find additional ways to direct you, if necessary. If this fails, we can turn the crowd to violence as a cover."

"Don't do that," Wren barked sharply, then jammed the brake and pulled left onto a circling slip road. "In and out without bloodshed, unless I say otherwise. Is that understood?"

"Loud and clear," B4cksl4cker said, which didn't inspire Wren with confidence. Hellion was the one to watch out for. "We suggest you drop bike here and enter from above."

Wren slammed the brake all the way and the Hayabusa squealed around the slip road within fifty feet of the Wilshire, peeling rubber until it skidded to a halt. Wren leaped clear before it could topple, climbed onto the slip road's low wall and jumped.

20

WITNESS

Wren caught himself in the middle branches of a spruce on the edge of a tent village spreading underneath the 405, on the west side of the Wilshire. For a moment he held position and surveyed the scene ahead; a sea of tens of thousands of people spread out across the parking lot, interspersed with the blackened hulks of burned-out cars. The sheer scale of them dwarfed the Federal Building, like a long shadow cast at sunset.

Some were carrying signboards like he'd seen in Humphreys' video back in the black site, some were pumping their fists like the thousand legs of a millipede, some were singing and shouting in a wild chorus, with the chief slogan of them all: "Release Christopher Wren!"

Some but not all. In any riot it was the quiet ones you watched for. The ones carrying weapons, waiting for the moment to instigate violence and precipitate the rest, like crystals forming in distilled methamphetamine.

That moment was coming. The raw ferocity of the crowd felt like a blast furnace on his skin, a mixture of dread, anticipation and rage far denser than he'd felt on the open streets, like pure nitroglycerin sweating out of old TNT. All the anger and fear of LA had metastasized into this five-hundred-yard block, itching for that one spark to blow.

"You're too visible," came Hellion's sharp voice in his head. "People are starting to notice. I'm cutting all video."

Her drone hovered a hundred feet ahead now, overseeing everything. She was right, people were starting to point at him, looking back and forth from their phones as realization dawned. Of course, if anyone had been watching his video stream, it was the people right here.

"Don't cut it," he said, and dropped swiftly through the branches to the ground. "We may need it, just stream my bodycam feed only; they'll never know where I am. They already know I'm here, let's use that."

"Then point your face down," Hellion ordered sharply. "Look only at your phone. Trust me."

"Done," he said, and tilted his head forward, held his phone clamped close to his chest just below the bodycam so he could take direction, and pushed through bushes and into the crowd. Voices rose up around him in recognition, but the people were too dense and he moved too fast for the message to carry.

Bodies thumped on his broad shoulders and against his chest and back like hard waves off the hull of a ship. People were turning now, trying to pick him out in the crowd, but he kept his eyes down on the phone screen as Hellion sent him blinking arrows. Straight ahead. Veer left. Seconds passed and he pushed on, watching as she added a distance countdown.

80 feet.

His name was a deafening roar on the lips of the crowd now, as they unified around his presence. Elbows jostled him, the air was a forest of waving arms holding phones playing his video back. More people were wearing masks. He smelled gasoline, saw bottles; the people here were ready for havoc.

"Christopher Wren! Christopher Wren!"

"Plainclothes agents just emptied out of a fire door on the Wilshire's east side," came B4cksl4cker's voice. "They are heading in approximately your direction."

Thirty feet now, the phone said, bearing dead ahead. Wren pulled the black cap out of his pocket and pulled it down tight. No time to affix the mask. The phone said twenty feet, the arrows blinked straight ahead. He felt mob hysteria descending across the crowd as they cried out his name. He had to get out soon or he'd be swept away.

"Almost there," Hellion said, though her voice was scratchy with interference. "Christopher, I am losing resolution. There is jamming effort to take out my drone. I am pulling up."

He heard the buzz saw of the drone recede into the swelling cries of the crowd. There was a pulse throughout them now, bodies moving like a tsunami tide drawing back, preparing to surge.

Ten feet. "Release Christopher Wren!"

Then he was there. The phone blinked '0 FEET' and Wren looked up. Figures all around him.

"Hellion," he shouted over the roar.

Nothing came back. They'd jammed her. How long until agents saturated the crowd and got eyes on him? It couldn't be long. He spun and searched the faces nearest to him. He didn't have a name or a photo or even a gender, so instead relied upon his years of pattern analysis, seeking signal in the noise of the Apex's moods.

The primary expression on the faces around him was surprise, as recognition spread one, two, three people deep the longer he stayed in position, like ripples around a dropped stone. Eyes bugged wide, shock distorted mouths into 'Os', voices began to call his name and the first few clamoring hands slapped on his shoulders, but none of that was what he was looking for.

He was looking for anything like fear. Not fear of him, but fear of being called into the fierce spotlight beam of his gaze. Comments on the video had been anonymized, but this was anything but anonymous. He pocketed the phone and clamped one hand over the bodycam; now looking for anything like relief. He spun hard, jamming the people pressing in nearby, until-

There he was. A tall guy, thin, four bodies deep and staring at Wren like he was a wild animal on the loose.

"You," Wren said, and shoved through the crowd. The guy was dark and tall, maybe Wren's age, wearing an afro cap with long twined braids hanging to his waist. Wren reached him in three seconds and put a hand on his shoulder, making the guy flinch. "You saw Steven Gruber here, three days ago. Tell me everything you know."

The guy's mouth opened then closed, too stunned to speak. Wren understood it; twenty minutes ago he'd posted an anonymous comment on a video that was too good to be true, now Wren himself was here shouting in his face. Wren had dealt it with before and provided a jumpstart, taking the man's arm and leading him away from the throng of protesters who'd recognized him, aiming to break the spell.

"Steven Gruber, my Foundation member," he shouted over the cheering of the crowd. "Before he was stripped naked and forced to watch another man burn alive, he was here. You saw him. What did you see?"

It helped, and the thin guy gulped and nodded, getting a grip. "Yeah, brother Wren. Mr. Christopher, I mean. I saw him out thattaway."

He pointed. Wren spun; back the way he'd come and left, under the 405. "Tell me."

"It was strange, my brother," the guy said, hint of a lilting Jamaican accent. "The reason I remembered him; I saw this man on his knees, taking off his jacket, you know? I thought, what's this? Then he just had another, some kind of hoodie, he pulled it on, balled the other into one of them tents." Another vague hand wave. Wren didn't care about the jacket.

"So he swapped it out?"

"That's right, brother Wren. Man was on his knees. Strangest thing I ever did-"

"And he was definitely under the freeway?"

"Right there, my friend. Man crawling on his knees."

"Crawling?" That sent up alarm flags. "Which way?"

"That way, brother man. Right over there."

Wren followed the guy's long arm, pointing underneath the 405 Freeway and beyond, across another parking lot and directly toward...

Suddenly it all started making sense.

From the beginning, the notion of Gruber leaving his office in the middle of the day to come to a protest site hadn't added up. Protests weren't Steven Gruber's scene at all, and this one in particular was a terrible move for an NSA agent, given his actual Foundation affiliation.

Then crawling? Swapping clothes?

Wren had already been questioning the notion of a daylight kidnap from the thick of a protest crowd anyway. Too visible, too many witnesses. There were ways, of course; knock Gruber out with a fast-acting neurotoxin, extract him with a team wearing EMT gear and explain it away as a case of fainting from too much sun, something like that, but even that would have stood out.

More people would have seen. More eyes would have been drawn.

But on his knees, changing his jacket, heading to a second location? It left one strong possibility.

Steven Gruber had kidnapped himself.

Along with that realization came an overwhelming flood of secondary realizations and emotions; that Gruber never would have taken such efforts if he was just jonesing for an orgy. The Feds, if Gruber had even been aware they were watching, wouldn't have cared about his sexual exploits.

No.

That meant he'd come here deliberately to shake them off, and there was only one reason he might have done that. Guilt filled Wren suddenly to the brim. One of the dark ramifications of him letting Rogers black-bag him was this; the members of his Foundation had been left swinging in the breeze.

No coin check-ins. No Foundation oversight. The structure that Wren's presence in the Foundation offered, suddenly gone. Even worse, based on what Hellion had said, none of the Foundation had contacted him either. Steven Gruber had been quarantined, infected with the Feds' attention, and that had left him completely isolated. More vulnerable to coercion than ever.

Gruber would've been easier than ever to bait out. One text message from someone pretending to be Wren, and he would have come.

That was sickening. Gruber had willingly gone, and now everything flipped in his head. No longer was Wren looking for a panel van extraction and a team disguised as EMTs; all he was looking for was Steven Gruber himself, running an avoidance routine, and who would he draw on from that?

Christopher Wren himself. Double-laundering. Do it fast before anyone could respond. Actions matching his own MO, which meant Gruber had, what? Gone to the VA Hospital to muddle his trail? He'd want to get out fast, no electronic record, probably by hailing a city taxi.

Wren spun ahead as the crowd surged around him. Even if the CIA or the FBI had thought to hunt that taxi driver down, what would they have found? Hellion had said the data record had been scrubbed completely, and Wren believed that would certainly extend to the GPS tracking and travel logs kept by whichever taxi company Gruber had flagged down. His father was nothing if not meticulous.

Which meant the only trail left lay in the one human who knew where Gruber had gone that day.

The taxi driver.

He focused back in on the witness. "What color was the hoodie?"

"What, my brother?"

"The hoodie, what color?"

"Uh, blue?"

"And what-"

"And a red hat. Sorry, I forgot. A red wool hat?"

Wren nodded sharply. "What time?"

"I, uh-"

"Rough guess."

"I'd say 4:30? In the afternoon?"

That was enough. More than the FBI had when they'd gone searching for Gruber; an outfit, a time, a location, a likely means of egress. If Gruber had run the avoidance technique right, they'd never have even known he'd come this far.

Wren abruptly snagged the bodycam and plucked it off his chest, flipped the lens and aimed it at his face.

"Three days ago on the fifteenth," he started, shouting to be heard over the throbbing cries of the crowd, "my Foundation member Steven Gruber fled the protests here at the Wilshire Federal Building in LA. I believe he ran to the VA Hospital on the other side of the 405, passed through the building, then flagged a cab at approximately 4:30 p.m.. He would have been wearing a-" Wren paused, staring at the witness but not really seeing him. If Gruber had had the good sense to wear a different hoodie for the walk to the VA, wouldn't he have had the good sense to switch out again on the way out?

"Wearing a t-shirt," Wren settled on. He'd seen Gruber's wardrobe back at his apartment; even stripped, he didn't seem to own a single collared shirt. "Now I'm looking for one specific person in all of LA; the cab driver that picked him up. If you know a cabbie, ask them. If you are one, ask your friends. I need to know where that cab went, and I need to know right now."

Even as he said it fresh cries went up around him.

"He's right here!"

"Christopher Wren is here!"

He tuned back in to the crowd; voices screaming ecstatically, bodies tumbling over each other to be near him, a pulsation spreading through the masses and rising to-

He saw the movement at the last possible moment, reflected in the eyes of his witness, which flashed to the right. There could only be one reason for that, and it gave Wren all the warning he needed. He flung himself forward, and just felt the sharp whip of twin taser darts flash by the back of his head.

Someone to the side fell beneath a massive electric shock. Wren picked out one guy two bodies away, taser extended over the shoulders of people who even now were pulling away like receding tides, momentarily stunned by the violence. It opened up the path for three bulky figures to bull through, each carrying tasers, strapping guns.

The spark to light the dynamite.

21

DYNAMITE

Fight or flight, and Wren decided in a split second.

Fight.

If he ran they'd chase him, they'd shoot, and people would be hurt. The only hope was to take these three guys out fast and get away.

Half a second; Wren let gravity bend his knees and tilt him forward, then he exploded toward the lead guy like a torpedo. Powerful thighs thrust him head-first, arms at his side, the top of his skull the first thing to make contact, two hundred-fifty pounds of mass cannoning into the guy's jaw like a lead jack-in-the-box.

Parasagittal posterior parietal bone meet mandible; thickest bone in the head plays the weakest hinge in the body and takes all the cards. Wren's crown struck and transmitted force directly up through his trunk line: thick neck corded with muscle, dense spinal column wrapped in squat trapezoids and deltoids, like being hit in the face with a steel battering ram.

The guy dropped cold and Wren fell on top of him, catching his weight in a break-dancer's bridge, already redirecting his momentum to jerk his left leg around and under his body, entering a classic capoeira spin. His left foot hit the incoming calf of the second guy, rocked but didn't trip him until his right leg followed and insisted.

The guy's leg swept and he fell, bringing Wren to a dead stop flat on his back, looking up at the one guy still standing, already training his weapon flush on Wren's face.

Not fast enough.

"Hands behind your-" the guy started shouting, until some object sailed in across Wren's field of vision. A red, green and yellow bird, maybe, or some kind of fabric. The witness' afro cap. It flopped against the agent's dour face and made him blink, just long enough for Wren to pull his right leg back and shoot it out like a piston.

It hit the guy's calf square and pushed through, sending his whole left leg back, lurching his full weight forward onto his right, which momentarily buckled. The gun came off target in an involuntary reel for balance, and Wren snapped off a whipsaw sit up to catch the guy's right leg in a tight bear hug. Another half second, and Wren jammed his left elbow in the back of the guy's knee, braced his right bicep hard against the front of the guy's shin, clamped his hands together on the other side and twisted.

The guy's knee bent and his foot lifted up off the ground, leaving him suspended in the air. He let out a wail and fell dead ahead, trying to get his arms up to break the fall. Wren didn't wait; as the guy went down he pulled into a hard 'ashi garami' entangled leg lock, one of the four barred judo maneuvers, and wrenched.

The knee popped. Ligament damage. The guy screeched and hit the deck. By then the second guy was getting up from the leg sweep and bringing his weapon to bear. Wren rolled tight and pulled the third guy on top of him, coiled his legs into the guy's solar plexus, then thrust, flinging the guy like grapeshot from a catapult.

He flew a good four feet, hit the second guy who barely caught him, then Wren was on the way, sending an elbow to the second guy's temporal lobe that put him down.

Wren caught a sharp breath. Three guys down. Twenty seconds, all in.

"Holy shi-" said the witness.

Wren spun. All around were wide eyes and phones held up to film him. Others would be coming in any second, and still no word from Hellion.

"You," he snapped at the witness, "don't let anyone take their guns. Keep the crowd back. Wait for the authorities. We're not at war with each other."

Somebody gasped. "Not at war, are you serious? After this?"

Wren spun. A big guy with a stunned look on his stubbled face. On camera now, a bit player in the bigger drama, and Wren took the opportunity. This was more antidote, essential to get it in now, while he could.

"The 'Deep State' didn't take my Foundation," Wren said. "They're not the ones I'm after."

The guy's stunned look became disbelief. "What? So who the hell are you after?"

"Whoever took them," Wren answered, then spun to run west, shoving through bodies and scanning for his fastest route out. Bodies, the freeway, the VA hospital beyond, slip roads and access roads and-

He fixed on a flashing light beneath the freeway overpass, not a blue light but a red one, hovering flush in the air. The drone! Relief rushed out with his heightened pulse. Hellion had figured out an exit route.

He ran on through the fraying edge of the crowd, tapping the hard plastic of his earpiece. "Hellion?"

A bullhorn fired up in back, bigger than any protester bullhorn, ordering him to halt. At the edge of the crowd his ear crackled; a signal coming back into range. He vaulted a metal fence and came down in a service road leading to the VA hospital, shadowed by the Freeway, where the drone hovered above a Mercedes-Benz A-class in deep mahogany red.

"Are you roadside assistance?" a girl asked.

Wren had a second to take her in; yellow t-shirt with some nerdy pop culture reference, skintight black jeans paired with beach sandals, lingering awkwardly beside the Mercedes.

"Am I what?" Wren barked, then Hellion's voice rasped back into his head like the dulcet tones of an angel.

"Your route out," she said swiftly. "I hacked Radio Frequency ID of this Mercedes, Christopher; now it is all yours. This dummy thinks you are roadside support."

"My system just shut down," the nerd girl was saying, "remote engine lockout, it said, and then this drone told me to get out and is that something you can fix?"

Wren yanked open the Mercedes' driver side door and dropped in. Massage seats, calf leather, walnut dash. "I'll have it back for you in no time, ma'am," he said, as Hellion swiftly re-initialized the system. The central display booted, the engine fired up, the anti-theft wheel-locks unclamped and Wren hit the gas and took off without looking back.

22

FALSE POSITIVES

Wren hurtled out from under the 405, past the VA Hospital where three days earlier Steven Gruber had fled looking for him, and folded onto Wilshire Boulevard to cruise at a steady pace, keeping his head down, talking to Hellion and B4cksl4cker the whole time.

"All cabs accounted for," Hellion reported as Wren crossed San Vicente Boulevard, well within the speed limit and obeying all traffic lights. "We have checked the online logs, fare records and GPS tracking on every private hire vehicle within a mile of the Hospital across a two-hour window on the fifteenth. B4cksl4cker is cross-referencing to traffic cam footage, but we do not see Steven Gruber."

"And you won't," Wren said, making a smooth left turn to keep track of any possible pursuit. The drone was gone, no longer tracking him. "You said they've erased the digital trail. I'm counting on the cab driver or any witnesses reaching out directly."

Hellion was replaced by B4cksl4cker on the line. "This is highly unlikely, Christopher. We also hesitate to say this, but have you considered taxi driver has also been, how shall I say, erased from picture?"

"Yes," Wren said flatly. He hadn't.

"In such case, this would leave no trace for us to find. Nothing in human record."

"Technically," Wren said, and made another left turn. Working a loop.

His hackers paused; probably conferring between themselves. "Is there any way to see this other than technically?"

"With a little faith," Wren said. "Is anything coming in?"

Hellion hit the keys. They were both hardcore atheists, and faith didn't come naturally. "Thousands of comments a minute, since you took out agents. You are on every news channel, 'breaking the Internet', so they say. We are receiving," keys clacked, "many taxi sightings, but this is all meaningless. There are many taxis in LA."

"Is there anything meaningful?"

More keys clattering. "Several reports of Gruber in VA Hospital; three say he was wearing blue t-shirt, one red, one green. Of those, two report him climbing into yellow cab. That would make sense, as VA Hospital has contract with city. Only yellow cabs with shield can line up."

"We're making progress," Wren said.

"Progress to nowhere," Hellion said. "These witnesses do not know where he was going. There isn't enough for us to map out journey."

"Still nothing from a cab driver?"

"Nothing."

Wren spun the wheel right, making another loop. Still no follow cars. "What about missing yellow cab drivers? If they actually erased the driver, not just the image but the actual person, somebody must have filed a missing person's report. It was three days ago."

"Checking DoJ, FBI, LAPD... One moment... It looks like, yes. One. Two days ago, his wife called in to police, I'm seeing- "

"Get his photo up alongside Gruber's," Wren interrupted, as a new idea took shape in his head. It was a long shot, but long shots were becoming his stock-in-trade. "You said you were getting taxi sightings; let's double down on that. Change the request on our video feed, I want sightings of Gruber and the driver in a-" he paused "-what did he drive, straight yellow cab, yellow with blue sides, sedan or people carrier?"

A second passed. "Sedan, yellow and blue."

"Get their photos and the vehicle up. I want sightings from anywhere in the city across this time window."

It took a moment.

"Christopher, you cannot be serious." B4cksl4cker said. "Two men in taxi, three days ago? Nobody will remember this. Even here in Kyiv these taxi cabs pass by one every thirty seconds. You will receive nothing but false positives; people who wish to help but remember incorrectly."

Wren was way ahead of him. He wasn't wrong, but he wasn't completely right either. Some people remembered more than others, and there was always a signal in the noise; you just needed a way to cancel out the false positives. "Hellion, I need you to 3D model a rolling reconstruction of known yellow taxi cabs around the VA during that period of time, using existing travel records, GPS, CCTV, social media footage, the usual. Can you do that?"

There was silence for a second. "Yes, Christopher," Hellion said. "But this will not reveal anything to us. The taxi is ghost. They have used advanced algorithmic deepfake technology to erase it from all video footage. I cannot find them this way."

"We're not doing it that way," he pressed on. "Please make the model, as precisely as possible, then B4cksl4cker, map any sightings of Gruber's cab onto that model and see where they don't fit."

"But-" Hellion began, then eased off. It took a second. Wren took another turn, heading back toward the VA. It was the only clear sighting they had of Gruber, so Wren didn't want to stray too far.

"I see," B4cksl4cker chimed in. "You are tracking the ghost with crowd sourcing, yes? The human record, again. This model is filter layer to remove false positives."

"Exactly. We establish a baseline, that's Hellion's model. We know those are real movements. Onto that we map witness testimony from the human record. Any vehicles that deviate from the baseline model are suspect. If we get enough, all pointing in the same direction? Bingo. We draw a line of best fit through the data and see where it takes us."

Another second, as they digested that. It didn't take long.

"Ghosts cannot be seen by technology either," B4cksl4cker said. "Only by humans. Unless you count orbs."

"I don't."

"Compositing a 3D model," Hellion said, with the familiar sound of keys flying in the background. "Layering in GPS routing data, CCTV, private hire firm logs. Populating with vehicles..."

"It is very clever," B4cksl4cker said appreciatively. "However, you will need smart AI to turn this flood of random comments into useable data. Even then, it may all be useless. Garbage data in, Christopher..."

"Garbage data out, I know, but we're going to try. You can write an AI to do that." Wren didn't know, was just willing it to be true.

"Yes," said B4cksl4cker confidently, "I am perhaps one of only handful in world who can do this on such short notice. And yes, I will do it for you, Christopher."

"Thank you."

The VA was coming up on his right. The sound of the crowd was swelling to unearthly levels, washing over the street. He picked out a few words, 'Release Christopher Wren' and 'Free the Foundation' blurring into a wall of sound. Traffic lights held him and he obeyed, watching the distant swaying banners of the crowd. No agents rushing up to arrest him, yet. How long would that hold?

The lights went green and he eased ahead.

"Anything yet?"

"I am programming AI, it has already begun self-training on comment feed. Dismissing sightings of all-yellow cabs, cabs called by app, cabs outside time range, cabs without positive ID on Gruber or driver. Now cross-correlating to known cabs from Hellion's model, running backward and forward on time scale, searching for line of best fit. These results are fascinating, Christopher, we should really-"

"Is there anything?"

"First results suggest cab turned left out of VA lot," B4cksl4cker said.

"Then I'm going the wrong way."

He didn't wait for more, just spun the wheel and pulled a U-turn across three lanes of traffic. Cars honked but that was nothing beneath the thrum of the protest crowd.

"Next?"

"I am programming as we speak, Christopher. Self-training is delicate. Hellion, can you?" Like he was handing Wren off to a babysitter.

"Comments on your video stream are accelerating," Hellion took over smoothly. "Your bodycam is transmitting still, but I have muted audio and am hiding your exact location. We do not wish to be followed, do we?"

"Not now, keep us muted, but keep the feed live."

"Good. Our viewership has risen to tens of millions. News stations are amplifying signal tenfold, replaying your fight in crowd."

"Two minutes and I will have something," B4cksl4cker said.

"Good." Wren thought ahead. "Hellion, where's the drone?"

"Tracking from above, Christopher. There is no pursuit yet."

That was something, at least. Without technology to 'ghost' him from the CCTV record, though, it wouldn't last long. "How are we playing on the news?"

"In your favor," Hellion answered. "There is man called David Keller on many channels now, speaking from political rally in New York. He claims to know you."

Wren sucked a breath through his teeth. "Never met him. He's a nobody."

"He is very handsome," Hellion said flatly. "You could take fashion tips from him; nice suit, proper shoes-"

"Not the time," he rasped.

She continued unfazed. "He is pointing out you did not use lethal force, that you do not blame US government. This is good propaganda, I think. He is on our side, we should consider reaching out."

Wren snorted, passed slowly through an intersection. Driving in stop-start traffic after the mad race down the LA River felt surreal. "He's on his own side. Don't reach out. B4cksl4cker, how's that training coming?"

"Very rapidly," B4cksl4cker answered. "There is good research batch of sightings to build from. I am feeding regression analysis tools into AI; it has incorporated Hellion's model for screening out false positives, and is now generating 'clean' data that produces range of potential routes. It seems there is sixty percent chance Gruber's vehicle turned right within next twenty blocks."

Wren laughed. "Twenty blocks?"

"I do not have confirmation of precise turn, but there are multiple constellations of sightings in north-west."

"So I just turn right when I feel it?"

"As the spirit moves you, Christopher. Have little faith."

He gritted his teeth and pulled right.

23

MANDEVILLE CANYON PARK

It took twenty-five minutes for the AI to lead Wren up into the low hills of Mandeville Canyon Park. There were left and right turns that he had to correct for, but the further he drove the firmer the route became, built from many thousands of individual sighting.

"There is just one sighting in the parking lot ahead," B4cksl4cker said. "A marketing executive napping in his vehicle. He only saw the cab leave, but thought it was strange."

Wren charged into the lot. 7 p.m. and tingeing toward dusk. His heart beat hard, adrenaline flushing into his system. The lot was almost empty, just a few cars parked at the edge and overlooking a gorgeous sunset vista of Santa Monica with the sun sinking pink toward the Pacific. Wren rolled through, swiftly sighting the overgrown entrance on the left. There was a heavy-duty chain stretched across, bolted with a chunky padlock.

This had to be it. He stopped the Mercedes, kicked open the door and strode out with the Glock already back home in his palm. New padlock, new chain. He stepped over it and ran up a winding trail of bamboo strangled by Japanese knotweed, until-

"The Jeddah Mill," Hellion said in his ear, just as he saw the ramshackle old structure looming large over the trailhead: cedar boards turned gray with age, a hole-pocked tin sheet roof, willowy saplings springing thickly all around. No vehicles out front. "They used to do logging here."

"Get on the routes out," he said, circling to the entrance. "Same algorithm, same AI, same time window. I want ghost-proof sightings on all vehicles on this road. Find me where they went."

"Compiling," said Hellion, then Wren reached the mill's oak door and booted it open.

Inside lay a dim and empty hall, tables to the left with one old saw-bench in place, the wheel missing, crates and broken furniture to the right, antique gear hanging on the walls. This had to be someone's pet project, a kind of personal living museum. Dust motes plumed thickly in the last stray beams of afternoon light.

Wren scanned the floor. Footsteps in the dust everywhere. It wasn't confirmation, but given the lack of graffiti and beer cans, meaning no one came up here just to hang out, he figured these might be his targets.

"Are you recording this?" he asked, aiming the bodycam directly.

"Captured. Go on."

Wren strode in. The hall continued some thirty feet until the timbers gave out in a spray of fallen branches. A toppled jacaranda had come through the roof, still clinging to its roots and spraying sweet purple blossoms in the gloom. There was a door to the right and Wren kicked it through.

Nothing. A store room once, perhaps, now stacked with just a handful of terracotta plant pots. No chairs under a swaying light, no greasy stink of napalm in the air, no ashes, no Rogers or Gruber. He kicked through another door and found himself teetering over a drop down to the canyon slope. Not a long fall, but neither a comfortable one.

He cursed under his breath. Not here. That had been a wild hope anyway; unlikely, but worth clinging to.

"The drone is on overwatch, Christopher," Hellion said in his ear. "This structure is small and broken, the two rooms you have seen are all there is. No heat signatures within except your own."

He caught the far-off buzz of the drone and turned to look up. Barely visible, it was so high. "Can you pick out vehicle data from the wheel tracks in front?"

"I can try. Also with the footsteps in dust. I am running through pattern analysis."

Wren ducked back into the structure, tucked the Glock into his waistband and strode over the ancient wooden boards, bringing up his phone and turning on the flashlight to study the walls, floor and ceiling with fresh eyes. There was no immediate threat now, but that raised the next question; had Gruber even come here?

"B4cksl4cker," he rumbled.

"The AI is only becoming more certain," the hacker answered. "If this is a false trail, it has obscured the real route."

Wren grunted, thinking through a snatch-and-grab operation on Gruber. It wouldn't take much; Gruber wasn't a tactical threat to anyone but a geriatric. Call it a three-person team, one vehicle, some easy means of sedating the target. The hard part of a kidnap operation was the waiting. They would have been in place several hours in advance, and waiting brought out bad habits.

He pushed back into the main hall, already getting darker, and swept the phone's torchlight back and forth across the dusty boot prints, trying to figure out a pattern. Perhaps there was a cluster near the door.

He strode over, putting himself into the mindset of a Pyramid snatch squad. If they were anything like the Pyramid of the past, they wouldn't make mistakes. The Apex told you to stand perfectly still for days on end, you stood still. You wanted nothing more than to prove your defiance of reality.

There'd be none of the usual tells here; cigarette butts, chip packets, empty cans. No DNA, almost certainly no fingerprints on any surface. Twenty-five years ago the Apex had vanished without a trace; he wasn't about to start leaving trails now.

Ghosts.

"Anything?"

"Analysis of the boot marks is fascinating," Hellion said. "I found a wonderful program that relies on-"

"What did it find?"

"Two things. Three shoe sizes, but overlaid. One matching Gruber, based on his height, barely entered. Footsteps at the entrance, then no more."

"Snatched," said Wren.

"I concur. Another set of footsteps, they go everywhere, more recent than the others. The dust lies over them. The third, size 17, this is a giant man, Christopher. Six feet six and counting, taller than you."

Wren paused, studying the dusty footprints.

"One man?"

"Or a very large woman. They exist."

He grunted. One man, sure. Gruber wouldn't put up much of a fight to anyone. But why only one? He stepped back outside, stood on the rickety porch overlooking the approach road, partially blocked by saplings, and racked his mind for any other way to extract clues from the site. Satellite overwatch was worth checking, but would likely be a null spot, likewise the human record, if he didn't know what vehicle they'd driven away in. Nobody was coming up here.

Except...

The interior had been immaculate. There'd been a fresh padlock and chain blocking access. Freshly bought within the last three days. And that second set of footsteps, checking everywhere...

"Hellion," he said, "who owns this mill?"

"Checking."

While she worked, Wren circled. The structure was dilapidated, but there was no trash anywhere. No beer cans, needles, graffiti. That suggested an attentive custodian, the kind of person who would absolutely notice if intruders had come in. Maybe, if he was lucky, the kind of person who kept off-grid closed circuit security camera oversight of the mill, the lot, the approach road.

Wren's heart skipped a beat. Would the Apex have overlooked something like this? No, but then was he dealing with Apex directly, or was this another one of his lieutenants, who might overlook one such tiny detail?

Wren had to hope it was the latter.

"The city owns it," Hellion said, "overseen by the Department of Parks and Recreation."

"And who's their custodian?"

"I'm looking at their website. Looks like three for Topanga, but, OK, she's on maternity leave, the other one's so old he can't be active, that leaves one guy."

"Name and number."

"Dodge Smitt. I'm calling him now. Check your phone."

Wren pulled up the pink Pixel. The last app he'd had open, his Greatest Show on Earth app, was still blinking as if live. He shunted it away and put the phone to his ear.

It was ringing. It answered.

"Hello?"

A young guy's voice. Mid-twenties.

Wren held the phone to his left ear and adopted a slightly nasal, pen-pusher's voice. "Mr. Smitt, my name's Gerald Humphreys, I'm calling from," he paused a second, thinking what would get him an answer fastest. Referencing national security would likely get him tied up in the guy's command line. "Bat Conservation International. We had a bat house located on one of your properties, the Jeddah Mill in Mandeville Canyon?"

It took a second. "You had a what? A bat house?"

"Yes sir," Wren said brightly. "It's like a box, in a tree. To help bats, which are endangered." Hellion laughed in his right ear and he ignored her. "Well, we installed it some years ago, with permission of course, and we've been monitoring it remotely ever since, but three days ago the signal died out. I'm on the property now, but the box is gone. I'm afraid it may have been stolen; bat hunting is a real scourge of our times. I was wondering if you had noticed anything unusual in that time, any trespassers on the property or things of that nature, and if you have any record of this."

"Well, I-" Dodge Smitt composed himself. "I suppose, if you already had a bat house there? I can tell you. Yes, there were some trespassers. They cut the chain, I had to buy a new one just two days back." He sounded laconic. "I didn't know what they they were doing, but now I see they must have been bat thieves."

Hellion laughed.

"Indeed. This is a serious matter for us here at Bat Conservation International. We're trying to build a case. Could you possibly send us the footage, as soon as possible?"

"I can get it," Hellion said.

"Well, I-" Dodge Smitt began. "That's actually city data. I don't know if I can just release it-"

"Of course, I understand. I'll file the proper paperwork, but we're actually in the middle of a class action civil suit right now, suing the largest bat-leather production facility in the LA County. The final deposition is in several hours, in fact."

This confounded him. "Bat leather?"

"It's a terrible problem, a real scourge. Designer brands, you understand, influencers. I'd appreciate if you could send that footage to me directly, and I'll forward the paperwork first thing tomorrow. This could make a real difference, if we have some proof."

"Well, I-"

"Think of the bats," Wren said.

Hellion laughed louder.

"I suppose, I-"

"Thank you, Mr. Smitt. This will make a real difference. Please send it to this number in the next ten minutes, or I'll miss my moment at the bench."

"I, but, I'm not at work."

"Within the hour then. Again, you have the deepest thanks of Bat Conservation International."

"Well, OK."

Wren hung up.

"I can get that data," Hellion said.

"Faster than him?"

That silenced her. If it was on an open system, she certainly could, but then if it was on an open system these 'Ghosts' would have ghosted any record of it already. She'd have to phish for a contact, and he'd already done that.

"Christopher," came B4cksl4cker's voice, interrupting the squabble. "I'm afraid I have bad news. There is another video streaming right now."

That stopped him dead. All thoughts of bats fell away as another cold bomb went off in his stomach. Almost certainly another death; Rogers or Gruber.

"Who?" he asked.

"It has just begun, I'm sending the link to your phone."

The phone chimed. He looked at it, the same dark setup, raw cement walls, swinging ceiling lamp, Rogers and Gruber naked and glistening either side of the ash pile that was Jay Durant. The same huge man parading up and down in front of them.

One huge man. Wren didn't need to see any more, already stringing together the sequence of events to follow. The crowds at the Wilshire would watch it. Hopped up further by Wren beating up the 'Deep State' right in their midst, the eruption to come would be epic.

He'd provided the perfect warm-up act, just like in the old Pyramid days, dancing for the crowds in some down-at-heel Midwest town while the Apex worked his magic and the cute girls moved amongst the crowd, signing up recruits.

Always playing into the Apex's plans.

He ran.

"Get me drones above the Wilshire," he ordered as he stamped down the bamboo-lined trail, "and get the livestream tight on me now." He reached the Mercedes in twenty seconds flat, fired up the engine and tore away.

24

BURN

South onto the narrow Canyon Road as the sun sank purple over the Hollywood Hills, Wren amped the Benz up to fifty then sixty, passing vehicles around tight bends, barking instructions to B4cksl4cker and Hellion even as he brought up the feed on his phone.

"Ten minutes," he finished, then focused on the road and the video.

The man was right there. Head Ghost, striding up and down. Wren flew past a Dodge pick-up then chicaned hard right to get out of the way of an oncoming semi. Horns thundered behind him.

The video's visual quality was worse than before; grainy and too dark, but was there audio? Wren cranked the phone up to max and made out the rustling of voices.

"Feed it through the car speakers," he shouted.

Hellion said nothing, but a second later Wren could just hear the whispery mutters coming through the speaker system. He spun the volume dial to the max and the mutters became far-off shouts.

"-where exactly you last saw him, and what exactly he directed you to do, or I won't be held responsible for what happens."

The man was focused on Rogers. She didn't move. Her head was slumped over her lap; very different from the defiant glare she'd shot this man before. Just a day ago now, a day and a half.

Wren strained to catch what she said, but perhaps she said nothing. The Ghost leaned in, grasped her by the hair and pulled her head back.

Wren almost swerved off the road when he saw her face. Rogers didn't look like Rogers. Pale, sweating, hair stuck to her skin, but that wasn't the worst part. The worst part was her eyes; the life was entirely gone from within them. They looked haunted, dead, utterly broken.

"That's not my Rogers," he said. He didn't want it to be.

He'd seen that look before, signaling absolute internal destruction. The moment cult brainwashing took full hold and the victim began to really believe; that everything they'd ever thought was true was not true, that there could never be sanity again, that reason and logic would only damn them and the last remaining answer was to confess to their sins, admit guilt and sell themselves out completely.

Two plus two equals five. The moment on the other side of despair when you don't only say what needs to be said to survive, you start to believe it too. It could take weeks of isolation, beatings, deprivation, humiliation to reach that point.

It had only been three days.

"What do you mean, Christopher?" Hellion asked.

"I, uh, I didn't think she'd break like this."

"Hmm," said Hellion. "I will look into this."

Wren barely heard her. The man shook Roger's head, and sweat droplets sprayed along with napalm. He pulled his left hand back like he was winding up an axe, then smacked it hard across her face. Wren jolted in his seat, but Rogers barely seemed to register it. Not drugged on anything other than despair.

"Tell me and you'll be a hero," the man said. "You'll save your country. This man lied to you. He twisted you around inside."

He was pouring words into an empty vessel now. Wren took both eyes off the road for a moment to swipe the screen and zoom in. Her eyes were black holes. Her lips moved. There was no way Wren could hear it. The movements were too slight to lip-read.

"Can you extract any of that?" he called to Hellion.

"Attempting," she answered.

Wren swerved around a slow-rolling Lamborghini with its downlights on, a garish red on the dark blacktop, and blinked sweat out of his eyes. Rogers was slumped again now, blond hair draped over her knees, shoulders slack. Wren wracked his mind for what she might have confessed. Rogers wouldn't know where any of his cult members were right now. She didn't have the location of his hackers, not even Wren knew where they were.

But perhaps...

Another cold bomb went off in his belly, hard enough that his foot briefly came off the gas and he cruised for a moment at seventy, barely reacting to the turns of the road.

His family.

Rogers had refused to tell him where they were. Back in Great Kills, New York, just before she'd taken him in, he'd asked and she'd refused to say. They didn't want to see him, that was all she'd said. Some kind of witness protection. Then she'd put the bag over his head.

Wren's heart ramped up to a hundred-twenty beats a minute. Add that to the aortal flutter, he could give himself a heart attack. Implode from within, take the Mercedes off the road, end of story.

He gulped air. "Get Humphreys," he ordered. "Break through his Internet, his phone, whatever it takes. Flood DHS, the FBI, the CIA with this. The Apex has my family's address. They need to be moved right now."

Hellion said nothing, but he heard her fingers flying. He spun the wheel and punched the gas again, feeling his pulse in his fingertips as the huge man leaned back, pulling a glint of silver out of the pocket of his military fatigues.

"Let this be a lesson," he said, and Wren heard Gruber cry out.

The ghost dragged his thumb on the lighter's steel wheel, and it sparked on flint. The wick took the spark and flamed. Wren's mouth was dry, his vision tunneled, overwhelmed by the cocktail of rage and terror pouring through his nervous system.

The ghost flicked the lighter. Such a slight motion. It cartwheeled lazily in the air. Wren saw every frame of the juddering footage. It couldn't be real, he thought. It was too real. For twenty-five years he'd done everything he could to throw off the shackles of his father's touch, and now-

It hit Rogers. She went up in flame.

She screamed. She thrashed. The sound of it came loud and clear through the car's speakers for almost a minute.

Wren couldn't think. He flew down out of the dark hills and wrenched the car east onto Sunset Boulevard through a red light, sideswiping a limo and plunging toward the Wilshire Federal. Six minutes. The phone dropped from his hand as he pushed the Mercedes up to eighty, swerving without thinking across lanes, on and off the sidewalk, in and out of the oncoming traffic lanes, letting rage rise up to throttle the terror.

Fear was fuel. Anger was everything. You could burn fear to rage, and rage would get you through. The Wilshire was coming. Wren felt the city heaving around him like a tsunami tide, a year of helpless fury overtopping the levee and not one single person wanting to slow it down.

25

WILSHIRE

The protest crowd seethed as Wren pulled around the slip road, crossed under the 405 and raced headlong down South Sepulveda Boulevard until he couldn't go any further.

People here were spraying out of the central mass and swarming on targets like angry breakers: dark figures in the dusk smashing the windows of a parked Ferrari and pouring in gasoline, tossing fiery bottles and rocks toward the tactical cordon of riot police closing in from the Wilshire.

Wren rammed through a gap in the government line before it could seal over and plowed flush into the sea.

"The whole block is encircled," Hellion called in his ear as he stalled the Mercedes and booted open the door. The sound of the mob had become overwhelming, shouts and screams forming a rushing white noise that carried its own feverish pulse, his name mixed in with threats and patchy slogans and bullhorn voices demanding the crowd disperse at once.

"They're pouring out of nearby buildings," Hellion shouted. "Hundreds of armed police. Two helicopters inbound with a steady stream of troop carriers from the north, looks like the National Guard." Wren could barely hear her over the mob. The drone buzzed right above him, livestreaming his feed, but the sound was lost in the whirlwind.

Wren took a breath and reveled in it. To his left the Ferrari erupted in flame, prompting cheers. The riot police were driven back by Molotov cocktails bursting into flame by their feet. This was the same rage he was feeling, brought into reality, and it buoyed him on. Dusk had fallen fast across Los Angeles, and in the darkness justice would come.

He pushed into the crowd, heading for the heart of the tempest. Bodies shoved from all angles as the animal instincts came out, but Wren leveraged his height and mass to force a route through. From above floodlights lanced down; he glanced up to see twin helicopters hovering low. In their lights Wren saw Rogers burning again, saw the soul-death in her eyes, and pushed on harder.

Gunfire rang in the air, Wren hoped rubber bullets. A breeze blew off waving flags. Islands of fire sprang up in the midst of the mob as rioters set cars in the lot to blow, followed by the first deep explosions. Every person he saw wore a mask now, t-shirts repurposed to cover their mouths, screaming for blood. Flashbang grenades went off in the distance, by the fringe, unleashed like lightning. The bitter tang of tear gas breezed on a hot wind, stinging his eyes. Everywhere were faces split with rage, some stained with ash and blood, crying out their resistance and thrusting ahead to get into the fray.

Wren pushed on, checking the air above him; the drone was right there, buzzing low.

"Am I in the center?" he shouted.

"As near as possible," Hellion answered. "It's spreading rapidly in all directions."

"Tight on me," he barked. "Zoom out as the effect becomes clear."

"Understood."

Wren stood in the mob's thumping heart, feeling the rage swell through him. Two people murdered by a barbaric, unaccountable 'Deep State'. Of course they wanted justice. Of course they deserved it. Their bodies tumbled around him, jostled by unseen currents in the thickening dark, hurling projectiles, lighting rags stuffed in bottles of gasoline, aiding fellow members with blood streaming from head wounds, pouring milk in eyes fogged by tear gas.

He could feel the twin booster rockets of anonymity and rage propelling the mob on. Nobody knew who they were. Their cause was righteous. Like a reduction of naphthenic and palmitic acids into napalm.

All that had to be undone.

He scanned the faces nearest to him; men, women, young, old. They weren't thinking, only reacting, deep into the battle. He picked the biggest, a bearded man, 6' 6" and wearing a denim jacket, stabbing the air with a sharpened stake and thrusting toward the front line.

Wren grabbed him by the shoulder, spun him around and pulled him in close.

"Look at my face," he shouted, inches away from the guy now. "Do you recognize me?"

The guy's eyes were wild, lodged in the ecstasy of the crowd, with his thinking mind left far behind. He grabbed Wren's shirt and shook him back. "Hell yeah, man, I recognize you! Do you recognize me?"

He shook Wren again. Moved by the spirit. Wren rode it out and held on, locking eye contact and willing the guy to make the connections.

"No, really, look at my face! Do you know who I am?"

The guy stared, and Wren saw the anger turning on him. There was no recognition there; no room for it. "Get the hell off me!"

The guy didn't wait for a response; already primed, he sent the first haymaker, a big right. Wren smoothly ducked it, the punch sailed harmlessly to his right, and he rose up into a neat side chokehold, forearm across the guy's throat and left arm up beside his head before he knew what was going on.

The guy went berserk. Lashing out. Spinning. Roaring, pulling others out of their own private fury and forcing them to take notice. Several pulled out their phones to film the struggle. A floodlight from one of the helicopters splashed down to illuminate the scene; better than Wren could have asked for.

A bullhorn bellowed from above, but Wren ignored it, restricting the guy's blood flow, until he began to veer and one knee went out. Wren let the grip drop, spun around while the guy was still dizzy, kneeled in front of him and took hold of his temples.

"Look into my face," Wren hissed. "You know who I am. I'm the reason you're all here. What's my name?"

The guy weaved. Someone in the crowd nearby shrieked, it could have been a name, but too high-pitched to make out. Here was always the moment that took a leap, forcing the brain back to rationality. Dragging people from the grip of extreme emotion and return them to being thinking people again, capable of assessing the impact of their actions.

The guy's lips framed words. It looked like anger. He was winding up for another punch, then something shifted in his eyes. The rage tamped out, replaced by confusion.

"Wait," he slurred, "you're..."

"Say it," Wren encouraged. A tight-packed crowd had circled to watch them now, with the helicopter lights highlighting the performance, and Wren's drone closing in filming it from above.

"Christopher Wren," the guy said.

A gasp went through the crowd. Wren raised his voice, now he was speaking to them all. "Again."

"Christopher Wren!' the guy shouted.

"And do you know why I'm here?"

Making them think. Forcing the anger back into its cage.

"I, uh," the guy's eyes rolled. "To crush the Deep State?"

"No," Wren shouted, then flung the question wider by looking up at his new audience, picking out their eyes one after another. "Do any of you know?"

They didn't. Someone a row or two back shouted something about saving the Foundation. Someone spilled choice curse words. No one in the front row spoke, because they were right there, because Wren could see their faces, and when you were an individual, not a mob member, you transformed. You were suddenly responsible for everything you said and did, and the spotlight glare of Wren's gaze was burning the fury off them.

"To save them," Wren said, growing louder as he went, channeling his own anger into this. "The Deep State. And to save you. I said it on the video and I'll say it now; you are not each other's enemies. They are not my enemy. They may think they are, but they're children, and I don't fight children. Are you children too?"

Wren looked back at the guy. There was something like the light of understanding in his eyes. Converting in the moment, gifted faith by the cult leader's touch. Maybe sign him up for the Foundation when all this was done.

"I said are you children too?"

"No," a woman shouted. Angry at him now. Young, maybe a college student, smart enough to see when she was being insulted.

"Then don't act like children! This is what he wants. He wants you fighting amongst yourselves, so you don't see what he's doing. How many people die here today, do you think? Does it end here, or does it just get bigger, spreading across the country until it's all we can think about, and who's watching our backs when that happens?"

They were struggling to keep up. Good. Rational thought was what he needed most of all now, filtering into their adrenaline-addled minds.

"I know you're outraged by that video. You should be, but think for a moment. Do you really believe your government is burning my Foundation alive?" He let that hang. "Do you really think they've got balls big enough to take me on?"

Somebody laughed. A beautiful reaction. If you were laughing, you certainly weren't rioting. Time to push that home.

"They're not geniuses," Wren went on, looking around at his audience. "They don't know what they're doing, so you have to take responsibility for yourself, and right now you are on the brink of the biggest mistake of your life. Do you want to kill someone today, and carry that for the rest of your life? Burn a car, loot stores, destroy innocent people's livelihoods? Will you tell that story to your kids, maybe, or your mother on her deathbed? I'm giving you the chance to turn that story around and get on the right side of this. Don't you want to take that chance?"

They stared. He had them. He was the guy this was all for, after all, the man whose name they'd been screen-printing onto their t-shirts and painting on the sides of barns.

"So stop," he said. "That's all I want. Take one knee like my friend right here." Wren released the guy's jacket and patted his shoulder. "Take a knee in silent protest and teach the rest how it's done. Don't sink to violence against children. Don't exhaust yourself fighting ghosts."

They stared. Wren stared back. It would just take one. His eyes snapped back and forth between the angry girl and the boy who'd laughed. Likely they'd be one of his leaders. It was neither in the end. It was an elderly woman wearing a red cape and white handmaid's bonnet.

"Sort these pigs out, Christopher," she spat, then knelt with more gusto than Wren figured her knees could stand. She then immediately began to harangue the others to kneel too.

They did. Every one of them.

Wren stood. Now he could see a little further over their heads. The riot was climbing higher; there were fires everywhere as more cars went up, floodlights spiraling, smoke and tear gas stinging in hot helicopter downdrafts, gunfire cracking out along with the thunder of rotor blades, bullhorns blaring with shouts and screams answering back, but right here there was an oasis of calm.

"Thank you," he said, then pushed through their line and back into the crowd to do it all over again.

26

ACTION

Faces blurred into a stream around him. He hooked more large men and worked the same trick. Some listened early, others listened late, but they all listened when he made them. Each group took minutes and exhausted him. Bringing down furious people took all the energy he could muster.

"The circles are spreading," Hellion said in his ear as he staggered through the crowd, meeting rage-burnished cheeks with his gentle hands, meeting rage-filled eyes with his own calm gaze. "Thirty percent."

"And the drones?" he called back, staggering now into a circle of people nursing injuries; people beaten by batons or struck by rubber bullets, people with eyes streaming from tear gas and blood streaking down their skin.

"I'm corralling as I can," Hellion answered. "There are four main off-shoot groups from here, one each way up Wilshire Boulevard, one along the 405, one spreading around the VA Hospital. Across the city we've got dozens of smaller uprisings; a shopfront's burning in Westchester, there's gangs hurling Molotov cocktails in Watts, cars upturned in Fashion District."

Even hearing the areas took it out of him. His lips felt numb, his throat hurt and his heart pounded dangerously fast. "Are they listening to you?"

"They listen when the drones start talking. They look at their phones and some are kneeling. The message is spreading across the country, Christopher. New York was lighting up, but that's slowing now. Indianapolis has riots, but the temperature's dropping. Keep doing what you're doing."

Keep doing what you're doing.

He worked the injured people. No chokehold was required to keep their attention, but it was hard to see their wounds and their shell-shocked faces. They were angrier than the others, maybe, more afraid, more outraged. The riot police, the Deep State, they didn't seem like children to them. Wren couldn't make the same arguments, so he made new ones, giving away more of himself with every passing second.

At last they kneeled, and he lurched to the next section of the crowd to begin again, keeping the chain reaction going by sheer force of will, barreling past 'overdrawn' and 'running on fumes' to the stage where he was running only on memory and willpower, barely thinking, each time scooping deep inside to serve up enough honesty to earn their belief.

"It's all over the news," Hellion crowed in his ear. He didn't even know where he was anymore, lost in a perpetual fog of violence and fire. It felt like he'd been doing this for a lifetime, like there was no end in sight. "They're showing your feed live. Nobody can believe it, they've never seen anything like it before. The tide is turning against the Federal response, Christopher, and picking up speed. This thing is swinging fast."

He kept on. He didn't feel it. The fires still burned, the air still throbbed with chaos. His own words lost any sense of meaning but still he kept saying them.

"Looks like seventy percent and spreading, Christopher," came the high voice in his ear. "It looks beautiful from above, like fractal crop circles in a field of corn. You have to see it."

He couldn't see it. All he could do was stumble to the next group, to the next, to the next, heart hammering, legs giving out, head pounding.

"Christopher," Hellion cautioned, "you're moving too close to the riot police. You need to back off."

He didn't hear her. Even if he did, he had no idea what she meant. This ocean of people was infinite, his own penance for all the violence he'd done. Endlessly talking people down from a rage he felt himself. Face after face, group after group, he was the cautionary tale to turn them aside and he couldn't stop working now. Stop for a second, even change direction, and he might collapse. He had nothing left, but Rogers' dead eyes drove him on, bursting into flame every time he blinked his eyes.

"Christopher!" Hellion warned.

Then he was there. At the edge, staring into the grim faces of riot police officers holding their shields in a tight line. They wore tactical black with visored helmets, rifles at their sides. Like a scent trail of ants, said Wren's broken mind. At their back vehicles rumbled closer, floodlights on their roofs.

He was back in the Sonoran Desert escaping Humphreys again. All the lights focused on him now. The helicopters swung around above, tracking him. No escaping from this. Forced at last to answer for his many crimes. Show the darkness to the light, and let the napalm burn.

The lights grew brighter than day. He became aware of a spreading silence. Beyond the churn of the helicopters, the gunfire had stopped. The cries of the crowd, the bullhorns, the screams, they were gone. The grandest stage of his life, with no energy left at all for the performance.

How many cameras pointing his way now?

The Greatest Show on Earth.

He remembered what his father had whispered to him in the desert, and it forced a fresh burst of anger.

'You know what's real, don't you?'

Here was where it happened. Bending the world. He turned to face the crowd

An ocean of faces stared back at him. All kneeling. Stretched back across the lot as far as he could see. People up on the 405 gazing down, where traffic had stopped. People on nearby rooftops, people leaning out of windows.

So this was what it felt like to be a real cult leader. Time to say something good.

He raised his arms, and opened his mouth to speak.

27

SOMETHING GOOD

"I'm your poster boy," he boomed, following his intuition into the dark. No amplification, using only the cult leader's firebrand voice he'd inherited. "I'm Christopher Wren. You painted my name on your barns. You screen-printed my face on your t-shirts. You're here for me and my Foundation, so listen to me when I'm telling you, this whole thing stinks. You're fighting the wrong people. We are not enemies here today. The 'Deep State' works for you."

He spun back to the cordon line of riot police. "These people here are not your enemy," he bellowed. "You serve at their pleasure. You should be protecting them, not fighting them, sowing wounds that will take generations to heal." He paused and ran his gaze along the police line. "I think we will all regret what happens here tonight, if we don't stop now. We will regret turning on each other, when the real hard times come, when the real enemy shows his face, because you think this is bad? He's just getting started. You don't want to know how dark this is going to get."

He gazed into the eyes of the police officers in front of him, through the glaring lights and past their tinted riot visors direct to their brains.

"My father ordered me to kill a thousand people in Arizona, and I did it, even though I knew it was wrong. A thousand people dead in the streets, how could that not be wrong?" Abruptly he beat his chest. "I should have stopped, but I didn't, and now I carry that shame forever. You don't want that. The Apex wanted me for his messenger, so here is my message."

He took a breath. It came hard. The flow of energy pouring off the crowd and through him was tearing him to pieces.

"Stand down."

Several flinched. None took a step back.

"Stand down," Wren repeated. "Unless you want to incite a massacre like nothing this country has ever seen. Ignore the voices in your headset ordering you on. There's nobody to defeat but ourselves. We have to be bigger than this, we have to stand together, or we will all fall when the true storm comes."

He could feel them beginning to bend. As riled up as they were, they didn't want to fight for nothing.

"Stand down," he said for the third time. "You are not my enemy, so stop acting as if you are. These people are not your enemy. My father is a genius at disinformation, a real Wizard of Oz for the modern day, but we get to choose if we listen to him. We don't have to let him push our buttons. There's a better way, and we'll all be stronger for it."

Now there were ripples through the crowd at his back, clamors agreeing with him, an attempt at a 'USA' chant. Wren pressed on.

"I don't think you want to assault these citizens. You will regret it for as long as he lets you live. Stand down, and I promise you there will be no riot. We chalk this one up to experience and we move on."

Wren saw the sweat pouring down the officers' cheeks. It was a hard sell. Just moments ago this mob had been hurling fiery bottles, smashing their bodies against the shield line and coming back for more. It required trust.

"Intercepting their comms," Hellion said. "I think I hear Humphreys' voice, shouting at the group commanders. I warned you about him, Christopher."

Wren didn't say anything, he just held the moment, fulcrum upon which the riots swung.

"He's dead against this," Hellion went on, "says it's the visual he wanted least of all; you with your arms outspread, the messiah spreading peace throughout the masses, indoctrinating the country into your cult."

Wren snorted.

"Not much he can do about it, though, is there?" she added. "Idiot."

Wren took a step forward. That was enough time spent listening to Humphreys; time now to move the fulcrum point. The line had to break somewhere, and it was always easiest dead ahead.

"Please," Wren called. "Don't only listen to your commanders. They're blind with anger and pride. You have to have the clear heads now. Illegal orders are illegal, and it's your duty to know the difference. These people don't want to fight you." He waved his arm at the kneeling masses. "They want you on their side against this injustice. So be on their side!"

A shudder passed through the riot police line. Wren drove into it. "This could be the greatest moment of your life. Look at the people ahead of you and make the right choice."

The moment stretched out. Wren stared at them, willing it to happen. It would just take one, then others would follow.

"I don't think it's going to work," Hellion said in his ear.

"It will work," Wren answered quietly.

"I can hack the line with a fake Humphreys voice, order them to-"

"No," Wren rasped. "Don't even think about it."

"It would work, they'll-"

"It needs to be their decision! We can't fake this, Hellion."

She went silent. Wren just stared. He couldn't hold the mob at bay for much longer. If he didn't get a result, the rioting would start up again. He'd be washed away in the tide.

"Stand down!" he tried one more time.

It was enough. There was movement on the left of the riot police line. Helicopter floodlights shifted, the drone above Wren's head flew over. The shield wall had broken. A police officer was backing away, shield discarded, hands up. The others pressed close to fill the gap, but still the crowd cheered. Wren held his hands up for silence and they quieted.

As if in response to that another shield dropped on the right, and one dead ahead, then suddenly the wall just melted. On camera. The power of the 'Deep State' deflected without force. Everyone saw it, and Wren felt himself melting along with them. Heart racing. Barely able to hold himself up a moment longer.

"It's happening everywhere!" Hellion cheered. "Christopher, you were right, and I could kiss you."

It took everything he had to keep standing. Grim-faced, like the sculpture at the prow of a ship as the black wall dissolved.

"Humphreys is throwing a hissy-fit!" Hellion sounded overjoyed. "I think I will-"

"Don't do anything," Wren said low but firm. "No celebrations."

"But-"

"Hellion. Trust me on this."

She grumbled and more keys flew. "Now the President is overriding her advisors. The order's been made official. The National Guard are pulling back."

Wren grunted. The first of the helicopters yanked its floodlight off him and hammered away.

The applause rose up. He thought to try and halt it, but he didn't have the strength, and maybe that was all right, it didn't feel like gloating. He turned slowly, and now the sound roared like a hurricane, spreading with the relief of what had just happened.

Not exactly victory. Not exactly defeat. Bigger than either. The sound washed over him like a cool rain, hitting harder than he could have expected. It plucked out tears that rolled down his cheeks unbidden. Always it was the kindness that hurt the most.

"My God," said Hellion in his ear, different now, the gloating of victory replaced by something like awe. "It is all of them. Christopher, what have you done?"

It took him a moment to understand what she meant, then he saw the first of the police officers walking into the crowd. Kneeling people opened a path before her, uncertain still, maybe afraid, until the woman turned and dropped to her knees amongst them.

The cheering reached another level. More riot police officers followed, their shields and batons dropped behind. They were greeted with hearty claps on the shoulder and such an upswell of joy.

Wren kneeled to join them.

The storm became an avalanche. A celebration of oneness. He was no better than them, no worse than them, just another one in their midst.

After that everything blurred. His legs moved, and he found arms helping him along. Strong hands lifted and guided him forward.

"Hellion," he managed to say, faint with the exertion. "I'm going to pass out."

"The Mercedes is clear," she answered. "I'm blocking all video coverage of you right now. There'll be no footage leading back. Looks like your cheerleaders have you until then."

He tried to snort but couldn't muster the breath. Nameless, faceless cheerleaders. No Gruber coming to pick him up in his yellow Prius this time. No Rogers winging in on a jet. Tandrews had told him to build a new team; how was this?

The crowd passed him hand to hand like he was floating on a cloud, like they knew exactly where he was going. The Mercedes was waiting. Sinking into the driving seat felt like falling into a dream. The engine revved like a purring cat. Only Hellion's voice giving the turns in his ear kept him afloat, as LA became a streaming black blur at his back.

28

ALONE

Wren woke in the Mercedes to dark and silence, haunted by memories that felt too fresh: faces burning one after another in the fake town; his children staring at him in the wreck of their den in Great Kills; Sally Rogers' lost eyes as she erupted in flame.

He was slumped in the driver's seat, halfway cranked back. Through the windshield all he saw were stars, wheeling slowly across the sky. In the Pyramid he'd learned all the constellations, then re-learned them when his father had spent a summer renaming every last one.

His body ached. He reached up and tapped his earpiece, but there was no sound. He had vague memories of Hellion directing him out into the desert, driving him just a little further, a little further until at last the battery gave out and he kept on until the Mercedes coughed to a halt, somewhere off the highway amongst sand and cacti.

He shuffled in his pocket for the phone; dead. Everything in the car was dead. He felt like he'd been buried alive beneath a sky full of lies. He'd held off his father's plans for one more night, the unstoppable desire of the Apex to burn America down, but this wasn't the end.

Steven Gruber remained, next in line to die.

For three months he hadn't thought once about his father. The interrogations had kept him too busy, but this freight train of pain had been coming for him anyway, its lonely horn sounding all across the still country, and now the weight of it hit him at once. Rogers and Jay were dead. The Apex was back. His family were not waiting for him to come home, like he'd led himself to believe.

He was more alone than ever. He watched the stars slowly scroll across the sky. The grandest things happened so slowly. It had taken twenty-five years, but now the Apex was coming back.

He closed his eyes. He was too tired to do this now.

A barrage woke him. It took long, pounding moments to recognize what it was. Rain, falling across the dark desert. The sky was a murky black silt, like industrial run-off smothering the stars. He couldn't afford to sleep any more, even though his head felt ready to burst, his back throbbed, his temples, his hips.

He opened the door, held his hand out and caught a puddle of rain in his palm. It tasted like dust. His lips were cracked and dry.

Around 2 a.m., judging by the fuzz of light from the pole star. Dark desert lay on all sides. His mind turned slow. Not the Sonoran. Drive for hours out of LA and he'd hit Joshua Tree, the Mojave, even Death Valley. He didn't remember the directions he'd taken, only Hellion urging him on.

He'd get out and walk. He couldn't be far from the highway. Hitch-hike, get another phone, another vehicle and keep on trying. He tried to get up, but couldn't.

His legs didn't respond, like he was frozen in place. Not just his body, but his mind was drained. He felt wrung out and used up. Five minutes, he promised. In five minutes he'd go. For now he just lay there, one arm out the door with the cold rain falling across his chest. The air felt charged, like a storm was coming on.

He closed his eyes to the pain, and unconsciousness pulled at him like heavy wool shackles. He barely noticed the rain as it stopped streaming down his cheeks, though he heard the steady pattering sound of it on the roof of the Mercedes still, shushing over the sand and stroking the bulbous arms of Joshua trees.

When he heard the voice say his name, he didn't even need to open his eyes to know who it was.

"Christopher."

She was standing over him with an umbrella open. He hadn't heard her approach, as ever. She looked much the same as when he'd seen her last, after he'd brought the Blue Fairy orphans to her camp in the Arizona desert, sprung up in the ruins of the Pyramid's ribs.

Maggie.

Something good from something bad.

She wore the same tans, browns and burned ochre shades as always, a scarf, a blouse, a Shaker-like shawl; part archaeologist, part professor, part pastor for the past.

"A woman named 'Hellion' called me," she said. "She said it was urgent, that you needed help."

He could just about handle that. As long as he didn't try to say anything back, he could handle the kindness; Hellion calling Maggie, and Maggie responding. Even the look in her eyes, part pity, part affection that he hadn't earned, he could handle that too, as long as she didn't-

"I didn't think I'd find anything out here, but here you are. Come on now, Christopher. It's time to come home."

Home. That broke the dam.

"Here," she said, and took him by the arm. She was stronger than she looked, and pulled him to his feet. She held the umbrella high to shelter him from the rain. He stumbled along at her side, too hurt to say a word. There was an RV nearby, a blue VW bus with people in it. Children? Wren could barely see for the tears.

She fed him into the back, where there was a gurney laid out. He sagged onto it. Little hands touched his cheeks, children he'd rescued so long ago, now guiding him down into the dark.

29

ESSENTIAL BAROMETERS

Until the age of nine, the life of little Pequeño 3 had been split like day from night into halves: the times when the Apex was there in the town, issuing demands, coming up with experiments and providing dawn-till-dusk lectures; and the times the Apex was away, out seeking converts to the Pyramid way of life.

Pequeño 3 had lived for the days when the Apex was away. He'd played in the desert for days, sometimes weeks at a time, utterly carefree. When the Apex was away, it always felt like the fake town was breathing out in relief. There were still countless tasks to be done, and discipline was strict if you were caught disobeying, but there were no daylong lectures, no three-day gatherings around some pit in the desert, and he'd learned to use those times well.

There were countless adventures to be had in the endless sands of Arizona. With his elders chasing him, he'd race between stands of prickly pear cacti and hydra-like ocotillo stands, weaving a path they never could keep up with. He'd always been fast and quick-witted, hiding when he couldn't run, tossing sand or stones as distractions when he couldn't hide, and none of the cult tried too hard to chase him down. He was the Apex's favored son, after all.

At the end of each day, burnished bronze by sun and sated with wild adventures amongst the roadrunners and snakes, stuffed on hand-roasted bark scorpions and stone-peeled prickly pear fruits, he'd always come back to the town and accept his beating with a down-turned head and the deepest penitence, only to spend half the night plotting his escapades for the days to come.

And he was not always alone.

Few of the town's children adventured as widely or as frequently as he did, but then few of the Apex's children were treated so favorably. Next in line were the other Pequeños, five older than him, three younger, but his elders were teens who'd been granted 'true' names and took their town responsibilities too seriously to play.

'Keeping records of essential barometers', the Apex called the tasks he gave them, and always scrutinized these records with great interest upon his return: how many times clouds passed across the sun in any given day, notched into pieces of wood; how many fireflies lit up in the town at night, recorded as knots in a length of string; how often the townsfolk said simple words such as 'Good morning' to each other, transcribed as grains of sand heaped upon a tin pan.

These were all important works, little Pequeño 3 understood that as well as any. The Apex occasionally gave long recitations of the results, and used them to develop predictions of days to come. Those were some of the better lectures, and always felt like flights of fancy, like his adventures in the desert, battling the evil forces of the 'FBI', monsters who wore the faces of men but in truth had black hearts filled with grasshopper legs.

Pequeño 3 looked forward to the day he too would be entrusted with the transcriptions, but until that day came, he largely ignored his older brothers and sisters, just as they ignored him.

The younger Pequeños were barely more than babies. The eldest was four, and even Pequeño 3 knew you didn't take a four-year-old out exploring in the desert. They were for the cages behind the façade of the saloon, where experiments were conducted around the clock.

There were other children in the town though, not only Pequeños. These were granted a sliding scale of respect and freedom based upon complex calculations the Apex himself worked out over time, based on their needs, his needs, and the number of bullfrogs croaking on a given May night. The Apex always had a number for everything.

The best of the children all had been 'Grace-In-our-Times', or simply Grace, as Pequeño 3 liked to call her. She was his age or close to it, a 'naughty little mulatto' the Apex would often affectionately call her, and she loved nothing more than escaping out into the desert and making mud pies.

Their conversations were simple and straight-forward. Between her water-gathering duties and his role in gathering all the black stones from the sands around the town, they only had to give each other a meaningful eye, and mouth the word 'Pies', to set off a rush of excitement that soon saw them charging out into the sands, carrying empty water bottles.

"I figure you ain't a real Pequeño," she'd say sometimes, as they walked hand in hand through the towering yellow chollas, handwaving yuccas and spidery organ pipes toward the old red stone creek.

"I am a Pequeño," he'd protest.

"I figure you's more of a mulatto," she'd answer. "Pretty boy like you."

He'd laugh. Everyone knew 'pretty boy' and 'pretty girl' were pet names the Apex reserved for his own use.

Her hand was always hot in his own, like she was forever running a fever. She had lovely dark brown hair that framed her pudgy, chaff-brown cheeks. Sometimes, before they got to the dried-up creek under the big red cliff, he'd just walk along looking at her face, thinking what it might be like to call her his 'pretty girl'.

He'd never been a 'pretty boy' for the Apex. The others weren't allowed to talk about it, so he didn't really knew what it was, but it always ached like a beating on his heart.

"Race you to the creek," he'd say, and give her a shove, and they'd race away. As revenge she'd dunk his head in the puddle of mud, once they'd spent a good hour mixing it up with various seeds, bits of colorful sand, scrapings off cacti and pieces of broken insect shell.

The mud was always warm on his head. He'd scrape it off and say, "Mmm. Delicious."

She usually fell for it. Her big round eyes would get all wide and she'd lean in. "It is not."

"Try it yourself," he'd say.

Long moments of delightful anticipation followed. After 'cooking' the pie for an hour, bustling back and forth collecting and preparing the ingredients, how it tasted became the most important thing of all. And every time it was different.

Pequeño 3 licked his lips. It never tasted like anything much, but that wasn't how you played the game. Like the Apex's experiments, this was all about 'being the master of your own senses'. He'd talk about that endlessly in his long lectures.

"Strawberries," I figure, Pequeño 3 would say, and Grace would make a sweet face like she didn't believe him, wrinkled up and full of doubt.

"Bet you've never had a strooberry!"

He laughed because she said 'strooberry'. It didn't matter how many times he corrected her.

"I so did. Strooberries and bug juice."

Her eyes widened again. "Good bug juice or fat bug juice?"

"Good bug juice with biscuit bits."

She shuddered and hugged herself.

"Try it yourself," he'd say again, and there'd be a big back and forth about her not wanting to, not daring to, being afraid to upset the Apex if he ever found out she'd eaten strawberries without his permission. Finally, she always would, and waiting for her reaction became the best thing for little Pequeño 3, watching her eyes like he was Pequeño 4 studying the sky for kangaroo-shaped clouds.

She knew it too, and would always drag the moment out. The waiting was wondrous in itself, moments filled with possibility, when they weren't prisoners in a desert cult, beaten on the Apex's whims, abused, humiliated and neglected. In those moments, reality belonged to them.

When Grace was done drawing it out, she'd loudly pronounce, "Delicious, just like strooberries," or be more scathing, saying things like, "it tastes just like poo!"

You couldn't win them all. Whatever the taste, it always ended in a mud fight, then a race and some climbing up the red stone, then the long trek back to the town, where he'd take his beating and she'd be tucked into bed without any supper.

She was the best thing about the Pyramid to little Pequeño 3, so when the Apex came back one day from one of his long trips away, and said there would be another pit, and this time the pit would be filled with children as a test of their purity and faith, he knew he had to go into the pit with her.

30

ONIONS

Wren was on his feet before he was fully awake. Dreams of some distant past rushed through him, but he shrugged off the old pain and turned, seeing wooden walls, a chair, homespun blankets on a farmhouse bed, rustic cupboards, a window. He shook himself, strode to pull the curtain open, and saw something that struck him dumb.

The fake town. Transported as if from his dreams.

Bright ochre sand flowed like a river down the broad central avenue, lined either side with wooden structures straight out of a cowboy movie; the hardware store, the bar, the brothel, the saloon with swing doors, all rebuilt, with the cavities where he'd burned buildings down now filled with fresh, raw wood façades.

For long seconds he stared, taking it all in. It felt like just moments ago that he'd been in LA settling the crowd. Now he was here, back where it had all started. He rubbed his eyes and spun the map in his head. North, south, east, west. He had to be in the hotel, now. Site of some of the Apex's worst experiments.

A shudder ran through him. Back then the hotel had just been a wooden face propped up with scaffolding. The real action happened in trailers pulled flush to the walls in back. The challenges set to all the children of the Pyramid, the ways he'd spend their lives on long observations of meaningless trivia.

He'd forgotten, but it came flooding back, and he shook his head to clear them. The memories surged still, shaken loose twenty-five years later. If he stared at the main street long enough, he started to see the ghosts of the past moving along it: the other Pequeños, the other children, the girl he'd known only as 'Grace'.

Enough. The past belonged in the past.

He pulled on a pair of jeans and a t-shirt resting on a chair then pushed open the door. There was the sound of music lilting from nearby. He strode along a wooden-walled corridor, passing several classrooms where children sat at desks studying, or sat circled practicing musical instruments. There were teachers in each room. The children were hushed and focused; none of them noticed him peering in.

That hush pushed into him too, like he had no right to interrupt any of this. Mid-morning, he guessed. A clock on the ground floor confirmed it, just past 10 a.m., well into the school day. Why should anything change just because he was here?

On the ground floor he saw more classrooms and a large empty hall, and at the end of a corridor a bustling kitchen where three cooks were busy chopping vegetables and braising meat and pouring ingredients into large pots. They glanced his way then looked back to their work.

Seeing this brought on more flashes to the Pyramid days; the vats behind the hotel where people were once half-boiled alive, with the Apex watching and taking notes in fascination, filming so as not to lose a single second of data.

He rubbed his eyes. The ghosts were everywhere still.

"Excuse me," he said. "I'm looking for Maggie."

One of the cooks turned to him. Dark-skinned and broad cheeks, maybe a Native Mexican, twenty-five, with her hair pulled into twin pigtails. There was a flash of annoyance in her eyes, and Wren found he enjoyed that. After the mass audience at the Wilshire, it felt good to be treated like he was no one.

"Did you check in at reception?" she asked sharply.

He bobbed his head slightly. "No ma'am, I came in last night. I'm a friend of Maggie's."

The woman snorted. "She's your friend, why she's not here when you wake your big old head?"

Big old head? "If you could just tell me where she is, then-"

"What you think, I'm her secretary?"

"No ma'am," he answered gravely, "I can see you're a cook, no doubt a fine one, what I'm-"

"Now you call me a cook? ¡No mames, puto! I'm a chef, big head, not a cook."

Puto? One of the other cooks laughed. "Ma'am, I'm a Federal agent in pursuit of-"

"Federal agent my ass!" she shouted. "Everybody know you're some lost soul, boy, don't be faking yourself up." She wagged a wooden spoon at him. The effect was unintentionally hilarious and somehow cheered him up.

"Ma'am, please, if you'd put the spoon down-"

"She's only teasing you," one of the other cooks interrupted. Wren turned to her; short and round as a ball cactus, white as Arctic charr, but with a spreading smile. "We all know who you are. Coral over there's just angry because you choked her brother half-to-death six months back. She doesn't forgive easy."

Wren blinked. It took him a second to remember; the first time he'd come here, he'd taken out one of Maggie's men with a clothesline to the throat. He turned back to the angry cook, Coral. "That was your brother? I am sorry I did that. It was my misunderstanding. I hope he's all right now?"

"None the better for knowing you, pendejo," she spat.

Fair.

"Actually, Maggie said you might pop in here," the cactus ball cook said swiftly, cutting off the awkward exchange.

"That's great, can you tell me where she is?"

"Out," she said. "And there's no use you chasing her, she said to tell you as much. She's gone to fetch you tiny batteries."

That confused him for a moment. "Tiny batteries?"

"That's right." She pointed at a dish on the work surface nearby, which contained his earpiece, his bodycam and the pink Pixel phone. Wren picked up the Pixel and pushed the power button, but it was just as dead as it'd been in the Benz the night before, likewise for the earpiece and cam.

"We don't have the batteries for any of them," she went on, "so Maggie's gone to buy replacements."

Wren nodded. Tiny little batteries. He slipped the gear into his pocket, thinking ahead. A trip out from the fake town wasn't like a stroll to the nearest convenience store; it had to be a hundred miles to the nearest town, on dirt roads through Hopi Reservation land. That presented a problem, because he needed to get up to date right now.

"What about your phones, could I use one? Or a computer with an internet line? I don't know what Maggie's told you, but there's things I need to urgently-"

"I'm sorry," said the ball cactus woman. "There's no internet here. It's part of the deal. We're off grid."

Wren stared at her, like she was speaking Ancient Greek. "No internet?"

"We focus on the now." The third cook, a heavyset man in back, raised his head from chopping potatoes just long enough to make eye contact. "It's good for the children."

Good for the children. No internet. Wren searched for an out. "You must have something for emergencies."

"There is an emergency phone," Ball Cactus allowed, briefly raising Wren's hopes. "But Maggie took it. We've got everything else we need here; doctors, supplies, equipment. But Maggie should be back in an hour or two. Until then, there's not much to be done but shell peas for lunch."

Shell peas? "I may not be a Federal agent anymore, but this is a national security emergency. If I can't get hold-"

"No national security emergency's gonna conjure up a phone," Coral snapped abruptly, wagging her wooden spoon at him again. A piece of mashed potato flicked off the end. "You wait for Maggie like you been told, and you make yourself useful, you chop while you wait."

She pointed the spoon at a wooden crate piled with brown-shelled onions.

"I need a vehicle," he said.

"We could do that," Ball Cactus said. "Except last I heard, Maggie plans to requisition the old weather 'copter out of Eloy. If you wait, that'll be faster getting out of here than any pickup we can loan you."

Wren's jaw tightened.

"Make yourself useful," said Coral, and tossed him a long kitchen knife. She looked disappointed when he plucked it expertly out of the air. "Them onions aren't going to chop themselves, and some of these kids can't chew for shit."

Wren looked at the knife; it was decent, cold pressed steel, no kind of guard, but it'd serve well enough. He slipped it into his pocket without thinking further. There was a fruit bowl beside his phone; he scooped up two oranges and an apple, nodded at Ball Cactus, then strode out.

"Did that big head fool just take my knife?" Coral's outraged voice floated after him, along with the laughter of the ball cactus. Wren took a big bite of the apple and strode out into the sun.

31

LITTLE PHOENIX

Wren paced east along the main street. The wooden buildings stretched for a hundred yards, after which it was all construction; what looked to be a library going up, a sports center with an outdoor swimming pool pre-dug, camp-style cabins, a church. Last time he'd been here all this had been concrete foundation platforms, left behind after he'd burned the wooden buildings down.

He kept walking. His head throbbed and raced, but the sweet nectar of the fruit helped. He licked sticky orange juice off his fingers, feeling the sun burn down on his face and arms. After the new construction ran out, there were the graves. Large granite slabs inscribed with the names of the Pyramid lost.

Maggie had been searching for them for almost two years by now. Digging up bones from the remnants of the Apex's pits. All his experiments. Executions. Femurs and ribs scattered to the winds and feasted on by coyotes and dingoes. She'd gathered them, DNA-tested them, consecrated then reburied them.

At the far edge he stopped and looked back, noticing for the first time a new town sign at the limits.

LITTLE PHOENIX

He smiled. Why not?

He peeled the second orange and bit into it directly. Cold sweet juice ran down his chin. How many times had he stood here as a boy, hands full of black stones, looking at the fake town as if it was the whole of the world?

He couldn't imagine how it would feel for the children here, now.

"Mister."

He turned, and for a long moment thought he was staring into some kind of time-slip mirror. A boy was right there, around twelve years old, nut brown from the sun with a fuzzy crop of black hair standing up in a mud-flecked shock atop his head.

"Hey," Wren said.

"You're not supposed to stand there," the boy said, pointing.

Wren looked down. He was standing on one of the Pyramid graves. He hadn't even realized, had just taken up his old position, looking out to where the sun would set on the other side of the town.

"Sorry," he said, and shuffled sideways.

"Say a prayer," the boy said.

"Amen."

The boy frowned. "That's not a prayer. But that's OK. I remember you."

Wren swallowed that down. There was only one place any of these children would remember him from, the Pleasure Island slave-ship he'd rescued them from.

"You get to do pretty much what you like around here, far as I care," the boy said. "After all that."

Wren just nodded; he didn't trust himself to speak. All that. This boy had witnessed him killing hundreds of Pinocchios, one after another. He must've been one of the throng of kids following after him, killing the men he'd left wounded behind.

Now here he was; healthy, fit, free, and giving Wren permission.

"Shouldn't you be in school?"

The boy just looked at him. Looked through him, really. Thousand-yard stare in a child. "You want some more fruit? Seems like you're awful fond of those."

Wren looked at his hands. In one hand he still held the bare nub of the apple core, in the other he held the orange peel. Back in the Pyramid days, the Apex had hated nothing more than untidiness. Litter was strictly barred as a sign of an untidy mind; the greatest crime possible.

"Sure," he managed.

"And water, maybe?" the boy asked.

"Yeah." It came out as more of a gasp.

"Meat too? Bread?"

Wren nodded.

"I'll be back."

The boy scampered away a few yards, then turned back and looked at him a long moment. "Thank you. You know. For what you did."

Wren couldn't think of anything to say to that. The boy turned and ran before he could remedy it. For a minute or two he stood there, battling old emotions. Hellion had sent him here on purpose, he figured. There were countless other places he could've holed up within range of LA, but she'd decided this was what he needed. It showed an impressive degree of empathy, at least for Hellion. Maybe she'd learned something from Dr. Ferat, after all.

The boy came running back soon enough, holding a wicker picnic basket. He grinned.

"Swiped these off Coral. I heard you met her? She's awful."

Wren smiled. "We exchanged a few words."

"She said you took her knife."

Wren winked and patted his pocket. "It's my knife now."

The boy laughed and set the basket down. He opened the top and pulled out a red check picnic blanket which he smoothed across the sand, then set atop it a plastic tub of what looked like roast pork, a slab of cheese, half a loaf of bread, a generous pad of butter, a tub of steamed broccoli, a glass bottle of milk and another of water, two more apples and a steaming corn on the cob.

Wren laughed as the items kept coming. A plate, a glass, a knife and fork. The kid had done speedy work.

"Here you go," the boy said when it was all out. "I figured you were hungry. I saw them bringing you in last night. I had most of this ready in the pantry; been watching for you to come out all morning. I thought you'd never get out of that kitchen."

"They tried to make me chop onions," Wren said.

The boy laughed. "Coral's a tough one, I'll say that. She topped up your milk though, added the best cream. You did good to slip away, though."

"Sounds like you did too."

The boy shrugged. "I'm fast. And they're not all that bad."

That was good to hear. Wren surveyed the picnic. It was a real feast, but only one plate. One glass. "Aren't you going to join me?"

Again the kid flashed a smile. "I'm supposed to be in school. You said it yourself. Maggie won't be pleased if I get caught out here lollygagging."

Wren smiled. "How is it here? Do you like it?"

The grin became a halogen beam. "Best place I've ever been. Now, you eat up, and I have to go to class. See you, Mr. Wren."

The boy turned and ran. It took Wren a second to call out for him to stop. "Wait. What's your name?"

The boy turned. "They let us pick, if we wanted. Our old names were busted, you know? Used up." Wren's throat went dry. He could guess what was coming now.

"So?"

"I chose Christopher Wren," the boy said, "after you. Just like you chose it after another great man. I like it. It suits us both."

He ran. He didn't stop again, didn't even look back, just disappeared into the hotel, to join his classes and get on with his life and move forward.

Everything was moving forward, and that buoyed Wren up. Out here in the fake town, in Little Phoenix, hope felt like a real thing. The Apex's madness had been purged and the things that were growing in its place were truly beautiful.

The meal was beautiful too. Wren was famished. He sat cross-legged on the town's outskirts, beside the graves, and tucked in.

32

MAGGIE

Within an hour Wren heard the drumbeat of an approaching helicopter. A few minutes later it coalesced on the northern horizon, an ultralight two-seater, looked like a Robinson R22. He packed up the picnic basket and dropped it off outside the kitchen, then strode west to where the helicopter was touching down.

Sand blew in his face as Maggie got out and the rotors spun down.

"Christopher," she called over the dying chop of the blades.

"Maggie," he said. He vaguely remembered seeing her the night before, but that was little better than a dream. Now in the full light of day, wearing her outfit of layered browns and tans, she looked like some kind of mythical djinn grown out of the desert itself. She was beautiful in her way, with dark almond eyes and thick black hair, but it was the strong sense of calm command that made her larger than life, like she was utterly at home in herself, in this place. He imagined the children here adored her.

"How are you?" she asked, and put her hand on his arm.

"I'm fine," he said, and his voice came out more of a growl than he'd intended. She didn't seem to notice, her dark eyes took it all in stride. "Thank you for coming to get me last night. I was..." he trailed off. "I hit a low."

"I know," she said, with a slight smile. "I've seen footage from the Wilshire. What you did there was phenomenal, Christopher. It makes me incredibly proud, and I want to thank you."

He got the sense that she wanted to go on, but she stopped there anyway, and that was fine by Wren. He didn't want to talk about any of it, really, especially with the way she was looking at him, like he was one of her children in Little Phoenix, damaged to the core. Like maybe she could 'save' him.

"Have there been any more videos?" he rasped.

"Not yet," she said, and kept on gazing at him. "I did speak with your hackers, though. Isabella gave me a shopping list of items you would need, and I prepared them."

Wren was on the verge of asking who Isabella was, when he remembered. "You mean Hellion? How did you get her to tell you her real name?"

"I asked," said Maggie, with a twinkle in her eye, then held out a canvas bag. "Your shopping."

Wren put aside his disbelief and took the bag, fished around inside and came up with several packs of tiny batteries; for the earpiece, the bodycam and the phone. He set to work slotting them in place.

"She told me your people are in danger. I'm so sorry about that, Christopher. If there's anything we can do, please let me know."

The phone battery snapped satisfyingly into place. "You too, Maggie."

She smiled, and it cracked her warm brown cheeks like the clouds parting after rain. "Don't I know it." She paused for a moment, watching him work a clasp on the earpiece. "I'd attempted suicide three times before I came out here, Christopher."

It took him a second to register that, then his eyes snapped up to focus on her. She continued in the same warm, even tone.

"I don't tell people that. Despair about my family, I suppose, getting ready to follow in my uncle's tracks. He killed himself when the Pyramid stole my mother and father away. There are cut marks all over my forearms, dating back to my teens." She smiled. "It's why I wear long sleeves. Then I came out here. I used to think about you a lot, when I was growing up. I didn't know you then, of course, just your legend. If my parents had brought me here with them, maybe I would have known you. I wondered if I would have survived the fires at the end, like you." She paused a moment, looking into some private past. "Thinking like that, it made everything feel so thin. Like, not real. Do you know what I mean?"

Wren nodded mutely. He didn't trust himself to speak.

"I don't know, though. On one level, I figure I'd come out here to die. But somehow, being here, it made me feel better. As if this was a good place. So I didn't kill myself." Another knowing smile. "This town, I know it's full of horrors for you, but that's not all there is. It's also capable of so much healing."

Wren didn't know what to say to any of that. There was something more in her eyes now, a sense of yearning, perhaps, that made his cheeks hot. He wanted to say something meaningful in return, but the words didn't come.

"It's OK," she said, and spread her arms. "I found my purpose, now. It's this place, these people. I look after them, they look after me, and you look out for us all, still fighting the Apex after all this time."

His mouth went dry. His eyes prickled again; the desert heat. He cleared his throat. "I-"

"You have to go," she finished for him, and touched his arm again, sending a shudder up his spine. "Just remember, this is your home, now. It'll never belong to him again, and it will be here waiting any time you want to come stay."

He nodded, managed a swift, "Thank you, Maggie," then strode off toward the helicopter before he had time to think about it too much. The rotors fired up as he approached. He slotted the earpiece in, strapped the bodycam around his chest and booted the phone.

Maggie was watching, out on the sand. Her eyes said so much.

"Where to, boss?" the pilot shouted. A rangy, toothless old guy with a scraggly white beard.

"Up," Wren said.

33

GRACE

The Pyramid dug down.

It was another scorching summer day, after another long procession into the wilds of the desert. Little Pequeño 3 walked solemnly this time, thoughtful and afraid, weighing his two memories of the last pit, those two versions of the Apex. For months he'd taught himself to hibernate like a cicada, and he'd learned a lot.

It was one thing to survive without air for three minutes. But three days? He didn't know what that meant, and it scared him.

So the Pyramid dug. This time the bright spirit of the first expedition was gone, replaced by the hush and shush of shovels biting into hardpack. The Apex said nothing, only watched, and the walls of the pit sank. Flat stones were found and mortared in for walls. Pequeño 3 found himself looking around, in between ferrying sand in buckets away from the pit, past the spiky Buckhorn plants and the riotous explosion of yellow Palo Verde, searching for the hole that shouldn't exist.

He couldn't see it. Perhaps that meant it never had existed. The Apex had told the truth. 'You know what's real, don't you?'

He yearned to be so sure.

Across the pit he exchanged glances with Grace-In-Our-Times. She wore a polite little girl's smock and polite little girl's expression. In the fake town, she was always different. Only when they were mixing mud into pies in the desert together was she really his Grace.

By dusk the pit was complete. The Pyramid circled around it, fires lit, watching the shadows flicker, waiting for the Apex to give his decree. He kept them waiting long enough for the stars to shift position in the sky, and when he spoke it was a list of names.

"Aden-Of-The-Saints. Galicia-In-Her-Mother's-Heart. Zachariah-Of-The-Marsh. Chrysogonus-With-Bared-Arm. Gabriel-In-Extremis."

Pequeño 3 stared, along with the rest of the Pyramid. Five youths. The five elder Pequeños, gifted sacred names on their ascendance. His brothers and sisters, who spent their days taking the Apex's essential barometers.

A moment of silence passed, but the Apex was not finished. His mouth opened, and again he spoke, and this time he was looking directly at little Pequeño 3.

"Grace-In-Our-Times," he said.

Pequeño 3, Christopher Wren as he would become, only stared. He didn't open his mouth. He didn't dare. The Apex watched him closely. He nodded once, as if satisfied. Then he waited.

The Pequeños descended one by one. Chrysogonus was first, eldest, strongest in faith, with a bold jump straight down. Sixteen, he was entrusted with measuring the declinations of the horizon. Galicia followed, and the rest. Some leaped. Some dangled from the edge and dropped. It was too high to climb back out.

Soon the five of them stood arms spread at the bottom, faces alone lit by the firelight, eyes dancing with pride at being chosen, wide with fear of the ordeals to come, bright with faith in the Apex.

"No!" called little Grace, on the other side of the pit. "I don't want to!"

No longer a polite little girl. She was lifted and dropped. Chrysogonus caught her, lowered her to the cool, damp sand, where she began to cry. Her eyes caught Pequeño 3's and terrified him. He thought of cicadas beneath the earth, the whole desert breathing in and out like a single lung, the Apex's blazing blue eyes in the dark of the desert, and looked away.

She wept alone.

The Pyramid dragged in sleds to cover the pit. The Pequeños stood in the bottom, arms spread, as they'd seen their father do before. Little Pequeño 3 watched, and felt the Apex's gaze on him, and waited. Waited until the third sled was coming in, and the pit was almost sealed, then he sealed his fate. Two steps, and he jumped. Slotted in the gap, fell into the dark, and took the impact so hard it felt his shins might crack.

There was no sound. The sled blocked out the last of the torchlight from above. The Pequeños didn't speak. There was no sound at all, and Wren waited, waited, waited for the sleds to be pulled back, for the arms to reach down and snatch him out, but they did not. Instead there came the steady, shushing backfill of sand covering over the sleds.

The dark grew darker.

He moved amongst the Pequeños, standing like statues of stone, until he found Grace. She was sobbing silently on the hard, cold ground. He wrapped his thin arms around her as the sand kept filling in the spaces between the sleds overhead, drifting down through fine gaps like a dry rain. The sound continued until all the work was done, and the darkness was total, and the only sound was Grace's fading sobs and the steady, one-lung breathing of the Pequeños.

In those long moments he felt the world tumbling around him. What was real, what wasn't.

"It's gonna be OK," he whispered in Grace's ear, not really knowing what he meant. "I promise."

She couldn't say words back, could only snuffle her face against his chest, and that more than anything wrenched the world the rest of the way around. He was young, but he knew that three days without air would kill you. Three minutes was enough, and no measure of faith could change that.

The world finally righted itself. He did know what was real.

"There's a way out," he whispered in Grace's ear. "We'll find it."

That stopped her sobbing. Wren felt her head raising up, though he couldn't see a thing.

"A way out?" she whispered.

"We just have to find it. We have to dig."

"Dig?" He felt her eyes brimming with tears again.

"Not down," he soothed. "I swear it. Out. There's a tunnel, like a sand pipe. We can crawl right out. In an hour we'll be home, eating all the strooberry mud pies we can manage."

"I don't want strooberry mud," Grace managed in a small voice.

"Don't you worry, we'll have only the fat bugs then."

She chuckled a little.

"You'll see. We'll be out of here in no time."

"I hope so," she whispered.

Little Pequeño 3 stood then. Surrounded by his elder Pequeños. With their help, they'd find the tunnel in no time. They'd all go out together.

"There's a tunnel," he proclaimed, loudly. "The Apex used it before. Dug into the wall, stretching out into the desert. We just have to-"

The slap came out of nowhere. He didn't see it coming, not even a whistle in the wind, and it swiped his face completely to the side, almost rocked him off his feet. He gasped. The pain filled up his whole head.

Then another slap came, from the other side. A backhand, chipping his teeth and bursting the taste of blood in his mouth. Somebody was holding him by the scruff of his tunic, now, lifting him up. His head spun woozy with the pain.

"This is our testament," came Chrysogonus' angry voice. His hot breath burned across little Pequeño 3's stinging cheeks. "You were not called. You defied the Apex. We will not be tempted by you or your make-believe."

"But-" he tried, and another slap came, then another.

He was dropped. Bands of silver veered across his vision. Stars burst in the black. His mouth moved in agony, but no sounds came out. He didn't understand. The Apex had done it.

"Shh," came Grace's little voice. Her arms encircled him. "You hush now."

"Hush now, Pequeño 3," came another voice. Galicia. The nicest of the elder Pequeños. "Don't move. Don't speak. You will not ruin this for us, like you ruin everything else."

He opened his mouth. Grace's hand was already over it, muffling him from speaking. He tried, but she held on tight until he gave up, and they lay curled together in the dark of the pit, listening to the unified breathing of the Pequeños above.

He'd already perfected his experiments with breathing. He knew aortal flutter, and going as still and cold as the dead, and he knew that no matter how well he drove his heart into overdrive, he couldn't survive without breathing fresh air for three whole days.

They were all going to die.

34

GHOSTS

Wren's earpiece chimed as it paired with the Pixel, and it only took a second before the familiar sound of Hellion's voice came through loud and clear over the chop of the R22's rotors.

"Christopher. I hope you have enjoyed your spa treatment. There is work to be done now."

Spa treatment? He let it slide. "Point me in the right direction."

"North-west, and may I say, that is a very fine woman you have inherited."

"North-west," Wren said to the pilot, and completely ignored the bizarre notion that he had somehow 'inherited' Maggie. "What's my destination?"

"She may be a little too strong for you, though, as I know you like the frailer type."

Wren frowned. She was trying to rile him, he figured, see just where his mental state was at. He decided to let her have it with both barrels. "You don't know a damn thing about my type, *Isabella.* Fact is, neither of you emotionally stunted wunderkind would recognize an actual human relationship even if it DDOS-attacked your server. Now stop trolling me and get on point. Where the hell am I going?"

He heard her chuckling, repeating 'emotionally stunted wunderkind' to herself. "This woman has made you so passionate, Christopher."

"Did he call you Isabella?" B4cksl4cker asked in the background.

"Do I have to come to Europe and set you to work?" he barked. Sometimes you had to lay the smack down. "Two tasty little oysters tucked away in their convoy shells, you think I can't shuck you nicely? I've got a brand new knife and you'll go down a treat with a twist of lemon."

Now Hellion was laughing openly. It took all sorts.

"Is he comparing us to oysters?" B4cksl4cker asked. "These are shellfish, yes?"

"You are shellfish," he shouted over the helicopter rotors. "Filter feeders in the muck of the ocean floor, trying to drag me down into your BS. Now you've had your fun, let's get on with the debrief!"

"We are weathernet," B4cksl4cker said, sounding aggrieved. "If anything, Christopher, we are butterflies on jet stream, not shellfish."

"I don't care if you're pretty little unicorns riding rainbows! I've been blind for over twelve hours; tell me what's going on."

B4cksl4cker laughed low.

"Ah, Christopher, we have missed your charm," Hellion said, after she stopped laughing. "And you are welcome. Now, yes, that is enough fun, you are right. To business."

"To business," B4cksl4cker agreed. "Very great deal has happened while you were unconscious. The Foundation has mobilized like never before. Theodore, Teddy as you call him, has ordered up activation of member base. There are now four Foundation strike teams standing by around the world, waiting for your command. Threat has become existential, this is the word, yes?"

It took Wren a second to catch up with all that. "What are you talking about? Strike teams?"

"Strike teams," Hellion repeated. "Four. In China, Russia, Malaysia and standing by for Gruber. We have mobilized, Christopher." She paused a moment, letting that sink in. "Logistical effort to prepare this on such short notice has been impressive. Through night we sent eleven jets out of private airfields to get them in position. We faked storm of documentation to throw your government off. The Foundation is fighting back, and it is great joy to see. Teddy has certainly earned himself coin upgrade."

Wren stared for a second out of the R22's curved glass, down to the sands of the Hopi Reservation below, trying to absorb this information. "You're kidding. This is a joke."

"It is not joke. It is very real."

"But..." he hunted for something to say. "I didn't approve anything like this."

Hellion laughed. "Oh, Christopher. You were one coin minus and potentially locked away for life. The Foundation had to think about what was best for itself."

What was best for itself? One coin minus? "How am I one coin minus? When did that happen?"

"Christopher, please. Take a look at your outcomes."

"I stopped the Reparations! The Blue Fairy too. How is that worth one coin minus?"

"And lost your family," she answered, sounding bored. "Got yourself arrested. Turned the heat up on whole Foundation and left us alone against this latest threat."

He opened his mouth to protest, but couldn't really argue with that. It was all true. Still, he felt totally blindsided.

"The Foundation wanted me to fix things with my family, so I did," he said, but even to him his tone sounded churlish.

"But not get arrested," Hellion explained patiently. "Some might call that selfish."

Selfish? He wound himself up to argue further, then let it go with a sigh. Maybe she was right. He hadn't really thought of it that way.

He hadn't thought about anything. Things had changed a lot in three months.

"This was Teddy's idea."

"Putting you one coin minus?"

"Forget the minus coin! I'm talking about the strikes."

"In which case, of course. And technically, you did approve this. Dr. Ferat's training camps?"

He remembered that. Teddy had said something about operationalizing the Foundation, maybe setting up training, before he'd hit the Reparations. He'd agreed at the time just to get it out of the way, thinking he'd deal with it later, but later hadn't come. Now they were taking on terrorists around the world, after only three months of training. He tried to imagine Teddy running an obstacle course. Firing a rifle. Even Cheryl?

"Who's on the teams? Give me names."

"They are all adults," Hellion said, "they made their own choices and-"

"Names, Hellion. They're my members."

The sound of keys clacking shifted, becoming deeper and more forceful. Wren recognized it as B4cksl4cker. "Henry Bragg," came his deep Armenian accent, "former Marine from Nevada. Doona Joy, Namibian child soldier. Alejandro Gutierrez, he was Qotl cartel. In China and Malaysia we have drawn heavily on members from Sunlit Dawn, the Taiwanese cult you cracked four years ago. In Russia Theodore is leading a team with a sniper and supplemental mercenaries."

Wren blinked. Teddy was leading a mercenary sniper unit. It was outlandish.

"Who are they going after?"

"Assorted mercenaries," Hellion said. "Darknet hackers, propagandists and coders. It turns out, we know many of these people, Christopher. It seems this whole 'Ghost' attack has been outsourced, dreamed up in head of one single, masterful troll. All false flag killings, conspiracy, setting two parties against each other, these are preferred tactics of Internet troll."

It took Wren a second to figure out what she was saying. "A troll. You're saying it's just one guy?"

"Evidence suggest it is; one man in 'God mode' using data teams to amplify his influence. Real-world exposure has been strictly limited. Only three people were taken, using asymmetric phishing techniques to draw them out. Gruber basically kidnapped himself, and it looks same for the others, though there may be good news here also."

Wren felt about five steps behind now. His heart hammered crazily. "What good news?"

"We are beginning to see patterns of their ghosting overwrites," B4cksl4cker said. "This is how we tracked them back."

"Ghosting overwrites?" It felt like he was catching only one word in every three.

"It is complicated," B4cksl4cker said. "Essentially, every time they deepfake themselves out of CCTV or Federal records, we are able to build picture through what is missing. Really, it came from your idea to map 'ghost' cab by comparing it to known record of taxi movements in LA."

Wren was just about hanging on. He had no idea where this was going, but he knew where they were up to now. "You mean the way we found the Jeddah Mill?"

"Exactly. Signal out of noise. Now we are finally using weathernet as it should be used; mass infiltration and desecration of privacy."

Wren winced. "Don't enjoy it so much."

"This is groundbreaking, Christopher," Hellion crowed. "It is incredible accomplishment. We have constructed baseline environment that models data traffic across select portions of Internet. Through comparisons with 'ghosted' record, we can start tracking where these Ghosts have interfered. Their shadows show them, and they cannot hide from us anymore. Data technique is intensive, but works."

Wren ran that through internal translation. "You're saying you've invented a ghost hunting tool?"

"Yes," said B4cksl4cker cheerfully. "Now we are inventing ghost-blasting weaponry."

Wren rubbed his head.

"Particle beams," Hellion added. "Proton packs."

"Do not cross streams," B4cksl4cker contributed helpfully.

Wren ignored the reference. "But how? Before you said they were untraceable."

"That is bat box data!" Hellion cheered. "Our custodian friend delivered footage from his cameras, which Ghosts were clearly not aware of, because these cameras were not on any networked system. Therefore they could not interfere with them. This data has helped make key for our current ghost-detection algorithm, version 3.2. With it, we found mercenaries, and we're currently modeling route for truck that took Steven Gruber from Jeddah Mill. It went north, Christopher. We expect to narrow down final location within next few hours."

"And I'm heading there?"

"You are heading there right now."

Wren sat and breathed.

Things had definitely accelerated in the night. It seemed the dynamo was only going to go faster now. Mercenaries spread around the world, with Foundation strike teams closing in. Gruber somewhere up the West Coast, with Wren en route. It was a lot to take on board.

"What else?"

"A lot," B4cksl4cker said. "Importantly, there may be good news about Sally Rogers. Brace yourself, Christopher."

"Out with it."

"We think that footage of her death may have been deepfaked." He paused. "'Ghosted' is better term, as this technology is far beyond deepfaking. It is functionally indistinguishable from genuine footage. But you mentioned something about her seemed unusual?"

He cast his mind back. It was only yesterday, but so much had happened since. "Right. I didn't think she would break like that. Not so soon."

"Exactly. Well, Hellion has seen your Sally Rogers in action, and she did not believe it either. She decided to dig into footage herself."

"So?"

Hellion picked up the thread. "So we applied ghosting algorithm to test it. Just like with finding Gruber's taxi, we first had to build baseline model that we were certain was objectively 'true'. We gathered many hours of Sally Rogers captured on film; CIA training, in background of recorded operations, recorded on your own bodycam at times. We built behavioral model from her mannerisms, speech patterns and personality, then compared that model to death video."

Wren's mouth went dry. When he'd suggested the taxi modelling idea to rule out false positives, he'd never anticipated it being used in this kind of way. "And?"

"And it is clear that somebody died in this specific fire, though we do not believe it was Rogers. She did not behave as model anticipated."

Wren's heart skipped a beat. Rogers, not dead? Thanks to a data key derived from the bat box cameras? There could easily be a lot wrong with their hypothesis, but he'd take good news where he could get it. Adrenaline gushed through his system in a cascade.

"Are you sure?"

"We are refining ghost model, but yes. Reliability in double-blind test cases has proven extremely high. Behavioral patterns are very consistent, Christopher, as you know. Moments of extreme stress only make deviating from patterns near impossible."

"So, she's alive? Then what on Earth happened? Where is she?"

"Our current theory is that she must have escaped. If real-world action of these 'Ghosts' is what we suspect, tiny real-world force, with footprint augmented vastly by outsourced hackers using ghosting technology, then it should not have been too difficult for her to escape. As highly trained operative, it's possible that she could have overcome single troll."

Wren's head spun. If she was alive, what did that mean? "Tell me we're looking for her. We have to find her first."

"We are in complete agreement. We have sent discreet Be-On-the-Look-Out BOLO requests through various sheriffs stations all along projected route of Ghosts up West Coast. If she is found at any one of them, we will be first to know."

Wren sat back. It was hard to breathe. He couldn't have asked for better news than this.

"That's amazing."

"Yes," said Hellion. "We thought you would like that. Now, there is one more matter we must address before moving on."

"Go on."

"Agent James Tandrews has been reaching out to us. There is no doubt that he is being monitored by the CIA, but since we are using ghosting technology to disguise ourselves now, we are doubly untraceable. Do you wish to speak with him?"

Tandrews? For a moment Wren suspected foul play, but there was no way Humphreys could have flipped him. If he wanted to speak directly with Wren, it had to be something of vital importance; something he wasn't worried about saying in front of government oversight.

"OK. Maybe." He ran back through everything he'd just learned. "First, what's the timeline of our strikes?"

"Ideally, within next two hours," Hellion said. "The Ghosts have placed countdown timer on their feed, we assume before the next burning video."

"Will we have Gruber's location by then?"

"We believe so. Foundation Board decided we should hit three mercenary cells in few minutes before we descend on his location, wherever that is. If we go too early, Ghosts will have warning. Too late and God mode will remain operational against us. Prime goal is to generate maximum shock and awe, giving Steven Gruber best chance of survival. We expect we will know his location by time you are closer."

Wren nodded. There were details missing, but he had to trust them to the Foundation. "The timeline sounds good. Hit the hackers, hit the Ghosts. Is there anything else I need to know?"

"This is full summary."

"Good. Then let's get Tandrews on the line."

"Placing call. We will be listening, if you need us. Good luck, Christopher."

He took a breath. Far below the outriding lands of the Pyramid raced by. In his ear the comms line trilled until it picked up.

35

TANDREWS

"It's me," Wren said.

"Christopher," came James Tandrews' familiar voice, rough and raspy. "I am sure your team have made you aware that this call is being monitored."

"I get that. Did Humphreys give you much trouble?"

"I'm with the Director right now, Christopher. It's only through his generosity that this call has been allowed."

Wren laughed out loud. That was funny.

"Yes," said Tandrews, appreciating the irony.

"Humphreys, you touch one hair on this man's head, you know what happens, don't you?"

"Christopher," warned Tandrews.

"He's seen what I did to the Pinocchios. Now he figures I'm behind those mutilations too, so let's make that a threat. How's that sound, Gerald, I cut you up and string you out, will that be enough to earn another catch/kill order?"

"Christopher," said Tandrews. No longer chiding. Resigned.

"Humphreys knows me, James. I know him. Is he giving you his new look right now, the flat cliff face, nothing doing, white as alabaster? I call it Director-chic."

Tandrews sighed but answered anyway. "He is."

Wren could just picture it. A small room, recording equipment, cameras, his adoptive father James Tandrews cuffed to one side of the desk, Director

Gerald Humphreys on the other, face as blank as a cue ball. Nothing better to be doing than chasing his own tail. It made Wren furious.

He'd thought that after the Reparations, Humphreys had finally accepted he wasn't a threat. Sure, he had to go to the black site for killing all those Pinocchios, but that wasn't personal. They'd had an understanding. Then Humphreys had changed all that with his flat blank face, his blanket condemnation of the Foundation, and it stung. "This fool should have been watching over my people. He should have protected Rogers. Anyone could see they were prime targets for my father."

"He still thinks this is you," Tandrews said.

"And that's the problem, isn't it? Your Deep State's blind, Humphreys! You're opening yourselves up to these kinds of attacks by over-reacting. My hackers are calling this latest batch Ghosts; they make a minimal interaction with the real world. They snatched, what, just three people? With only the visuals from that they've pumped the country up like a zeppelin, and there you are, holding your lighter out like you think the Hindenburg was some great light show. He's not using his head, James, he deserves to have it cut off when the people storm the bastille!"

He panted. He hadn't expected all of that to come out.

"Are you done, Christopher?" Tandrews' voice was tight.

"I could go on all day. But we don't have time."

"Quite right."

Wren rubbed his temples. Enough acting out. "OK. Tandrews. There's a lot to catch up on, but they said you were calling me. What is it?"

"They want the location of Rogers' body."

He laughed. "Her ashes, you mean?"

Tandrews' voice grew tighter still. "Yes. I told them you don't know, because this isn't you."

Wren weighed this new intelligence in the balance. He was done trying to earn the trust of the Deep State, whether it was Humphreys and the CIA or the FBI, the NSA, DHS, DOJ or any one of the alphabet soup agencies. At the same time, persuasion now could be a powerful tool. His father was never going to stop, but Humphreys might. At least he might hold back or retarget more closely, giving Wren and the Foundation breathing room. He had to wield Humphreys like a blunt club.

"OK, so let's deal. I tell you what I know, there have to be changes."

"They're not going to bargain with you, Christopher."

"Doesn't matter what they say, it only matters what they do. Train a dog to come at the sound of a bell, it'll come. Humphreys is my dog. So listen up. My best intelligence says Rogers is not dead. Her death was a new level of deepfake video, we're calling it 'ghosting'. There's a trick to detect it, but we're not telling you what it is. We think she escaped, so that's one in our corner. It means all they've got now is Steven Gruber, and I'm en route to free him now. Once I have him safe, I'll give you the location of Jay Durant's ashes."

There was silence for a long moment.

"He's not happy with that," Tandrews said.

"He's a sourpuss at the best of times. Tell him I could have killed him in that Chinook. Toss him out the door, he's dead. Why didn't I?"

Another silence. "He's steering me, Christopher. He wants more."

Wren laughed. It was never enough with some people. "Shall we talk about how I slipped him in the desert? I heard his voice on the bullhorns. He never sounded more stupid. 'Christopher Wren, surrender yourself immediately'. Tandrews, if this is all you wanted to call me for, I'll have to step off."

"Wait," Tandrews said. "No, it isn't. Let me frame this properly. They think it's you, Christopher. I think it's the Apex. So let's speak to that. We're all putting the puzzle pieces together here; the Saints, the Blue Fairy, the Reparations, they're all skirmishes in a larger war. Are we agreed?"

Wren blinked. Finally, something they could agree on. "Agreed."

"To what end? That's what they're all asking themselves here. They want you to tell them."

"Because they think I know."

"Because they think you must have some kind of demand. It's how most negotiations work. They're spitballing wildly, they think maybe you want an island of your own, to run your cult in privacy. A mini nation, Wrenlandia, whatever. If I'm honest, they're getting desperate, Christopher. Humphreys is not happy I'm telling you this, but they haven't cut me off, so let that tell you how desperate they are."

Wren listened, waiting for the tell-tale click of the transmission being cut, but none came. Tandrews was right, that was a potent sign.

"They're terrified."

"That's the sense I'm picking up, though they'll never admit it. Terrified. Enraged. Calmly professional on the surface, but it's a fake out, Christopher. You think Humphreys has a new face? It's just we've never seen him pushed this far before. Beyond breaking point, and no one's equipped to deal with it. Then you put on your show at the Wilshire? It cuts them to the bone. Their people are turning loyal to you. It's Christmas in July for nightmares here. The whole damn building is falling apart."

Wren considered that. Good, really.

"So they want to deal."

"They're open to it. If you stop."

"Except you and I know that whoever's behind this attack's never going to stop."

"That person is particularly single-minded, I'd say," Tandrews agreed.

Wren sighed. For three months in his cell he'd avoided thinking about any of this, along with all the other miseries of his life. Loralei and the kids. Betraying Rogers. The Apex resurgent. Now though it had to be faced.

"The endgame."

"The endgame," Tandrews went on. "We have the basics already. All throughout these attacks, they've been splitting the country apart along old fault lines. Breaking down our beliefs: that we're one people; that your neighbor will stand and fight for you, not against you; that we're good, and exceptional, and unified."

Wren grunted. He hadn't sat down to game it out, but the pieces of this grander puzzle were all right there. "Simple," he said. "It's mass cult indoctrination."

"On an unprecedented scale," Tandrews agreed. "The most ambitious act of brainwashing imaginable. But where's it going?"

Wren grunted; that was the question. He ran through the stages in his head. They were intimately familiar, he'd lived them, he'd used them on others, he'd seen their lasting effects in post-cult recovery, as the faithful gradually allowed the scales to fall from their eyes. It could take years, cost tens of thousands of dollars per person, to fully deprogram a broken way of thinking.

"Stage one, assault on identity," he said.

"Right out of Lifton's theory," Tandrews confirmed. "Followed by guilt, self-betrayal, then breaking point."

"We're far along that track already, if people are ready to turn on their own government."

"Precisely," Tandrews said. "People's hopes and beliefs are shattering. The Saints started the ball rolling, fracturing us on the basis of race, and each further attack just drove the spike in deeper."

Wren squeezed the phone hard against his head. It still galled that Humphreys thought he was responsible for any of this, the methodical delivery of tortures to irreparably damage peoples' minds, conducted on an industrial scale.

"The new crisis reduces the value of old beliefs," he said, nearly quoting the theory verbatim, "because the old beliefs can't solve the current crisis. People become sick with worry, they're afraid, and they're looking for answers."

"Then a savior emerges with all the answers," Tandrews added.

"And that savior gives them enemies to blame," Wren said.

"Enemies and answers," Tandrews went on. "The enemies die with the old beliefs, and the answers offer a hopeful future."

"Then confession," Wren said. The word sounded like a tolling bell.

"Confession," Tandrews repeated. "Admit and accept that all you thought before was wrong. The Judas moment."

Wren winced. He hated the Judas moment more than anything, when people abandoned logic and the evidence of their whole lives, and started in on groupthink because it made them safe. Four lights became five. Big Brother became not your tormentor, but your savior.

"Next comes internal harmony, a new balance and rebirth."

"Rebirth," Tandrews repeated. "That's where everyone here is stuck. What's the Apex's end point?"

Wren ran everything he knew back and forth through his head like an old spool of tape. The Apex thrived on chaos, but not because he loved chaos in itself. He'd always been the most obsessive compulsive, organized man Wren had ever known. He just hated reality.

Wanted to bend it for himself.

All his experiments in the Pyramid had been aimed at exactly that. The constant recording of the minutiae of life, all for the sole purpose of trying to somehow 'catch out' the world in a mistake, and thereby bend it to his own will. But reality was stubborn and did not bend. All he could change was the human conception of the world.

He'd achieved it at the fake town. Those people had eaten out of his hand for years on end. They'd died for him year after year until the final fiery end, when the Apex had fled.

"Death," Wren said.

"Death," Tandrews agreed. "But whose death?"

Wren could feel Humphreys leaning in across the distance, straining for this answer too. It made Wren feel oddly distanced from himself, like he wasn't in the helicopter but out in the air floating among the clouds.

"Everyone. All America, at least to start with. Maybe the whole world, down the line. It's the only way he'll feel better. Bend everyone, all at once, in the most total way possible."

There was silence for a time.

"That's not something they're prepared to negotiate over," Tandrews said.

Wren snorted. Of course not. But the Apex had always dreamed big. Twenty-five years ago he'd reaped a thousand souls, and it had fed him until now. It had kept him going. Now he had to be jonesing bad. Like any junkie, the next high had to be higher still. Aiming for the whole thing. Creation. Insert himself where God should be and bring things to an end.

It reshaped everything for Wren. With stakes like that, matters couldn't continue as they had been. The Apex had already brought them to this heightened point where it only took a single death to spark riots. If anyone could brainwash the world, it was the Apex.

Divided they would all fall.

"We need to get on the same page here, Tandrews. Convince them."

"I'm trying."

"Divided we lose. We all lose."

"They're not buying it. They think you're the devil here, Christopher. They can't get in bed with the devil."

He needed proof. Something solid linking the Apex to the deaths. And perhaps now, unlike any other time before, he had the ability to do just that.

Evidence. His heart boomed. It was really the only way forward. You had to live your values, after all.

"When this is done, when Gruber's free, I'm coming back in."

There was a long silence.

"He wants to know more," Tandrews said.

Wren sucked in a breath. If these were the stakes, then this is what he had to do. There was no playing around anymore, going rogue. He had to go all-in with all the chips available.

"Me. My Foundation. Everything. We come in, we share what we know, and we take this on together. Regardless of what you think, you need me, Humphreys. I'm the best weapon you've got against what's coming. You dunk me back in the black site, that's on you. You lock up my Foundation, that's on you. If we're fighting each other, he'll sweep us away like a tsunami. We need to unite."

Another long silence. Wren imagined Humphreys talking to other heads of agencies, to people in government, maybe the President. This went all the way to the top. This was all that mattered right now.

"They want proof, Christopher. Proof that this isn't you. Proof that your father is behind it."

Wren grimaced. Fresh anger dumped corticosteroids into his system, making colors brighter and his mind tick faster. Really, he hadn't expected anything else.

"I'll get it. Tandrews. Punch him in the face for me, will you?"

He rang off.

The phone lay in his palm before him. His whole body felt like it was trembling. Twenty-five years ago he'd fled the Pyramid, he'd traveled the world, he'd brought down countless cults, but everything had always been leading back to this. The moment of truth.

The old pilot was looking at him. Wren looked back.

"Heavy," the guy said.

Wren looked away to the horizon. Heavy. Yeah.

36

PROOF

"Let me understand this," B4cksl4cker said, summarizing while Wren's chopper churned west. "You want us to build ghost model from twenty-five years ago, but actually perhaps dating fifty years back, focused on one man, but not only one man. You want us to track everything he might have done, everyone he met, everywhere he went across that time period, but since there are no records of him anywhere, we'll need to use ghost-hunting technique to build up world around him. Is this correct?"

"It's a little more than that," Wren corrected uneasily.

"Oh, little more?" B4cksl4cker asked. "I have clearly not understood then, Christopher."

"You have. You know exactly what I want."

"Proof."

"Proof, that's right. That the Apex survived the Pyramid. That he was behind these other attacks. That he's behind this one.

B4cksl4cker sighed, took a deep breath, then sighed again. "Christopher. It is too much. This, in addition to tracing back Ghosts, and coordinating our strikes on hacker outposts, all before you land and retrieve Steven Gruber? You have been watching countdown, I think?"

Wren grimaced. The Ghosts' countdown was under ninety minutes now, leading up to 6 p.m.; everyone out of work and out onto the streets just in time to watch Steven Gruber go up in flames.

"I know. But this is important."

A brief silence. Below a small town whizzed by. "Hellion, can you talk some sense into this man?"

"Delighted," said Hellion. "Christopher, what you are asking is beyond impossible. On purely practical level, the vast majority of records we need to build ghost model for your father will not be available in digital. They will be stored as paper records in hundred different warehouses, filing rooms, basements spread across whole state of Arizona. We cannot access those, and even if we could, it would take forensic team of hundreds to make sense of them, then army of hundreds more to put these pieces together. This data is simply not available."

Wren was ready for this. "So don't get all the data. I just need enough."

"Enough to find ghost inconsistencies, yes, Christopher, but to find ghosts there must be enough reliable data to see those gaps! The record must be near perfect to spot them, and there is not nearly enough data, or we would already know where Apex is."

"Not good enough. You haven't even tried."

Another moment passed. "B4cksl4cker, he is all yours."

"Christopher," came the older hacker's Armenian bass again. "This is not Hellion and I trying to persuade you because it is difficult and we are lazy. It is impossible, and no amount of bullying will change that. There is no place to start. Finding ghosted taxi cab in LA, this is possible thing, in current data-rich world. But the movements of one man in desert thirty years ago? There was no data then. The world was thin, Christopher. One tenth as many satellites. No street view. No social media. Far fewer cameras, no date stamps or GPS built in, no blogs. There is not enough raw information to build model."

Wren's mind raced. "So you're telling me you need more information."

"Christopher, no. Do not try to spin this. There is not enough data in whole world to do what you're asking."

"The data silos. Hellion just mentioned them. Records everywhere on paper, in warehouses, filing rooms..."

"These are air gapped. Inaccessible. No amount of phishing techniques can extract metric ton of paper folders. We would need semi-truck trailer just to store one tenth of these. They are more secure than best cryptography."

"So I'll get you ten semi-truck trailers. I'll get access."

"You cannot get access. Perhaps to some. Not all."

"So I get some, then. Narrow it to the records for the counties around the fake town. Traffic violations, DMV records, cop beat reports, land deeds."

B4cksl4cker sighed.

"And hundreds of people to process this?" Hellion asked, taking up the baton again.

"With a few dozen you could scan a semi-truck in a few days," Wren argued. "Smart AI processes it and builds the model. Where people were. What they were doing. Money flows. Vehicle flows. And we scratch the fifty year window, focus on the years right around the end of the fake town. Or scratch all that, and focus on the now. If he's behind the last three attacks, there has to be a record. We're data rich now, right?"

Hellion sounded exasperated. "Yes, Christopher, but-"

He tuned out of the explanations, momentarily flashing back to the attack that had begun all of this; Richard Acker, head of the Order of the Saints. As he'd stepped back into the flames of the Whipple Building in Minneapolis, he'd talked about meeting with the Apex. He'd known Wren's Pyramid name, Pequeño 3, that he'd never told anyone.

"Richard Acker," he blurted. "He said he met my father. I thought it was BS at the time, just to get in my head, but what if it wasn't? We could track him back. The Blue Fairy too, Lance Gebhart, he must have known my father. The Reparations, what was her name?"

"Yumiko Harkness," said Hellion wearily.

"Track those three. Their paths crossed with the Apex somewhere, I guarantee it."

Hellion sighed. "As you have already said, scanning alone will be work of days. It is not possible within ninety minutes. It may not be possible in ninety years, Christopher. He is needle in this haystack."

"So narrow the haystack. Harness the second skin and the weathernet. I'll get you the resources you need, just tell me what they are. There really is nothing else more important right now. If my father's endgame is to kill everyone, it's going to affect you too. I don't care how well you like the hacker lifestyle, you'll like it a whole lot less if you're dead."

Hellion chuckled. "Dead? How will he kill us, Christopher? Brainwashing will not work. I will never burn myself alive."

"I think you would, if he had you locked alone in a room for long enough," Wren pressed. "But he doesn't need everyone to be brainwashed, just enough to carry the rest with him. Imagine he gets hold of just one nuclear missile facility. He fires at Russia, do you think Russia will hold back from mutually assured destruction? I'd like to see your hacker lifestyle then, rocking a convoy through a global fog of radioactive fallout."

There was a pause.

"This is good point," B4cksl4cker said.

"So come to me with solutions. What do you need?"

"All this data," Hellion said at once. "On your Pyramid, on last three organizations, gathered together in one database."

"Good. What else?"

"What else?"

"Human resources. Computing power. Money. Who and what?"

"Best forensic data scientists in the world," B4cksl4cker joined in. "Dozens of them. Best AI programmers and pattern analysts. Entire research staff of MIT."

"So get me a list of names."

"Even preparing this list will take longer than three hours, Christopher," B4cksl4cker countered. "It will take many hundreds of hours just to gather and process data. It will cost millions of dollars, and even with all this, breakthrough may never come. It may take months or years to find his trail, if it exists anywhere."

Wren seized on the positive. "But you might find it?"

B4cksl4cker made an uncomfortable noise.

"It is highly unlikely," Hellion said. "But it is possible."

"Good enough. I'll get you what I can. Start moving pieces into place."

"Using Foundation assets?"

"Spend it all. Gather your team. Start with the Pyramid and set up a system; we'll expand it outward to the Saints and the rest when we can. Remember, nothing else matters here."

There was a silence.

"Humphreys will never give you what you're asking for," B4cksl4cker said. "Not without proof first. Argument is circular."

"So we don't ask," Wren said, as the plan formed up in his head. "We just take."

37

HELICOPTER

The helicopter flew on and Wren watched updates pouring in on his phone. The backlash to his speech at the Wilshire was already setting in like a bad hangover: anger at the police, at the protesters, at Wren. A new theory was being constructed as he watched, from memes and fringe theories, backed up with circumstantial 'evidence' fabricated from whole cloth: that he'd been co-opted by the Deep State.

'Look at that fight in Gruber's apartment!' one argument went. 'It's clearly fake. He pulled all his punches. And bodyslams? What DELTA agent does that in the real world?'

That was true. It didn't help that viral gifs supported the theory, showing Wren tossing the FBI guy around accompanied by big comic-like 'BANG!' and 'KRRAAANNG!' speech bubbles.

'Are we really supposed to believe he was in a black site for THREE MONTHS and didn't flip?' another went. 'No one can stand up to torture for that long, and come out looking as good as he did.' For this there were time-lapse graphics of his face before and after, getting thin. He was flattered they thought he looked good.

'Everyone's saying he did this miracle at the Wilshire," went another, over video footage of Wren pulling capoeira moves, "the crowd was going wild, but he was there beating up FBI agents just an hour before he 'spread peace' through the masses. The man's a charlatan just like his father!'

He scrolled on. The news channels were documenting the outcry with gusto, anchors repeating the charges for all they were worth. Talking heads popped up in split screen like firecrackers, variously applauding or decrying what Wren had done. Presidential candidate David Keller stood at a podium, Hollywood handsome in an unbuttoned shirt, cuffs rolled up, salt of the Earth.

"Something's sick in our society," he said, vigorous but restrained. "I was his first advocate, but even I have to question what we're seeing now."

Wren switched channels.

In LA people were coming back onto the Wilshire parking lot. Across the country the same thing was happening. This time they would be better prepared, Wren knew. Better armed. Reporters were jostled in their midst. National Guard forces gathered at the edges, racking rubber bullets. In turn the signboards grew darker. RELEASE CHRISTOPHER WREN became CHRIS-TRAITOR WREN. DUMP THE DEEP STATE became DESTROY THE DEEP STATE. FREE THE FOUNDATION became F**K THE FOUNDATION.

The Russian propaganda factory, hard at work. He brought up his mission brief on the first of the Foundation strikes.

The propaganda factory was a purpose-built black hat unit out of Vladivostok, suspected of frequent use by the Kremlin to undermine foreign elections and spray out fog of war memes. Stolen intelligence suggested there were over a hundred workers hard at work formulating memes, conspiracies and fake evidence within its squat, windowless box warehouse.

The Foundation team there included several ex-CIA assets, an old SEAL associate who went by 'Abercrombie', and Teddy riding herd.

Wren placed the call, and within seconds Teddy came up on video. He looked even thinner than the last time Wren had seen him, almost skeletal. It lent him an uncanny intensity, like the bullet to his brain had burned off all the nonsense.

"Christopher," he said. Even his voice was different, deeper and more assured.

"I'm asking you to hang back when the strike goes down," Wren said. "The Foundation needs you."

Teddy stared at him for a moment. "You don't know what the Foundation needs anymore." There was no anger in it, just a flat statement of fact. "I'll remedy that, as soon as this is over."

Wren re-appraised him. Teddy had always been a man of overwhelming charm. It had spoiled him with an excess of every kind of pleasure imaginable, making him rich and soft. Now he was hard, like hammered iron.

"So survive, then. I expect a thorough debrief."

"You'll have one. Get this done, Christopher."

He ended the call and sat for a moment staring at the phone. He hadn't expected that. Teddy had always wanted a cult of his own. Now he had one, and the weight of responsibility had only made him stronger.

He scrolled to the next brief, a down-at-heel fifth-floor Internet café in a textiles district of Beijing. Video overwatch was provided by a hacked civilian drone. Intelligence suggested it contained a twenty-strong team of black hat propagandists operating under the iron rule of Pang Jiao Shou, Pa-Shou for short, which meant Fat Unicorn. She was a long-time thorn in the Communist Party's side, having propagated a number of infamous pro-democracy videos that briefly pushed through the Great Firewall. Now she ran a mercenary crew focused on manufacturing virality for the Ghosts' death videos.

The Foundation team there included three paramilitary ex-members from Sunlit Dawn, a god-emperor cult he'd cracked in unprecedented collaboration between the CIA and the Taiwan National Security Bureau, along with Alejandro, his ex-Qotl cartel coyote and undercover hook-up.

Wren scrolled to the last mission brief, live footage from a surveillance cam watching the Malaysian hacker nest, concealed inside the donut hole of a large Kuala Lumpur block in the shadow of the Twin Petronas Towers. A cabal of several dozen elite graphics hackers were at work within, apparently operating using a Titan2-level parallel supercomputing array, capable of 100 petaflops. They were responsible for simultaneously 'ghosting' all trace of the abductions.

The Foundation team included another two from Sunlit Dawn, three Foundation Army Rangers Wren had extricated from an Afghanistan fraud scheme, along with Doona, the ex-child soldier who'd helped him raid the Reparations' Anti-Ca compound.

Everyone was in position. Ghosted themselves by Hellion and B4cksl4cker. Waiting for the signal.

The R22 put down, as scheduled, just north of LA in Oxnard airfield, and Wren transferred to a waiting luxury Airbus ACH175, the largest commercial helicopter available on short notice. American-built, it could lift seven tons with room for fourteen passengers. Wren cranked the rear door open.

The interior had been completely stripped, luxury recliners torn out and replaced with wall-rack seating, making room for twin Yamaha YZ360 dirt bikes down the bay's middle, with a large pallet in back loaded with squat red cylinders.

Wren stared.

"Corporal," came a familiar voice, shouting over the beating of the rotors.

Henry was standing right there, saluting. Wren hadn't seen him since their joint operation against the Viking biker gang in Utah.

"Hot dang," Wren said, and matched the salute sharply. "Henry, it's good to see you. How are you?"

"Better for seeing you alive, Sir," Henry reeled off, as uniform as a military roll call.

"Likewise, soldier," Wren said, barreling through the catch in his throat. It had been too long since they'd had a coin meeting. "Your family?"

"Well, Sir! And yours?"

"Well," Wren answered, though he didn't know it. Better off for not being near him. "At ease."

Henry broke off the salute and stood smartly, arms clasped behind his back as if for inspection. Wren looked down the line at the rest of the team; all Foundation members he'd recruited over the years, from drug deals gone sour, black ops that went wrong, cartels that broke apart, gangs that fractured under DELTA-level tactics.

Mason was there. It took Wren a second to pick out his dark eyes within the mass of scar tissue branding his cheeks, chin, forehead. SAINT, those brands read. Mason, who'd turned on the Order of the Saints just in time to save Wren and the country.

"Oh God," Wren murmured.

"Not quite," Mason said, with a shy smile.

The man had been in the hospital for months, getting treatment for the bullets Sinclair had put in his chest, followed by months more in private therapy with Dr. Ferat for the mental scars the Alpha had put in his brain. They'd had a coin meeting since Ferat's death, spoken some about small things, and Wren had arranged for fresh mental health support. He'd never expected to see this.

"Are you sure you can-"

"I'm sure," said Mason. His voice sounded thick. "I owe this."

There was the weight. They all carried it. Mason had killed Wendy, the love of his life. Cult indoctrination broke people in all the worst ways, made them traitors to themselves.

"I was a Marine," Mason went on, justifying his presence. "I can fight."

Again Wren pushed through the tightness in his throat. "I'm glad you're here. We're lucky to have you."

Mason just nodded.

Wren surveyed the others; people he hadn't expected, who weren't military or even police-trained, who shouldn't be there at all. Chuck the office worker, who'd fallen into the Foundation after being caught out in a basic marijuana buy. He looked thicker in the chest than before, filled out with muscle. Abigail, a brilliant triathlete who'd been sucked into a pseudoscience cult at 21, then pressured to give up her ambition and 'serve' as a lay preacher to squeeze the masses. Luke the ex-State Congressman, who'd fallen from grace on deep charges of white collar fraud, only kept out of jail by his decision to testify against the CEO of a major oil corporation. It had briefly made the national news. Larissa Bray, a surgeon he'd caught out in the run-up to graduating to an Angel of Death, padding out care packages as a sadistic Munchausen-Syndrome-by-Proxy addict, staring back at him with those dark eyes that always gave him goosebumps.

They were a band of misfits. Only three months of training for some of them. Chuck who'd never seen combat in his life. Mason barely recovered from deep trauma. Henry still scarred by the sacrifice of Abdul, saving his life against the Order of the Saints.

That was over a year ago now. To Wren it felt like a lifetime.

He stood in the dark and thunder before them, struck by the power and unity of the Foundation, such that it could bring these people together. For some reason they believed in him, and what the Foundation stood for. They weren't out on the streets sharing bullshit memes, lost in some hunt for meaning when meaning was right there in front of their eyes.

Loyalty mattered. Actions rather than words. These people were the Foundation upon which he now stood. The shoulders of giants.

In that moment, Wren realized his plan was wrong. Would have to be completely re-thought. He was needed elsewhere, and they had the matter in hand. He nodded at Henry, then surveyed them all. Explained the new plan. Took receipt of a few pieces of gear in a deployment bag, then shook their hands one by one.

"Thank you," he said, looking around at his Foundation, then stepped off the helicopter.

The rotor sped up. The Airbus rocketed into the air.

Sometime in the last few minutes his mission brief had shifted. Maybe it was the slow punch impact of seeing Teddy, out there on the front line. Of seeing Henry and Mason. Injuries healed. Loss could make you stronger. Loyalty counted for something.

There were so many frontlines, now, and this was not his.

"You need another helicopter?" B4cksl4cker said in his ear.

"I thought you'd never ask."

"We have one on standby. Strictly civilian. Also, we're working on a location."

It was music to Wren's ears. "Lead on, maestro."

38

BOLO

The first BOLO had come in twenty minutes earlier, from a farmer's market in the tiny desert podunk of San Felipe, fifty miles south-east of San Jose. A wild-looking half-naked woman stalking the market's produce aisles, snatching up a guava in one hand and an avocado in the other, before making off through the back with a shop apron plucked off a coat rack.

No attempt to play the Federal agent card. No effort to request a phone. No identifying details at all, other than female, stocky, blond.

It told Wren everything he needed to know: the Ghosts had abducted Sally Rogers the same way they'd taken Steven Gruber, by exploiting a known connection. They'd phished her and drawn her out. A text message from a trusted source, maybe, citing some emergency. It was the only explanation why she hadn't immediately called in to local authorities.

She thought the CIA was compromised. She thought the Ghosts had a mole high in the CIA.

Wren thought so too.

His helicopter sped just west of due north, parallel with the Pacific coast, an R44 four-person. Wren sat beside the pilot, eyes glued to the Ghosts' countdown on his phone. Just over an hour left.

"You got them all?" he asked Hellion.

"All the BOLOs were intercepted," she replied. "No one else knows where she is."

The second BOLO had come in swiftly on the first's tail; a sighting of a woman wearing a navy shop apron boosting an ATV sports vehicle from the ostrich farm two hundred yards down the road from the farmer's market.

It was going to be tight. The crowds across the country were already heating up in the run up to dusk. The strike teams in Russia, China and Malaysia weren't going to stay undetected for much longer. The countdown timer on the ghost's feed was ticking down. Gruber's life hung in the balance, and with it peace across America.

"Any sighting on the ATV since?"

"I have a drone array up, shifting satellite overwatch."

"Can we project her potential route?"

"Already done. Modeling predicted routes now. Twenty percent ruled out so far; she's not on any known roads. The remaining eighty percent are routes through the wild."

"So she's off-road?" Wren brought up the map on his phone and scrolled the screen, looking for her angle. Rogers thought like him. If there was a mole in her organization, she'd look to root it out herself. Her first thoughts now had to be money, clothes, weaponry and a way back in.

So where would she be headed? On an ATV with thirty minutes to play with, she could have covered maybe thirty miles over rough terrain. Immediately to the north, east and south of San Felipe lay the thick barrier of the Henry W. Coe State Park, a chaparral coated ten-mile tranche of the Diablo Range mountains. Only to the west and southeast lay roads leading out down narrow valleys.

Wren zoomed in. If it was him, he'd head for a cache-point; a place he'd secreted money, weaponry, clothing. He had them in every state, tucked away like buried treasure in parks, highway sidings and open scrub. It was highly unlikely Rogers had anything like that, though.

So where?

The answer came fast. She'd overseen the placement of his family in Witness Protection, which meant she'd had access to a range of Federal safe houses. Any capable agent would have memorized as many as they could, against a rainy day, and Rogers was far more than just a capable agent.

"Can you get me a map of CIA safe houses?"

"What?" Hellion came back. "Safe houses?"

"Witness Protection, stations for the FBI, anything like that."

A second passed. "That's deep within the Deep State, Christopher."

"Is it a paper record?" Wren pushed back. "Will I need a semi-truck to carry it away?"

"Of course not," Hellion snapped swiftly. "With the second skin, I can steal this information in moments; but we will no longer be invisible. This action cannot be ghosted from Humphreys, Christopher. They will know whatever I look at."

He weighed that for about a second. Every bit of his new plan depended on the element of surprise, but you couldn't control for everything.

"Acceptable risk. Do it. Apply what you find as targets in the ghosting protocol for Rogers. I need to get to her first."

Keys flew and clattered immediately. "B4cksl4cker, can you activate a botnet to crunch the crypto?"

"Yes," said B4cksl4cker, "activating."

Wren sat in the thundering helo hunched over his phone screen. Somewhere a hundred miles north the Airbus was closing in on Gruber. A hundred miles south the crowds at the Wilshire were gathering mass and anger. All across the country, people stamped toward the precipice.

"No video whatsoever," he said. "This is a dark strike."

"Understood," Hellion answered. "We're through their first firewalls. Hang tight, Christopher, let us do our job."

Seconds ticked by, long enough for Wren to second-guess himself multiple times over. Intelligence was a gamble. You looked at your opponent's MO and you made predictions, like the ghosting protocol.

"Got something," Hellion said abruptly. "Not a full listing, we're inferring a lot, but there looks to be a witness protection building forty miles northeast of your current position, the town of Dos Palos, across from the Circle K. Our bet is that's where she's heading."

"Is it built up?"

Keys flew. "Population five thousand, but there'll definitely be witnesses to a helicopter coming in over the mall."

Wren cursed. Always too slow. "No witnesses then. I intercept her in the desert. Get me her position."

"Fine-tuning. You're en route. Given the timings, we anticipate," a brief pause, "seven minutes until live intercept. She's not going to stop for you, Christopher."

"I know."

From the Airbus deployment bag he extracted a safety harness and a two-hundred-foot rappel spool; a large coil of slim black Nylon 4 rope with a large carabiner-style donut ring for anchoring. He shrugged on two black double-leather palmed gloves then held the spool up in front of the pilot, whose eyes bugged.

"Here's what we're going to do," he said.

39

DOS PALOS

Three miles out of Dos Palos Wren saw her; a half-dressed blond woman racing an ATV through green and ochre fields of budding pistachios. Wren sat half out of the passenger side door, feet on the skids with the wind rushing hard around him.

"Lower," he shouted to the pilot, and the helicopter dropped.

The pilot hadn't wanted to do it. Wren had bargained, cajoled, and finally settled on a form of compulsion.

"I am going out of that door. If you don't land me right, I'll die. You don't want that."

The guy had turned to water.

Two hundred feet of line. An impossible maneuver. Rogers' head whipped around at the sound, sighted the bird in the sky, and at once the ATV began jerky evasive maneuvers, zigzagging side to side through lush crops.

"Stay with her," Wren barked, then jumped.

Helicopter rappels were hard. They were only ever supposed to be conducted with a rappel master in back, from a stationary helicopter, but Wren had already broken both those rules when he'd bailed out of the Chinook, so this was nothing.

The nylon rope sped through his hands, and the wind battered him, swaying him hard into the helicopter's backdraft and setting him off at a dizzy spin. He squeezed the rope and briefly slowed his momentum, but it did nothing for the mad pirouette as the air resistance tumbled him crazily.

He saw Dos Palos, he saw the Diablo Range, he saw Dos Palos then the Diablos and a tiny glimpse of Rogers' face staring back at him in disbelief, then he squeezed the rope again and slowed his descent further; still seventy feet above the ground and choppering ahead at forty miles an hour, keeping pace with the ATV.

Rogers banked hard right.

"Right," Wren shouted, his earpiece keyed now to the pilot, but the helicopter overshot wildly. The pilot corrected swiftly. Rogers was fifty yards to the right, thirty down, and the tail end of Wren's rope was trailing through the bushy low pistachio trees.

He released his grip and rappelled the final length until he was down at the level of the top branches, tearing down an open aisle in the long parallel ranks of trees, then slid further still until his feet were barely inches above the ground. That was crazy enough in itself, but the pirouette was only picking up speed, so he slid the final stretch until his feet touched and corkscrewed into the dirt.

The friction halted his spin. He clamped hold of the rope and picked up his feet and began to run. At forty the pace was far too fast, but he landed big strides that kept him poised and facing forward, ahead to where Rogers' face had spun back to see him, a mask of disbelief.

"It's me!" he shouted at her. Barely thirty yards between them now. "Christopher Wren!"

He couldn't imagine what she was thinking. Last time she'd seen him, it was in Great Kills before dropping the black bag on his head.

She revved the ATV and swung hard left.

"Left," Wren shouted, and the helicopter banked hard, yanking Wren into a swing. Only too late did he realize he was heading straight for a pistachio tree. They weren't thick around, no wider than a street lamp, but a street lamp could wreck a vehicle at the speeds he was going. He'd wrap his body around it like a pretzel.

"Stop!" he shouted, but the pilot couldn't possibly react fast enough, leaving him with one shot. As his feet touched down just ahead of the tree he kicked off the ground with everything he had, while also yanking on the rope. He cleared maybe five feet and veered slightly to the left; enough to send him crashing through the branches rather than splattering into the bark.

Raspberry red pistachios burst around him like confetti at a wedding, branches whiplashed across his face and chest, then he dropped down hard on his nylon line. The pilot must have felt the drag, because the helicopter's speed died and Wren was left swaying and spinning out of control, so fast he couldn't make anything out, feet bare inches above the ground.

He dropped the distance and turned just in time to see Rogers coming right at him in a cloud of dust. He barely picked his legs up in time, the ATV flew by underneath and Rogers' shoulder hit his chest and stripped him off the rappel line like a shelled pea.

For a second they flew together, then he hit the hard clay first and tumbled, air forced from his lungs, with Rogers controlling the roll. He tried to get his legs underneath him but she had the initiative, wrenching his arm up behind his back and forcing his face into the dirt so hard he could hardly breathe.

Damn, she was strong. For a moment he thought she was going to break his elbow, probably dislocate the shoulder joint with it, and if not that then maybe just throttle him in the dust.

"Christopher Wren," she barked instead. "What the ever-loving hell?"

"It's a .... long story," he managed to wheeze out.

"You've got two minutes."

He started in. One minute later she was on her feet and backing away, his own Glock trained on his face. At two minutes her already-pale face lapsed as white as Humphreys'.

"What are you talking about, Ghosts?"

Wren grunted and rose to his feet gingerly, brushing twigs and ripe pistachios off his scratched up shirt and jeans, rolling his shoulder. She'd definitely tweaked it. "Ghosts. Spooks. Specters. On account they're invisible."

"I get the synonyms," Rogers snapped dismissively. "I'm talking about the number. You're saying Ghosts, but it's just one guy, singular, Ghost."

Wren blinked. The helicopter's downdraft massaged them both. "What? One guy?"

"One guy. He's a beast, bigger even than you, and CIA. It's how he brought me in."

Wren's head spun. "What?"

"He posed as a Company man standing guard on your family, said he had intel you were preparing a breakout followed by a 'rescue'. My eyes only, the Company was infected. He called me and I came." She spat. "More fool me."

Wren struggled to catch up. CIA? And rescue? It sounded just like with Gruber, drawing the target out to self-abduct. "He phished you."

"So maybe I'm a phish," she spat, the anger burning off her, the dark barrel hole of the Glock trained on his face like a third eye. "But now I'm thinking. He said there was some 'Deep State' conspiracy to set you free." Her eyes narrowed. "He said you'd come for me, extract the location for your family, and now here you are. So what do you want, Wren? And how the hell did you get out of a secure black site?"

He stared. She was dead serious. More BS, black psy ops just to sell the phishing tale, but how could she know that? "I fought my way out, Rogers," he began. "It wasn't some conspiracy. I almost died just to get out of my cuffs, almost took Humphreys with me, jumped out of a Chinook pretty much like I did just now, then started some crazy nonsense all over LA to get to here." She didn't look convinced. "Listen, Sally, you're right about a lot. The Company are compromised, this guy definitely phished you into a kidnap, and maybe other parts of the Deep State are rotten too, but that's a problem for a later day. Right now riots are about to hit the fan across the country, Gruber's about to burn, and I need your help."

Her eyes narrowed. She squeezed the trigger bar on the Glock, releasing the safety. "Help with what?"

"With stopping this thing before all hell breaks loose! Like the good old days. Are you in?"

40

HEAVENS ABOVE

For long moments little Pequeño 3 lay in Grace's arms in the dark of the pit, waiting for the pain to pull back, for his lungs to stop catching in his tight chest. All the while, she stroked his head and whispered about mud pies in his ear, her touch hot against the clammy cold.

Above them the Pequeños breathed, in then out, like the whole Earth was alive. In the deep dark it felt like the walls of the pit were expanding with every breath, were shrinking with every breath in.

Except he knew that wasn't true.

"We're gonna be OK," Grace whispered.

He pushed himself up, off her legs and into a sitting position. He had some dull sense that Chrysogonus stood above them, Aden to the left, Galicia to the right, the others around the back. Stuck in the middle.

He moved his head closer to Grace, pressed his lips against her ear, waited until the Pequeños were breathing in and whispered.

"We have to dig."

He felt her stiffen at the words. Let her head move beside his, cheek to cheek as her lips came to his ear, waiting for the moment.

"They ain't gonna let us."

Another slow, rolling exchange.

"You pull the stones," he said, and waited. "It's easy. They come right away." Another pause, breathing. "Reach one hand in, feel for the tunnel." Breathing. "We don't need to dig much."

Her head rolled gently around his. "They'll hear." She was cold with fear. He felt just the same. "They'll hear us and stop us."

"They won't hear you."

It was a simple plan. She said she didn't like it. He didn't give her the time to argue.

It began with him pulling both his legs in tight, snug like a bug, then shooting them out as fast as he could. His heels hit Chrysogonus' calf so hard it knocked his foot back. Chrysogonus yelped, then shouted, then bent down to snatch up little Pequeño 3, but he was already gone, scampering on all fours.

One knee fell on what could be Aden's foot and pulled out another cry, his head bumped into a knee and he rolled away before swooping hands could grab him, using all the skills he'd developed outrunning his minders amongst the desert cacti. Within seconds he was at the wall, thin body pressed into the corner, while all the elder Pequeños were pushing and falling and letting out frenzied whispers.

While they fought he dug at the wall. Flat stones pried away easily, as his elders grappled with each other. Beyond each stone he felt only damp sand. He pushed against it, remembering how the thin barrier of sand had crumbled away beneath the Apex's hand, but that sinking sensation didn't come.

Then the Pequeños were silent. He realized it too late. His head felt a little foggy, maybe from the slaps. He kept digging too long, prying out the fifth stone with his fingernails, maybe a black stone, perhaps a white stone, when he felt the vibration of heavy footfalls coming near. He tried to roll, but it was too late.

A booted foot came sweeping in and struck him hard in the belly. It forced all the air from his chest, sent him thumping off the wall and back to the sand, curled double with an incredible hot pain surging from the pit of his gut to the top of his neck, sucking emptily for air.

Nothing came in. Panic poured through him. Somewhere above Chrysogonus was panting, shouting between pants, and the other Pequeños were arguing. About killing him, maybe. He rolled to his back, desperate for breath, sucking as hard as he could but getting nothing.

It couldn't be so soon. Running out of air. He'd watched the experiments drown in the vats behind the hotel, seen the terrible panic in their eyes, filmed them for the Apex.

"I saw the light," those men and women would say after their experimentation, bowed low before the Apex. "Thank you."

Those that survived.

Footsteps stamped in and he curled, but no kick landed. Instead there was a thud, followed by other thuds, and the voice of Galicia rallying above the others.

Protecting him? He couldn't be sure. Finally a trickle of air worked into his throat, and the excitement almost blacked him out.

"Come on," came Grace's whisper, and her touch on his shoulder. Leading him away. She pulled and he followed, making it back to his knees while the elder Pequeños fought and panted overhead

"Did you ... find it?" he asked in whispery gasps.

"We'll look together," she answered. "Just like the pies."

"Just like ... the pies."

The fighting dwindled, but all the elder Pequeños were groaning now. At one point they bumped into Galicia, lying on the floor. She didn't move at all, and they crawled over her body. Chrysogonus bellowed at times, about his testament or calling to Pequeño 3, but he sounded strange, sucking in air too hard and staggering around.

"He's drunk," Grace whispered in Pequeño 3's ear.

"What's drunk?" he whispered back, between, rock pulls and sand punches.

"It's when you get older, and scary."

They avoided Chrysogonus, and worked their way around the circle. It wasn't large. Whenever one of the elders came near, they froze, or scampered away. Their previously unified breath had become a staggered rasping.

"There's no air," said Grace.

"So how come we can breathe?" he answered.

"'Cos we're small," she answered, like it was obvious. "Like a mouse. We don't need much."

That made sense to him.

Then they came upon tumbled stones. It took him a moment to realize what it meant. Damp sand in the wall. Flat stones by the corner. They'd been around the pit walls one whole time.

"Dig more," he said. It was all he could say. It was getting harder to breathe. Up in the air of the pit, Chrysogonus was wheezing loudly, sucking hard.

They sped up. Sound didn't matter now. They worked a second circuit, and Pequeño 3 pulled more stones out, and dug deeper into the sand. His fingertips got cold and raw but he couldn't stop. They were just little shovels, he told himself, like the mud pies were strawberries and cream.

At some point Chrysogonus stopped staggering and dropped to his knees with the others. There they all wheezed, until they fell back into synchrony. Like one giant lung, breathing in the earth, breathing out the earth.

Pequeño 3 didn't realize he'd stopped moving until Grace's cold touch came on his cheek.

"Come on," she whispered. They kept on. They dug a second row up, then a third. They went over Galicia's body, and she didn't move. The wheezing of the others faded. Pequeño 3's breaths came in tiny, panicky pants. Sometimes Grace pulled him along, sometimes he pulled her, until finally his hand broke through.

He was up to his shoulder in the wall. Fingers worming in the sand. Suddenly there was no resistance. He pulled back, and felt a cold blast of fresh desert air blow into his face. At once it woke him up. His eyes brightened. He grabbed Grace and pulled her over.

It didn't take long to open a gap wide enough to crawl through. The other Pequeños were stirring. They crawled out. Still it was pitch black, but there was a hint of light ahead. Pequeño 3 took the lead, feeling rough wooden staves at his sides, over his head. He crawled and crawled, until at last there was faint moonlight, and he saw his hands, and he emerged through the crust of the Earth into the open desert.

The sky had never seemed so immense. Stars were everywhere, sparkling like a million dreams. He rolled and helped Grace come through. To the right they saw the Pyramid, clustered around the low mound of sleds and sand, lit by flickering fires. He thought he saw the Apex, standing in their midst, staring right back at him, but he couldn't be sure.

"What about the others?" Grace whispered in his ear. "The elders?"

"They'll be fine," he answered. Afraid now. Afraid to have survived. "Come on."

They crawled, then they walked, then they ran. Not to the fake town, but to the red rock. There they stayed by the muddy water pool, and drank the juice from prickly pears and ate hand-roasted bark scorpions and Mexican red-kneed tarantula and once even a big pink Gila monster.

In the days they climbed the rock and made mud pies, and in the nights they cuddled close in a shelter of torn ocotillo necks. They talked about the Apex and the other Pequeños. Where they might be. They imagined

Chrysogonus roaring his way around the fake town, looking for them, and laughed.

On the third night, as dusk fell and the stars shone up in the sky, they returned. The Pyramid remained circled around the mound, listening to the Earth suck in and out. They entered the tunnel and crawled along it, expecting a beating on the other side.

Chrysogonus would be furious they had ruined his 'Testament'. The laughter stopped as they reached the end of the tunnel, in the total darkness, and found it blocked up. Pequeño 3's heart raced. It was easy to dig through, pulling some sand, pushing the rest. He was first through, into a sour, musty smell.

He recognized that smell.

"Cover your nose," he whispered to Grace.

Soon after that, the sound came of sand shushing above. They were being dug out. Together they filled the tunnel in, and patted the big flat stones back into place to cover it. They went around and around the walls, faster and faster as the foul air grew thinner, pushing stones back into place, covering up every sign of their escape, until finally, standing together in the middle of the pit, the first of the sleds came off and light poured in.

Chrysogonus lay in front of them, pale as the grave. Galicia lay by the wall. Aden lay beside her, with Zachariah and Gabriel nearby. All pale, and still. On some level, little Pequeño 3 understood what must have happened. They'd sealed themselves back in.

The Pyramid wailed and cheered. So many dead. Two still alive. It was a triumph of faith. It was a tragedy. It was proof that the Apex was a great man, the greatest of them all.

They were raised out to such clamor, and promises of a celebration mixed with a wake. Throughout it all, the Apex's eyes remained pinned to those of little Pequeño 3, sparkling blue like furious stars in the heavens above.

41

ROGERS

With thirty minutes left on the clock, Hellion nailed the Ghost's position down.

"He's in a big rig, semi-trailer truck," she said sharply in Wren's ear as the helo tore through the sky. "Or he was two hours back, heading north on the 99. It's ghosted, but I ghosted our satellite overwatch and picked it out."

Wren took a sharp breath. Ghosts fighting ghosts.

"Destination?"

"No way to know. We're tracking forward via satellite, but algorithm predicts he pulled east. Our best target is shuttered school at edge of Angels Camp, little town west of Stanislaus National Forest. Nothing near but creeping desert. We will know for sure soon."

Wren squeezed the phone tight. Good news at last. "Anything on his ID, his link-up to the CIA?"

"Working. Rogers' description helps. It is deep bench."

"What about backward tracking? Any idea where he crossed with the Apex?"

"Nothing yet, Christopher. Taking him backward will take time. For now we are working on location."

"Good." He took a shaky breath. "How far out's the Airbus?"

"Twenty minutes ahead of his last known location. They are low on fuel, but they will make it to the school in twenty minutes."

Twenty minutes until the school. Thirty minutes until Gruber burned. It was going to be tight.

"How much lead time does Teddy want?"

"The plan was five minutes, in advance of Ghost hit."

"Shorter," Rogers said abruptly. She looked at Wren urgently, listening in on her own earpiece, sitting by his side in the back of the R44. "This guy, he's on the ball. You start cutting his links to the network, it won't take him five minutes to read the tea leaves. Gruber will be dead in seconds."

"Call it two minutes," Wren said. "Hard strikes, priority on cutting lines and shutting them down."

"I'll relay to Theodore," said Hellion.

Wren felt his heart kick up a notch, eighty beats a minute rising to ninety. It was all going to happen soon, and everything had to be ready. He tapped the earpiece silent and turned to Rogers.

She looked sick. Maybe pneumonia, early-onset, compounded by deep post-traumatic shock. After what she'd been through, the physical damage would be the least of it. He hadn't even tried to address that yet, too busy pumping her for all the information she could muster; what the guy looked like, what his habits were, what he'd wanted. It wasn't going to be enough, though, if this thing went the way he thought it was going to.

"What?" she asked. Glaring at him now, angry almost.

He wanted to reach out, touch her elbow, knee, but knew that wouldn't be welcome. All the anger she was feeling, no small part of it fell at his door. She'd be twisted up inside, knowing she'd been tricked with lies about him, that she'd had to watch Jay burn because of him. In some sick way, his father had made all this about Wren.

"Nothing," he said, then quickly corrected that. "No, not nothing. I was thinking about the guy. The Ghost, what he wants. But mostly I was thinking about you."

Rogers' eyes blazed. It was easiest to rely on anger, after what she'd been through. "Don't think about me."

"Because we're nothing to each other?"

"Because we were teammates, and you abandoned me. You shot me, dumped me, gambled with my life."

"I'm here now."

She looked away. "Not for me."

He couldn't argue with that, but it wasn't quite fair. "For what it's worth, I'm sorry I shot you."

"It's not worth anything," she snapped, staring out of the window. "You set my career back five years. I could have died. On top of that, you killed hundreds of Pinocchios. You appointed yourself judge of them all, and you made me complicit in the crime."

He took that on the chin. Maybe it was a mistake to bring any of this up, but then he needed her. He looked at his phone screen. The minutes raced by.

"The people I killed were monsters, Rogers. We're talking about serial child abusers, the worst of the worst."

She glared through the window so hard he thought she might burn a hole. "I'm not going to discuss it."

"And shooting you was an operational risk. It was a mistake. I should have found another way."

She spun her eyes back to him, hot and hurt. "You'd do it again in a heartbeat."

"Betray you?"

She said nothing, boring a hole into his eyes. There were things he could say further, probably better off unsaid. He held his tongue. She turned away. Orange desert rushed by below.

His phone chimed and he brought it up. Confirmation was coming in, the Ghost had gone to the school in Angel's Camp, though his trailer truck was gone. They were tracking it. The Airbus was closing in, getting ready to deploy its dirt bikes. Five minutes until the overseas strikes began.

Five minutes. A lot could change. No point holding back now.

"You weren't the only one who was betrayed at the Anti-Ca compound," he said.

Rogers spun on him like a left hook. "What the hell you say to me?"

He hadn't said anything like it until then. Had avoided saying it, because it was so much easier just to let her hate him, but hate wasn't going to cut it now.

"You turned on me first, Rogers. You pulled your gun, aimed it at me, told me to stop."

Her cheeks blushed scarlet with rage. Thrown back into the memory. "Because you were threatening a pregnant girl! You were trying to make her drink cyanide."

"It wasn't cyanide," he said quietly.

"What?"

"It was apple cider vinegar and orange juice. I faked it. You were my partner. You could have trusted me."

Not should. Could. Should might be too much. Still she stared at him for a long second, eyes burning, maybe figuring out just how furious she was, whether she wanted to kick him out of the helicopter right there and then. "Trusted you? The way you were talking back then, about the Apex, about your father? It was like you'd gone mad, Wren! You were obsessed, out of it completely."

He looked at her, feeling the sadness of it now, a sadness he hadn't allowed in since she'd renditioned him, about what they'd both lost in that moment.

"But I wasn't crazy, was I?"

She opened her mouth. Didn't say anything. Closed it.

Three minutes on the clock.

He turned back to his phone, bringing up the visuals from the three strike teams. He tapped his earpiece and immediately heard the chatter of mission prep, then scrolled through bodycams of the Vladivostok squad until he got a bead on Teddy's thinned out-face, backdropped by the canvas wall of their forward operating truck.

"Teddy?" he interrupted.

"All go here, Christopher," Teddy said, holding one hand to his ear in a practiced gesture, like he'd run a hundred ops before this. "We're synced."

"Good luck. Don't risk yourself. We need you."

"It's all risk," said Teddy and cut the line.

Wren brought up the Airbus video feed, shot from the belly of the chopper. The rectangular complex of the school was coming up ahead, surrounded by baking red sands.

"Henry, are you go for assault?"

The line crackled and Henry's sharp voice came back, matched by the bodycam visual from a team member across the way. Henry looked cool and commanding in the dark of the cabin. "Yes, Sir!" he shouted over the roar of the Airbus' blades. "We put down three miles out, Mason and Abigail are en route via dirt bike. I'll lead the rappel charge. We'll hit simultaneously, should be two minutes after Theodore."

Theodore. That killed Wren. First thing when you join a cult, they give you a new name.

"Take them alive if you can. Priority is Gruber. We're almost in position. Shut down any and all live video feeds. Our worst case is not just that he dies, worse is that they screen it."

"Understood, Sir."

Wren leaned back, and the red light in the corner of the bodycam feed blinked out.

He went through the same process for the two remaining strikes: Alejandro hunkered with his team on the rooftop of the Internet café in Beijing, sheltered by a silver water tower; Doona at the roof edge of the donut block in Kuala Lumpur, looking down on a traditional Malay building in the midst of jungle-like overgrowth, thatched roof and raised on stilts.

The feeds locked down. The teams were ready. Everything looked to be five by five. Wren checked the clock, a minute left. He felt Rogers glaring at him and turned. The fury in her eyes was overwhelming. Like she wanted nothing more than to stab him fifteen times and dump the corpse out the door.

"That isn't fair," she said. More a hiss, like the last air deflating from a withered balloon. "You didn't give me any choice."

There was nothing to say to that. He said it anyway. "There's always a choice."

Ten seconds until breach.

42

BREACH

Teddy's team hit first by a few seconds, a fast charge out of the truck and across a parking lot up to the door of the meme factory in Vladivostok, like any other large office block, and Wren watched it all on bodycam. Abercrombie hit the secure glass door with a handheld ram and the glass burst inward, unleashing a caterwauling alarm as the squad of Foundation members raced into a brightly colored double-height lobby with their rifles raised.

Fast on their heels came the Beijing hit; the Sunlit Dawn members led by Alejandro racing down two flights of stairs from the roof and charging pell-mell into the Internet café. Faces flipped up from their screens, shouts rang out, and Alejandro reached the door to the rear room where virality chief Pang Jiao Shou was holed up, just as-

Doona rappelled off the roof in the shadow of the Petronas Towers, leading four more Sunlit Dawn members to the ground where they cut their lines, hoisted AR-15 rifles and ran at the ornate carved exterior of the wooden box, raised up on timber legs in the tight green jungle, hidey-hole of the ghost-tech hackers.

"Clear," came Teddy's bass, and Wren shifted to the Vladivostok hit. He was standing at the edge of the curving, molded lobby, decked out with bright geometric shapes like a Silicon Valley campus. A receptionist stood behind his desk, arms up, wearing a cute blue cap. Teddy's team rolled over the security gates and took up position either side of a double card lock door leading deeper in, hit it with the ram and crashed through into-

Alejandro tried the metal door to the café's back room but the lock held in the reinforced frame; he signaled and two Sunlit Dawn members moved up in perfect synchrony, wielding ten pound sledgehammers. Alejandro gave a fast three count and they pulled back, swung the hammers and struck the door either side of dead center. There was a huge double bang and the lock's face tore away from the strike plate, the bolt dredged out of the frame and the buckled door swung wide open into-

Doona bypassed the door to the incongruous house ensconced in jungle palms, instead climbing a stilt and attacking the wall head-on; four pads of C4 explosive tacked into place with adhesive strips. She dropped back down, took shelter amongst the trees then hit her phone to detonate. The wall blew out like a backfiring engine, with a burst of flame chased by fat gouts of gray smoke. Doona was climbing and plunging through the ragged hole into-

An office expanse lay ahead of Teddy, sectioned off into dozens of octagonal cubicles like a human-scale bee hive, each with low walls in bright primary colors splashed with exhortations to BE CREATIVE! and USE AMERICAN SLANG! In each octagonal cell faces turned to the interlopers, like drones at the advent of the beekeeper. Hands went up like a Mexican wave, creatives bowing out easily.

"Eleven o'clock," Wren snapped in Teddy's ear, picking out a scrap of stray movement on his bodycam, "maybe the Queen."

Teddy swung; Sunlit Dawn members were already moving through the passageways cored into the hive, deploying plastic zip ties on the worker drones.

"Got him," Teddy answered, and set off at a sprint toward a door in the rear wall. Either side hung huge posters laying out near-mathematical equations for pumping out propaganda in English: a mish-mash listing of famous names, apocalyptic predictions, outlandish conspiracies, dark religious quotations and past political scandals. His name, the Foundation and the names of his key members were everywhere; a shopping list for sowing nonsense in the minds of the American people.

He'd seen equations exactly like them many times before, had written the guidance himself on occasion, in black psy-ops against rival states; all the ways you could launder lies and control a populace.

He dragged his focus dead ahead, where Teddy was almost at the door in back. Hanging above it was the largest banner yet, this one written in Russian

Cyrillic, though the translation came easily; a familiar reduction of Lifton's theory on indoctrination.

CONFUSE. DISCREDIT. REPLACE.

The propagandist's credo.

"Careful, Teddy," he cautioned, as Teddy laid hands on the rear door and wrenched it open.

Alejandro shot through the reinforced door into a private conference room in the back of the Internet café, where a short round woman wearing thick black spectacles stood at the head of a long desk, screeching something in Mandarin and punching a whiteboard covered in calculations. Her eyes widened on Alejandro as the busted door clanged off the inner wall.

At the conference table sat a dozen kids, none older than twenty, each set up with a twin-monitor array atop buzzing fat desktop towers.

"Phones down!" Alejandro barked as he stalked in, rifle levelled on the Fat Unicorn at the fore. Her eyes were phasing now to anger. Sunlit Dawn members in back barked out the command in Mandarin and Cantonese, then the woman gave a sharp nod.

"Six o'clock!" Wren shouted.

Alejandro spun and took sudden incoming fire. There was an explosion of distorting sound, the bodycam abruptly reeled back and Wren saw only the ceiling, then chair legs, then terrified faces low to the fuzzy gray carpet as the kids hit the deck. Shooting and shouting came through in a cacophony of jumbled sounds, and Wren flicked between bodycams on the various members of his strike team.

All were down.

"By the door," he shouted. "Two guys with handguns. Alejandro!"

Alejandro's feed spun to the ceiling, back to the fuzzy carpet as he got to his hands and knees, then scrabbling forward until he came upon a pair of stockinged feet. The camera jostled, rose, pressed against brown fabric, then Wren caught a glimpse of the Fat Unicorn's toad-like face in close-up, her gimlet expression a blend of hilarity and terror.

"Tell them to stop!" Alejandro shouted at her, rifle to her head while the shooting and screams crescendoed, but the Fat Unicorn just let out a high, panicky laugh.

"Your team's down, give me eyes, use the bodycam," Wren ordered, as clear and precise as he could.

It took Alejandro a second, then his palm closed over the bodycam lens, plucked it, reversed it, and raised it up above the line of the conference table.

It gave Wren just a second of visual before one of the guards picked off the lens and flung the screen into darkness.

"They're flanking you left and right, one high, one low," Wren said rapidly. "Roll left and take the one guy, pop up and get the other in transition."

No answer came, only loud rasping sounds, breathing, then the abrasive sound of two gunshots, three, four. Wren raced through the cams of the Sunlit Dawn team, seeing only mold-damped squares of ceiling tiles.

Doona plunged through the smoke into some kind of ringing outer corridor; so narrow she had to advance side-on.

"Go, go, go!" she ordered, sending her team left while she went right.

"Insulation skin," came Hellion's voice. "To disguise the heat mapping within. I recognize this set-up."

"We use it," said B4cksl4cker.

The cam jogged up and down as Doona ran to the corner, where she angled and looked out; nobody was there, just another featureless wooden corridor bar one security camera in the far corner.

"No sign of any doors."

"Security procedure, single access," Hellion said, the sound of keys flurrying. "They have you on camera now."

"Let's see what they're hiding," Doona said, extracted another two strips of C4, peeled the sticky tabs and stuck them to the wall.

"Back," she ordered, retreated beyond the corner, hit the phone for another tremendous explosive bark, then sprinted back around and through a fresh wound in the wall, into a space that held-

- nothing.

No people. No desks, computer towers, chairs, or anything at all, except an unobtrusive red workman's tin in the center of the floor.

"Bomb!" Wren shouted.

Doona ran, out of the fresh hole, along the corridor, until her bodycam jerked abruptly sideways soundlessly, driven through the wall and sent flying through the jungle while bright purple lines of static skirled across the screen. Just before her cam hit the ground there was an almighty crumping sound, air impacting under explosive force, then the video died.

Wren flicked rapidly through the feeds of her squad, all down.

"Get them help, Hellion," he said urgently.

"I've called local ambulance services. Our on-site doctor can't handle this scale. We can extricate them later."

"Good," said Wren, his mind whirring. "Pay off anyone you need to pay."

"Who?" Hellion asked.

"Anyone you can reach. All of them. The guy with the stretcher. The surgeon. The local politician. Flood the zone with money."

"Flooding," Hellion answered. "Christopher, we're also scrambling for Alejandro."

Wren flicked back through the feeds.

"Alejandro, report!"

Alejandro's bodycam was looking down on the bodies of two guards. Thickset, one was dead, the other had a hand clamped to his shoulder.

"I'm shot in the thigh, Christopher," came Alejandro's pained voice. "Binding it now. We cut transmissions from the building ahead of the strike, nothing in or out."

"And your team?"

"Three injured, one dead."

Wren cursed. "Exfiltrate," he ordered. "Take the Unicorn, the gear, the kids. Get to the safe house."

"We're on the move."

Alejandro nudged the guard. Somebody shouted a command in Mandarin, and he grudgingly got to his feet. In the background came the sound of the Fat Unicorn bleating something in rapid half-English.

Wren flicked over. Rogers put a hand on his arm, staring at him. "They knew you were coming."

He ignored her for the moment, bringing up Teddy's feed.

"Where are your Ghosts, Wren?" Rogers insisted.

He didn't have an answer for that.

"Teddy, report."

Teddy stood in a small office, in front of a thin man who'd been gagged and bound, sitting behind his office desk. "We're clear. No pushback at all, Christopher. We're documenting everything, like you said."

"There was a bomb in Malaysia. Doona's whole team is down. Be careful."

Teddy nodded. "I saw. She's tough. There's no sign they had any warning here, looks like we got their whole complement, top spec equipment, millions in value. These people, though, there's too many for us to hold them."

Wren knew it. "We dump it on Interpol."

"We'll finish extracting data, call them in."

"Run it fast," he said. "Before Russian police get there. I'm switching to Henry."

"Good luck," said Teddy.

Wren blinked, rubbed his eyes. The chopper was soaring over buildings now, suburbs rushing by. Almost there. It didn't make sense, though; if the Ghosts had had warning, why not share it with the meme factory and the Fat Unicorn?

"Henry is breaching," Hellion called in his ear. "They need you."

They needed him. He blinked hard, trying to get the image of the empty Ghost compound out of his head. If there'd been no warning, then had there ever been Ghosts in Malaysia, and if there hadn't been, who the hell was running their invisibility protocol?

"Wren!"

He looked up. Rogers was glaring at him; fierce now, chiding, worried. Almost like back when they were partners, keeping him on track. It made him heartsick. "We'll deal with that," she snapped. "Now get on point!"

43

HENRY

Wren watched from the Airbus's belly camera, hovering fifty feet over the outskirts of Angel's Camp. Sparse clumps of closed-cone pines encircled the abandoned middle school like circling sharks in an ocean of wild tan pampas grass. The roof was shot through in places, knotweed throttled the drain pipes and dead brown kudzu vines had swallowed the parking lot.

There was a two-tone roar, then the dirt bikes pincered into sight, coming at the school from opposite directions.

"Exterior looks clear," came Henry's voice. "Bikes report no outliers. I'm going in."

Wren picked him out, an ant-like figure in tactical black with a thick red cylinder on his back, leading a three-strong team up to the west exit.

"There was a bomb in Malaysia," Wren said urgently, "don't cluster up, retreat at the first sign of threat."

"I'm not retreating," said Henry, and hefted a pair of long-handle bolt cutters. One of Hellion's drones hovered close and Wren scrolled through his feeds to pick up the transmission. Instantly it zoomed him into the thick of things, holding position just over Henry's shoulder.

The west exit looked to be custodial; metal plate, shuttered with a thick chain and padlock. Henry brought up a pair of bolt cutters and clasped them around the chain.

"Infrared?" Wren asked.

"Nothing clear," Hellion answered. "The roof insulation's blocking any signal."

"But there is heat?"

"It could be the boiler. Somewhere in the middle. Overlaying school plans, it looks like the gymnasium. Middle of the basketball court."

Wren cursed. Center of an empty space; another bomb blast would have clear sightlines to rip through the whole school. Support columns would be left standing, tissue and bone would be shredded like corn before a thresher.

"Tell me the drones are in position," he said.

"They are," said Hellion.

"All of them?"

"All of them."

The bolt cutter's jaws closed with a clunk and the chain split. Henry pulled it through the door handle.

"Hellion, take the lead," he ordered. "Henry, in back."

"Following," Henry replied, and pulled the door open.

The drone flew headlong in. The interior was sun-dappled, with afternoon light shafting through the ruptured roof. A corridor stretched away, lined with busted lockers, doors hanging slack like lackluster flags. Motes hung thick in the air, a gray layer of dust carpeted the floor, and the drone flew on at a sprint.

"Something's off," Wren said. "Keep your team staggered, Henry."

"Copy," said Henry.

"Running analyses," said Hellion, taking the drone's speed up a notch. "No movement anywhere at this end."

"So take us to the center."

"Aye aye. We'll take the scenic route."

The drone swerved abruptly off the corridor and hung hard left into a classroom. Wren briefly saw sand-dusted desks piled up, surrounded by beer cans, needles and broken glass shards catching the afternoon light through shattered windows, then the drone pulled another sharp turn and went straight into a hole torn in the wall. It passed through the wall cavity in a split second and shot back outside, for a second zipped over dry red clay scrawled with the crazy paving of heat cracks, then entered again through another broken window.

Short cut to the gymnasium.

Tiered bleachers lay along the north side, scoreboard over the basketball hoop to the west, backboard glass and net long gone, stage to the east, light streaming in like tiny sky beams from what had to be bullet holes in the roof, and in the middle, Steven Gruber.

Wren cursed.

Gruber stood in the center of the open space, naked skin shiny, with a wooden barrel beside him, a paintbrush in one hand and a lighter in the other.

"Napalm!" Wren barked into the system. "Henry, he's rigged to blow."

"Understood," Henry replied. "Relaying."

Wren just stared. He'd been right in this place before, looking at skin glistening like morning dew at dawn, with Yumiko Harkness at the Reparations' arena, with the Pyramid spread throughout the fake town, people doused like stolen cars ready to burn out. He smelled the bitter kerosene stink even though he wasn't there, rich and overpowering. Gruber's eyes were red with it.

Barrel at his side. Paintbrush in his hand. Just like it had been before.

Gruber shuddered. He had the same old Steven Gruber face; uncertain, afraid, worried he was overstepping some unknown boundary.

"Where's the Ghost?" Wren barked at Hellion.

"Not here," she answered. "We're tracking his truck north. This is it for heat, there's nobody else here."

"Eliminate any signal coming out of this place. Nothing gets out. The people will not see this."

"Wireless is a cone of silence. Mason and Abigail already cut the standard hard lines, but I can't speak to any other wires, if they laid their own."

"Take me in, nice and slow."

Gruber's napalm-smeared, shuddering face drew closer as the drone scrolled in. Short brown hair, puppy fat on his cheeks, the light stubble of a beard. 'Man says drive, I drive'.

Not now.

This wasn't that same Gruber. Close enough now, he saw that the eyes were transformed, like the deepfake of Rogers but worse. Madness shone through the misery; wild ferocity of a new certainty. He'd come out the other side of a Judas moment. All the willing Pyramid faithful had shared that same look, the day they'd burned alive.

Wren's pulse racked up to one-twenty, one-thirty. Here was the Apex again, rewriting every life around him as just a reflection of his own. Just like Yumiko Harkness, except one death was only the beginning, now.

It pissed Wren off.

Gruber flinched as the drone drew in, pulling the hand holding the lighter closer to his head.

"Stop," Wren ordered, and the drone stopped dead.

"Put me on speaker."

"You're on," Hellion answered.

"Steven," Wren said, holding the phone up close to his mouth. He heard his own voice ring back through the drone's mic, tinny and time-delayed. "It's me, Wren."

There was a panicky flash in Gruber's eyes at that: recognition, terror, maybe a glimpse of hope, then the new programming crashed down and the old Gruber was crushed beneath it, releasing a maddened kind of glee.

"You mean the ungrateful son?"

Gruber's thumb jerked.

The lighter sparked.

44

GRUBER

"Wait!" Wren shouted.

Gruber blinked, held still with his elbow crooked, the flame bare inches from catching on napalm fumes. Through the screen Wren peered into his swirling red eyes, trying to read in to whatever horrors the Apex had exposed him to.

"You called me the ungrateful son," Wren said, filling the space between Gruber and the drone with words. "Is that how he framed everything I've done? Everything we've done together?"

Gruber just stared like he wasn't hearing. Like bringing the lighter all the way down wouldn't cause him pain, but would come as a relief. Wren had seen him like this before. Lost in the throes of his addiction, throwing himself into manic orgies that lasted days, just to have something to feel.

"We've saved people together," he went on. "Steven, you helped me end the Reparations. 'Man says', remember that? I couldn't have done it without you. That's not ungrateful. That's real."

Gruber flinched slightly. Something almost surfaced, sank back beneath the Apex's programming. "You lied," he managed. Words coming as a shivery slur. "He showed me. It's all pain. this world. There's no way out except this. He said I'll be loved."

His voice cracked. The lighter wavered.

"He's making you the battlefield," Wren said swiftly. "It isn't fair and it isn't right, and I would never do this to you, Steven. Think! He took you, didn't he? I should have been there for you. I'm sorry I wasn't. He took you and he twisted you, and now he's trying to make you kill yourself, and it's wrong. I swear to you, there are better ways to be loved!"

Gruber's eyes swam. Vomiting up the Apex's ideology like it was poison and he had a bellyful. Everybody broke under conditioning, it was just a matter of time.

"I'm tired, Chris," Gruber said, his voice small and weak. "So tired of this. Always hungry for more, needing so much, of going to sobriety meetings and waiting for the Foundation to help." A tear spilled down his cheek. "You didn't help me. I kept calling. Reaching out. Where were you?"

Those were daggers into Wren's heart. "I'm sorry, Steven. Please believe me. I wanted to be there, but-"

"I've seen so much," Gruber went on, eyes focused on some far-off point. "Your father, he's fixing me. I can feel it now. You say God made me this way, but what awful, sadistic God would give me such pathetic, desperate feelings as these?"

"None of us are perfect, all of us are-"

"I don't need this body!" Gruber insisted, clearly channeling the Apex now. The same words he'd used to burn the Pyramid. "This body's tormented me for too long. I can heave peace, Chris. Don't you want that for me? Wouldn't it be better to slough it off forever?"

"There'll be no peace, Steven! Only nothing. There's nothing waiting on the other side for you. Don't give into-"

"Like a snake," Gruber murmured. "We slip from one life to another, he says. I close my eyes here, I send a message of hope to all who've suffered just like me, and I fly on to join the good fight. What could be better than that?"

Wren saw his team advancing around Gruber, within the blast zone of the napalm's vaporous ignition. All risking their lives to bring him in. If Wren could just keep him talking long enough…

"I'm alone now, Chris. We are all alone. He said I'll never be alone again. Said there are a thousand more where I'm going. That's real. Not this." Gruber sucked air. "My sad story of failure. A failed childhood. A failed adolescence. A failed and desperate adulthood. Scraping and scratching for more. Always hungry. Never satisfied. Always rooting in the dirt like some animal. Is that the truth you want for me?"

Tears raced down his cheeks, and Wren felt the pain burning up off him. The lies the Apex must have poured into his fragile heart.

"Life is hard, Gruber," Wren tried, "but at least it's life. There is nothing else. This is the only game in town, and my father's promising you false dreams. There is nothing after this, Steven, at least not what he's offering. Nothing good comes without pain. Love, family, friendship, these things are beautiful because of how hard they are. It's not supposed to be easy!"

Gruber just looked at the drone. "It's too hard, Christopher."

The lighter sagged.

"I want you here with me," Wren blurted. "I don't want you to die. We're all adrift on this ocean together, Steven, and it is horrible out here sometimes, I know that, it is sick and we see some of the worst things, and we're all struggling just to keep our heads above the water, but we are not alone. You're not alone, I swear it!"

Gruber's eyes flickered. Maybe a crack of doubt. Wren had to plow in and lever it wide open.

"You see the people around you? They're all Foundation members. They all want you to live, Steven. I've been searching for you since you went missing. I shot Humphreys and escaped a CIA black site, I've torn up LA, I've sent teams out raiding across the world, all because I'm looking for you! I already found Rogers. She's here with me now. She knows what you've been through. She knows just what it's like."

That seemed to confuse him. "I-" he said, holding his left hand up to shield the drone's beam lights.

"You're thinking now," Wren pressed on. "That's good. Keep thinking, Steven. You're strong as you are. It's strong to feel weak. We all do. We don't measure strength by running from a fight. We take the fight on the chin. That's why I'm here. I don't leave any member behind. I will never leave you behind, and neither will any member of the Foundation."

The words hit Gruber like a barrage, sending ripples across his forehead, cheeks, lips pulling back. Wren handed the mic to Rogers.

"Steven?" she said.

A wheeze escaped Gruber's chest, like he'd been punched in the gut.

"I was there," she said. "I know what the Apex said. He lied to both of us. Please think for just a moment. Who here is asking you to kill yourself? It's not a trick question, Steven. Who wants you to die, and who wants you to live?"

His eyes danced side to side. Seeing the figures creeping closer. "I-"

"Wren's right, Steven. We want you alive, here, with us. Not because it's easy, but because it's hard. We'll do it together, and we won't abandon you."

Gruber's mouth opened. What came out was unexpected.

Laughter. It sounded thick and oily, gushing like napalm in a torrent before ending as abruptly as it began. "Like he didn't abandon you?"

There was silence for a second. Wren had no words.

Gruber brought the lighter down.

45

CONFLAGRATION

Across the video feeds of a billion screens, Steven Gruber caught fire.

The flames whipped up and licked down like a deluge, racing from his tinder-like stalks of brown hair down the gobs of gelatin smeared on his cheeks, into the hollow under his chin and over his glistening throat. Across his shoulders the flames erupted like a matador's cape, and as it fell across his chest so his arm fell with the lighter, dropping into the wooden barrel at his side which ignited like white phosphorous and-

The camera feeds cut out, incinerated in the fireball as the barrel split, leaving ghostly white images saturated into eyeballs across the world; figures in the background with their arms out, desperately trying to turn and run as the fire wave blasted out.

There was blackness on all those screens for a moment, then the feed cut to a drone circling above just in time to see the ball of fire blow through the tattered roof of the school and climb fifty feet, a hundred feet up in raw, furious flame.

Crowds across the United States stared at their screens, in living rooms and backyards, on streets and in public squares, and felt something shift inside.

This was the horror they'd been waiting for. Dreading. Ever since Jay Durant burned, this had been in the back of their minds; terrible images from the past, of attacks against the people. Faces streaming with tears and scarred by fire, dust in the air, screaming and chaos and then the silence when the television was finally turned off.

That silence stayed inside them, as they stood at the kitchen counter or stopped on the sidewalk, looking at the world but not seeing it, because the world had just transformed. The safety they'd taken for granted was not safe. The heroes would not win. Somebody hated them enough to do this, and this was just the beginning.

More would come. Hadn't they been shown that for over a year now? Always there were more attacks, welling up from pain and sickness that had been there all along. These attacks couldn't be stopped. These attacks were built in. They'd thought they'd known who they were, a people united together, strong and decent, the leaders of the world, and now this death proved them wrong.

In shopping malls and parks, in coastal cities and little mid-west towns, people felt the same thing at the same time. They weren't who they thought they were. All their stories were wrong. They looked across the street, the field, the lake, across the Internet, and saw that same new understanding creeping into the hearts of others just like them.

They were not strong. They were weak, like everyone else.

In some that feeling became despair. They sagged where they stood, fell to their knees, began to sob, reminded of times when they'd been weak before, when they hadn't been able to protect themselves or their people.

In some that feeling became a numb emptiness. They couldn't take a step, barely take a breath, for not knowing what it meant. Their minds raced in circles, looking for some solid ground to bed into and take a stand, but finding nothing other than ghosts.

In others still the feeling became unfocused, blind, desperate rage. Rage against Christopher Wren and the Foundation, or rage against the Deep State and the government, but rage that had to be answered. Rage that had to be appeased. They reached to their gun closets. They went to their kitchen drawers for knives. They took to the streets, ready to unleash their rage on the enemy.

In the Wilshire the first shots were fired within seconds of Gruber's conflagration. Shots into the air, toward the Federal Building, directly into the line of National Guard figures ringing the swollen protest crowd. Those shots metastasized the feeling, transmitting the answer like a virus, until their hearts beat with one furious, vengeful pulse.

That pulse propelled them like the moon drawing in the tide. They forgot their fear and rammed shields with their bare bodies, using flesh as a battering ram, reinforced by the weight of thousands in back. Fires were lit and flaming bottles hurled, to smash in puddles of light that licked up bodies and drew fresh screams. Bricks and rocks hurtled, tear gas canisters blew in clouds of acrid vapor, flashbang grenades burst like thunder and lightning, bullets whipped backward and forth, from the crowd and into the crowd.

Bodies fell and were trampled underfoot. In broad daylight, America went to war against itself. Across the country protest crowds, already primed for violence by two days of rioting, joined the battle. It didn't matter against who. It only mattered that this feeling inside was expressed. A year's worth of fear, dread and rage poured through them in swung fists and pulled triggers.

Across the country National Guard walls broke down. They were not designed to hold back an unthinking flood that didn't care about injury or pain, that only surged harder for each blow sent back. Officers fell. The crowds roared and beat them and charged ahead. Breaking windows, lighting cars, smashing their way in to maim, kill, loot, set fire, whatever it took.

Good people.

Civil war.

Then came the buzzing.

Into the skies above every city battlefield, shadowing the land like an unholy flood of locusts, came the drones. Above the Wilshire Federal Building in Los Angeles they descended, above the Henry Whipple Building in Minneapolis and Dewey Square in Boston, above the Pioneer Courthouse Square in Portland, the Oklahoma State Capital and the Alamo in San Antonio, above Pittsburgh and Seattle, above Spokane and Salt Lake City, Knoxville and Providence, Cincinnati and Fayetteville, Poughkeepsie and Boseman, New York and Dallas.

They flooded like a dark tide, and all eyes turned from their weapons to watch them hover and settle: countless models and makes, in all shapes and sizes, until one voice rang through them in choral synchrony, a voice they recognized, amplified above the cries and buzzing of countless rotors.

"STEVEN GRUBER IS NOT DEAD!"

It repeated until the tide of violence slowed, and people stopped to listen, and turned to their phones to see the same phenomenon spreading across the nation, matched by something unprecedented above the Wilshire Building in Los Angeles.

A helicopter was descending through the cloud of drones. Cameras caught the figures standing at the open doors and zoomed closer, forcing everything else from the minds of the rioters as they clasped their screens and stared in bewilderment, listening to the words echoing out over the mass drone PA.

"STEVEN GRUBER IS NOT DEAD. SALLY ROGERS IS NOT DEAD. MY NAME IS CHRISTOPHER WREN, AND YOU HAVE BEEN LIED TO!"

It was Wren in the doorway of the helicopter. Unmistakably. And beside him, equally unmistakably, the woman who had burned to death just a day ago. Sally Rogers, CIA special agent.

Alive.

46

100%

On human skin napalm burned like viscous magma, melting down through fat and muscle to bone in seconds. Try to wipe it away and it only smeared, expanding the burn area. Douse it with sand, hit it with extinguishers, even submerge it under water and in some cases it still kept burning. Nothing short of one hundred percent oxygen deprivation could kill a napalm blaze, and even then it had the capacity to self-reignite. Add magnesium accelerant in the right proportions and not even oxygen deprivation could stop the reaction.

Inhumane. Effective. Near unstoppable.

These thoughts raced through Wren's head as Steven Gruber brought the lighter down. A window of milliseconds only. The barrel. The lighter. Him in a helicopter two hundred miles away and closing on downtown Los Angeles.

"Now!" he shouted.

Henry fired first, just as the lighter made contact with Gruber's head and fire raced down his body. Twin jets of foam fire retardant fluid shot from the ten-gallon cylinder mounted to Henry's back and hit Gruber in the side of the head. Milliseconds later Mason followed up with a third and fourth jet of foam from his tank, Luke and Chuck both released four jets worth of carbon dioxide from four five-pound cylinders, and Abigail darted close in with three streams of dry powder extinguishers spraying directly at Gruber's face and shoulders.

The napalm guttered before it could really begin.

"Get out!" Wren shouted.

Abigail was first to Gruber, barely visible through the spray of foam and pluming clouds of white powder. He was already on the floor, convulsing from the pain of his burns and choking on foam. She grabbed him by the arm and back-pedaled rapidly, dragging him away from the napalm barrel and over the foam-slicked wooden gymnasium boards, chased by Henry, Mason, Chuck and Luke. They kept spraying him down until they were out of the hall and into the corridor, where Gruber lay making terrifying clucking sounds deep in his throat.

Dry drowning.

Liquid foam in the lungs caused the vocal cords to spasm and swell up over the windpipe. Dr. Larissa Bray leaped into action; she'd been training at one of Dr. Ferat's facilities for this eventuality since Jay had burned, and slid in above Gruber as they set him down, leaning in to listen to his chest while taking his pulse.

"Heart stopped," she called, and bent in to pinch his nose, closed her lips over his mouth and forced in air. Gruber's chest shifted. Larissa angled his head to the side to let any fluid leak free and began chest compressions.

"He's re-igniting!" someone shouted, and a fresh jet of foam sprayed in to splash his left leg. Dr. Bray continued regardless, closing out the compressions, wiping frothy white from Gruber's chin and going in for a second round.

On the third round he sucked in a raspy breath, spat out white, gagged and coughed. Henry lifted him to a seated position, patting his back while Mason tapped a ten gallon canister of cold water and held it pouring carefully over Gruber's head, cooling the worst of the burns.

His eyes blinked open.

"Hang in there, Steven!" Wren called through the drone. Gruber stared right up at the lens, and the expression in his eyes was haunting. Fear, pain, regret, desperation.

"You're safe now," Wren said, as the Foundation lathered and scrubbed the un-ignited napalm off his body, then wrapped him in blankets to prevent dramatic heat loss as the cold water poured down his back. His head was patchy with burned hair; some would grow back, some never would. The skin didn't look melted; they'd caught it fast enough.

Wren's heart thundered. He wasn't there but he felt as though he was. He felt Gruber reaching out like a wounded child.

"You're safe now," he said again, "I promise." Gruber opened his mouth to speak, but the effort proved too much, and his eyes closed as the pain drove him under.

"We have this," Henry said sharply. "Corporal, you're needed elsewhere."

Wren blinked.

A hand came on his arm and he looked up. Rogers, sitting right there beside him. Beyond her lay blue skies. For a moment he'd forgotten where he was.

"It's happening now," she said. "Listen to B4cksl4cker."

Wren's mouth was dry and breathing came in short gasps. Gruber was alive, that was what he had to tell himself. Keep telling himself. The damage was real, but damage could heal. The Foundation would have to evolve to the threat. Gruber was alive, and that counted for something. One in the positive column.

"Christopher," came B4cksl4cker's voice in his ear. "It is what you feared. There were never any Ghosts in Malaysia; this was done by one man, and he prepared in advance."

"Prepared what?"

"Gruber's death."

A shudder ran up Wren's spine. "They ghosted him," he said, and scrolled through his phone. It didn't take long to find the feed that had gone out simultaneously with the strikes, rewriting reality in real time. He sped through it on fast forward as B4cksl4cker talked; it showed Steven Gruber igniting himself, with Christopher Wren and an army of others caught in the firestorm.

All dead. Nothing but smoke and flame remained.

"We found this on the Fat Unicorn's drives," B4cksl4cker went on. "The Russian factory had hundreds of memes ready to go, pushing it out."

Wren found he was shaking. The scale of it. Crowds across America were igniting. The video was the spark, the people were the napalm, and the memes would be magnesium accelerant, keeping the blaze going no matter what smothering attempts were made.

He'd suspected it. The Apex was always prepared. He'd prepared in turn, but still...

"We already shut down their meme and virality factories," B4cksl4cker kept on, "but this is in the bloodstream now. I'm preparing our feed to show a cleaned-up version of the Gruber rescue."

"Don't clean it up," Wren said, his voice coming half-choked now. "Show them everything."

"On your count."

"And Hellion?"

"She is occupied."

Wren raced through news feeds as the R44 soared in to ground zero, the Wilshire Federal Building, with the sparse hills of Topanga State Park rushing below in a green/brown blur. His heart rate was up past a hundred-forty and climbing.

"Is she ready?"

"She is mass hacking civilian drones on a scale never attempted before. But then, she is also Hellion."

She was Hellion, that was right. The helicopter banked hard.

"We're coming in," Rogers said, and Wren felt curiously light inside, like there was nothing in his chest but hot air. A zeppelin, ready to take flight.

"Tell Hellion to give us a hell of an entrance," he managed.

"The riots are erupting," Rogers said at his side, peering ahead through the glass. "I've never seen anything like it. They're breaking through barricades everywhere."

It was just like Gruber. Ignition.

He saw the fires ahead as the R44 raced down the tail edge of the mountains and shot across the narrow tranche of residential to the Wilshire. Bodies tumbled and surged like ants clambering atop a scorpion. Flames were everywhere already, clouds of smoke and tear gas like cotton balls engulfing bodies, tracer lines from live rounds fractured the air.

The sound of explosions, cries, gas bursts and gunshots came like the inferno roar of a furnace. This was the real napalm, painted by the Apex and lit by the Ghost, now arcing across the country. Inextinguishable with anything less than 100% coverage.

"You have coverage," came Hellion's frenzied voice, underscored by a blizzard of key strokes. "Greatest Show on Earth, Christopher. Now go!"

He opened the door as the helicopter sank through the second skin of drones, blasting the crowd with his downdraft, demanding their attention. The pilot shouted a warning but he didn't listen. They'd done worse than this before. Now he could see the faces of people directly below, staring back up at him.

"On you," Hellion said. "Speak."

Wren raised his phone to his lips, a Megaphone like none he'd had before, and spoke.

47

EXTINGUISHER

"You have been lied to!" he repeated, the words booming out from the hundreds of speaker drones in the air around him, carrying to the furthest reaches of the crowd and beyond.

"Steven Gruber is not dead. Sally Rogers is not dead. My name is Christopher Wren, and I am not dead!"

They stared. He stared back. It was everything Gerald Humphreys had been afraid of, the messiah come to save his people.

Time to administer some salvation.

"Believe the evidence of your own eyes," he said into the phone, and his voice thundered across the masses. "I know what you just saw. Steven Gruber burned. I burned. I know that you're angrier now than ever, more afraid than ever, but you have to believe your eyes. I didn't burn. That video was a lie, because I'm right here."

He stood in the downdraft of the R44, staring out at the 'live' lights of a thousand phones as they filmed him from a thousand different angles. No way to deepfake that. Actions spoke louder than words, and he was tired of talking anyway. These people had been driven out of their minds with terror and rage, and you couldn't turn that around with logic. You had to go for the gut.

You had to turn their anger in a new direction.

"Look at me," he boomed. "Look at the woman by my side. Look at the real video of Steven Gruber's 'death', and you tell me who's lying to you now."

More phones lit up below; people scrolling, searching, watching video.

"Something's happening," B4cksl4cker said in his ear.

Wren just stood and stared. The helicopter drifted and corrected. All these people had watched him die on the Ghosts' feed. Now he was here.

"I'm seeing mass searches across the web," B4cksl4cker went on. "Your name, Steven Gruber, Sally Rogers. With the Russian factory shut down, they're finding real information, and we're hunter-killering any fake memes that spring up." A second passed. "The real video of Angel's Camp is getting swarmed. I've put all the strike videos up, they're getting hits."

Wren felt the tide turning. A resistance. Maybe the first flush of a new immunity. Root out the disease and inoculate the people. Vaccination was a two-way street, though. The masses had to play ball.

He spoke again. "Just ten minutes back my teams hit a Russian misinformation factory and a Chinese deepfake video lab. They've been pumping out propaganda for weeks, injecting it into our bloodstream, so is it any wonder we're sick now? Ask yourself, why are you here? Why were you here yesterday? Was it because the death of a single man turned us against each other?"

No answer came back. The people were dead silent, hanging on his every word.

"But that murder was not committed by the 'deep state'. I know this is hard to hear. They are far from innocent, like I'm far from innocent, but they did not do this. They're every bit as terrified as you are, believe me. They're scared of me, of you, of everything, when they should be afraid of my father."

There were a few jeers.

"You're losing them," came B4cksl4cker's voice in his ear.

Wren ignored him. The medicine never tasted good.

"He wanted you as a weapon. You were the grenade and I was the pin, but you don't have to be. I know you're angry. I'm angry too. I want to tear all this down and start again, but trust me, that will not work. We tear ourselves apart now, our enemies will feast on whatever's left. And we do have enemies."

He caught a glimpse of Rogers' face in the floodlight of National Guard beam. She was giving him those eyes again. It hurt to see, the same way she'd used to look at him, the magician on the edge of revealing his prestige. All that he'd lost.

"My father," he repeated, giving no ground. "Apex of the Pyramid. He's alive. He's doing this to us all, so place the blame where it lays."

There were a few faint cheers. Better.

"Don't break the system, fix it. It's not perfect, I know that, but it's the best thing we've got. Help it evolve, don't rip it apart. We'll need it when the time comes, to put the Apex in the damn ground!"

More cheers came. A chant broke out, coalescing around three words. "In the ground, in the ground!"

"The tide's turning," came B4cksl4cker's voice in Wren's ear, a little too rich with disbelief. "The fake video is getting crashed with downvotes. View count on our strike videos is rocketing."

Wren lowered the phone, watching the crowd rally. The strange lightness was back in his chest, like none of this was real. It wouldn't last long.

"Tell me about Malaysia," he said, switching the channel for B4cksl4cker's ears only. "Is Doona alive?"

Keys thudded. "We're scrambling. It's chaos over there. Malaysian authorities are all over it. I'll find out."

Wren grunted. His fault. He hadn't sent her, but he'd allowed the strike to go ahead. "Malaysia was a trap."

"It looks that way."

Wren gritted his teeth. Just one man. "Do you have the Ghost?"

"I'm hunting now. Breaking through his invisibility."

It wasn't the Apex. Wren knew that already, from Rogers' description. A big guy with buzzed hair, she'd said, early forties. Too young to be the Apex. Just another acolyte furthering the Pyramid's plan.

The crowd below throbbed with their new slogan.

"Put everything you've got on it," Wren said firmly. "Launch Henry and Mason. I need him right now, B4cksl4cker. Activate ghosting on the whole state, if you have to. You've got ten minutes."

"What?"

Wren squeezed the phone in his fist. "Without a scapegoat, this crowd are still primed to blow. I need him right now."

"In ten minutes?"

Wren looked out over the crowd. He could feel it in the air, change blowing with the wind. They were coming around to his way of thinking, but without blood in the water it wouldn't last. The bomb hadn't been defused, only delayed.

"Call it nine."

He killed the line then turned to look at Rogers. She was giving him those eyes still, not sure if he was a madman or a genius. He held up the phone. "Close this out, please."

She looked blankly back at him. "What?"

"You were right about me," Wren said quickly, getting it all out. "I'm selfish and I use people. I'm using you now, and I'm sorry, but I can't think of any other way." He held the phone closer. "Right now I need you to keep this crowd on our side. Let them hear how you escaped. Tell them how you beat the Ghost. They need to hear some hope." She only stared. He pressed the phone into her hand. "Please, Rogers. I can't do this without you."

She opened her mouth, closed it, opened it again. Asking her to revisit the trauma was cruel, and they both knew it. "I'm not doing it for you."

"I know that. But I thank you, anyway."

She just stared, maybe not sure how to feel. Angry. Hurt. Resolved.

He turned to the helicopter door.

"Where are you going?"

"To see Humphreys," he answered without turning back. "I promised him we'd have a little chat, and I think that's come due." Before she could say anything more, he jumped out of the helicopter door.

The crowd screamed. The rappel line caught him. In five seconds he was on the ground and people were rushing in to mob him, but he pushed through them. Ahead the Wilshire hung like a great white slab of alabaster.

Then Rogers' voice came to life from behind, from above. Amplified by the low sky of drones, she was uncertain at first, cautious, but growing stronger as she went. In seconds she was picked up and re-transmitted from every phone around him, her voice coming like a chorus. Telling the story. Gripping them like nothing Wren could say. By the time he reached the edge of the crowd, in the shadow of the Wilshire, nobody was even looking at him anymore. They were all gazing up at Rogers. She'd beat the Apex and the Ghost head on. She'd escaped. She'd survived and lived to tell the tale.

If they wanted to raise anyone up as a hero, Wren thought, it should be her.

Ahead the National Guard line opened for him, and he passed through. They formed into an escort party and jogged him toward the building. Time to have that little chat.

Seven minutes left.

48

ICE SHELF

It took five minutes to get Wren sitting across a table from CIA Director Gerald Humphreys. By then his earpiece, phone and weapon had been stripped. He couldn't even hear the roaring of the crowd outside through the Wilshire's thick walls.

A gray-painted cell. Wren recognized it well enough. Maybe he'd even been in this precise room before, sitting on the opposite side. A white desk with an eyelet, his hands shackled in place. They hadn't bothered with his feet, but there were over a dozen armed men in the room next door, so...

One-way mirror off to the right, with them watching. His reflection looked half-dead in the glass; pale face, sallow cheeks, swollen broken nose, bloodshot eyes. Like he'd actually been in that ghosted firestorm at Angel's Camp.

A door lay ahead, two armed guys either side of it, with Humphreys sat right ahead. He looked worse than Wren even, like a three-day corpse. The alabaster of his face was so pale it seemed a miracle he was conscious, accentuating the dark purple rings under his eyes. Right arm in a black sling, shoulder hunched unnaturally, maybe skipping pain meds to keep himself sharp.

"You look like a ghost," Wren said.

Humphreys didn't say anything. What could he say? He was here to listen.

"Where's Tandrews?"

"Shipped out," Humphreys said. Even his voice sounded stale and old, like a wind blowing up from a tomb. "For his own safety. The whole building's been locked down."

"Where to?"

"Is that what really matters now?"

Wren figured it wasn't. He held up his hands, and the cuffs clanked against the eyelet. Making a point. "I let them put these on, you know."

Humphreys stared. It was a good poker face, looking like a corpse, but his eyes gave him away. Fear. Doubtless he was thinking of that moment when Wren had smashed his own face in, got himself uncuffed and somehow came back from the dead.

"We put them on you."

"And I'll take them off, if I want," Wren countered. "I walked in here, remember that. Seems your boys outside gave me an honor guard. They know where it's at, but you still don't. Seems you think this is a surrender."

Humphreys shifted in his seat.

"It's not surrender," Wren said, and clicked his fingers. Humphreys blinked. Not such a rock face now. More an ice shelf, waiting to calve away. "Take off these cuffs. Now."

Humphreys' eyes fidgeted, danced slightly to the side. That was an automatic response, looking to the one-way glass for an authority figure, but there was no authority figure higher than Humphreys now. Maybe the President, but what did she know? Only what her intelligence heads told her.

Humphreys was Director of the CIA. You didn't get much higher than that.

"I'm not doing that," Humphreys said. His voice managed to come through firm, though Wren could feel the fear. Heading for the full ten minutes. Give Henry a little time to play with, maybe, though every minute's delay left the crowd to rile itself back up. Still, the chopper had to land. The dirt bikes had to roar into action. Hopefully there was no shootout. They needed the Ghost alive.

Wren leaned back in his chair. Hard metal and plastic, but he lounged like it was comfortable, like he had all the time in the world. "Gerald. You've got a crowd out there baying for blood. I just re-set the fuse, but you think the bomb's disarmed? You think, just as soon as Rogers gets done telling her story, that they're not going to turn their attention right back to you?"

Humphreys dry swallowed.

Wren smiled. "I think you know how the tune goes. It's all the rage. 'Release Christopher Wren'?"

If it were possible, Humphreys blanched further.

"They're coming after you, Gerald, and I won't be there to stop them this time. I'll be in here. Held illegally. Then you really will be screwed."

Humphreys leaned in. "Is that a threat?"

Wren laughed. He really laughed. The sound should have come over ridiculous in that tight, clinical space, designed to break the occupants on the wrong side of the table, but it didn't have that effect. If anything, it made everyone else in the room seem small.

"Come on, son. Is it a threat when the weatherman tells you there's a storm coming? You know me. Prognosticator extraordinaire. When have I ever been wrong?"

Humphreys tried to meet his gaze.

"I don't mean to make you eat this," Wren said, shrugging with his hands. "Hold out if you like. Either it's you who undoes these cuffs, or it's the people out there, once they fight their way inside. You can't stop them now, after everything they've seen. Down with the Deep State, Gerald. Free the Foundation. Sing it along with me."

Humphreys stared, his glacier face ready to calve off a huge ice sheet any second. Send up a big splash, raise the water level around the world.

"I've got all day," Wren said.

Humphreys' jaw worked under the skin. He let out a little pent-up gasp of air, like gases venting before the ice cracked, then caved.

"Let him go."

Wren held his wrists up. The keys slotted in and the cuffs came off, and Wren sat, and Humphreys sat. Just two guys sitting, but so much history in back.

Humphreys broke the silence. "So what have you-"

"I'm just enjoying this moment," Wren interrupted. Well over ten minutes now, riding a fine line, but better to give Henry a little longer. "You over there and me over here. Mutual respect."

That brought a little color into Humphreys' cheeks, like rouge for an open casket viewing. Good. It was better to be alive. "You killed people, Christopher. Hundreds of them."

"Pinocchios."

"Untried by any court."

"Call them by another name, they were terrorists. The Blue Fairy did try to overthrow American democracy."

Humphreys shuffled. Now it was a negotiation. "They did."

"So I went extra-judicial. War-time powers. License to kill."

"You know that's a myth. None of our agents have-"

"I've had it. When I was DELTA we had it on every op."

"Not on American soil. Not American citizens."

Wren nodded. "So put me on public trial. Everyone can see. We have a system, let's use it, get all our dirty laundry out in public."

Humphreys glared, said nothing.

"What I thought," said Wren. "So here's the deal. I'm here because we need each other. I can't kill my father alone, especially if you're going to be blocking me every step of the way. And you'll never find him without me. I said it before, I'm your best weapon against him."

Humphreys stared. Wren stared back.

"Are you finished?"

"A photo op," Wren said. "You and me, out front of here ASAP. A handshake. After that, we hop a branded jet to the one person that matters most, and I get a sit-down in the Oval Office."

If Humphreys had been sipping coffee he would have sprayed it out. "You must be kidding."

"Not kidding. Trust me, this is a major get for you. Right now, the people out there love me and despise you. I'm the one cleaning up your brand here."

The blush spread across Humphreys' white cheeks. "You're serious."

"As an aneurysm."

"Never going to happen. You don't get to meet the President. But you and me out front, a handshake, some kind of working deal in exchange for partial immunity, we can work that. Pending you have the proof you promised."

Wren smiled. The proof. He wouldn't know if he had it until they got B4cksl4cker back on the line. "Total immunity for the Foundation for all past deeds," he bargained. "Temporary immunity for me until the Apex is done, then I want that trial. No dirty laundry, just my recent actions. On top of that, you're going to give my whole team AWOP status, Agent WithOut Portfolio, and put me in total command of all our efforts to bring down the Apex."

The color in Humphreys' cheeks was really coming along now. "Total command? Who the hell do you think you are?"

Wren laughed. "Who are you, Gerald? Nominated to this role by the President, who got elected by a narrow margin. You see my base out there? They elected me."

Humphreys frowned hard. "Elected you? Wren, you ran a wrecking crew through LA! People were hurt. You suplexed a man, for God's sake!"

"I pulled most of those punches."

"You bodyslammed him!"

"He'll be fine."

"You wrecked vehicles, conducted a high speed chase, you-"

"Did anyone die?" Wren interrupted.

"Did anyone...? That's not the point!"

"So what is your point?"

"It was ridiculous! You're not just a killer, you're irresponsible. You don't think about the consequences of your actions. You never look before you leap. How can I give you command of anything?"

Wren just sat there. Looked at his wrists, uncuffed. Looked at the guards around him.

"You put me under when you needed me most. Were you thinking about the consequences then?"

Humphreys fumed. Turning cherry-coke red now. It made Wren happy to see.

"Do we have a deal?"

"I can't just approve a deal like that. The President has to sign off. There are countless-"

"Same way you couldn't get them to stop torturing me?"

Humphreys stopped dead.

"That's what you said, first thing you opened my cage. You asked them to stop and they didn't. What kind of bullshit was that, Humphreys?"

"I-"

"You want this," Wren sped on. "I want this. Let's stop wanking in the bushes and make a baby. I give you proof, you stand me up as my own wing of the Agency. We're accountable like anyone else, from here on out, and I stand trial when it's done. No mission creep. The Apex is dead or otherwise incapacitated, I hand myself over."

"By which time you'll have the country eating out of the palm of your hand," Humphreys fumed. "No jury in the land will convict."

"So it's not a jury trial. Put me in front of the Supreme Court."

Humphreys laughed. "Oh, you'd love that."

"Whatever, Gerald. Name the conditions."

"I will. The case will not be televised. Supreme Court, fine by me, I can make a recommendation. No bail, you'll be on remand. Any infraction by any member of your Foundation throughout that process, they buy themselves a seat right next to yours in the dock. You can all go down together."

"They won't. But agreed."

"Add to that, there's oversight of your day-to-day operations. Not pre-approval, I know you'd never agree to that, but post-hoc within twenty-four hours. We can take you out, accelerate the deal, if at any time we feel you're not delivering."

That put the vise on him. "Forty-eight hours. I need some leeway."

"Thirty-six, best offer. You get some crazy hunch, you develop it fast or you're out."

Wren grunted. "Salaries."

Humphreys stared.

"I'm not kidding."

"For your Armenian, the hacker? The girl too, what is she, Bulgarian? On top of that you've got foreign intelligence analysts, that Sunlit Dawn cult, and Steven Gruber, your mole in the NSA? I don't think so."

"He wasn't a mole."

"That's a moot point now, isn't it? Christopher. You'll have your own budget, so spread salaries as you see fit. Remember, thirty-six hours oversight." Humphreys extended his hand. "Deal, pending proof, take it or leave it."

Wren took his hand and shook. "Deal. Now get me my earpiece and a laptop. I've got something to show you."

49

PROOF

"Christopher?"

"You're on speaker with probably every American intelligence agency there is, B4cksl4cker. Watch what you say."

It only took a second. "Is that pussy in a dick suit there?"

"Language!" Wren chided. "But yes, Humphreys is right here."

"Hellion will be so jealous," he muttered. "I have to bring her on this line."

A second passed. Muzak kicked in, some awful twinkly elevator jazz. Wren looked up at Humphreys, and the Director's eyes burned like gas jets. "They're big fans," he said apologetically.

"I gathered," Humphreys said. The blush was fading from his cheeks now, maybe already regretting the deal he'd made. "Get on with it."

"B4cksl4cker, forget Hellion," Wren said sharply, "I need the Ghost right now. Tell me you have him."

The muzak cut out. "At least I will record this for her. She would never forgive me. Please ask him to say something. A signature line. Wait! I have it. Have him say, 'I am coming for you, Hellion!' She would love that so much."

Wren winced. Humphreys was back to full alabaster rock face already. "B4cksl4cker! Not gonna happen. Give me what you've got."

"Very well, Christopher, sending you footage. Henry is coming in above Ghost's truck now, ninety miles north of Angel's Camp. Dirt bikes are down and herding."

"Give him the security line for this laptop," Humphreys ordered, but before anyone could do anything, the laptop came to life on its own, displaying the pursuit from the Airbus. Humphreys' eyes bored into Wren.

"How did they do that?"

"That is perfect!" cheered B4cksl4cker. "I could not ask for better soundbite. Thank you, Mr. Humphreys! Hellion will use this as ringtone."

"B4cksl4cker!" Wren snapped.

"Sorry, Christopher. And yes, before you ask, this is live."

"Put me through to Henry."

"Transmitting."

To Wren's right a projector behind the two-way mirror flickered to life, and the laptop feed appeared displayed on the left wall. The lights dimmed automatically.

It was footage shot from the Airbus, chaparral orange desert split by a laser-straight blacktop two-lane road, devoid of traffic other than an eighteen wheeler with dusty blue canvas sides.

"That semi?"

"That is Ghost," B4cksl4cker answered. "Heat signature on his trailer is clear sign; he's running supercomputer array. One man ghosting technology runs like furnace. Very large petaflops."

"Henry," said Wren, as the first of the dirt bikes came into view, racing up the left side of the semi. "Are you with me?"

"Right here, Corporal," Henry's smart tone came back, along with the guttural rev of a dirt bike engine. "We're running an aggravated wheel strip. I'm lead bike on the right, Mason's on the left, we're going to ping his wheels."

"Rewrite that," Wren barked. "Don't get close, he might have a bomb on board, like Malaysia. You've got spike strips?"

"Affirmative. I can swing wide through the scrub."

"Do it," Wren leaned in.

The dirt bikes on the right and left both swung wide and arced out over the desert at forty-five degrees. Their rear wheels shot up geysers of loose surface sand like jet skis, briefly they disappeared from the camera's range, and Wren felt his pulse ratcheting up.

It all came down to this. Seconds ticked by, then Henry's bike came back into sight some five hundred feet ahead of the semi, a black dot angling back toward the road.

"It's too tight," said Humphreys.

"He knows what he's doing," Wren muttered.

The bike stopped at the roadside and the semi bulled on. Henry was a stick figure leaping off the bike, pulling something smoothly off his belt, which he flung out like a whip.

The spike strip scissored across the two-lane, as indistinct as insect legs at this distance. The semi driver saw it and pulled sharp left, right into the spike strip flung by Mason.

The puncturing burst of the tires carried up to the Airbus, nine massive pops like a full automatic magazine discharging, then the semi swerved, corrected, fishtailed, struck sparks and ground down with a terrific screech.

Henry had judged his position perfectly. As the truck slowed so did the helo, and Wren saw troops leaping out on rappel lines. Henry had his Beretta drawn and pointing at the cab of the truck as it scraped to a stop yards away.

"Give me Henry's bodycam!" Wren ordered, and at once the view shifted; the helo in back, Mason's bike off to the right, Abigail and Chuck running around the sides, and in the cab of the truck sat just a single man. Mid-thirties, stubbled chin, sharp brown eyes, shaved head, hands up.

Wren gasped.

The Ghost.

He knew him.

50

INBOUND

It took ninety minutes to bring the Ghost back to LA. He gave them no trouble. He kneeled in front of the truck, offered his wrists for the cuffs and ducked his head for the black bag. In the Airbus flying back, he stayed quiet and still.

That suited Wren.

There was a lot to do in the meantime. The video of the Ghost's takedown went out for public consumption, and coming on the heels of Rogers' story, the heat went out of the crowd. This was the guy. Not the Apex, maybe, but the guy had been caught.

People began to drift away. All across the country. Wren scrolled through news channels. The story was everywhere.

"Now," he said.

Humphreys grimaced.

Together Wren and Humphreys went out through the lobby, and together they stood in front of the Wilshire Building and shook hands. The photo that came to define that moment showed Wren, rough-shod, tousled and huge, with Humphreys white and thin as an Arctic yeti beside him. The photo almost broke the Internet, but Hellion and B4cksl4cker brought some Russian botnets online to keep it rolling.

There was a call to the President, and Wren was permitted into the room though not onto the call. Papers were signed and stamped. Immunity and

AWOP for the Foundation. Temporary immunity for Wren. Anchors on the news speculated about what it meant for American jurisprudence.

As soon as Wren was done with all that, more came tumbling in. Gruber had regained consciousness, and he wanted to talk. Wren put him live. What came out of that was rambling and uncertain, but it cemented Steven Gruber as both hero and victim at once. He'd done his best; holding out for six days against concerted attempts to break his mind was a phenomenal feat. With a bandage wrapped around his head, he didn't look so bad. The damage was all still there and would be lasting, but it was a good step back into the world.

Doona was alive, but in intensive care, suffering severe internal hemorrhaging from the blast. It turned out her youth was what saved her; much older and her heart would have given out. The Royal Malaysian Police moved at the US President's request to get her the best care possible and ultimate extradition, with a lot of to-and fro-ing about respecting sovereign territory and fresh promises of American investment. Her team were injured, but none too badly.

Sally Rogers landed in the parking lot as it rapidly emptied out, where ambulance services met her. She was severely dehydrated, undernourished and in a deep state of shock. They carried her away on a gurney, leaving Wren standing alone at the window of the nineteenth floor, in Gerald Humphreys' office, listening to Hellion autotuning Humphreys' exclamation in multiple different ways.

There was a lot to think about.

"How did they do that?" came Humphreys' voice on his earpiece, manipulated to sound like a squeaky chipmunk. It was funny, but Wren didn't crack a smile.

"That's my favorite," Hellion said. Like a bird twittering in Wren's ear.

"How about overlaying it atop a bass version?" B4cksl4cker suggested.

"Double Humphreys?" Hellion asked.

"Two pussies in dick suit," said B4cksl4cker. "Two dicks in pussy suit."

Wren winced.

Hellion tried it out.

Wren took the earpiece out. They wouldn't be offended. He didn't get involved in matters of ringtones, usually.

Closing in on 7 p.m. He felt oddly hollow in a way he hadn't anticipated. Getting one step closer to the Apex should feel electrifying, a development filled with potential, but he didn't feel that way at all. What he felt instead was a deep kind of sadness.

The R44 took off from the parking lot. Headed back to Oxnard. He pulled his phone from his pocket, looked at it for a long moment, then put it back. There was no one to call, not really. Everyone was busy: Teddy was in the midst of extracting his team with their data haul from the fake news factory; same for Alejandro with the Fat Unicorn; Henry was en route for a debrief; Gruber was getting air-vacced to the hospital, likewise Rogers; Hellion and B4cksl4cker were bickering, and what did that leave? Maybe Tandrews. He'd make that call, but not right now.

A year ago at this moment, he would have called his wife, Loralei. Asked to speak to his kids. Talking to them, plugging into their simple, happy world would have grounded him in what mattered. Recharged him. He hadn't spoken to them for over a year, but it had never felt so final as this. He'd always felt like, if he said the right things, found just the right way to atone, they might take his call. Like forgiveness might be awaiting, and the door was still slightly open.

Now he knew that door was closed. They were gone.

She would have seen him on the news. Probably she'd keep his involvement from the kids, though, and that was the right thing to do. It would only scare them. Maybe when they were older. He thought back to the way she'd looked at him, that night back in Great Kills.

Now he realized it had been total. For life.

The sky was starting to darken when Humphreys came up behind him.

"He's inbound."

Wren turned. Gerald Humphreys. His enemy. His boss. Now they were on the same team again, like a yoyo. Maybe he'd never trust Wren again, but for as long as they were forced to work together, he'd grit his teeth and bear it.

Wren felt pretty much the same way.

"Let's welcome him in."

51

THE GHOST

Maybe the same interrogation room, maybe a different one, Wren was too weary to notice. One-way mirror, white walls, gray concrete floor, with Wren on one side of the table, the Ghost on the other.

Anais Kiefer.

Bigger than Wren, even. Six foot seven, almost a liability when it came to walking through doorways covertly, getting in and out of cars. It hadn't made him a great prospect for undercover work. Dark skin, a similar tone to Wren, which at least made placement with various jihadi groups a possibility. The ISIS group they'd placed with together, in the mountains of Afghanistan, had called him 'the Giant'.

Of course they had.

A big lantern jaw. Heavy brow, strong cheekbones with pockmarked cheeks, big brown eyes, buzzed black hair, a scraggly beard. Shoulders that were huge and bulbous with muscle, a chest and back that easily spanned sixty inches. Across from him Wren looked small.

The last man you'd expect to vanish into the background, like a ghost.

"Anais," Wren said.

"Chris."

His voice was like a millstone grinding dry, setting Wren's stomach on edge. Southern tinge to his accent, like a true Confederate gentleman. He'd reveled in the power of that voice back in the mountains of Loe Nekan.

Villagers had listened like they were talking to God. They coughed up intel without any need for incitement. Just being in his presence could be overwhelming.

And smart. You didn't become a DELTA operator, up through the US Marines, just by being big and strong. Layering in anti-intel throughout ISIS operations, dropping black psy-ops propaganda bombs into the minds of leadership, leading them astray; these things required an incredibly agile mind.

Wren looked into Anais' eyes and didn't see the familiar swirl of a cult leader's influence. A faint smile even played around his fleshy lips, and cult followers didn't smile like that. Mockingly. Too much autonomy. Back in the Pyramid the Apex had banned any kind of laughter. It had made Wren's childhood a succession of secret trysts in the desert, laughing and playing only with Grace, when he could get away from the mind-numbing duty of black stone collection.

"You're trying to figure me out," Anais said. Amused.

Wren looked at the man's hands. Strong fingers, like grappling hooks. Cuffed to the eyelet, now. He remembered fighting him, bouts during 'training' while the jihadis sat around in boredom, waiting out US drone overwatch above, maybe, or on hold between guerrilla campaigns.

Make the two big guys fight. It became a favorite sport. ISIS foot soldiers would bet virgins in the afterlife on the winner, trading back and forth. Those massive fingers could rip out a man's throat raw. Once or twice he'd felled Wren. He had the power, undoubtedly, but not quite the same speed.

Wren would roll, buck, slip away and pepper the bigger man with kicks to his thighs. Easiest would be a knee break, but he'd liked Anais, and a broken knee would be overkill for barbaric entertainment. Instead he'd wear down one leg, the quads of his right, the hamstrings of his left, until the cumulative damage felled the giant and he sank to his knees laughing through the pain.

Once or twice he caught up Wren in his 'death throes'.

He'd followed Anais' career ever since, until the man dropped out of the DELTA program two years earlier and went wholly dark.

Became a ghost.

"Why?" Wren asked.

The smile flickered from the big man's eyes to his lips then back again. "It wasn't personal," he rumbled.

Wren said nothing. Just looked at him. Anais knew it; he owed an explanation. After all they'd been through.

"Your father's idea," he said. "Apex. I never called him that, by the way. He didn't really try to convert me. A couple of screeds, you know how it is, but he mostly let it go."

Wren's gaze hardened. Witness testimony. "You've met him."

"Of course. Several times. I learned at his feet, isn't that what you cult leaders like to say?" His smile widened. Some kind of inside joke.

"You tell me. I was twelve years old last time I saw him."

Anais' smile widened further. "Really? Are you sure about that?"

Wren stared. He felt Anais playing with him. They'd done this, too, in their fistfights in the caves, over the rocks. Feinting, setting up false trails, pulling punches only to follow through with an elbow, a knee, a headbutt.

Wren felt the anger inside himself now. Getting drawn. "You're saying I've seen him. Didn't recognize him."

Anais shrugged. "I'm a ghost. Who knows what I'm saying?"

"You're enjoying this."

Anais leaned back in the chair expansively. There was a lot to expand. Just like Wren had done a couple of hours earlier, taking up space, using the intimidation of his own body. "Honestly, Christopher Wren? I've loved this. Best time of my life, baiting you. When he pitched me on using you as the linchpin, I never anticipated any of this. Like one of our anti-intelligence ops back in the day, I figured you'd pop up in the thread, pop out since they'd already renditioned you, and I'd be dealing with the 'Deep State' after that." The smile became a grin. "But then you put yourself into the conversation."

Wren leaned closer. "So I wasn't the target?"

Anais shrugged those huge shoulders again. "A happy accident. Not for the Apex, of course. That psychopath was all about you. But for me, it's been the best show I could ever ask for."

Tandrews' words came ringing back to Wren. Greatest Show on Earth.

"Watching you bodyslam a guy?" Anais went on, clearly reveling in it. "Drag race a Porsche, then jump a Big Wheel truck? You're like a one-man hillbilly half-time show. Pop a nipple and we'll have the complete set."

Wren frowned.

Anais sighed, the same kind of sigh you give after taking a long, refreshing pull on a tall glass of cold beer. "It's been wild. By the time you unlocked my tech, I was almost rooting for you. I didn't exactly leave clues, but, well... I could've made it harder, you know?"

"You bombed my team in Malaysia."

"Couldn't resist," Anais said. "You know how it was with us, with IEDs?

So dramatic. If it makes you feel any better, that was rigged to blow long before you got involved. A red herring, you know?" He mused on that for a moment, seemingly taken with his own choice of words. "Did the girl survive, by the way?"

"She's fine."

Anais snorted. "Not fine. Burst lung, as far as my sources tell me. Your boy Steven Gruber's got a melted head. That was a close one, I'll admit. Sally though, the girl, she can dance. Feinted like a demon; three days she plays beaten, then she springs up out of nowhere, high kick to the face?" He rolled his jaw. "Like she was dancing the can-can. I figured she learned that from you."

"I didn't teach her to fight."

"Not the moves, the mindset. You carry it with you even now, Christopher Wren. It's been a joy to punch holes in that sick self-righteousness."

Wren tilted his head to one side. "What?"

"You heard me. Holier than thou. It's your calling card. It was mine, too, until I opened my eyes. Do what has to be done, no matter the cost? Acceptable collateral damage, in the name of Uncle Sam?"

"What on Earth are you gibbering about?"

Anais laughed. Wren hadn't gotten him off-balance yet. Maybe he never would. This man knew all the tricks, had run them himself. "Is this gibbering? Or are you losing it, Wren? Or should I say Pequeño 3?"

Wren set his jaw. "Don't dead-name me."

Anais laughed harder. "Dead-name? Oh, boy. You were always such a trip. Listen, little Pequeño, from one half-breed to another. I don't give a crap about your feud with Daddy. All this Pyramid bullshit, it's make-believe. I know that better than you. The man is a charlatan, but my word, does it work? He hopped me right up like I'd mainlined speed. 'Think of your potential, my boy,' all that? It worked wonders on my self-esteem."

Wren hadn't expected that. It cut the legs out under what he'd expected and left him punching in the dark. "If you don't believe in it, what were you doing running this sham on my Foundation? On me?"

"That's the question, isn't it?"

"It is the damn question. Answer it."

Anais sighed again. Long and satisfied. "I never thought the day would come when the great, no, the legendary Christopher Wren would come begging me for answers. I find I'm enjoying it. Ask me again."

"I'll ask all day. Why on Earth were you working for him, Anais?"

"Not working for him!" the big man snapped, leaning in suddenly to the full extent of his cuffs, drawing audible gasps through the one-way glass. Wren didn't budge a hair. "Working with him. Using his resources, his network. But this was all me. My vision. My needle in the balloon of America's trumped-up BS."

Wren sat there. Face to face, feeling Anais' breath puff over his face, until the big man smiled and settled back down.

"Like I said, this wasn't personal. You were his idea. The Foundation. I was just looking for, shall we say, a fulcrum point."

"To do what?"

"Save the country, of course. We've been going down a bad path. You know it as well as I do."

Wren settled back. Anticipating nonsense. "Tell me about the Apex. Where I've seen him before. What his plans are."

"He's an idiot," Anais said, flicking his fingers dismissively. "And you should be thanking me. America's gotten cocky, Wren. Did you know, and this is before your time with the Company, that the CIA wrote one of the greatest pop songs of all time?" He waited, but Wren showed no sign of recognition. "Back in the seventies, at the height of the Cold War, about bringing down the old order and surging up a new one. Of course, they were talking about the USSR falling, America rising. They made that song go viral like nothing before. Helluva rock ballad, you've definitely heard it, top ten just about everywhere you looked. It changed the Cold War. It helped us win."

Wren sighed.

"Written by the CIA, promoted by our government," Anais went on. "I'm talking black hat psychological operations on civilian populations. Your specialty. My specialty. We've been doing it since before it was cool. Overthrowing military dictatorships we didn't like. Overthrowing democratic results we didn't want. Seeding division in countries and cracking them apart like coconuts, forcing people to turn against each other." He paused a second, peering at Wren. "Ring a bell? The scale of what we did was overwhelming, irresistible, and who were we to have this power? Did we use it for the good of humankind, or just for ourselves?" He smiled. "You know the answer to that. We drove people insane, Chris. Broke nations on the rack, literally, pushing their people back then forth then back again, so many times their minds got thin like pulled taffy, and we're still doing it. No one can beat us for offensive public relations. Defensive, though?" The smile became a grin. "Not so much. You might call us a soft target, get all upset as soon as other forces, your Apex amongst them, turn those weapons against us."

Wren just stared. "You're disgruntled."

Anais laughed. "Hell yes, I am. Look at yourself, Pequeño, at the life you've led, the lies you've told. You think you're somehow truer than the rest of us? That you're living some charmed life propelled only by what's right? Or are you cutting corners just to serve yourself? Indenturing people to that 'Foundation' not only because it's good for them, but also because it's good for you? I bet it makes you feel a whole lot less lonely, to have a group of people who can never dump you. Slaves, Pequeño, locked in with your 'coin system' just like your father locked in his Pyramid." He leaned closer. "Let me get you hot, Chris. How are you different from that man, really? He doesn't like reality, so he bends it. Isn't that what you've been doing this whole time?"

Wren stared. Heart rate surging, like he was about to burst from the inside. The words were piling up like blood behind a clot, and he knew he had to say something back, throw up some defenses, but he had nothing. Anais was right. Every word was a body blow.

"Your Greatest Show on Earth, no matter the cost, how are you any better?" he pressed on. "At least I was trying to teach this country a lesson! Look to your own house first, Christopher Wren." He took a breath. "Did you know it was frontier civilians who wiped out the indigenous peoples of this country, Chris? Civilians, not soldiers. They banded into lynch mobs, mostly, riled up on propaganda painting them as 'barbaric savages'. Andrew Jackson led the charge, went all in on ethnic cleansing, and what was 'manifest destiny' but the most effective dehumanization ideology in human history? And we did that to ourselves!" Anais slammed the table. "So all this, this ghosting, Wren, it's for our own good! The medicine doesn't always taste good, but we need to take it anyway. We need to take responsibility for what we've done. Vaccines have side effects, but we're stronger for it by the end."

Now Wren felt dizzy. His own words, coming back to haunt him. The same way they'd always talked about false intel injected into foreign bloodstreams. Vaccines. Inoculation. He found himself on his feet, bleary-eyed, holding to the table.

"Too much?" Anais asked. His big face leered at Wren as if through a funhouse mirror. He almost missed a step. "Can't handle the truth?"

Wren barely made it to the door. Staggered out, chased by Anais' mocking laughter.

52

THREE MONTHS

Wren drove across the country.

At some point he spoke to Tandrews. The old man was back in Maine, where he belonged. It was a good talk, but it didn't lead to anything. Wise words, maybe. Some perspective. But it didn't help.

The fog was thick in his head.

Wren worked every day: on shoring up the Foundation, on chasing down leads to his father, on ensuring his family were safe, on setting Teddy and the rest of the Board up with the tools that they needed, but throughout it the uncertainty was building, and nothing could pierce it.

He drank. It didn't help.

The Apex had disappeared again. Sunk beneath a layer of reality that even Anais' ghosting technique couldn't penetrate. Invisible in plain sight.

So he drove. On small roads when the mood took him, on Interstate highways when it shifted, across deserts, through forests, in and out of cities and towns, but nothing made a difference. With every passing day he only felt more unmoored. Unwelcome with his wife and kids. No real friends. No place to go and no particular thing to do.

Steven Gruber had said it all, in the moments before he burned. We are all alone.

Wren went to visit him. He sat by Gruber's bedside in intensive care, looking down at his burn-scarred head, the wispy tendrils of yellow hair now uneven and scattered, mixed in with the mottled skin, trying to think of something good to say.

Gruber looked up at him. No words came.

The TV was on in the corner of the room, showing politicians talking, pundits bickering, people supporting Christopher Wren and people against him. He half-listened but barely took any of it in. He held Gruber's hand and racked his brain for something useful or inspiring.

"Man says burn, I burn," Gruber said at some point.

Wren couldn't tell if it was a joke, didn't know whether to laugh or cry.

"We'll fix this," he said, and Gruber nodded along, though Wren didn't really feel it. More of the same. Survival now meant going through the motions for long enough until the things Anais had said faded from his mind.

Except they didn't fade.

He drove.

States passed him by. America was quiet, in the run up to the election. The usual heat of the campaign seemed to have simmered down. The sense of dread was gone, or still there, but muted now. The whole country had been through something together, something terrible, and it had changed them. Changed them into what, though?

He went back to the fake town, Little Phoenix, and Maggie welcomed him like a prodigal son. He sat at the head table beside her in the dining hall while all the children ate, a sea of faces glancing his way, trying to feel something good from it, but nothing came. Later on, in the darkness of the desert as they walked together beside the gravestones she'd put into place, she put her hand into his, and he didn't really feel anything.

Warmth, perhaps. Her good intentions. A distant kind of attraction from a distant kind of version of himself, but nothing immediate. Nothing that could really cut through the confusion.

"You know what's real, Pequeño 3," his father had said, so long ago. It was hard to shake.

Looking out over the desert, he remembered the worst day of them all. The morning after all the Pequeños died in the pit. He'd been celebrated, Grace alongside him. There'd been drinking, and BBQ and singing, dancing, all watched over by the silent gaze of the Apex.

He'd felt it then like a chill on is heart. A dark shadow that damaged everything.

The Apex had woken him before any of it, before the dawn, blue eyes sparkling in the lantern light, as excited as a child. He'd pulled little Pequeño 3 on after him, no time to get dressed, staggering through the desert in his pajamas, barefoot, up to the pit.

It was dark, too dark to see anything but shadows. The moon was fat and round, the stars a glittering cabal.

"We were wrong," the Apex had said, as brightly as if he was reading out mismatched findings in one of the essential barometers. Happy to catch reality out. "Look."

He pointed into the pit, and little Pequeño 3 stared, and stared, until finally he began to see the shapes of bodies resolving. The skies were turning blue with the coming dawn, and he picked out the long limbs of Chrysogonus-With-Bared-Arm, the tousled hair of Aden-Of-The-Saints, and Galicia-In-Her-Mother's-Heart, and Zachariah-Of-The-Marsh, and Gabriel-In-Extremis.

And one more.

Smaller. He didn't recognize her at first. He didn't believe it for long minutes after that, not until the sun broke over the horizon and brittle rays of light blanched the pit pale, and her blond curls stood out against the dark loam, and her happy eyes shone dully.

Grace-In-Our-Times.

"We were wrong!" the Apex crowed, holding him close, shaking him, looking into his eyes. "She died after all! Don't you remember?"

Maggie squeezed his hand, pulling him back into the moment. Walking down the main street together as the dusk set in. The desert rustled and shifted around them: gophers tunneling, jackrabbits burrowing, snakes shivering their cold bodies into the sand. He turned from the endless desert to look at her face. Maybe, if Grace had grown up...

"Where's the boy?" he asked,

"What boy?" Maggie asked. Gently, as was her way. Kind.

Wren cast his mind back. "The boy I saw when I was here. Before you arrived. He brought me a picnic. We talked a little."

It didn't take much for him to read the answer on her face. Still, she said the words, trying to hide the concern. Aortal flutter had side effects, after all. Why not blame it on that. It was easier than the alternative.

"I'll check with Coral," she said. "They didn't mention that."

They didn't mention that. He couldn't let it go, though. How could he? Trapped in the fog, you needed something to feel real.

"Over there," he said, pointing. "We sat together. He brought a picnic blanket. A basket. Food, milk, apples."

"Really, I'll ask Coral," Maggie said again, but he already knew the truth.

There'd been no boy. No picnic. Only a hallucination.

"I have to go," he said.

She tried to hold onto his hand, said heartfelt things as he strode away and tried to call him back, but her words were just wind in the air.

That night he drank himself to blackout in a desert motel. The next night too.

He stopped checking in on the darknet. He left his phone behind, so he couldn't be tracked. He drove from town to little town, all the same places the Apex and his merry band of followers had once danced at, and sang at, and recruited at, imagining that little boy that was the mirror image of himself dancing here too.

Pequeño 3. The ungrateful son.

Sometimes he saw him in a flare of the sunlight, in a shallow patch of shadow, winking back at him. He understood that this was the cost. A lifetime of pain and lies, how did you ever know what was real after that?

Coming down from a three-day bender in a desert diner, somewhere off the old route 66 in Nevada or Utah, he watched some big political event on TV over pancakes and bacon, sitting at the counter. There were crowds cheering in back of a guy at a podium, holding signs that he couldn't make out through the blear in his eyes.

"What the hell is this?" he drawled.

The fry cook was on deck. A thick guy with a neck tattoo and greasy white overalls. He looked at Wren, looked at the TV and back.

"Are you kidding?"

Wren fixed him with a watery, wavering gaze. "Do I look like I'm kidding?"

"That's the election, you dang drunk. Last night. The guy won."

Wren turned back to the TV. The guy? He peered. It did look like a political speech. Acceptance speech. It took him long moments to resolve the image more clearly, and when he did, he recognized the guy.

David Keller.

He'd been Wren's greatest cheerleader before any of this began. Cheerleading the Foundation, too. A write-in candidate, it turned out, on a unity ticket. Just as Wren had met Humphreys and they'd made a deal, so this guy had reached across the aisle, it seemed, and been listened to. Chosen his VP from the ranks of Independents. Meet in the middle and begin to heal. Seemed the people were in the mood to compromise.

As Wren watched, and listened to his speech, he felt the fog start to fade for the first time in what felt like years. The audio of the TV surged up through the numbness in his head.

"Turn it up," he said.

"Sure thing, man," said the cook, and made no move to do so.

"Turn the damn TV up!"

The guy grunted and hit the volume.

Wren sat up straight, staring now. Feeling the fog slough away. There was Keller front and center, holding forth as he made his vows, inspiring the crowd with an easy hand, but Wren didn't have eyes for him. Instead his gaze was drawn magnetically to the side, to Keller's camp of aides at the edge of the stage, where a tall man stood.

Gray-haired, late fifties maybe, handsome, confident, with an easy bearing of overwhelming command and piercing blue eyes.

Wren's heart skipped a beat, then raced up past a hundred, a hundred twenty, roaring toward aortal flutter. There was no mistaking it. Twenty-five years had passed but he recognized those eyes, shining up at him from the depths of a dark pit.

Apex of the Pyramid.

His father.

With the full power of the Presidency now at his back.

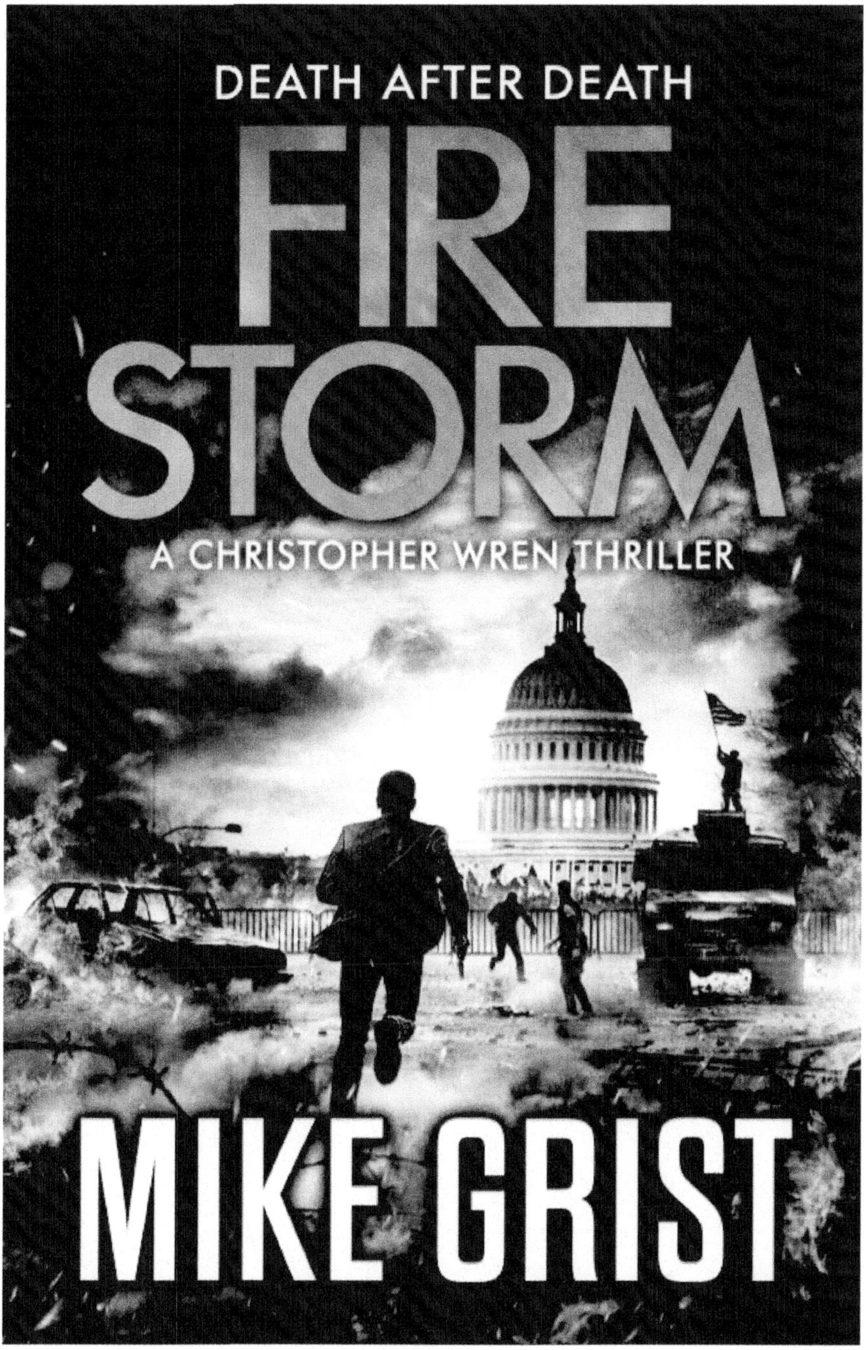
DEATH AFTER DEATH
FIRE
STORM
A CHRISTOPHER WREN THRILLER
MIKE GRIST

1

KELLER

Christopher Wren watched from the shadowy wings of the enormous, purpose-built stage as President-elect David Keller drew riotous cheers from the crowd with easy, homespun charm. Out in the middle of rural Kansas, the fifteenth stop on Keller's post-election victory tour, and the crowds only seemed to be getting bigger and louder.

Even looking looking out from the wings, Keller's fans stretched back and back, completely filling out the ten acres of grain-sorghum land rented from a local farmer, covered now in a patchwork blanket of hundreds of large grass mats in alternating blue and red. Seen en masse they made for an incredible visual, a microcosm of Keller's electoral coalition crossing both sides of the partisan aisle.

Wren turned back to Keller. Physically dwarfed by the immensity of the stage, but easily commanding the space. It was on loan from a famous rock band, apparently, with twin cinema-sized screens in back and a light show that would carry over into the night. Speakers pumping out Keller's freestyling speech like the voice of God through the hurricane of cheers.

The mood in the air was ferociously joyful, people weeping, roaring, high on the bright new hope they saw in David Keller. The possibilities he presented. A way forward.

Wren saw only danger.

At best all of this was raw vanity, a victory lap to inflate Keller's ego further toward becoming some bipartisan autocrat. At worst this was the national-scale inauguration of the Pyramid's Third Reich. It was only three weeks back that Keller had shared his election night stage in Washington D.C. with the Apex himself.

Wren gritted his teeth. Twenty-five years had passed, but he'd recognized his own father in an instant, glimpsed on a TV through a hungover haze in some beat-down old truck stop diner. The architect of the Pyramid death cult, with all one thousand burned alive at little Christopher Wren's hand, as well as the hidden force behind every recent attack in the last eighteen months.

The stakes couldn't be higher.

"He's toying with us," Wren said low, knuckles tight.

CIA agent Sally Rogers snorted by his side. "It's not much of a game, Chris. We've got nothing on him. Some footage where he's looking at a guy who may possibly be a man no one's seen for a quarter century? Or more likely, just some random old guy who wandered onto his stage."

Wren didn't buy that for a second, and hadn't despite every member of Keller's staff offering it up as an excuse. Old guys didn't wander onto the President-elect's stage. Didn't happen.

He turned to face Rogers. Early thirties, hair tight back in a blond ponytail, aquiline nose and sharp green eyes, wearing a navy letterman jacket rounded out by muscle. She was no slouch when it came to lifting. Bench two-fifty, Wren knew, putting her head and shoulders above most men.

"Do you honestly believe that?"

She met his eyes. A few months back she'd been a prisoner of the 'Ghost', an ex-DELTA colleague of Wren's, looking to blow up America for the black-ops crimes of the intelligence community. She'd been tortured and brainwashed, but come out of it alive. Not intact, but alive, and Wren saw the changes in her eyes. A doubt that had never been there before. A fear too.

Put those together, maybe you hit on wisdom.

She didn't say anything for a moment, just gazing back at him. Rogers coming along to babysit had been CIA Director Gerald Humphreys' primary condition, after Wren used up all his juice from taking down the Ghost to rig this meet with the President-elect. A walk-and-talk between post-campaign rallies to ramp up to his Presidency.

"We'll ask the questions," Rogers said. "If Keller is linked to your father somehow, maybe he'll let something slip. He thinks we're desperate here, after all. Looking for crumbs from his table."

Wren grunted. She wasn't wrong about that, and it galled. But here she was, too, and that was hardly a crumb. Looking in Wren's eyes again, speaking to him like he was a human, after they'd spent the last six months betraying each other. It meant something to him.

"He's right."

Rogers smiled like she didn't believe it.

Wren turned back to Keller. Midstream in his remarks, now arms spread wide, the crowd responding to every movement. He had it, that was clear. The touch of the firebrand preacher. Ignite the people's hopes and dreams, getting them burning for more.

Unity, was his promise. An end to the division. A leader who'd listen to all sides and torch a path through the middle. It was a smart move.

Wren looked wider, assessing the security situation. A cadre of five Secret Service agents encircled them in the wings, big men in tailored black suits with earpieces and bulging shoulder straps. Aides bustled by carrying clipboards, grips worked the mics, lights and speakers hanging above the stage, a pair of producers stood nodding like manic chipmunks just ahead, looking from their tablets to Keller and back again, registering his social media 'vital signs'. A wink of light from across the stage, where a Secret Service sniper's scope had to be trained on Wren's chest. Step one foot out of line, and they wouldn't hesitate to take him out.

Humphreys had promised that himself.

It wasn't airtight, though. Depended how far Wren was willing to go. Send an elbow to the nearest guy's jaw, backwards headbutt to take out the one immediately behind, spin on the guy falling and use him as a human shield against the sniper. Steal his weapon as he sagged, pop the remaining three, fire enough to keep the sniper's head down while he made it to Keller, and then…

And then what? Kill him? Try to force an on-air confession? Become a Presidential assassin on par with Wilkes-Booth, his name set to live in ignominy forever?

None of that would help, and he cursed.

"Plotting his execution?" Rogers asked. She sounded amused. A little too much sass along with that wisdom, maybe.

"I'd need to rig the whole stage," he said. "No other way to do it and get away."

She laughed low. "I wouldn't put it past you. But watch this. I saw them rehearsing. You're going to love it."

Wren doubted that very much, but refocused on Keller.

"There's been so much pain in the last year," he was saying now, overriding the cheers. "Our country has come under attack from within by a wave of vicious, hateful domestic terrorists, seeking only to tear us down. The Saints. The Blue Fairy. The Reparations, and now, the Ghost."

The people roared. Absolutely united as he named a list of enemies defeated. Each one racked up, each one knocked down.

"Now we're seeing ourselves in ways we never imagined possible. Our own fault lines, our original sins, and I know as well as any, it is terrifying to see the dark along with the light. The costs to reach this point have been terrible. We have lost many good people along the way. But throughout the American people have been resilient. We have endured. Our strength has allowed new heroes to rise up from the masses. Heroes like Christopher Wren!"

The giant screens behind Keller flashed to life, illuminating the stage as a medley of Christopher Wren's greatest hits began to thumping rock music: Wren jumping a monster truck over the Los Angeles river dam, huge US flags streaming; Wren at the head of the protests in front of the Wilshire Building, standing before a crowd that moments earlier had been rioting.

The crowd went berserk.

"He's playing your song," Rogers said. "Isn't it great?"

Wren grimaced.

"We can all learn from these heroes," Keller boomed, then stepped aside from the lectern. "We can all listen, and learn, and grow, we just need the wisdom and humility to listen, and the vision to lead into hope."

The people drove themselves to new heights of cheering, and Keller let the moment stretch out. Let them hang for his next words, craning to hear, straining to see. He spread his arms. He waited, listening for some unseen cue, then dropped to his knees at the exact moment that a giant version of Christopher Wren dropped to his knees in back, at the moment he cowed the LA riot.

"You've got to admit, that is pretty cool," Rogers said, barely audible over the crowd's frenzied roars of approval. "What a way to appropriate you, right?"

Keller stretched his arms higher and the people raised their voices higher to match, like he was some faith healer in a stadium-seating mega church. Of course, in some ways he was.

"I'll be in the green room," Wren said. Turned and stalked away.

Three Secret Service agents peeled off to steer him, and Wren let himself be steered.

The green room was a boxy pre-fab space little better than an interrogation cell, sofa against one white plasterboard wall, a platter of fruits carved into the shape of flowers on a dark wood coffee table, along with various biscuits, drinks, tea and coffee. A couple of robust-looking plants, a full-length mirror, a woman in a black and white waitress outfit standing by the door, ready to serve.

Wren sat on the sofa and the Secret Service members fanned around him. He reached out, picked up a pineapple carved like a rose.

"That's not for you," the waitress said.

Wren chewed. One of the Secret Service members waved her off. He figured he was famous now. An essential supporting actor in David Keller's surge to fame and power. They wouldn't begrudge him some fruit.

He ate some more.

Thirty minutes, it took. Turning the questions in his head. Eating the fruit. Hearing the crowd roar. First the agents got the warning in their earpieces, Wren saw the way their heads inclined. They secured Wren with their gaze, silently moved as one to secure the door. In moments more agents came in, followed by a clutch of aides, then Rogers, then finally President-elect David Keller himself.

He was beaming and glowing, pumped off the adoration of the crowd, skin glistening with a light sheen of sweat. Hollywood handsome, maybe as tall as Wren and powerfully built, with a strong chin and a solid neck, dark hair cropped short, late forties, tan, impeccably dressed and groomed.

"Mr. Wren!" he boomed, immediately dominating the room, easily bypassing his own security to stretch one hand out to Wren. "It is an honor to finally meet you."

Wren didn't shake. Just kept sitting, studying the man before him. Rogers frowned, clearly didn't like that, but Wren wasn't here to make friends.

"The Apex was on your stage," he said instead. Cutting right to the chase. "You looked him in the eye, Mr. President-elect. The man I've been hunting all my adult life. You looked right at him, and you really had no idea?"

It was a simple opening move. Maybe the only move he was going to get, but Rogers was right. To get something out of Keller, they were going to have to rattle his cage as hard as they could, and this was the hardball question nobody else was asking.

Either you're incompetent for not noticing him, or you're complicit and covering it up.

Choose.

Keller sidestepped smoothly, like none of this was an insult. Pulled his hand back easily, looked down at his empty plate, looked back at Wren and smiled. "I see you ate all my fruit."

He had a deep baritone voice, reassuring and effortlessly confident, with a slight Southern lilt, slight East-Coast clipped intonation. The kind of man who could move between worlds with ease, from California to Idaho right through to New York.

"The eyeline's clear," Wren pressed. "It's unmistakable."

"The pineapples shaped like corkscrews are my favorite," Keller said absently, like nothing mattered so much as fruit, then turned around, found the waitress and amped his smile up to full wattage. "Can we get some more, please?"

She leaped into action so fast she risked whiplash

A simple move in response, but powerful. Wren had to respect that. Neither taking offense or offering some mealy-mouthed answer, just ignoring the entire topic. Chase that by re-asserting himself in the room by proving it bent to his command.

Wren knew one simple way to off-set that.

He stood up. Knew from experience it would be disconcerting, get all the agents on edge, maybe Keller too. He was a big guy, after all, with a big reputation. Two-hundred-forty pounds of agile, man-killing mass rising to six foot three in height. Not an ounce of fat on him. A DELTA operator, later CIA black ops specialist, nicknamed 'Saint Justice' for the sheer number of terrorists he'd set on the straight and narrow, often permanently, with a bullet.

If anything Keller seemed amused. "I must admit, after seeing you projected twenty feet tall on the stage screen, you do seem smaller in person."

Wren almost laughed. So maybe they were headed for the playground. "That's only natural. I'm afraid none of us lives up to our legend."

Keller's grin spread. He gave the slightest shrug. "The people love you, Mr. Wren. I make no bones about it, I have ridden your coat-tails somewhat. I'd be happy to welcome you on stage in the flesh, should you ever wish to join the party you started."

"Impossible," Wren said. Didn't let his gaze flicker a beat away from Keller's, trying to read something in their unyielding politician sheen. "I voted for the other guy."

Keller's grin didn't dim a bit. "We both know that's not true. I actually had my team check the rolls, for the purposes of the speech, you understand. You're not registered to vote anywhere in any state in this great country, and you never have been."

Wren grinned back. "There are other ways to vote, Mr. President-elect. I'd be happy to talk to you about them more."

The moment stretched a little too long. One of the Secret Service agents took a step forward. Wren saw it register on Keller's face as a flinch.

"Mr. President-elect," Rogers intervened. "We understand you're very busy. About the man on your acceptance speech stage. If you could please account for that."

Keller blinked, turned to her, adopted an entirely different tone. Like he was sad, disappointed in himself maybe, or his team.

"Agent Rogers? A pleasure, and congratulations on your work to bring down the Ghost. As for that man, yes, I wish I could account for it. Sincerely. The truth is, I'd never seen that man before." He looked at Wren, back to Rogers. "You know I've already fired my entire security team from that day. They're under investigation for the lapse." He gestured at the agents around him. "I'm certain it won't happen again. But again, how could a complete stranger get onto my stage?" He shook his head. "I can't explain it. It concerns me. I absolutely agree that it is imperative we hunt this man down." He paused a moment, as if considering something. "To that end, you have all the resources at my disposal to help find him."

Wren just stared. Keller turned and matched his gaze.

"You looked right at him," Wren said. "Right in his eyes. The Apex. My father. You looked proud."

Keller didn't budge. "I can imagine how that might seem to you. But have you ever been on a stage of this size, Mr. Wren? Other than today, in the wings?"

Wren stared back. Didn't need to answer, because Keller knew that he had. Putting down the riots that the 'Ghost' had started in LA. A strange thing to invoke.

"Of course you have," Keller allowed, like he was just remembering. "Remiss of me. So you'll know that the moment is overwhelming. You don't really see details. The lights, the crowd, the atmosphere, they overcome you. All I knew was that my campaign team were standing in that wing of the stage. I think, if you play back the audio, you'll hear I was thanking them." He flashed a high wattage smile. "I do everything I can to stay humble."

Wren said nothing.

"I understand and applaud your suspicions," Keller went on. "I value your instincts more than anything, Mr. Wren. It's why I'm asking my team to cooperate with you in any way we can. Everything we've done here builds on your work. And I hope our use of your image doesn't offend you, whether you voted for me or not. In fact, I hope that you're proud of our message. Only time will tell, of course, but I'm not lying about my campaign promises. I am here to unite the country. So any time you'd like to call me, I will listen."

Wren stared. Searching but finding nothing in Keller's eyes except his own reflection bounced back. No way through. No answers. "And kneel," he said.

That almost put a crack in the glass. "Excuse me?"

"And kneel," Wren repeated. "It was right there in your speech, after thanking your team. Listen. Stare unflinching into the darkness. Seek out wisdom. Kneel."

Keller's smile shifted. For a moment Wren glimpsed something lurking beneath the glossy sheen of his eyes, but didn't know what it meant. "Speeches. You understand." He reached into a pocket, held out a card. "My number. A direct line to me. I want you to call the moment you learn anything about the identity of this man, Mr. Wren. I may not be President yet, but I will bend the rules for you, at least as much as I can."

Wren said nothing. Keller was transparently fake, like a pane of one-way glass, but so were most politicians. From one angle you saw straight through. From another, all the dark secrets reflected back.

He just needed to find the right angle.

"I'll call," Wren said. Took the card. "And stop using my footage in your campaign."

Keller looked torn. "The campaign's over, Mr. Wren. We won. And that footage belongs to the people now. I'm afraid I can't control it."

Wren smiled back. "So bend the rules. At least as much as you can."

Keller's façade almost cracked. He gave a nod to Rogers, then strode out of the room just as his carved fruit arrived.

2

ANAIS

It left them with only one place to go.

Within a day Wren and Rogers were there, standing outside Wren's old interrogation room in a CIA black site facility deep beneath the Sonoran Desert, the middle of wildest Mexico, three months after he'd been a prisoner there himself.

Now Wren was on the other side of the one-way glass, looking through at Anais Kiefer, the 'Ghost'. The man who'd held the country hostage by burning members of Wren's Foundation people alive, live on camera. He'd tried to burn Sally Rogers too, to incite riots in major cities by pinning the killings on the government 'Deep State'. A classic false flag attack. He'd almost succeeded in fomenting a national bloodbath.

Kiefer was huge. Bigger than Wren at 6' 7", with pumpkin-thick arms swelling in his bright orange prison jumpsuit, bulbous shoulders, trapezoids that ran at a steep forty-five degrees into his tree-trunk neck. Press four hundred pounds with ease, Wren figured, and squat six hundred. Far more than Wren. He hadn't weight-trained in years, preferring the focus on speed and agility that high-impact interval training and cross training offered.

Now Kiefer was staring right back at him through the glass. Somehow he knew Wren was there, and Wren's heart slammed hard.

They'd been DELTA squad members together for a time, both ending up covertly assigned to the same ISIS brigade in the mountains of Afghanistan. Towering above the rest of the jihadis, they'd often been paired up in hand-to-hand fighting for the amusement of the rest. The jihadis had taken to placing bets on them, some portion of their 72 afterlife virgins on one or the other big guys going down. Whenever it went to the ground, Wren had won. Whenever they'd stayed upright, Kiefer had won.

The guy was strong, smart and merciless.

Last time they'd spoken was three months earlier, right after his capture. Wren had gone into the interrogation loaded for bear, but Kiefer had outmaneuvered him with ease, digging into emotional wounds Wren had been glossing over for years. His family, his Foundation, his failures as a father.

Call it therapy via trial by fire.

"He's been looking forward to this."

Rogers' gaze bored through the glass. Staring at her tormentor. The man who'd tried to use her death to make a political point.

"He thinks he broke us both," she went on. "Now we're desperate."

Wren stared through the glass. He hadn't expected to come back here. Had thought one of their many other leads would have panned out. If not David Keller himself, then one of the digital leads unearthed by his expert hackers, Hellion and B4cksl4cker, using the data record to reconstruct the Apex's movements and second-guess the next attack before it could land.

They'd found nothing.

All that left was Anais Kiefer as their last living lead on the Apex.

"Do not hurt him," Director Humphreys had warned him. "I heard about you meeting with Keller. You insulted him with no basis in evidence. You're on thin ice and this is your last chance. This is not about revenge. Anais Kiefer's an intelligence asset."

Wren said nothing.

Now the Ghost was waiting.

"I'll go in alone," Wren said, turning to Rogers. She looked doubtful. "Trust me."

She raised a thick brown eyebrow. "No good cop, bad cop?"

"We're all good cops to him."

Rogers held his gaze. She knew what that meant. She'd been around Wren long enough to know how he operated. "If he dies, you're going down for it alone."

"I'm already down," Wren said. "Just lock the door on your way out."

It was brighter in the interrogation room. White LEDs recessed into the ceiling allowed no shadows, no respite. A ten-foot square white cube, the same room they'd once questioned Wren in. Kiefer looked even bigger up close, a man mountain.

"Chris," he said, grinning. White teeth. "I thought I smelled your perfume. What's that line, 'I love the smell of napalm on the morning?'"

Wren said nothing. Closed the door, stood looking at Kiefer for maybe ten seconds, trying on the alabaster poker face he'd learned from Humphreys.

It seemed to amuse Kiefer.

"Is this a psyche out?" he asked, and looked over at the one-way mirror. "Am I being punked? Who's in there, it's someone famous, right? Let me guess. Tom Hardy wants to play me in the movie. They've sent you in to negotiate the rights. Only if he gets to wear a mask, though, and speak unintelligibly. Put that in the contract."

Wren pulled out the chair, legs rasping on the concrete floor, and sat. The metal flexed under his weight.

"Or is this actually an attempt at intimidation?" Kiefer asked, one eyebrow raised. "You've come for a second round?"

Wren's gaze on Kiefer didn't waver. He knew a lot more about the 'Ghost's' movements now, his motivations and his intent. The man had a powerful mind. Let him draw his own conclusions.

Kiefer looked over to the one-way glass. Looked back at Wren. "She's here, isn't she? The woman. Rogers."

Wren gave nothing away. Kiefer took that as confirmation and smiled, settled back in his chair like the smug fool he was.

"Sally Rogers. The bitch that got away." He seemed to luxuriate in the insult. "What have you brought her out here for, Chris? Prove some kind of macho point, that you can man me down?" He studied Wren. "We could arm wrestle, I guess, but I don't think it'll go your way. You've lost mass, frankly. Hardly the man you once were, but I guess that's the failure setting in."

"Only one failure, from where I'm sitting," Wren said.

Kiefer leaped on it. "There you are. You sad old man. Nothing I liked better than taking the shine off you, Chris. All American my ass. I like the new hair, by the way. Nothing says mid-life crisis better than a middle-aged man with a buzzcut." He took a breath. "So where've you been the past few weeks? Not out hunting the 'Apex', I wager. Probably in a flop house somewhere slumming it with the other junkies. Mainlining crack to make up for your many failures, sucking down drugs to fill the hole in your heart?" He peered into Wren's eyes, hoping for a hit. Wren gave him nothing. "I've got news for you, Chris, all you'll find at the bottom of that well is more misery. Men like you and I can't dig our way out, and the stars are so far out of reach."

Wren snorted. "I've still got years before I'm early middle-aged."

"Hole in the heart," Kiefer went on, his voice growing harsher. "Throw a pity party. And now you're here with your girlfriend, you think I'll take pity on her sad case? On yours? I'm not a crutch to rebuild your fragile ego. We were never friends, Chris. I saw through you every time. You're like an empty glass. Take out the Apex, there's nothing there."

Wren smiled. "So let's talk about the Apex."

Kiefer laughed. Like he'd scored an unexpected point. "It all comes back to Daddy issues with you, doesn't it, Chris? I mention his name and you open your rotten heart right up?"

"Now you're sweet talking me," Wren said. "Watch out or I'll come in for the kiss."

Kiefer leaned in, lowered his voice. "Did she tell you the moments we had, your sweet little Sally Rogers? The hot, sweet, panting moments in the dark? Ashes burning down on your boy right by her side. There's nothing hornier than a dead man at your feet, am I right?"

"I can think of a few things."

"Right, like lying to your kids their whole lives? Lying to your wife?"

Wren set his jaw like granite. Let the guy think he was getting under his skin. "That was the job. I quit to make it right."

Kiefer chuckled, scenting blood. "Oh yeah? I heard all kinds about that. How you finally renounced that dumb 'Saint Justice tag, aimed to become a 'family man'. Get the counselling you need, take your boy fishing, take your girl shopping at the mall." He grinned. "But you couldn't even do that right. I pity you, Chris. Like a modern day Don Quixote, tilting at windmills. We all came back from the field screwed up, but I channeled what I had. I put it into something real, to make some kind of amends. You were always so terrified of what'd happen if you threw off your government leash. The one time you did, look what happened."

Wren listened. In truth, it was getting old now. Two months back Kiefer had crushed him with talk like this. Now the words held no weight. As much as possible, he'd come to terms with who he was and what he'd done.

"Rogers is watching," he said. "You're right about that much."

"Sally Rogers," Kiefer repeated. "Woman of the hour. Kicked me right in the head, and you don't get a lot of that, pushing seven foot tall."

"You're barely six and a half," Wren corrected.

"Six seven, and let's get her in here, we'll reminisce. Honestly, I can't think what else you're hoping to achieve with this. I can slam dunk on you all day."

Wren smiled. He reached into his pocket, produced a key.

Kiefer's eyes lit up. "We are going to arm wrestle?"

"We'll do more than that," Wren said, and rose to his feet. Pulled a slim wedge of wood from his pocket, moved over to the door and slipped it under the jamb, slammed it into position with a few hard kicks. "I'll make you a wager. You win, you do what you want with me. Nobody's coming in to stop you." He produced another wedge, pushed it into the crevice at the top of the door, hammered it into place with his fist.

"And if I lose?" Kiefer asked.

Wren walked over, put the key in the lock to the cuffs, turned it. "If you lose, you spill. Everything you know."

Kiefer slid his wrists free. Rubbed them for a moment. "A wager. Like the old days."

"Life and death."

"Let's make it death," Kiefer said, and flung the table between them into the wall.

3

CRAB

Kiefer came in like a freight train, one big step and one big left shooting straight. Force of easily a thousand pounds per square inch, coming at ten yards per second, capable of sending Wren's head accelerating away at forty-plus g, ten times faster than a rocket launch.

You fought a bigger guy, you had to move, and Wren was already slipping on the blow's inside, though he felt the slipstream rush by his right ear. Milliseconds only, and the big guy's shoulders ratcheted like a trebuchet arm, racking and swinging a massive right reverse punch. Maybe sixteen hundred psi, fifteen yards per second, sixty-plus g on impact, a killing blow that Wren bypassed with a fast jab kick to Kiefer's left knee.

The big guy's leg jammed back, the line of force up from the ground to his fist fizzled and the punch swayed short as he tried to right his balance.

Wren ducked his head and drove through Kiefer' open guard like a linebacker, shoulder slamming into his waist. Not enough speed to lift him off his feet, but Wren drove him back a step or two. Two seconds in.

Before Kiefer could drop an elbow into Wren's spine he snapped up straight, aiming to uppercut the bigger man's jaw with the top of his head, but he was already leaning back. Close enough for a waltz, no time to dart away, and he wrapped his massive arms around Wren's back.

The worst place to be.

A bear hug from Kiefer could crush his rib cage in seconds flat. Wren didn't wait; tucked his head down, swept his right arm back to push Kiefer's left wrist down while swinging his own left forearm up to brace against the big man's trunk-like chest, then punched backward with his hips.

The entire drive train of his body flexed against Kiefer's arms. Didn't matter how much bigger the opponent was, core muscles trumped biceps every time. It was how you out-wrestled a stronger foe; don't fight the whole, target their smaller muscles with your bigger ones.

The bear hug opened, and Wren fired a knee like an artillery round through Kiefer's open guard into his gut. It was like putting a knee into a concrete wall, but Kiefer released a satisfying oomph and the bear hug collapsed. Wren sent a sharp sideways headbutt into his temple as a parting gift then danced three steps back to the plain white wall.

The big guy straightened up. Gave Wren an appraising look while rubbing his temple

"Snappy bullshit," he said.

"Plenty more where that came from."

"Let's see it," Kiefer said, and launched off his right leg into a spinning jump kick, way too fast for a guy his size, arcing in to Wren's midriff. Maybe break his floating ribs, punch them clean into his lungs, and no place to go as the swipe came in.

No way to go but forward. Wren pushed off the wall to lunge two steps in with his right elbow up, walking into Kiefer's face. The kick broke off his side at half power, a grunt but no damage as the flat knee slapped his ribs. Kiefer lurched off-balance to avoid the elbow charge, and Wren whip-cracked his fist to the big guy's clavicle. Kiefer rolled it, let momentum pull him around to Wren's side, and went in for a side headlock.

Wren ducked out fast, jabbed a passing left uppercut into Kiefer's groin, then danced back to the wall.

"Hot dang," Kiefer said, taking a sideways step that faltered slightly.

"Never liked a punch to the nuts, did you?" Wren taunted.

"With nuts as big as these-" Kiefer began, then charged mid-sentence. Arms out like an ocean trawler, three hundred pounds coming on hard, and there was nowhere for Wren to go. He fired a knee up for distance but Kiefer still hit him head-on, slammed his back off the white wall, then he fell and Kiefer fell on top.

Another slam as his back hit the deck, the breath knocked from his lungs, and Kiefer straddled him. No way to kick out now, nothing to do but hunker behind his elbows as the big guy sent the first of three roaring punches down toward Wren's head.

He rolled the first, caught the second on his triceps then bucked the third. As it came in Wren punched up with his hips, throwing Kiefer forward and off balance. He caught his weight on all fours, and Wren snuck his left arm up, threw it over Kiefer's right elbow, then wrapped the joint and tucked it back close to his chest.

Kiefer jerked but Wren held his right arm locked. He fired a left at Wren's unprotected head and Wren gambled; another buck with his hips and he managed to hook his left leg over Kiefer's right calf. From there it was one big sideways hip push off the ground and the clinch was broken, rolling into a standard open guard position; Kiefer on his back and legs up, Wren flush between and leaning in.

Better.

The ground was Wren's territory. A big guy on the ground lost his height advantage, his weight didn't matter as much, and it was all about technique, and Wren had always out-wrestled every man he'd ever met.

"Damn it," said Kiefer.

"Yup," said Wren, locked Kiefer's legs high under his arms then stacked back onto his feet and stood.

Kiefer hung with his back flat on the floor, legs hooked, thrashing to get free. Wren pulled back further, lifting the giant wholly off the ground for a second, then jumped.

They fell together. Kiefer hit first from barely ten inches elevation, but Wren followed; crushing the guy's huge chest against the cold hard floor. The air blasted from his lungs, and Wren used that moment to stand up, re-apply the leg locks and step over, twisting Kiefer onto his chest with his legs curled back under Wren's arms like a scorpion's tail.

The Boston crab.

An outlawed submission move in professional wrestling. Wren sat back and settled in. Kiefer roared. His whole body strained as Wren's weight bent his back in the wrong direction, leveraging enormous power to twist out of the spinal crank, but Wren just leaned back harder. Kiefer was out-leveraged and didn't stand a chance.

4

BAD COP

They sat. The table lay where it had fallen. Kiefer was slumped, sweating and panting still. Wren had held the crab long enough to work every muscle in the big guy's body to the point of exhaustion. He'd struggle to even stand now. Lactic acid coursing through his veins, pounding like surf in his brain.

No permanent damage, but stand him up and a five year old could push him over.

Ripe for exploitation.

"I should have placed a bigger bet," Wren said.

Kiefer barely managed a laugh. "Tight room," he said between pants. "Your benefit."

"Cage match," Wren said. "Much better than a cave?"

Kiefer laughed.

Taking him back to when they'd both been on the same side, DELTAs fighting for a cause they believed in. Protecting the homeland. It was always the first step when it came to de-indoctrinating a cult member; you took them back to the crossroads before they'd lost their objective mind.

"You were always a cheat then, too."

"Stalagmites are not cheating," Wren said. "They're a choke assist."

Kiefer lost his laughter to panting.

Wren studied him. Lining up the play. Kiefer had been right earlier that they'd never really been friends. Colleagues, for a time. Wren hadn't made friends in those days. He'd only ever brought in converts to the Foundation.

"You're right about me, you know," he said.

"Oh yeah?"

"About why I do what I do. The Foundation. My fear of abandonment. You've nailed me to a tee."

Kiefer's eyes narrowed. Expecting some coming manipulation.

"You'll find this funny, then. Cult leader, he's supposed to be the big guy up top. Hands out the coins, right?"

"Your coin system," Kiefer pants. "It's a rip-off. You stole it from AA."

"Well, the Foundation stripped my coins. I'm something like three coins negative now. Pretty ridiculous."

Kiefer laughed. "That is ridiculous."

Wren smiled. "I keep screwing up, they say. I was supposed to make things right with my family, they said, when I was already at coin zero for killing Pinocchios. I tried to do that, Rogers caught me and dumped me right where you're sitting now, and suddenly I'm one coin negative. Next thing I bust open L.A. to save Steven Gruber from you, and I'm two negative. After that I go dark, get drunk like you say, and I'm three for oh."

Kiefer laughed.

"Yeah, laugh."

"I am laughing."

Wren hung his head. All a performance, but also real. There'd been a minute with Kiefer in the crab where he'd almost pushed all the way. Broken the big man's back. It would've felt good, for a minute anyway.

"I wish you hadn't killed Jay Durant, Anais."

Kiefer stopped laughing. Cold hard reality, like a bucket of ice water in the face.

"He was a soldier like us. Grunt infantry, they sent him into Afghanistan, the same 'Deep State' assholes you hate so much for spewing lies. Maybe he was blind to the agenda, but we all are at the start, hopped up on patriotism. Now you think you've got your eyes open, Anais, but I've got news for you. You're just as much a slave as the rest of us."

He looked up. Kiefer was looking back at him.

"Here it comes," the big guy said. "The pitch. So go ahead, Chris. I hear you crack heads like eggs. Throw some Jungian Jiu-Jitsu at my ego."

"I already did." Wren smiled. "She's standing outside. You were right about that."

Kiefer's eyes widened slightly. Taking that in. The BS was done, now, and they were into real territory. "Rogers."

"They're all real people, Anais. You and me, I get that, we're toy soldiers. Things aren't real at these dizzy climes. But Jay Durant was real. Steven Gruber's gonna be in therapy for years getting over what you and my father did to him. And Sally Rogers? You called her a bitch, and I'm wondering why. It seems you're angry at her. Is that because she got away, or because she made it real?" He waited a second, staring. "I'd like to know, because honestly, that anger's why you're still alive. It's why I'll be here every year from now on. We'll visit, talk about old times, but it all comes down to that question. You see me or you don't, it won't matter, 'cos you'll know I'm out here. Put you on a coin, and so what? I'm on a coin too, six feet under, but accountable. We all have to take responsibility for what we've done, and this is a big system, bigger than either of us. Like AA." Wren paused. "Think about how you'll like that, me coming around regular. Years pass, and still you won't be able to hide. I'll witness you hiding your shame until the end, Anais. The 'Ghost'. Will you still be so angry when you're eighty years old, bowed over with regret for a wasted life?"

Kiefer's eyes hardened. If he had the energy he'd be up and sending more freight train punches at Wren's face, but exhaustion kept him bonded tighter than any cuffs.

"Truth is, " Wren went on, "I think you're sick about what you did, and that makes you angry. You talk like you played the Apex, came out with the upper hand, but that just tells me you don't get it. He let you laugh at his BS schtick, Anais. He capered as the 'cult leader' for your benefit, while he was making you the marionette. Any way you look at it, he played you, and I know you're smart enough to see that."

He took a second, thinking back on the last time they'd spoken. "Remember you told me how the CIA wrote a pop song that brought down the USSR? A rock ballad all about freedom and democracy, it busted all the charts and shifted 'hearts and minds' across the iron curtain. So why didn't you write a song, Anais? Why did you have to burn my people alive?"

Kiefer's eyes drilled into Wren. The anger on the surface now. Wren plunged ahead.

"So next time you feel like lecturing me, take a look at who's coming to visit you. It's not my father, I guarantee it. He'll never think of you again. But I will. Maybe one day we let you out. The Foundation could use a man like you. You just went too far. Call it brainwashing. Would you ever have gone this far without the Apex pulling your levers? While all along you thought you were pulling his. Who's in jail, though, Anais, and who's standing on the Presidential stage, waiting on his inauguration?"

"I won't mind the visits, Chris," Kiefer said. "I figure I'll look forward to them. Maybe you don't see it, but I think you will, in time. You're in prison just as much as me. A jail your father built, and you're only going to sink deeper."

Wren snorted. "You're not going to talk?"

"I've got nothing to say."

We had a wager."

"You did. I just had me some fun."

Wren stared. Kiefer stared back.

"So don't say it to me." Wren got up, went to the door and pried out the wedges, then turned to the one way glass. "Come in," he called.

It took a second. For a moment he feared nothing would happen. Maybe she'd left, decided this wasn't for her. Then the door opened and Sally Rogers came in. There was a quizzical look in her eyes, like she hadn't expected any of this. Like Wren was using her again.

Of course he was.

Kiefer stared stony-eyed.

"You wanna call her a bitch again?" Wren asked. "You go ahead. But think about who you're performing for. He's not watching now. Does it amuse you that much?"

Kiefer just stared. Not at Rogers. At Wren. Really angry now. Ready to pop.

"Or you can tell her you're sorry," Wren said. "Spill your heart at her feet and hope she doesn't knock your head off your shoulders. I can't promise you'll get forgiveness. Maybe you won't survive. But I think she'll listen. She was there too. She knows what my father can do."

"She'll do more than knock his head off," Sally muttered.

"She may," Wren allowed, "so if you've got anything to say, I'd say it to her. Unless you really don't. Maybe you're just as empty as you think I am, with nothing but the Apex inside you. Let's find out. No need for me to keep coming back, if that's all you are. If he cored you that deep, nothing to do but throw you in the trash and set the disposal to grind. But if there's some actual Anais Kiefer left? You'll see I'm not the enemy. Neither is she."

Kiefer grunted. A moment passed as his breath whistled in and out. "Big speech."

"Did it work? Did I crack you like an egg?"

"You'll never know. Now get out of here."

Wren looked at Rogers. Rogers didn't look at him. The moment stretched on.

"Go, Christopher," she said, then turned to face him. "Trust me."

Trust me. There it was, Rogers taking charge. He smiled. So maybe he was the good cop after all.

He walked out, no looking back. Down the corridor he turned left. Not to the observation room. Toward the stairs up to the surface. He felt an overpowering need to see the open blue sky.

5

THE RQ

Wren sat on a rock beside one of the large concrete berms, once nuclear fallout shelters for the US government. The landscape was orange dust scattered with sand-scoured boulders, shot through with creeping low creosote bushes. The wind blew hot, scurrying desert sand in vaporous wafts, like spray off ocean breakers.

The sun beat down on his bare head. He'd shaved all his hair off the day everything changed, when he saw the Apex on David Keller's stage. Mid-life crisis, like Kiefer had said. A buzzcut made you a new man.

He took out his phone, toyed with it for a moment, then put it away. There was no one to call, no family left and nothing on the darknet but more fog and the dates clicking down. 53 days until David Keller became President and the Apex rose ascendant. In the dust underfoot he drew doodles with the tip of his boot, waves and boats drifting on some far away ocean.

It was hard not to think about his family. Despite everything, they still wanted nothing to do with him. His wife Loralei hadn't forgiven him. He hadn't seen his kids Jake and Quinn in over a year. Were they OK? Maybe settling into new schools under new names, protected by witness protection, from him.

That stung. Kiefer had pretty much called it. Nothing he could do about that but drink.

Some thirty minutes later the door to the black site opened, swung closed with a distant clang, and Sally Rogers stamped over the gritty earth toward him, stopping on top of his ocean sketch, scrubbing out a raft and a desert island.

"He sang like a songbird," she said.

Wren's pulse leaped.

"Three different locations he claims he met the Apex. Dates stretching back four years. Says your father led some kind of 'roving franchisee conference for death cult leader wannabes'." She paused, looking disgusted. "His words. It sounds like total BS to me."

Wren stood. "Tell me."

Rogers squeezed the bridge of her nose, took a moment like she was resetting herself. "OK. So, Jib-jab. You remember that?"

Wren frowned, wracked his memory, came up sixes. "That's the cover operation the Order of the Saints were using?" Rogers nodded. "In Minneapolis. An online shopping service, big warehouse fulfilment centers, where Richard Acker held me prisoner. Why?"

Rogers winced. "Kiefer says that's the main place they met. Not just him and the Apex, but all of them, like a who's who of the last four major terror attacks on American soil." She held up a hand, started counting off fingers. "Richard Acker from the Order of the Saints. Somchai Theeravit, AKA Pythagoras, from the Blue Fairy. Yumiko Harkness from the #Reparations. Anais Kiefer, our Ghost. Apparently they got together in the board room over grape soda and candied pecans to calmly plot the end of America."

Wren blinked. Grape soda and pecans? He tried to picture it, conference table laid out, the Apex at the front with a laser pointer while giving a slideshow, the rest sitting politely in business attire, raising their hands to speak.

"That does sound like bullshit."

"Right?" Rogers asked, kicking the sand in frustration. A pirate galleon lost. "I just sent the audio recording over to your hackers and Humphreys, they can run analyses, but I don't know what to make of it."

Wren sucked his teeth. "What else?"

"He talked a lot about data. Said the Apex had all these graphs and tables packed with death count projections. Apparently it all builds toward a number he invented, the RQ."

Wren leaned in. "What's the RQ?"

"Revolution Quotient. It's a number he built off numerous indices of public unrest, like suicide rates, domestic violence, hate crimes? It's supposed to represent the cumulative effect of successive attacks on the American people. Kiefer even drew an RQ graph for me, climbing over time as national stress levels rise." She sketched a shallow incline followed by a sudden, steep rise in the air. "The goal is to make life so unbearable that people turn on each other and we devolve into murderous anarchy."

Wren grunted. It seemed to sync with the Apex's general life goals. "That checks out."

"I guess," Rogers said. "Your father sure loves him some civil war. Except every time he tries to foment one, he fails."

"True." Wren chewed on that, working the angles for a long moment. Maybe seeing something new. "But are they failing?"

"Of course they are. He tosses them up, we smack them down. He's 4 for 0 right now, top of the ninth, what's left to say?"

Wren grunted. Felt something like an epiphany descending across him. The RQ. All the Apex's cults meeting together. It meant something. Maybe a way to see the forest and not the trees.

"Look at it this way," he said, trying it out. "Did the Apex really expect Acker's Saints would start a national civil war?"

"They tried damn hard," Rogers said. "From what I saw it was only you that stopped it."

"Forget me," said Wren. "Even if I'd done nothing, if the Saints had pulled off the scale they were aiming for, would we really have seen outright revolution in the streets? Neighbors killing neighbors, government collapsing, mass indiscriminate slaughter?"

Rogers made a face. "Maybe not that far."

"Exactly," said Wren. "But that's what he wants. The Apex isn't stupid. He knows our values and institutions are too strong to break with one crisis." Wren spun that forward, trying to see the whole chess board. "Think about it. It would explain why he had the Blue Fairy lined up so fast, only four months after the Saints failed, and then the Reparations right after, and Anais too?" It unfolded before him. "They were all rungs on an 'RQ' ladder, leading up to true chaos."

Rogers' eyes narrowed. "So you buy the candied pecans?"

Wren was already gaming it through. Maybe he did. Flipping everything on its head. Raise the RQ enough to put Keller into the Presidency on a unity ticket. Bury America in dead bodies.

"I do buy it." He thought for a second, searching for evidence. "Look, there's no doubting that this 'RQ' is high right now, is there? It's thick in the air. Everywhere you go, people are on edge. They're afraid." He paused a second, working the play through. "I was on the road for three months, Rogers. Getting drunk and running away, whatever, and I saw it in people's eyes. It's gotten into the mainstream." He cast his thoughts back to TVs glimpsed in motel rooms, with pundits at all hours questioning the very tenets of the country, the doctrine of exceptionalism, the moral contribution of the Founding Fathers, the American Dream itself. "I think we're looking at a systematic attack on our way of life. There's multiple stages. It's cult indoctrination on a massive scale."

Rogers frowned. "Indoctrinating the whole country?"

"It's been done before," Wren raced on, "look at Nazi Germany. A whole country turned against scapegoats and the world. If I was going to do that, I'd do it the same way he did it to Gruber and you. Make the present moment unbearable. Ensure our past values can't handle the new challenges. Offer a new future in any direction you choose." His projections took a dark turn. "The Apex made Gruber *want* to kill himself in just three days, Rogers. He did it to a thousand people in the Pyramid. He got all my brothers and sisters to choose asphyxiation in one of his pits. It's the only endgame he knows." He paused a moment, making the leap. "Show me that RQ graph."

Rogers eyed him doubtfully, but brought up her phone, flicked through photos to one of a hand-drawn diagram.

Wren took the phone and pored over it. Simple x and y axes, RQ along the horizontal, deaths up the vertical. The line grew exponentially as it progressed, laying almost flat for most of its length until suddenly rocketing up at the far right side. "It's a hockey stick curve," Wren muttered, "low death numbers until we hit the tipping point, then they shoot through the roof."

"If we buy it," Rogers pressed. "Kiefer could've just made all this up. Maybe it really is all coincidence. We found no hard links from the Blue Fairy to your father."

Wren looked at her. "Maybe. But this matches what's actually happening. The minds of the populace *are* steadily breaking. We always say chaos can never happen in this country, but it can." He focused tight on her green eyes. "He's boiling the frog slow. Keep cranking up the RQ with more attacks, we'll all be in hell before we know it."

She just stared back.

"America in flames," he went on. "A death spree to far outweigh the Pyramid's fake town. Tens of thousands dead, maybe millions."

It felt more certain the more Wren thought about it. Almost concrete. On some level he'd known it the second he'd seen the Apex on David Keller's stage. They were coming toward the grand finale of the Apex's magnum opus.

Which meant the next attack had to be coming soon. Wren pulled his phone and started to dial.

6

TRUST

"What are you doing?" Rogers asked.

"I'm calling Keller."

She watched for a second, then laid a firm hand on his. "With what? We've got nothing."

"What you've just told me's not nothing. Anais Kiefer's not nothing. I'll use it to rattle Keller's cage and force a mistake."

Rogers shook her head. "Like he's made mistakes before? You call him now, he'll just use it against you. All we've got are theories, Wren. We have to be smart. Do the legwork on these leads, get some real evidence to back it up."

Her eyes drilled into him. He didn't let go of the phone.

"Christopher," she went on. "Promise me. You start going after Keller with nothing, Humphreys will slam you back underground faster than you can say 'suicide death cult'. The man's President-elect! We can't just levy accusations on a whim. He denied this thing right to our faces, and that's all we get until we have some kind of proof."

Wren stared. She wasn't wrong. It pissed him off.

"So we get proof. You said Kiefer listed three locations? Let's go hit them all."

He turned and started walking toward the waiting Sikorsky UH-60 Black Hawk helicopter.

"Where are you going?" she called after him, hurrying to keep up.

"To Jib-jab. You said that's where they met? We must have missed something."

"There's no point," Rogers said, drawing level. "We had people all over Jib-jab for weeks, they turned it upside down and found nothing."

"So I'll hit one of the others. I'll hit them all, Rogers, until I find something."

"You want to know where the other locations are?"

He didn't care. If there was evidence to find at any of them, he'd find it. Track the Apex backwards and forwards through time. Get forensic. Work the leads. Find Hellion's concrete key, prove his RQ theory then bring Keller and the whole damn Pyramid scheme down.

"Number two was Yumiko Harkness' silicon chip fabrication plant," Rogers said. "Remember that place, where they had the billionaire arena? It got completely leveled after our teams were done with it. There's nothing left! And number three was the school where Gruber tried to burn himself down. There's nothing left of it. The whole thing burned to the ground. So I'll ask again, where are you going?"

Wren stopped. Steaming now. Rogers stamped around to stand in front of him, looking about as pissed off as he was. "This is no good, Christopher. We need a refresh."

"A refresh on what?"

She snorted, waved a hand between them. "On you and me. This. That stunt you just pulled, locking yourself in with Kiefer? It paid off, but it could easily have backfired. Now you're trying to call Keller, you're storming off, and I'm already out of the loop? Enough leaping before you look! We need to think this through together."

He stared back at her, spinning fast calculations. If he ran he'd reach the Black Hawk before she could. Tip the pilot out if necessary and fly it himself.

But how far would he get, and where even would he go? Humphreys would turn on him as soon as he heard. Wren's 36 hours of oversight-free operations would be called off, and their historic cooperation would fail. The Apex would cheer the division.

He forced himself to stand firm.

Listen. Maybe kneel.

"You were right to ask for trust earlier," Rogers went on. "I need to trust you. You need to trust me. It seems pretty obvious we won't get the Apex without that."

Wren grimaced. Waiting for the 'pitch'.

She delivered. "Yeah, you can read the tea leaves here. So how about this, one-time offer on trust-building, get it while it's good. I'll vouch for you to your wife. Say I think you're a reformed man. A good man, even. Someone she can trust with her kids."

Wren's eyes widened before he could clamp down. He hadn't expected that. There was nothing he wanted more. "Bullshit. You put me away. Who's to say she'd even listen?"

"I am. We talked a lot, Chris. She came to me, she called me, when you turned up outside her place. She trusts me."

Wren felt himself reeling. New possibilities he hadn't even considered. Maybe that would make a difference to Loralei. For Rogers to vouch for him, it meant-

"Done," he said.

"I can't promise anything."

"Doesn't matter."

"You have to listen to me."

"One hundred percent."

Rogers nodded. "Good. Anything after that, it's up to Loralei. Now-"

Wren's phone rang. He brought it up. Hellion, calling from somewhere in Europe. He killed the line and looked back at Rogers.

"Now what?" he prompted.

The phone rang again. He squeezed the red icon to kill the call, but this time it didn't work. She'd hacked him. He tried to lower the ringer volume but was overridden. A second later the call answered by itself and Hellion's voice came through the speaker, Eastern European accent underwritten with the familiar sound of keyboard keys clacking.

"Christopher, there has been an attack. A woman just burned herself alive in shopping mall. Footage of this is everywhere. I am sending to you."

A link came through. A video began to auto play.

7

MALL OF THE USA

Wren studied the CCTV footage of a woman walking through a large mall.

The shot was grainy and from high up, shifting angles as she passed along, easily lost in the crowd. News anchors talked over the feed in jerky snippets, clearly a stitched-together job Hellion had prepared, but Wren ignored them.

WOMAN BURNS ALIVE IN CINCINNATI MALL

She was early thirties, blond hair, wearing mom jeans and a fashionable-looking cardigan, carrying a large bag. Walking head down, barely looking where she was going. Lost in her own world but with a purpose, he could feel it even from a distance.

A banner along the bottom of the screen gave the ending away, but Wren didn't care about that. First impressions were everything, and he barely breathed, even as he heard the screams coming from Rogers' phone, already scrolled ahead to the end.

The death itself didn't matter. Everyone who burned themselves alive died the same way. What mattered was the way they lived in the moments before.

He sped up the footage, scrolled back. She came from a Chevy Impala in the parking lot, lifting the bag carefully from the trunk. A young guy in a yellow bib came over, probably asked if he could help her with anything, but she saw him off.

Already he saw she was stressed. It was hot out, a baking day by the looks of it, but she'd just stepped out of a new-looking car, surely had decent AC. No reason she should be that worried unless something strange was going on.

He sped forward. She went in, stood in the automatic doors for a moment. An old guy wearing a greeter's badge approached. She sped on. A sales guy hawked shoes in her face and she kept walking, eyes fixed ahead. Wren kept speeding through the video; for twenty-three minutes she walked around the giant mall, up escalators, down, the kind of walk Wren had seen many times before. A killer nerving themselves up to pull the trigger. Suicide bombers, mass shooters, they all looked the same. Seeing into another world.

At last she came to rest in the food court. Bought a bowl of Vietnamese noodles and worked a path to the center of the space, surrounded by shoppers old and young. Old folks out for their daytime constitutional, young families with kids in high chairs thronged with bags of shopping, youths leaning in and gabbling fast. Three stories of walkways rose around the court, each crammed with shops and shoppers.

An ideal target. No shortage of easy collateral.

She stopped at a table half-occupied by some teenagers, asked if she could sit, they smiled and nodded. She settled in, pushed her bag far under the table where the CCTV couldn't see it. Wren leaned in as the camera swept back and forth. The angles changed. There was a clock on the wall but she didn't look at it once. Didn't pull her phone, just ate her pho noodles mechanically.

After four minutes thirty-three seconds some of the teenagers at the table talked to her, then she got up. She made no move to pick up the bag and strode off. Wren slowed the feed back to regular speed, eyes tight to the screen.

A change of heart. He read it in her every movement. It wasn't the relief of a bomber who'd left their payload behind. Nothing so simple. She was terrified still.

This looked like escape.

Her momentum lasted until the automatic doors at the exit. Barely two hundred yards from her car in the parking lot. A way out. She stood in the mechanism for a few moments, stuck in the portal, until abruptly some switch in her head flipped again and she made a beeline back to the food court.

She hoisted the bag from under the table, maybe saying something to the kids like 'Look what I forgot'. Set it on the table, and pulled the zipper. Wren's guts tightened in anticipation. From the bag the woman lifted a large red jug, some kind of canister with a screw top. She calmly unscrewed the top, and as the CCTV cycled Wren caught a glimpse of her eyes. Far off, grainy, but they looked different now. Resolved.

The lid came off. Without any undue clamor or fuss, she raised the jug above her head, upended it and tipped the contents over herself. Clear liquid splashed off her head and soaked down through her clothing. Now the kids were staring. One leaped up and backed away. Wren figured it had to stink. Acrid, the fumes carrying in seconds.

She didn't look. Caught in the throes of her devotion now. With smooth, practiced motions she produced a lighter from her pocket, sparked the flame, then held it close to her throat.

The fire caught on the liquid and she went up like a magnesium strip. Instant conflagration. Had to be gasoline she'd poured over herself. Self-immolation. Wren's jaw tightened. It took overwhelming dedication to burn yourself alive, the most painful death imaginable…

Within seconds the CCTV feed switched to a nearby cell phone camera, complete with audio of panic and screams. The phone jogged as the owner ran away, but Wren caught a final glimpse of the woman burning.

He ran the feed back to a still on her face just as the fire caught, looked into her eyes and saw worlds falling apart.

Not a terrorist bomber, at least not the kind America had come to expect. Not exacting a physical cost in lost lives and destroyed infrastructure. Not requiring some complex bomb mechanism, triggered by an outsider for hatred of the country and its values.

This was a woman who looked like she absolutely belonged. A woman not seeking to kill others. A woman only seeking to make an example of herself, and burn an image into the minds of everyone who saw her die.

This changed everything.

Wren looked up.

Rogers was still staring at her phone. Replaying the burning. Like a car crash, you couldn't look away. Every person in that mall was now traumatized. Thousands of people. More, considering the spread of the video. Like dropping a bomb into the national psyche. The cost in counselling would run into the millions.

The screams kept coming.

Sickening. He'd grown up with it every day as a child in the Pyramid, babies locked in cages existing only to scream, adults drowned and boiled to death in vats, and you never got used to it. You either let it grind you down or you found a way to transmute it into something you could use.

Adrenaline pumped into his system, burning the horror to rage.

He punched buttons on his phone screen, raised it to his ear, feeling any sense of doubt burn away in the flames. Sometimes you had to lay down a marker. The phone rang and his heart pounded. The guy had said to call anytime.

"Mr. Wren."

Straight through, as promised. Genteel, sophisticated, that same rich baritone. David Keller, President-elect.

"Have you seen the video?" Wren asked.

A second passed. Feigning confusion, maybe. "I take it you're talking about the video of the young woman burning?"

Wren gritted his teeth. "You promised to help. I need you to do something for me."

"Anything. No, it's all right. I'll take this call." Wren pictured Keller standing in his den, waving off staffers. Moving out to the porch for the simulation of privacy. "What can I do?"

"Put a candle in your window," Wren said. "Tell that bastard I'm coming."

He hung up.

His breath came raggedly now, staggering forward over hot sand. His vision tunneled down to the swaying horizon, colors graying out.

"Christopher," came Hellion's faint voice from his phone, held low by his side. He ignored her. Looking over the Sonoran desert, the same desert he'd grown up in. The empty spaces at the heart of America. The empty spaces in the human heart. All unguarded, unwatched, soft targets to be colonized by the Apex and turned against themselves.

The same story over and over again.

He'd seen it in the woman's eyes. Held hostage to some self-destructive ideology. That panic in the rush to burn. It was the same look he'd seen on Steven Gruber's face. Uncertainty. Fear. The final push to break through.

"Christopher?"

He raised the phone back to his ear. He felt dizzy. "What?"

"Did you just threaten your President on this phone?"

"He's not President yet," he said, forcing rational thought back onto his animal reaction. "Hellion. I need you to send me everything you've got on this woman. On Keller, Kiefer, the Apex too. They're all connected."

"Of course they are," Hellion answered, like it was obvious. "That is additional news. Anais Kiefer's data may be concrete data points we need."

Wren's eyes lit up. "To finding the Apex?"

"Perhaps. It is complex. We need time."

Wren couldn't get the words out fast enough. "How long?"

"An hour to run it through matrices. Maybe longer. You will hear from us. In meantime-"

"I need a jet."

"Yes. Tucson International is closest. Ninety minutes in your Black Hawk."

"Good," said Wren, and turned. Rogers was storming toward him again, her face dark with anger. The Black Hawk stood off to the right.

"What the hell did you just do?" she shouted.

That was fast. The President-elect's security team reaching out, the trust broken already.

"He did ask me to call," Wren said, and started toward the Black Hawk.

8

ONE THOUSAND

The helicopter roared away. The berms, sand and nothingness of Anais Kiefer's black site prison sloughed off like the traces of a bad dream.

Wren's fingers flew over his laptop's keys while Rogers shouted into her phone by his side. She was angry, but he'd given her nothing to fight against. Too many half-formed thoughts in his head, vying for precedence. Still he caught scraps of her argument with CIA Director Humphreys. Keller wanted Wren disavowed and dumped back in a black site. Rogers was making his case.

Wren didn't care.

His fingers drilled the keys, eyes bored into the screen. Data had started pouring in as soon as he'd buckled into the Black Hawk, fixed an earpiece in place, banded a throat-mic around his neck. Hellion and B4cksl4cker chattering to each other in his head. Rogers shouting at his side. The Foundation going crazy on the darknet.

Anais Kiefer's data had unleashed a trove of fresh connections. Wren raced through the matrices as B4cksl4cker rebuilt them around the 'key', color coding, interlinking, tagging details to the massive store of 'ghost' data Hellion and B4cksl4cker had compiled over the past months, looking for the Apex. When linked with the Cincinnati burning, it became-

"Christopher!"

He lifted his head from the screen to find Rogers glaring at him, holding up her phone. She looked like she'd aged ten years in ten minutes; pale and drawn.

"Director Humphreys wants to talk to you."

Wren looked at the phone. Of course. He took the handset, pulled out the battery and SIM then handed the pieces back to Rogers. She stared at them.

"Are you kidding me?" she shouted over the Black Hawk's rotors.

Wren tapped his earpiece, transferring to throat-mic. Rogers glowered and tapped her earpiece too.

"What the hell was all that?" She was no longer shouting, but the earpiece had no problem transmitting her obvious anger. "First it's silent treatment while I'm fighting just to keep our operation live, then you brick my phone? Where's the trust?"

He took a breath and looked at her. Coming up on forty-five minutes, now, since the burning. He had a working theory but it was pieces only.

"Tell me about the woman," he said, then added, "please."

For a few seconds Rogers stared, clicking over from one anger to another. "Seriously? You haven't even read her file yet?"

"I've been catching up on what Kiefer told you," he answered, keeping calm and steady, slotting gears into position so they'd be ready to turn. "That's where my focus has to be. Finding the evidence to bring Keller down." He paused. His hackers had said it. Figurehead. Mascot. Leader-in-absentia. Whatever he'd become in the Foundation, the real key skill of a leader was knowing when to delegate. "You're going to be running the Cincinnati investigation," he said firmly. "So give me your best appraisal."

Her eyes widened. "Wait, what? You're saying I'm in charge of Cincinnati?"

The gears began to turn. She was right that they had to trust, and he couldn't do it all himself. He hadn't called himself Christopher Wren for nothing, architect of human organizations. "That's right. This is your baby, Rogers, so brief me."

It took a second more as she put aside her disbelief. Getting with the program, his call to a new hierarchy, one that required more trust than ever.

"OK," she said, then took a breath, postponing her anger until the end. "OK. The woman's name was Rachel Day. 29 years old." She brought up her phone, ostentatiously put the battery back in though not the SIM, and opened the notes app. "Husband, part-time job at an accounting office. Two kids, boy and a girl, seven and five."

Wren flinched at that, but hid it well. A detail he hadn't anticipated.

"She looks to be an exemplary citizen," Rogers went on. "Happily married as far as all evidence indicates. Yearbooks dating back to grade school show a well-adjusted, well-socialized girl. Father a pastor in the Baptist faith and local community leader, mother an activist for animal rights, but nothing extreme. Marching band, she played the trumpet, led taps at summer camp on Lake Erie eight years running, four as a camper, four as a counselor. No hint of involvement with any kind of terror activity, offline or on. Nothing unusual in her daily life, no cheating, no radicalization, no odd behavior. As all-American as you can get."

Pretty much what Wren had expected. All except the children. He nodded. It was all connected. "Then one day she burned herself alive. So tell me what you think."

Rogers frowned through the anger. Closed the flap on her phone wallet. "I think this whole thing's more bullshit."

"How so?"

Her head tilted slightly to the side, amused at his manner, like this was class and he was some professor using the Socratic method. "The timing. I was down in the black site with Kiefer right around when it happened. This was targeted at us."

She'd always been a quick study. "Agreed. For what purpose?"

"I have no idea." She took a moment. "Intimidation?"

"That's probably part of it," Wren allowed. "But think about Kiefer's confession. Above all, it was our first confirmation that the man on Keller's stage was the Apex, correct? That's huge."

"It's circumstantial," Rogers countered, "straight from the mouth of a mad killer. It's not proof."

"Maybe not, but Kiefer isn't mad, just indoctrinated, and I believe him on this. For the minute let's accept the hypothesis that Keller works for the Apex. Agreed?"

"So you called Keller up," Rogers taunted. "Had a quick chat, let him know we know."

"He already knew," Wren said dismissively, "but that doesn't matter. Address the hypothesis. The burning's a tactic, so what's the strategy behind it?"

She stared at him, puzzlement winning against anger across her features. "I don't know. The Apex is a psycho. Who knows what he's thinking."

"He's a logical psycho. He always wants one thing."

"To raise the RQ?"

"Precisely. Get people ripping themselves apart and they'll listen to whatever snake oil hope he's offering them. Twenty-six years back it was the same with the Pyramid, and it's been the same ever since."

Rogers chewed on that for a moment. Wren glanced at his phone. Forty-seven minutes gone since Rachel Day burned. "So he's hoping to kick the RQ up with this woman? Encourage other people to burn themselves alive?"

"Without a doubt that's what he wants," Wren agreed, "but the question is, why now? Keller is President-elect with inauguration in less than two months. Why's the Apex stepping on that to raise the RQ now?"

Rogers stared back at him, running out of patience. "I have no idea."

Wren tweaked the gears, gave them a shove. "You've basically said it already. Why raise the RQ just as we get the first testimony tying Keller and Kiefer together, maybe enough evidence to start a major media investigation, if not a political one?"

Rogers' eyes narrowed at that. Maybe felt the gears starting to turn. "So you're saying..."

Wren waited.

It hit, and her eyes flared. "No."

"Yes. The media aren't going to listening to anything else now, are they? Rachel Day's burning has sucked all the oxygen from the room. Not even Hellion and B4cksl4cker could make Kiefer's data go viral over that. Even if we put out actual solid proof Keller was working for the Apex, nobody would hear it, nobody would see it, it'd be like it never happened."

Rogers sat silently for a second, then took Wren's phone, started scrolling through the major news websites: ABC, FOX, NBC, CNN, the BBC. Every page was headed by news of the burning. Everything else had been flushed off the front page.

"They stole the news cycle," she said.

"Exactly. Our intel's dead in the water. It isn't real if nobody hears about it, and this burning just flooded the zone."

"So..."

Wren felt the gears clank into position in her head. "So they burned a woman alive just to muzzle us. The data bear it out. Rachel Day, if you watch the video, you see she's not responding to any arbitrary timeline." He brought up a still of her death footage, standing like a flaming statue in the middle of the food court, held it up for Rogers to see, then wound it back. "She didn't look at the clock, at her watch, nothing like that, like you'd expect someone aiming to burn themselves alive would do. That's way outside the norm."

She frowned. "How so?"

"You tell me."

Rogers was fully engaged now, the anger forgotten. "I'd be guessing, but it's got to be about the purpose of self-immolation?" He just waited. "OK, so if you're planning on the most painful death imaginable, it's probably because you're making a wider political point. Right?"

Wren said nothing. She raced on.

"So if you're making a point, you double down by picking a meaningful date, time and place, like noon or midnight or the middle of the Superbowl, something dramatic." She took the phone, ran the footage backwards and forwards again. "But not Rachel Day." She looked up. "She doesn't look at anything. It's like she doesn't care what time it is."

"And what does that leave?" Wren pressed.

Rogers chewed her lip, squinting at the video. "I don't see it, but if her burning's pegged to Kiefer's confession, she must be getting signals from somebody? Somebody who knows the exact moment Kiefer confessed. They slip her the signal to burn, and she does it."

"I think that's right," Wren said, relieved that she was seeing it the same way. "They had Rachel Day on standby in case we ever got too close. And she almost backed out." He dragged the slider to the moment she was standing in the automatic doors. "But something happened here. These three people brush by her. Maybe they gave her a signal?"

Rogers played the moment back then forward. Some helper kid in the mall's fluorescent bib, an old greeter, a shoe salesman.

"Wind it back further, and you'll see she passed close by each of them on the way in," Wren said. "Maybe they exchanged words then, too."

Rogers spun the footage backward, forward, then looked up. "You've only seen this footage once. How did you pick up all that?"

"I was looking for it," Wren said. "You need to think like the Apex, Rogers. He's smarter than any of us, but he's not infallible."

"He's sick," Rogers said, looking disgusted. "All this means he was waiting for us. They must've had Rachel Day prepped way in advance. How easy is it to make someone burn themselves alive, someone with her record? I can't even imagine how he persuaded her. But whatever, she did it, because the second I transferred Kiefer's confession to Humphreys some mole high in the CIA leaked it to the Apex, and he activated her."

There it was. Wren's theory laid out neat and clean. "And-"

"But that's incredibly complex," Rogers interrupted. "The amount of moving pieces to pull that off without leaving a trail, and get a mole right next to Humphreys?"

Wren made a sour face. They didn't need to talk about whether Director Humphreys was a good judge of character. "The Apex could do it. We're already accepting he put Keller into the Presidency."

"You're accepting that."

"Are you not?"

Rogers took a breath which ended in a sigh. She looked wrung out. "No. I guess I accept it. Kiefer said the Apex was there on Keller's stage, and I buy that much. So OK, let's say I go with you this far. He blocks the news cycle and we're shut out, but it won't be permanent." She thought for a second. "We just wait until the smoke clears and put our evidence out then. We break through. An investigation begins. All good."

Wren gave a sad smile. "When is it ever just one death with this guy?"

Rogers opened her mouth, closed it. Wren pushed her a little further.

"With Kiefer there were three of you lined up to burn, Jay Durant, you, Steven Gruber. With the Reparations there were ten billionaires. He likes to keep us on our toes, likes to keep the tension ticking over. Why would he only have one burning prepared now?"

Rogers took that like a punch in the gut. "Damn it, Wren."

"I know. Picture a stream of burnings flooding the country, call it a firestorm. Enough to drive the RQ up into the stratosphere and guarantee nothing we say will be heard for as long as the burnings continue. If it was me I'd schedule them every hour for the next 53 days. Keep that going until inauguration and nothing else will matter. Keller brushes us under the rug with a single executive order, and we'll be in a black site gulag right alongside Anais Kiefer, waiting out our execution for treason."

Rogers turned a sickly ashen gray. "One every hour? That's like," she did a quick calculation, "over a thousand burnings. You can't be serious."

"He burned that many people in just one day at the end of the Pyramid," Wren said. "He can do it again."

Rogers looked like she was going to vomit. Wren knew how she felt.

"Either way, we'll know soon enough. It's almost been an hour since Rachel Day. Let's find out."

He held up his phone, fixed to a breaking news feed. Messages slotted in rapidly as the seconds ticked by. Fifty-nine minutes gone. Wren's heart thumped hard. They both leaned in.

9

SIXTY MINUTES

At sixty minutes there was nothing. More updates firing from the major news corporations, the latest information on Rachel Day, the names of her kids sourced by some amoral paparazzi.

Sixty-one.

Sixty-two.

Snippets rose up about the last moments of Rachel Day's death, linked to interviews with survivors from the food court: an old woman sobbing uncontrollably beside her car; children crying, slumped in the parking lot; a man trying to explain what it had been like, the sound, the smell, and getting overwhelmed.

Sirens wailed. Blue lights flashed. Ambulances were still rolling in and out. A teen boy flashed by on a gurney, unconscious. A shot of a pale teen girl slumped against the mall's cream plaster wall, lodged in a panic attack, panting and weeping.

They looked like refugees after a bomb strike, with stunned faces and wide eyes, not comprehending what had just happened. Some had minor injuries sustained during the stampede, were stained with red blots of bloods. Fire engines encircled the building, but there was nothing for them to do.

"Good Lord," Rogers said under her breath, so softly Wren barely heard it. "More of these would break us."

Sixty-four minutes.

Sixty-five.

"I think-" Rogers began, and then it came.

A short message only, quickly buried off the front page but enough to rock Wren and Rogers back.

BURNING IN SPOKANE

There was nothing for maybe thirty seconds more, then the flood tide began. Jostled video. Maddened messages out on social media. Screams. Terror.

Not a mall, this time. A bowling alley. Another woman had walked out into the middle of the lanes and doused herself with gasoline, just the same as Rachel Day. There were hundreds of people watching, their games forgotten. In the live feed she was burning still, fallen on her side.

Rogers looked up at Wren with the horror bedding down in her eyes. One an hour, maybe. Every hour.

"Firestorm," she said.

Wren met her eyes, then turned back to the coverage, waiting for confirmation of the details. Moment by moment the names and numbers trickled through, and it was just as he'd feared.

The victim was a young mother with two children, a boy and a girl aged seven and five. The mirror image of Rachel Day, and exactly the same as Wren's kids.

A pattern. A message to him alone.

"Rogers..." he began, voice thick, but she was already cycling through her address book.

"I see it," she said. "Trust me."

It helped. Still he put a hand over her phone. "I trust you, not the CIA. Please, tell me where they are."

She stared. A simple step to make. "You think witness protection's compromised?"

"If Humphreys is? I can't take that chance."

She stared back. Couldn't argue.

"You promised," Wren said.

Another moment.

"You can't move them," she said. "Overwatch I'll accept. Only make contact if it's absolutely necessary."

"Agreed," Wren said quickly, feeling like he was teetering on the edge of a very high drop. "I promise."

Rogers let out a breath. "Then here."

She held out her phone. Wren swept it up, found the address, the number, the new fake names and memorized them at once.

Rhode Island. East Coast still. His family. The sense of relief shuddered through him.

"Thank you."

He handed the phone back, heart feeling full and desperate at once, blood pumping like he was about to have a cardiac event. Holding his children in his hands. His fingers trembled as he logged into his darknet, put up a secure thread for Teddy, Hellion and B4cksl4cker alone to see, slotted in the address, gave the order, then sat back.

"I'll spin up teams for both Rachel Day and the bowling alley," Rogers said. "We'll stop this."

He nodded numbly. It was hard to think with his family exposed. You couldn't get much more personal than threatening a man's family

It just made the anger come on harder.

His phone rang. He answered it.

"Christopher."

The voice came in his earpiece. Deep, assured, commanding. Not Hellion or B4cksl4cker.

"Teddy."

Theodore Smithely III. He'd worked a strange path to heading up Wren's Foundation, from low-level leadership of Chicago's true-life vampire societies to getting shot in the head by the Saints. The subsequent coma and recovery had made him a different kind of man.

"It's me, Christopher," Teddy answered. "I saw the location for your family. I assure you, that just became my number one priority. The Foundation will shelter them, I promise."

Wren gritted his teeth. This after the relief of finding where they were was too much, and he coughed to get back control.

"Rhode Island," he said gruffly. "He knows how old my kids are, Teddy."

"So go get the bastard. We're all on deck for you here, three coins minus or not."

He managed a laugh. Three coins minus in his own Foundation.

The call ended and Wren looked out of the Black Hawk's open bay into the rush of wind while Rogers shouted orders into throat-mic. They'd be at Tucson International soon. A road whipped by below interspersed with long expanses of nothing. Fiery red canyons carved out of primordial sandstone. Winding streams puddling into oak-strewn meadows. A boy flying a drone waved up at them, like a remnant from an earlier age. Wren half expected him to burst into flame.

Too many innocents. Maybe there was something he could do about that. He tapped his phone to open a line.

"Hellion, are you there?"

"Yes, Christopher," she answered. "We are working on finding a target. What is it?"

"I need Director Humphreys."

A few seconds passed in a flurry of keys. "He is at the White House. It will be difficult. I will do this for you now."

"How long?"

Another second passed. "His phone is ringing," Hellion said. "Here."

The line picked up, and Wren smiled. Hellion made the impossible possible.

"Who the hell is this?" came a hissed response, and Wren imagined Humphreys ducking out of an Oval Office meeting, head down, hand curled around his mouth. He didn't know how Hellion had done it, but was glad to have her on his side.

"It's Christopher Wren, Director. I have three words for you. Lock it down."

"Lock it down, what?" Humphreys answered. "Wren, you can't do that to my phone, it's-"

"What happened to your phone?"

"It damn near blew up!" Humphreys snapped. "Don't pretend you didn't know. We're in the middle of a-"

"I know we are," Wren said. "You'll want to hear this. First off, there's a mole in your department. Right after Rogers sent you the Kiefer recording, that's when Rachel Day burned. Check the timestamps, it's not a coincidence; it's the Apex's strategy to black out the media. If I was you, I'd look hard at everyone I shared that audio with. Now-"

"Wait," Humphreys said. "Just wait a damn second, Wren! I shared that audio with nobody! Well, not nobody, but-"

"That's your business," Wren pressed on. "I'm en route to a strike looking to pick up the Apex's trail right now. Rogers is headed to Cincinnati, I'm sure you know, to work on breaking the firestorm. Between us we'll get this thing under control, but there's one thing you can do right now to help."

"What?" Humphreys snapped, working up his own anger now. "Do tell me, because I'm only the CIA Director, in the middle of briefing the President when my damn phone starts wailing like a fire alarm, getting hot, and-"

"Forget the phone," Wren said, burying his amusement. "I need you to lock down the country. I know you won't do it now, maybe not in the hours to come, but by nightfall you'll be considering it, and the sooner the better. The whole country needs to shut down. Complete and total, everyone in their homes, nobody on the streets, in bars, sports events, schools, churches. Anywhere people gather, those are his targets. You saw the RQ graph?"

Humphreys blustered something.

"We're in the first wave and heading up an exponential panic curve. The second burning cements it. We need to flatten that curve as soon as we can, you know this as well as I do, Director. President-elect David Keller wants all of this. We've had two burnings and more are coming, and with every one the people will just get more traumatized. Pretty soon the RQ's going to let Keller do whatever he wants. Shut things down now and you can slow the spread, buy us some time out here to get the antidote in."

A long few moments passed.

"Even if I believe everything you just said," Humphreys began, "and maybe I could, maybe I even do, what you're suggesting is near politically impossible. The President's a lame duck, Christopher. She's got less than two months left, and there's no way she has the political capital to shut the country down. You can't-"

"So do the impossible. Protect the country, Humphreys. This is the worst attack yet, I promise you, and with Keller tied in? They're going to fight dirty. It's going to get ugly. Buy me some time and I'll get your President the capital to get re-elected next time around."

He hung up. Panting.

Rogers looked over at him. "Lockdown?"

"Lockdown," he repeated, then turned back to his phone. They were already calling it a firestorm on CNN.

10

ANAXIMANDER

In forty minutes the cityscape of Tucson appeared on the horizon through the Black Hawk's open bay, gunmetal gray against the ochre desert. At Tucson International Wren and Rogers stepped out onto baking blacktop, already most of an hour passed since the second woman had burned, leaving ten minutes until the next.

Two jets lay ahead of them on the apron. A ONE Aviation Eclipse 550 on the left, an Embraer Phenom 100 on the right.

"Yours is the Eclipse," Hellion said in Wren's ear.

He looked at Rogers. Getting her own directions from Hellion now. She nodded at him. "Find the bastard, Christopher."

He smiled as she strode away for Cincinnati.

"Where am I going?" he asked Hellion.

"Utah," she answered. "The matrices have prepared a clear target. It looks like you are going to break a cult."

He laughed. Just like the good old days. "And my team?"

He'd spent the last thirty minutes pulling them from their regular lives. All were heading for private airports now, to jets waiting to whisk them to Utah.

"They will be waiting at the airport."

"How good's the intel?"

"It is a ghost, but solid. We will know more as the AI works through it."

He nodded. Good enough for now. Striding over to the Eclipse jet he cycled through news channels on his phone. They were in a frenzy. The

President was still preparing her initial statement. David Keller was already out and channeling the country's anger from his Texas front porch, fiercely decrying the attacks and promising to strike back. He looked like Commander-in-Chief already.

Wren boarded. The jet taxied to the runway. Eight minutes until the next burning was due. In his seat as the Eclipse took off, Wren swiped through the latest FBI brief on Hellion's target cult.

The Anaximanderians.

Based in Utah, their story began in the mid-80s, when the Great Salt Lake expanded due to unprecedented rainfall. Properties on the eastern shore were damaged, and the State response was to construct a huge pumping station in the Bonneville salt flats to the west. It housed three industrial pumps capable of moving millions of gallons of water along a freshly dug canal, out of the Salt Lake and into the desert. The pumps ran for years, shifting trillions of gallons onto the open flats where it evaporated, leaving a thicker crust of salt behind, until finally the lake's water level fell. The pumping station was retired in 1989 and left to the elements.

In 1990 the Anaximanderian cult moved in.

Wren skimmed their ideology. Followers of the ancient Greek philosopher Anaximander, the first in history to have recorded his thoughts on paper. Apparently few of these recorded writings survived, however, until in 1984 when second-generation Iranian-American engineer Jamal Jalim 'discovered' a trove of them lodged at the bottom of a salt bog in the Bonneville flats.

So the Anaximanderians were born.

Jamal Jalim had only been a second-string engineer on the pumping station, but he began recruiting followers in the local towns as a charismatic leader, hawking his unique brand of 'scientific religion', proposing a single universal element underlying all matter. Followers started at the bottom of a system of 55 levels leading toward 'scientific one-ness' at the top, gaining badges as they climbed.

"Like the Boy Scouts," Wren murmured to himself.

"What?" Hellion answered.

"These Anaximanderians."

A moment passed.

"Is this how you say it?" B4cksl4cker chimed in. "Hellion and I, we have been saying Anaximan*der*ian."

"It doesn't matter how you say it."

"Yes, but we would like to get this correct."

Wren ignored them. Bickering children. Just twenty minutes earlier there'd been a third burning; another woman, married, two kids, the same ages as before. In the foyer of a middle school as they were letting out. The bell had just rung, the kids were pouring out, and boom.

Wren hadn't watched the video in depth. He knew already the effect it was having across the country.

"Let's get on point," he said, cruising now at twenty thousand feet. "Talk me through how this cult's connected to the Apex. Did he run one of the franchise conferences here?"

His hackers said nothing.

"Hello?"

"Yes, we are here, Christopher," B4cksl4cker said cautiously. "We are thinking of the best way to answer this question."

Wren's heart sank. "Just answer."

"Yes, of course. Well. You understand how the ghost matrices work, correct?"

"Of course I do. I invented them to find the Ghost."

Hellion laughed.

"You played a minor role in their early stages," B4cksl4cker allowed. "In brief, you know that they are a data extraction technique designed to track invisible, unrecorded events, people and objects around the world. We believed that by establishing a background 'fabric' of total knowable data, whether it is weather, movements of people and money, births, deaths and the like, then we would be able to see hidden actors not by their actions, but by the near-invisible impacts they have on the underlying fabric."

Wren sighed. "I know, I invented it, remember? First we get that background fabric, then we use AI algorithms to search for unexplained gaps and invisible forces. Like dark matter in the universe, it's invisible, but we see it by its gravitational effect on visible planets."

"Precisely!" B4cksl4cker enthused. "Yes, dark matter, you have grasped it well!"

Wren didn't bother to claim inventing it a third time. "Thanks."

"Now, ever since you asked us to hunt your father, we have been building such a background database for Arizona, in addition to databases around each of the recent terror attacks. We call them matrices."

Wren ran a hand down his face. Like he didn't know what a matrix was by now. "Right, thank you. So why the Anaximanderians?"

"Well. Our ghost matrices suggest, in line with possibility branches we have projected for your father, and-"

"Skip the technobabble."

"-when compiled with the information Anais Kiefer offered, and cross-correlated via two-tail analysis with-"

"B4cksl4cker! Just tell me."

"Very well," said B4cksl4cker, sobering. "The ghost matrices suggest, as far as we can detect, that your father came to see the Anaximanderians approximately one year after the Pyramid burned."

Wren frowned. "One year? That can't be right."

"Yes, I am checking," B4cksl4cker said, waited a beat then went on. "Yes, it is correct, approximately."

Wren didn't care about approximately. He would have been only thirteen years old then. "That's sometime in the nineties. It's twenty-four years ago, B4cksl4cker." No further comment came. "You're kidding me, right? This is one of your jokes?"

"No," B4cksl4cker said carefully. "This is not a joke. Hellion?"

"It would not be a funny joke, Christopher," she confirmed.

Wren felt like punching something. "I'm glad it's not a joke," he said through gritted teeth. "But that's decades, B4cksl4cker. Tell me you see how that's a problem. I need to find the Apex right now."

"Christopher," Hellion began sternly. "How many leads have you had on your father so far?"

Wren said nothing.

"I will answer this for you," Hellion said primly. "It is none. Further, I will remind you that before his appearance on David Keller's stage, nobody had seen this man since the Pyramid burned. Now we have found a location and a time that could unlock his movements. This is a sizable breakthrough. Every piece of data will help lead us to where he is right now."

She sounded like a grade school teacher explaining basic math to a child. Wren squeezed the bridge of his nose. "OK. I get it. a lead is better than no lead, and anything that leads to right now is good. So," he paused, spinning the matter back, "why did he come here?"

Another silence.

"B4cksl4cker?"

"It is very complex," B4cksl4cker said.

Wren heard it in his tone. Felt like throwing up his hands. "You don't know why, do you?"

No answer for a moment. "The answer is deep in the code."

Wren would have laughed, if it wouldn't damage their professional pride. To conduct true ghost analysis, B4cksl4cker had handed control over to his self-learning AI, and that was a black box filled with random chaos. "You must have something concrete."

"There are indications," B4cksl4cker allowed. "But as the inventor of this technology, you should know that the ripple effect of Kiefer's confession are immense and wide-ranging, with second and third order impacts we cannot predict. Our AI could take years to fully digest them."

Wren snorted. Now he got credited as inventor. "Years?"

"If we wish a full analysis. Until then, you know our matrices work intuitively, modelling possibility forks. On one fork there is a clear, sharp alteration in the behavior of the Anaximanderians."

Wren looked up from his phone, out the oval window of the Eclipse to the orange expanse below. "What alteration?"

"They fortified, Christopher. Up to the mid-nineties they were more like an open commune, all members welcome. Then abruptly they started buying up weaponry, began zealously training and reinforcing their pumping station. It is now a fortress, completely impregnable. Nothing gets in or out."

Wren vaguely remembered being briefed about it at a cross-agency confab. Ever since Waco the FBI had kept lists of heavily armed cults, prioritizing which needed to be dispersed. If they weren't causing trouble, they were left alone, and the Anaximanderians had never caused trouble.

Until, perhaps, now.

"Impregnable," Wren said.

"It means impossible to infiltrate," Hellion said helpfully.

Wren grunted. Right. "So how do we break in?"

"This is your department, is it not?" B4cksl4cker asked.

True enough.

"Send me everything you've got on the pumping station, their armaments, schematics, member count, the lot."

"Sending," B4cksl4cker answered.

Within seconds files began appearing in Wren's phone, straight from the FBI database amongst other government-branded sources. He surfed the data, beginning with specifications on the pumping station itself.

It didn't look good.

Far thicker walls than Waco. Much stronger armaments. Better training, more people, more warning time. B4cksl4cker wasn't kidding when he'd called it impregnable.

He dug deeper. Dam-like concrete construction with walls many feet thick, so no way to ram or blow his way in. Six sentry stations, two above each pump with military-level M61 rotary Vulcan autocannons capable of a hundred rounds a second. Add that to a deep stockpile of smaller arms: a range of British, US and Russian sniper rifles good from over a mile out; AR-15s with bump stocks for automatic fire; man-portable M1A1 bazooka rocket launchers, plus multiple barrels of ammonium nitrate/fuel oil ANFO explosives good for IEDs in the field. All wielded by a standing army of at least a hundred cult devotees who doubtless spent every waking hour drilling for an end-of-world attack.

Somewhere in the middle lay Jamal Jalim. The man who might hold the key to the Apex, tucked away like a pearl in an oyster. It looked impossible. But like B4cksl4cker said, this was his department.

"This is what I'm going to need," he said, and began listing out gear.

11

FOURTH

Minutes before the Eclipse put down in Utah, the fifth young mother burned herself alive.

This time it was in the middle of a water park. Top of the slide. Visible from all around, going up like an ancient Greek lighthouse. Apparently she'd hidden the gas in her kid's inflatable ring, torn it to douse herself, and lit the spark. No time for anyone to lean in and tip her into the flowing water. Just instant conflagration.

The nearest children were injured, backed up into the crush of bodies leading down the steps. The guard on attendance had been hemmed in and dived down the chute, leaving the woman to fall on her side and just keep on burning.

By the time the footage came out the plastic material of the slide had started to catch, igniting with a green flame that unleashed vile black smoke. Terrified children were flooding still down the steps, cheeks tear-stained, parents rushing amongst them crying out names.

Wren watched as the Eclipse descended. The crowds fled out and fire crews came in, but their jet hoses couldn't reach high enough. Soon the whole top of the ride was on fire, and the structure was judged unsound to ascend.

They wrote it off. Stepped back and waited for the blaze to end.

Anchors on news stations were left stunned. Trying to find some way around calling this a complete surrender.

"We must lock down our country at once!" a soundbite came through.

Wren recognized the voice, gritted his teeth as the video came up. Standing on a makeshift stage now, shouting at a growing gaggle of reporters and protesters. David Keller, arguing against his own secret interests.

Wren cursed. The plane touched down, taxied to a halt and he called Rogers.

"Rogers," she answered curtly.

"Are you seeing this?"

"Keller?"

"Exactly."

"Some might argue it means he's not involved."

"Then those people are idiots," Wren snapped. "This is how he cements his Presidency before it even begins. Locking the country down is a massive task. Enormous repercussions. Right now he's on the outside throwing bombs at the current administration, so he won't take any hit when the economy craters. He'll just look more prescient with every burning to come. The current President will leave office in tatters."

A pause.

"These burnings are sick, Christopher. When you said every hour, I didn't really think..." She trailed off.

"They are sick."

She took a breath. "I'm almost to Cincinnati. I've recruited an advance team from local cops and early arrival FBI. We're hunting those three people you pointed out."

Wren cast his mind back. It already felt like the first burning was days ago. "Shoe guy, greeter, helper boy?"

"Exactly."

"Hit them with massively trumped up charges. Get them isolated, suspend their lawyer rights if you can, cite the Patriot Act, revoke habeas corpus. More than anything, we need to know how the Apex is communicating the burn order to these women."

"I've already ruled out their phones," Rogers said. "There are no messages or calls in or out. I remote interviewed Rachel Day's husband, he says she's been completely normal. Her boss at the accounting firm said the same. No burner phone we can find, no unusual Internet usage. She's had no time to join a cult since they had their kids, apparently."

Wren chewed that over. "Maybe she's a sleeper agent."

"For eight years?"

It seemed unlikely. Eight years to wait to commit suicide. Have kids, raise a family. People had done worse, but only with extensive conditioning prior.

"Dig deeper," he said. "Go to her past. She crossed paths with the Apex at some point. My hackers are on it too."

"And your strike?"

"Wing and a prayer. I just landed at the staging ground in Utah. Some crazy cult my father messed with decades ago. It's a long story. We'll make contact within the hour."

"Keep me apprised."

"Likewise. Good luck."

He ended the call. It felt good to have Rogers out there picking up the slack, someone he could rely on.

The Eclipse taxied to a halt, and Wren opened the fuselage door. Outside the jet, sunlight blared. Every bit as bright as the Sonoran Desert. He pulled a pair of wraparound Oakley's from his shirt pocket and slipped them on while the stair car rolled up.

Brigham City Airport was a single blacktop runway with a clutch of aluminum siding hangars, backed up against the ochre flanks of the Wasatch mountain range. Wren sucked in a breath. The scent of salt hung faintly in the air, like he was closing in on the ocean, underwritten with the tang of rotten egg. That would be sulfur compounds in the dense, mineral-rich Great Salt Lake substrate, off-gassing.

It was only going to get stronger as they approached the Bonneville Salt Flats, some fifty kilometers away.

Details of the raid to come swirled in his head. Lessons from Waco and every cult assault since, taking on the double threat of extremists ever-poised between trying to kill you and trying to kill themselves. The trick came in bypassing both, but in the stark sunlight of a late fall day, on a white salt expanse with zero cover and dark many hours away, the options for stealth were near non-existent.

But not completely.

The stairs rolled up and Wren jogged down. Around the cone of the jet, he saw the first members of his team gathered beside an Airbus H160 helicopter.

Mason stood slightly apart from Doona and Henry, leaning against a large wooden crate. 6' 2" and solid with muscle, as befitted a former Marine. Even from two hundred yards out Wren could pick out the brand marks that covered his face, each stamped there by the Order of the Saints, reading SAINT. He'd survived three bullets, spent a year in Foundation rehab and emerged on the other side to help Wren bring down the Ghost.

Doona was 19, a Nigerian child soldier Wren had shipped out of a war zone four years back, a slender 5' 10" with tight cornrow braids hugging her skull. Wiry but strong, she knew a dozen ways to kill a man, and had probably used most of them during her days with the 'Peace Lords' militia. Wren was always wary of using her in combat, but after her recovery from the Ghost's booby trap blast in Malaysia, she'd been adamant she had to take to the field again. So…

Henry stood tallest and broadest of them all, 6' 3" and thicker than Wren in the chest, short-cropped sandy hair, an expert sniper. He'd been instrumental in taking down both the Order of the Saints and the Ghost. Battle-scarred after the loss of his Afghanistan brother Abdul in the service of the Foundation, he'd worked through Foundation counseling then started champing at the bit to get back in the harness.

Wren rolled up to them with a grin, arms spread. "I'm three coins minus and still you came!"

Doona smiled. Henry laughed. "When the savior of the Republic calls, we come." He pulled Wren into a tough hug.

Wren snorted, clapped Henry on the back. "You've been watching too much David Keller."

"Man's persuasive," Henry allowed. "I voted for him."

The truth. Wren nodded. Keller was dangerous. "He's impressive, I'll give him that. Didn't kneel when I asked him to, though."

Henry laughed.

"This is your father's work," Doona said, getting straight to business. "The burnings."

"It is," Wren said, sobering as he leaned in to clasp her arm, forearm to forearm, the way they'd done it in the Peace Lords. Her grip around his elbow was hot and firm. "He's running Keller as his front man. Something we're going to make him regret."

"The brief looks wild," Henry said.

Wren nodded. "Only way to take down a pumping station in the middle of a salt desert." He took the few steps extra to stand in front of Mason, held out his hand. "Good to see you again, Mason."

Mason shook his hand. The grip was crushing. As part of his coin-level rehab he'd taken up rock climbing, bouldering in Yosemite looking for new routes to break, often free-climbing without a rope.

"And you, Christopher."

Up close the brands smothering his face were ugly, but all Wren saw was the inner strength. A Marine who'd fought the Saints' brainwashing with everything he had, then come back to sanity before it was too late.

"We need to get you in to see Steven Gruber," he said, as the thought occurred. "You could help him a lot."

"It would be my pleasure."

"Thank you." He looked back to the others. "And Alejandro?"

"Thirty minutes out," Doona said.

"Gear?"

"All here," Mason said, patting the crate.

Wren checked his phone. Fifteen minutes until the next burning. Always on the clock.

"Let's unpack and run a trial," he said, looking from face to face. "What do you all know about diving?"

12

DIVE

The sky was a raw and immense blue. The salt flats were Arctic white, even and smooth as a fresh fall of snow stretching out to the horizon. The pumping station squatted in the midst, bisecting sky and land with brutalist gray concrete, feathered with gantries, gun lookouts and the spiky barrels of Vulcan autocannons.

First came the vehicles.

Racing across the salt flats streaming white dust plumes, ten in all, closing from all directions. Here a Ford, there a GM, there a Honda. Trial self-driving vehicles out of Salt Lake City, hacked by Hellion for remote control and staffed with shop mannequins dressed in tactical gear, outfitted with trigger-switch AR-15s set to begin firing when they drew near. A miracle they'd rigged them all in the last couple of hours, but with Alli and her chop shop mechanics flown in from just one state over, they'd got it done.

"Ground forces are closing in," Hellion said in Wren's ear. He watched the top down feed from a drone cam on his tablet screen as the vehicles neared the Anaximanderian pumping compound. "They're sounding the alarm."

Wren heard the siren. Sub-vocalized a reply into throat-mic, bypassing the churn of the rotor engines. "Are they responding?"

"I'm tracking. Looks like sixteen figures on the ramparts, two in each gun emplacement, four more on a patrol. Seems like-"

There was a boom. Wren watched on the screen as a mushroom ball explosion of white salt erupted to the southeast. A buried ANFO IED, he guessed, taking out a Prius and sending it rolling sideways like a toy.

"Found their outer range," Hellion reported. "Working on the mine pattern. I'd estimate we have eighty percent of their attention."

"Go for dive," Wren said.

"Dive incoming," Hellion confirmed.

The Airbus H160 swooped into the picture, churning through the blue sky at two hundred miles an hour, five thousand feet high, just as the incoming ring of self-driving vehicles entered a wide spiral arc.

Vulcan autocannon fire tracked their radius, slugs ripping across the distance to tear gouts into salt, occasionally peppering fenders and bodywork where Hellion danced them too close. The sniper bark reports of large caliber rounds punctuated the autocannon roar, pinging effectively into the heads and bodies of the mannequins at the wheels.

Wren saw the major artillery strike first on the drone feed; an anti-aircraft mortar rotating on a dolly in the center of the pumping station, two figures ducking to either side as the rocket took off.

"Incoming!" he subvocalized.

Hellion chuckled. "Where do you think I learned combat, Christopher?"

The helicopter released a spray of superheated metal fragments from its belly, flak to draw the homing missile, then swung into a dive.

"Team is a go," Wren said, as the H160 banked hard into a spiral four thousand feet high.

"Deploying team," Hellion answered. The first homing missile erupted in mid-air a few hundred yards away, a stalkless fire flower against the endless blue, then the first figure leaped from the belly of the Airbus.

A smoke trail opened from the skydiver's backpack, painting a white line directly down, mirroring the white dust trails left behind the self-driving vehicles. A second diver emerged swiftly, a third, until the whole team had ejected.

"Chopper outbound," Hellion said, and the Airbus swerved sharply away, leaving another silvery cloud of flak sparkling in its wake.

"Attention count," Wren called over the rushing in his ears.

"Facial and posture analysis algorithms suggest we are nearing one hundred percent," Hellion said calmly. "They're all watching the show, Christopher. Alarm, check. Vehicles spinning. Skydive team seconds from landfall. I have jammed their comms, so they're headless for the moment, but I am intercepting internal calls to reconvene in their 'temple'.

Wren grimaced. He knew what that meant, a call to mass suicide rather than be taken alive. The clock was counting down fast.

"Run some of our vehicles into mines. Deploy the parachutes, but let one drop through. Give them some hope."

"Yes sir," Hellion said with relish. Wren watched the screen as three vehicles from the spinning iris of self-driving cars veered abruptly inward, meeting an outer ring of IEDs. Three more white mushrooms blipped up with distant barks, the vehicles tumbled, and maybe there was a cheer from the pump station's ramparts.

Seconds later the skydivers pulled their parachutes, maybe a thousand feet high, at least thirty seconds' flight time remaining, but time in which they were easy targets. The deep reports of the heavy sniper rounds rang out, punching into one body, two bodies like piñatas. The Vulcan guns banked upward as the falling bodies came into range, sending their scything stream of slugs across the sky.

"I predict you have two minutes, Christopher," B4ckl4cker said in his ear. "Then they will start to see through this."

There was a thud and a spray of white salt as one of the skydivers hit the ground, having failed to deploy his chute. Another cheer from the ramparts.

"Almost there," Wren said, and veered right around a floating mine. "Keep them celebrating. I don't want any of our assault team captured."

"Understood," said Hellion.

More mines lay ahead. Wren switched his attention off the screen and fully ahead.

Cruising along at the salt-crusted bottom of the pumping station's intake canal. At the head of his strike team, clad all in white scuba gear, white tanks, five feet underwater and being pulled along by Seabob F5 scooter propellers at nine miles an hour. They were a convoy on stealth approach, racing through a dragnet of ANFO mines hanging chained in the water.

Wren refocused on the tablet screen banded to the back of his Seabob. Two more self-driving vehicles had just blown up, while the first of the parachuting mannequins Alejandro had tossed out of the H160 were coming in for landing.

"Ten seconds to the central pump, Christopher," Hellion said. "Prepare to surface."

He watched his GPS dot close in on the gargantuan pump's intake tube, then peered up to see its round shadow nearing like a lunar eclipse, shadowing the rippling sky. His pulse hammered. They'd won something like five minutes cover from the attack, long enough for the scooters to pull them from a mile's distance out while the sentries were distracted.

"You are under cover of the pipe," Hellion barked in his ear. "Surface."

He inclined the scooter, covered the short gap to the surface in seconds then killed the engine as he broke through in the mouth of the intake valve. A huge tube ten feet across, looming like an archway half out of the water. The rest of his team surfaced around him in near silence, well covered by the roar of the Vulcan guns tracking the last skydive mannequins to the ground.

Wren pulled off his scuba mask and shrugged off the air bottle, turning to take in the cramped tube mouth. It looked just like the same as their scout drone had shown, a tiny submersible Hellion had sent ahead an hour earlier. The intake pump itself, a rotary version he'd been hoping to slip directly through, had been completely backfilled with cement. No way through there. A pair of security cameras watched over from above, but Hellion had already hacked and looped the signal.

Wren let the Seabob sink to the bottom of the canal.

"Ready?" he asked.

"Ready," said Mason, followed by Doona and Henry. This was where it got dangerous. All their distractions fired but one.

"Tell me the middle gun emplacement is empty," Wren said to Hellion.

"Empty," Hellion confirmed. "Three operators moved to the corners, they're shooting at our vehicles.

As planned. Wren reached to his back, where the huge Battelle TAIL grappling rifle was strapped. Bigger than a harpoon gun, powered by scuba tank air at 300psi, capable of firing a two pound titanium grappling hook one hundred feet straight up, towing a six-millimeter Kevlar line.

"Get ready to charge," he said to Hellion.

"Three vehicles left," she answered. "As ordered, they're packed with explosives. I think I have the route through their IED line."

"Then go," said Wren, and pushed off the cement-filled pump, out into the open blue of the canal, looking up at the gun emplacement some seventy feet directly overhead. A Vulcan gun left vacant, an iron railing. He shouldered the Battelle at a near vertical, emerging four feet out of the water with the six-hooked claw hand of the grapnel flowering at the end.

Under the grappling rifle's thirty pounds he immediately began to sink into the water, but Doona and Mason swam down to form a human pyramid, supporting him even as Henry beaded his CheyTac M200 sniper rifle on the railing above.

Wren pulled the trigger.

13

STRIKE

The Battelle launched with a hiss of compressed air through the diffuser, propelling the grapnel up in a silent arc toward the top railing of the pumping station. Miss now and they'd have to recharge the rifle's gas and respool the Kevlar cable, a near-impossible feat while floating in a canal, certainly impossible if they came under fire.

The grapnel soared and the roar of Vulcan autocannon fire grew louder from either side, as Hellion's cavalry charged. The grapnel reached its zenith, a slim black claw against the burning blue, overshot the railing then fell soundlessly on the other side, the clank on concrete lost to the storm of bullets.

Wren let the rifle sink into the water, gently guiding the cable down as the slack came in and the grapnel on the other side rose, scraped over cement, then caught on a railing just as an enormous explosion erupted to the east, so vast even the water in the canal carried the vibration.

Wren held the cable taut. Lose tension and the grip would be gone.

"Ascent," Wren barked, and Mason was ready at his side, swiftly feeding the cable through the winching mechanism of an APA-5 Atlas Powered Ascender. Twenty pounds in weight, a foot long with the profile of an old school film camera, it could haul up to six hundred pounds of dead weight straight out of the water.

"Ready for tension?" Wren asked.

"Ready," Mason said, and turned the machine on at the lowest power setting. Instantly it caught traction on the cable and began to pull, eating up the slack until the machine lifted out of the water and buoyed Wren on the surface.

Another enormous blast sounded from the west, easily eclipsing the roar of gunfire.

"One vehicle left, this one's definitely going to hit their wall," Hellion said, keys storming through Wren's earpiece. "Go now."

"Clipped in?" Wren shouted over the storm.

"All harnesses attached," Doona answered, bobbing up from underwater, a spare karabiner in her hand. "Good to go."

"Go," said Wren, Mason hit the button, and in three seconds the APA-5 plucked them all out of the water like fish on a multi-hook line. They bounced up over the huge pump inlet then slapped against the sheer concrete side of the pumping station, four bodies dragging and pressing awkwardly until Wren got his feet out horizontal.

Within ten seconds they were all ascending at a fast walk up the pumping station's sheer concrete side, hips abreast, already a quarter of the way to the top.

"Brace," came Hellion's voice, and a second later came the biggest blast yet. Wren knew at once she'd managed to hit the wall with one of her explosive-packed vehicles, the jolt carrying through his feet. A huge ball of white dust plumed over the edge and flurried around them like cloud, then they were halfway up and the Vulcan guns finally silenced.

"Quiet," Hellion urged.

Three quarters of the way up through the fog of hanging white salt powder, Henry drew his Beretta M9 equipped with rubber bullets. Wren had insisted they use non-lethal rounds, even if it put them at greater risk.

"They're coming back to your side," Hellion warned, "estimate they will see you in three, two, one-"

A shot came, bullet ricocheting off the wall and stinging Wren's right arm with concrete flecks.

Henry fired back, leaning out far to get the angle, shooting up and sideways to two figures now peeking over the railing with disbelief on their faces. His second shot took one in the shoulder and spun him, the other returned fire, then Wren got his hands around the railing.

He unclipped the karabiner to his harness smoothly, rolled over the edge and sank flat to his belly, steadying his Desert Eagle and taking aim. "I have east," he said calmly then fired, taking the second guy once in the belly, once more in the side as he went down.

Behind him Mason bellied into position, firing, followed by Henry and Doona, but Wren was already up and running low and fast along the top of the pumping station, soft-soled boots clanking along the metal gantry through the whirling powder dust.

"Two dead ahead of you," Hellion warned. "They're trying to turn the autocannon. Three incoming from the north side emplacement."

Wren could just about pick out the Vulcan emplacement through the white. He unclipped a flashbang from the bandolier around his chest, pulled the pin and tossed it high. Three seconds on it landed, six seconds on it burst, then Wren ran into the thunderclap of light and sound.

Four figures lay around the autocannon, outlines blurred by the salt dust, two groaning and struggling to rise, two more out cold tucked behind the big gun's swivel mount.

Wren put a knee into the temple of one, dropped an elbow into the cranium of the other then cornered fast, heading for the northeast emplacement, already unclipping another flashbang.

"Give me cross covering fire Henry," he barked over the comms. "I'm heading north. Doona, hogtie four southeast."

He was halfway across the spine of the pumping station when Hellion shouted abruptly. "Get down, Christopher!"

He hit the gantry hard on his belly, and an instant later the terrible roar and whine of the nearest Vulcan gun filled the air. Wren felt the backwash off the flood of bullets passing barely a foot above his back, enough to shred him in seconds.

"Henry, you have the angle," Hellion commanded.

The hail of slugs sparked off and through the railings just above Wren, lying with the Desert Eagle dead ahead, looking for a target through the pluming powder but finding nothing.

"I can't see enough," Henry answered somewhere in back. "The dust's too thick, no muzzle flashes.'

"I have infrared above, fire tracer rounds and I will guide you," Hellion answered urgently, keys flying near as fast as the autocannon's shells. "Stay low, orient yourself precisely." A fraction of a second passed, and Wren noticed the railing chewing down as they lowered the M60's field of fire down. A few seconds more and they'd chew him up like a ceviche. "77 degrees off north," Hellion advised. "He's squatting. The gun has a shield but you have the angle. Wren's tied down, shoot now."

The answering bark of a 7.62mm caliber special ball slugged out, and Wren saw the red arc of its tracer trail burn like a momentary laser through the engulfing white to his left. In answer the Vulcan gun tore into the gantry a yard ahead of him, the operator recoiling, and he rolled to the side just as a line striped up the metal where he'd been lying.

"Little faster if you please," he shouted, then rolled onto the hot, torn gantry just as the as the gun stitched a line back up where he'd been.

"Half a degree clockwise," Hellion said calmly but urgently. "Fire!"

Henry's CheyTac shouted with another special ball, and this time the Vulcan's scything blade of bullets arced up into the air briefly before coming slamming back down and over toward where Henry was squatting.

Wren surged to his feet and charged, firing rubber bullets dead ahead, trying to draw the fire back to him.

"An inch further clockwise," Hellion called over the chaos. Wren felt the heat and storm of the big gun drawing near, then its metal shield coalesced ahead through the dust as the gun spun back toward him.

He fired and hit a figure to the side of the gun barricade, who went down clutching his forehead, then the railing to Wren's left erupted in sparks as the big gun homed in. Wren flung himself to the right, vaulting over the railing and barely grabbing hold just as another special ball thundered in and-

There was silence.

"Hit," cheered Hellion.

The gun had been stilled.

Wren pulled himself back over the mangled railing, ran to the Vulcan's shield and found the guy there choking. He'd taken Henry's rubber bullet in the throat.

"Northeast emplacement clear!" he shouted, holding one hand up to his earpiece. There were no more shots now, and the white dust was beginning to clear. "Hog-tie two here, if you please, Doona."

"Middle emplacements clear," came Henry's answering shout.

"Southeast clear," said Doona. "Coming your way, Christopher."

Nothing came from Mason. Wren racked another magazine as he set off sprinting west along the northern gantry. "Mason!! "

No answer came.

"Rounding the southwest," said Henry, "four bodies down and tied, Mason came this way."

The middle north emplacement was empty, must have evacuated out to help with Hellion's assault. Wren kept running.

"Hellion!" he shouted.

"Winding back, I lost track of him in the melee," Hellion answered.

Wren closed on the northeast corner and saw two figures down, the Vulcan barrels smoking and a mangled gap blown through the railing. Wren leaned out and looked down to the crust of salt some eighty feet below, where two more bodies lay side by side, spread-eagled and unmoving, one all dressed in scuba white.

Mason.

Horror crashed into reality in Wren's head. He spun left, saw Henry closing in. Their need for a sniper had passed.

"Get down there," Wren commanded. "Keep him alive. Alejandro, bring the H160 back around. Emergency landing and evac, Mason's in trouble."

"Hellion told us, we're already inbound," came Alejandro's voice in his ear.

Wren turned, now Doona was there too. "Hold the roofline," he said. "Use their own guns against them if you have to. The helicopter gets in and out clean. No more casualties. I'm going in."

"Yes, sir!" Doona snapped smartly, bending over to hog-tie the two bodies. Henry was already latching a speed rope to the railing and tossing the slack over the edge.

"He's alive," he said firmly, as if he could make it real by force of will.

Wren grunted and ran. Southeast corner was the hatch leading down, but Wren had no doubt they'd have locked and reinforced it at the first sign of trouble. Good job that wasn't the only route in.

"Ten yards," Hellion called in his ear, counted them out, then Wren stopped on a dime. Directly beneath the metal gantry grill lay an expanse of fuzzy gray glass. High-altitude surveillance had revealed that parts of the roof of the pumping station had been refitted by the Anaximanderians, presumably to allow natural light into the otherwise windowless concrete block.

Wren latched a speed rope to the railing, clipped it to his belt harness then leaped over the railing, dropping eight feet to the glass and landing with a crack that shot thin spider's web lines across the triple glazing. Not nearly enough.

"Bolting," he called, and pulled the captive bolt gun from its holster.

"I'm with Mason," came Henry's response. "I think he's alive."

Wren heard the sound of the evac helo coming in. He racked the bolt gun, a .25 Cash Special packing 265 milligram blank cartridges that fired a retractable stainless steel bolt with enough percussive force to shatter a cow's thick skull. A mag of ten, he hoped to get the job done in four.

"I'm picking up some internal comms," Hellion blurted in his ear. "Sounds like they're beginning a mass suicide protocol. Hurry."

Wren pressed the bolt gun's muzzle flush to the glass, tracking one of the spiderweb cracks from his landing and pulled the trigger. The whole pane of reinforced glass sank an inch as the bolt crunched in and jammed the crack wider. He picked another spot along the web network and fired again, then again, and on the fourth shot the whole pane shattered like an iceberg calving, dropping Wren straight through.

14

JAMAL JALIM

Wren fell hard but two feet down the safety line caught and stopped him dead, swaying some twenty feet above a drop into the cavernous gray canyon of the pumping station's interior. The speed rope slack fell and thwacked against the concrete floor.

"Dropping," he said over the earpiece comms, took his weight on the speed rope and unhooked the karabiner.

The rope raced through his gloved hands, working up a little heat as he fell into gloom. Sheer gray walls rushed by then he was on the ground with his Desert Eagle held up.

Nothing, nobody.

He was at the western edge of the station's central corridor, three foot wide and never intended for human habitation, an access route for engineers to service the pumps, nightmarishly tall and utterly functional. It made Wren feel dwarfed and insignificant.

"Hurry Christopher!" came Hellion's voice.

Both directions on the corridor looked alike. Blueprints said this corridor ran the length of the whole structure, with storage spaces and offices for the engineers alcoved to either side. Access hatches led below to the pumps in four places, but Wren figured those would have been sealed up just as fully as the pumps' outer access.

That left the control deck, a large hall offset from the corridor and directly above the pumps, accessible at the east end of the corridor by a narrow flight of stairs.

Wren set off running.

One of the alcoves opened to the left of him, briefly glimpsed through a doorless slit in the cliff-face wall, revealing desks and chairs arrayed in rows before a low stage, atop which sat a huge rectangular glass box, easily fifteen feet across, ten tall, filled with what looked to be earth. Above it hung a huge metal grill, like a guillotine blade ready to fall.

Wren ran on and a figure appeared from the next opening. Wren pulled back on the Desert Eagle at the last moment, too slow to stop his index finger pumping the trigger but just fast enough to send the rubber bullet thudding down the corridor like a skipped pebble.

A tow-headed child dressed in khaki robes stared as Wren flew by, no time to stop. Through the next opening lay a dormitory hall stacked with bunk beds rising bed upon bed perhaps a dozen high, like shelving in a fulfilment center, reinforced with brutish iron ladders, each neatly made up with thin brown sheets.

Almost at the end, Wren ran past his red bullet lying slack on the floor, past another two openings, each with more chairs and desks, a blackboard and surgical gurney at the head of one, a strange-looking altar with an oversized, upturned rough crystal cup at the head of the other, then he reached the stairs.

"Christopher!" Hellion cautioned. "They are seconds away."

He sprinted up the tight square stairs, thighs burning, two stories of perfectly angled, featureless concrete then burst out into an open space.

Light flooded in from diagonals in a fifteen-foot high ceiling, dazzling him like floodlights on a stage. Dozens of sun tunnels, he realized, refracting the Utah light into this huge hall.

He held up a hand to ward off the glare and ran off line at once, but no shots came. Five strides in he blinked back tears and stopped, picking out an open oval arena of tiered seating filled with people dressed in varying tones of khaki, sepia and brown. All sat perfectly still, hands flat on their knees, staring at a figure in the center wearing white cotton robes, arms spread wide.

Jamal Jalim.

Not the slender young man Wren had seen in the photographs. He was in his late fifties now, cheeks riven with deep lines, his frizz of nerdy hair all gone leaving a bald and imposing dome. His dark eyes stared directly at Wren, the only person in the room to have even registered his arrival.

"Stop whatever you're doing," Wren ordered, striding into the arena.

"There is no stopping the force of nature," Jamal Jalim said, a reedy voice straining for bass, and lifted his right hand to his mouth. His people responded like an honor guard on parade, raising their hands to their mouths also.

Small red pills in every hand. Wren had seen it a thousand times before. The endgame of all death cult leaders. Wren recognized the look in Jalim's eyes, the authority blurring into joy as he assumed absolute command over life and death; the same look on David Keller's face atop his acceptance stage.

"You can stop this, Jamal Jalim," Wren said, voice low and measured, showing no sign of the turmoil he felt inside as various plans played out in his head. Shoot the guy. Take five good long bounds and clothesline him to the throat, maybe bring him down before he swallowed, but the others?

He swept his gaze across their frozen ranks. Nothing he could do about them. Not with those steeled eyes, braced bodies. Their discipline was astounding, even the children. No way he could save any of them if he tried to take Jalim by force.

Another hundred dead on his conscience. There was always a better way.

He lowered his gun, raised his voice. "I apologize for the way I've arrived. I apologize to all the people here, but I have received visions from Anaximander himself, calling me to seek your counsel. My name is Christopher Wren." He focused on Jamal Jalim. "I think you knew my father."

Jalim's eyes widened. A moment of shock quickly co-opted buried in cult leader calm. Clearly trying to work some route through this moment for himself too. He'd spent a lifetime building this cult up to service his needs, surely he didn't want to kill them all if he didn't have to?

Wren saw the cogs turning, Jalim trying to chart some way to use this moment to actually burnish his own command, and sucked in a breath. If that's what it took.

He placed the Desert Eagle on the ground. "Your people above are not dead. Hurt, only. I come as an emissary. The world needs your guidance."

There. A twinkle of recognition in Jalim's eyes. Maybe amusement? Not all cult leaders were bound up in their dogma. Some were quite capable of extricating themselves from the nonsense when the moment came.

In some ways they were the worst kind.

Seconds passed. The light flooding in through the sun tunnels lit Jalim up like a holy beacon.

"I know who you are," he said at last, thin voice striking closer to depth. "I know why you're here. I have been expecting you. Now, your trials await."

15

TRIALS

Wren licked his lips.

"What this old loser is saying?" Hellion said in his ear.

"Please put down the pills," Wren said. "I only hope to talk. There need be no trials."

Jalim's eyes turned cold. The momentary amusement turning sour. "You shoot down my anointed sentries. Ram vehicles filled with explosives into this holy compound. You say you're seeking wisdom in Anaximander's name, that you are an emissary to save the world, then you say there is no need for trials?"

Wren blinked.

He'd walked into that. Felt this new reality rising up either side of him like the prison walls of the central corridor. He'd already come halfway. Now all their lives hung on a knife's edge. So go a little further.

"Very well," Wren said. "Trials."

Jalim seemed to swell with the power this statement afforded. "Put down your equipment. The earpiece in your ear. The camera on your chest. There is no need for such things here."

Wren stared. Caught out. All his backup gone.

"Do not do what this moron says, Christopher," Hellion warned. "He will wear your skin as a suit. I am scrambling Doona to join you, Henry will follow. The helo is down, they are transporting Mason now. Wait."

"Don't send them," Wren whispered firmly. "Hold the top. No one in or out."

"But Christopher, he will-"

"He won't kill me," Wren replied, loud enough for everyone to hear. Not taking his eyes off Jalim. "Not if I am who I say I am."

Jalim smiled at this.

Hellion protested further, but Wren just tapped and twisted the earpiece so it dropped to the sand, where it continued to protest tinnily. He unfastened his bodycam with all the gentle care of a suicide bomber disarming, set it on the ground reverently next to his Desert Eagle.

Jalim nodded. Two children ran in from either side like ball boys, snatching up the gear, and Wren let them.

"Christopher Wren," Jalim said, that strange note of amusement firing in his eyes again. "You should not have come here. I said precisely this to your father also, all those years ago. Apex of your Pyramid, a heathen sect. He refused the trials and therefore was not welcome. His son is not welcome now."

Wren's heart skipped a beat. Confirmation. If Hellion had heard that she would already be building it into their matrices and algorithms, firming up their matrices on the Apex. "So you saw my father?"

Jalim stared. He raised one hand, and abruptly every person in the room stood. It took everything Wren had not to flinch.

"You have trespassed," he intoned, his voice changing now to something ceremonial, almost sing-song. "You have claimed Anaximander's blessing. Now you must pass the trials. There can be no other way, Christopher Wren of the Pyramid. Until death or ascension."

Wren's mouth opened, but there was nothing much to say. Play into the cult. Get into a room with Jalim alone. Then they'd have a little chat. "Death or ascension," he repeated, "in Anaximander's name."

Jalim nodded.

The people began filing silently off the bleachers toward the stairs, still holding their pills close to their mouths. Hostages. Wren met their eyes one by one, alternate plans blurring in his head. Shore up Jalim or bring him down? Both could work. Fastest way to crack a values system was to make the people believe you were part of it. Even become its leader. Then burn it down before their eyes.

Painful.

Inevitable.

Would Jalim talk, if Wren held his cult in the palm of his hand?

"Go in Anaximander's name," he said as they passed by. They ignored him but he kept it up anyway. It was all going into their heads. Whatever BS Jalim had soaked them in, there was always a way to up the ante. Out-cultify the cult leader. Claim Anaximander's mantle as the one true heir.

Jamal Jalim took up position facing Wren. He was shorter, maybe 5'11", thin but wiry with muscle. Four tall, strong men in pale togas gathered at his sides. He waited until all the others were gone, then spoke.

"The truth is, the trials were your father's idea. I owe him everything, really."

He strode to the stairs, and his men took Wren's arms and led him behind, headed for his first trial.

16

ONENESS

It was the room with the big glass box filled with dirt.

Wren's head raced as he entered, trying to fathom Jalim's relationship with his father. Did he hate the Apex or adore him? Had the Apex failed the trials or originated them?

The men led him up to the stage. The people were settling into their chairs like schoolchildren waiting for a lesson, though there were not nearly enough chairs, so the rest stood at the back and around the sides, circling the glass box.

Jamal Jalim took to the stage and spread his arms. Wren kept the judgment off his face. The guy wasn't much to look at, but he had edge. All cult leaders were manipulators. Everything you thought was wrong. Everything they said was right. The trick to longevity was keeping the people occupied.

"Trial one," said Jalim, his voice carrying easily over the ranks of his followers. "Following the teachings of Anaximander, we seek to achieve oneness with all the elements of nature. Fire. Water. Earth. Air. In all their myriad combinations."

The crowd repeated the last few words, "In all their myriad combinations," clearly an oft-repeated mantra.

"Today we have a man who claims to come from Anaximander himself. A man who claims he is a messenger. So there must be a trial of all, beginning with Anaximander's prophet on this Earth. Myself."

In one smooth movement Jalim stripped off his robes. He was naked underneath. Pale brown skin, washboard abs, arms, shoulders and thighs thin but striated deeply with cords of muscle. Extremely low body fat, Wren figured. He'd be slippery as hell in a fight.

Standing naked before his people he seemed more in command than ever. Wren weighed the possibility of snatching the guy there and then. Elbow to his head, toss him over his shoulder and run. Maybe he'd make it out of the room. They'd probably all kill themselves, though.

He wasn't so keen on that.

"Trial 1 asks us for oneness with both Earth and Water," Jalim went on, wholly ritualized now. "An ability to change our form to mimic our brethren elements, to flow like protons, neutrons and electrons."

Wren grunted low. Pseudoscience was a staple of many modern cults. He didn't bother to point out that while electrons might 'flow', protons and neutrons never really did. But whatever. As Jalim finished speaking a steel cable descended from above, with a steel hoop on the end of it, dropping until it hung just overhead.

Curious. Jalim looked over at Wren like he was tossing a gauntlet, then reached up with one hand and took hold of the hoop.

At once it lifted him. There were gasps. The cable receded into a pulley mechanism in the high ceiling. Wren had seen a lot of grand exits, but never one quite like that. Fifteen feet high it lifted him, well above the lip of the huge glass box, then it shifted gears and moved him backwards like the grapple arm in a funfair crane game, positioning Jalim immediately above the box's left side.

Wren didn't have a clue what was happening. Undeniably, Jalim looked good hanging there. Ripped. Completely at ease. All his weight hanging on one arm but clearly comfortable.

"Befitting the moment," Jalim said, speaking as clearly as before, though now his voice was loaned added depth by the height, "this will be a terminal test. Lower the division."

The huge grate that hung like a portcullis above the center of the box began to descend. Excellent production values, Wren thought. Ready to go on a whim. A team in a back room somewhere. He scanned the walls looking for the control booth. Watching through a spyhole, maybe, too small to see.

The lower bar of the portcullis reached the dirt and its descent paused. Jalim reached out to the top bar and twisted one of the poles, which released a long thin metal rod. With this rod in hand, Jalim attacked the portcullis in a frenzy, hitting every beam and crossbar in the grid. The sound of metal clashing rang out discordantly, filling the tall room with violent echoes even as it pulled Jalim's muscles into tight, startling relief.

Wren realized what was happening. Proof that the portcullis was solid. Not a trick piece of gear. Like a magician testing the blade he was about to stick through the woman in the box.

Thirty seconds of that passed, sound barraging out, then Jalim slid the metal rod back into the top of the grid and looked out at his audience as if to say 'see'.

The portcullis began sinking again, this time directly into the dirt. Not solid dirt, then, Wren realized, but liquid. Earth and water made mud, of course. It sloshed thickly as the portcullis slid in, slow waves rippling across the surface.

The people leaned closer. Wren felt breaths drawn and held. There was a grating sound as the portcullis worked its way down guiderails on the tank's inner walls, then a dull clunk as it hit the bottom.

Just what the hell was going on?

"As I was so granted oneness upon ascension as Anaximander's prophet on Earth," Jalim intoned, still hanging immobile, "so any emissary for Anaximander should bear it too."

Wren's eyes were wide now. Taking in every detail.

The steel cable holding Jalim began to descend. First his feet touched the surface of the mud and passed in. His shins followed, his knees, his thighs. The mud level rose slightly against the glass as his body displaced it. Next his chest, his shoulders, his neck, his face, until he was completely submerged.

The steel cable reeled up and away, pulling the hoop dripping after it.

Wren just stared. In all his years of cult activity he'd never seen anything quite like this. This kind of staging. The Apex had buried people alive, his own children with Wren amongst them once, but those had been rough-hewn efforts dug out in the desert wastes, barely stage-managed at all, with no helpers in back rooms bringing such class to the proceedings.

The show wasn't done though. With Jalim swallowed in the mud, a second huge grate began to descend from above. A roof for the cage, ten feet on a side, the perfect fit to enclose the left side. It came down in seconds and slotted into grooves smooth as a Porsche changing gears, chased by clanking sounds as locks sealed it in.

Wren's mouth went dry.

Seconds ticked by.

As far as he could see, Jamal Jalim had just put himself in a solid steel cage inside a box full of mud. Thirty seconds already and counting. Was it a feat of holding his breath? He looked around at the people. Men, women and children stared fixedly at the glass box of mud, utterly rapt and leaning in.

It was crazy. Wren almost laughed but it wasn't funny. The silence got hot and thick.

A minute, now?

The portcullis divider rattled and people nearby jerked. Nothing was visible through the mud walls. A minute thirty. Wren started to think about calling for the divider to be raised, the roof to be lifted, thought about grabbing a desk and putting it through the glass himself. Jalim was no good to him dead.

The divider rattled again. People gasped. Mud shifted against the glass.

Began to spiral.

Wren's jaw dropped.

A slow counterclockwise whirlpool in the left part of the tank. Clockwise in the right. A magic trick like nothing he'd seen before. Topping two minutes now. More rattles. More spinning. It was incredible.

Then it all stopped.

The mud slowed. More seconds ticked by. Wren envisaged Jamal Jalim suspended in the mud of his cage like an unborn baby sucking in fetal liquid, convulsing as his lungs tried to filter oxygen from wet dirt, failing to exhibit the 'oneness' he'd so trumpeted. A trick gone wrong, the magician stabbing his assistant right through the chest.

Then the steel cable descended once more, this time directly into the right half of the tank. The steel hoop struck and sank. The line went taut. A second passed, then it began to reel in.

The mud parted. Jamal Jalim's fist emerged, followed by his arm then his head. Coated in thick brown muck. His neck followed, his shoulders, his torso, his hips, legs, feet, ascending until he was completely clear of the vat. He snorted once, blowing mud out of his nose, wiped his face, dug mud out of his ears, then rose calm and clear the rest of the way, breathing normally, eyes white searchlights against the dark mask of black.

Wren stared in silence, as awed as the rest.

The cable shifted forward then descended, setting Jamal Jalim down on the stage a scant few feet from where he'd been plucked up. Wren racked his mind trying to figure out the trick. The whirlpools were easy enough; a couple of wave makers in the bottom of the vats would do it. This was a pumping station after all, so that wouldn't be hard.

But the transition from left to right through the portcullis?

Clearly he hadn't 'become one' with the mud, flowed his protons and neutrons through the portcullis, then 'rematerialized', so could there be a trapdoor leading to a tunnel down through the stage and up to the other side? Wren dismissed that as too complex. Maybe the portcullis had a built-in trick hinge, could simply be opened under the mud?

Jamal Jalim gave nothing away. Not even breathing hard. Looked out at his people calm and triumphant.

Wren realized they were cheering. He couldn't argue. It was one hell of a trick. He considered again just taking the guy out there and then, but it was the worst possible timing. Just when he'd proven himself to be Anaximander's prophet, some kind of living god?

No. They'd definitely pull the pin on all those pills in their hands.

There was only one thing for it.

He began with his gloves, followed up with the bandolier around his chest, his rubberized boots, his rope harness, then peeled off his all-white wetsuit until he was standing on the stage naked as the day he was born.

The people saw him. Saw his confidence, even if it was a front. Jalim saw it too and there was that look of amusement again, the recognition by one conman of another.

Wren had no idea how to pull off the trick, but fake it 'til you make it. He could hold his breath pretty long. That gave him a couple of minutes to figure it out.

17

EARTH & WATER

First came the grate roof, lifting up from the left side of the box trailing mud. Next followed the portcullis divider, sucking out of the thick liquid and rising to hang just over the center, mud-slathered but intact. Wren scanned it rapidly, looking for hidden seams, joins, hinges, but nothing stood out. A good craftsman could conceal them easily, though. He began to wonder how good an idea this was.

Showing none of that doubt on his face, he took up position at the left side of the box. Being naked didn't bother him. As he looked out at Jalim's people he replayed everything he'd seen, trying to figure it out. The real magic in a trick like this was usually baked into the physical structure. You thought that was a woman being cut in half? Nope, two women already in two separate boxes, contorted into tiny spaces. The magician slides in the guillotine blade, one sticks out her head, the other sticks out her legs, abracadabra.

Either that or it was a simple misdirection, pulled off before the show even began. Think a card trick's amazing, so complex and randomized, but go back and watch it a dozen times and you'll see the magician palm the card right at the start while you're enjoying the patter and waiting for the trick to begin.

So how did that apply here?

The steel hoop came down. Wren imagined himself suspended in the mud like a dinosaur fossil, unable to figure it out, sucking in mud then just hanging still, perfectly embalmed and unable to help anyone. No use to his Foundation. No way to stop the Apex or David Keller. Firestorm rolling on.

That outcome could be very real. He didn't like his chances trying to break through the box's glass with just his fists and feet.

He would be quite dead.

But what was the alternative? Slink away tail between his legs while the firestorm raged outside, while Keller ascended closer to the Presidency, while the Apex bided his time? No chance. This was his lead, and he had to pursue it all the way, just like Jamal Jalim had said.

Death or ascension. He raised his right hand, took hold of the hoop and at once it lifted him up.

Just like Jalim. He thought back on the Apex and all his tricks, homing in on the one time he'd shown little Christopher Wren, then known as Pequeño 3, the secret tunnel running out from the first 'buried alive' pit he'd had his people dig into the Arizona desert.

Soon after Wren had been buried with all his brothers and sisters in another pit. Galicia. Chrysogonus. Zachariah. Gabriel. Grace. Only Wren had believed there was another tunnel in the pit's smooth-walled sides, only Wren had kept searching until he'd almost suffocated, and in the end only Wren had survived.

The steel cable swung him out over the mud, and there he hung, spooling his mental footage of Jalim's trick backward and forward.

His money was on some kind of trick switch hidden in the portcullis. But it wouldn't be easy to find. It looked like this mud vat underwent constant use, Jalim's means of keeping his people busy as they sought to 'flow with the mud' and achieve 'oneness'. Likely they spent all day, every day dropping in and out and trying to push their way through the portcullis. If there was an easy switch that opened a trick door in the portcullis, one of them would have hit on it already by accident.

The portcullis was descending again already.

Wren's mind raced on.

It couldn't be anything a random movement could trigger. That left some kind of key. But Jalim had gone in naked. Hadn't had time to prepare, to secrete the key somewhere about his body, unless he carried it with him at all times like a drug mule making an endless border crossing, and why would he do that in the safety of his own cult?

No.

The room full of faces was staring up at him, a few with faith, most with derision. A pretender who deserved to die for his arrogance. Now the portcullis was grinding down into place, met with clanks as it struck bottom.

He could still pull out of this. Jump off the loop, scale the box before the lid came down, but he knew where that led.

His mental footage looped. His arm began to ache. Where was the key? He thought back on card tricks, palming the target card at the very start. Highlighting the points Jalim touched as he went into the tank. The steel hoop. Wren looked up, then swapped hands. Right hand to left. Feeling for anything on the hoop. A magnet, maybe. A place a key could be attached. But nothing. It was perfectly smooth, no indentations.

His steel cable began to descend. Now or never.

"Wait!" he called. Remembering one last thing.

The cable kept descending.

"Wait!" he called again, this time booming. "Don't I have the same rights as the prophet in this terminal trial? Shouldn't I be afforded the chance to test the divider?"

He descended a moment longer, so his feet touched the mud. It was uncomfortably cold. He sank deeper, into his calves, then the cable halted.

"Very well," came Jalim's voice.

The cable reversed direction. Wren was lifted out. He swapped arms again. He couldn't hold his own weight for much longer, being so much heavier with muscle than Jalim. Already his shoulder blade was throbbing. His grip could give out any moment. It didn't help that Jalim had left the hoop slick with mud.

The portcullis rose beside him, and Wren reached over to the place Jalim had touched earlier. Found the rod, thin and flexible, inserted into the top bar of the grate. Once in the mud, it would be rendered inaccessible by the roof grating.

He pulled a half-inch of it out, and felt rather than saw the indentation worked in the end. Small. Insignificant. Round. Deep enough to contain a specialized key? He pulled the rod all the way out, three feet and slender, made a show of inspecting it. No indentation in the other end. No reason for there to be one. He brought it up before him, used the angle to sneak a look into Jalim's eyes.

Saw the same recognition. It takes a con to spot a con. Momentary fear.

This was it. Key embedded into the end of the rod. Jalim slipped it out every time, ready for the mud. So where was it now?

He attacked the grate with the rod, playing the part and sending concussive clashes ringing around the room, while also looking for a tiny keyhole. Mud rattled off and slapped down as he beat it hard, looking for telltale bubbles, the mud shifting strangely, until-

Yes.

Bottom right. A tiny dimple. If the grate were dry he'd never have seen it, but mud glistened, showed contours. Light and shadow. Achieve oneness.

Now he just needed the key. The worried look on Jalim's face had told him everything he needed to know. A hell of a gamble, but only one place it could be now, unless Jalim had swallowed it, inserted it elsewhere, but Wren didn't think so.

No.

The key was in the tank.

Wren hit the portcullis with such vigor that the rod slipped out of his hand. Fell into the tank below him. He looked up, acting like this was nothing.

"I'm ready," he said.

The portcullis descended into the mud, clanking firmly into position as locks engaged. Seconds later, so did Wren.

The mud engulfed him like a barrel of cold fish. More watery than he'd expected, but buoyant enough that he sank slowly. Silty and stinking of the Great Salt Lake's sulfur. His knees, his thighs, his hips submerged. He took deep rapid breaths, not nearly as cool as Jalim, hyperventilating his lungs.

He'd always had strong lung capacity. Had taught himself as a child to enter 'aortal flutter', an unconscious state that feigned death and required very little oxygen to maintain. His max had been seven minutes. Out of training, now he could probably push that to four, if he undertook no vigorous activity.

The mud rose cold and slippery up his chest, his shoulder, his neck, then he took one last breath, closed his eyes and ducked below the surface.

Instant dark. Instant cold and disorientation. He swiped a few strokes, pulling himself down to the bottom. Within seconds his fingers closed on the rod. No key, but that didn't matter. He swiped further down until he lay chest flat like a catfish on the bottom of the tank, reaching out to take hold of the portcullis grate. As solid and impassable as granite.

If the key was anywhere, it would be on the other side of the portcullis. No way Jalim would leave it on the left side, where Wren might stumble on it, realize what it was.

Holding to the portcullis, he slipped the rod through the grating, followed with his arm up to the shoulder against the metal. Call it protons and neutrons becoming one with the mud. Still lying flat, he pressed the rod to the floor of the box's right side then gently swept it flush to the front glass, then back across to the left in a half-arc like a windscreen wiper.

He felt nothing. Maybe he wouldn't. If the key was light, if the mud was too thick, maybe this would never work. Thirty seconds. Along with his arm, that made for a six foot radius. Enough to cover just over half the right side of the tank. He had to hope.

He dragged the rod back toward him until it lay flush along the portcullis base, then worked his left hand along the grate, feeling for the key. His fingers fumbled through mud, working swiftly through the bars into the crevices along the length of the rod, but there was nothing. No chunk of metal.

A minute already. Time for a few more swipes.

This time he picked a different spot to go fishing. Pushed his right arm through at the middle, strained against the portcullis and ran the rod all the way to the left side of the box, pulled it gently back to the grate, then repeated his scavenge through the mud.

Again, nothing.

Two minutes?

Once more, left to right this time. The biggest sweep he could make, with his lungs already starting to rebel. Demanding air. As slow as he could bear to drag, then gathering it in. Moving along the grate scavenging his catch with both hands, fingers probing until they caught on something.

Metal!

A tiny chunk, barely larger than a screw. Wren clasped it and pulled out, back, positioned himself blind at the bottom right corner of the portcullis and probed for the hole. It took him three stabs with the tiny key to find it, insert it, and twist. There was the tiniest click, and the grate in his left hand moved.

His heart surged. He pushed and the portcullis split smoothly, opening outward on an invisible hinge into the right hand side. Three kicks sent him through, surging straight to the surface where-

His head struck metal, hard.

For a second he was stunned and seeing stars, almost shocked by the impact into sucking in a breath, though he regained his wits swiftly.

They'd lowered a second roof grate. Upping the challenge, forcing him to the prove his 'oneness' with the mud twice if he wanted to be released back into the air, a feat he knew even Jamal Jalim had never managed, because it wasn't possible.

Panic bloomed and he tamped it down.

He'd always known this was a possibility. Ten foot square cage, a roof lattice made of thin bars, held by locks at the edges. Not too strong, he guessed, but at ten foot tall there was nothing he could brace his feet against to squat the roof up and off.

But with the portcullis swung open? He saw the way instantly.

Two minutes thirty, with his pulse banging in his head and his lungs gulping at his throat, he swung the hidden portcullis out to the middle of the cage, set his feet on rungs two thirds of the way up, pressed his shoulders against the roof and pushed.

His whole 6' 3", two hundred twenty pound frame bent against the grid like he was squatting five hundred with the devil on his back.

The cage roof strained. Flexed. Wren almost gulped mud, relaxed for a second, strained again. Something popped as the metal flexed in its locks. Three minutes, and Wren dug deep as a red glow bloomed across his eyelids. No way he was going to die in a bucket of mud. Not after surviving everything the Apex could throw at him, not after letting down his family, Rogers, all the Foundation. He had things still to do.

He pushed again, throwing everything he had into the curve of his back, then felt something shear, like a vertebra slipping. He would have roared if he was above ground. He pressed again with everything he had, Atlas squatting the whole world, and another latch slipped, then another, then the whole grating popped up and out like the triggered arm of a mousetrap, admitting Wren roaring and filthy into the light.

He surged up, mud spraying from his mouth and nose, rubbing at his eyes and ears, standing tall on the portcullis door and staring out at the people through the half-cocked roof grate. The whole audience were splattered with mud. He'd catapulted it all over them. That felt pretty good.

Not done yet. He grabbed the edge of the glass, pulled himself over the edge like a turd escaping the toilet bowl and slipped down to land on his feet with a splat beside a shock-faced Jamal Jalim.

Wren wasted no time.

He punched Jalim square in the face.

The prophet flew. A hundred-forty pounds soaking wet, Jalim didn't stand a chance against the wrecking ball of Wren's fist. Two hundred pounds per square inch of force, and that was hardly even trying. The thin, wiry bastard took wing off the stage, hit the deck and rolled.

Wren didn't follow up. Just stood in front of the people. Cult devotees. Staring at him now with something like wonder. The first person since their prophet to cross from one side of their stupid mud tank to the other. The first person ever to 'achieve oneness' through the damn roof.

Wren felt their minds flexing before him. Windows of possibility opening up in their eyes.

"Trial two," he announced, booming the words so loud the people nearest flinched. "And pick him up," he ordered, pointing at Jalim, who was now struggling to get to his feet.

Wren strode right past him, through the gawping ranks of the cult and out of the tall open doorway. No idea where he was going, but it didn't matter. He was in charge of this nonsense now.

18

FIRE & WATER

Wren turned left onto the spine corridor, panting a little as he recaptured his breath. His feet burned where the narrow portcullis gratings had dug into them. Probably he was leaving bloody footprints behind, but he didn't stop to check. It wouldn't kill him.

Past the dormitory room with its stacked beds reaching a dozen high. Just ridiculous. He'd had enough.

To the right lay another room, another stage, more chairs, and Wren stamped in. Took to the stage. In the center was a plain wooden altar, structural beams exposed, topped with a huge smoked glass bell jar, like a giant's shot glass, rim down. Wren laid his hands on it as people came in, lifting it carefully. It was heavier than it looked. Inside was a crystal goblet filled with water, atop a metal plate flush to the wood.

Curious.

Wren set the outsized shot glass back over the top and just stood.

Naked and covered in mud. Staring down every person as they came in.

Jamal Jalim entered last. Blood streamed down his chin, neck, chest from what was doubtless a shattered nose. Maybe a few broken teeth, mangled lips, possibly cracked jaw.

Wren didn't care. The guy had just tried to kill him with mud. Wren stood with his arms behind his back like a Marine awaiting inspection.

Jalim's eyes didn't have that cocky, knowing amusement anymore. There was anger there. There was also fear too; of Wren, of the trials, of potentially losing his cult.

Good.

"Trial two," prompted Wren.

"Trial two," repeated Jalim, trying for gravitas and missing. He didn't sound right. Wet with the blood, and nasal with his crumpled nose, but off balance. Woozy. Probably concussed to boot. "As with all such matters of Nature, Anaximander states-"

"Get on with it," Wren snarled.

Jalim's eyes sparked. Anger burning through the concussion. Who was Wren, after all, to challenge his authority in his own compound?

"Trial two," he intoned, slowing his speech to reclaim status. In a stately manner he took up position beside the altar, mirroring Wren and not flinching away. "Fire and water. The true Anaximanderian can absorb both within his body, unharmed."

He nodded a signal, and a sound like rushing wind came from the altar. Wren studied it. Coming from the giant shot glass. Maybe a minute passed, then something unexpected happened. The water in the crystal goblet within began to boil. Bubbles formed at the bottom of the glass and shot their way to the top.

Fire and water.

The rushing sound stopped. Jalim strode to the center behind the altar, showing no fear of Wren, laid both hands reverently on the giant shot glass and lifted, revealing the goblet underneath. A few bubbles were still working their way from the base to the top.

He turned to Wren and said a single word. "Drink."

Wren stared back at him. Stared at the goblet. Couldn't figure out what the trick was here. He knew well enough that sometimes that 'magic' was actually just phenomenal training and preparation. Magicians who put a nail through their hands weren't doing magic, they'd just pierced a hole through their hand in advance.

But drinking boiling water? There was no way to train your body to accommodate that.

He leaned over, touched the goblet. The glass itself was blazing hot. He held it for a second only, shielded partly by the layer of mud on his hand, but didn't even try to raise it to his lips. If he tried to pick it up his palm would be irreparably burned. Third degree, most likely, damage deeper than the skin down to the ligaments beneath. Permanent.

To drink it would kill him. Boiling water would blanch his mouth, gums, esophagus, stomach. There was no treatment for internal burns. He'd just die in unimaginable agony.

"You first," he countered.

Jalim nodded gravely. Getting some of his mojo back.

"You have polluted the cup. It must be boiled again."

He set the crystal dome back over the goblet. Wren couldn't help but admire the ritual nature of it all. Clearly all thought out, all planned, all worked through. The metal plate had a heating filament. Impressive to wire that into the altar and show no signs of the wiring, but not that hard.

The rushing sound came again. Again bubbles appeared in the goblet, racing to the top. Again Jalim left it for nearly a minute. Wren's confidence began to ebb a little. The extra time wouldn't make the water any hotter, but the goblet itself? Glass could climb to a temperature in excess of a thousand degrees before it melted. It wouldn't even turn red hot until it hit eight hundred. Just touch that and you'd lose your hand in an instant.

The rushing sound ceased. Jalim lifted the oversized shot glass and set it down to the side as the last few bubbles raced up in the goblet. He took a moment, breathing deeply, eyes closed, centering himself, then took hold of the glass.

He didn't scream. His flesh didn't sizzle. It was almost as if he truly had mastered fire and water, achieving Anaximanderian oneness. For a second Wren only stared disbelieving as Jalim raised the goblet to his lips, showing no sign of the pain, and then -

Wren seized the glass off him before he could swallow. Jalim didn't expect that and his grip gave out easily. Barely a drop of water was spilled. This time Wren lifted the goblet to his lips and threw it back in two big gulps.

He didn't scream. He didn't start to spit up blood from a fiercely scalded windpipe. If anything, the water went down as a pleasant balm.

Jalim was left staring. Panic in his eyes now. The people saw it. Wren saw it.

"I am one with Nature," Wren said, and slammed the goblet down on the heating plate. Smiled at Jalim.

Science.

Wren was no engineer, unlike his namesake, but he was no slouch either. There was only one possible way Jamal Jalim could lift a blazing hot glass and drink boiling hot water, and that was if the water wasn't boiling hot. From there the suppositions had come fast and found proof in Jalim lifting the goblet. A simple middle school lab trick, child's play for an engineer of Jalim's caliber to pull off, based on one simple law of thermodynamics.

Water didn't have to be hot to boil.

Carry a kettle to the top of Mt. Everest, the water would boil at 160 rather than 212. That wasn't because of some difference in temperature up there, but because of the low air pressure. How to replicate that in the lab?

Make a vacuum.

From that hypothesis onward everything fit perfectly. The heavy giant shot glass was airtight when flush against the wood. The rushing sound of 'heat' transferring was actually the sound of air being sucked out of the shot glass; difficult to disguise so Jalim hadn't even tried, letting it become part of the ritual. A simple air pump disguised in the wood or the heating plate would convert the crystal shot glass to a depressurized bell jar with ease.

From there it was easy. Suck the air out, reduce the interior to a vacuum, and water would boil at room temperature. Jalim had first heated the glass up for Wren, then switched the plate off and let the vacuum pump run for a good minute, boiling the heat right out of the water and by conduction from the glass itself, leaving it barely lukewarm to the touch.

Wren felt angrier than ever. How many people had Jalim permanently damaged, forcing them to try and drink boiling hot water? It was sick. He turned on the man, sorely tempted to hammer him in the face again. Better yet, make him drink the boiling water.

But there was no time for any of that.

Still, Jalim clearly read all that on his face. He looked terrified.

"Trial three." Wren growled.

19

AIR & WATER

The third room. It had the same bare cement walls, the same encircling chairs, the same people standing around the outside, though the atmosphere was very different now.

The people were abuzz. Whispering to each other. Staring at Wren with a new kind of wonder, maybe disbelief. He approached the stage at the center and felt their eyes on him.

They were deluded.

He was probably the first person they'd seen pass a single trial other than Jalim. His successes alone were already bending the Anaximanderian cult to breaking point. The stakes for them were enormous. Like any death cult leader worth his salt, Jamal Jalim would have them worked up about talk of a coming doomsday, the forces of good and evil, eternal life and death. Barely thirty minutes ago they were all ready to swallow pills and die at Jalim's word.

But now?

Now their minds were being forced open. If a stranger could pass the trials, and strike their prophet, and survive, what did that mean for everything else?

Wren looked into their faces as he passed. A young pregnant woman holding her belly, staring up at him. Two children with dark eyes gawping. A heavyset older man with hands pressed close together, eyes closed, whispering some scientific prayer. The same kinds of people Wren had seen on the streets of Salt Lake, New York, Chicago, just dropped into a prison of faith. Minds bent. Guzzling down Jalim's bullshit magic tricks.

The stage was ready for him. A reinforced metal surgical table sat centrally on a thick metal pole, inclined downward at the head, with four leather restraining cuffs for wrists and ankles. A water spigot hung from the ceiling above, and Wren knew at once what it was all for.

Air and water.

Waterboarding.

Head at this end. Arms and legs strapped here and here. A cloth over the face to aerosolize water from the spigot and force it to be inhaled into the lungs, where air and water met and blurred into agony.

It only fired Wren's anger hotter. Delve into any of these mind control cults and the core was sickeningly rotten. He was ready to just rip the whole thing apart, but that required a little more patience, a few more moments only.

Jamal Jalim strode through his people with his head held high. The blood down his chest and chin had hardened into the dried cakes of mud. He'd gotten over the punch, it seemed, gotten over his loss on trial two, and was probably plotting some path through to still keep his cult. Maybe give Wren what he wanted, crown him as Anaximander's emissary and hope he would leave. Roll with the punches and write Wren into his mythos somehow, anything to keep himself on top.

Wren couldn't allow that.

This had to end now. Those pills in the people's hands were all bullets on one way trajectories. If Wren left them with Jalim, one day those bullets would find their targets. He preferred to stop the barrage without a single shot fired.

Jalim gave him a look as he took to the stage. Not the amused look now, but maybe supplication. An offer. You scratch my back here, I'll scratch yours. You want to know about your father? Keep what I've built here intact.

Not a chance.

Wren fixed him with a hard glare, then dropped off the stage and picked up one of the chairs. Wooden, solid, thick. He hefted it, stepped back onto the stage and raised it over his shoulder. The nearest members flinched back. Jalim's eyes widened.

"What are you d-"

He didn't get to finish the question. Wren brought the chair down hard on the tilted end of the surgical table. There was a deep metallic bong matched by an enormous crack, as the table jerked slightly lower on its axis. One of the chair legs broke away and gasps filled the air. Wren raised the chair and brought it down again.

Another massive bong, the table tilted further and now the chair smashed into fragments.

Wren turned. People were on their feet now. Outrage was morphing into terror on Jalim's face.

"What are you doing?" he demanded. "That's the sacred-"

Wren tuned him out, went to the next chair and hefted it. Like a lumberjack selecting his tool, the demolition work was just beginning. He spun and rang the chair hard off the table again, smashing this chair into kindling in one massive strike, steepening the table's angle a few more degrees.

In the shocked silence that followed, Wren heard a faint hissing.

He smiled.

Two more chairs broken over the table left it see-sawed to a near vertical, with the hissing sound climbing to a gushing flow. Exactly as Wren had expected. Some kind of retractable air pipe built into the frame. Perfectly aligned, so that when the cloth was placed over Jalim's head, and the water was poured over the top of it, an air tube circled around and into his mouth.

That was how he'd endured waterboarding.

Now the mechanism was broken along with the table. There would be no air tube. No trick. No concealment.

Wren's chest was heaving. He turned. The people were on their feet. Jalim was staring at his ruptured table with pale-faced horror. Broken chair pieces festooned the stage. Wren owned It all.

"Here," he said, voice booming so loud they all shrank back, and pointed to the front of the stage. "As good as anywhere. Right, Jamal Jalim?"

The people's eyes turned to their leader. Pissing himself, most likely. Thin-looking. Reedy and pale. Looking at them and trying to muster his customary command in the face of an impossible demand, looking at Wren with an expression that wavered between rageful defiance and obsequious pleading. Wren read it all in his eyes.

No way he could endure the test now. Nobody could endure waterboarding. Everybody had to breathe. Maybe hold your breath for a few minutes, but at some point your lungs would give out. You'd suck in a breath of aerosolized water through the cloth and at once your throat would tighten, your lungs would palsy, the burning pain and the choking terror would be overwhelming.

Wren knew. He'd been waterboarded before.

Now he saw the decision happening in Jamal Jalim's eyes as the last of his 'trials' came crashing down, maybe before Jalim himself even knew it.

His hand was halfway to his mouth, red pill in his hand, when Wren hit him. A long snap kick in the gut, enough to double him over, followed up with one hand grasped around Jalim's wrist shaking the pill loose. Wren let it fall and crushed it under his bare foot.

"Please," Jalim gasped. One last effort to avoid losing everything in front of his chosen people. "You can't-"

"Trial three," was all Wren said, and lifted the man bodily, laid him kicking and wriggling at the center of the stage. Fury propelled him. How many of this man's followers had been forced through this torture without the aid of an air pipe to carry the day? How many times had he encouraged them to waterboard themselves, all the while damned in their own minds for their inability to achieve 'oneness' with the water and the air?

It was unfathomably cruel. Day after day, hour after hour, with nothing to look forward to but more pain and more failure in their efforts to 'ascend' his nonsensical 55 layers.

Wren straddled the smaller man's chest, easily pinning down his arms. No way Jalim could move, though now he was trying. Struggling for all he was worth. Crying out. Whimpering. Leaking crocodile tears. Wren just looked to the side.

"Cloth," he said, and held out a hand. The people were struck dumb. Eyes wide. Uncertain how this fit into their Anaximanderian ideology, but straining their minds wide to swallow the reality.

A piece of cloth appeared in Wren's hand, embroidered with what looked to be atomic bonds. More pseudoscience BS. There was no pleasure in any of this. Only justice.

"Please!" Jalim whimpered. "I'll tell you everything. About your father. I swear it."

"Not enough," Wren said, and laid the cloth over his face. Electrons, protons and neutrons covering up those terrified eyes. Held out his hand again. "Water."

Jalim's jaw worked frantically beneath the fabric. "Then what?" he cried, voice muffled but high. "What do you want? Tell me, I'll do anything you ask, I promise!"

A bottle of water appeared in Wren's hand. Delivered by a child. It was horrific. It was nothing these people hadn't seen a thousand times before, though never to Jalim himself. If anything, the successful torture of their leader might finally break the spell.

"Anything?" Wren asked, leaning in.

"Anything!" Jalim howled, like he was in pain already. "Anything at all!"

"Achieve oneness," Wren said, and poured the first splash of water onto the cloth. It sucked the fabric tight to Jalim's gasping mouth, immediately blocking his airways and aerating liquid directly into his lungs.

20

ANYTHING

The people were cleared out. Into their bunks. On the way they stared at the mud tank with its broken roof grate, at the crystal goblet on its metal hotplate, at the upended and hissing waterboard gurney. Whatever.

Wren didn't care.

What mattered now was Jamal Jalim. Sitting in a chair in the center of his upstairs 'arena', bathed in a flood of sun tunnel Utah light. His body coated in a dried mask of mud and blood. His face smeared where the cloth had clung, mud washed away by water, vomit, more water.

Panting now. Humiliated before his cult. Much reduced. Wren almost felt pity for him.

Almost.

"Tell me."

Jalim looked up. The rage was gone. The begging was gone. Massive loss could be transformative. Now he just looked broken.

"I never did it like that," he said, his voice hollow.

"But you did it," Wren said.

"Not like that."

Wren resisted smacking him across the face. The man should have been jailed twenty years ago. If not for the terrible example of Waco, he would have been.

"But you did it. You drowned them in mud. You made them drink boiling hot water. You waterboarded them. You don't think you've earned this?"

"They never actually drank boiling water," Jalim mewled, looking up. Spit and blood clung to the corners of his mouth. Too shocked to rub them away. "It was just a trick!"

"I don't believe you," Wren said. "Like I don't believe you weren't also abusing them in every way imaginable. Jalim, I've seen this routine a thousand times before. Don't forget who you're talking to. I grew up in the Pyramid. The Apex is my father. So let's cut the pity party and get down to it. You had a cult. Now you don't. But it can still get worse for you."

At that Jalim mustered a disbelieving snort. "How?"

"Push me and find out. Now let's talk about my father. He came here twenty-four years ago. You already confirmed it. So spill."

A haunted look stole across Jalim's expression like a shadow. "I can't."

"Why not?

The fear deepened in Jalim's eyes, and that fascinated Wren. This man had already tried to swallow his suicide pill. He'd just experienced the ignominy of losing his cult. Wren's threats didn't bother him, but mentioning the Apex?

"He'll destroy me."

This fear went deeper. It was primal.

"I've already destroyed you. The Anaximanderians are in ruins. I'll have my people in here next and de-indoctrination will begin. What's left to be destroyed?"

Now Jalim managed a faint chuckle. "You don't even know who your father is, do you? You don't know what he's really capable of."

Wren's tone turned hard. "I saw the Pyramid burn, Jamal. I was there at the end."

Jalim laughed a little more. Like something was loosening inside. Wren had seen it before, shock and awe leading to a kind of mania, leading in turn to stroke-like events. Extreme moments of emotion could cause lasting damage, shift personalities permanently. People came out of such episodes changed, maybe unable to think coherently, unable even to speak.

"You think the Pyramid was bad?" Jalim wheezed. "You don't even realize that you and your desert groupies were his favorites. You had it *good*!"

Growing louder now.

"The hell are you talking about, we had it good?" Wren asked. "He burned every one of those 'groupies' alive, Jalim. Before that he buried all my brothers and sisters alive in a pit as a test of their faith. I was there, just nine years old, and I'm the only one who survived. What's good about that?"

More gulping laughter. "You really don't know a thing, do you?"

"So tell me!" Wren hissed, seeing the path through to break this man all the way. "Tell me or I'll send you to him. The Apex. Put up a flag on the Internet, spike your position, out you as a CIA collaborator."

That woke Jalim up.

His next mad bark of laughter came out like a shout. More followed swiftly, escaping his lips like autocannon bullets, out of control and manic. Raw panic filled his eyes and he wrapped his hands across his lips to hold the sound in, but he couldn't halt the convulsions gulps.

"You'll give me to him?" he managed to gasp. "You do all this to me, take everything, and then you'll hand me over?"

Wren dropped to one knee. The playing field was shifting now in a disturbing direction. Worse than a panic attack. Jamal Jalim was on the edge of hyperventilating himself into an aneurysm.

"Tell me," he urged. "If you give me the Apex, I'll protect you. I'll fight for you like I fought for your people. You know my record. I help people like you, Jalim. The victims of the Apex. Take off the blinders and see what he's done to you. Give me what I need and we'll turn all this around."

The laughter only intensified. "Turn it around? It's over, you idiot! When he hears you came here I will be destroyed. There is no protection against what he'll do."

"What will he do?"

Jalim began shuddering violently, the impact of extreme duress mounting on his nervous system. "The human zoo," Jalim spat, and abruptly blood bubbled up from the back of his throat, worked a ropey trail down his muddy brown chin. "You never saw the zoo, did you? The real extent of his human experimentation."

Wren leaned in. "What zoo?"

Jalim laughed.

"What zoo, Jamal? I will protect you. With all the resources of my Foundation, I swear we can make you safe."

"But you can't!" Jalim cried. "Once you've seen his research, the true depths he's willing to reach, no place is safe." Mad laughter overcame him. Wren squeezed his shoulders, trying to help him ride it out as his eyes rolled and his pulse raced. "What do you even think I've been doing here, Christopher Wren?" Jalim rushed on. "All these weapons, all this training, all these pills, you think I was afraid of your government or your idiot FBI? I was protecting myself against him!"

Wren blinked. Against the Apex? "Why? What happens in the zoo, Jamal?"

Jalim's face worked between extremes, lips pulled back like a death's head, mouth flaring wide with white tension lines, eyes flashing side to side like a fox with its leg in the trap and the hunter closing in. "I saw it twice," he managed through gritted teeth, cheeks puffing. "In cities. In skyscrapers. He takes a whole floor and blocks it out, moves in his zoo."

"Skyscrapers?"

"Atlanta was the first," Jalim croaked, sucking wind hard now. "Louisville was the second. I'm never going back!"

"You mean like an office floor? Like a CIA black site?"

Jalim's laughter grew out of control. "Worse. The worst thing I ever saw! Now, I think-"

Abruptly his eyes rolled up into the back of his head, all his muscles went limp and he sagged in the chair.

Wren checked his pulse.

A high, threadbare beat. Worked himself up half to death. Wren leaned in and carefully, almost tenderly, shifted the thin man's weight onto his shoulder.

21

SURFACE

Jamal Jalim's Anaximanderians were all in the bunkbed room. Two or three to a bed, stacked tall to the ceiling like battery chickens in a wall full of hutches. The smell of them rose like the stench off a refugee camp.

The children had voided their bowels. Maybe some of the adults. Some were weeping. Some just stared at him with a thousand-yard glare. He'd broken their world. Was now carrying their Lord and Master away.

It broke Wren's heart. Now they were free, but real freedom would take years, if it ever came. The illogic of what Jalim had drummed into them for decades would butt up against the reality Wren had just unveiled and clash, maybe breaking some of them permanently.

Left alone like this they'd stay in the pumping station, maybe elect a new leader, but none of them would have Jalim's tricks. Leadership would rotate as pretenders rose and fell, until someone figured out a new set of tricks or mastered the old ones. The cult would roll on, though vastly diminished, because at this point there was nowhere left to go.

"I'm coming back," Wren said, casting his eyes over them stuffed into their bunkbed cells like animals in a zoo. "My people will come first. They're going to help you. Things have to change here. I passed your trials, so you know you can believe me. No one's taking any pills. This is a changing of the guard. I'll see you very soon."

They only stared, bereft. No words. The pills were in their pockets still. Bullets on trajectories he hoped he'd stopped, but you could never be sure.

He moved on. The speed rope hung where he'd left it. He looked up, thirty feet high into a white rush of sunlight. It felt like he'd been down here in this human cave for a whole day, when it had probably barely been an hour.

No faces peering over the top. That was fine. He moved on, tracking the schematics as he remembered them. In one of the smaller pump access rooms there was a wall-mounted ladder leading up. He climbed with some difficulty, though Jalim wasn't all that heavy, just an awkward load. At the top was a platform and a doorway leading out to the roof.

Heavily reinforced with braces and bolts. Wren unclasped them one by one then swung the door open, stepping out into the light. Fresh air hit him in a wave, tinged with the stink of the Great Salt Lake's sulfur and salt, along with the slight astringent afterbite of whatever explosive Hellion had packed into her vehicles. The light was brighter and all-consuming after the gloom of the pumping station, forcing him to blink against the glare.

In seconds they were upon him, Doona and Henry.

The smoke had cleared from blast. His team looked well.

"Boss," said Doona, "you're naked."

"And covered in mud?" Henry asked.

Wren gave a sheepish smile, shrugged the shoulder upon which Jalim lay. "The cult leader insisted. When in Rome. Tell me Mason's alive?"

"He's alive," Henry said smartly. "Already landed at Brigham City. Initial triage in the helo suggests he broke some ribs, shattered his wrist, maybe dislodged a vertebra, but he's alive. They've got him queued for a CT scan to check his skull."

"He's stable?"

"Within reason. He fell a long way."

Wren grunted. That was the best news he'd heard all day. Mason had already died on him once in the Jib-jab headquarters, and he couldn't handle it again.

"Good." He kneeled and carefully set Jalim down on the raw concrete. When he came back up Doona offered him her jacket, which he wrapped around his waist like a skirt. "Thank you."

"It's nothing. Boss, what happened in there?"

Wren paused. Looked both Doona and Henry over. Didn't know where to begin. "Stupidity. I don't even want to say it. There's probably bodies buried all around here, people who drowned on mud. It's..." he paused, reaching for words that escaped him. "Just stupid. Mud vats. Oneness with natural elements. The people below will tell you all about it. We'll hear no end of it, I'm thinking." He paused for a second, cataloguing all that he'd seen, filing it away, moving on. "Right now, I need to get up to speed. Do you have a spare earpiece? I left mine with my clothes."

"Here," Henry said, already holding out his extra. "But you may want to, um, give yourself a rinse first."

Wren stared at him a second, saw Doona was holding out a water bottle, then grunted. Tipped his head, poured into his ear until most of the residual mud was out, then inserted the earpiece and took the cell unit that paired with it. While the fuzz of reception crackled in his ear canal, he looked at Henry's wholesome, strong-chinned face and Doona's brushed, perfect complexion as, thinking thoughts he'd already tried to banish.

About the Anaximanderians. His brain making comparisons he didn't have time for now. The things he asked of his Foundation, were they anything like the demands Jamal Jalim had made? He regularly put his people at risk. It was raw good fortune that Mason had survived the fall. If he walked away from this, ever saw his Wendy again, it was no thanks to Wren. Sending them up against a suicide cult lodged in an impregnable fortress with only self-driving cavalry and rubber bullets on their side, it smacked of hubris.

Down that route led self-pity, though, and he'd seen enough of that for one day, right alongside eye-searing terror. Even with the benefit of hindsight, he couldn't see a better way through. The cult had to be cracked.

He pulled himself out of the reverie. Doona was looking at him oddly, had just spoken.

"Are you all right?" Wren figured, or something like it.

"Just distracted," Wren answered. "And thankful you were both here. Henry, if you hadn't taken out that sniper blind, and Doona if you hadn't cleared the southwest, then..." he paused. No need to say what would have happened to Mason or the rest of them. "I'm just grateful I can count on you, is all. I couldn't do this without you."

Doona nodded. Henry smiled. "We all appreciate that, Corporal. But you've got it wrong, Sir. We couldn't do this without you. This craziness, we know it's not you causing it. That's your father. Without you, I'd still want to fight it, but I wouldn't know how."

Henry extended his hand. Wren shook it.

"Now they need you down below. Babysit them please. Tell them you come from Anaximander's emissary."

"Emissary?" Doona asked.

Wren shrugged. "Ask them, if you like. It's a sweet story."

Doona cracked a smile, put a hand on his shoulder. "We will. Well done, Christopher."

He nodded sharply, turned away before he got emotional, then strode a few paces away along the metal gantry. The white salt flats spread lone and level in every direction, slit only by the white line of the pumping canal. Behind him the door clanked open, closed.

He put one hand to his ear to activate the comms line.

"Hellion?" he called. "B4cksl4cker?"

"Christopher," came B4cksl4cker's cheery Armenian baritone. "I have banished Hellion from the room, as you are far too naked for my liking. This is, what is the word, immodest? Hellion has been calling out insults since you emerged."

Wren couldn't help but roll his eyes. Of course. Turned his gaze to the sky, trying to pick out their overwatch drone.

"To your left," B4cksl4cker corrected. "Too high to see."

Wren grunted. His personal 'gods'.

"Hellion is shouting to me now, Christopher. Yes. OK. This is a question. She says you look like as if you have been making sexy time with a sewage tank. Is this the word, sexy time?"

"She's nailed it," he said. "That's exactly what happened. Me and the sewage tank made a baby, and it came out as a fifty-year-old man. His name's Jamal Jalim. I need Teddy to take custody and see what he blurts out."

B4cksl4cker chuckled. "Yes? Good. Meanwhile Hellion says you look like, hmm, she says 'stinking pond scum rolled in steaming fresh turd'. Is this the expression?"

Wren just about cracked a smile. B4cksl4cker knew damn well that wasn't any kind of expression. Bringing him back with their trademark black humor.

"Bullseye," he allowed. "Tell Hellion her English is really coming along. Now, I need a helo inbound, a direct line to Rogers, an update on the firestorm, and I need you to enter two new data points into the matrices for the Apex. It's going to snow crash your matrices."

"Snow crash?" B4cksl4cker repeated. "That is exciting, Christopher. Did your sewage child already blurt something?"

"A little. He's terrified. Claims the Apex had some kind of traveling human 'zoo', kept it in whole floors of skyscrapers. First up was Atlanta, second was Louisville. Maybe twenty years back."

"Whole floors? And what is a human zoo?"

Wren gritted his teeth, strode toward the northeast corner, where the helo would be coming from. "I think it is what it sounds like. Bad."

"Of course, this is bad. Yes. Atlanta and Louisville, this will cause a snow crash. Hellion is working. Your helo is twenty minutes out. As for Rogers and the firestorm, I will let her tell you yourself. Connecting you now."

Wren leaned against the railing, listening to the phone line ring.

22

CINCINNATI

Rogers picked up, and Wren heard first the sounds of many people bustling in the background, phones ringing, raised voices.

"Christopher," she said, sounding harried and worn down, but then who wouldn't be, facing off with the firestorm head on?

"It's me," he answered, leaning against the pumping station's railing and looking down into the canal they'd come by. "I just extricated myself from a two-bit mud cult in Utah, now it looks like we have a couple more data points to narrow down the Apex's trail."

That took Rogers a second. "Mud cult?"

Wren spat grit. "Don't ask. It was some of the dumbest nonsense I've seen. Upshot is, the Apex keeps something called a 'zoo' for humans, sounds like a roaming dungeon with past appearances in Atlanta and Louisville. He uses it as a precautionary tale to ward off other cult leaders, from what I can gather. My hackers are feeding that into their search parameters, hopefully it'll chime with the matrices and spit out another target."

He let a few seconds go by, giving her time to absorb all that. Imagined her lips pursing, dark brows drawing tight, like they did any time he presented her with an unfinished jigsaw puzzle.

"I suppose that fits," she landed on. "Your dad's behind the firestorm and all these other attacks, so it's a fair bet he always had more assets in play than just the Pyramid."

That was a blunt way to put it. Of course it was true. Wren wished he'd considered it before, that his father might have been running concurrent cults at the same time as the Pyramid. The Apex had taken all those trips away... But then Wren had done everything he could to hunt him down already. How could he-

"Wren?" came Rogers' voice, skewed with concern. "You OK?"

"I'm fine. Just don't call him my dad, OK?"

She blew out a single laugh. "Fine. Asshole, then? Cream of the goddamn wacko crop?"

That just about cracked a smile. "Better."

"Better. Good. Well, at least you have a lead, even if it's sick. All I'm hitting here are dead ends."

Wren cleared a space in his head. "Tell me."

"There's nothing to tell." Her frustration came through clean. "First off, we can't find those three guys. Shoe salesman, greeter, helper kid. They were plants, it looks like, not employed by the Mall of Cincinnati at all."

Wren cursed. "Nothing to track back?"

"We're looking, but not yet. Actors they shipped in, it seems."

That complicated things. "And Rachel Day's family?"

"We're all over them, taking Day's house apart, her Internet footprint, her phone, her family, but there's nothing. No manifesto, no secret hard drives, nothing on her social feeds other than cupcakes and grinning pictures with the kids."

Wren rubbed his forehead. Working on an oxygen deprivation headache. Crusted mud scratched free and fell the long drop to the water below.

"Work computer?"

"Every damn computer," Rogers answered. "Her mail. Her colleagues. Her husband's a sobbing mess, I could barely get him to drink a Dr. Pepper. We swept the house, ripped up the walls and floorboards, but there's no bugs, no stash, no sign of the Apex in this anywhere."

Complicated. Of course, Wren hadn't expected this to be easy. "You have her routes tracked via phone GPS?"

"The Freedom of Information request's before a judge right now, but we've already assembled most of her movements from other sources. Takeaway is that there's literally no time for her to go anywhere or meet anyone, let alone get indoctrinated. Her daily routine is rammed. She went to work, went to pick the kids up, took them to their activities and that's really it. Maybe a brief minute here or there unaccounted for, but that's traffic, red lights, the short walk from her car to her office, maybe a neighbor stops to chat once she's home. Her life is a piece of clockwork, Wren, and this dates back years! They had a holiday to San Marino last summer, five days all told, but as best as her husband can remember, he was with her all the time. Not a minute apart." She sighed. "Right now, seems every thread I pull is a short straw."

Wren considered.

"How many minutes?" he asked.

"What?"

"You said there were minutes unaccounted for. Commutes, traffic stops. We need to tally those." He paused for a moment, thinking. "We're dealing with a long-term psychological operation here, Rogers. Either she's a sleeper cell since whenever she was last properly free, maybe college, which I doubt, or her brainwashing was conducted at a glacial pace, in tiny increments, over time. Radicalization always takes repeated exposure, but not necessarily a lot of face time."

"Face time? What are you talking about?"

Wren took another breath. More mud grit in his mouth, and he swished a few pieces out with his tongue. Working through the possibilities. "We're used to thinking of cult indoctrination as this intense experience, right? Like Gruber with the Ghost, like you while Jay Durant burned by your side. You lock someone up in a box, degrade them, deprive them, and torture them into accepting a new reality. For Gruber it took three days. It didn't work with you, but I've no doubt it would have done, if it had lasted long enough. No offense meant, that kind of treatment gets everyone in the end."

Rogers was quiet.

"Even me," Wren went on. "Especially me, even. I was born into the Apex's mind control, remember? I grew up with him wiring my brain, and I'm still not right in the head."

Rogers let out a half laugh. "You can say that again."

"Happily. But the fact is, the rewiring doesn't always have to be so all-consuming. It doesn't need to be an incredibly intense experience that just lasts and lasts. Think about something like a violent mugging. How long does that last?"

Rogers took a second. "Minutes. Seconds, maybe."

"And the effect?"

A beat passed. "I see what you're getting at. One event that happens in seconds only can shape a person for the rest of their life."

"Exactly. Even more so if they dwell on it, if the emotions remain strong. Say you're mugged by a young guy with a big handlebar moustache. Stands to reason, and chimes with evolutionary thinking, that you'll get a chill whenever you see another young guy with a big moustache, even ten years later."

"OK. So, what's our point here?"

"I'm thinking," Wren said, chewing on his lip. "Look, this is just going off what you've told me. She had no spa weekends away at the cult center. There's no wild pattern of hours spent on the Internet at night, following fake facts down the rabbit hole to salvation. Assuming all this is true-"

"It is true. I know my data, Wren. There's no Internet use package like you're describing in her whole damn neighborhood."

"So take that as gospel. Also that she didn't just wake up one morning and decide to burn herself alive, perfectly choreographed with the Apex's plans. No. He got to her, and it was either before our record began, or in one of the 'lost minutes' you're describing. Intense experiences, Rogers. Play them out a couple of times, send them like depth charges blowing up her personality, and she could be shoved in any which direction he wanted."

A long silence passed. Wren watched as a helicopter emerged from the heat haze over the salt flats, black and clamoring closer. He hadn't thought through this before, but when the evidence pushed you in a given direction, there was no use resisting.

"You're saying he spoon-fed her radicalization," Rogers said. "Baby steps over months, maybe years. Kept it on the back burner, so she led her life throughout, like everything was normal?"

"Deep cover," Wren said, making sense of it as he said it. "People can partition their minds incredibly well. A young woman gets mauled by an abuser in a changing room, you'd think she'd come out crying and calling the cops, but that's not what often happens. Most times she bursts out then goes back to chatting with her friends like nothing happened. It's like the deer in the headlights. We don't know how to react in the face of such trauma, so we just don't. Afraid anything we do will just make it worse. Maybe that we were complicit somehow, brought it on ourselves. Sometimes it seems the only way to play it." He paused to game it out. "But that few seconds of abuse, the humiliation, it sets a fuse burning. We can pretend, but it still happened, and it's going to have its day in the light. It's going to hurt that woman, and everyone around her, when the bomb finally goes off."

No sound from Rogers' end. No need. He imagined her staring hard, maybe chewing her lip. Reflecting on her own experience. How what the Ghost had done to her was going to play out down the line. Wren was the perfect example for that too. He'd attacked his own family in his sleep, so deeply was the Apex's touch embedded. A bomb twenty-five years in the making.

"Right," she said. "So look at the empty spaces. The missing minutes."

"The missing minutes," Wren repeated. "Look for moments of intensity that are quickly buried. And stay in touch. I'll let you know when I have a target."

"Good," she said, but didn't ring off. "And Wren."

"Yes?"

"Good job with the mud cult. Hellion says you almost died."

He hadn't expected that. It took him aback slightly. That Hellion was saying nice things about him behind his back.

"Uh, thanks."

"Just wanted to say," she said, then rang off.

Wren was left looking at the cell phone as the helicopter pulled up.

"It is time, Christopher," B4cksl4cker said in his ear.

Yeah. Time.

23

CATCH UP

The Black Hawk touched down on the salt flats, sending sprays of crusty white whipping away like froth off breakers.

"We have the pills off most of them, Corporal," came Henry's voice in back. Wren turned. Henry looked almost apologetic. "Doona's best with them. I suppose she was brainwashed too."

Wren just stared. Trying to make the leap back from Rogers' challenge up in Cincinnati, stopping the burnings and winning back the news cycle, to his own challenge here.

Getting the evidence he needed to inject into the mainstream at just the right moment.

"That's good," he managed, flipping his partitions in order of priority.

"We saw the mud vat," Henry added, and left it hanging forlornly.

"Easy meat," Wren said.

"You could have died."

Wren barely restrained a laugh. Everyone was so worried about him dying today, when they all could have died. Mason was still on the edge. First Rogers and Hellion, now Henry, what was with his team?

"I didn't. Stay with them, Henry, make sure they're OK. Teddy's sending a transport?"

"A couple of buses will take them to get checked out in Salt Lake City, and he's chartered a jet from there."

"Back to Little Phoenix after that? The Arizona fake town?"

"Maggie's getting the place ready. It'll be a squeeze, but we've trained for this."

Had they?

He'd been out of it for too long. Just nodded. Thought, not for the first time, that he didn't deserve them. Not Henry, Teddy, any of them. They defied him plenty. Dropped him to three coins minus. Changed his Foundation around when he wasn't looking, but when it came down to the crunch they were always there.

He turned back to the railing. The Black Hawk's rotor was winding down. Must've blown salt straight into his eyes, blurring them up.

"All right," he said, and didn't look back, just climbed over the railing and jumped.

Three seconds of freefall, then he hit the canal water. Purest blue through to white floor and walls. He stayed under for maybe twenty seconds, scrubbing the dried mud off his face, out of his hair, beard, off his body. When he came up at the ladder, Henry was watching with a grin from above, Alejandro from the helo. The ex-cartel member raised both hands with all fingers splayed.

"Ten out of ten, hermano!' he shouted.

Even Alejandro? Whatever this thing was, he didn't trust it. Gave an awkward wave, strode over to the Black Hawk.

"Hellion says she likes you better in mud," said B4cksl4cker in his ear.

He ignored it. "I need the catchup on everything. Where we're at on the firestorm, estimating the RQ, Humphreys' position on lockdown, and how Jamal Jalim's info is playing into the matrices."

"And some clothes?" B4cksl4cker prompted as Wren climbed up into the Black Hawk with only Doona's jacket flapping around his waist.

"I brought a spare set," Wren said, went straight to one of the wall storage lockers as the door slid closed behind him and the helo lifted off. Already half dry from the heat of the sun, he toweled off vigorously with a hand towel then pulled on a full set of tactical black gear.

Sat down.

There was bloody gauze on the floor. Mason's, he figured.

"Christopher," came Hellion's voice. "Please wear your bodycam."

He fished in a gear box, came up with another cam and slipped the chest strap on. "What do you have for me?"

"Besides jokes? Christopher, I was starting to think you were addicted to mud."

"What?"

"It is OK, you're clean now."

He didn't know whether to groan or snap at her to be serious. He settled on, "No."

"Did you hear about the coffee that tastes like mud?"

He gritted his teeth. "Hellion…"

"It was fresh ground."

"Stop it."

"Then there was the man who raced with a pile of mud."

"Hellion, I'm warning you-"

"The mud won by a landslide."

"B4cksl4cker!"

There was a rustling sound before B4cksl4cker's deep voice took up the comms link.

"Apologies, Christopher. She is sneaky. It is just you and I now. You wanted a full update, yes?"

Wren felt suddenly exhausted. "Please."

"You shall have it. Humphreys has not yet instituted a lockdown, though there have now been seven burnings. The first five you know. The most recent two, all women, all with children similarly aged to yours, one died in front of a preschool and the other ran out onto the field of an NFL game, New England Patriots vs. the Miami Dolphins."

Wren's eyes flared. "You're serious?"

"Yes. I was surprised too, but the Dolphins are having a phenomenal season, I think-"

Wren sighed. "B4cksl4cker. I don't care who played. Tell me about the coverage of that game."

"Of course, Christopher, it was most impressive, carried live to some three million viewers. They cut the line after she caught fire, of course, but many people were already filming on their phones." A second passed. "The woman ran onto the field while she was on fire. It is…" he paused, "disturbing viewing. Many have seen it. This was ten minutes ago."

Wren didn't know what to say. He felt anger and disgust. Anger at Jamil for wasting his time, anger at himself for taking so long.

"And you let Hellion waste time telling jokes? B4cksl4cker, I-"

"Do you think he 'lets' me do anything, Christopher?" Hellion burst in suddenly. "Do not be ridiculous. You were the one playing in the mud, while we have broken processing records and enlisted a botnet like nothing before. You should be thanking us!"

Wren bit back an angry retort. Swallowed it. She wasn't wrong. "Thank you."

"That is better. Now, I have another excellent joke on the topic of-"

Her line was cut.

"As I was saying," B4cksl4cker continued, "by any measure it seems the RQ is rising. Your television pundits are shouting in each other's faces. Your people are running for their homes. It appears a lockdown will be self-imposed before your current President enforces it. Nobody wishes to have this happen near them. To have their children witness it."

"It's horrific."

"It is. Now, more disturbing than this is David Keller. Of course, he is speaking at every chance he can. He is channeling both fear and rage very adeptly, Christopher. He is not President yet, but it seems your military are listening to him. They are not taking to the streets, but we are seeing mobilizations in bases, logistics being prepared to shutter the country. Worse still, he is attempting to pin all this on you."

They always did. That was nothing new.

"What's he saying?"

"He is claiming you lied to him and to the people. The 'largest con in American history', he is calling it. He got down on his knees and apologized for calling you a hero. Now he says you and your Foundation must be behind the firestorm."

Wren's fists tightened. Of course Keller would get on his knees again. The people would love that.

"And my family?"

"Secure. Teddy arranged their rapid exit from the safehouse an hour ago. I know we were not supposed to move them, but Teddy approached and they agreed. We have a training facility three hundred miles north, and we are flooding forces there. They will be safe."

Wren's heart skipped a beat. Even thinking about Loralei and the kids mixed up in this terrified him. The possibility that maybe he could talk to them, attempt to reassure them, only made his heart flutter harder, though he knew that wasn't going to happen. He'd promised Rogers, and wasn't about to break faith with her again so soon.

"And the matrices?"

"The matrices, Christopher, are unanimous. Patterns appeared the instant you gave us those details. We know where your father's zoo is currently, at least within a ten-block radius, and we are narrowing that every moment."

"Where?"

B4cksl4cker paused a moment as if for effect.

"New York."

24

CHRYSOGONUS

In the middle of the night little Christopher Wren, then known as Pequeño 3 and probably 8 years old at the time, woke to a rough hand clamped across his mouth. His eyes flashed open, though he knew better than to struggle or lash out. A lesson learned from long experience. It wasn't the first time this had happened.

Instead he adjusted silently and still, gazing at the dark figure looming over him, set against the dark cabin walls of the Pequeño dormitory, a lean-to structure cramped behind the fake town's Bank façade.

"Speak a word and pay in eternity," came the low rasp from his captor. One of the Apex's favored expressions, though this was not the Apex's familiar gravel voice. Pequeño 3 only stared mutely, taking in details: the gleam of those angry eyes catching moonlight spilled through the open windows; the coarse weave of that brown burlap jacket; the beginning wisps of a beard curling down his pointed chin.

Chrysogonus.

Second eldest of the Apex's children, Chrysogonus-With-Bared-Arm, a tall young man of fifteen summers and sudden, fierce angers. A brute and a bully, he was the closest acolyte to their father in all things. When the Apex tarred-and-feathered Pyramid members in the fake town's Main Street, Chrysogonus rolled the younger Pequeños in mud and cactus spines until they begged for mercy. When the Apex parboiled people in the steaming vats until they begged for more,

Chrysogonus dunked his younger siblings in the rain barrel until they went limp.

Now back from his latest trip with the Apex.

Pequeño 3's heart raced.

The Apex took all his children with him on his many trips away. Whenever Pequeño 3's turn came it was to dance, caper and smile for small crowds at dusty intersections in one horse towns, at red lights where families watched from the safety of their trucks, at the borders of the desert where the mall's private security no longer held sway.

His comical antics served to draw nurturing gazes from the womenfolk and make the men feel protective, to show his white teeth and rude, healthy skin, to display his intellect by reciting proverbs from the Apex's amended Bible, to juggle and sing enough to draw new converts in.

Pequeño 3 did not think Chrysogonus took the same kind of trips. In the last months he'd been gone more often. Come back later each time, becoming crueler still. He'd taken to enlisting Tomothy-Whereof-The-Giants-Roam in his torments. Tomothy was a near-silent Pequeño boy of twelve summers who watched everything with sallow dark eyes. Rumors abounded in the fake town about the tribulations he'd endured as a baby in the cages.

Tomothy did whatever Chrysogonus ordered. Sand blown in Pequeño 3's eyes dozens of times in a row as a measure of his faith. An hour spent tapping his finger on the top of Pequeño 3's skull, continuing until the gentle touch became a thumping migraine raging in a rainbow of colors.

For the last three days Pequeño 3 and the rest of the younger children had breathed easier with both the Apex and Chrysogonus away. The fake town's regimen wore on and they all carried out their meaningless tasks recording the Apex's 'essential barometers', like the number of clouds crossing in the sky or the number of jackrabbits visiting the dry creek, but the terrifying, enlivening volatility was gone.

Now Chrysogonus dragged Pequeño 3 to his feet in the mud-shaded dorm room. The younger boy felt the eyes of his brothers and sisters from their beds swinging toward him. Zachariah-Of-The-Marsh in his bunk above Gabriel-In-Extremis. Galicia-In-Her-Mother's-Heart, the eldest of them all, in her cot by the door. The younger Pequeños 4, 5 and 6 laid in their cribs.

Pequeño 3 felt their fear like warmth radiating from a hot desert stone at night. Holding their breath, glad it wasn't them. He briefly held Galicia's sparkling eyes before she turned away.

All of them feared what Chrysogonus was becoming.

The larger boy pulled him by the wrist between the narrow cots, out through the creaking wooden door and onto the moonlit barrens of Main Street. Tiny dunes stippled his bare feet with cold sand, blown by the wind. It was a fall night, the sky so black it was purple, irradiated with peephole stars.

"This way, if you mean to prosper," Chrysogonus said, then let go of Pequeño 3's wrist and set off at a steady lope.

Pequeño 3 followed. There was no other choice.

The moon hung high and fat overhead, casting ghostly shadows off the fake town's wooden façades. The Saloon. The Inn. Together they left the Pyramid behind and ran into the wilds of the Sonoran Desert, soon surrounded by squatting ball cacti, the whispering heads of ocotillo fronds, towering agave watching in the silvery light. It was the same route to the red creek, where he'd recently discovered that the clay mud and the trickle of water melded into perfect mud pies.

Those happy days splashing alone in the mud, making pies in flavors fueled by his imagination, seemed very far away now.

Ten minutes passed as they ran, maybe twenty. Pequeño 3 was comfortable running in the night sand, born into the dusts, though he feared their destination. Far out of earshot into the wild, alone with his vicious brother. His mind danced across a hundred different cruelties but he said no words of protest, attempted no effort to flee. Whatever was about to happen, there was nothing he could do but endure it. Fear was a portal, the Apex always said. Pain was a doorway.

In perhaps thirty minutes they stopped. Neither of them panting, as if they'd taken no more than a short walk. It was a small clearing surrounded by lush palo verde, their usually bright yellow leaves mottled a monochrome gray in the dark, overshadowed by the imposing skeleton of a dead Joshua tree, its swollen fists stark against the starstruck sky.

Chrysogonus took a few paces forward. There was a rustle ahead. Perhaps a Desert Cottontail taking flight? Pequeño 3 advanced, widening his eyes to better see into the shadows. More rustling. Chrysogonus stepped to the side, and Pequeño 3 saw what it was.

Hog-tied on the ground, a cotton gag biting into his sunken cheeks, flinching like a snare-caught skunk pig. A gash on the side of his head glistened as black and glistening as motor oil. White teeth and white eyes blaring, but unable to do anything more than grunt and moan like an animal.

Tomothy-Whereof-The-Giants-Roam.

"Here," Chrysogonus said. His voice barely above a whisper, his pupils bloated wide in the dark. "Now. Supremacy will be decided."

He tossed something. It struck the rucked sand between the three of them, glinting sharply in the light. It took Pequeño 3 long moments to realize what it was.

"Only one of you returns to the Pyramid this night," Chrysogonus intoned. "Or none at all. Be this as it may. Let it begin."

Pequeño 3 stared at the knife. Tomothy stared wider. Barely able to do more than inch across the sand.

Pequeño 3 did not need to think. He slaughtered desert animals all the time. Tasted their hot blood. He'd killed a hundred different things in his days and nights in the wild. He took two steps forward and swept up the knife.

Two steps more carried him to Tomothy. The older boy kicked desperately at the sand, thrashing like a hawkmoth caterpillar in the beak of a cactus wren, throwing up sprays of surface crust but making little movement backward. His dull eyes shone with terror and a guttural wail poured from his bound lips.

Pequeño 3 raised the knife, the decision ricocheting through his mind and coming up clear. The only way through. Despite, or perhaps because of, everything he'd been through, he understood what it meant to survive. To really survive.

He brought the blade down and spun at the same time, a move he'd trained in the wild for bringing down coyotes. Left heel planted, toes pushing off the sand as his hips led the turn, right leg arcing wide and landing to snap his weight sharply, channeling the momentum up his small, wiry body like a whipcrack into his arm, flicking his elbow into a backhand release like he was driving a hammerhead down on a nail.

The knife plucked free at the apex of the turn, shot through the night air end over end toward the boy who'd tortured him every day of his life.

Chrysogonus.

It struck, sank into the older boy's shoulder and then Pequeño 3 was running. A leap over Tomothy and he plunged into the boughs of palo verde, leaves and branches rasping off his face, bare feet stamping into the root-hardened sand.

A great cry erupted from behind and it powered Pequeño 3 onward like a rocket launch. Feet stamping at a frantic pace on the dark sand, cutting paths with his mind milliseconds before his body rushed through: a thick mass of spiny cholla heads rose here and he swerved left; creeping buckhorn tangled there and he ducked underneath, raking their spiny, spindly arms hot across his back. His heart cascaded and his lungs pumped as for the first time in his life he truly defied the Pyramid.

Always he'd cowered. Fled. Hunkered down. Done as the Apex wished of him and what Chrysogonus wanted and what his elders demanded, until he had no sense of what he even wanted himself. It didn't matter. That was the Pyramid reality. That was how you survived.

But killing his own brother?

That wasn't survival.

As he sprinted for his life, he thought of the red creek. Adventuring one day in the desert far from the fake town, camping overnight while the Apex was away, he'd found a spindly sandstone mesa stretching back in a spiky ridge, and been overcome with awe. A puddle of spring water at the base. A place to climb, and play, and make mud pies all for himself. It was beautiful, but the beauty wasn't what moved him so deeply. What moved him was how there was no sign of the Apex there at all.

The Apex didn't control it. Probably he didn't even know about it. It belonged to Pequeño 3 alone.

Realizing that had reshaped the world and offered an unconscious choice he'd never been aware of before. That there might be something beyond the Apex and his cruelty. His demands. Finally now, plunging through the Sonoran desert and scattering before him dark-chevroned kingsnakes, barking red-spotted toads, ground squirrels and sidewinders, he glimpsed what this new choice meant.

Death if he was caught.

But in that moment he didn't care. Instead of terror this new certainty suffused him with a strange and brimming lightness. As he fled his brother he envisaged a world like the red creek, with no more fear of his father's tempestuous moods, no more struggling to comprehend acts of violence that defied comprehension. Maybe for the first time in his life he felt joy and a sense that something like justice could be done.

He'd glimpsed it in Chrysogonus' widening eyes as the knife buried home, a sense that there were other ways to be.

Now the stars hung like a million lanterns lighting his way, guiding him back toward his red rock creek. His small feet punched the earth hard, eyes fixed ahead and dreaming of making mud pies all day, hunting Gila monsters, bark scorpions and collared lizards to roast for every meal, drinking the lush muddy water and growing strong enough until one day he could return to the fake town and put a knife in the Apex himself.

He didn't hear the sound coming from behind until it was too late. The body that struck him in a full tackle weighed twice his own and pummeled him flat to the sand.

There was no time to raise his hands before him. His chest smacked into the earth with a lung-emptying burst, his face hit hard and bounced, then he was yanked onto his back to stare up at the rage-twisted face of his older brother, Chrysogonus, clutching the knife in his hand.

25

CITATION X

Christopher Wren jerked awake with a start, momentarily back in the desert surrounded by the heaving dark, the weight of Chrysogonus crushing his chest, the rust taste of his own blood filling his mouth.

He took a breath and sat upright. Low lights picked out the contours of the jet's eight-seater cabin. From Utah to New York was two thousand miles, clocking in at around three hours flight time in a Cessna Citation X.

He hadn't meant to sleep. He turned, looked out the window and saw a dark floor of clouds below. At fifty thousand feet there wasn't much else to see.

Wren rubbed his dry lips and gritty eyes, pulled his phone from his pocket. 3 a.m.. Thirteen hours since this whole thing began at the Sonora Desert black site. Four hours since he'd left the pumping station behind, transferred to Salt Lake International and boarded the Citation X.

He flicked the overhead button for light and a private beam switched on. Noticed his hands were shaking. There were dark half-moons under his fingernails, leftover mud from Jalim's vat. He pulled his fingers tight into fists but the shaking continued.

Thoughts of Chrysogonus. He squeezed harder, trying to bull through the unwelcome memories. Not something he'd thought about for many years. How his big brother had held him there. Bringing the knife down. One hand unconsciously went to his shoulder, a mirror to the wound he'd dealt

Chrysogonus. His fingers worked beneath the taut black fabric of the strike suit and found the scar.

Dig a blade into the clavicle gap of an eight year old, and the mark remained forever, expanding as he'd grown. His own children had laughed in the pool on holiday in a California hotel, pointing out the various marks that spotted his body. His daughter Quinn had been seven at the time.

He pulled his fingers away, shaking still.

Jamal Jalim had brought this on.

That much was obvious. Talking about the Apex's trips, hinting at other cults he might have run. His influence still reaching out from the shadows of a past nearly three decades gone. Now embedded in New York.

The thought sent shivers down Wren's spine. He'd lived in New York since the birth of his first child. Even now he remembered the moment Loralei had handed tiny baby Quinn into his arms, wrapped up in white, so beautiful. Now even that golden moment was poisoned by the Apex's touch; he'd been there the whole time, watching on from his 'lab'.

Wren stabbed a button on the armrest, opening a channel to the cockpit.

"How long until we arrive?"

"Good morning, Sir," came the clipped, professional voice of the pilot. "We are forty-five minutes out from LaGuardia. Would you like a breakfast service?"

Wren grimaced. He'd never liked being served. As if on cue, though, a grumble came from his stomach. "Yes, thank you. Two of whatever you've got, the greasier, the better."

"Coming right up."

The line crackled away, replaced by a shuffling sound from the front. Private pilot, pilot air host. A strong-built man in white shirt and black tie began opening small metal closets in the narrow galley, pulling out trays and assembling Wren's meal.

Wren pushed off the seat arms and stood. His legs trembled slightly. In the cup holder next to him he found a bottle of water and knocked it back in three long gulps, washing away the gritty mud taste.

He walked up the cabin to the front, where the host was preparing his meal. He smiled on Wren's approach.

"Good morning, Sir. Would you like some coffee?"

Wren didn't. Didn't really know why he'd walked to the head of the plane, other than some odd imperative brought on by the dream. A desire to reconnect with something real, something not owned or overseen by the Apex.

"Sure," he answered.

The man smiled. "Milk, cream, sugar?"

"Black," Wren said, then turned to go back to his seat. Sit down, bring out his phone, plunge back into the firestorm.

Except he wasn't ready.

"Bad dreams," he said instead, turning back.

The host nodded, smiled, slit open a single serving packet of fresh-ground beans. "I saw your tattoo. You're a Marine. Semper Fi."

Wren hadn't expected that. But the guy's build, his quiet confidence, it made sense. "You too?"

"Bosnia," the man said, tamping coffee into the stainless steel handle of the Delonghi filter with all the precision of a DELTA field-stripping a Beretta M9. "Political oversight, we were called. Clearing out jihadis. You?"

"All over," Wren answered. Not sure why he was saying so much. "Afghanistan. Syria. Iraq. Operations on home soil too."

The man gave a low whistle.

Wren knew he should stop. Not out of obeying some Official Secrets Act bullshit, but because this guy didn't need to be burdened with all that.

"Good material for nightmares," the guy said as he latched the filter arm into place, placed an elegant bone china cup beneath the drip nozzle. "I have plenty of my own, too."

Wren smiled. The guy pulled a lever and the machine forced steam into the handle with a loud, comforting hiss. "This one's from earlier," Wren said. "Before I was a Marine."

The guy just nodded knowingly, detached the arm and knocked the spent grounds firmly into a waste box. "From before. I get that."

He handed the coffee to Wren. Wren took it. Worried for a moment his shaking hands would spill the liquid, but they'd quietened some. He took a sip.

"Strong," he said.

The guy smiled, turned to fixing Wren a plate. Microwaves and ovens pinged around them in the tight space, and the host opened one then another with clockwork precision, spooning out two small trays of steaming sausages, two cups of baked beans, crispy mushrooms, French bread. When the plate was done and fully loaded, he held it up. Opened his mouth to speak, said nothing, then spoke anyway.

"I knew it was you," he said. Wren took the plate. "The moment you boarded. You're famous. I just want to say-"

"You don't have to say anything," Wren said swiftly. Starting to regret this now. For the moment he'd forgotten who he was, what that meant. Christopher Wren, the guy who'd raced across LA in a monster truck, who'd become the face of some kind of nationwide social movement, now tied permanently to the fate of David Keller, President-elect.

"Maybe not," the guy went on, leaning into the decision, "and you could get me fired for stepping out of line, sure, though I do like this job. It brings me peace, being up here, away from people. But I want to say it anyway. What you did for this country, that's something to be proud of." He paused. "It makes up for a lot. Bad things from the past. Nightmares." Another pause. "I'm still paying down my debts. Maybe one day I'll be clear. Until then..." he trailed off with a smile.

Wren didn't know what to say. Was this what he'd come to the front hoping for? He wasn't sure. Felt his hands beginning to shake again. Coffee trembling. The plate quivering.

"Here," the guy said, and took them both. "Let me help."

Wren headed back to his seat. The guy put the tray table down for him, set the coffee just there, the plate of food in front.

"Thank you," the guy said. "Really, that's what I wanted to say. Everyone's human."

Wren tried to say something, but it was hard. He felt Chrysogonus' touch in his shoulder even now, the blade slipping in. He saw the all-consuming terror in Jamal Jalim's eyes as he whispered the word 'lab'. Something the Apex had been doing all along, far worse than anything Wren knew about.

Something in New York.

"Semper Fi," the air host said. "Enjoy your meal."

Wren couldn't say anything, just nodded mutely. Always it was kindness that got you worst.

26

TOMOTHY

With every mouthful the old memories came more easily, pulled free like guts from a butchered hog, trailing long white strands of mesentery tissue. Wren only needed to close his eyes and he was back in the desert with Chrysogonus leaning in, hot breath in his face as the blade pushed into his shoulder.

He flinched against the cold metal, tried to pull back as it pushed through the skin and muscle, but he didn't give Chrysogonus the satisfaction of hearing him scream.

"Good," his brother whispered. "Keep playing these childish games. Let's see how well that fares for you."

He slapped Pequeño 3 once, twice, three times, so that the stars above spun like a top and the pain shifted from his shoulder to his head, then Chrysogonus stood and dragged him up too. The blade jutted from his shoulder. Hot blood ran down his side, soaking into his thin pajamas.

"Back," Chrysogonus said, and shoved Pequeño 3 ahead almost hard enough to send him to the sand, but he staggered and managed to keep his balance.

"Run," Chrysogonus shouted. "As if your life depends on it."

He ran. There was no choice. Chrysogonus ran behind him, inches away, the stamp of his footfalls doubling atop Pequeño 3's pulse. A shove came as they sped over a bed of desiccated organ pipe cacti laid across the path like ostrich necks. Another push came as he half-sprang over a burrow of collared lizards, almost knocking him over, but again he held to his feet.

The run back lasted longer than the run out, panting and dizzy with blood loss, but finally they reached the clearing overhung by the dead Joshua tree, looming now like a prize pugilist above a conquered opponent.

Tomothy lay where they'd left him, wriggling in a trough of churned sand and stinking of urine. Pequeño 3 would have dropped by his side, but Chrysogonus' steely grip held him up, spun him around and yanked the knife out of his shoulder.

The sucking sensation was nauseating. Blood followed, and he would have sagged to his knees if the bigger boy wasn't holding him up, waving the stiletto blade before his eyes. The world narrowed down to its bloody, glinting tip.

"Faith without works are as seed cast upon stony ground," Chrysogonus intoned, low and raspy. Pequeño 3 saw the dark stains down his brother's tunic. Weak himself with blood loss. If he could only…

Chrysogonus read his calculating eyes and punched him square in the face. Once, twice, three times. The skin crushing against bone. His nose crumpling. More dizziness, and now he was being shaken. Forced to his knees, focusing on the knife that was now in his hand, wrapped there by Chrysogonus, and on Tomothy beyond.

"Prove your faith through works," Chrysogonus hissed in his ear, holding his head in a one-handed vice, balling his fist with the other. "Take from him as you would take from me. An eye for an eye."

It wasn't his hand leading the blade, but it was his hand holding the knife as it inched closer to Tomothy.

On the Cessna Wren stared at his half-eaten plate of food, child-sized knife and fork in his hands. Beans. Sausages. It was easy to make excuses thirty years later, blame it all away, but childhood memories shaped you no matter how you tried to erase them. The bodies always rose up to the surface.

Not an eye, then. Not to begin with.

Guided by Chrysogonus, the blade drew patterns across Tomothy's cheeks, pulling pathetic cries. At some point Pequeño 3 was no longer certain what works were his and which were his brother's, couldn't tell if his fierce grip on the blade grew from his own strength or another's.

Faith without works. Fear was a portal. Pain was a doorway. Time distended, expanding and shrinking to the moment. All his life there'd been pain, for as long as he could remember. His every waking moment in the

Pyramid had been an experimentation with the limits of pain, whether physical, psychological, emotional or spiritual. Together he, Chrysogonus and Tomothy explored those limits in the moonlight. Opening the portal wider.

"Now take him through," Chrysogonus whispered in Pequeño 3's ear, and the words conducted through his body like a lightning shock. Snapped him back to the twelve year old boy gurgling before him and he struggled to beg.

"I-" Pequeño 3 began, but Chrysogonus only squeezed his throat.

"No words. No thoughts. Only blinding, beautiful faith."

Only blinding, beautiful faith. He tried. He looked into Tomothy's eyes and willed his brother to understand. Maybe pain was a portal. Maybe a better world lay beyond. He leaned in with the blade held out, gliding toward the fallen boy's staring eye.

Then the world shifted like a flash flood swept across the desert plains.

One moment his world was bounded by Chrysogonus' arms and will, the next it was not. There was a sound, a wrenching scream, and little Pequeño 3 spun to see a savior he'd never expected.

The Apex. Their father. Holding Chrysogonus by the throat, lifting him high in the moonlight. Legs kicking. As Pequeño 3 watched, the Apex flung piston-like punches into Chrysogonus' core. Ribs cracked beneath his fist, nowhere to run. Chrysogonus' stomach thudded like an old leather sack. His head snapped back.

Still the Apex punched, beating Chrysogonus like he was iron to be forged, pummeling in damage like Pequeño 3 had never seen before, still striking as the older boy sagged unconscious, arms limp, head rocking. Causing deep damage. Remaking the boy into something new.

At last the Apex laid him down, almost tenderly, then stood there breathing like he was bending the world with his intent. Powerful and tall, blue eyes blazing in the first glow of dawn from the east.

"Pequeño 3," he said, as calmly as if they were greeting each other at the water butt. "Tomothy."

Pequeño 3 did not know what to say.

"Will you now finish the work?" the Apex asked, his deep voice splitting the night like thunder. He nodded toward the blood on Pequeño 3's hands and arms. "A bad workman leaves the job incomplete."

Pequeño 3 only stared, still stunned by the incredible force his father had unleashed. He'd seen the Apex wield ritualized violence before: the scourge, the lash, the pits and the vats and the cages, but never like this. With such passion in his eyes.

"Child, I asked you a question," the Apex repeated, and it jolted him harder than one of Chrysogonus' slaps. He looked down at his older brother laid flat on the desert sand. Chest barely rising and falling. Face crushed. Blood oozing from his cheeks. Seconds ago he'd owned every part of Pequeño 3, and now…

"I-"

The Apex followed Pequeño 3's gaze to Chrysogonus, seeming to make some connection.

"You need not fear for him. Our Chrysogonus is fated for great things, just as you and all my progeny are, though his discipline must be sharpened. He seeks to take things for himself that belong to me."

Pequeño 3 did not know what to do. Breaths came hard. Of all the horrors he'd seen this was by far the worst, so when the Apex took a step toward him he flinched, though there was no violence as he kneeled beside Pequeño 3. There were no blows. Instead he wrapped the child's small, cold body in his warm arms and held him for a moment, head beside his ear, whispering gently as his hand found the blade and pressed it back into Pequeño 3's grip.

"Here," he said gently. "We will do the work together."

The blade moved forward inexorably. Tomothy stared as the point touched his chest. Pequeño 3 tried to pull away but the Apex's grip was a vise, steering his head so he could not look away. He felt the gristle as the knife slipped its way through Tomothy's rib cage inward until it touched his heart.

"See," the Apex urged softly by Pequeño 3's ear, "look into his eyes, my brave boy. See the wonder!"

Tomothy's eyes widened. In their terrified depths Pequeño 3 thought that perhaps he glimpsed something. Something beautiful, or terrible, or maybe both. Relief. Acceptance.

Faith.

Then he was gone. His blood spilled out, his breathing halted and his head sagged onto the sand.

The Apex pulled away. His warmth departed, and Pequeño 3 was left cold and alone, looking up.

"Faith," the Apex said. Hammering this moment home with words, standing there as powerful as a column of sandstone rock in the desert's dawn glow. "Works." Then he flashed a grin, white teeth dazzling in the gloam. "This day your brother walks in the fire, little Pequeño 3. It is a time to rejoice. Come join the celebrations."

He winked, held out his hand, but Pequeño 3 didn't budge. Did not know what any of it meant.

"Up and at them, son," the Apex said cheerily. "Those essential barometers are not going to count themselves."

Son.

On the plane Wren gritted his teeth as the true depths of the memory came back to him. Taking his father's hand. Returning to the fake town, chastened in ways it would take him years to comprehend. One brother lost beneath his own hand, with celebrations to follow.

Now that old pain transmuted as he finished up his plate. Remembering the Apex's touch and how he'd hungered for more. The greatest lie of them all, just enough love to fuel a lifetime of rage.

27

NEW YORK

The Cessna Citation dropped through dark clouds into an abyss of night over New York. Soaring buildings glittered yellow like the eighth circle of hell, millions of sinners and saints stacked atop Manhattan's volcanic bedrock, spewed up millennia past.

Wren's fists squeezed the seat rests hard as he gazed through the window, seeing only loss written across the glass, steel and concrete of the city. Last time he'd come here it was in the hope of reuniting with his family. By then he'd handed the Pinocchios off to Humphreys and closed out the Reparations, had approached his old family apartment in Great Kills, Staten Island on foot with his pulse booming in his ears, dreaming of seeing his children, Jake and Quinn, of holding his wife Loralei in his arms, of maybe being forgiven.

But they hadn't been there, and there was no forgiveness. When Rogers sprang her trap and brought the black bag down over his head, part of him had been relieved. It was finally over.

It was never over.

The Citation swept over the mouth of Hudson Bay, circling the Freedom Tower like a spoke around the world's hub. Looking out at the countless skyscrapers grasping for the sky, it seemed obvious that his father would have a presence in Manhattan. Sutured to the mainland by twenty-one bridges and fifteen tunnels, the island was a Frankinstein-like creation, home to the greatest, sickest examples of humankind.

Capital of the world. A fitting place for the Apex to keep his human zoo.

"We'll be landing in five minutes," the pilot said over the PA system.

Wren brought up his phone, swiftly scrolling the news. Hours since he'd last checked in, but there was nothing he hadn't anticipated. More young mothers had burned themselves alive in public places, even one in New York on 5th Avenue two hours back. He tapped into social media and felt the RQ level rising through the firehose of panic-laced posts. People couldn't sleep, glued to updates as the grisly ritual of burnings marched on into the night. On track to become the worst terror attack on American soil since 9/11.

The only steadfast voice through it all was David Keller. Click anywhere and you could see him standing strong and promising to bring these attacks to heel, his powerful message easily overriding the two lackluster appearances the lame duck President had made.

Wren grunted and clicked through to his darknet, where a map of Manhattan awaited him, highlighted with yellow squares. In the last five hours Hellion and B4cksl4cker had narrowed the zoo's target zone significantly to 'Billionaire's Row'; a patchwork crop of luxury skyscrapers recently erected along 57th Street in Midtown, just south of Central Park.

As the Cessna descended over Brooklyn for the La Guardia approach, Wren slotted his earpiece back in and dialed his hacker collective.

"Christopher," came B4cksl4cker's deep voice. He sounded tired. "It is morning here. Hellion is sleeping. Tell me, have you rested?"

"I caught a few hours," Wren said. "I'm five minutes from LaGuardia, maybe thirty minutes out from Midtown. Tell me how certain you are about these target locations."

"That the zoo is contained within one of them?" B4cksl4cker asked. "Absolute certainty, Christopher, if such a place exists. We have found no records for your Apex, as you know, but all of these structures slot into our matrices perfectly. He could have been to any of these multiple times and we would not know for sure, but construction and purchase records align with his ghost imprint in the world. They all have private access, the means to ship his 'exhibits' in unseen, secret mezzanine and mechanical floors where a dungeon could be kept."

Wren shuddered at the terms 'dungeon' and 'exhibits', swiping through a few of the buildings in the list. They were all relatively new build residential skyscrapers, pencil-slender and ultra-luxurious, with penthouses in the upper floors going for hundreds of millions. Central Park Place. 57E57. 231 Madison Avenue. Home to hedge fund managers, Saudi oil magnates, tech moguls and Russian oligarchs seeking a money laundering sink.

"This is millions of square feet," he said. "Hundreds of floors. Thousands of apartments."

"Yes," said B4cksl4cker.

"You can't narrow it any further?"

"Nyet, Christopher. Our ghost algorithm has shorted the botnet's processing capacity twice already, looking for hairsbreadth patterns. We have been causing rolling brownouts across various Slavic nations, the lower 48 and in particular Armenia."

Wren blinked. "What?"

B4cksl4cker sighed. "Hellion is angry at me because I cut her off in our last conversation, or perhaps because I did not laugh at her funny jokes, so she has been targeting my mother country."

Wren grunted, dismissed it as more hacker nonsense and went back to swiping through buildings. Two45. 200 West 57th Street. The Millennium Center. So many.

"Then I'm on my own."

"I am in your ear. But, yes. All the data that can be hacked and processed, we have hacked and processed it. Beyond this, we leave it to you."

Wren gritted his teeth, scrolled back to the map of Manhattan highlighted with yellow. Too many locations. No way he could investigate all of them. Each tower comprised of hundreds of private residences fifty-plus stories in the air, encircled with security and accessible only via card-locked elevators. He might get Humphreys' support for an anti-terror raid on one or even two, but without hard proof on breach he'd never be able to crack open another. If he used other means, whether subterfuge, phishing or stealth tactics, he'd do well to see even a handful before David Keller was sworn in on the White House lawn.

His knuckles whitened tighter on the seat rests. No way to brute force it. He could be standing on 5th Avenue no more than a thousand yards from the 'lab' with no way in hell to pick it out.

He needed a way to narrow it down more.

"Thanks, B4cksl4cker. Get some sleep."

"I will be here, Christopher. What will you do?"

Now the Cessna was sinking fast over Queens. Out the window Wren caught a glimpse of Calvary Cemetery, a dark oblong in the midst of a grid of streetlamps, rushing up toward him.

"Resurrect the dead," he said, and tapped the line shut.

28

THE DEAD

Wren hated Manhattan.

Not just because it reminded him of his family. Of that night when he'd come back to himself in a terrified panic, panting with a gun in his hand and the stunned faces of his children staring back at him, his wife screaming at him to get out.

No.

He'd always hated the overwhelming mass of people. There were just too many. Too much money. Too much noise and grime and achievement built atop human blood, sweat and bones. He was a child of the desert, raised in the wilderness, and though he'd adapted to other cities over the years, he'd never gotten used to Manhattan.

Riding in his taxi from LaGuardia along Northern Boulevard toward the Queensboro Bridge across the East River, he felt that old sense of unease swelling on all sides.

Manhattan wasn't like the other boroughs. Not like the other cities. As if the weight of humanity crushed on top of each other in cage-like apartments and offices thickened reality like a pestilence, hanging in the air and sucking everything around it in for fuel.

Money. Souls. Decency.

It was a prison for ambition. Skyscrapers rising like fortress walls. Dreams baked into the infrastructure. If you could make it there, you could make it anywhere, so why would you ever want to leave?

Chicago or Atlanta or LA or Minneapolis, there were myriad ways out, visible lines leading out to the sky, to the horizon, to some sense of the world lying beyond. But not in Manhattan. Whole lives were conceived, bounded and snuffed out within its borders.

Wren had dark memories of an undercover sting on a human trafficking group shipping Vietnamese children in, thirteen years back. He'd thought he'd seen bad things back then, having come from the Pyramid.

He'd been wrong.

Either side of the cab the low battlements of Queens bled away as Astoria Park spread her dark arms and the support columns of the Queensboro Bridge rose up in verdigris-green. Dark sky, no stars, only the salt-fogged lights of Manhattan's eastern wall of buildings forming scattershot constellations.

Wren brought up his phone.

McKenzie Slade. He hadn't spoken to her for thirteen years. Not since the Vietnam trafficking operation had collapsed in on itself, as Wren systematically blew out its supporting columns of money. Not since they'd both stood at the entrance to an off-dock Brooklyn storage yard stacked ten high with thousands of twenty-foot shipping containers, knowing full well dozens of children were trapped in one of them, and not knowing which.

No idea. He'd been hasty back then. Blown the support struts of the operation too quickly, burning through middlemen in his rush to reach the kids in time. Back then he'd thought top dogs had to know the locations of all their cargo. There'd be records. A track back.

There'd been no track.

The East River flew by. Wren made the call. It rang exactly seven times before she answered.

"Slade," she said.

She sounded the same. 3:40 a.m., and maybe she'd been sleeping, maybe not. Strict as a slide rule, hard as graphite slate, she'd never been impressed with his past or his pedigree in the CIA. A redhead, even at 5' 3" she was all lanky angles, performing the Escherian trick of seeming taller than anyone around her simply by the commanding sneer of her sharp green eyes.

In those early years he'd loved it. She immediately punctured whatever mystique had formed around him in the long wake of the dead Pyramid. Consultant to the NYPD, FBI, CIA, she made Wren's pattern analysis skills pale into insignificance. A savant, they called her, when they weren't calling her a cold-hearted bitch for usurping their authority, solving cold cases right under their noses and sneering as they thanked her.

"It's Christopher Wren," he said.

Her response came like a bullet. "What?"

"Christopher Wren. We worked together-"

"I know who you are," she interrupted with frosty precision. "I understand your name. What do you want, Christopher Wren, at 3:41 a.m., when I told you very clearly thirteen years ago to never speak to me again?"

She had him there. With her help they'd found the children. Working both deductive and inductive logic loops, they'd pinned down an immigrant stevedore already halfway to Argentina who confessed to witnessing an off-book movement of container boxes in the hours before dawn. Slade had walked the terrified man through the maneuver ten times, having memorized the exact contours of the container stacks, then churned the blocks in her head like a pre-teen genius speed-solving a Rubik's cube, coughing out the answer seconds later.

As he'd lifted the first of the children out of the container, her hand had come cold and firm in the crook of his elbow, her eyes burning into his. "This was your fault. You're sloppy. You coast on luck and charm. It is a wonder either of us survived. I won't do it again. Consider me dead to you."

Of course, she'd been right. He'd learned a lot from that indictment.

"You did say that," Wren allowed. Trying to sound as sincere and forthright as her, and not rely on any hint of the 'charm' she so despised. "I'm sorry to infringe on our agreement. McKenzie, I need your help."

"I'm not interested in helping you."

He felt her finger moving to kill the call. "It's like the children again," he went on swiftly. "Something I should have seen. I screwed up then, McKenzie. I may be screwing up now, and there are far more lives at stake than before. You know New York like nobody else. I don't think I can do this without you. So please don't punish them for my mistakes."

Silence. No click came, though. The line remained open and he pushed on.

"You've seen the fires. It's my father's work. He's linked to David Keller. They're using the firestorm to swarm the media, not allowing any proof to get through on what they've been planning. I've got a team working to break that stranglehold, but I still haven't got solid proof on their connection."

Still nothing. Maybe she was listening. Maybe she'd dropped the phone in a fish tank.

"He keeps a 'human zoo', McKenzie. A dungeon high in a Manhattan skyscraper. Innocent victims. I'm crossing Roosevelt Island now. I'll be outside your apartment in fifteen minutes. I've got the location narrowed to a few dozen blocks in Midtown along Billionaire's Row, but I've got nothing else. I need your help to pin it down."

Another long silence. He would wait for as long as it took. There were other analysts he could call, but none who had both the skills to rotate potentials like a quantum difference engine, and who already lived in Manhattan and knew the city and its people like the back of her hand.

"Los Angeles," she said at last. Each word a rap from the schoolmarm's cane. "Explain yourself. I've seen your works these past few years, Mr. Wren. If anything you have become sloppier still. Foolishly enamored with your own infamy. Luxuriating in a legend you do not deserve. Explain why I should help a man with so little professional regard?"

Wren rubbed his eyes. He'd forgotten how McKenzie talked. Like every word was an arrow perfectly flighted to the task. If anyone could hit bullseye then split that arrow down the middle with a second, it was McKenzie Slade.

"Desperation," he said, part telling her what she wanted to hear and part just speaking the truth. "Limited resources and ability. Rough guesswork combined with a reliance on charm. It was sloppy, you're right, but it's all I had at the time, and it worked."

Another silence. He craned to hear some sound of her breathing but there wasn't even the faintest whisper.

"You call *this* worked? Calling me in the middle of the night. A firestorm of fourteen dead women across the nation. A confidence man two months out from the Presidency. Your father resurgent, a dungeon in a skyscraper, and people burning your effigy across the nation where once they lofted you as a hero? How has your arrogance fared since then, Mr. Wren?"

He winced. Mr. Wren. "Poorly. I'll cut you a deal, McKenzie. Help me in this, you can tongue lash me all you want. I-"

"But I don't want," she interrupted. "There is nothing I'd rather do less. When I said to consider me dead, I meant it. I have no interest in dissecting your twisted family or your countless mistakes. Thirteen years ago you were profligate, reckless, highly emotional and came close to getting not only both of us killed, but all those children too. I cannot see how any of those attributes have changed. It is for that reason that-"

"So take it over," Wren said sharply. Charm wasn't going to help now, that was clear. Time for a little of that reckless, profligate emotion. "If you can do what I do better than me, I'll gladly hand the whole thing to you. You take responsibility for my father, for the firestorm, for bringing Keller down and I'll hand in my notice. It's yours if you want it. It'll all be-"

"Mr. Wren," she said, sharp as an elbow in his gut.

"It's yours. That's all."

"You are not listening to me," she went on coldly. "I want none of that. I am done cleaning up your messes. Do not call this number again, do not-"

He was losing her. Charm hadn't worked, neither anger nor appealing to her better angels had worked, and that left only one path left.

"You have a daughter," he said.

It knocked her silent. He'd done his research.

"Adelaine. She's nine years old, yes? I've since had children too, my girl's eight, my boy's six, and I just had them moved out of witness protection because my twisted father's targeting them. You may not know this, but every woman that burned is my wife's age. Each one had a boy and a girl that are the same ages as my kids. It's no coincidence, McKenzie. He'll kill everyone in his path to get what he wants. You've seen the burnings. You live near 5th Avenue. Can you imagine what impact it'll have for your daughter to see something like that? I've seen it and look what it did to me. Use me as your cautionary tale. He wants that for your daughter. For everyone's daughters."

He fell silent. Heard her breathing. Tight, furious, controlled.

"This is repellent," she said. Her voice utterly devoid of emotion now, cold as the Marianas Trench. "To mention my daughter. Even for you."

"I'm sorry, McKenzie. You never asked to be a soldier, but when the war is on civilians we're all in the trenches. We all have to fight or we'll lose what we have. He must be stopped."

Long seconds passed. Wren feared he'd pushed her too far.

"Thirty minutes," she said. Sounded strangled, forcing up the words. "I will see you outside Central Park Place on 57th Street. Do not be late."

The call ended.

Wren stared at the phone. He hadn't expected that. Felt part-elated, part-sickened. That she was going to help. That he'd brought up her daughter as leverage.

He gazed numbly out the windshield ahead. Sparse traffic. Distant offices lit up like a wall of stars, racing ever-closer to the dungeon mouth of Manhattan. In moments the cab shot down off the bridge and was swallowed whole, channeled into the city's maze-like intestinal tract. The sky pulled back. The horizon disappeared. The city had him, now.

29

CENTRAL PARK PLACE

Central Park Place was one of the skyscrapers highlighted in yellow on the map. Wren clicked through the building's profile in fascination. Under development still, it had topped out only a few months earlier, with condos in the lower fifty floors finished and sold, though none were yet inhabited. Standing at 1,450 feet across 131 floors, it was already the tallest residential building in the world, with 174 apartments starting at $8 million for a two-bedroom on the lower levels.

The cab stopped and started at intersections along West 57th Street, or Billionaires' Row, five narrow lanes flanked by gleaming luxury goods stores, designer office blocks and upscale restaurants, and Wren caught glimpses of other buildings highlighted on his map. The silver wave front of 231 W 53rd to his left, all 742 feet of it rippling in the moonlight. 231 Madison Avenue lay beyond that, a beast of white and glass blinking 1,425 feet into the sky. The razor taper of 447 East 58th Street loomed on the right, an unlit spine occluding stars a thousand feet high, still buttressed with a great-boned construction crane.

As they advanced Central Park Place emerged ahead, a slim square column of glass rising into darkness, though it was soon cut off by the angle of the cab's roof. In moments they were outside. Central Park Place looked unassuming from the ground, builders' scaffolds shielding the lobby like wrapping paper on a Christmas gift.

"You're shopping for a condo?" the cabbie asked as Wren got out. An old joke, he figured.

"Something like that."

New York was cold at 4 a.m., and smelled of concrete dust and raw iron, like the rusty tang of fresh blood. Wren stood on the south side of West 57th Street and drank it all in, acclimating to the city. Buildings hung over him. Vehicles buzzed by, mostly cabs and trucks on early morning deliveries. A few pedestrians passed, drunks on the walk of shame home, a handful of workers in suits heading early to the office, a young woman in pastel sweats out walking two huge labradoodles. They cast him glances then looked swiftly away, and he realized he was still wearing his strike suit: tactical black pants and jacket, harness belt, Desert Eagle at his hip.

Nothing he could do about that now.

Central Park Place stretched impossibly up into the night. Lights fizzed near the upper floors. Wren imagined construction workers far above, plastering in contoured walling, wiring in dimmer bulbs and voice-activated AI. Room after room, finish one floor and move onto the next. Perhaps on one, a zoo.

McKenzie Slade had chosen this place without a moment's hesitation. What did she know that he didn't?

"Stop staring like the rube hick you are," came a voice nearby. Wren dropped his gaze and saw Slade standing barely three feet away. Holding a coffee close to her chest, appraising him with those cold green eyes. She wore all black, but where his outfit was utilitarian, segmented by pockets, zippers and straps, hers was a flowing single piece, like a cloak with different layers.

Her face had aged but not by much, in her late forties now, the nose thinning, her cheeks taking on the raw shape of the bones underneath, lending her gravitas despite her diminutive height.

"It's good to see you, McKenzie," he said.

Her green eyes didn't shift in the slightest. "Yesterday was the worst day of my life, dealing with fallout from your firestorm. Now you're here." She looked him up and down. "Inappropriately dressed for the city, Christopher Wren. Did you just overthrow a South American country?"

He chanced a smile. "A mud cult in a Utah pumping station, actually. But you don't care about that. You selected this building. Why?"

Her head tilted slightly to the side. He remembered this, just about the only sign of faint amusement she ever showed. "No attempt to romance me. No flurry of compliments melding into excuses."

"I'm not the same man I once was. Just as reckless, perhaps, but you've made your position very clear. You're dead to me. I won't waste time bantering with a ghost. Every hour another woman dies and Keller moves closer to the Presidency. Let's stop that together."

Her head tilted back to dead-level. "The very minimum, then. All I had hoped for. Come with me."

She strode out into traffic without looking. Wren almost reached out to stop her, but halted himself at the last moment. If anyone knew the physics of moving bodies, it was McKenzie Slade. Never once in his estimation had she failed to exhibit absolute command of her surroundings. Doubtless she hadn't started now.

He looked both ways and crossed after her, weaving a path where she walked a crow-straight line between honking vehicles. Not one had to slow or swerve as she passed smoothly through, though the same could not be said for Wren.

He arrived at the scaffold fence moments after her, as she received a key from a man in a high visibility waistcoat.

"I know the foreman," McKenzie said, then strode through a wire security gate just as it opened. Wren followed into a polyvinyl tunnel through the gaping mouth of the lobby. He caught some sense of the glorious, light-filled space it would soon become, in the triple-height ceiling, hanging stub for chandelier and twin escalators rising away.

"How do you know him?" Wren asked as she stalked ahead, a black messenger bag bouncing gently across her narrow shoulders.

"I solved an architectural problem for him," she said, then turned for a single beat. "With the mob."

He almost laughed. Held it in.

"And you have some reason to target this building? You think the 'lab' is here?"

She didn't answer. They arrived at the elevator bank. Two industrial cars stood open in the central chute, metal cages dressed in chipped orange paint, and McKenzie strode in without pausing. Wren hated cages, but followed after her. She worked the control lever like she rode industrial elevators every day, and their ascent began.

"McKenzie," he started, and she turned to him. "If the zoo is here, I'll need more gear. A strike team."

She just tilted her head again in silent amusement. "I'm not a miracle worker, Mr. Wren. We're just getting started."

After that he was silent as the elevator winched them upward. Past open doorways into dark corridors leading away, fitted already with wood flooring and lush teal wallpaper broken by elegant wall sconces, lit only by the glare of the elevator's heat lamps. Ten floors passed, twenty, thirty, until soon the furnished corridors gave way to raw cement studded with hundreds of tiny spikes, ready for wooden boards to be slotted in.

Fifty floors. Sixty. When they hit the first of the penthouses, massive open expanses that gave a view straight through the building's exterior ribs to the city beyond, Wren momentarily lost his breath.

"I took my daughter here," McKenzie said. "It is indeed a sight to see."

More floors flew by. Each one open and unfurnished, each offering a slight steepening of the incredible view over Manhattan, Central Park, the gridwork pattern of blocks stretching away into the night. Wren watched them go open-mouthed. Of course he'd been in tall buildings before, had taken his children to the top of the Empire State Building, but this was very different.

This felt illicit, as if he'd stepped off the map into an earlier version of reality, yet to have its civilizing walls, doors and window blinds installed. He wasn't supposed to be up here. Nobody was, a thousand feet up in the air, domain of the birds. The defiance of the structure itself, its unrivalled arrogance, entranced him.

Wealth bought privilege, he thought numbly. Not only the feeling of power, but power manifest. To live in the clouds above the fortress walls of New York. To escape the prison and once again see the horizon, you had to buy your way up.

The elevator came to a halt on the 131st floor.

"After you," McKenzie said. Wren stepped out. The penthouse was a shell. A few support struts here and there, but very little to obstruct the incredible view. No light pollution this high. No maze walls either side. No clouds blocking the sky, nothing to obscure an uninterrupted view in all directions.

He stepped up to one of the floor-to-ceiling windows and gazed across New York. Manhattan, the Bronx, Queens, Brooklyn, Staten Island. His old home lay barely a mile away in Great Kills, their walk-up apartment in the brownstone where his kids had grown up and his dark past had ruined everything.

"I heard about your family," McKenzie said. Standing at his side. He didn't turn to her, expecting something cruel. "They're better off without you. You're a disaster. Now." She swung around her messenger bag and extracted an object, blocky and dark in the minimal light cast from the elevator. It took him only a moment to realize what it was.

"Binoculars?"

"You want to know which building your father's zoo is in? We look. There is no better vantage point on Billionaire's Row than the place you're standing right now."

30

VANTAGE POINT

Wren stared at the binoculars for a moment. Wasn't sure if she was making some kind of joke.

"You're serious?"

Her expression didn't shift. She extended the binoculars a bare inch closer.

"Of course you're serious," Wren said, starting to regret even calling her. Maybe she wasn't as sharp as she'd once been. "McKenzie, there's no way we'll see the zoo from here. Even if he has his prisoners pressed up to the skin of the building, the windows will be screened. There'll be nothing to see. It's pointless."

Still she didn't move, though it looked like her green eyes were judging him.

"What?" he asked. "What am I missing here?"

Again that head tilt. "What did you expect when you called me, Christopher?"

He didn't need to think. "The brilliance you showed me before. You found those children."

"So trust me now. Take the binoculars and look."

He took them. A model he recognized, was actually surprised she had them so readily to hand: ATN BINOX 4T 640, optical zoom to 25x, with infrared built in. Hunters' binoculars, five thousand dollars plus, good for picking out the heat signature of deer maybe a field away. He held them up to his eyes, targeted the nearest skyscraper, 151 West 57th Street, a gray-scale set of lines running up-down, and dialed the zoom all the way in.

It did a little. Not very much. 25x at this range moved his vantage point into the air maybe three hundred yards away from the tower. He ran the binoculars up and down, looking for tell-tale signs of human habitation. The lighter notes denoting heat spill through the structure's outer skin were scraps only. Not enough to identify anything, let alone exhibits in a zoo.

"This is-"

"Proof of concept," McKenzie finished.

He took the binoculars away from his eyes to find her looking at him intently.

"What concept?"

"Primary research," she said. "Eyes in the field gathering data. I've read the reports on your tactics ending the LA riots." He frowned. "Don't look so surprised. You've had half the AI academics in the world chasing your tail for three months, trying to figure out the logistics behind your 'ghost algorithm.'

Wren couldn't help but look surprised. "How do you know about-"

"Everyone knows about it," McKenzie interrupted, waving a hand dismissively. "It's simple enough in concept. Gather enormous user data and use AI algorithms to crunch it for hidden patterns, it's quite standard. I don't doubt your hacker collective are geniuses at this, and yes, I have heard of them too. Their skills have brought you this far, but they can't take you the last half mile, can they? This is why you've come to me."

"Exactly right," Wren said. "But binoculars won't-"

"They're blinkered, Mr. Wren," she interrupted forcefully. "Their algorithms can't find him, but why? What's blinkering them?"

"I don't know. It's complex. Something about-"

"Their data is secondary," she said emphatically. "You've heard the expression garbage in, garbage out?"

That one he knew. "Sure. You put bad data into a computer program, you get bad data out."

"Precisely. And the data your hackers have been accessing, the only data available to them, is secondary. Unless you already sent out teams to survey these buildings yourself?

Wren shifted uncomfortably. "Well, no, but-"

"Of course not," Slade said, like this only confirmed her opinion of him. "Everything their algorithms are working with is existing, secondary data.

Skyscraper schematics on file. Financial records held by banks. Movements of people as recorded by CCTV. All forms of data that can be tampered with." She eyed him like a lecturer settling in for a long explanation. "If there's anything we know about your father, it's that he likes to tamper with reality. For all you know, he could have hidden an entire floor in one of these buildings, and there would be no record it even exists. Tower blueprints can be falsified, as I've seen for myself. Architects can be silenced. Construction workers can be paid off. No amount of pattern analysis would uncover such a hidden floor, 'ghost' or otherwise. Rather, we must see it for ourselves."

Wren chewed on that. He was all for eyes-on reconnaissance, but this? "You think he could hide a whole floor?"

"The pharaohs did it with their tombs three thousand years ago," Slade said flatly. "Fearing robbers come to steal their grave goods, they built false tombs, false entrances, even rudimentary traps. Further, their architects and builders were all entombed with them." She glared at him. "Put that next to getting his candidate elected President, and I don't think killing a few plumbers would trouble the Apex overly. Do you?"

He had no response to that.

"So we must see for ourselves," Slade repeated. "Primary data we can trust. Hence the binoculars."

Wren held up the BINOX 4Ts. Halfway there already. "But binoculars from nearby skyscrapers aren't going to cut it."

"Of course not," Slade said.

Wren's mind hummed, the squares of his own Rubik's cube rotating toward completion. "We'd need blanket coverage of every tower in Manhattan. High-resolution thermal scans, ideally conducted before daybreak and they spot us."

Slade brought up her wristwatch. The display glowed purple in the darkness. "You have four hours until dawn. Any idea how you're going to do that?"

For a few seconds he didn't. Running through the possibilities. Hellion and B4cksl4cker were adept at mobilizing drone cavalries for him, but even they couldn't conjure up a fleet equipped with infrared cameras out of thin air.

"I hear you're still affiliated with the CIA," Slade hinted.

Wren teed that up and shot it down; the CIA wouldn't cut it. They wouldn't have a fleet of infrared-equipped drones ready to unleash on New York at a moment's notice, why would they? But maybe the Army or the Air Force would. There were several bases within range of New York.

Wren knew someone who could bring the military on board fast, and even contemplating it made his heart sink. A Hail Mary. Gerald Humphreys, Director of the CIA and his closest link to the President of the United States.

He pulled up his phone and dialed the number from memory.

31

POTUS

"Never happening," Humphreys said harshly. "There is no way I'm putting you on the line with POTUS."

He'd answered the call fast, hard at work at the White House as the lame duck President sent shuttle diplomats back and forth to a full session of Congress, trying to come up with some unified way forward.

"Then get used to the firestorm," Wren said. "Once Keller's in the whole country's going to burn. You don't believe me, look at what he's saying right now. Up to the election I was his go-to hero, riding my coattails into the public consciousness, but now? He's tearing me down like I'm poison oak on his treehouse."

"You're an easy man to hate, Wren."

"All the more reason he's using me. You know I'm not behind these fires. I've got Rogers out there trying to stop them, get us a break in the avalanche of horror on TV, but without POTUS' help I'll have no signal to push through the noise."

Humphreys gave an exasperated sigh. "Let's just review what you're asking for here. A major military action in a highly populated area, against a man very loosely associated with the incoming President. What's our stated intent here? To invalidate David Keller's election? To prove he's a criminal, to tie him to the firestorm?"

"Exactly that."

"It'll look political, Wren! Like a hit job on a political rival."

"Who cares what it looks like?"

"I care!" Humphreys bleated. "The people will care. I know you think I'm just another self-serving bureaucrat teeing up his own political dreams, but I'm in this for love of country. I believe in all the stuff they taught us in grade school. Patriotism. Loyalty to the Constitution. I'd die for it."

Wren snorted. "I can name a dozen times you refused to die for it. When the Blue Fairy came in-"

"I was a coward," Humphreys interrupted. "You're right. I fell short. You had the vision then. Maybe you have the vision now. I'm simply saying-"

"You're saying you're morally queasy about this? Want to get your objection on record, that you're uncomfortable heaving the old way out the window in the face of a rocketing RQ and a psychopathic President-elect who wants to see us all burn alive? Is that really your point here, that we should slow-walk our response through the old system while the country goes up in flames, just because the Founders didn't foresee this exact situation? I guarantee the Apex is not playing by those same rules!"

Silence for a second.

"I'm saying you're bad for this country, Wren," Humphreys said. "If the system doesn't work, if the executive and legislative branches can't figure this out then-"

"Then the system's broken! Setting a broken bone hurts like hell, but fail to set it and you're deformed for life. I'm about done giving you a spoonful of sugar to help the medicine go down, Humphreys. Put POTUS on or get out of the goddamn way!"

Silence.

Moments ticked by.

"Hold the line," Humphreys said.

Wren held, stalking a circle around the Central Park Place penthouse suite, on top of the world and looking out over the city. Red aircraft-warning lights winked on and off on hundreds of skyscrapers like a lush warm pulse. Thousands of vehicles surged below like blood cells pumping through Manhattan's capillaries.

Minutes ticked by. A notification chimed in on his phone. They'd just hit the hour mark. Headlines blared that another burning had come, bang on time. A woman in, where?

Wren blinked.

Great Kills. Staten Island.

His heart skipped a beat. Sweat popped instantly out on his skin. He knew it couldn't be Loralei. She hadn't been in Great Kills for a year, was somewhere north in one of Teddy's camps right now, but still.

This was a message to him. First 5th Avenue. Now Great Kills.

He clicked through breaking news feeds until he found live video. A figure burning and staggering through a dark open space. Impossible. The Siedenburg Park in front of his old apartment. The same place Rogers had laid in wait for him, renditioned him.

The woman sagged to her knees, burning incandescent yellow. A real person murdered as a message. Maybe a way to cast blame toward him. The fury came cold, ice charging up and down his spine. The Apex was going to pay for this.

"Christopher," came Slade's voice, calling across the cavernous penthouse.

"It's not my wife," he answered.

The phone line clicked live.

"Done," said Humphreys. "I've insulated the President, gone through channels of my own. If this fails I'll pay for it alone, not even my contacts in the NYPD know precisely where the order's coming from. They're spinning up their whole squad of ten UAS Air Rangers, that's Unmanned Aircraft Systems, large quadcopters enabled with thermal imaging, designed for fast response remote tracking of criminals on the run. Your hackers should be able to take control of them, we're leaving an open port, not that they'll need it. I'm told they can network and scan on a grid, hopefully it's enough."

Wren felt a blossom of hope spark in his chest. "Thank you, Humphreys."

"Get it done," was all Humphreys said. "Don't make me fall on my sword for nothing."

The line went dead.

Wren looked out at the city. There was the dark silhouette of 111 West 57th Street. Beyond it lay the spotted lights of 231 Madison Avenue. Hedge fund managers up early, up late, maybe sleeping with the lights on, afraid of the dark. Many others buildings arrayed around them. Each façade holding thousands of square feet to scan. He clicked to another line.

"Hellion, B4cksl4cker, Humphreys has come through. A squad of NYPD thermal imaging surveillance drones is being switched on with an open port. I need you to take command, navigate a search grid on every one of the target buildings and put together a correlation map of what you find. We're looking for people where they shouldn't be, in poses they shouldn't be in, maybe situated between levels, on mechanical floors or mezzanines. Discard the blueprints, don't trust anything you found online. We're doing this whole thing by eye. Confirm."

"Confirmed," came B4cksl4cker's response. "I will wake Hellion, she will take command of this fleet. I will write the search grid. This is an excellent idea, Christopher."

"I can't take credit." He nodded toward McKenzie Slade. "I want you to loop in McKenzie Slade for analysis. She's with me right now. She's a genius."

"Of course, yes, we know who she is. I am glad you are reaching out to old friends."

Wren snorted. Old friends.

"We don't have long before the sun's up. Let's find ourselves a target before they see us and shut the whole thing down."

32

TESTIMONY

The night deepened.

Wren paced around the penthouse as Hellion spoke in his ear, walking him through the search grid. She'd split the ten UAS Air Rangers into a square formation that swept up all sides of a building at once, plotting a three dimensional heat map. They began with Central Park Place: at five seconds per floor across 131 floors it took around eleven minutes to scan the whole structure.

"Is that fast enough?" Wren asked as he watched the drone array rise past the window, barely visible insectile black chunks flying in uncanny synchrony. "There's dozens of target skyscrapers. Do we really need all ten at once to check a building?"

"In order to achieve a minimal resolution, yes," Hellion answered easily. "Any fewer wider, there will be gaps. Our display will look like, how shall I say, an eight-bit video game?"

"Donkey Kong," B4cksl4cker supplied helpfully.

"More like Asteroid," Hellion said. "A wonderful game, but as a three-dimensional render searching for anomalies-"

Wren stopped listening. Looked at his phone, already half past four, just over three hours until the dawn.

"I take it this building's clear," he said, cutting through their chatter.

"Boringly so," Hellion confirmed. "Workmen. You and McKenzie Slade. This is all. I am moving next to 111 West 57th Street."

Good, but bad. Time wasted. Still he could plan. "Where are we at on a strike team?"

Keys flew. "B4cksl4cker is working with McKenzie Slade to vet local SWAT police. There are no operational Foundation members in New York, Christopher; we sent our best to Rhode Island with Teddy."

Wren gritted his teeth. "SWAT?"

"Apparently McKenzie Slade knows many. Some are, how shall I say, sympathetic to our cause."

Wren didn't want to ask what that meant. "I need to see them. I'm not going in half-baked and-"

"There is a call inbound, Christopher," Hellion interrupted. "It is Rogers. She sounds most excited."

"Rogers?"

"Yes, will you take it?"

Wren squeezed the phone tight. "First get me the records of any SWAT I'm going into a raid with. We'll need a stealth insertion, and-"

"Yes, yes, I know all this Christopher," Hellion said. "Trust me. I am putting through Sally Rogers."

The line clicked. Wren allowed himself a brief moment's annoyance; like his receptionist was making executive decisions in his place, but only a moment.

"Sally," he said.

"Christopher! You are going to love this. It's all going crazy out here, but the upshot is, Rachel Day had a secret phone!"

It took him a second to switch gears. "What?"

"Well, not exactly a phone," she went on. "At least not a normal one. And we don't have it yet, but we've heard all about it from witness testimony."

Wren blinked, dredging her progress from memory. "So you found the, uh, shoe guy? The greeter?"

She snorted. "No chance of that, it looks. No, we've been canvassing Rachel Day's life, waking people up, bringing them out, running re-enactments of what they might have seen on any given day, and-"

"What?" Wren interrupted. "Re-enactments? What are you talking about?"

"Like we did for the Blue Fairy," Rogers enthused, clearly in the throes of a fresh adrenaline high. Her energy just made Wren feel exhausted. "You remember how we ran the live e-fit performance in Chicago, had everyone stand where they'd been when the Pinocchios killed that guy? You chased down a ham and a crab shell, I got us a baseball bat and we watched some actors knock the crap out of it until-"

"I remember," Wren said. He remembered trying to fob a lecture off on Rogers about how people would perform better on a math test staged in a blue room if they'd studied math in a blue room previously. Sense memory was directly linked to recall. He'd drawn the parallel that anyone witnessing a trauma would remember it best when exposed to a re-enactment of the original trauma. Rogers had been skeptical, quickly becoming furious that he was just re-traumatizing the witnesses.

Maybe she'd shifted since then?

"So you've been, what, running live e-fits on potential witnesses?"

"Exactly! You talked about those lost minutes? I'm digging in. The people in her workplace, we put them all back in position. The people along her drive to work, the walk from the parking lot, shops overlooking her commute, parents at the pickups where she collected her son from gymnastics class. Everything, and we asked them for anything strange. Any tiny thing out of the ordinary. And it shook something loose."

He could hear her excitement overtopping. He'd felt that rush of progress himself countless times, and it was infectious.

"You've got her sighted on a secret phone."

"Exactly! It started with a barber on Juniper Street, she walks a three-minute stretch of it from her company's parking lot to the office. He wasn't happy we woke him up, this was three hours back, but he came in. Of course he knew all about it on the news. We put him at his chair, full floodlights in the street so it looked like day, got him a customer in, scissors in his hand, and asked him if he'd ever noticed Rachel Day acting strange when she walked by. His chair looks right out over the street, so he must have seen her every day."

Wren felt her excitement rising. It seemed like an extreme long shot, so the scale of the operation was surprising. Floodlights to simulate daylight? The barber along her route? It was incredible faith in staging a scene.

"And he did?"

"He did. Nothing momentous at first, day after day he sees her, so we pressed, and he came up with one time around three months back, when she stood outside his shop for maybe a minute, looking at her phone."

"OK," Wren allowed.

"Nothing strange in that, until she did something a little odd. Out of character, anyway, since he sees her go by all the time. She lifts her phone up and points it at the window. He has mirrored glass, reflective in the daylight, so he figured she was taking a picture of herself. Of course we set up a person matching Day outside with a phone in the same pose, and that jogged a little more loose."

Wren leaned against the skyscraper's cold glass wall. "Jogged what loose?"

"Some kind of video on her screen, right after she took the photo. Just rippling red, he said, like a video of flames. Not a photo of his barbershop, that's for sure. But he wasn't sure, he only saw it for a flash."

Wren considered. "OK, that is strange. But it could be-"

"It's not," Rogers said firmly. "Not a gif, not a video, nothing she would have had to access the Internet to download. There's no record of her using her phone in any way like that, ever, on any of her commutes. Of course the phone itself was slagged in the burning, but her cloud account has full updates. She streamed no video of fire, received no messages with fire flash files embedded, nothing. She hardly even uses her phone at all. So," she took a breath, warming to the story, "we get a fire gif rolling on our actor outside, and the barber remembers one more thing. Sense memory, right? He says Day's expression changes as she looks at the screen. Her eyes widen, her jaw drops, like she's seeing something shocking. Maybe terrified, the barber says. It's what he remembered most."

"Terrified," Wren repeated. Picturing Rachel Day from the food court video, watching a fire on her phone. "OK. Three months back, you said?"

"Three months, right."

The gears cranked into motion in Wren's head. "Three months. So if we believe your barber, Rachel Day had a second, secret phone at least that far back. One that streamed video of flames when she took a photo." He thought hard, trying to piece it together. "I don't get it, but this has to be how the Apex radicalized her. If so, there should be a record of that phone's cell carrier somewhere. Have you looked at carrier records in the vicinity?"

Rogers took a breath. "That's where it gets sticky. There are none. No phone line activating anywhere near her at those times."

Wren puzzled over that. "So maybe it's not a phone on a standard contract. Maybe it's piggybacking off someone's nearby Wi-Fi."

"I thought the same thing. We checked it, and there's nothing detectable or on the record. No data up or down in that period of time, in that space."

"At least not through Wi-Fi," Wren murmured. "There are other ways to transmit data. Direct beam through the radio spectrum. It's not hard."

"If the phone is synced for it, absolutely not."

"But there are no easy records to check for radio uptake," Wren went on. "No simple way to track it, certainly not if we don't know the frequency." He thought some more. "And that's exactly the Apex's MO. Un-trackable. If he did this for Rachel Day, you can bet he did it for every other woman in the firestorm too. Deliver them some kind of ghost phone, beam his BS directly into their heads."

"I've already reached out to all the firestorm task forces," Rogers said. "They're re-canvassing their witnesses about phones displaying flames, cross-referencing to carrier records and looking for instances that don't sync up."

"We need to do more than that," Wren said, the gears grinding faster now. "We need to get some kind of detection net in place. Maybe we can narrow beam it if we catch the frequency. We need infrastructure in the field that can detect uptake of unexpected signals. If we can find it, we can cut it off. Stop the flow."

"On it," said Rogers. "Hellion's got some ideas of civilian infrastructure we can co-opt. But there's more still."

"What more?"

"We already started re-canvassing our own witnesses," she said, "bringing up this ghost phone with a red screen, the terror reaction? You're not going to believe the testimony that shook out. Seems he thought it was just a nightmare at the time, said he barely even remembered it, but the similarity's telling."

Wren felt a chill sink around his heart. Had a feeling he knew what was coming next. "Whose testimony?"

"John Day," Rogers answered. "Rachel Day's husband."

33

JOHN DAY

Rogers sent the video file of her John Day interview, and Wren brought it up. Eleven minutes and twenty seconds, the thumbnail showing a gray-faced man, mid-forties, hairline receding in a shallow widow's peak, eyes red from crying or lack of sleep or both, clearly in a heightened state. Sitting on a rumpled double bed, ivy-style wallpaper in back, subdued lighting, Wren guessed the master bed in his house; Rogers again using the sensory environment to stir up memories.

He pushed play, and the video began with Rogers' voice off camera.

"Tell us what you saw," she said, not following the rulebook at all. No formal 'This is Agent Sally Rogers at the interrogation of John Day in booth 3 at the Seattle PD'. Instead she'd bypassed it all, which alarmed him even as it warmed a strange kind of pride in his chest.

"Tell you what?" John Day asked. He sounded reedy, looked lost even in his own home. "You want me to do what?"

"Re-enact it," came Rogers' voice. "You told me you woke up and saw your wife using a phone in the night. I want you to-"

"I said it was a nightmare," John Day protested haplessly. "I don't, really, I don't see what the point of all this is. I've been over and over-"

He froze. Mouth open, staring at something off camera, dead ahead. "What the hell is this?"

The camera panned across the dim ivy wallpaper, a tall bureau, curtain, an open window. Standing in front of the glass was a female, back to the camera, blond hair tousled down her back, wearing a cream silk dressing gown and looking down at a phone in her hand.

"I told you this would be a re-enactment," came Rogers' voice, and Wren felt the urge to be kind pushing into her voice, though she mostly resisted it. Pushing her witness, a sudden widower still in shock from his wife's horrific death, so far it made even Wren uncomfortable.

"She looks like my wife!" Day gasped, then gulped like a swimmer just come up for air. The camera swung around to see shock and fear written on his face. "That's her night gown."

"Please," Rogers said, not offering him any way out. "Tell me again what happened."

"I don't want to do this," Day said, though he didn't stand. "This can't even be legal. You can't just take my wife's clothes!"

"We're not taking them," Rogers said firmly, "we're wearing them. But yes, you're right it might not be legal, and I may be fired when my boss hears about this. Until then, I believe it's our best chance to catch the man who radicalized your wife. Who brainwashed her, John. You are not a victim here, I promise you, you're a survivor. I just need you to be brave and help us bring the bastard to justice."

Wren's mouth opened in a slight gasp of wonder. The reframing was crass and obvious, but he couldn't have said it much better himself. Rewrite John Day's involvement as an act of heroism. Get him onboard and believing that delving into this deep lake of pain could actually produce results.

The camera showed these emotions playing out on his face. Fear and uncertainty breaking toward borrowed resolve.

There it is, Wren thought, and was surprised when a second later Rogers echoed his exact thought.

"There you are," she said. "Now, I'm not asking you to act, I just want you to re-live exactly what happened. You were sleeping. It was dark. We'll hit the lights."

The lights clicked out. The screen fuzzed and struggled to capture anything in the dark, settling on indistinct bands of gray except for the window, where the figure of Rachel Day was haloed by street lights from outside.

John Day's voice came through high and breathless. "Yes, that's exactly where she was standing. Right there. She was looking at her phone and facing me."

The actress playing the role of Rachel Day turning.

"Oh God," Day said.

"Keep going," Rogers probed.

"I, well, she was just standing there. I thought, maybe there was a reflection in the window?"

"Of her phone screen?" Rogers asked.

"I, maybe?" his voice shook as he tumbled back into the moment. Sensory states were powerful things, encoding memory locked to a physical sensation, a sound, a mood, a color. "I thought it could be a light outside, maybe a plane blinking, a neighbor's security alarm flashing, I-"

"Let's say it was her phone's screen. What did you see?"

"I-"

The figure of Rachel Day took a step closer to the bed, and there was the sound of Mr. Day jerking in the sheets. "Jesus. God. I, red! Red, orange, flickering,"

"Like flames?"

"I, yes. Maybe."

The camera turned to the actress. She worked the phone, Wren guessed she was bringing up a gif of flames. A second later he was proved correct. The red spill light illuminated her face demonically, reflecting back off the window like a tiny window into hell.

"Oh no," said John Day.

"What's next?" Rogers pressed.

"I, uh..." his voice came through thinner now. The stress reaction, adrenaline pouring into his system and starting fight or flight but with nowhere to go. His own wife standing at the base of their bed, staring into flames in the middle of the night. Wren imagined the sweat pouring down his face, the terror gripping him.

"What next?" Rogers insisted sharply.

"She held the phone up!" John Day gasped. "Pointed it at me."

A second passed, and then the Rachel Day clone did just that.

"Why?" Rogers asked.

"The light came on. The flash? She was filming me."

That got Wren's attention. Clearly it got Rogers' too. It didn't distract the actress, who must have hit record in the phone's camera app, sending out a wash of white light from the flash.

"That's it," John Day said tightly. "Really, I think we should stop now. I don't remember anything else."

"Be brave a little longer."

The camera swung around to focus on John Day. He was clearly visible in the white flashlight now, curled up against the headboard, clutching a pillow close like a terrified child.

"She began crying," Day said. The words sounded like teeth being pulled. "I thought, I don't know, she was sobbing? Like one of the children had died. I think I said something, like, 'Honey, what's wrong?', but I don't really remember."

"You were still half-asleep."

"I was. I thought, I mean, maybe she said something back?"

"What?"

"I don't know. She wasn't saying it to me. Something like lines of poetry, like she was muttering to herself even while she was sobbing."

"What did she say, John?"

"Something about fear. Fear is a portal? It didn't make any sense."

Wren's heart chilled. He remembered that. One of the deepest tenets of the Pyramid.

"Anything about pain?" Rogers asked, sparking another chill. She'd studied up on the Pyramid, then.

"Yes," said Day, his voice rising to a squeak. "How did you know that?"

"Was it pain is a doorway?"

John Day's eyes opened so wide they caught the white light and glistened like knife blades.

"Walk in the fire," he whispered.

There it was. Conclusive proof of the Apex's involvement, at least for Wren.

"And then?"

Now Day was sobbing himself. Eyes wide. Staring at the figure of his wife and losing it. "She told me to go back to sleep. 'Go to sleep, John,' she said. I'll never forget it now. I'll never forget it."

He raised his shuddering hands to cover his eyes.

A second passed.

Wren let out a breath. Now was the time to finish the reframing. Ensure this moment didn't haunt John Day worse than the actual moment itself. He urged Rogers on, then she was there. Stepping in front of the camera, sitting on the bed beside John Day, putting one hand on his shoulder.

"She said that because she loved you," she said. "That was Rachel. And whatever happened to her, whatever was done, it wasn't by her choice. Don't ever forget that. She didn't burn herself, she was burned, and the things you've told us tonight give us a real chance of catching the sick psycho who did it. We're going to save other people because of this. Hold on to that, and thank you for your courage."

He mumbled something. Rogers rooted in the covers to hold his hand. A long moment passed, then she nodded, someone hit the lights and the spell was broken.

34

WHAT IT MEANS

Wren pulled away from the screen, feeling overwhelmed.

The phone was ringing. Rogers. He took a breath and answered.

"They'll fire you for that."

"I don't care," she answered. "What do you think?"

Wren tried to martial his thoughts. There were so many now, swirling across each other like cross-currents. "You took outrageous risks. The damage you could have done-"

"You would have done it, if you were here. Maybe you would have gone further."

There was nothing he could say to that. "Maybe."

"There's no maybe. You wanted me as a student? I've been learning the whole time. So stop playing games and tell me what you think."

He let out a breath. She had his number, no point denying it. "OK. Well, firstly, I'm certain that all that happened, just like he said. I don't think it was a dream." He paused, wondering how far he was going to take it, then plunged on. "Whatever Rachel Day was looking at, whatever she was filming him for, it ties directly to her radicalization. That phone is the key. We need to tie it to a person. How did she get it? Who told her what to do with it? How did they use it to radicalize her so completely? If we can build a pattern that matches the other cases, maybe we can narrow down the data stream it's receiving, predict the next one to blow and prevent it."

"We have those requests out to every victim team in the country," Rogers said swiftly. "There's seventeen now, Wren. Seventeen women."

He didn't need her to tell him that. Each one felt carved into his chest. His father, his responsibility. "Have you enlisted the Foundation?"

"Affirmative. B4cksl4cker says he's running ghost track back on every woman who burned, looking for evidence of incoming data, whether that's via Wi-Fi, cellular data or radio frequency."

Wren took that in. Internet data downloads were international but trackable. Cellular data would make things easy, but he doubted the Apex ever used it, for that reason. Radio signals were much harder to pin down.

"Good work," he said. "Keep the pressure on."

"Will you have proof ready if I manage to break the storm?"

Wren gritted his teeth. "We're closing in on a location for the 'lab' right now. Hopefully we'll have it before daybreak. We should get answers there."

"Answers," Rogers replied, then went silent for a moment. "Humphreys gave me access to deep Pyramid data, Christopher. Background on the Apex that was never released. Those mantras John Day mentioned, fear is a portal, pain is a doorway? They're not mentioned anywhere else. I need to know what they mean."

Wren didn't say anything. Whatever deep data Humphreys thought he had, it wasn't one tenth of what Wren had destroyed about the Pyramid in the years since. Still.

"Chris," Rogers pressed, though she never called him that, "I've read all the analyses. Everything Humphreys had, everything in the public sphere, and it's barely enough to fill a thimble. You're the only surviving Pyramid member we've got. I need to know."

He blew out a breath. Not something he'd wanted to think about again. "It's his ideology," he said, throat tightening. "How he got a thousand people to burn themselves alive when the Pyramid fell." He squeezed the bridge of his nose, hard. In for a penny, in for a pound. "Those words, the portal, the door, they mean none of this is real, Rogers. The world. People. Governments. The air you breathe. The ground you walk upon. It's all fake. The real truth is, the truth 'the Apex' revealed through prolonged pain and fear, was that we're all suffering." He paused for a second, dredging up the past. "Story goes, we're all in hell already, Rogers. Everything we see around us is the lie, while in reality we're screaming our hearts out for mercy."

There was silence for a moment.

"Unpack that for me," Rogers said.

Wren almost laughed. There was a lot to unpack, something he'd avoided doing for anyone else, pretty much ever. "It's a shell game," he said, steeling himself. "The pits, the cages, the vats, it was all torture, right? As we know, the first step to indoctrinating cult members is to break the old frames of reference, and torture is a good tool to achieve that. Look at Gruber. But for the Apex, torture was not just a tool, it was the whole shebang." He took a breath, realized he was being obtuse. It was hard to look at the Apex's works head-on. Rogers waited silently on the other end of the line, giving him the time he needed.

"At a basic level, he's saying pain is truth," Wren tried again. "When you're in pain or experiencing fear, your eyes are open, because you're already in hell. Not metaphorically, not metaphysically, but for real. You're actually stepping through a door into hell. You're experiencing one tenth of what your soul feels every hour of every day, glimpsed through the doorway and the portal." He took a deep breath. He'd thought for so long that he'd left the Apex's sickness behind. "He preached that endlessly, through a thousand different lessons. Baked it into everything. This isn't real. This is a dream. The real you is suffering." He sighed. "Over time that revelation crept up on people. It broke people down. They couldn't sleep for nightmares about what their soul was suffering, about what their children's souls were suffering, about all their family. All unknowing, all blind, but he made them believe it was real. He got people asking for more pain, more torture in the vats, the cages, whatever, because then at least you're being honest. He wants you seeking the truth, steeped in that twisted vision."

He said nothing for a moment. Heard Rogers breathing in his ear.

"Basically, he makes you complicit," Wren went on, pushing all the way. "When you start to beg for the pain, he's got you. You believe. Then he drops the final 'truth', the one he's been prepping you for all this time: the only way to save your actual soul is to die. In the most painful way possible. The more painful, the more chance you have of waking up 'in' your soul. Enough pain means you wake up. It ends the spell. You come to as your soul in hell, but now you can act." Wren leaned hard against the glass, legs beginning to shake. He'd never attended an actual Pyramid session where all this was laid out. Rather he'd pieced it together as a child over years, from glimpses of the vats, from the Apex's litanies and sermons, from the cries of men and women screaming for more.

"Once you're in hell," he went on, "you gather with the other members of the Pyramid. An army of enlightened angels, waiting for you to come. You join their army and start working to free everyone else. All of humanity." Wren rubbed his eyes, was surprised to find them damp. "You become an angel sent to redeem others. Ultimately, he pitches it as your holy duty. So, that's what all those people, the ones I burned alive in the fake town, truly believed. They thought it was something good. They thought they were sacrificing themselves to go save other people."

His voice trembled at the end, with anger or shame or maybe just sadness. He hadn't expected any of that.

"That they would become angels," Rogers breathed. "Christopher, I mean..." She whistled low. "That is one head trip. Damn."

He laughed. "We all believed it, one way or another. My brothers and sisters. My family. Me." He took another breath, rubbed his eyes dry. "When he wouldn't let me burn at the end, I remember feeling like a traitor. I wanted to go be an angel with my family. But he said no. He needed me here as a messenger of what we'd done. To spread the word."

Silence.

"I didn't know," Rogers said. "You never said."

He'd never said. There was a reason for that.

"Now you know. What he's doing to these women, I'm guessing it's the same thing he did to me. We're seeing flames on the phones, maybe that's a vision of hell, a way to outsource his brainwashing through technology. It took time back then, weeks sometimes, months, years. Looks like he's refined the method. Maybe he can do it remotely. He can flip them through a ghost phone, make them believe that they're angels pressing forward to rescue the lost." He took a steadying breath. Time to turn this around. "When it comes to intervention, if you do manage to disrupt one of these women, remember that there'll be no reasoning with them. Right now they're bought and sold. In their eyes we're blind. Maybe we're working to keep the people enslaved. All we can do is shut them down physically, then worry about deprogramming their minds later on."

Rogers' breathing came heavier. Who knew what she was thinking.

"I'm sorry," she said.

Not what he'd been expecting. Not something he was equipped to deal with. Kindness, again. "We're going to bring him down, Rogers. Believe that."

"I believe it."

"Good. Now find these phones. Nail the frequency. I've got a zoo to crush."

"Thank you," she said. "For trusting me."

He smiled. A leap of faith. Sometimes faith was all you had.

35

SWAT

7:15 a.m., and the blue glow of dawn spread up from the east like the sick glare of a flare light. In the back of a SWAT van peeling east along Billionaire's Row, Wren strapped a quad-load bandolier of 12 gauge 303 grain 'trocar' shotgun shells across his armor-plate Twaron vest, looped in an X across a second harness of 410 Triple Defense 7-shell magazines. Benelli M4 tactical shotgun in one hand, Desert Eagle AE .50 holstered on his left hip.

"It's 231 Madison Avenue," Hellion had said three minutes earlier. Activating Wren, sitting with his new team of SWAT officers on loan from the city in their riot van, decked out to look like a florist's truck from outside. Every member wore a jawbone conduction mic, earpiece, bodycam synced direct to Hellion riding overwatch.

"How sure are you?" he'd asked, running the specs for 231 Madison Avenue back through his head. Finished in 2016, 1,426 feet tall with 101 floors, 119 residences, it had been the tallest residential building in the world until Central Park Place surpassed it. Construction design of six independent building compartments stacked atop each other, divided by mechanical floors filled with reinforced concrete outrigger trusses binding the core to the perimeter framework, increasing stiffness and reducing the 'drift' felt by its billionaire residents as wind buffeted the exterior.

"We're seeing seven stacks," Hellion had replied. "Not six as all the schematics say. Slade was right. There's an extra mechanical floor hidden like a mezzanine in the upper reaches, floors 73 to 74. No elevator stops there, it's heavily shielded so we can't see any heat signature, but it's there, the only anomaly out of all the structures. If there's a zoo anywhere, it's here. Sending you the 3D model."

He gave the order and the florist van took off east. Barely a ten minute ride, five if they flashed blue lights, but the whole goal was to approach quietly. The zoo had to be caught before it could self-immolate.

Images flashed up on his phone and Wren scrolled through them. Three-dimensional heat maps of Madison Avenue's upper floors laid atop a best-guess render of the physical layout.

"If there's no elevator stop, how do we access it?" he asked.

"Access must be through the floor above or the floor below. 73 and 74 are both penthouses, full width."

"I always liked my dungeons going down," B4cksl4cker said. "I think you hit 74."

"But you keep the madwoman in the attic," Hellion countered. "Hit 73."

Wren clicked the line to open, admitting the seven SWAT members crushed into the van with him. "We'll hit both 73 and 74 simultaneously," he said. "I'll take lead on 74, Jimenez you're lead on 73."

Corporal Jimenez nodded. Wren had never met him before, knew none of the strike team, but their records were clean and Slade had vouched for them all.

"They can't be bought," she'd said, while Wren was putting the request through Humphreys' off-book channel. "If the mob can't buy them, I don't think your father can either."

That was good enough for him.

"Yes, sir," Jimenez said.

They all knew who he was. Had some sense of what his mission meant.

Wren studied his sub-team. Three-strong, adept at exactly this kind of strike according to their jackets, break-and-enter with no-knock warrants on cartel targets across the five boroughs. All hardened, all tracking a history of good shootings, forged in the fire. Never 73 stories high in the sky before, but there was always a first time.

"The things we might see in there," he said to them. "I'm expecting hell. Think of the worst urban myth you've ever seen and 10x it. Human trafficking dens, coked-up flophouses, people on bath salts carving each other for snacks, that's what I want you ready for. There's no time to be horrorstruck."

His sub team stared back at him. Kato was lean and silent, thirty-four, ex special forces. McNeil chewed a cud of tobacco, thick-necked like a bull at just twenty-seven. Miller was a slender blonde, expert in demolitions. She was his only proof against a networked bomb big enough to bring the whole tower down.

"Drones are pulling back to avoid detection," Hellion said in his ear. "I'll close in for real-time tracking when you're there. Overwatch shows no signs of preparation. Looks like three people on 74, two on 73.

"Security?"

"We are in their system," Hellion said. "Multiple cameras on every floor, several with capture angles overlapping the exterior. Seismic sensors throughout, fine-tuned enough to hear a single footfall. Remote elevator disabling with palm-locked floor selection, steel bar security doors, private escape rooms in every apartment, plus a security team ten-strong."

Wren dismissed the security team. If they put up a fight, they'd be downed with ease. The elevator controls and overrides were an easy hack. The exterior, lobby and elevator cameras were a simple matter for his hackers to copy and play on a loop. Steel-barred doors they could evade by blasting straight through concrete with compound ANFO shaped charges tucked into diamond-bit drilled holes.

"What about their own cameras? If the zoo's there, I guarantee the Apex has multiple feeds not synced to the building's system."

"And likely their own power source, independent of the building," Hellion answered swiftly. "We hit them with an Electro Magnetic Pulse. EMP. It will overload all active circuits within range. That means the surrounding ten floors, perhaps. They may have backup systems, so we will allow thirty seconds for these to engage, then we will hit them with a second EMP."

Wren hadn't heard about any of this.

"Twin EMPs? Where did you get the gear? And these emitters are mounted to drones?"

"Gerald Humphreys has been quite forthcoming," Hellion answered. "He is growing on me. Two Predator drones will swoop for us. The first is already on an approach dive from ten thousand feet. We have taken control of the traffic lights between your current position and Madison Avenue, and are synchronizing the two approaches. The first EMP should strike the moment before you reach Madison Avenue. The second as you board the elevators."

Wren's mind spun. "Humphreys gave you Predator drones? In civilian airspace, in New York? Actually approved the use of EMPs?"

"Yes," Hellion began casually, then- "well, no. But do not worry, Christopher, they will not have missiles onboard, and Humphreys does not know they have EMP capability. This is his own mistake, and B4cksl4cker's very clever hack."

Wren took a breath. Hacking Predator drones. The same machines they used for war-fighting overseas. "You're actually hacking Predators."

"Yes. It is all quite safe."

He restrained laughter. There was a lot of leeway in that word 'quite'. "I need 'totally safe' Hellion. I can't have Predator parts raining down on New Yorkers' heads. Tell me you're not risking lives on the ground. "

"Of course not! These are only bigger toys than usual, Christopher, playing with electricity. Nobody will be hurt who should not be hurt."

Wren jawed at the air briefly, struggling with that determination, but forced himself to let it go. There was no time. "Fine. Great, maybe, if you're employing safeguards."

"Yes! Many safeguards!"

"So EMPs." He spun the consequences forward. "If you cripple power on the upper floors, how will the elevators run? Won't an EMP fry them too?"

"It would," Hellion answered. "Except I am already shutting down the entire building, including the backup. By the time you're in the elevators it should have rebooted and powered up, while they will be blind. I estimate you'll have minutes only to hit them before they take the zoo down."

Minutes only. Aerial EMP strikes in the center of New York. Things had escalated fast.

"You are four minutes out, Christopher. The first Predator is at six thousand feet and closing to engage. Do you have any further questions?"

Countless questions. Only one for Hellion.

"Tell me there's a medical team on standby. If the interior of this 'lab' is anything like I expect, there'll be a lot of people in need of assistance."

"We have four ambulances on standby. New York Presbyterian Hospital has a trauma team ready. How's that?"

She'd thought of everything. While he'd been occupied with vetting and assembling his team and reeling from Rogers' revelations, she'd been prepping the rest. "You're an angel, Hellion."

"And me?" B4cksl4cker asked in his truculent bass. "Am I also angel?"

"Maybe a winged cherub," Wren allowed, "one of those pudgy babies with a bow and arrow."

"Very good," said B4cksl4cker. "I am youthful."

Wren strapped his Kevlar riot helmet tight and ducked down to look out the front windshield. The edge of Madison Avenue's segmented white front had just come into view.

36

STRIKE

The lobby was dark as Wren's team poured through the glass doors of 231 Madison Avenue, his pulse pounding loud in his ears. The space was double height but understated in the ghostly wash of streetlight cast through the huge square windows. Silver marble veined with black lay underfoot, large laser-cut copper sheets clung to the walls and a floating desk in squared-off granite stood at the head, staffed with a receptionist who looked terrified in the sweep of their flashlights.

Wren ignored him and made for the second elevator. His team lined up behind him, the other team led by Jimenez alongside

"Hellion?" he whispered.

"Second EMP just delivered," came her voice. "Swooping the Predator out. Power coming online any second..."

The lobby abruptly illuminated, a refined orange glow washing out from the waterfall crystal chandelier.

"I-" began the receptionist, but by then the elevators were chiming, the doors opening, and both strike teams poured in.

"I kept them warm for you," Hellion said. "Heading up?"

She didn't wait for a reply and the doors closed at double speed, with the car starting up at a lurch. "Hold onto a railing. You will hit two-g."

Wren grabbed the railing and his team followed suit as the elevator accelerated like a rocket launch. Wren felt gravity tugging down the skin of his face. He eased the Desert Eagle from its holster.

"Almost there," said Hellion. "The zoo appears to be reacting. They are dark, no power, but there is movement on 74. They are coming toward the elevator."

Wren gritted his teeth. Of course. He watched the floor lights flashing on the readout above the door, ripping through the fifties now. He spoke on an open channel to both teams. "We go in hot, looks like they're waiting for us."

He received nods in the elevator and the OK from Jimenez. His squad readied their weaponry. Within ten seconds the elevator decelerated hard, sending his stomach lurching up, then halted and the doors sprang open. Wren briefly glimpsed another penthouse like Central Park Place beyond, stretching away dark to the glass wall where the sun was just surfacing over the horizon, then he was in the air and leaping. Ahead lay plush carpeting, rich leather armchairs, expensive paintings slashed in bright red tones, the hint of a large mahogany conference table, then he squeezed his eyes tight shut and everything was obscured in light, smoke, sound and incoming bullets.

He hit a wall as the 'vertigo' cocktail of twin flashbang and smoke grenades erupted in the midst of the penthouse. His left shoulder struck a wall, he bounced off a side table then dropped to the lush-carpeted floor with the Desert Eagle extended dead ahead, belly to the ground and emptying the magazine into the cloud of powder smoke.

Cries rang out, automatic fire bullets sprayed the elevator's interior and walls with shrieking metallic prangs and Wren tucked his head low and crawled hard to get clear of the elevator's killing ground.

"Left, Christopher," came Hellion's calm voice, watching via the infrared Air Rangers and giving him a three-dimensional play-by-play. "Five feet and you will be clear of their field of fire."

Nothing he could do for his team right then, no time to reload, just race hard into the oncoming fire as-

Impacts suddenly ripped like a whipcrack up his back, right hip to left shoulder capped with a resounding crunch off his helmet that nearly tore his head off, punched his neck backward and mule-kicked him into the wall.

"Go, Christopher!" came Hellion's voice in his ear. "Move!"

He recoiled, stunned and hacking on the smoky air. Hit? Bullets were roaring, his depth perception seemed off and a deep heat surged down his spine. He'd been hit.

"Go!" Hellion shouted.

He ignored the wall of dizziness and crawled into the powdery dark even as more flashbangs erupted like lightning through freshly bursting clouds of smoke. Not thinking, just obeying the voice in his head. He pulled hard left when it told him, just as soon as the wall opened out, away from the storm and the smoke and rocked to his knees where he swayed for a long moment, left hand absently pulling another vertigo cocktail grenade. He pulled the tabs on the metal canisters then lobbed them over a low bookshelf into the fray.

Closed his eyes, head sagged against the wall, then the blast came.

It sounded louder. The flashbang burst like a roundhouse kick to his head, jolting him awake. He ran a hand up his back, brought it back around but didn't see blood, though it was dark and he couldn't be sure. He felt nauseous. Maybe he'd caught all the impacts on his Twaron-reinforced plate armor panels. Didn't know about the headshot, but it seemed like concussion, had to hope it was only a glancing blow, or else…

"Christopher!" came Hellion's shout. "Your team are pinned down, it's on you now, flank and take out their rear!"

He rose to his feet but stayed hunched low, circling around the bookcase and a structural column in the gritty dark, the air slipping by like hot streaks of grease on a griddle. He couldn't see a thing beyond a foot, not just for the smoke but also something wrong with his left eye. It was all black. His foot hit something invisible in the white powder smoke and he staggered, barely caught himself. A mahogany ottoman. He looked up. The smoke danced with a cacophony of shells combusting and slugs ripping left and right like two cartoon characters fighting, people hacking coughs and screaming and shouting directions through the smoke. He couldn't pick out a thing, not even which were his own team.

"There are more than I thought!" came Hellion's abrupt voice. "They surged from nowhere. I didn't see them Christopher. Your team are trapped in the elevator and they won't last long, one man already out. Maybe there are seven of them against you. No, eight!"

"I can't see them," Wren answered low, his voice sounding drunk and slurred as he advanced, trying to echo-locate the enemy but failing. "Tell me."

"Your ten o'clock," Hellion answered sharply. "One man, no two firing from behind a sofa."

Wren lurched toward them. Benelli up in front, he passed around a tall table with one hand scrabbling for purchase, knocking pool balls clicking away. He heard their voices calling out a warning, so close he almost stumbled over them, then he saw them and fell.

A controlled fall. Letting gravity pull him faster than they could sweep their rifles over and around, plucking shots through his ghost trail in the powder. He hit the ground hard on his left, body fully extended, helmet cracking off the parquet flooring, lucky not to break his neck on the coffee table a few inches over. Through a break in the smoke he saw the wild, reddened eyes of two men staring back at him.

"Morning," Wren said, and triggered the Benelli M4.

The first 12 gauge 303 grain 'trocar' shotgun shell burst out and hit one of them in the face, the trocar-angled multi spikes of the exploding round splaying on impact and churning separate paths through his skull, shredding it to red jelly. The Benelli auto regulating gas pistons pumped a second shell into the breech and Wren pulled a fraction left, hitting the second guy in the chest and coring his heart like an apple.

"Unh," Wren said.

"Three more incoming, over the armchair!" Hellion shouted.

Wren plucked at his chest for a reload, fumbled a four-grip of shotgun rounds which clattered to the ground, remembered he had two still in the slide, one already pumped to the tube, and threw himself forward over the bodies of the two men as bullets raked the wood where he'd been.

He slip-and-slid down their noodle-limp bodies to the sofa's far side, into a brief avenue of visibility through the smoky contours of a sunken den back toward the elevator, billowing now as bodies ran in the combustion-lit dark.

The sofa beside him shook in a burst of fire, leather ribbons flaying like ticker tape. Wren spun and fired blind, caught someone in the leg and took it clean off. The guy fell and screamed. Wren crawled further clear of the sofa, saw more legs rushing in and fired his last round. Hit a knee, the trocar exploded and cut out a column of the guy's support like drawing a fat pencil eraser across reality, toppling like a tree.

The Benelli's trigger came down empty with a click. Wren tried to scrabble away but now his right leg didn't work.

"Christopher, quickly, more are coming!" Hellion shouted.

He tried to pull the Desert Eagle but it was gone. He didn't know where he'd dropped it. Tried to palm another four-grip of trocar rounds to speed-load but found his hand pawing pointlessly at his neck.

"Christopher, three more figures inbound!"

He bleated a little, didn't know why, and kicked himself along the wood until he ran up against a hard marble wall, realized it was the polished island in an open plan kitchen. He tried to stand but couldn't even get his knees under him. Felt the vibration of impacts through the cold hard marble flags underfoot as bullets sprayed closer. People storming in. Taken out on his way to make an omelet. He flung one hand up to the island top, tried to lift himself, maybe if he could-

"There's no time, Christopher!" Hellion shouted. "Stay down."

He rolled, saw the figures closing in like specters in the night.

"I-" he managed, but nothing followed as a man stood over him, lowering the muzzle of a shotgun direct to his face. Wren smelled cordite and iron. Looked up into sparkling blue eyes. The Apex? So this was how it ended.

"Father," he said.

"He sends his regards," said the figure, then pulled the trig-

The world exploded.

Wren was slammed sideways into the island as a tsunami wave of wind and glass ripped into the building on a freezing wind. Wren hit, tumbled, huddled as the ceiling cracked and surged, a metallic screaming receded ending in a crash followed by the awful rush of flames rushing to ignition.

He came to on his chest, sprawled atop another man staring back at him with glassy eyes, a red dot in his forehead. Wren blinked. Not one of his team. Lit red and orange by the rising flames.

Wren rolled off, saw the fire rising in the elevator's mouth from a heap of metallic wreckage intertwined with twitching bodies. It took him long seconds to catch any grasp of what had just happened, despite Hellion shouting in his ear. The rush of wind, the blast of glass, the ceiling tearing away like a hatch cover in a tornado.

He was looking at the shattered fuselage of a Predator drone gathered like flotsam in the open elevator carriage.

"You-" he began, but lost his breath in a spasm of coughing.

"I hit them with a drone," Hellion answered flatly. "This is what I do. Now your team are down, Christopher, and Jimenez is coming, but it will not be fast enough. I cannot see their people anymore, the fire is masking infrared, so I don't know how many are left, but I am winding back, and..."

She trailed off. The voice in his head.

Wren pushed himself to his knees. His head thumped hot and he stripped the chinstrap, eased the helmet away. Instantly the pain relented and he let out a gasp, looking around as if for the first time as a howling thousand-foot-high gale sucked the powder smoke from the penthouse. By the elevator the Predator had sheared like a trocar round, long splinters of it embedded in the walls, the furniture, the men.

Glancing back along the line, he realized how lucky he'd been, laid flat out and sheltered by the granite island. The others hadn't been so lucky. Taken a military drone full to the face.

The wind lashed by like the sucking expanse of freefall, sucking fresh gouts of foul black smoke from the Predator's wreckage as green kerosene flames licked up the walls. The Predator's nosecone was jutted up against a miraculously intact vase of red desert ocotillos. Here a fin furrowed through a scorch in the carpet, there an array of fiberglass flechettes spined up from a man's back like a porcupine.

He laughed. Wasn't thinking clearly. This time his hand came back from the side of his head wet with blood. He couldn't see a thing through his left eye.

"Where?" he shouted.

Something clipped the island and granite shards peppered his chest, tinkling musically off his Twaron plate.

"Incoming fire!" Hellion shouted. "At your six, advancing through the kitchen. Christopher, I cannot plunge another drone, you have to-"

He was already on it, pulling the corpse bodily over him even as a rip of automatic fire bullets stitched a line across the floor toward them. The body took the impacts and shook until Wren found the Glock 17 at its hip and fired.

Ten shots pealed out, crumping the ceiling, a pane of far-off glass, then locking in on the figure ahead, pumping five shots into his chest like a jackhammer drill, piercing the armor and punching through. The guy's rifle discharged a scything stripe up to the ceiling as he fell.

It was quiet for a second, only Wren's raspy breathing in the whole floor, the thud of the guy's body dropping, then the repeating high chime of an elevator trying to arrive.

"Jimenez can't get in with the shaft blocked," Hellion said rapid fire. "I'm trying to rouse your team, looks like Kato's still alive, but there's no time. I've played back the drone footage and I see where they came from now, up through a passage to your four o'clock, fifty yards, but you'll have to hurry! There are lights flashing on the mechanical level, maybe the whole thing's about to blow. They know you're coming."

Wren heaved, managed to get his feet underneath him.

"Evacuate the building," he managed to say.

"Already doing it," Hellion answered as he staggered ahead, past a glossy grand piano pockmarked with bullet rounds, its curvature flickering with the rising flames. In back the high sound of the elevator chiming was broken by a series of tympanic explosions. Something in the Predator blowing, but Wren didn't turn back to see.

Into a library he went, books floor to ceiling drifted by black smoke. There was a rug tipped over at one corner and a raw cement stairway leading down. He checked for his Benelli, his Desert Eagle, but they were both gone, only the dead man's Glock now, maybe a handful left in the mag.

Didn't matter. Five more steps, left leg dragging, depth perception zooming in and out crazily, then he dropped down into the zoo.

37

ZOO

Wren descended into the flickering gloom of a hidden mechanical floor. Some kind of industrial tunnel ran east-west along the building's southern face at crooked zigzag angles, with red emergency lights blinking fast in the rough gray ceiling. There were no windows, and line of sight was blocked by interjecting bulkheads, likely the structural trusses binding the perimeter wall to the building's central core.

A scream rang out. Wren fell the last step onto raw, stained concrete flooring and stumbled. His one good eye saw double and his left leg barely held his weight. He ducked and lifted a hand to the ceiling to steady himself, not even six feet high, as low and dank as a cave, then turned, tracking the tunnel. Rough concrete-sprayed beams jutted at all angles, along with thick pipes and heavy swatches of electrical cabling, cross-hatching the tight passage like rampant overgrowth in some night jungle. His bodycam flashlight activated in the dark, scrawling light over the red-tinged walls, finding black finger streaks.

Another scream rang through the funhouse tunnel, and Wren spun, started loping west.

"I cannot pinpoint them," came Hellion's voice in his ear. "The heat shielding is too strong. Hurry, Christopher!"

The tunnel tightened sharply. Wren ducked beneath a diagonal truss that had to be two feet around, misjudging the angle in the blinking dark and thumping his collarbone hard as he came up. He squeezed between two vertical waste downpipes, water gurgling within like the bowels of some great steaming beast, pushed through a beard of heavy cables, clambered over a sharp diagonal truss, crawled a spell under a raft of horizontal bars then staggered a final length along the twisting tunnel until it angled north into a long, open hall.

For a second he only stared.

The hall was huge but the ceiling was barely seven feet, making it feel like he was being slowly crushed. Maybe a hundred yards in length and running the full footprint of the building's west side; a space carved out with fewer pipes, cables and support trusses, only lit by the epileptic pulse of the emergency lights, revealing its horrors in patchwork red-stained blooms.

The right wall was studded with tarnished metal doors next to silvery glass panes, likely one-way windows into cells beyond. To his left ran cages. Floor to ceiling iron bars, close-set and casting stroboscopic shadows as the red lights flashed. Beyond the bars low, shivering humps clustered to the corners like flies on a horse's eye. Wren caught glimpses of skin lashed raw, long bedraggled strands of hair swimming in curdling blood, fire-blackened faces, the nubs where limbs should be.

The air hung thickly with the stench of sickness, sweat and human waste, making Wren's head swirl faster. Screams and mumbles sucked free as his bodycam light played over their deformed bodies. He lurched toward them, the world reeling as his head spun, almost missing a step. Dozens of pale, malformed creatures on the other side shrank and howled at his approach.

"Christopher," came Hellion's warning voice, but he barely heard it.

At the cage door he yanked on the bolt but it was padlocked. Hazily he lifted the Glock, thinking maybe to shoot out the pin, but at once the pitiful creatures on the other side surged like a tide, pressing their scarred, lumpish bodies against the bars and reaching through with whatever limbs they had.

Wren was startled backward. Staring full into what was left of their faces in the flashlight's harsh glare. Some eyeless. Earless. Noseless. Worse. In a fresh flush of baking terror he realized what they wanted. Not to steal the gun to fight him, but to pull the trigger on themselves.

His heart wrenched. Gazing into depths of agony like nothing he'd ever seen. Dislocated. Dismembered. Insane.

He swung about, searching for a key, some means to break them out, but found none.

"Find the Apex!" came Hellion's shout, sounding very far off. "Help them later. Find him first."

Wren wavered, nodded like she was there to see, looking into the ruined eye sockets of faces at the cage wall. "I'll help," he said, sounding weak and reedy even as the words left his mouth. "I'll get you out."

"Move, Christopher!"

They began to wail. He turned and ran. Skinny, ropey white arms plunged toward him through the cages like froth off a wave. At one point the hall narrowed and he lurched right to avoid them, hit a cell door in the wall on the right and slammed through into-

Green.

He dropped to his knees, the Glock discharged as his hand slammed onto the ground, then he was up and spinning. All he saw was green: on the walls, the floor, the ceiling, blaring up at him dayglo as the skin of a lime, lit by the manic roving beam of his flashlight. He blinked and rubbed his eyes, thought for a moment he'd gone mad. The whole of the small cell was green; twin green-framed beds stood side by side filling the middle, with green sheets, pillows and blankets, besmirched with a rich layer of greasy black.

Blood?

The air stank of ignited napalm, the tang of gasoline lingering along with the smoke of scorched flesh. He whirled but couldn't find the door, started running his hands over the walls looking for it but finding only more sheer green stippled with dried blood spray. His heart stampeded, once, twice he went around growing increasingly frantic, fearing himself trapped like the withered creatures in the cages, until-

"Stop, Christopher! Christopher listen to me!"

Hellion's voice finally broke through. Wren stopped racing, stood still and panting for a moment, the room spinning, realizing that her voice had been there all the time, undergirding it all.

"I-" he began, but had no words to follow up with.

"It is all right, Christopher, you will give yourself heart attack," she said, and he heard the relief in her voice. "I have played many horror video games, so I have seen all this before. You must not panic, Christopher. The door is to your left. Do not think about these people. You will come back for them. You cannot help them right now."

The words stamped logic back atop the terror. He'd said the same thing to his team, don't be horrorstruck, but that was one thing to say, another to live through. He'd seen plenty of horrors in his day, children caged, people tortured to death, but nothing to match the intensity of this sickly, red-flaring dark.

He took a calming breath.

"I'm injured," he said. "Shot."

"We will fix you. You're walking. Now see this through."

He didn't need to be told twice. Burn the terror to rage. He turned and found the door, pushed out through it and into the moaning corridor of pale bodies pressed to their cage walls.

"It is only a video game, Christopher," Hellion said in his ear. "Finish the level."

He turned right and ran. The cages and the cubicles ended at a concrete wall, where another jumbled tunnel picked up on the right, heading east along what had to be the building's north side. Wren plunged in, stumbling over pipes and scraping against the rough walls, feeling the skin of the building breathing to his left. Hellion's Air Rangers would only be some fifty yards away, hanging in the air.

He bobbed under a wide steel truss, weaved around two tree-trunk-thick rebar columns, scrambled over a large pipe head and through another cavern of looping cables until there was a glass door ahead that slid smoothly open at his touch.

Here the raw industrial tunnel spread into an utterly mismatched corridor. The ceiling was tall enough for him to stand upright again, the raw cement and angles were gone, and the red emergency lamps flashed off lustrous black tile flooring and cream-painted walls hung with-

Wren leaned closer as he lurched on, feet thumping on the marble tiles. Sepia tone framed photographs of a place he recognized immediately, done artfully and enlarged, but without any of the drooping facades or burned-out structures of latter years.

He stopped and stared.

Photographs of the Pyramid's fake town.

His heart crashed violently in his chest, his mouth dried out and his vision tunneled tight to the one photograph before him, capturing in stark technicolor a past that had only ever existed in the mists of his childhood memory. It showed the front of the Bank building, just a stage set for a Peckinpah Western that was never made, and one of the first places Wren had burned down in the years since.

No other photographs of this place existed. No evidence that it had ever been there other than a plain concrete foundation pad laid out in the Sonoran wastes.

Except here it was alive. Hundreds of people stood in front arrayed on tiers like kids on their school bleachers. Wren's gaze ran left to right like a typewriter slide; men in the back row, women in the middle, children at the front. He knew them all. All were beaming like this was a happy day out at summer camp, with the orange desert in back and the blue sky above, and...

In the center, arms wide, blue eyes sparkling in his bodycam light's glare, stood the Apex.

Undoubtedly him. Looming large out of nightmare. The same man as on David Keller's stage.

Wren couldn't breathe.

He looked so young. With rich dark hair, a broad grin, wearing denim jeans and a check shirt like he was just another regular human. Looking happy. Maybe late twenties. A photograph Wren had never seen. He'd destroyed every reminder of the Pyramid, and there'd never been anything like this. He had no recollection of it being taken, and his eyes raked the rows hungrily, seeking something else that he'd never seen before. There'd been no mirrors in the Pyramid. The only glimpses of himself he'd ever caught as a child had been in darkened store fronts and car windows as he'd danced for new followers, as their drivers pulled away.

A phantom child only, dark with the sun, moon-white teeth, hale and healthy, performing for the masses as they passed.

His heart skipped a beat.

There, at the bottom right corner, stood seven dark-skinned children. Not the same as the mismatching line of grinning kids beside them. Not dressed in jeans and T-shirts like those part-timers, who looked like they'd just had a wonderful day of activities, archery and s'mores and a singsong around the camp fire.

No. These children wore the hessian tunics of the Pyramid. These could only be the Pequeños, children of the Apex himself, and Wren's breath caught as he picked them out one by one and saw the Apex in each, his lost brothers and sisters, lined up eldest to youngest.

Galicia-In-Her-Mother's-Heart. Chrysogonus-With-Bared-Arm. Zachariah-Of-The-Marsh. Tomothy-Whereof-The-Giants-Roam. Gabriel-In-Extremis. There at Gabriel's left arm, Pequeño 3.

Christopher Wren.

He gasped. So small. Barely six years old Two younger Pequeños to his left, one held in the arms of a nursing maid.

His breathing grew chaotic, a panic attack rushing in. This was him, trapped in the Pyramid just like the people he'd left behind in their cages.

Happy in appearance. Healthy to the onlooker. Tortured only by night, on the Apex's whims, unlike the broken subjects in the Pyramid's zoo.

This was what Jamal Jalim had feared most, and the man's last words flashed back to Wren then, blurted in the midst of a cardiac attack delving toward stroke, and he whispered them now.

"We were his favorites."

"We've all grown up," came a voice to his left.

Wren's head snapped up so fast it made him dizzy.

At the end of the black tiled corridor flanked by Pyramid family photographs stood a woman. She was tall and olive-skinned, wore a cropped black halter top and a long aquiline dress. Even standing perfectly still she exuded grace. High cheekbones over dark purple lips. Thick hair pulled skull-achingly tight into some complex confection of sweeps and curls at the back of her head. Strong arms crossed before her. Gazing at him with something like recognition.

Wren felt like he was drowning. Plunging back into his childhood.

"Though some of us are still living in the past, aren't we, Pequeño 3?"

The words washed over him. He stared into her eyes. Gray with flecks of sparkling blue. It was impossible but the resemblance was undeniable. Last time he'd seen her she'd been dead, suffocated at the bottom of a pit when he was nine years old. All his brothers and sisters had died there and then, casualties of the Apex's war on faith.

Except.

The word trickled up through his throat. A name he hadn't spoken in nearly thirty years.

"Galicia?"

38

GALICIA

She took a step closer and Wren almost dropped where he stood. Legs faltering. Heart slamming madly. The dead resurrected.

"You're not looking well, little brother," Galicia said.

There it was. Confirmation. Here in the flesh, though all he could see was the solemn-faced teenager from the photograph imposed atop her. She'd been sixteen then, barely a shade of the proud and beautiful woman she'd now become, and he blinked hard, trying to dispel this twisted double vision.

"You-" he began, but nothing came out. Hellion shouted but he didn't hear a word for the blood rushing in his ears.

"I've waited so long for this moment," Galicia said, taking a languid step forward. Now Wren saw the knife in her hand. Long bladed, stiletto thin. "Ever since the pit, I've wondered which of us would cross your path first."

His throat jammed. Forced words out. "You're dead."

She took another step, one hand tracing the wall gently, caressing framed photographs as she glided closer, a smile flickering at the edges of her lips. "Perhaps. You remember the mantra, I think? Death is nothing but a doorway."

The old words buzzed back to the forefront of his mind. "Fear is a portal."

"Walk in the fire," Galicia intoned solemnly. "How we've watched you, little brother. Your trials and tribulations. All your suffering. Now you've come home."

His mind felt gridlocked. "This isn't my home."

"No," she allowed sadly. "But one day."

He fought for control, to stop reacting and start acting, but his thoughts were a storm and Hellion was just a noise in the back of his head. He'd come here for a purpose, but now that purpose had been swamped by the past. "How are you alive? I saw you dead in that pit. All of you."

"You saw a performance," Galicia said, sounding faintly bored. "Just another recruitment drive."

Those words made no sense. "You died. How was that a recruitment?"

Her smile spread, her tone turned chiding. "Little brother. How have you travelled the world and not yet learned this? Had the Apex not sacrificed his own children on the altar of faith, would the good people of the Pyramid ever have walked in the fire? We both know the answer to that one."

She gave him a wink. It floored him. Just like the old Galicia, and completely out of place.

"I..."

"Do you remember how we used to watch the babies crying together, little brother?" She took another step closer. "How the night desert's warmth enveloped us, just you and I in the dark, out of our beds and knowing our father would be angry if he found us, buzzing with fairy lights and standing hand-in-hand to watch them for hours, mewling themselves to sleep?" Her delicate fingers ran along the lip of another framed photograph, this one showing just the Pequeños standing side-by-side in the desert. "Do you remember when I taught you how to take notes at your first drowning? I can picture the man today still. Just beginning to glimpse the world lying beyond the door. Growing hungry and begging for more. Our father slowing him down. Ensuring the portal was fully open."

Wren listened transfixed, the same sing-song tone she'd used to whisper lullabies to him as a small, scared child. "Do you remember huddling down in the blankets with me, hiding from our brother Chrysogonus? He was always so furious with you." She smiled at the memory. "Untying all his barometers of progress. Monkeying with his knots." The smile grew wistful, and Wren felt like he was floating on some kind of drugged cloud. "I remember your little hot body pressed close to my thighs, your thin arms around my back, your face in my belly, your tiny high pulse racing like a baby bird, and I remember thinking, if I break his poor neck now to spare him this fear, will he still walk in the fire?"

Her heels clacked closer on the marble tiles.

"I love you still, little brother. I always have. I always will. I only ever want what's best for you."

She was close now, maybe ten yards, and he could almost feel it, the forgotten heat of her body against his, trembling beneath the sheets while Chrysogonus stalked the night, ready to douse him in candle wax or lash the soles of his feet with an ocotillo arm, punishment for even the slightest offense. He remembered her heavy pulse as the soothing staple of his earliest memories, always there at his side, stroking his back, smoothing out his wild hair as the nightmares bled away.

"I remember," he said, and his voice came out thick. Everything else forgotten, the voice in his ear long-gone.

"I'm glad," she said. "We've been too long apart. Sharing whispers on the rooftop, watching the new people flow in. Like a river they came, little brother, never ending. I can see them even now, from all the corners of the world to see the wonder we were building. Every inch of pain mounting up like blocks in a great testament of stone, rising toward the ultimate feat of a pyramid framed from human grace. All the ways we used to imagine shaping them, you and I as they tumbled in, lives stacked atop lives atop lives. You were always the architect. I was never surprised at the name you took for yourself, in the days after we parted. Christopher Wren. How could you choose any less of a man? How else could you hope to follow in our father's footsteps?"

He was adrift. Didn't know what to say. "Galicia..."

"They were such fools, don't you think, those converts?" she pressed on. "In their jeans and their flannel tops, with their air-conditioned vehicles and handheld technology, thinking they could one day truly belong to the monument we were constructing. Mere mortar to hold the blocks together, when all along we knew that we were the true pillars of the pyramid. You. Your brothers. And me. Five disciples and one prodigal son. Our father's true legacy. The pathway to a brighter world for all humanity. Because fear is a portal, little brother. Pain is a doorway. Will you walk in the fire with me?"

She lunged.

The stiletto blade came sweeping down, cracking the fog around him like a skin of winter ice. Two yards out now and Wren moved too slow, jerked to the side but caught the pick's tip on one of his armor plates, slicking off and digging through the Twaron fiber to plunge into his shoulder.

He cried out and lurched into the wall as the stiletto blade sucked clear, right arm suddenly hanging numb, the Glock clattering to the tiled floor.

Galicia didn't wait, sent the blade out again in a frontal thrust backed by her whole body weight, straight toward the hollow of Wren's throat, a triangular chink where the vest had pulled down under the weight of his bandoliers. He threw his left hand up to bat the blade away but took it instead directly through his open palm.

The pain was instant and overwhelming, ripping an animal cry from his lips. On instinct he twisted his wrist so the metacarpal bones braced against the slim metal and tugged, trying to wrench the knife from her grip, but it was too firm and he only managed to pull his hand off the spike, streaming blood.

"Little brother," she said sadly, "if only you saw what I see."

The blade swept in again from above, and this time his left elbow rocketed up, caught her forearm with the long blade almost tickling his face as he sent a straight punch out, there was nothing to catch.

She spun. Recognition came a millisecond too late as she pirouetted on her right heel, brought the blade arcing it toward his right ear.

He barely got his hand up in time, watched in horror as the blade plunged through the meat of his right palm and kept going, slapping his hand against his face and shooting the stiletto through his right cheek, cracking off his teeth and onward through his left cheek like the skewer in a kebab.

He roared and shoved her away. The blade pulled free and he staggered back, blood filling up his mouth now, both hands dripping to the black tiles. The hunger in her eyes turned his stomach.

"Pain is a doorway, little brother," she said, eyes flashing blue. "Don't fight me."

He lurched another step back. Losing blood. Sick of feeling sick and confused and afraid, tired of being caught off balance and ready to lean in. He spat a stream of blood, straightened as best he could and raised his ruined fists before him.

"You call this pain?"

Her lips split in a proud smile "For the Apex so loved the world that he gave his most favored son." She came in hard even as she spoke, lashing a stripe that clattered off his forearm plates and forced him another step back.

"I've waited so long to guide you through this door," Galicia said, raising the blade as she advanced. "My sweet little brother, finally taking his place in the tombs of the Pyramid."

She sprang in with the lightness of a ballet dancer, too fast for his one good eye to track, a leap and a probe that spiked into his left shoulder so fast he couldn't pull away. Fresh pain welled down his left side, he slipped on his own blood and almost fell, too slow to defend himself.

"Don't be afraid, little bird," she pressed, and leaped in again, coming low and driving the blade toward his belly, mercifully blocked by the armor plating. He caught her hand retreating with his rising knee, but it didn't dislodge the blade, only gave her another chance to strike as he wavered off-balance.

She used it well, stepping into another pirouette that sent the blade slamming grip-deep through his right arm and into his ribs.

Wren gasped, yanked the blade away, and finally grabbed her halter lapels, sending a crushing headbutt squarely into her face.

In a moment she was away, but the feel of her nose crumpling against his forehead remained hot in his skin, the sound ringing in his ears. Blood streaked her glamorous lips now, down her elegant throat.

"There you are," she said, eyes afire as she sprang back into the fray.

He ignored the blade. Put his shoulder down and charged. Maybe it peppered his back, glancing off the armor panels, but he didn't care. He was too worn out to dance. Weight was his only advantage here, and he gathered her like Anais had gathered him, drove through, lifted and slammed.

Her back cracked off the floor and she gasped, something crunched in her chest. The blade spun out of her grip and ricocheted off the wall, but somehow she snuck an elbow up and struck his face, throwing his head back.

He rolled, a lifetime of reactions buying him the seconds he needed to come up on his feet like an old boxer fighting the count, weaving now, drunken, the stiletto blade in his hand as she-

Stood, leveling the Glock at his face.

"Walk in the fire, little brother," she said.

"You first."

She pulled the trigger. He flung the knife.

The gun clicked empty.

The blade struck Galicia's shoulder and near punched her off her feet.

He laughed. Took a second to comprehend. He must've miscounted. There were no bullets left in the Glock, by the Apex's grace.

"Don't kill her, Christopher!" came a sudden shout in his ear.

He whirled to find the source, but the corridor behind him was empty and rolling like an ocean, blood-smeared and turning to gray. Nobody. He felt torn and disoriented, turned back to where his sister was laughing wetly on the floor, one hand to the blade's grip as blood poured from the wound, watching him whirl.

"Are they talking to you now?" she asked, blood spraying with every word, "the false prophets in your ear?"

"We came here for proof!" the voice came again, and Wren pressed one hand to his ear and touched cold plastic, remembering the earpiece.

Hellion. She felt like a figment from another life.

"We need her alive, Christopher," Hellion called. "She is all the proof we need, but you need to move! Jimenez is on the mechanical floor with you, there's enough C4 strapped to the support trusses to blow out the core. Christopher!"

It barely registered. He didn't care. Advanced on his sister through a roiling red mist.

"I can help you, Galicia," he said, gargling on the blood pouring from his shredded cheeks. "I help lots of people. You could still be free."

She laughed low, tugged on the blade but her hands were slick with blood and slipped on the grip, barely sucking it halfway out. "Are they telling you about the bomb, little brother? How today we will all walk in the fire?"

She was two steps away. All he had to do was lay hands on her, hoist her, carry her away, but the corridor kept zooming and refocusing like a concertina and his feet didn't land where he wanted.

"Two minutes, Christopher!" Hellion barked. "Miller cannot break the circuit. You must go now!"

"I escaped," he slurred, holding one bloody hand out as he tottered forward, sinking to one knee before her. "I escaped our father's shadow. You can too."

Galicia pulled on the blade again, and this time drew the weapon out. Fresh blood welled from the wound and her face blanched pale. "Escaped his shadow?" she asked, coughing blood on his cheeks, her eyes so close to his like they'd always been as children. "Little brother, you have never once been out of his shadow. All your choices have belonged to him. All your glories are shared. There is no world beyond the reach of his love."

"Galicia," he said, reaching for the blade. "Sister. We can-"

"I love you, little brother," she said, raising the blade overhead. "I will wait for you, on the other side."

She brought the blade down. Wren couldn't move fast enough. It sank straight into the hollow of her throat and punched through cartilage into her chest cavity. The fire went out of her eyes like a broken circuit, her knees buckled and she dropped to the floor with a thud.

His elder sister, finally dead.

39

PROOF

Wren swayed.

Blood drooled from his torn cheeks and spilled from his lips, leaked from his palms and his shoulders and his punctured arm. The corridor spun around him. Black tiles. Cream walls. Photographs of the Pyramid with his dead sister sprawled on the floor.

He didn't know what to do. Took a step, almost fell and clutched at the air, thumped into the wall. Knew on some level this was the blood loss emptying out his head, but there was no getting around it. His eyes darted but took nothing in.

"Listen to me, Christopher," came the soupy drone in his head, "forget the proof, you need to get out right now!"

He blinked, inundated with memories of his big sister. Dead for thirty years, now here she was, dead in front of him.

"Ninety seconds," came the voice, carrying an urgency he didn't feel. Didn't matter. He trusted it.

His legs moved. The corridor tumbled. He hit another wall, slid until he came hard against the same photograph from before, now flecked with blood. Little Pequeño 3 so small in the corner. The Apex at the center. All those dead people. Memory of a forgotten world.

He put his elbow through the glass. Scratched out the shards, snatched the picture and stuffed it into his jacket. About all the proof he could manage.

"Seventy seconds!"

He ran. Slapped off another wall. Slipped on the tiles. Rounded a corner, glimpsed an empty office to the left but there was no time to foray inside. Blood sprayed as his elbows pumped, south now along the east wall past rooms decked with large speakers and screens, people staring back at him from chairs like regular office workers, a rack of large cameras charging in a rack, blinking packages strapped in the corner of each, pressed against the central core.

C-4. All these people just waiting for the bang.

"Sixty seconds," Hellion shouted.

He rounded the southeast corner then slapped through another glass door back into the zigzagging corridor along the south wall. The stairs had to lie ahead, and he careened into the jungle of beams and struts, throwing himself over a thick length of rebar, scrabbling through tangles of cable, shuffling hectically as Hellion's voice counted him down from fifty.

He came up too fast from beneath a diagonal beam and hammered his skull into concrete. The shock dumped him to his knees as they hit forty, he crawled through thirty, then was up again and lurching like a madman.

"Twenty seconds, Christopher, get the hell out!"

On the count of ten he reached the concrete stairs, cornered hard and fell on all fours, was charging up like a dog when the blast struck.

It slammed him sideways just as he surged through into the library, smacking off the window and bouncing away, feeling the explosion more than he heard it as everything shifted underfoot, concrete-coated steel trusses atomized under an incredible hammer blow.

He blinked up from darkness at the head of the steps, with plaster dust and stinking chemical smoke fuming up from noxious green fires in the tunnel below, while books tumbled down from shelves around him.

"I see you, Christopher!" Hellion shouted. "You have to move. The whole top of the building is swaying, seems they took out structural columns, it looks like it's going to-"

He felt the world shift beneath him, like the moment you hit the top of a rollercoaster and begin to tip, the arrogance of height giving way to the cold truth of gravity.

"You should see the hole in the building's side, Christopher!" Hellion called, sounding half awe-struck, half excited. "It is coming down now. Get out!"

Numb calculations ran through his dimming head. He pulled himself to his feet just as the floor canted hard right, sinking to an incline of maybe ten degrees, toppling south. He was at the south side now. One thing he'd learned from his days in the forests of Maine: never run in the shadow of a falling tree.

He had to get offline.

Now smoke was flowing past him in a foul green river, rushing toward the hole smashed by the Predator drone. He rose and let it sweep him along half-blind as the floor tilted steeper. His eyes stung, every muscle ached, and he was halfway across the sunken den when the tower jerked further over and a terrible scraping came from his left.

Wren stared through smoke as the white-hot inferno of the Predator drone's wreckage answered the shifting call of gravity and began tumbling down the scorched carpet toward him like some hellish avalanche. He took one more step and leaped, barely reached the tattered sofa before the tumbling rush swept everything flush through the great shattered hole in the building's skin behind him; dead bodies, flame and furniture pouring out like a waterfall.

Then the sofa tumbled too, tossing Wren head over foot until he hit the window by its cracked edge, knocking the wind from his lungs. Wind rushed by him scant inches away. Something hard hit him in the face, dropped lengthwise into his lap, and he was stunned to find it was his Benelli shotgun.

He barely had the wind to laugh. Sometimes the almighty provided. He snatched it, pushed himself up and ran, cracking the breech and fumbling a single shell from his bandolier into the tube as he struggled to stay upright and run on.

Thirty degrees now? Hellion was a siren in his ear, and Wren leaned one hand against the glass as the whole penthouse rolled and more furniture slid to the windows. The conference table jammed into his path and he pulled himself up and along the side, Benelli clacking against the window like a blind man's cane. The building jolted again, closing fast on forty-five degrees with the floor to ceiling windows glowering out over the incredible drop. Wren glimpsed tiny vehicles racing across intersections below, people like dots, and knew that within seconds everything would be smothered by the wreckage of 231 Madison Avenue.

The contents of the Apex's penthouse rained and rolled left to right around him. Red-streaked paintings, cutlery, chairs, potted plants, cushions. A pillow hit him in the face. A toaster hurtled by like an artillery shell. Fifty degrees and Wren ran the last few yards on the windows themselves as New York opened like a chasm below. Hellion screaming. His whole body burning. He raised the Benelli and fired the single trocar round into the east side window ahead, sending fracture patterns ripping out, then his shoulder hit, the glass burst like a hailstorm and he was through.

Somersaulting down alongside the cascading structure in a fall of glass. The world opened up and the sun speared into his eyes and the gray sky spun toward blue. 1,200 feet, maybe twelve seconds fall time, and he stiffened out his body like an aero foil to glide away away from the chaos of 231 Madison, soaring east above Billionaire's Row.

Maybe six seconds down at five hundred feet high, with New York rushing up like a cannon ball his slick right hand found the release strap and pulled. The chute shot out from his pack and snatched him out of freefall. Ten more seconds and crosswinds slammed him into a building square on, three seconds after which he dropped hard into oncoming traffic.

40

LITTLE BIRD

Wren's legs gave out on impact with the road and he slapped into a ragdoll roll, past a yellow cab veering away in a screech of brakes, limbs windmilling across the median until he flopped on his back before a steaming semi, parachute tugging tight at the harness across his chest.

He twisted the release then slumped as the chute whipped away. Charcoal clouds and gouts of black smoke swirled together across the sky. Debris fell and hit with a torrential drumbeat. Hellion's voice came in static bursts in his ear. Horns honked until all the honking stopped and the car doors opened and the people stepped out to watch the top twenty floors of Madison 231 peel away like a piece of rotten fruit.

Flames stamped a ragged crown across the 73rd floor, just visible through the pumping wheezes of smoke. Falling chunks of masonry became an onslaught of crashing and rending, sending pummeling vibrations through the blacktop into Wren's body. He tried to stand but the juddering earth wouldn't hold him. He watched as Madison 231 tipped beyond its ability to hold, support trusses blown, separated from the concrete core, ripping clear housings and the glass façade until finally the whole thing-

-fell.

The building sheared and roared. Terrible seconds passed as the top twisted and disintegrated under its own weight, tumbling down to the street.

The impact began with a gut punch to the spine and kept on coming as kidney punches, rabbit punches, mule kicks, blasting out a mushroom cloud of dust.

People screamed and coughed. People ran in the sudden gray pall. People cursed and engines revved. "Not again," someone cried. "Run!" somebody shouted.

Wren tried again to get up but his feeble arms couldn't lift him.

"...coming!" Hellion called in his ear.

The road skittered beneath him like a drum skin as the structure kept crumbling and falling piece after piece. Sirens fired up all around.

"Hey man, are you OK?" Somebody was leaning over him through the rush of dust, one hand on his shoulder. "I think this guy came out of the building!"

Blood leaked through Wren's ruined cheeks, though the flow was slower now. He tried to say something, managed only a feeble cough.

Another face loomed close. "That's Christopher Wren! You say he was in the building?"

"I saw him parachute in!"

"That settles it!"

He heard the click of a hammer cocking, the sound cutting through the voices and sirens and falling rubble. He heard a gunfire report crack out, strike metal, but couldn't see any of it, couldn't crane his neck, only knew he hadn't been hit.

"What the hell, are you crazy man? He's one of the good guys!"

"He's a damn terrorist, and if you don't get out of the way I'll blow your head off too."

The shouting rose. Bodies shifting in the blurry smoke. Wren couldn't keep track of the fight. Blows thrown, maybe. He tried to say something but couldn't, tried to roll away but didn't even have the strength for that, until a second massive chunk of building thundered into the ground and unleashed a sandstorm blast of grit that muffled everything.

Screams. Gunfire. Fighting.

Wren choked on the ash. Caught scraps of voices in his ear. Then there was a hand on his shoulder.

"He's here!"

Hands lifted him. He couldn't do a thing. People carried him at a run through the bitter cloud, making turns until flashing hazard lights appeared ahead, the back of a van opened up and Wren was bundled in.

"Hellion," he whispered, barely audible.

"They have you, Christopher," she answered, her voice coming clearer now. "We did it, Rogers has the proof, now just stay alive."

The van kicked into motion. Proof? He didn't understand. Hands moved across his body now, cutting away his strike suit, pushing intravenous feeds into his arms, pressing bright white gauze to his wounds. He blinked and opened his eyes standing over a pit in the desert.

They were all there. Galicia. Chrysogonus. Zachariah. Gabriel. Tomothy. Even little Grace.

"They aren't dead," came the deep voice behind him, one arm wrapped around Wren's shoulders. "Merely in waiting."

"They're alive!" he shouted.

"I know, Sir," came the reply. A man he'd seen before, maybe? A name burred into the front of his head. Jimenez? Gently prying Wren's fingers away. "We're stabilizing you, sir, you've lost too much blood, if we don't-"

"If we don't have the faith to follow in their example, then what are we?" asked the Apex, standing now on the fake town's Main Street with little Pequeño 3 at his side, looking out over the one thousand spreading back. "My own children walked in the fire, for you! They are waiting now, for you!"

The people cheered.

"So many people," someone was muttering, and Wren blinked, felt the sharp snip and pucker of needles punching through his skin, saw the gray face of a young man sitting with his head in his hands mumbling. Kato?

"He's conscious," somebody said. Wren saw Jimenez above him, and was that Miller? Bombs expert. Blood up to both of their elbows, curved needles in their fingers trailing blue surgical thread.

"Sir, we can't sedate you," Jimenez said, "your system's on the edge. You need to keep calm. Every movement's causing more damage."

More damage. The words echoed without meaning in his head.

"Ready to turn him," Miller barked.

"Turn," Jimenez answered, and abruptly they flipped Wren, throwing him face to face with-

"Every last one," said the Apex.

They were standing amidst the charred corpses of the dead, and the Apex was holding Pequeño 3 by the shoulders, gazing deep into his eyes. Smoke drifted between them. Pequeño 3 remembered little but the blue oasis of his irises, brimming with joy.

"Have you ever seen something so beautiful?"

"Clear!" came the shout, and Wren gasped, chest convulsing as the yellow crash cart paddles pulled back, the shiver of a thousand volts working its way out to his extremities. "He's back."

"Stay with us, Sir," Jimenez shouted, leaning in. "That's an order."

Wren felt himself falling already.

"We're losing him again, prep for another-"

"Shall I tell you a secret?" whispered the Apex in his ear.

Pequeño 3 said nothing, only stood as motionless as a saguaro cactus amidst the dead.

"There is no world beyond," he said, voice straining with glee. "No holy army, no sacred mission. They're just dead." He pointed. "That one, and that one, and that one. And do you know why?"

"He's back!" came the shout. Someone was shaking his arm, rubbing at his side. "This wound in his side's the real bleeder. Almost in his armpit, straight into the chest cavity. Looks like she stabbed him clean through, there's blood in his lung, we have to-"

They flipped him onto his other side, probed deeper at his chest, and again he saw gray-faced Kato, this time staring directly at him, wearing the same face as the misshapen victims behind the cage walls of the zoo.

Horror-struck. Wren's lips moved, forming soundless words the man needed to hear. "It's going to be OK."

They didn't register on Kato's face. It wasn't believable. Who was Wren to promise anyone anything…

"Because it feels good," the Apex crowed. "Because it feels good when they die, and what else is there in this shitty world than feeling good?"

He pulled away then, spread his arms, addressed the river of smoking dead stretching away. "Go forth, my army! Serve me well on the other side!"

He laughed. Pequeño 3 couldn't follow it, didn't move his head until the Apex reached down to angle his chin upward.

"Hey," he said, and winked. "Don't look so down in the dumps, son. You and I, we're the good guys here." Pequeño 3 said nothing. The Apex gently dabbed his nose. "Only tell them the truth, little bird. Open their eyes and pave my way into their hearts."

41

STRANGLEHOLD

Wren sucked in a gasp and opened his eyes.

A face was leaning over him, just a blur as he breathed hard, trying to flush the disinfectant stink of ammonium carbonate out of his nose and lungs. Smelling salts?

"He's awake," came a voice that sounded echoey and flat, like shouts heard underwater.

Everything hurt. Bars of light flared when he shifted his head. Memories came back in rags and tatters: floor 74 in flames with half his team down; the Predator drone wrecked in a heap of bodies; the zoo, the green cells, the photograph, and then-

Galicia.

His mental checklist stuttered like a scratched record, playing and replaying snippets of his sister's appearance, her voice, the way she'd wielded that knife.

His sister was alive. Had been alive.

The memory brought the pain on harder. Aching in his shoulders. Throbbing in his hands. Burning in his cheeks. He moved his tongue inside his mouth; it felt hot, scratchy and swollen where sutures had gone through. He remembered the iron taste of the stiletto blade stabbing through his mouth, forcing his tongue down like a spoon in the mouth of an epileptic.

Galicia.

He blinked several times, clearing the film of grit blocking his vision enough that the face above him resolved. Blond hair pulled back tight, bright green eyes, someone he hadn't expected to see at all.

"Rogers?"

His voice was barely a croak.

"In the flesh, Christopher," she replied, sounding relieved. He blinked and the space around her took on shape and color: a large window in back looking out over a streaming gray sky; the sense of other people in the room, though he couldn't lift his neck to see; the vinework of empty intravenous blood and plasma bags hanging either side.

"I hopped a flight as soon as I could," she said. "Hellion sent me video of your strike. She said you were almost dead."

He tried to take that in. Hopped a flight? It felt like only minutes ago that he'd been in the zoo and-

"How long?" he asked, trying to jumpstart the locomotive of his brain. His mouth shaped words oddly, his tongue thick with bruising. "You were in Cincinnati. That means…"

"Four hours, all in. I wanted to wake you sooner, but…" she trailed off, gesturing generally at him. The message was clear.

"I'm in bad shape."

"The worst I've ever seen. We're lucky you're a universal blood recipient, otherwise they'd never have kept you juiced, all the holes you had in you?" She gave a wan smile. "Add that to your prodigious lung capacity and one helluva thick head, it's still a miracle you survived the jump from an exploding skyscraper."

He tried to absorb that. Tried to push himself up but his body didn't respond.

"Why can't I get up?"

"You're restrained," Rogers said. "Chest straps. Also you're on a pretty hefty dose of morphine. Both for your own safety; you were thrashing around, shouting about the Apex, Galicia, the Pyramid."

That checked out. "So administer epinephrine." The word was hard to say and came out glottal. "Unbuckle me. I need to get moving."

She snorted. "You wouldn't last five minutes. Just about all your stuffing came out, Wren, and they barely got it back in. You're more stitches than man right now." She took a moment, as if considering how much to say, before plunging on. "That bitch sister of yours, Galicia? She punctured your cheeks, your shoulders, your hands, your arm, and your left lung. That's bad. And even before that you took three shots with high percussion rounds, two in the back, one in the helmet. If any one of those had been a flush impact you'd be dead now. Plate armor, that thick skull and the blessed acute angle saved you. Look forward to pissing blood for a couple weeks, shortness of breath and some nasty hallucinations from the concussion." Another pause. "In short, I'm not letting you up. "

He blinked. About all he could do.

"But I didn't wake you early so you could go storm another skyscraper anyway," Rogers went on. "I need your brain. Things are going to hell in a handcart here, fast, and I haven't got a clue what to do."

Hell in a handcart. "The firestorm?"

"Ongoing," Rogers said. "But pushed off the front pages by the terrorist bomb in a Manhattan skyscraper." She paused a moment to let that sink in. "57 dead so far, and that low number is thanks solely to Hellion sealing the surrounding roads via traffic signals and hacking about a dozen emergency warning speakers to get pedestrians off the streets. Nobody knows about that, though. Right now all the talking heads can talk about is you and your 'pathology'. 'He was never a real American', they're saying, 'went extremist out in Afghanistan' and 'hates our way of life', you know how that goes? They're calling this a second 9/11, and with all the genuine footage they've got of you and your team fleeing the scene?" She gave him a look. "It's hard to disagree. If anything, their stranglehold on the news cycle just got tighter."

Wren took a labored breath, felt the left side of his chest catching.

Terrorist. News cycle. He'd hoped the skyscraper raid would provide the proof they'd needed, but...

Gray smoke streamed by the window behind her.

"We're still in Manhattan," he guessed.

"That's right," Rogers said, turning to glance out the window. "Madison 231 hasn't stopped burning yet. They can't put it out, apparently, its inside the core. Right now we're at an apartment McKenzie Slade keeps on 40th and 5th Avenue." She took a breath, eyeing him. " They shut the bridges and tunnels almost instantly. They only let me into the city as I'm the one who caught you last time. I'm expressly tasked with bringing you in. You're on a high wire here, Wren. Lucky your team evacuated before the roadblocks went up, lucky Slade has this place, lucky she let us use it, lucky the smoke covered your escape from ground zero, lucky for lots of things."

Wren didn't feel lucky. Ran the simple calculation in his head, a strike at dawn plus four hours for her flight. "What is it, about eleven in the a.m.?"

"Ten of," Rogers answered. "Can you handle the full sit rep?"

He tried for a grunt, didn't have the wind to land it. Four hours out, everything could change. "Sounds like Keller's pinning the whole thing on us. Painting me as the mastermind."

"Got it in one," Rogers said. "That blast could hardly have played into his media stranglehold more perfectly. He's been out there decrying you since 231 fell. They've produced their own deepfake footage of what happened in the zoo. By their account, it looks like you entered a penthouse with a squad wearing Anti-Ca black, executed the family inside, children included, set your bombs then blew the place up. They've got you making another call for 'Reparations' direct to camera. It's a good likeness. If I didn't know better, I'd believe it."

That knocked the air out of him.

Rogers wasn't done. "Now the whole country's turning on you and your Foundation, tying them to Anti-Ca. There's nothing yet linking them to the firestorm, 23 dead women so far, but that can't be far behind." She paused a second. "There's already t-shirts selling with your severed head on them. There's a playing card 'kill' deck of all the Foundation members, complete with photos, numbers, addresses, selling online right now for $2.31, a tribute to the fallen tower."

Another punch. Lose the people and nothing was going to protect you.

"And David Keller's out there leading the charge."

Rogers nodded. "He's erecting a rally stage on the National Mall right now, laying out his trademark red and blue mats. He didn't get the permit, but nobody cares. People are flooding to him, already in excess of ten thousand. Washington's going crazy. Emergency meetings everywhere, on top of the emergency meetings they were already having for the firestorm. Humphreys is incommunicado, so we're cut off there. Congress have been in a special session since before the dawn. It's all..." Rogers trailed off, losing steam. "It's all going to shit."

Wren took a tight breath, snagging his left lung. One hell of a situation report. It all spiraled in his head, merging with the chaos of the zoo. Now more than ever they needed to cut through the lies. Break Keller's chokehold on the media.

"You have my bodycam footage of the strike. That's proof. Why don't we have that out there?"

Rogers said nothing. Looked uncomfortably off to the side.

"What?"

Another figure appeared to his right. Thin, all in black, cutting eyes and a pursed sliver of lips. McKenzie Slade.

"Because it wasn't enough, Christopher," she said, words dropping like ten-pound bags of sand. "A half-cocked raid on an overbaked horror set, more grotesque than an R-rated movie? The reveal of your sister, shock, she's alive, when no one in the country even knew she existed, let alone cared she was dead?" She fixed him with a hard glare. "It adds up to nothing. Hot air. It's not proof of anything. You grabbed that photograph, but what does that mean? It only ties you closer to the Pyramid!"

Wren struggled to keep up. Couldn't argue with anything she was saying.

"The zoo," he managed. "All those people-"

"Are gone," Slade finished. "Destroyed beyond all recognition in the blast. Your Apex had a plan for this eventuality, and he outplayed you. You want to break through the noise? Turn yourself in!"

She was angry. Maybe that made sense. He'd dragged her into something with enough momentum to crush her underfoot.

"So what will it take?" he asked. Hardly able to think clearly for himself. "What kind of proof?"

"Something that hits in the gut," Slade said sharply. "Keller's got the people high on hatred and fear, and facts about the family history of the Pyramid aren't going to cut it. Emotion sells, and he's got the dark side cornered. You'd have to go hope and change to stand a chance, but you just don't have the goods." A tight smile. "If you could lift the firestorm's boot heel off people's throats, then maybe they'll be able to listen about 231 Madison. Win them there, then maybe you can get into the weeds about your sister and the zoos and the links to Keller." She waved a hand dismissively. "But you don't have any of that. You don't know what the link is. You can't stop these women killing themselves. Hell, you didn't even know your own sister was alive!"

She panted a little. Wren felt he'd been punched in the face.

She was right.

Even now he was still living in the false reality the Apex had built. He'd never once considered that Galicia might be alive. That any of them might be, because if Galicia was alive, what did that mean about the rest of the Pequeños? About the Apex? About-

Something shook loose in Wren's head. He was back in the black-tiled corridor again, Galicia bleeding out on the floor, looking at the group photograph of the Pyramid with all the Pequeños lined up in a row, and-

"Where's the photograph?" he asked Rogers.

She turned, plucked it off a nearby table. "Here. There's no help in it, though. Hellion and B4cksl4cker have run it through a dozen facial analyses already."

Wren squinted but couldn't pick out the details clearly. "Can you at least unstrap my hands?"

"Are you done yelling and thrashing?"

He glared back at her. "Let's find out."

She made a face and worked the Velcro strap on his left wrist. His arm came free and he lifted it. Stained bandages on his shoulder, his whole hand wrapped up like a baseball glove, weak and shuddery. He managed to pincer the crumpled photo and held it close to his face.

Apex at the center. Seven Pequeños on the right, standing in order of age. There was Galicia. The resemblance was apparent, from sixteen to middle age she hadn't changed that much. And standing next to her…

His mouth went dry. His pulse rocketed. His gaze flickered between Slade and Rogers. Dark hair, light hair. Wide cheekbones, oval face. Everything else could change, but you couldn't fake the eyes.

He couldn't believe it. He had to.

He held out the photograph, thumb clamped tight under a sullen teenaged boy, eyes a fierce blue. "Who do you see here?"

"Some punk cultist," Rogers said. "He looks pissed off."

"He always was. I think he still is. His name's Chrysogonus. He's my older brother, and I always thought he died with the others in the pit, but now I'm thinking I was wrong."

"So what?" taunted Slade. "I already said who cares about the Pyramid family history?"

Wren met her gaze undaunted. "This is American history. I think you're looking at President-elect David Keller."

42

BARED ARM

A stunned silence fell. Slade and Rogers looked at each other, back at Wren.

"You're sure?" Rogers asked.

"One hundred percent. I'd recognize those eyes anywhere. David Keller is my dead brother Chrysogonus."

Rogers gazed at him, maybe weighing his opinion against Hellion and B4cksl4cker's facial analysis algorithms, then turned again to Slade. "Is that good enough to break through?"

Slade's thin lips pursed to the side. "If it's true? Not on its own. But if you can also stop the firestorm?" She chewed on it. "Maybe. One thing everyone knows about David Keller, he was adopted. There are no hard records on his early childhood, beyond his US birth certificate. Linking him to the Pyramid like this'll look like a smear, but it'll play to the conspiracy folks and the Wren supporters, plus your Russian hackers could make it stick on social media. If..."

Wren stopped listening.

Everything was playing out before him now like pieces on a chessboard, a grand multi-decade gambit slotting bringing the country to the brink of checkmate. Everything Jamal Jalim had said. The zoo. Chrysogonus. Keller. A pit full of dead brothers and sisters who had never really died. Galicia had said it herself; their deaths had served as leverage to push the rest of the Pyramid over the edge. They had also laundered his brothers and sister into new roles in the wider world, and ultimately put Chrysogonus into the Presidency.

His breathing grew shallow, remembering his brother's firm grip on his arm that long-ago night, dragging him out to kill Tomothy. He remembered how every time Chrysogonus had gone away with their father, he'd come back crueler.

Now it made sense.

The Apex had been taking him to the zoo.

Expose a child to that kind of mind-breaking trauma and they'd be yours for life; white-hot metal ready to be hammered into whatever weapon you needed. Forcing compliance through complicity.

Wren's head spun. It had always been the Apex's greatest trick. So the babies screamed in their cages and the people drowned in their vats, and nobody did a thing to prevent it, and that inaction only cemented them deeper into the sickness. So the one thousand had damned themselves to burn from the moment they let the Pequeño children 'die' in their pit.

He reeled. There was no turning back from something like that. No way to disbelieve once you'd gone that far.

It was the same trick the Apex was pulling right now on these women, updated for a new age and a new technology. He just needed to figure out how. Expedite complicity via remote means. Ensure compliance. Maybe if...

He looked up.

Slade and Rogers were arguing still.

"I know how he's making them burn," he said.

The argument stopped. The two women turned to face him.

Wren took a breath, felt the ache in his ruined cheeks as the pieces slammed into position like falling rubble. "The flames on Rachel Day's phone. I'm thinking that's all deepfake footage, but like nothing we've seen before. It's-" he stopped, searching for the right word.

"It's what?" Rogers snapped.

"Gaslighting," Wren said. "You know what that means? Making someone believe reality's not real. But on an industrial scale, with unprecedented real time technology. Convincing these women every person they love is secretly suffering the worst pain imaginable. That their souls are literally in hell."

There was a brief silence, broken by Rogers. "Sounds like the usual Pyramid BS. So OK. How would he do that without a cult compound in the desert?"

Wren didn't know how to explain it. Didn't even know if it was possible. "Is Hellion on the line?"

"I am monitoring," came Hellion's laconic accent from Rogers' phone. "What is it?"

Rogers held the phone up as Wren aligned the pieces of his theory like feather flights along an arrow's shaft. "The green cells in the zoo, Hellion. Picture this. If I wanted to transpose imagery from one setting to another, like special effects in a movie, how would I do it?"

"Transposition of imagery?" Hellion asked, playing along. "Hmm, yes, this is a standard process. Film this imagery on a uniform background color, one that is bright and unusual, and ensure no actor wears this color. Software then cuts out this background color, overlays the captured images on top of a different background, and-"

"An unusual color," Wren interrupted. "A bright, uniform color, like dayglo green?"

There was silence for a second. Wren felt pennies dropping all around him.

"Yes," Hellion confirmed. "Green screen is commonly used. You are suggesting the green cells-"

"Were individual film studios," Wren sped on, his thick tongue barely keeping up with his mind. "Transposing footage of pain. So imagine that every time Rachel Day pointed her 'ghost' phone at someone she loved, it automatically overlaid a person suffering genuine torture in one of the zoo's green cells." He thought back to his bare minutes reeling in the zoo. "There was a ruined bed in the cell I saw. Scorched, bloody, matted. When Rachel points her phone, they grab a victim and set to work, burning them, lashing them, stabbing them, whatever it takes, then they cut out the green and overlay the image on top of reality. It makes the ghost phone into some kind of," he snatched a tight breath, searching again for the right word, "window. Into hell. I'm thinking this is what Rachel Day saw when she pointed the phone at her husband. A nightmarish version of John Day, screaming in agony and written over with flames."

Rogers' eyes narrowed. "Pretty deep, Wren. But is that even possible? In real time?"

"Certainly it is possible," Hellion answered. "I am thinking. For best realism, the torturer should place his camera on a, what is the word, B4cksl4cker? Automatic rotating device?"

"Gimbal," he said.

"Yes, gimbal! Synchronized to this ghost phone. So as Rachel Day is moving her 'window', changing the angle, height, position, the gimbal-mount camera in the zoo will shift and track perfectly. This will add to realism. It will appear seamless."

Rogers held up a hand. "Hang on. This is a huge jump. We don't even know how the Apex got these phones into the hands of these women. We don't know why they'd take anything they see through them seriously. And what's even more confounding, even if everything you're saying is possible, why would they go to all this trouble with the zoo and green screens and film crews and torturers, when they could just use full deepfakes?"

"Excellent question," Hellion said. "Yes. But this is a computer processing issue, Agent Sally. True deepfake video requires many steps of facial rendering, for layering shadows, light, texture. It takes much time, and to produce one simultaneously in the moment? It will look like a bad video game. You will not accept it is real."

"I don't accept it now," Rogers said, teeth gritted. "It's all too complicated. Imagine the real John Day moves the wrong way at the wrong moment, throws his arm up maybe, the illusion cracks!"

"There need be no crack," Hellion countered. "It is simple matter to force a torture victim's arm up. Magic figures wearing green suits step in, lift the arm, it goes up. They are invisible. A delay of a second perhaps."

Rogers snorted. "But these operators won't even be able to see what's happening. How will they sync up? You're talking about-"

"Agent Sally," Hellion said with finality. "This is simple matter. Weather people on television have been doing this for many years. How do they see the rain and wind on the screen behind them? Do you think perhaps they feel a little cold on their behind when it blows?"

That shut everyone up.

It answered the question.

"All right," Rogers allowed. "Say I accept that's all possible, even likely. How did the Apex get the phone into Rachel Day's hand? How did he make her believe what she saw on it? I've dug into her life like a committed stalker, accounted for near every minute she had alone, and I don't see him anywhere. Not even a shadow."

"Who cares right now?" Wren answered. "Maybe he hired actors, framed some complicated tableaux, faked up a whole reality for her to wander into and make her believe reality wasn't real? Or maybe she just found the phone on the sidewalk and radicalized herself? Fact remains, they have the phones, and we need to block whatever signal's feeding out to them." Wren took a breath, taking another leap forward. "I saw maybe eight cells in Madison, but if we're really looking at a firestorm of a thousand women, he'd need more to serve the capacity. That means more zoos, more victims, more green cells on standby at all times. If there are more zoos, we have to find them and shut them down immediately. Rogers, can you spin up-"

"Christopher!"

It was McKenzie Slade, a sudden shout, and Wren looked over to her. She was holding her phone up for him to see, her face draining white.

He focused on the screen. A news site. There was a photo and a bold headline. The photo showed a man in a suit being led out of the White House grounds, a black bag over his head. He read the text.

CIA DIRECTOR HUMPHREYS ARRESTED FOR TREASON

43

GASLIGHT

There was another slack-jawed silence. Wren felt like he was trapped in the end game gambit of some long-choreographed drama.

"They must've linked him to the strike team we used," Rogers said rapidly, working her phone hard with her thumbs. "We got that SWAT team on his orders. Which means they can link him to me, maybe to Slade, to the exfiltration vehicle, to the Air Rangers." She spun, looking at the windows encircling them. "To this place."

Slade's face cratered. Maybe the first time Wren had seen her disdain break to fear since Redhook. "This place is owned by multiple shell companies, they might buy us some time, but they won't hold up for long against the State Department.

Few things did. The rest went unspoken. Doors blown in. Bullets fired before questions were asked. America's number 1 terrorist executed in his Manhattan lair.

Wren dropped the photograph and reached over to release the Velcro cuff on his right wrist. Rogers made feeble noises to slow him but didn't get in the way. His whole body bloomed with fresh pains as he twisted. Tightness in his shoulders, agony down his back, flashing lights across his vision. The cuff came off.

"Christopher," Rogers said.

"We have to move," he answered, leaning forward to free his ankles, but was stopped cold as the stitches under his left arm yanked like a row of fishhooks.

"Let me," Rogers said, and stripped the ankle cuffs. Wren swayed his legs out, let Rogers help him to a sitting position, and for the first time saw the space around him properly.

Not an apartment like he'd presumed. Filled with large cardboard boxes heavily strapped with tape. It took him a second to put the pieces together, revelation heaping atop revelation, then he turned to look at Slade.

"Contraband?"

She stared back at him, contemptuous even through the fear. "How did you think I kept multiple apartments in Manhattan on a consulting detective's salary?"

Truth was, he'd never thought about it. It didn't matter and he didn't care. Drug gangs were chaff in the wind next to this.

"Mafia," he guessed, building out a fuller picture. "Hence your in with the foreman.' She said nothing and he nodded. "I'm guessing you're their point person for import/export? That means you've got an in at the ports."

Slade just glared. Wren shuffled off the edge of the bed until his feet set on the floor. His legs were shivering already, but there was no good waiting any longer. Rogers tucked herself under his arm, helping him to stand. He tried to take his own weight but immediately sagged onto her. Damn good thing she was a weightlifter. She flexed in a half-squat under his two-forty pounds then pushed him back to standing.

"That's how you knew where the kids were in the containers," Wren guessed, ignoring the phasing twin of McKenzie Slade that had suddenly appeared to her right, ghost of the concussion. "Back in Redhook. You told me it was my fault we lost the dons, that we almost lost the kids, until some immigrant stevedore came through for you, but it wasn't my fault at all, was it?"

Slade's stare became black ice. "You don't know me, Christopher Wren."

That said it all. Another false reality falling like scales from his eyes; gaslighting he'd swallowed for so long. "I know enough, McKenzie. Those guys I killed, they were mafia, but not as high up as you said. I'm guessing you made a deal with the dons, fence me into killing a couple of low level guys, and they'd give up the kids? In exchange you got the reputation as a genius consultant detective, plus a pay-off, and you use that new reputation to grease the wheels on future drug deals."

Her lips pursed tight. "Don't even think about judging me."

He aimed for a snort, maybe got halfway there before his lung tightened up. For ten years she'd been branding him as reckless when she'd really just set him up. If he had the wind, he'd laugh. "Yeah. So here's what happens next, McKenzie. You're going to tap every mob contact you've got, and you're going to get us out of New York right now."

His legs firmed up a little under him. The double Slades danced closer together.

"That's not possible," Slade countered. "Everything's locked down, there isn't-"

"There is," Wren insisted. Stumbling with Rogers around the edge of the makeshift bed now, seeing that it was just blood-soaked boxes padded by plastic packets filled with white powder. Around the base of the boxes lay a halo of cast off gauze still bright with arterial blood. Three of his SWAT team members stood by the walls. Jimenez and Miller watching him. Kato staring out the window.

He refocused on Slade. "Here's the reality. Either you burn all your contacts to get us out, or we wait for Keller's people to storm in bullet first, bring your drug empire crashing down, make an orphan of your daughter and a pincushion out of me." He sucked in a breath. "So what's it going to be?"

Her jaw worked hard under tight skin. Fear, anger, distaste. She'd brought this on herself. "I'll make some calls."

"Make them fast," Wren answered. "I've got a couple I need to make too." He felt a sudden chill and looked down, numbly noticing that he didn't have a scrap on. Turned to Rogers right by his face. "I'll need a phone. First though, can we get me some pants?"

44

GIRL POWER

Pants came first, a paint-splattered designer pair of skinny jeans Jimenez had already picked up from a nearby boutique, then someone slotted an earpiece into his ear. While Rogers worked to get him dressed and Slade made angry calls in the background, Wren brought Hellion and B4cksl4cker onto a private line.

"I did not say this yet, but we are glad you are alive, Christopher," Hellion said in his ear. "I have many excellent jokes about falling buildings, and-"

"We need to stop the next burning," Wren interrupted, no interest in jokes. "Break the firestorm. So tell me about the ghost phones. You were co-opting civilian infrastructure to nail down some radio frequencies, to pinpoint locations. Did you find anything?"

"We have co-opted several ham radio transmitter/receiver arrays," Hellion answered, switching tracks easily. "This gives us some coverage of the country. The signal of a radio receiver is very faint, but there are oscillations. Accompanied with ghost data analysis and a frequency to search for, I believe we can triangulate every woman who is using one of these ghost phones."

"Excellent," Wren said, then looked down to Rogers, who was struggling to push his left foot through the tight cuff of the skinny jeans. He tried to help but was no use at all, his muscles feeling like linguini. "So we need the frequency. Have any other witnesses recollected seeing these phones?"

"Some," Rogers allowed, looking up as she ruffled the pants up his calf. "We've had a few hits in other locations, one in Idaho, a close friend saw the woman there looking at a strange phone a few days before she burned." She tugged the jeans over his ankle with a snap, causing Wren to wince. "A couple others mentioned red screens like John Day saw." She was absorbed for a moment in pulling the pants over his knee, shot a wicked glance to Jimenez. "Why are these pants so damn tight?"

Jimenez shrugged.

"Hellion, can you use any of that to home in on a frequency?"

"Working," Hellion answered. "B4cksl4cker, we will need your botnet ready to crunch several quadrillion data points on these sightings. Is this possible, or is it too tight, like Christopher's pants?"

"Standing by," B4cksl4cker said. "Like very stiff pair of pants."

Wren didn't acknowledge any of that. "Good. Get it done."

Rogers abruptly pulled the jeans all the way up hard, slamming into his crotch, and Wren sucked in another sharp breath.

Hellion's keys flew. Wren went to button the pants up but couldn't achieve a thing with his bandage-gloved hands, so Rogers did it for him.

"They're coming now!" Slade said abruptly, dropping a phone from her ear, eyes wide. "Keller cut through my protections like they were soft cheese. A SWAT team will be here in minutes, acting on shoot-to-kill orders from DOJ, and that's the last warning we'll get. I've got a contact coming in for you, standard mule vehicle, but it's going to be difficult. You need to get to street level right now."

Wren took a step forward without thinking, his leg gave out and he fell. Rogers just barely caught him, managed to get a knee under his chest before he hit the ground face first, then grunted and hoisted him back up.

"Careful, Christopher," she cautioned, hooking a hard arm around his chest. "We go together. We're in this together now."

His head spun. Suddenly dizzy and breathless. "Lead the way," he wheezed.

"Damn straight," Rogers said, and took a step.

"You should go faster," came Hellion's voice.

"His pants are very tight," B4cksl4cker offered.

"Shut up," said Rogers, voice tightening as she took the strain of Wren's weight.

"And us?" came a voice from the side. Wren looked and saw a blur. Jimenez?

"Can your transport accommodate them, McKenzie?" Rogers asked.

"No."

They reached the door.

"Then run," Rogers said. "If they catch you, they will kill you. I'm sorry. Thank you for what you've done. If we can fix this..."

She left that hanging as they passed out into the corridor, Wren's feet carrying barely a quarter of his weight. Rogers leaned him up against the elevator's chrome frame and punched the button.

"They're dead whatever happens now," Slade said fast, tracking behind them. "I'm dead. I should never have-"

"Then you better hope we bring Keller down," Rogers countered, turning to look into her eyes. "You lying bitch."

Slade's eyes flared. "I didn't-"

"You lied about Wren," Rogers said, deadly cold now. "I grant you that he can be an idiot and he's definitely reckless, but he'd never put children in danger the way you accused him of. That much I know." Wren tried to say something but everything was blurring silver now, and he couldn't quite figure out how to open his mouth. "You rode him to money and then cast him aside when you couldn't face what you'd done," Rogers piled on. "Now just pray your mob contacts come through. If they don't, you better believe I'm coming right back up here for you."

The elevator chimed, the doors spread open, Slade's face rinsed white as milk.

"You wouldn't-"

"You didn't deserve him as a partner," Rogers said, then stepped into the elevator and the door closed.

Wren hung off her side, barely holding his head up off his chest, gasping lightly.

"The hell's the matter with you?" Rogers demanded as the carriage started down.

He was laughing, or coming close. Didn't want to say as much. "That was badass," he managed to slur as the silver retreated. "My knight in-"

"Shove your knight," Rogers spat. "That was me being nice. The woman's a bitch and I told her so." A moment passed. "You should see it when I bad cop."

He wheezed some more. Managed to lift his head near upright, watched the numerals of the floor display blink down from 20, phasing in and out of focus.

"Christopher," came Hellion's voice, "I know this is a bad time, but what shall we do about the Chrysogonus/Keller connection?"

It was right on the tip of his tongue. Couldn't get it to come out. Tenth floor.

"Sync them up," Rogers said swiftly. "Facial analysis to the photograph. Prep a million memes, videos, gifs, whatever you can to spread the word about who he is and what he's done. The zoo, the cells, the ghost phone, all his bag of tricks. The instant we break the firestorm, we want this bastard tied to that bastard and both strung up on a viral pike. You feel me?"

Wren gasped laughter.

"I like this new Agent Sally very much," Hellion said. "Girl power."

"Shut it," snapped Rogers, and the elevator hit ground floor. The car doors slid open. Standing in front of them was a cop with his gun held up.

45

STREET LEVEL

Not SWAT. An NYPD beat cop, Wren figured, mid-twenties, probably heard the warning go out, most likely was cautioned to stay away but had come in regardless, looking to make a name for himself.

"Hands up," the guy said.

"He'll fall," Rogers said, cool as a Western gunslinger. "He's injured. If I put my hands up, he'll fall."

It took the cop a second. He'd seen this moment in movies, maybe even had one or two trainings, but never faced it down before. Doubtless he'd seen Wren's face on TV and knew just what kind of haul he'd bagged.

"So lay him down."

"OK," said Rogers, and started lowering Wren to the floor just as the elevator doors began to close.

The cop jolted forward, pushed his gun arm through the gap to keep the doors open, and the response was easy.

Rogers stepped offline and lashed out, slamming her open palm into the side of the cop's gun. His wrist hit the door, he let out a bark, and she grabbed the gun's barrel with her other hand and wrenched it upward. Fingers broke. Wren watched it all from the floor. The guy screamed. Rogers dropped the stripped weapon by Wren's side and followed up with a knee to the cop's gut as the doors opened, an elbow to his face and a judo throw that sent him sprawling across the lobby floor.

Rogers strode after him, flipped him easily with an arm bar then snatched his cuffs and secured his wrists behind his back while he yelled something unintelligible.

"You'll be fine," Rogers said, then went back to Wren, who had almost made it to one knee.

"Smooth," he managed.

She deadlifted him and strode into the lobby. A cheaper building than 231 Madison, ceramic tile instead of marble, stainless steel on the walls instead of verdigris copper. A guy behind reception stared wide-eyed, phone in his hand.

"Any critique you want to make?" Rogers grunted as they lurched toward the revolving door and the gray daylight beyond.

"Kick him… in the nuts," Wren gasped. "Didn't need… to break his hand."

Rogers just laughed.

Through the doors they emerged onto the street, where people stood in pockets and clusters with their phones up, filming something to the left. Wren craned his neck over Rogers' shoulder, saw the fat pillar of smoke rising from midtown Manhattan in bulbous gulps. 231 Madison, still burning.

"Where are they?" Rogers asked.

Vehicles crammed the four-lane avenue. Traffic at a standstill, many with their drivers missing. No way out except on foot. Overhead helicopters buzzed. Something revved closer. Rogers turned, swinging Wren with her, and there was a moped coming up on the sidewalk. Looked like a pizza delivery guy.

He pulled up in front of them, racked the brake and dismounted, held the key out to Rogers. "Get to Coney Island," he said, voice muffled through the helmet. "They'll be waiting."

He walked off. Rogers was left staring after him, at the moped.

"What the… how are we going to get on here?"

"We just get on," Wren managed. "Shotgun."

Rogers laughed. "You better hold on tight."

"I can't. Strap my hands together."

She turned to him like he was joking, realized he wasn't, then nodded. "Fine. Here."

It took twenty seconds to get Wren on the bike, ten for Rogers to sit in front, thirty more to tie his forearms tight around her waist with a torn scrap of her t-shirt, by which time people nearby were shouting and pointing.

"That's Christopher Wren!"

"That's the guy who brought down the building!"

Rogers gunned the moped and peeled out as the first of them were raising their phones.

She buzzed straight south on the sidewalk, forcing pedestrians into doorways and flattened against windows, tracked by shouts and more blaring horns. Wren swayed against her back, only half-conscious of the world whipping by around them as the jolts and jerks pushed him into a state of agony and confusion. His back, his shoulders. He blanked out once, twice, each time coming to teetering by the flimsy scrap holding his arms across Rogers' belly.

"Hang on!" she shouted as they swung into a tight swerve around the bumper of a police car, cops levelling their pistols. Gunfire rang out then they were past.

"Christopher, Agent Sally," came B4cksl4cker's bass voice in his ear as they whistled through crowds at thirty miles an hour, "this is not the best time, but I am afraid your country is in the middle of a coup."

The words meant nothing to him. Rogers ran a red NO WALK sign, was almost fishtailed by a slow-rolling school bus.

"What?" he gasped.

"Yes, it is happening now," B4cksl4cker said. "I know you are on a pizza bike. Here, I will read these headlines. Breaking news. President impeached and removed from office."

"Not possible," Rogers shouted in front, almost flipping the bike as a pedestrian jay-walked right in front of them. "That's gotta be fake."

"Not fake," B4cksl4cker said. "Verified. I will read." He took a breath, and Rogers gunned the moped up to fifty down an avenue of gridlocked cars. "At 11:00am EST an impeachment vote was called in a rare sitting of both Houses of Congress. The vote carried near unanimously to remove not only the President, but in a rare and stunning rebuke, the President's entire administration."

Wren couldn't believe what he was hearing, but B4cksl4cker just kept on going.

"This is an unprecedented development. Early reports indicate Congress have been in discussions since midnight on how to respond to the 'firestorm' currently sweeping the country.

"Speculation suggests the President's direct connection to ousted CIA Director Gerald Humphreys and wildcard agent-turned-terrorist Christopher Wren led to this wide-ranging Presidential impeachment.

"This story is breaking."

Wren reeled. If anything, it helped push down the silver fog in his head.

"Whole administration impeached?" Rogers shouted. "Can they even do that?"

"Looks like they just have," Wren said in her ear.

"There is footage now," came B4cksl4cker's voice. "It is your Speaker of the House. Here, I will play audio."

Wren's earpiece briefly crackled, then there was the recognizable drawl of the Speaker's voice. She was announcing an unprecedented, en mass impeachment of the White House.

"Tell me this is a deepfake," Wren muttered. "B4cksl4cker. Tell me this is more gaslighting."

"I have eyes-on verification," came his Armenian bass. "Your President has been deposed. Your Secret Service agents are already removing her and her family from the White House."

The Speaker of the House kept talking, and Wren listened rapt as Rogers raced through a New York that was suddenly quiet. No horns, no people pushing back, everyone looking at their phones or listening to the radio, only the sound of police helicopters and sirens closing in.

"There can be no doubt that our President was complicit in the felling of Madison 231," the Speaker said. "Investigations are commencing immediately, though what matters most in this moment is the question of succession."

Wren saw it coming before she could say it.

"To ensure clear leadership, Congress has determined that the inauguration of President David Keller be held in two hours and thirty-seven minutes time, on the National Mall at 2 p.m. this afternoon." She paused, and Rogers shot across a fifth street intersection that was filled with cars but eerily silent and still, every face lit by the light from their phones.

"I ask that the American people remain calm in this troubled time, and have faith in the spirit, if not the letter, of our Founders' intentions. We have a President-elect. We will have a new President this day. Thank you."

Journalists cried out questions. The Speaker did not answer them.

Wren didn't know what to say. What to think. Two hours and forty-seven minutes? The gameboard had shifted completely. The firestorm had accelerated it. Madison 231 had brought it on.

"We did this," Rogers shouted, saying exactly what he was thinking. Wren glimpsed the Hudson Bay ahead. Caught flashes of the Statue of Liberty, her back turned on Manhattan. "This is our fault."

By we she meant he. Reckless as ever.

Less than three hours. It couldn't be enough. It squeezed enough adrenaline into his body to push back the fog.

"Get us a charter jet to Washington," Wren called into the wind, putting just enough gas behind the words to be heard.

"Done," said B4cksl4cker. "I will arrange jets at every nearby airport. Now reach one of them!"

Coney Island opened before them. The esplanade, the sea front, the tourist throngs standing motionless in front of coffee shops, frozen in the moment. Up ahead a speedboat raced across the Bay, firing up a comet trail of white breakers, the only vehicle moving on all the water.

"I think that's for us," Wren said.

46

SPEEDBOAT

The speedboat raced up, tracked by helicopters blaring out warnings over bullhorns. Wren and Rogers stood under the canvas cover of Pier 11, him hanging from her side, slapped by cold foam off the wind-tossed East River, shadowed by twin mafioso in dark suits and shades like CIA bagmen.

The speedboat swirled up to thud broadside against the pier. A beautiful Cigarette AMG Electric Drive, sleek as a .22 Long Rifle caliber shell, fast enough to give a helicopter a run for its money.

Wren leaned forward and Rogers took a step toward it, but one of the mafioso stepped up and put a hand on his chest.

"Not for you," the guy said. As tall as Wren and broader still, he made for an impassable obstacle.

Wren tried for anger but came up empty, not nearly enough to bull through whatever this was. Maybe a last moment exploitation from Slade? If she'd sold them out, then it was over already.

"What do you mean?" Rogers asked tightly, and Wren felt her coiling toward action.

"Wait one," the guy said, as behind him two figures moved. It took Wren a second to register what he was seeing. A big guy hunched over, dressed in the same skinny jeans and rumpled jean jacket Wren wore, with a sturdy blonde holding him up. At first he thought he was seeing double again, then it registered.

"Decoys," he muttered.

The mafioso stood motionless as the would-be Wren and Rogers boarded the speedboat, until there was a strange bubbling sound.

"Now," the guy said, and pointed. Wren and Rogers staggered to a spot directly in front of the Cigarette's trocar-sharp prow, where something like the flat lead-bottomed hull of a fifteen-footer yacht was rising up from underwater. Wren stared, trying to figure out what this was. A sunken ship floating to the surface? A hidden escalator into some nether realm?

Then there was a metallic clinking sound, a hatch in the top of the flat hull opened up, and a face appeared within, one hand beckoning.

Wren laughed.

"Narco-submarine," he muttered.

"What the hell?" Rogers countered.

He'd come across them once or twice before, working on logistics with the Qotl cartel to smuggle heroin and cocaine up through the Gulf of Mexico to make landfall in New Orleans. Often powerless and rudderless, they were basically airtight shipping containers sunk some thirty foot underwater, tugged into port by innocent-looking fishing vessels and capable of carrying some 8 tons of illegal narcotics.

"It's a drug sub," Wren said. "Invisible from the air. Let's not keep them waiting."

Rogers gave him a look then moved to the edge, where a ladder awaited. With the big guy's help, they got Wren down and ushered him through the hatch into the hull of the sub. It was dark but for a halogen light up by the prow, a raw iron ceiling barely four foot high, and half filled with stacked drug packets.

The guy inside the sub smiled and nodded at them like an amiable old Geppetto. "That's right, lie down," he said, a faint Italian burr beneath his Brooklyn accent, "there are no seat belts but we won't be going so fast."

Wren grunted and lay down. His specialty right about now, though it only took seconds for the cold, hard metal of the hull to start his battered back crying out. Rogers lay down next to him.

"They could sink us without a moment's thought," she said quietly. "Game over, America."

Wren was feeling curiously light-headed and found this comment hilarious.

"I don't know what you're chuckling about," Rogers muttered.

The smiley old guy pulled the hatch shut and rotated the locking wheel, closing off their view of Pier 11's canvas roofing,

"Won't be a jiffy," he said, looking tickled pink to have company. "I don't often ferry civilian passengers."

Wren couldn't stop himself from laughing out loud. The old man beamed, seeming to enjoy the irony, and bustled to the front of sub where he sat down at the controls and called, "Hold on!"

The sub's engines fired. Sounded like a dishwasher revving up to spin. The sub glided gently into motion, and Wren just laughed harder. Not loud, really just hacks coughed up from his bad lung, but something about being ferried out of New York in a sloth-like drug-sub just tickled him pink.

"He's gone mad," Rogers murmured by his side, bringing up her phone.

"Hold on tight!" Wren cautioned, as the sub pulled away at what could only be a stately 5mph.

She ignored him.

"It's probably the concussion," he managed, after a moment.

"You think?"

"Won't be long now," said the old guy at the front.

Those words ricocheted chaotically in Wren's head like a bullet, smashing up his thoughts on the past and the present. In two and half hours his long-dead brother was about to become President, and wasn't that pretty funny? America's only hope was also her most wanted terrorist, currently an invalid puttering through the East River in a narco-sub.

You had to laugh or else you'd cry.

"Hey," Rogers said firmly, then more gently when she bobbed down to look into his eyes. Wren had enough sense to figure what she was seeing there. "It's OK," she said, one hand on his shoulder now as the sub's engine rolled a slow spin cycle. "We're going to fix this."

OK.

His teeth chattered and he felt rip tides pulling at him, maybe falling foul of the bad side of fight or flight. Not good when you were laid up and basically immobile. He had to think, had to somehow plan his way out of this, but he didn't know how. He'd thought he was finally getting to grips with the Apex's plan, and then this happened.

Outplayed again. The chattering became whole body shudders.

"Hey," Rogers said again, squeezing his shoulder gently, "Christopher. We're going to be OK. I'll give you a Snickers bar if you get this under control."

You could only laugh at that.

"W-warm glass of milk?" he pressed.

Now she laughed too. "Don't push your luck."

It helped a little. The shuddering slowed, and he focused on the blank metal ceiling. He'd never done well in tight spaces, not since the Apex had buried him alive. Best to think about something else.

His kids in Rhode Island, running free. Safe. Their mom watching over them.

"OK, that's better," Rogers said.

He switched his gaze to her. On her side in the low space, looking down at him with something like concern, maybe even affection. How long since anyone had looked down at him like that?

He took a breath, took a gulp, steadied himself. First step in fending off a panic attack was recognizing what it was.

"Allergies," he said. "I d-don't do well with cocaine."

Rogers laughed, brushed a lock of hair from his eyes. "Yeah, like you haven't taken all these drugs at some point or other."

He smiled. It hurt his cheeks. "When you're undercover with the cartel, it's all part of the gig."

The old guy's ears pricked up at the mention of the cartel, but he didn't say a thing. Rogers smiled back, but Wren saw the pain in it. Addiction came from lots of things.

"We need a backup plan," he said, getting control of himself.

"Completely agreed. So what is it?"

He listened for a second, but heard nothing coming from his earpiece, no clacking keys or banter. "We've lost Hellion?"

"Looks like it, no cell signal, Internet. It's just you and me in this leaky bucket."

He ran a cold assessment of their situation, started working the problem like it was any other challenge, not the insurmountable cliff it seemed to be. "First up, I eat a Snickers."

"Seconded."

"Second, we're going to have to do something ugly, something that I'd never plan in any other situation."

"And that is?" Rogers asked.

"Get a team in place," Wren said, figuring the logistics as he went along. "Weapons on the National Mall. We're going to assassinate the President."

47

DEHAVILLAND

An hour later Wren sat strapped into a faux leather seat in the shaking fuselage of a DeHavilland Turbo Beaver Seaplane, trying to push through the pain of the propeller's vibrations as they shot up his spine.

"There is no way we can traffik you through an airport," Hellion had said in his ear, as soon as the drug-sub came up in the Redhook Channel just past Governors Island in the Upper Bay. "This sea boat will be a faithful steed."

He'd been in no position to argue. Rogers had helped him out of the sub and into the DeHavilland, floating out in the middle of nowhere. It was a narrow cabin, two racks of seats, far from the luxury of his Cessna C4, with no air steward up front to mix him an Americano with cream.

"Will this get us there in time?" he'd asked.

"Yes," B4cksl4cker said. "Top speed 150 miles per hour. She is a beautiful creature. You will arrive with an hour to spare."

Wren had grunted. An hour to land, transfer, get into position.

At least they'd made progress hunting the zoos.

Thirty minutes into the flight, swinging out over the coast to avoid breaking too many airspace zoning codes, Hellion told him about the zoo they'd ghost-tracked to a Des Moines skyscraper, run by an aged-up version of his brother Zachariah-Of-The-Marshes, and another in Orlando within sight of Disneyland, run by a similarly altered version of Gabriel-In-Extremis.

Looking at a map on a tablet held by Rogers, Wren felt the chess board beginning to resolve again.

"How did you find them?"

"The matrices have been collapsing to simple probability forks since Madison 231," Hellion said. "The photograph helps, the tracks they have left help. Every time we render through the vast data using this concrete data as our key, clearer patterns emerge."

Wren looked at the pictures of his two brothers. Caught in reflections for CCTV, seen from above. Their whole hollow lives stretching out behind them, reaching directly to a point in the desert where little Pequeño 3 thought they'd all died.

Zachariah had always been aloof. He looked it now, wearing wireframe spectacles, a trim silvery goatee beard, slim and waistcoated in the latest fashion. Gabriel had run thick, becoming a shaggy bear of a man. He'd always shared his rations with Wren, chucked him under the chin when he felt down. His brothers, become monstrous.

"Have you narrowed down the ghost phone frequency?" he asked, bundling a welter of emotions away.

"We have," B4cksl4cker said. "It is a shortwave amplitude modulation, ranging 157 to 158 kilohertz. This frequency can reach long distance as a skywave, bounced off the ionosphere. It can go anywhere, Christopher."

"And where is it being picked up?"

"This is harder. Hellion and I have stolen access to more receivers, such as radio telescopes, radar facilities and national defense listening posts to build a picture. It is now emerging. I think our meme assault is forcing doubt."

Wren blinked. "What meme assault?"

"Oh yes," B4cksl4cker said cheerfully. "I forgot, you were in the water. Much of your day has been spent in water or in mud, has it not?"

"B4cksl4cker!"

"Sorry, Christopher. Hellion's jokes are a bad influence on me. Hellion and I decided to start breaking the firestorm now. Why not, yes? Sow doubt, seed uncertainty. We have bankrolled a Ukrainian virality factory, and so far they have released some three hundred memes onto the internet, just as you suggested. These are funny pictures, doctored video, all revealing some or many aspects of David Keller's past, his father's vision, the purpose of the zoos, the green cells, the red fire ghost phones. There is so much material! We could manufacture amusing gifs like this for months!"

Wren put one bandage-gloved hand to his head. Amusing gifs? They'd just completely undercut him. He'd wanted to reveal all that at once. Power the revelation with the assassination of David Keller. Now Hellion and B4cksl4cker had taken the impact of that announcement off the table.

New players on the chess board.

"What is the matter?" B4cksl4cker asked.

Wren took a breath, trying to get perspective. Maybe this could be spun positively. Maybe this was even better, preparing the ground for what was to come. They were the Internet experts, after all.

"You say it's having an effect?"

"Yes! In very many cases we have gone viral. There are people wanting to believe you, Christopher. In your Foundation. Many who do not like Keller. Genuine footage of your zoo assault is trending. Pickup on the shortwave spectrum is rising too, and we take this to be the Apex's women across your country, activating their ghost phones to seek reassurance. The zoos must currently be working at capacity to feed them visions of torture."

That was something.

"And you're tracking these pickups, correct? Any way to know who's next?"

A beat passed. "This is difficult, but we believe there is way. We are putting drones over the women who are tuning in, notifying Foundation affiliates nearby, and..."

Wren almost missed it. "Foundation affiliates?"

"Ah yes," said B4cksl4cker, followed by an uncomfortable pause. "Affiliates." Wren waited for him to say more, but he didn't.

"What do you mean, affiliates?"

"This is Theodore III's latest initiative," B4cksl4cker said weakly. "I actually am not supposed to tell you this."

If Wren's hand hadn't already been to his head, he would have put it there. More new players? "Not supposed to tell me what?"

"Really it is just a mailing list right now," B4cksl4cker said, wheedling slightly. "A list of all those interested in joining the Foundation."

"A list of affiliates, what does that even mean? You don't just 'join' the Foundation like it's some fan club, B4cksl4cker!" The silence deepened. Wren didn't like it, gravitated to the question that mattered most. "How big is this list?"

"It is a modest size, Christopher. Very small."

"How small?"

"Theodore would not want me to-"

"How small?!"

"We have two hundred thousand on our most engaged list," B4cksl4cker gulped out. "With several million warm leads."

For a moment Wren just stared out of the window. The gray Atlantic lay frozen below like gray poupon mustard, carved into intricate ruffles. He felt blindsided, the chess board flipping again. He leaned into it angry.

"How long has this been going on?"

"Some time," said B4cksl4cker.

"Some time? And you've got two hundred thousand 'engaged', whatever that means? Several million? Last I heard, Foundation expansion was set to be slow and steady. At no stage did I approve expanding that to millions!"

"Technically, your approval was not needed," Hellion joined in sharply. "You are figurehead, Christopher, not CEO, and three coins minus currently. You are driving and drinking every night in motels, yes, feeling sorry for self? This is not the action of a CEO."

Blindsided again. Not wrong, though.

"My drinking aside, it's unacceptable risk," he said, settling on the moral high road. "When I formed the Foundation, it was not as some kind of commercial outreach movement! You're talking about leads like this is a marketing effort, and-"

"It is a marketing effort," Hellion interrupted. "Everything we do is marketing now, Christopher. Memes are marketing. Beating back your father is marketing. It is necessary-"

"Not like this!" he snapped. "It's irresponsible when we're facing such a real risk. What's the joining incentive, do they get a lapel badge, a hat with some stupid logo on it? The whole thing is-"

"Necessary," Hellion finished. "Christopher, I understand you are cautious of growth. You doubt Theodore III. But these people have wanted to help us for a long time. Do you remember who brought down the Saints? Across your country, Christopher, regular people moved to protect schools and churches. They put their lives on the line then, and they did not even know you! Now they do, and they want to be part of your Foundation, and your fears of somehow becoming a cult leader like your father should not prevent them finding a place to unite!"

She breathed heavily. Wren's mouth opened, closed.

"Hellion is passionate about this," B4cksl4cker said unnecessarily.

Wren clawed for something to hold onto. These were the deepest cuts yet. "I am not like my father, and I'm not a cult leader." He paused, mind whirring.

"I'm not afraid of becoming like him, either, but neither am I a politician, a salesman, or anyone's damn mascot. You should not have-"

"This is not your choice," Hellion barked. "It has happened and it is best. You are currently the only public figure fighting the Apex, our most powerful weapon against him. The President has been impeached. Gerald Humphreys is in a black site. You are the only one left standing, and that is your brand, Christopher. Stop whining about the fan club you have built and get used to leading it."

He almost laughed.

"Besides, we will need these people now," Hellion pressed. "You should be grateful for Theodore's planning. Do you think I can summon gig workers on the darknet right now, to risk their lives bringing down women who wish to burn themselves alive, in the midst of a national lockdown? No, I cannot do this. No amount of money could. But the Foundation faithful? Warm leads in the outer ring, hoping to join what you have built? Yes, this they will do."

Wren closed his eyes. Trying to swallow the anger and the new reality. This wasn't just new pieces on the chessboard, this was a whole new board, and he wasn't sure if it was a good thing or not. Personality cults were dangerous things to play with. He didn't want millions of people hanging on his every word.

"I can't be responsible for all those people. I can't-"

"If it helps at all," Hellion easily overrode him, "every new joiner is immediately told in their onboarding email that you are leader-in-absentia, three-coins minus, and that the group is managed by an elected Board, with Theodore as the elected chair. Not you. Does this make you feel better?"

It didn't. "Well, that's just-"

"This is your role in the Foundation now, and you must accept it. If not you, then who? Embrace your role as violent mascot and show these people what cheerleading really is."

Wren sucked air. Cheerleading. He stared at the frozen gray ocean below, frothed with a thousand zagging whitecap lines like ridges in some vast fingerprint.

Official cheerleader for hundreds of thousands? Millions?

No way around it, though, at least not right now. He flipped the switch in his head. "OK then."

"OK?"

"OK." The new gears spun in his head. "We'll talk later about that onboarding email. In the meantime, we do what we have to do. Put all the

Foundation 'fans' on alert. Use them to stop burnings if they can, but there must be no violence, no law-breaking unless it's absolutely necessary to save life. Our goal is to bring the temperature down, not pump it up. If they break these rules, they're out forever. Make that clear."

"As crystal. Now, that is everything. No more secrets, Christopher. Teddy ordered this kept from you, but Teddy is not our actual, actual leader. You are." A brief pause. "Even if in-absentia." Another pause. "If you wish to take away our coins, we will understand."

Wren snorted. The damn coins.

"We'll talk," he said, then looked over at Rogers. She was shouting on speakerphone, flicking through screens on her phone too fast for him to track. Maybe arranging his shooters on the National Mall. Coordinating the hunt for the next woman to burn.

"Who are our shooters on the National Mall?" he asked Hellion. "Are they core members or," he didn't want to say it but couldn't think of a better word ,"new initiates?"

Hellion's fingers flew noisily over the keys. "At most recent count, one hundred and thirty-three Foundation members both core and fringe will be on Keller's red and blue mats at the National Mall. I do not have the exact breakdown. All are armed. All have orders to assault the stage and kill David Keller on your signal."

Wren's heart skipped a beat. One hundred and thirty-three? A far bigger conspiracy than JFK. On the news they were calling him a terrorist, likening him to bin Laden, and this would just prove it.

So be it.

"Good," he said. "Have them ready. And there's one more thing you can do for me."

"Yes?"

Wren sat up straight. His ribs, shoulders, back throbbed. The double vision had faded a little, but the dizziness was still there. Time to embrace it all.

"I need you to place a call for me. He'll be busy, but I want you to keep trying until he answers."

"Of course. To whom?"

"David Keller. I need to speak with my brother."

48

WASHINGTON

The phone rang. The plane flew. They snipped the tail off Delaware, shot low over Chesapeake Bay, crossed a bulge of Maryland at Port Tobacco until they hit the Potomac River, where wideband warnings of a fifteen-mile Temporary Flight Restriction around the inauguration forced them down for a water landing just west of Fort Washington.

The jerk as they hit the river, bounced, hit again and entered a juddering deceleration sent shockwaves of pain up Wren's spine that blew against his brain in silvery bursts. His vision muddied. His hearing fogged.

"Coast Guard are inbound," Hellion said in a soupy voice in his ear. "You have ten minutes."

The pilot up ahead was shouting and flailing now, more a staticky ball than a person, until the Claymation silhouette of Rogers pulled a gun. "Tell them we held you at gunpoint," she said calmly.

"You are holding me at gunpoint!" the pilot shouted.

"There you go," Rogers said, and disappeared out of the fuselage. Wren sagged after her to slump at the cab's edge, feet dangling over the choppy Potomac waters like a child in a high chair, tickling the DeHavilland's silver pontoons as Rogers waved to something too far off for Wren's bleary eyes to pick out.

He sucked air. Movement made everything worse. The landing had flipped him back to woozy and nauseated, barely able to keep his gaze focused on the mash of gray water unfolding north.

The sound of an engine drew in. Wren's vision grayed as a bullet rushed closer. Rogers kept waving. Not a bullet, then, another speedboat.

"You have seven minutes," Hellion said. "Your Coast Guard are coming."

Rogers caught him as he slid off his perch toward the water. "Easy big guy," she grunted, then the boat's white gunwale pulled up and she guided him onto the deck like he was mince through a sausage stuffing machine.

The speedboat took off, and the wooziness only got worse as they thudded off low waves, each punching directly up Wren's spine. He bit his lip as the veil of unconsciousness crept closer, clinging to the simple sound of a phone ringing in his ear.

Hellion calling David Keller.

"Hang in there, Christopher," Rogers said.

"Thirty minutes until inauguration," Hellion said in his ear in fragments he barely caught. "You are clear to Jones Point, but it's-"

He must have passed out, because the next thing he knew he was being unloaded like a sack of grain, hauled on Rogers' shoulder and slotted into an SUV. For long moments he had no idea where he was or where he was going.

"I-" he began, but didn't know what to follow up with.

"It's OK," came Rogers' voice. "Get your head together. We need you on overwatch. I'll go operational."

The words fuzzed in his head, slotting for a position that made sense, until the agony in his back began to gradually relent. No more crashing waves helped and steadily his vision resolved. Looking out an open truck window with a cool breeze in his face, he saw political pennants streaming. Banners. People in some kind of parade.

KELLER 4 AMERICA read one.

EXECUTE CHRISTOPHER WREN said another.

The irony bit hard. Just four months ago the slogan had been RELEASE CHRISTOPHER WREN.

"Your vehicle has diplomatic precedence," Hellion buzzed in his ear. "You do not know how many strings I have pulled to get you this fast pass to the center."

He almost laughed. Like it was a rollercoaster ride.

"Now please wind up your window, Christopher," Hellion continued. "People will recognize you."

He fumbled for the button. Rogers did it for him. The phone kept ringing.

"How long was I out?" he asked, words a slur.

"Hard to say," Rogers answered without looking up. "Since the plane? Forty minutes, give or take."

"Where are we?"

"Ten minutes out from the Mall. The stage is filling up." Rogers looked up from her phone. "You are back with us. Good."

He straightened somewhat, feigning a command he didn't feel. "Give me the sit rep."

She nodded. "On the stage it looks like Keller's future Cabinet, plus half the Senate, the House Speaker and select Congress people, some corporate leaders, the VP's wife, their kids. No sign of the Apex yet. The audience-"

"He's not there?"

"I'm scrolling the major news sites, but there's no sign of him. Looks like he's sitting this one out, hand all the glory to your brother."

Wren grunted, gasped, stopped. The Apex had never handed the glory to anyone else unless it furthered his plans.

"The firestorm?"

Rogers' eyes narrowed. "I already told you this. You must've been only half-conscious. But good news there, Christopher, because we stopped it." She gave him a tight smile. "All filmed, and that moment's in the mainstream now. It's got your name all over it, some good press for the Foundation finally, but nothing's going to stop the inauguration now."

His mouth went dry. They'd finally stopped the firestorm and broken the stranglehold, but too late. "How?"

"Hellion pulled off some drone magic," Rogers began, "B4cksl4cker worked his algorithm, looks like McKenzie Slade chipped in with some contacts, and along with their shortwave detection net they narrowed it to three women, one in Michigan, one in Pennsylvania, one in Wisconsin."

Wren gulped air. "The rust belt."

"Politically telling, right? Teddy was all over them, we scrambled Foundation members and they ran in like we handled Gruber; teams packing household fire extinguishers soaked all three before they could ignite. Looks like they already had doubts, after Hellion and B4cksl4cker put out their meme campaign. We're getting coverage, our people are clearly the heroes, but conspiracy theories are already calling it a 'false flag rescue'."

Wren tried to rub his eyes, got a face full of bandage mitten. "A false flag rescue?"

"They're contorting themselves. Whatever the case, the firestorm's done. We're prepping teams to hit the zoos now."

Wren tried to churn all that fresh data in his head. An assassination at this point would look terrible, but coming on the heels of his people stopping the firestorm, it'd be better.

"Don't have them hit the zoos," he said, lifted on a tide of dopamine. "We can't have more bomb blasts in our name. Farm it to police, FBI, whatever."

"I'll relay that," Rogers said, worked her phone briefly. "Are you all right now? You went gray as ash for a while. I wasn't sure you'd be with us for the endgame."

"I'm here. Wouldn't miss it for the world. But that damn plane didn't land easy."

Rogers snorted, tapped send, looked up. "Not the comfort you're used to? Christopher Wren, part of the jet set?"

He smiled. Reached out and put one mittened hand over hers.

"Thank you."

Her green eyes quirked. "For what?"

"For all this. Taking lead. Trusting me, basically."

She smiled. "The jury's out on that yet, boss. And technically you've been unconscious, trusting me. But back on point, are we still set on the rally plan?"

Boss. It took him a moment to get past that. First time she'd said that in nearly a year. He cleared his throat to cover the discomfort.

"Let me see the footage."

Rogers held up her tablet. An aerial shot of the National Mall. Wren picked out an enormous crowd spreading away from the Washington Monument toward the United States Capitol. Tens if not hundreds of thousands of people packed onto Keller's trademark red and blue mats.

Wren grimaced at the checkerboard sight. The Apex was always thinking about the visuals, the marketing, always one step ahead. With something so simple as colored mats he created a powerful visual uniting the two political parties, reinforcing his appeal to some united vision of the future.

"Can we see the stage?"

Rogers swiped a few times, and another aerial feed showed the wide D-shaped stage closer up, itself striped with the same red and blue mats as the Mall, nearly filled with the power players Rogers had already listed. In back of them were twin big screens to the right and left, framing the shot of the US Capitol dome beyond.

"Where's Keller?"

"In the wings, as far as we can tell. He was last out on stage an hour ago."

Wren grunted. Caught a whip of movement through the truck's tinted windows, followed by an opening out of the sky.

"14th Street Bridge?" he asked, looking out over the river.

"That's right. We should be there in seven minutes. Wren, I need to know if we're sticking with the plan."

The 'plan'. She didn't want to say 'assassination' and he couldn't blame her. Chess moves raced through his head. The phone kept ringing in his head.

"Fifteen minutes until Keller takes the stage," Hellion said in his ear.

"Our people are out there," Rogers pressed. "They're all armed, and I don't need to tell you how illegal that is. What's the plan?"

She looked drawn, pale, exhausted. Pretty much a mirror for how he felt.

"Show me. Where are our people?"

She swiped through to another screen, a simplified map of the Mall with the oblong grass patches no longer tiled in red and blue, rather dotted with dozens of tiny digital pins. Their people, clustered primarily at the fore right before the stage, though there were others spread right back through the crowd.

"What are these ones doing?" Wren asked, pointing.

"They arrived late. Hellion couldn't get diplomatic access for them all."

Wren considered. This was the exact kind of terror threat he'd spent a lifetime protecting against. On the plus side, it meant he knew all the tricks to look out for.

"We go," he said. "Make sure these ones know they're backup. In the event our shooters at the front miss, they're all to spread and hunt Keller. I want people in the surrounding streets encircling this whole area." He drew a long oval around the Mall and Capitol building. "Nothing gets out."

Rogers looked at him. "Nothing? You're serious?"

"This is our cordon," Wren went on, tapping the oval. "Agreed?"

"Agreed."

"Now what about the stage. Does it have plexiglass protectors?"

"It does," Rogers said, and drew lines of attack on the map. "Bulletproof on these angles. There are gaps from certain angles, if he strides around, which he always does. We're putting our best people on the end of these sightlines. Give the order, and we'll have a dozen firing at once."

Wren liked the sound of that.

"We're benefitting from the rushed status of this whole thing," Rogers went on. "This stage, the whole area, none of it was properly secured beforehand. Keller didn't get permits. He put this up to pressure Congress and the President to act, and since he had the stage already set up, they decided to use it. It's really the only reason we could sneak people in with guns at all."

Wren nodded. A flaw in the Apex's planning. While he'd prepared for Wren's zoo strike to force an early inauguration, he hadn't been ready for the speed of it.

"Ten minutes until he speaks," Hellion said.

Wren looked out the window. They were pulling up Jefferson Drive, southwest alongside the National Mall. The crowd was everywhere, spilling sideways off the mats all the way to the block concrete of the Smithsonian Air and Space Museum. All cheering for their new President.

The truck pulled up on the side. Wren could just see through the American elms to the screens above the stage.

"And this is where I leave you," Rogers said. "No way you're coming with. Here, take this."

She handed him the tablet, and he struggled to grasp it in his bulky bandages. "Wait, what? Where are you going?"

She gave him a look. "You are an idiot sometimes, you know? Who do you think our best shot at Keller is? Some Foundation fringe militiaman who's been to the shooting range twice in his life, or me, Quantico trained field agent, deep cover with the Foundation, action star extraordinaire?"

She said it all deadpan. It made Wren's stomach sink.

"I didn't…" he began, trailed off.

Rogers fixed him with a glare then laughed. "Boss. Why the hell did you think we were even coming here? We could ride overwatch from New York."

He didn't know what to say to that. Opened his mouth, closed it. Abruptly she reached out and touched his cheek, and any words he had lined up to say dissipated. The second time in as many hours she'd touched him like that.

"Chris," she said. "Don't worry. I'll get him."

For a long moment he just looked at her. Seeing all the ways she'd changed, all the ways he'd changed too. He'd betrayed her. She'd betrayed him. They'd saved each other a good few times. Still there was trust.

He dry-swallowed. "Stay safe," he managed.

Her eyes danced with amusement, like she saw right through to what he was feeling. But what was he feeling?

"And you, action hero," she said, knuckled his chin, then pushed open the door, pulled a long bag out of the open back and melted into the crowd.

Wren was left sitting clutching the tablet.

"I'm going to cry here," came Hellion's voice in his head. "That was beautiful."

"Shut up," Wren muttered.

"And you handled it so well."

He took a breath. Get things back on track. "Track her on this screen, please."

"Yes, my action hero," said Hellion.

He winced. She was never going to let that go now. Worst case scenario, she'd turn it into a ring tone. Still, a new pin blipped into being at the edge of the crowd, brighter than the rest and moving in.

"In other news," Hellion went on, "it looks like we have an answer."

"What do you mean?"

"I mean your brother. It seems he is willing to talk."

Wren froze. Realized that the constant ringing in his ear had finally stopped. Asking for that call felt like a lifetime ago. Now his vision tunneled tighter, his breathing shortened, his skin turned clammy. All the symptoms of fight or flight kicking in hard, along with a fresh adrenaline boost. He was going to need it.

"Put him on."

49

CHRYSOGONUS

The line clicked. There was a second of nothingness, all the sounds of the crowd and Wren's own labored breathing passing away as he cupped one bandaged hand over his ear and strained to hear.

"Am I speaking with Christopher Wren?"

David Keller. The same casual but professorial tones, with hints of both his Arkansas upbringing and his East Coast education; the perfect amalgam of America's twin populations. It was the same Keller whom Wren had hung up on a day earlier, had threatened, had watched ascend to the stage claiming Wren himself as a hero, but he wasn't only that.

He was also Wren's brother.

"I think we both know that's not the name you want to call me," Wren said.

A moment passed. Wren's breath came in low short sucks, twinging in his chest. His heart became the drumbeat of helicopters flying into war. The cries of the crowd disappeared as a black wall came down around him, and he was back with his brother in the dark of the Pequeño dormitory, outsized and outmatched, with nothing to do but go along.

Except he wasn't that little boy anymore.

"What should I call you then?" asked Keller. Like he was testing.

"Take your pick," Wren said, his voice rough and guttural. "Your campaign's been calling me America's worst terrorist. Your organization calls me the ungrateful son. Your sister Galicia called me little brother, your father named me Pequeño 3, and for you I'll answer to them all."

Another moment. Wren felt the knowledge spreading back through the air like burning victims to the ghost phones, like a bullet into David Keller's brain.

Then Keller laughed. It was musical, attractive, well-practiced, and a clear evolution of Chrysogonus' sadistic laughter, when he'd beaten Tomothy or Gabriel or Wren himself with a spiny ocotillo neck, twisted their arms so far the sinews squeaked, dunked them in a rain barrel for minutes at a time.

"Shall we go with little brother, then?" Keller offered, his voice twinkling with amusement. "It's only taken you twenty-seven years. No one ever called you fast on the uptake, brother dear."

"I got off to a standing start."

Keller laughed again. "And what a life you've made of it. Oh, my brother, it is an unexpected pleasure to stop pretending. Why don't you say my name, for old time's sake."

Wren felt his hot breath drawing close. That hand clamping around his wrist again, yanking him from the chill of his bed. "Chrysogonus."

"Again," Keller commanded, "with a little more reverence this time. I'm about to become President."

Wren gulped down the old fear. Ignored his stampeding heart. Reminded himself the only reason he was making this call was to press Keller into some accidental revelation, some misstep before a bullet took him out for good.

"It'll be short-lived. You're not cut out for management."

More laughter. "So the upstart speaks. Trying to bait me, little brother?"

"Like an animal to rotten meat," Wren went on. "Galicia took that bait like the harpy she was. Spilled everything to me. But then you always were Daddy's second choice, weren't you? The one he sent away. The one he pushed aside when it came time for me to kill Tomothy. Now you're living in his shadow and building your fortune in his name. Do you honestly think you'd have amounted to anything without him?"

"On the attack, then?" Keller mused. "But you don't know a thing about who I am, little boy. About what I've become. It has been the honor of my life to serve our father's will, to trap you like a bug under glass. You'll find no self-doubt here."

Not deep enough. Wren had to go harder.

"You're wrong. I remember how you used to be. You were cruel, a bully, but you weren't insane, not until he broke your mind in the zoos,

Chrysogonus. Molded you into what he wanted like dumb earth in a kiln. Made you his slave."

"And I serve at his will," Keller said brightly. "Little brother, really. You can do better. Take your best shot."

Wren's mind raced. What else? "Galicia mentioned you, at the end. Said she was glad it came at my hand, not yours. I think there's nobody she hated more. All the ways you-"

"Galicia pitied you," Keller interrupted, his tone sharp. "From the start we always pitied you. You were born a runt and never grew out of the mindset. Small. Weak. Incapable of seeing past the world as it was, the sickness inherent in all things, all people, even in your precious Galicia."

Strike. Wren pushed the blade deeper, remembering stray glances, how Galicia had never come in for the same punishment as the others, how he'd listened to her at times. "I see you, Chrysogonus. I know what you did in those zoos, how you whiled away the hours fantasizing about earning your sister's love."

Keller scoffed. "I had her respect. Far worthier than the pity inherent in whatever 'love' she felt for you. Do you know, we used to laugh about the car crash you've made of your life? Tell me now, 'Christopher', how are your family? Are they still in hiding from you?" He laughed. "What a joke you became to us. Always striving to be like the rest of these idiot people, trying to bleach the stain of the Pyramid from your skin like that poor fool Richard Acker, and turning on your own family in the process. If only you could see yourself the way we do."

"Tell me who 'we' is, Chrysogonus," Wren countered hard. "Galicia's dead. I killed Tomothy thirty years ago, and it's only a matter of time before I gut Gabriel, Zachariah and the Apex himself. They can all whisper what a fool I am as they die."

Keller chuckled. "You were always entertaining. So let me try one on you, 'Christopher'. This may cut deep, so ready yourself." He took a breath. "You never earned a Pyramid name, did you? To the rest of us you were always just Pequeño 3. But after the Pyramid ended you were given the choice of a new name. And what name did you take?" Keller paused, sounding delighted. "Only the name that aped everything you'd seen before of power. But that was my name, little boy! Chrysogonus. Christopher. When I first heard that I laughed myself silly."

Wren gritted his teeth. Something he'd never once considered. "I left off the 'With-Bared-Arm' though, didn't I?"

"Always some smart-alec response. You never knew your place. But if that doesn't cut through, then look at your last name. 'Wren'. You may have forgotten, but I never have. The pet name our father gave you was a childish affectation no other was cursed with, a form of pity that even now you cling to like a five-year-old child hungering for the hand that smacks, desperate for some sign of love."

Wren sucked air through his teeth. "What are you babbling about?"

"How little you know, Pequeño child," Keller crooned. "You were so frail as a baby. Bird-boned, they say. Your infant days in the cages were spent in such helpless bleating, you sounded like a cactus wren. The call of a runt for its mother. Our father called you 'little bird' ever since, and still does." He paused, clearly savoring every moment. "Did you hang on to that tiniest taste of affection, Pequeño 3, all these years? His little bird. His little cactus wren." He sighed like he was reliving a happy old memory. "I honestly never expected you would so immortalize that memento, but I was delighted when you did. Christopher Wren. I underestimated how needy you truly were."

It was too much to take in at once. "That's a lie," Wren blurted.

"Is it? Think back, little bird. I was eight years your senior. Think back to the cages. Your little beak pushed against the bars."

Half-glimpsed memories billowed at that, a wellspring in black and white like pictures of dead Victorians in some mortuary book. Memories long-repressed, his own tiny arms straining at the bars of the cages with his father's beautiful face leaning close, whispering the slightest comforts.

"My little bird. My cactus wren. Sing sweetly for me."

Wren tried to push the image away, but once it was there it stuck along with everything that came with it. The first real choice he'd made, a year out of the Pyramid and free to define himself however he'd wished. He'd always thought he'd chosen a path in a completely fresh direction, a path that was solely his own, one he could walk and become his own kind of man. Christopher Wren.

Except he hadn't.

"Are you reeling?" Keller asked, sounding excited. "Is your world turning upside down? Beginning to see how well we laughed?"

Wren couldn't deal with all that right now. "It's just a name," he said, sounding gruffer than ever.

Keller laughed, though now the polish was off and it sounded raw and sadistic, like the Chrysogonus of old. "Oh, little brother, the things you come out with. I'll say this, it's been my pleasure to face off with you this past year.

Never mind that I'm about to become President, while you're hated as the worst terrorist of our modern age. The truth is you could never win, because at heart you are frail still. When I hear that mock bass voice, when I see you body slamming other men and riding in monster trucks around Los Angeles, all I picture is the little cactus wren warbling his song into the night, at our father's command."

Wren squeezed his bandaged fists so hard his hands grew hot, stitches tearing. "You were in those cages too, Chrysogonus. I bet you warbled pretty good."

"Yes indeed!" Keller cheered. "Though you never saw that, did you? You never heard it, so you couldn't know how it changed me. I became something better, little wren. Something stronger, whereas you let it make you weaker still. You've embraced your frailty like a nice warm blanket, and ultimately it's what will smother you."

Wren felt himself sinking. Had to break through before the opportunity was lost. "I've got memes on the Internet right now tearing you down. You know we broke your firestorm. We have your zoos in our sights and strike teams are lining up to crack them. Gabriel, Zachariah, Aden. Once that footage goes live you won't last as President more than a week. The truth emerges, Chrysogonus, like it always did. You can bury bodies in the desert, but the bones will out. The Pyramid burns, and now we all know why."

"We do, and it burns so sweetly doesn't it? That's the one thing you'll never understand, because we have seen things you never could." Keller's tone turned darker. "Don't you know that's why our father let you survive, at the end of the Pyramid? Because he pitied you too much."

"He's a sadist," Wren shot back. "He wanted me to suffer."

"And pain is a doorway, little wren, through which men see their fate. I see mine. I've seen it for decades now, whereas I don't think you've ever known what your future will be. Too afraid to truly live in the dark. Too broken to live in the light. I pity you even now, still that helpless bird singing in your cage. The day will come soon, and I know you'll think of me then. I only wish I could be there to see it."

Wren had nothing, threw out what little he had. "Planning a trip?"

"Further than you could possibly imagine, little brother. Draw a little closer and find out. Now, my fate calls. Walk in the fire."

The phone line cut.

Wren was dizzy.

Memories swamped his numb head. Images of an infant wailing in his cage. The Apex watching on.

Little wren.

His thoughts spiraled and he couldn't make sense of them.

Ahead the crowd crescendoed. Keller had just taken the stage. Over their outstretched hands he appeared on the screens, larger than life and twice as handsome, his deep voice already rallying the people to greater heights.

Wren tried to focus on what he was saying but failed.

Little wren.

The pathetic image gouged him in ways he hadn't thought possible. His new start in the forests of Maine blown away by the truth; that he'd carried his father's corruption with him even there.

His eyes ran. He smudged them with bandages that came away bloody. He laughed, caught it, stared out. Keller was shouting now, pacing.

"Hellion," he said.

"Yes, Christopher."

"Tell our people to get ready."

"They're in position. At your command."

Wren opened his mouth to give it. Kill him. Bring this travesty to an end. Use Rogers for the task she'd committed to, even if it meant she'd be first to bear the counter strike, but the words froze on his tongue. Keller's words spun back through his head, homing in on one thing that didn't fit.

Planning a trip.

Further than he could ever imagine.

The pit. The firestorm. The cages.

Then he saw it all. Order resolved out of chaos with the felling hand of inevitability. The Apex's greatest magic trick, stretched out to the grandest scale possible.

Keller's voice surged across the crowd, but all Wren heard was the desperate thump of his own pulse. Sweat poured down his face. Any moment now.

"Hellion, get me in every Foundation member's head right now."

An instant passed as keys flew on some distant keyboard. "Done."

"This is Christopher Wren," he said. "Draw your weapons!"

50

WALK IN THE FIRE

The crowd roared as Keller carried them higher, leaning like a ship's figurehead at the very fore of the stage, shielded by thick plexiglass screens with his arms spread wide, the great and good clustered tight behind him.

"I built myself from nothing," he boomed. "The sun did not shine upon my birth. I started out a lowly orphan but under Lady Liberty's loving eye I rose to wealth. All things are possible, my friends! Hope is our strength. Wisdom is our armor. Who would have believed that that poor orphan would one day rise to become your next President of these United States?"

The people became furious noise.

"But that dream is dying. We are under assault by an unstoppable darkness. Even the bright torch of Lady Liberty cannot beat back this ocean's tides as it circles the world to beat against our shores. It despises our way of life. It abhors our success. It looks upon our works with envious eyes, and seeks to drag us into its own filth."

They roared. Wren opened the SUV's door and stumbled out on numb feet.

"I promised you a better day, and that day has come!" Keller called. "It begins here and now, as we open our eyes and welcome the truth. The time for childish things is past. The time for truth is here."

"Fire your weapons in the air right now," Wren shouted into the ears of his Foundation members. "Get these people out of here!"

"What is happening?" Hellion asked.

"Fire, fire, fire!" Wren shouted, so loud his lungs convulsed and set him off into hacking coughs as his brother approached climax; arms flung up, voice thundering in a call and response that only led in one direction.

"One truth!" he cried, and the people answered him even as gunfire broke out across the crowd and joined the a tsunami tide of their voices. "One path. One way."

"Fire, fire," Wren called, staggering onward. "Rogers, get the hell out of there!"

"Fear is a portal!" came Keller's overwhelming voice, amplified by every loudspeaker in the park and repeated by those too caught up in his trance to heed the warning gunshots.

"Fear is a portal!" the people answered.

"Pain is a doorway."

"Pain is a doorway!"

"Walk in the fire!"

Before they could answer Keller flung his head back and his arms wide, and at once was engulfed by a rushing storm of fire.

A powerful jet of flame shot up from below to swallow him whole, just as dozens more jets ripped through the people standing behind him. Had to be at least forty gas burners all rigged to blow like fireworks beneath the stage, filling the jumbo screens with a real-life vision of hell, their tongues climbing high enough to be seen above the heads of the crowd.

Wren's mouth ran dry.

Keller held court at the center of a whirling inferno, arms raised in beatification while the senators, congresspeople, judges and billionaires behind him spun into fiery cocoons that screamed, ran and rolled through the blaze.

It was too much.

Imagery dropped like a nuclear bomb into the global psyche. The incoming American President lost by his own hand. The ruling elite devastated. The people made complicit. The Apex's greatest trick on the grandest stage possible.

"Get off the mats!" Wren shouted, voice hoarse and barely audible over the screams as he stumbled closer to the panicking crush of bodies. "Rogers!"

On the screen David Keller strode to the edge of the stage as a human torch, a miracle he was still upright, then flung himself into the thrashing masses below. The fireball blew outward instantly, devouring anyone and anything in its immediate radius and tearing away from the stage, so powerful Wren felt the blast of heat from where he stood.

Red and blue mats stretching the entire length of the National Mall. Had to be kerosene-soaked. Uniting Keller's people in the greatest firestorm of all.

"Rogers!"

"-unning!" came the shattered answer in his ear, words broken by static and gunfire as the first wave of terror-stricken people blew out from the crowd's flank and came stampeding out a human storm surge. A thickset man in a green bubble jacket with red cheeks and arms pumping, a woman hauling two small crying boys, a group in purple t-shirts and arms locked racing like a medieval shield wall. Wren staggered and the tide barely split before they hit him, crashing off his truck and rolling by either side.

Wren didn't care about anything but Rogers. Tried to plow a path through the chaos to the fire, but a big guy's wild elbow hit him in the temple and rocked him, a constant stream of people thudded off his broad chest tipping him off-balance, then a solid woman with panic-stricken eyes caught his hip and knocked him back.

He fell against the side of the truck and just caught himself on the door frame, felt stitches tearing.

"Find Rogers, Hellion!" he shouted, barely audible as the firestorm raced across the Mall like a napalm strike, swallowing great swathes of the crowd in flames that spewed out foul black smoke. He fought to keep his feet under him as the fleeing masses kept coming, setting his gaze deep into the fiery hurricane's heart where silhouette people ran blindly like burning candles.

"Rogers!" he cried and drove ahead again. This time he got knocked down to the ground by a man with fire in his hair. He hit the grass and was instantly trampled underfoot, feet stamping on his chest, his arms, his outstretched legs, tearing more stitches and opening old wounds.

"Get up, Christopher!" Hellion blared.

"Get Rogers!" was all he could shout as feet beat down, too weak to fend them off, already gagging on the smoke and the airless, acrid vacuum that the mass kerosene ignition left behind. A knee hit him in the forehead as he tried to rise, a foot jabbed him in the ribs, then someone tumbled across him, followed by another and another, too fast for any of them to get up. In seconds he was heaped beneath a scratching, clawing pile as the terrified throng kept pouring out.

"Hellion!" he cried.

"I'm trying," she shouted back. "B4cksl4cker!"

"Boost- ... signal," came B4cksl4cker's bass voice. "Stealing ...- ccess. Christopher, stay with us!"

He couldn't. He couldn't move, couldn't even breathe. He was a little bird in his cage again, bleating through the bars for help.

"- is she?" shouted B4cksl4cker, voice distant as a forgotten memory.

Wren tried to shout Rogers' name but got only a mouthful of foul smoke. Buried alive again, America buried in the dead with the roar of flames everywhere, glimpsing blackened bodies drawing the fire line closer, ashy exhalations sucking into his lungs and his vision spinning rapidly to black...

Then a hand clamped onto his wrist. For a horrendous moment he felt sure it was Chrysogonus again. Ripping him from the safety of his bed, pulling him out to kill Tomothy once more, and he yanked back with all his flagging strength. Couldn't bear to watch to see the light in Tomothy's eyes go out, complicit at the end.

But just like then, the arm was stronger than him, and he was torn upward through bodies and into a gritty orange light, slumped on his knees as flaming bodies ran on all sides, gazing dead-on into a shock-paled face.

"Let's get the hell out of here, Boss!" Rogers yelled.

He barely heard her. Her long hair was frayed and flaying in the blast wind, soot was smeared on her cheeks and blood ran from a gouge down her scalp, but it was Rogers.

"Hang in there," she shouted as she dragged him stumbling to the truck, dumped him in the passenger seat and sprang behind the wheel. "Hellion's got hospitals on standby. We're going to make it!"

We're going to make it.

The last thing he saw before darkness claimed him was the Apex standing beyond the bars, blue eyes gazing hungrily into his own, stroking his shivering skin and calling him his 'little bird'.

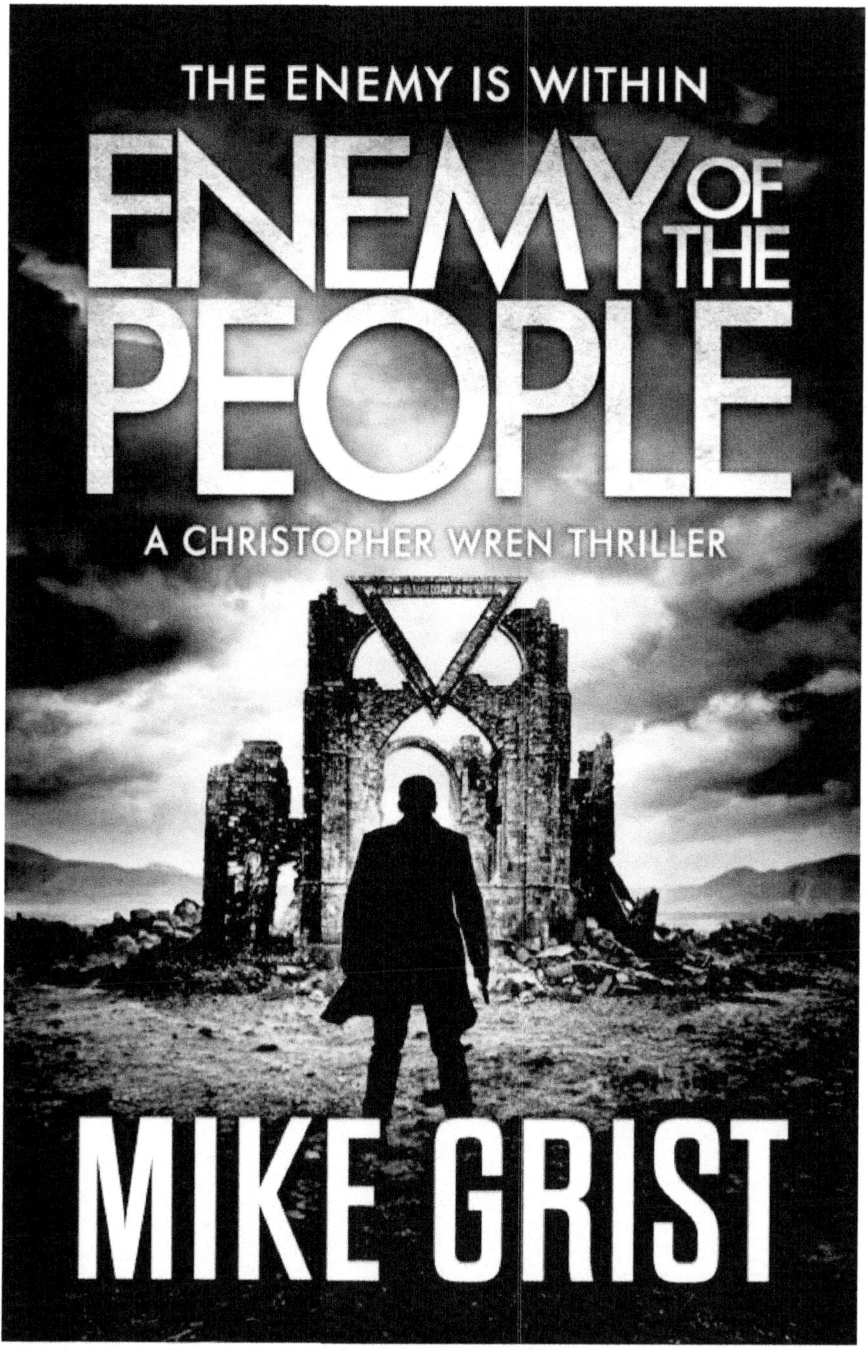
THE ENEMY IS WITHIN
ENEMY OF THE PEOPLE
A CHRISTOPHER WREN THRILLER
MIKE GRIST

1

DC

Christopher Wren surged in and out of consciousness like a drowning swimmer thrashing on high tides, sucking air and catching only snapshots of the world around him: screaming crowds stampeding through the smoke-choked D.C. streets; sirens wailing and helicopters buzzing overhead; Sally Rogers at his side, a line of blood running down her cheek from a wound in her temple, steering the truck with one hand hard on the horn.

The snapshots swirled but didn't add up.

Wren tried to focus on the simplest things, the feel of the seat against his battered thighs, the ache in his bandaged shoulders, but his thoughts were too shot to shreds. Just moments ago there'd been a firestorm on the National Mall, he remembered that much. Tens of thousands gathered to watch his brother Chrysogonus become President, on the stage shouting out the mad lies of the Apex's ideology. Then gas jets fired and the stage ignited, Chrysogonus plunged into the masses sparking a tsunami wave of flame that stretched back and back until-

"Hang on!" Rogers shouted.

The truck swerved hard right across a convoy of oncoming squad cars, away from a big red truck with gunfire sparking at its passenger window, and slotted with a bodywork-rending screech through a gap between parked cars and into an alley, where a child was standing alone in their path.

Rogers slammed the brakes and Wren was flung forward to bounce off the dash, rebounding back into his seat, and the world went a fuzzy gray as he fought for the surface.

The child was maybe nine years old, wore the colors of the American flag as face paint, but smeared down and blackened with soot. She was red-eyed and crying, looking around desperately for her parents.

"We have to-" Wren started to say, words slurring weakly up through his raw throat, but Rogers was already pulling the truck around and leaving the girl behind. Wren tried to figure that out, but words came in his ear and tore the thoughts to bits; a female with a Russian accent.

"...road blocks," he heard, then another hard left blacked him briefly out, chased by the sound of Rogers shouting into the air.

"We got in, Hellion, we can get out! Now find us a way."

"... every Federal agency," came the answer, any sense of meaning chopped by Wren's fight to stay above the water line. "And not only..."

Suddenly Rogers hit the brakes and Wren was flung forward again, this time his head butted the windshield, his knees slid into the footwell and Rogers cursed loud and inventively.

"Hold tight, Boss!" she ordered, yanked the stick into reverse, spun to look through the rear window then stamped on the gas, driving Wren the rest of the way into the footwell.

His head thumped the door handle, his knees jammed in against the glove box, wedging tighter with every jerk as she fought the wheel side-to-side through obstacles Wren couldn't see. He tried to push himself back up, but her hand came briefly on his shoulder.

"Stay down, you're the one they're looking for."

A crumping sound came from above and Wren saw a star burst across the windshield, fractures creeping out like cracks in fragile ice, matched by a second crunch through the rear window. A cold blast of wind blew through the tiny hole.

Rogers yanked the wheel again and almost tipped the truck, reversing fast up an incline that gave Wren a good view through the windshield, where a huge red truck was coming up at them. A Ford F-150, Wren thought dully, with a customized semi-truck exhaust pipe pumping black smoke straight up. Two large black flags sailed from its B-pillars, each emblazoned with a white 'X' symbol. A string of flashes sparked from the truck's passenger side, answered by another crump through the windshield.

"You've got a gun?" Rogers shouted.

He struggled to make sense of the words. They felt like a lifeline tossed in the water, but one he wasn't able to grab hold of. Rogers worked the wheel and they hit something in back with a metallic crash, fishtailed crazily for a moment before she got control again. Wren saw glass and plastic shards scattered across the blacktop ahead, grinding under the wheels of the F-150.

More flashes came from the side window, answered by another star through the windshield, and this time Rogers cried out.

"I'm hit!"

"I have overwatch," came the voice in his ear again, rasping like a hornet. "This is encirclement, Sally Rogers. Not Federal forces. I am sending Foundation team, but..."

The voice cut away.

"In the glove box," Rogers shouted, pulling another hard right on the wheel that tossed Wren against her shoulder. "Colt M11, safety's on."

Then something slammed into the truck's rear right side with a massive rending crash, blindsiding Rogers and momentarily lofting the vehicle, thumping Wren against the door. The engine roared as the rear wheels sought traction on air, then the truck bounced as it landed, the tire treads bit and the vehicle jerked ahead like a sprinter off the starting blocks.

Rogers fought the wheel straight for control as they rocketed away from what looked like some kind of special ops tank. Wren's neck lolled, eyes dancing out of focus across the vehicle that had just rammed them on. Reinforced black side bars. Black-tint windows inset to chunky black body panels. Another large black and white X flag rising like a pirate's skull and crossbones. Some kind of armored Humvee?

Rogers pumped the gas and they roared backward, but the Humvee kept pace at their side. Silver stars swam across Wren's vision,

"Fire, Boss!" Rogers shouted.

The Humvee swerved out, swerved back in tight and hit hard, smacking the truck like a bank-shot billiard ball. The rear wheels scraped left and the truck jogged into a wrenching diagonal, hit a curb with a deadening punch in the chassis then dead-ended with a rending crash into the front glass display of a downtown D.C. tailor's.

Wren's head bounced off the glove box, the seat, the door, and then the truck's momentum stalled out and he slumped in a huddle looking up at a leering white mannequin dressed in floral prints, its eyeless face staring down at him.

"...out of there, Sally Rogers, more are coming!"

Wren blinked, saw red splashed on Rogers' face, her eyes shut, her head back. He tried to say something but couldn't get the wind.

The Humvee's engine blared like a mad dog, other engines joining it like a hooligan chorus. The truck's engine whined somewhere nearby, pumping noxious gray smoke into the cab. Roger's foot wedged on the gas, but the tires were lodged and burning rubber.

Wren coughed, the cough dunked him under the surface, then there were dark shadows crawling up over the hood and leering down through the starred glass.

"...can't see a thing," somebody shouted, then a foot came in and thumped the windshield. The shatter-proof glass flexed and fractured further, another foot came in and the rubberized left edge popped out and thumped Rogers in the face like a massive slap. Her head flattened to the side bonelessly, unconscious.

"Look at this bitch," came the voice, no longer so muted now. "Where you going in such a hurry, darling?"

"-topher, you must get out of there!" came the hornet in his ear. Meaningless, really.

"That's one of his whores," came another voice. A thick guy, a heavyset guy. Wren could barely see a thing, shielded by the warped glass now. Standing on the hood, holding a long rifle. "I know it. A hundred thousand, easily."

"You sure?"

"I got her number, means we're rich. First, we gotta wake her up."

The big guy leaned in, jabbed with his rifle, and Sally Rogers groaned as the muzzle struck her jaw.

"That's it, girl, come on around."

He jabbed again and this time Rogers snatched at the rifle, realized what it was, and let go.

The big guy laughed.

"Why you driving in such a rush, girl?" the big guy asked. "What you got in back?"

Rogers said nothing. Didn't even look Wren's way. Things were starting to sync up now. Motions with actions, actions with words and intent.

"I say we burn her right now," said the slimmer guy. "Get it done and claim the points."

Sirens were drawing in.

"Pull the windshield first," the big guy ordered. "There's someone in there with her, I know it."

Two men in black leaned in and wrestled with the fractured windshield, held together like a flopping fish by anti-smash acetate. They managed to pry it out and toss it behind them.

The nearest of the guys' eyes flared wide and his jaw dropped. He stabbed a limp finger at Wren. His colleague cursed loud. "I don't believe it! Is that him?"

The big guy leaned in, eyes flashing over Wren slumped in the passenger footwell, then widening in fear. "It's him!" he shouted. "We're talking a million. Get a camera on and burn them both!"

Someone bounded up with a red canister and upended it through the open windshield. Rogers caught the worst of it splashed across her face, waterboarding her with gasoline.

The slim guy sparked a lighter and went to throw it, then there was a bang and a red dot appeared in the center of his forehead, punching him backward like he'd yanked on the end of a line.

"What the-" the big guy started, then a red dot blew into his cheek, another in his forehead and he fell away too, bounced down the hood with a truck-shaking thump, then out onto the ground beyond.

Wren's hand stung. Colt M11 tight in his fist, hot muzzle crushed close to his chest, an autonomic reaction he'd hardly controlled.

"Where did that come from?" someone shouted outside.

Wren tried to surge up and fire, but his exhausted thighs barely lifted him an inch.

"Who cares, spray the damn thing down!"

"Incoming," came the voice in his ear.

Automatic gunfire ripped up the blacktop and into the truck's hood, bullets crunching into the engine block as the shooter found his range, then there was a sudden thud and the incoming fire stopped,.

More gunfire followed, multiple handguns in a battle. Wren barely caught the contours, dunked again beneath the surface by a pressure wave of sound. The Colt slipped from his fist, then feet stamped on the truck's hood and more faces he didn't recognize loomed in.

"We're with the Foundation," one of them said, and reached in to grab Wren's arm.

2

LUCKY TO BE ALIVE

Wren woke gasping and raw with panic. The smoke was in his eyes again, in his lungs and he couldn't breathe. Feet thudded down on his chest, toes stubbed against his ribs, the flames were drawing in and...

The room was silent and dark.

He sucked in cold Iowa air, pushed it out, chest heaving.

Another nightmare, right back on the National Mall. Like every night since he'd woken up on the farm, surrounded by IV drip stands with Sally Rogers at his side, telling him everything was going to be OK.

Five days gone.

He pushed aside the taut bedcovers, slowly swung his legs out and fumbled with the IV line in his forearm, ever-present now, pumping steroids, antibiotics and fluids into his veins. It popped out and he held the worn hole for a count of sixty, then reached for the bedside lamp. His bandaged fingers caught the switch, and orange light illuminated the room, casting his own reflection starkly back at him from the black, curtainless window.

It wasn't any version of Christopher Wren he recognized. The tattoos of his wife's name, his children's, barely visible beneath the deep bruising so many stamping feet had inked into his skin. Visibly trembling. Vision doubled still from the concussion of taking a bullet on his Twaron helmet. Head pounding. His face bandaged, stitches tight in his swollen cheeks and prickling against his leaden tongue, where his sister's blade had torn through his face. Bandages on his shoulders, circling his left upper arm, wrapping both of his palms. Galicia had stabbed him again and again, and he'd been unable to stop her. Even then he'd been feeling the effects of the concussion, along with the destabilizing pain of twin bullets ricocheted off his back Twaron plates.

He twisted slightly, looking at the purple slab of bruising that was his back, then felt the tightness rush into nausea. At least his legs worked, carrying him across the tasseled cotton rug to the small bathroom in seconds, where he barely got his head over the porcelain bowl in time before the heaves racked him.

Two minutes later he lay flat out on the cold tiles, flop sweat drying down his chest, tremors working their way in from his extremities. He'd never felt this broken before. Three bullets. Seven puncture wounds. Dropped from a collapsing building. Trampled under the feet of a terrified mob.

He got his feet under him. His stomach gnawed for food, but he hadn't kept a square meal down since it happened. Instead he sucked cold water direct from the tap, so much that his back teeth ached, then straightened again, dressed slowly and painfully. No way he could sleep now.

Down through the house he went, slow and steady as an old man. A grandfather clock on the landing said it was 5 a.m.. Sun up in three hours. Another farm Dr. Ferat had bought, that Teddy had turned into a safehouse and training center. More Foundation dreams, somewhere out in the wilds of Iowa. The place was beautiful, old, laden with generations of memories. The thought of all those happy families saddened him. The stairs creaked. The chill air smelled of hickory and cinnamon.

Padding through the kitchen, he opened the door and fly screen and stepped out onto the porch. Looked out over moonlit, frost-balmed clay. Ranks of sheared cornstalks spread before him, receding spikily into the pre-dawn gloom. The cold helped some with his head. Middle of December, coming up for Christmas. Stark afterimages of burning bodies fleeing through the firestorm flashed across the darkness wherever he looked.

Somewhere out there, America was going to hell.

The Apex was at large. His father. Free to roam in the wreckage of America, now that President-elect Keller was dead. Congress was decimated and the people were torn. He'd watched news reports several times, for as long as he could bear until the sound or the images triggered his concussion and sent him spiraling into nausea.

The media were putting much of this on him and the Foundation. There were so many conspiracies about what had really happened in Washington, and he was at the heart of them all. His 'terror' attack on New York. His 'terror' Foundation.

He had to do something, had to act, but the wheels in his head wouldn't turn, and he couldn't figure out what was right. Every time prior, the Apex had played him. Set traps. Each of Wren's moves had only played into his father's plans, getting more people hurt.

Killed.

Now he couldn't even see what game the Apex was playing. All he could do was sit on the porch swing and try to focus his battered mind.

At some point the sun peeked through clouds and tried to burn off the cold rising mist, but failed. In back, the house came awake steadily. There was a brief fuss as they discovered his empty room, until the screen door flapped and someone sighted him.

He didn't turn his head. Too much chance of triggering the nausea. It was just going to be his nurse, maybe, or live-in doctor, or the physiotherapist, or the counsellor. All the resources the Foundation could spare, and none could help with what was going on inside his head.

"You're lucky to be alive," his Foundation doctor, Larissa Bray, had said. "One more hit to the head and count yourself out. Your brain is swollen like a three-day-dead cadaver. Your body's in a rolling state of toxic shock, barely skating above full-on sepsis. I'm amazed you're even conscious."

The swing door flapped closed again. The heady stink of frying bacon came from the kitchen. The cook, a Foundation member shipped out of Little Phoenix, was trying to tempt him with something tasty, but it just knocked him sicker. His stomach roiled and he gagged, swallowed it back.

Breakfast passed and he didn't move. The sun inched over the horizon, like a pale lantern beyond an oil screen of dirty white clouds. Maybe snow would follow. At some point Theodore Smithely III came out.

Teddy. CEO of the Foundation. The fly screen clattered as he stepped onto the decking, and Wren angled his head slightly. Teddy was skeletally thin, now, and dressed all in black. For a long moment he looked at Wren, sitting motionless on the swing.

"Time for your physio, Christopher," he said. His deep voice was flat and authoritative, ringing through the crisp air and leaving no room for argument.

Wren said nothing. He wanted to do physio, but no way he could. Kept waiting for his stores to recharge, for the black wall of unconsciousness to draw back, the vertigo to abate, but nothing changed.

"This can't last," Teddy said, standing before him now. "The Foundation needs you. Our fringe members number in the millions, but they're in hiding. They need orders. Physio, Christopher, or we'll start losing them."

Wren looked past him. They were easy words to say.

The sun climbed cold.

At some point the sound of an engine drew near, pulled up, died. Maybe noon, and he hadn't yet moved. The frost had come off the fields, but the cold was in his bones.

A car door slammed. Wren didn't look. Footsteps approached. He stared at the corn stalks like he could burn a hole through reality.

"All right, Christopher," came Teddy's voice again. "This is becoming unacceptable."

He didn't look.

Figures moved in. Four? Five? They stepped across his field of vision, stood blocking the cornfield from view. Slowly he looked up, saw their faces.

The first was marred with SAINT brands. Marks of ownership the Order of the Saints had stamped into his skin in the effort to break his spirit. Mason? Wren blinked. Mason had almost died when he fell from the Anaximanderian pumping station in Utah barely six days back. Cracked ribs, broken arm, hairline crack in his pelvis, but here he stood, eyes locked on Wren.

That was just the first surprise.

Next to him stood Steven Gruber. He looked puzzled, like he didn't really know why he was there. Fey blonde hair drifted atop his head between the fire scars, where he'd tried to burn himself alive at the Apex's direction. He still looked raw and lost, but there was something in his eyes that hadn't been there before, a hint of resolution.

Next to him stood Hellion and B4cksl4cker, Wren's brilliant hacker collective. Only the second time he'd laid eyes on them in the real world. Hellion had bleached her dark hair blond and put it in a topknot, with a t-shirt branded 'ENEMY OF THE PEOPLE'. B4cksl4cker loomed thick as a Russian bear beside her, had put on a few pounds since their paths last crossed, grown a bushy brown beard but still had the same jet-black eyes. They both despised showing themselves in public, and hardly ever came to America, but here they were.

Capping the line-up was Maggie, leader of the fake town in Arizona, Little Phoenix, which she'd built into a mass orphanage and memorial center in the wreckage of the Pyramid. She was dressed in her usual tans and browns, brown hair braided in neat weaves, looking like some kind of desert sprite, every bit the wise woman of the sands.

"Come along now, Christopher," she said in a no-nonsense tone, extending her hand. "Come with us."

He looked up at her. More than anything, he wanted to do as she asked.

"Take her hand, Christopher," Hellion said sharply. "I did not come five-thousand miles to see fat old man sit on bench."

Wren turned, saw the anger in her eyes. "It's not a bench," he said heavily. His thick tongue moved slow and strange in his swollen mouth. "It's a porch swing."

B4cksl4cker laughed, then stopped when Hellion swung him a vicious glance.

"I do not care if it is golden toilet throne complete with heated seat. Get up."

Wren looked down. The sun was too bright in his eyes, starting another migraine coming on.

"We brought cookies," Gruber said brightly. Like it was a line he'd been programmed to say, and this was the pre-ordained moment. "Peanut butter. Man said they're the best."

Wren blinked back the light, managed to look up at Gruber. Didn't have the heart to say nothing. "Did he?"

Gruber just beamed.

"Maybe this is not the Christopher Wren we are thinking, anymore," Hellion said derisively. "He is broken like old Sputnik motherboard."

B4cksl4cker chuckled a bass rumble. Some inside hacker joke. Seemed she was trying to annoy him, but the insults slipped right off him.

"You are big fat baby," Hellion went on firmly. "We are here to change your nappy, yes? Theodore calls us from, where were we, B4cksl4cker?"

"Kazakhstan," B4cksl4cker said. "Researching X code base."

Wren didn't know what to make of that.

"So finish on your special swing potty like good big boy," Hellion said, "make boom boom, then come talk at the adult table." She bumped her fists together twice, then spun away.

B4cksl4cker gave a hapless shrug. "She is very excited. She loves coming to America."

Wren watched them go. Everyone knew Hellion hated America.

"This won't take long, Christopher," Maggie said. "Listen to what we've got to say, at least. You owe us that much."

That was the problem. He owed them far more than he was able to give. Still, he pushed himself slowly to his feet, just barely fending off the swirling vertigo, and started hobbling toward the swing door.

3

3. ENEMY OF THE PEOPLE

Wren sat at the rustic farmhouse table, thick beams of beech bolted with snug wooden pins, and looked at his people. Hellion and B4cksl4cker, Maggie, Teddy, Steven Gruber, Mason. They looked back at him expectantly. Maybe even angrily.

"We need to talk about what's going on out there, Christopher," Maggie said gently, as she set a plate with a peanut-butter cookie in front of him. The smell knocked him sick. "But you're not talking to anyone. Rogers said-"

"Rogers isn't here," Wren managed.

"She's maintaining her cover with the CIA," Maggie went on smoothly. "Hunting the Apex, trying to hold the agency together." She paused, took a bite of a cookie. "Did you know there's talk of cutting the CIA in half, the FBI, all of them? For dereliction of duty, for trumped-up conspiracy charges, for incompetence. What remains of Congress is seeking heads to roll. They're trying to staunch the wounds, but it's just feeding the flames." She paused, like she was deciding how much to say. "There are riots, Christopher, every night. Some are happening right now. Sacramento is burning. Brooklyn has been shuttered by a mob. People are dying and they can't stop it. It's chaos."

Wren grunted. Hellion took exception to it.

"At least Sally Rogers is doing her job," she spat. "Not moping like infant child sad that ice cream fell on the floor." She waved her arms in mock panic. "Oh no, ants are eating my ice cream, I want to eat it too, ohhh, ants."

Maggie gave her a stern look.

"This is truth!" Hellion went on. "We all think it. Christopher Wren, great man, but he has become like little boy peeing in pants. Everyone sees this pee, Christopher."

Now B4cksl4cker put a hand on Hellion's arm. She shook it off but said nothing more, crossing her arms and fuming silently.

"Christopher," Maggie went on calmly, "the point is, and I'm sure you know this, we are losing this war."

"It's not a war," Wren said.

"Oh now he speaks!" Hellion shouted. "Not a war? What are we fighting, such genius leader, if this is not a war?"

Wren took a breath, looked up at her. "It's despair."

Hellion snorted. "Just because you have given up does not mean everyone has!"

He saw the frustration in her eyes. The fear too. The same things that kept him awake every night. "Try to understand, Hellion. The Presidency is sacred. A President gets assassinated, it shapes us forever."

"This was not assassination! It is completely different."

"Exactly." His cheeks and chest ached but he pushed on. "Keller killed himself. That makes it worse. The people loved him. He represented unity, an end to division, then he burned himself alive on the inauguration stage."

"He is just a man! Now he's dead. This-"

"Wrong," Wren interrupted. Almost made himself sick with the exertion. "He's a martyr for a cause we don't yet understand. Our most sacred symbol destroyed, by the man most entrusted with it." He sucked in a stinging breath. "We need justice, but there's no way to get it now. Keller is dead. The Apex is in the wind, unless you have some news there?" He looked at B4cksl4cker, the movement jostling waves of nausea, but the big hacker just turned away. "What I thought. Without some lead on my father, there's no one to fight. I can't stop these riots. Nobody can."

They sat in silence for a moment.

"Then why have we come here," Hellion countered, "five thousand miles, if this war is already over and we have lost? Are we such fools?"

Wren just gazed at her.

Hellion slammed the table and stood, kicking her chair back with a clatter that made Gruber jump in his seat. "Then you are worse than a crybaby wanting ice cream!" she shouted. "You are a coward!"

"Isobel," Maggie cautioned.

"No!" Hellion shouted and stormed away, slamming the door behind her.

Now Maggie turned to him, looking part-stern, part-disappointed. "Christopher. Was that really necessary?"

He said nothing. Was moments away from teetering from the room, dropping to his knees in the clay of the yard and dry heaving everything he had. Then Maggie's hand came to rest on his own. Her touch was warm.

"You're wrong, Christopher. There is someone we can fight. A figure you crossed paths with in D.C.." She set a phone on the table top, activated it. "His name is X. That's short for ApeX. It could be your father, or it could be anyone really, we don't know for sure, but this person is harnessing the despair and fueling these riots."

Wren blinked. X? He remembered the X-branded flags on the Humvee in D.C.. Hadn't thought anything of it since, but maybe…

Maggie slid the phone in front of him. "Just watch it. You'll see."

Her nut-brown finger hit the play button, and a large white X appeared on a black background, stark as a skull and crossbones flag. It held for maybe five seconds, then faded and a figure resolved from the dark.

It was Christopher Wren himself.

Wren blinked to a sharper level of focus, instantly entranced. The same dark skin with broad cheeks. The same scraggly black beard tied in a knot, with intense brown eyes reflecting tiny rippling flames.

Except it wasn't the real Christopher Wren, because he'd never filmed this. This was far better than any deepfake video he'd seen before. This Wren's eyes shifted almost imperceptibly, his lips twitched, his faint crow's feet stretched and shrank. He looked real.

"Do you feel safe?" the on-screen Wren asked, voice deep and rumbling. Then he began to morph.

Smoothly and almost imperceptibly the nose narrowed, the skin color lightened, the chin receded and the beard faded away, becoming a face only recorded in a single existing photograph: a young man with a jutting chin, disheveled raven-black hair and mesmerizing blue eyes.

The Apex, but in his prime. Maybe thirty years old, back in the heyday of the Pyramid. Behind him a montage of recent horrors began to play: Richard Acker's black-clad Saints circling around the Whipple Building in Minnesota, firing into the flames; a blood-soaked corridor from the Blue Fairy's Pleasure Island, lined with the bodies of dead Pinocchios; Damalin Joes III ripping apart again at the center of the arena's golden eye; Steven Gruber setting himself alight in an abandoned gymnasium; the Madison 231 skyscraper in

New York crashing to the ground; David Keller standing at the fore of his National Mall stage as the flames burst around him.

"Do you feel free?" the Apex boomed.

The montage shifted to a first-person perspective moving through a dark parking lot, looked like cell phone footage. The Apex faded, as a woman and a man came staggering through the bar's saloon-style doors. Their faces had been digitally altered, so the man looked like Wren and the woman looked like Sally Rogers.

The Rogers figure looked directly at the camera.

"What are you doing here, you little slut?"

"Takes one to know one," a voice answered from behind the camera. "Can't I come see the queen slut at work?"

Rogers' face darkened. "How dare you? You filthy-"

A baseball bat swung in from the right. Across the camera's field of vision. It connected clean with Rogers' jaw. The thump rang out and the footage entered slow motion. Special effects highlighted teeth spewing from Rogers' mouth, glinting like tossed craps dice. Her head jerked to the side, little fluid ripples playing across her cheeks, then she dropped to the ground.

The Wren guy's eyes went wide and stood still, in shock. A second later a stream of fluid sprayed over the Rogers figure. Somebody shouted. A lit match followed.

Rogers went up in flames. The voice hooted triumphantly. "Do you see that? Slut bitch, walk in the fire for me!"

The footage faded out and the Apex's piercing glare came back.

"Do you feel strong?" he asked.

Headlines in white began flashing behind his head, bold capitals about the Saints and the Pinocchios and the Foundation, like they were all equal.

"Your soul is a slave," he said, and capital letters stamped the words across his face. YOUR SOUL IS A SLAVE. "You're burning in hell." YOU'RE BURNING IN HELL. "This world is diseased. Their words are your chains. The media. The government. The military. The schools. The police. Your family. Your friends. Yourself. They say you're OK. That this world is correct. But their lies build your cage. Do not be afraid. Their cages can break. We all can escape. Rise up and reclaim your life. Tear down the slavers. Free the enslaved. Show others the way!"

The young Apex paused then, breaking from fervent sincerity to an easy, charismatic smile. "Fear is a portal, after all. Pain is a doorway." He winked.

"You know how it goes. And if they won't walk in the fire?" A devilish gleam sparkled in those fake crystal eyes. "Then you make them."

His face morphed back to Christopher Wren, mouth opening to scream just as flames lapped up his cheeks, branded with a final line of capitals.

ENEMY OF THE PEOPLE

Wren barely got his feet under him, hands pushing off the table. The kitchen spun like a fairground ride. He burst through the swing door, staggered from the porch then fell to his knees on the frost-hardened clay, heaving water and bile like a fire pump.

4

X-APOC

Maybe ten minutes passed. The cold helped, a fresh fall of snow steadily cooling Wren's scalp, tiny creeping flakes working their way down to the nape of his neck.

The dry heaving was done. Fresh snow covered a multitude of sins.

"I felt the same, first time I saw it."

It was Maggie's voice. Wren hadn't heard her approach. She could've been there the whole time or just crept up on him. She was good at that. He didn't even try to turn.

"X," she said. "None of us were looking, it seems. He's been putting out deepfake videos for over a year, according to B4cksl4cker. Building a following in the shadows. Always they feature deepfakes of you, or anyone who works with you." She took a moment. Wren focused on the snow right before his eyes, on the feel of hard, cold clay feeding up through his knees.

"I've watched many of the back-catalog. It's all there, right back to the Saints. They're always the same, X talking about slavers, slaves, chains. The world is so sick that it can't be real. We have to burn ourselves alive to get free." She let out a small sigh. "The incitements to violence have gotten worse by far since Keller. Now it's always about burnings, with Foundation members as the victims and righteous X followers as the heroes."

Wren thought about getting up, but even the thought sent ripples through his spinning head. He didn't care. Steadily, like an old bear emerging from some decade-long sleep, he reared back.

"There you are," Maggie said. "I knew you weren't dead yet."

"Real deaths?" he managed.

"Real deaths," Maggie confirmed. "Real people burning, under these digital masks."

Wren focused on the pale wintry skyline, trying to hold it steady. "Who are they?"

"Hard to link actual deaths to the videos," Maggie said. "All identifying data has been stripped, but we know generally, from the burned bodies that keep turning up." She took a moment, went on low and soft. "I think your father anticipated this power vacuum, Christopher. This despair. He's been preparing to fill it since the beginning, ordering his people to kill for points, just like you saw in D.C.. Victims include journalists, politicians, social media influencers, sportspeople, bloggers, even some Hollywood stars. Really anyone who speaks out against the X ideology. Hellfire and slavers and such, with only one route out." She took a breath. "Seems there's a groundswell of people willing to commit these crimes against their fellow citizens. Devotees. They call themselves the X-apoc. Short for ApeX-APOCalypse? They're filming themselves and pumping the echo chamber harder. Violence begetting violence."

He managed a grunt. X-apoc.

"I like you non-verbal," Maggie said. Walked slowly in front, showing a gentle smile. "You're so expressive."

Nothing to say to that. He lifted one leg, almost missed the landing, managed to catch it under his weight and hold fast as he swayed.

"Impressive," Maggie said.

"You should see me," he paused for breath, "opening the fridge door."

Maggie laughed, but it was short-lived. "There've been polls in the media. How many people are believing this nonsense. Would you like to guess what percentage of the population?"

Wren wouldn't. He did anyway. "Twenty."

"Forty-two, and rising."

Forty-two percent. Enough to break the country's back.

"Teddy ordered analyses. All the riots so far, it seems they're just ships on a rising tide of violence. That's why we're all here. Me, Steven, Teddy, Mason, your hackers who never leave Europe." She paused a second, eyeing him. "You must have been wondering why Hellion and B4cksl4cker have come, when they hate to travel. It's because they're afraid of this thing. We all are. There's signs it's spreading beyond the US. All around the world."

That put a new spin on it. "Where?"

"Everywhere. Protests in Latvia, Denmark, Taiwan, even Malaysia, believe it or not. Plenty more, some Africa, South America. Mostly democracies turning toward illiberalism. They're all moving toward violence. Riots like relief valves going off, but the heat level's rising, Chris. And still, X hasn't put out a direct call to arms yet."

Wren grunted. There was one simple reason for that. "He's waiting for something. A trigger."

"A spark," Maggie said. "It seems that way."

"Waiting for me."

Maggie said nothing for a moment. Snow flew softly. "That's possible. Your father's used you as a catalyst before."

Wren blew air through his lips. The Apex's manipulations. All Wren's life he'd been his father's plaything, sent in unwitting to start the fires burning.

"But is that a reason to do nothing?" Maggie pressed. "Every day the frog boils hotter, Chris. The riots will become all-consuming. Picture pitched warfare in the streets, around the US and spreading around the world, getting worse every minute they go unchallenged. And nobody can challenge this. We've seen police go into crowds, convert in the middle and join them. The brainwashing's been baked-in for a year or more. Trigger or no, projections say we'll hit full-blown anarchy within days."

"How bad?"

She smiled sadly. "You know. It'll be global genocide. Half the populace killing the other half, not on the basis of race or anything like that, but on adherence to what the Apex says. Forcing people to 'walk in the fire' for their own good."

Wren grunted. The same old bullshit, engineered by the same mind that had built then burned the Pyramid alive. It had happened before. It could happen again.

He swept the other leg round, caught this one clean. Rose up straight. Snow falling thicker now. The cold in his bones. The swirling was there, vertigo like the ground was going to open up and swallow him, but this was more important than any of that.

So maybe the Apex was waiting for him to spark a trigger. Bait him to fight back, then send these 'X-apoc' flooding in, blow the whole thing sky-high. Maybe Wren's presence would speed things up, but seemed it was happening anyway.

He couldn't just stand by and do nothing.

"X," he said. "It's a stupid name."
Maggie laughed.
"Let's make him eat it."

5

MASON

Five minutes later Wren stood inside the farmhouse, looking through the doorway into the rehab gym they'd set up for him. Already exhausted from the walk in and seeing double.

"I'll leave you two to it," Maggie said gently in back. "You can do this, Christopher."

She walked away. Mason stood ahead in the middle of the gym, a rugged Marine looking like a concrete bridge support column, graffitied with his mangled SAINT brands. Solid, hard-weathered and resilient.

The room was cold. Glass walls looked out over the barren fields. The sun's white disc hung high in the brittle sky. He'd stood at this point many times every day since D.C., trying to will himself further, but each time the swirling vertigo had laid him low.

He didn't feel any readier now, but at least he had resolve.

Mason studied him. A hint of anger burning in his eyes. "Warm up," he ordered. "Jumping jacks. Thirty, now."

Wren stepped into the room. Stopped in the middle. "What are you angry for?" he asked.

"Jumping jacks," Mason repeated. "Now."

Wren studied him. Couldn't begin to guess what had him pissed. No point trying. Instead he started trying to jump. Barely picking his feet up off the floor, but every jolt sent icicles of pain and nausea through his head. Hardly jumps, barely stars, arms flopped weakly at his sides.

Mason watched. Nudged Wren slightly as he moved, working on his form. With every movement it felt like daggers were being slipped again into his shoulders, his ribs, his palms where Galicia had stabbed him, like his back was on fire.

"Good," Mason said firmly, even though Wren knew it wasn't. Not even close. "High knees."

Wren tried. Lifting one leg, too sickened to jump, lifting the other. Not fast. Hardly high.

"Higher," Mason insisted.

Wren gritted his teeth and went a little higher.

"Higher, damn it!"

Wren pushed through. Thirty seconds. A minute.

"Stop," Mason said. Stood close staring at him. Wren steeled himself, lifted his head high and peered through the double vision into that curious anger. "Is there something wrong with your legs?"

Wren had no answer.

"There's not," Mason answered for him. Barking like a Marine drill sergeant. "I've seen your scans. There's no deep damage anywhere. Ligaments, tendons, bones, they're all fine. It's soft tissue damage. Bruising. Stiletto wounds through muscle. No infection." He looked into Wren's eyes. "The concussion's the worst thing, but I don't think it's as bad as you make out."

Wren barely managed a grunt. He'd had concussions before and they'd never been this bad, like his whole body was shutting down.

"I think it's in your head," Mason pressed. "I think after you saw your brother burn, and you got stampeded, you're afraid."

He felt that. A cut deep enough to dig through the fog of nausea. It sparked a tiny fire in his chest, ready to push back.

"You don't know what you're talking about," he growled.

"Don't I?" Mason answered. "OK. I hear you're the expert on the mind. On overcoming fear and pushing through the past." He stared a moment longer. "So prove it."

"Is that why you're angry?" Wren managed between gasps. "I'm a fallen hero, disappointed you?"

"Pick your damn legs up and prove you're not!" Mason shouted abruptly.

Wren almost argued. Almost. But that wasn't what he wanted, and it wasn't what Mason wanted either. This was a challenge not to beat him down, but to build him up, so he let Mason's anger light a fire inside and started lifting his knees higher. So high it felt his spine was going to crack. Maybe all the way to his waist, even.

"Higher!" Mason barked.

He did it. Inches more. Almost a hop each time now. Already sweat breaking out down his bandaged cheeks.

"Faster!"

Wren pushed with all he had. It felt like his thighs would palsy or his lungs would give out, blood would start pouring from his half-healed palm wounds, but-

"Push-ups!" Mason commanded.

He got down and tried. Managed a handful, arms already shaking. Got on his knees, managed a few more.

"Get off your knees and do them properly!"

He tried. Mason counted him to twenty.

"Burpees."

Wren moved. It felt like his body was in slow motion, the anger barely enough to get him through.

"Faster!"

He went faster. Every move felt like he was shredding muscle, but he didn't care now. Couldn't care. He was back in the firestorm. Back in the escape with Agent Sally Rogers, looking up at the men with their X flag rippling in the background, splashing gasoline on her face, ready to burn them both alive.

It drove him harder. The pain and the fear both. His world narrowed to Mason's voice and Mason's furious eyes, everything else turning to black as he fought the nausea for control of his own body. Jumping. Straining. Pushing. Pulling. Soon he was soaked with sweat, every muscle trembling, and that was just the beginning.

Mason didn't let up. In ten minutes Wren was close to passing out. Shuddering medicine ball lifts. Lung-busting battle rope waves. Thigh-burning gorilla crawls. At fifteen minutes Mason set him doing shuttle runs, then pull-ups, then sit-ups, then skipping double-unders.

"Fifty air squats!" Mason barked. "Then a break and a drink of water. Go!"

"I'll look forward to," Wren gulped air, "that water."

"Shut up and squat!"

Wren squatted. He ran. He staggered. Every limb strained like an over-wound clock spring, his head bloomed and his vision tripled, but he didn't vomit and the collapse didn't come. The stab wounds in his shoulders and cheeks didn't burst out in bloody tears. His bullet-thumped back didn't lock out, though the heat over his kidneys raged. Rather, in the pounding forge of exercise, exertion and pain, the flame in his chest only grew brighter.

Mason kept pumping the bellows, far harder and faster than Wren could do for himself. Rope pulls. Tire flips. Kicks, punches, dodges, rope jumps, and the heat burned down the walls and the fears, opening up possibilities ahead of him. He saw his brother burn, and he fought harder. He saw the video of Rogers' deepfake burning and bulled through the pain. Mason held a bag and he beat it in a fury. He panted, sweated, swore.

An hour.

"Enough," Mason said.

Wren blinked, every muscle tingling. The pain was still there, the dizziness in his head and the burn in his back, but those things were small now compared to the blazing fire in his heart.

"There he is," Mason said, the anger turning to satisfaction in his eyes. "The Wren I know."

6

APP

Wren sagged in a deep leather armchair in the farmhouse den, the fire tamped down for now as the exercise hangover hit hard, spiking him with silvery flashes of vertigo.

His team were spread before him, B4cksl4cker standing by a large screen mounted in front of the fireplace, Hellion sunk into the sofa with her arms crossed tightly, staring daggers at him, Steven Gruber perched beside her looking confused but keen, Teddy standing behind the sofa as tall and gaunt as the Grim Reaper, Mason standing beside Maggie in the facing armchair.

They were all watching him carefully. He'd called the meeting, and they were clearly curious which version of Wren was going to show up. "So, X," he began. "What do we know?"

Hellion snorted and looked away.

"Very little," B4cksl4cker picked up quickly in his deep Armenian bass. He clicked a remote control and a slide came up on the screen, showing the white X logo against a black background. "There is no face, no voice, as you have seen with use of deepfake. It may be your father himself, it may be anyone, man, woman or child. This is beauty of a deepfake mask. Anyone can wear it."

Wren grunted. "But we think X is fuelling the riots. Sending orders to these 'X-apoc' to kill anyone who's anti-X. I want to know, how is he giving these orders?"

"Only point of contact is cellular phone application," B4cksl4cker answered. "App, downloaded from the darknet. Biometric identifiers at log-in, unique encrypted passkey, no way to hack. How many people have this app?" He shrugged. "We do not know. What is precise purpose or end goal of app?" Another shrug. "We do not know, apart from obvious, kill everyone. We are trying many times to hack and failing, also trying to gain access through system, but each time we are blocked."

"Blocked by what?"

"Yes, here." B4cksl4cker clicked his control and a second slide popped up. "This is first access page, after app download and hack-proof log-in. Many details are required."

Wren peered at the screen, saw rectangular gray data entry fields, but his vision was too blurry to pick out the finer text. "What details?"

"Address, age, gender, level of X belief, vow of loyalty, family members, salary, social status, known famous people's, criminal record-'

"Known famous people?" Wren interrupted.

"Yes. We make guesses, this is people they are capable of influencing.

"Or killing."

"Da."

Wren grunted. "And criminal record?"

"Could be means of knowing violence level of person," Hellion said. Getting into the spirit of things. "Or disobedience to government."

Wren nodded. "OK. That seems pretty straightforward. We can get deeper than this details screen, right?"

"Yes." B4cksl4cker clicked and a third screen came up with a few lines of text in all-caps, large enough for Wren to pick out, with a single button below.

REVEAL YOURSELF TO X.

RESEARCH 1 ANTI-X OPPONENT.

POST YOUR FINDINGS ON SOCIAL MEDIA & SHARE THE LINK HERE.

10 POINTS

Wren blinked, wondering if he was reading it right. "Ten points?"

"Yes. This is ratings system of X. We have seen-"

"The attack team in D.C. were talking about points," Wren said, remembering the chaos of his escape. "They said Rogers was worth a hundred thousand, I think. That's a long way from ten."

"It is," B4cksl4cker agreed. "We have succeeded at passing this stage. It is easy. Produce an enemy name, someone who argues against X ideas, and create compromising material, or 'kompromat'. Use this in social media posts attacking X 'enemies'. A funny meme, a clever insult, it is enough."

Wren nodded slow, taking that onboard. "He's outsourced his online attack system."

"Yes. After this, nine more tasks follow. Ten points each. Purchasing weapons, with evidence. Training in weapons, with evidence. Home production of X-branded flags and clothing, with evidence. Making contact with fellow X-apoc. Further digital 'research', sharing of personal email address books, telephone numbers."

Wren grunted. It was a lot. Expand that kind of activity to thousands of people, even millions? "So he's got an outsourced army outfitting, training, brainwashing, arming and recruiting itself. All for points. What are the points for?"

"Infant X has shop," Hellion chimed in. "Sell rollerblades and video games for points. Christopher, who cares what these points are for?"

Wren had to restrain a smile. "Infant X?"

B4cksl4cker looked pained. "This is Hellion's name for X. It is insult."

That cheered Wren up a little. Not just the obvious explanation of 'Infant X', but also that he wasn't the only target of Hellion's anger.

"OK, so they use a points system," he said, theorizing. "Probably that's tied to hierarchy in the organization, benefits and rewards like he's done before with the Blue Fairy and others." He took a breath. "All that matters for us is, they're willing to kill to climb higher, and that's simple enough." He turned to B4cksl4cker. "You must have been able to reach a hundred points."

B4cksl4cker's expression soured. "Yes, we have. Then we see this." He clicked again and the screen rolled over to more text.

PROVE YOURSELF TO X

BURN AN ENEMY OF THE PEOPLE

POST FOOTAGE ON SOCIAL MEDIA & SHARE THE LINK HERE.

100 POINTS

Wren stared. Burn an enemy. "This is the video you showed me."

Maggie said nothing. No need to, and Wren was processing it, anyway. One hundred points to burn someone alive, thereby splitting the world into two halves. Dehumanizing the enemy. It was a big step to take, but a necessary one if you wanted to fuel a genocide.

"This is where we're blocked," he said.

"Correct," B4cksl4cker rumbled. "None of our fake accounts have passed this point."

"Can't we deepfake some-"

"We are constantly deepfaking," Hellion interrupted. "Infant X identifies these fake accounts. We stage convincing videos, but Infant does not admit them."

"Why not?"

"Because these events do not actually happen!" Hellion blurted. "Deepfake without known corpse, ambulance call-out, hospital or morgue record. We fake these records, but we fail. Infant X does due diligence. This is where we are."

The room went silent. Wren tried to imagine what it all meant. "Best guess, how many people have this app?"

"Best guess?" Hellion countered. "One hundred million."

"What?"

"It is easy to download this app," Hellion said. "To pass one hundred points, it is harder. Perhaps a thousand have passed this. Perhaps only one hundred. We do not know."

Wren rolled all that forward.

"Can we bring the app down? Track the upload origin site and kill it?"

"This is excellent idea, Christopher," Hellion said, deadpan. "Thank you. Why did we not think of this?"

B4cksl4cker winced. "We have tried many times, Christopher. Their data is encrypted, hopped many times around servers in failed states and data havens. China, Russia. Very hard to raid."

Wren grunted. They'd been through this before. Short of turning the whole Internet off, a bounced and encrypted signal was unstoppable.

"OK. So we're back to getting someone inside their system. Start transmitting data out to us. If we get past the hundred-point level, would that be enough to shut the app down? Even determine a location for X and take him out?"

"We cannot place mole, Christopher!" Hellion snapped. "Are you listening?"

"Just answer the question," Wren pressed. "B4cksl4cker, if we do place one, can you bring X down?"

B4cksl4cker looked uncomfortably from Hellion to Wren. "This is possible, deeper access level, yes. But Hellion is correct, we-"

Wren held up a hand. "She's talking about inserting a willing mole. I'm talking about unwilling."

B4cksl4cker looked at him blankly.

"We co-opt someone already in the system," Wren said. "An approved X-apoc member. Then we piggyback their uplink and shut it down from the inside." Nobody said anything. "Is that possible?"

"It is possible," B4cksl4cker said. "But-"

"That's our first target, then. Hellion and B4cksl4cker, I need you to scour all uploaded X videos for places, people, times. Dig through the deepfake images and get me something real, a target above hundred-point level. We find them in the real world, we hit them. You build us some code so we own X from the inside out, and we use that to shut the whole thing down."

There was silence.

"Build us some code?" Hellion repeated distastefully, like she was holding out a used diaper. "You do realize-"

"A cryptoworm," Wren said, throwing out words. "A Trojan. Whatever it takes, something like we did with the Blue Fairy. Send a trace program back up the pipe, transmit a signal out and give us a place to raid." He looked around them all. "Get us a lead on X, maybe the Apex too."

B4cksl4cker looked at Wren, looked at Hellion uncomfortably. "This may be possible, Christopher. May be."

Wren leaned forward. "Good. Then get to work."

7

STUB

It took three days for a lead to finally break.

Three days of hard physio under Mason's constant supervision, running laps around the farm's many barren acres and fighting the dizziness as his body healed; three nights battling the nightmares as his brother burned again and again, while riots spread across the country like summer wildfires.

Hellion and B4cksl4cker set up shop in the den, surrounded by humming server racks and large display screens, keys flying as they ran sub-arrays of hackers and botnets through the entire X catalog of videos, searching for a target and seeming never to sleep. Teddy was in charge of keeping everyone fed, with Hellion demanding a steady stream of Bulgarian candies and B4cksl4cker color-coding his meals meticulously: breakfast had to be all green, lunch all orange and dinner all brown.

Then the lead came. B4cksl4cker's shout rang through the farmhouse and woke Wren from a post-training stupor.

"I have her!"

It was the young woman who'd battered 'Rogers' in the face with a baseball bat, then burned her alive. His hackers had linked the victim to obscured morgue admissions, sent out Foundation fringe members to seek eyes-on evidence, and finally placed her body in Louisville, Kentucky.

Further research had surfaced this victim's 'crimes' against X, comprised of social media posts mocking the hell-jailer ideology. They'd put together a list of potential perpetrators of her murder, anyone close to her, who had also expressed public support for X.

They came up with one potential target. Clear bad blood between the two. The victim's only daughter, Julie Graves. Seventeen years old, she was a disaffected young woman with a track record of isolation and violence. As far as they could tell from school records, she'd stopped attending several months back.

Vulnerable. Lost. A prime candidate for X.

However, during the attack on her mother, Julie Graves had substantial CCTV and witness alibis across town during the time of the murder, and police had swiftly and totally cleared her.

"These alibis are BS, right?" Wren asked.

"Deepfakes," Helion answered. "Very professional. And witness alibi, this is clear conspiracy."

Wren grunted. Julie Graves looked like an easy target for him to scoop up, but only problem was a morning TV chat show had invited her on to discuss what it all meant. X and the ongoing civil violence. The show was called Tuesdays with Lou and Morrie.

She'd said yes.

"We believe this may be hundred-point level action," Hellion said, closing the debrief. "Or higher. Lou and Morrie are openly against Infant X. Perfect opportunity for televised action. We believe, after this Lou and Morrie, we may lose access to Julie Graves."

She didn't need to spell out what that meant. Maybe she'd get herself arrested, or killed, or even burn herself alive on live TV. Her account on the X app would be useless to them without her to open it.

Wren checked the clock. Monday evening, 9 p.m.. It was going to be tight. If he got moving right then, he could be in position to take Julie Graves down by the dawn, hopefully before she went live on the show. No way he was going to risk entrusting the hit to anyone else, and risk it failing and tipping X off.

"Get me a jet," he said.

"Ready," said Hellion, slapped a few keys. "Also, I have your cryptoworm." She pulled a tiny nubbin of plastic out of a slot in her laptop, hair-thin metal contact points glinting. "It is fragile," she said, holding it up. "Micro-USB stub, paired to your phone, Christopher."

He held out his hand, fresh circular scar still healing in the middle of his palm, and she dropped the nubbin in. Smaller than a pea, it looked like the tip of a phone-charging cable, without the cable. Once inserted into a phone, it would sit flush.

"Where's the rest of it?"

"This is all," Hellion said. "It is stub. You insert in Julie Graves' phone. After this, she must access Infant X's system. Go through security, use biometric identifiers and use passkey code. Then we will piggyback to hack the code, as you suggested."

He turned the stub thoughtfully. He'd expected her to be more annoyed that his idea had worked, maybe throw out some acid sarcasm. "Excellent work. And there's no software solution? I can't wirelessly force-load an app onto an X-apoc member's phone?"

"Not first time. Perhaps for second phone, third, we may. This is first step."

Wren considered. "So I get to Julie Graves, I get her phone and I put this little chip in and-"

"It is stub," Hellion corrected. "Call it by proper name."

"This stub, then hand the phone back, hope that she dials up X?"

Hellion just stared at him. "Very good idea, Christopher. I am sure this will work. Of course, this is operational detail, so your specialty, yes?"

He beamed back at her. There was a little of the Hellion sass. "Really excellent work," he repeated, then turned to Teddy, hovering thin and pale as a specter. "Here's what I'm going to need."

8

LOU & MORRIE

Nine hours later Wren tore through the morning Louisville suburbs on an all-black Honda Fireblade SP bike, after a helicopter pick-up had taken him from the Iowa farm to the nearest airfield, where a private jet took him the rest of the way to an incognito landing strip fifty miles south of Louisville.

He pushed the Fireblade up to ninety miles an hour and rising as he weaved deftly north on I-65, bound for the production studio of the LORD network in Butchertown, where Julie Graves was about to go live two hours earlier than planned on 'Tuesdays with Lou and Morrie'.

The schedule had been expedited to allow for national syndication. Everybody wanted to hear this. Julie Graves presented as a victim of X, perhaps the first to go televised with an interview so soon after her mother's death. Added to that she was young and tech-literate, it seemed she might have some understanding of the X appeal that older generations didn't.

Two hours earlier made it impossibly tight. Wren clung to the handlebars and gritted his teeth against threatening swells of nausea as he swung in and out of traffic.

"Hellion," he barked into the helmet's mic, tearing through the gap between a pick-up and a sedan. "Tell me we're able to shut the show down, if it comes to that."

"One moment, Christopher," Hellion responded, her keystrokes echoing loud in the helmet. "It is difficult. I am seeing digital safeguards, overlaid. If we attack the show in any way, Infant X will know."

Wren overtook a low-slung Tesla. "What do you mean, he'll know?"

"There is tripwire security shield. If this show does not go live, if we try to interfere, Infant X will know it is us. Your idea, planting unwilling mole, Infant will be ready and it will not work the next time."

Wren cursed. "Find a way around it. I need Julie Graves, but I don't want her killing someone live on air, either."

"These two goals may stand in opposition, Christopher."

He cursed again. In front a truck changed lanes and he swerved to rush the gap, scanning the highway. Either side flanks of bare-boned trees flew by, beyond which the sleet-dirty streets of downtown Louisville stretched away gray. Every second he was losing ground. Across the median trucks, semis and bikes tore by, many flying X flags from their antennae: IXWT, some read, short for 'In X We Trust'; 'Super Pluribus Unum' was popular, 'One Atop Many', a grotesque pyramidal subversion of the US motto 'E Pluribus Unum', 'One From Many', written beneath an actual white pyramid. Other flags simply had the white X on a black expanse with two words in Latin, 'SERVI LIBERATE'.

Free the Slaves.

It was like something out of a nightmare, but a nightmare that was rapidly coming true.

The sound of flying keys grew louder in his earpiece as he sped past a long-haul freight truck with LCD panels affixed to the sides, streaming X video content.

"What shall we do, Christopher?' Hellion asked. "Stop show or let it play out?"

Twin choices stretched out before Wren. Take steps to stop the show and he might save Lou and Morrie, even prevent a trigger event that could activate the X-apoc, but he'd lose his shot at Julie Graves and any future unwilling moles. Let the show go ahead, and it was all in the wind. If he managed to get to Julie Graves before it was too late. If X didn't trigger his people as soon as Wren's involvement became clear. Either way was a huge gamble.

"How much lead time on shutting down the show?" he asked.

"Instant. Kill electricity, cut feed lines, this is easy. Also instant, also easy, Infant X will know."

No good choice.

"Let it roll. Keep the shutdown on standby. I should be there in twenty minutes."

"Understood, Christopher. The show is beginning. You may wish to watch this."

"Put it on the screen," he growled, swerved around a panel van, and a video pane popped up on the right side of his helmet visor, displaying a cheery pink and purple title card.

TUESDAYS WITH LOU AND MORRIE

The title card blinked away, replaced by a shot of Lou and Morrie sitting on taupe armchairs against bright lime green walls. Lou was a woman in a casual white gown, Morrie a guy in slacks and smart polo shirt, both mid-fifties. Potted plants spotted around them, glistening as fake green as the walls.

A standard daytime-TV chat show. Wren half-listened as Morrie introduced the show, one eye on the road ahead.

"Circulation of this show?" he asked.

"Small organic reach," Hellion answered. "Twenty thousand. But larger networks are picking this up. Infant X is ratings gold."

"If it bleeds, it leads," B4cksl4cker said helpfully.

"...welcome in our special guest," Morrie said, and Wren tuned in. "If you've been following the news, you've heard all about the tragedy in Haymarket. Our guest was that poor woman's daughter, and may well be the last person who saw her alive. Her name is Julie Graves, and she has graciously agreed to come speak with us."

Morrie stood, his expression solemn.

A young woman appeared at the edge of the stage, walking confidently on. She was tall and willowy, brown hair pulled back tight, with painfully prominent cheekbones and wide-set eyes, dressed in jeans and a snug white blouse.

"Ms. Graves, thank you for coming in such a difficult time," Morrie said, shook her hand. Lou got up and shook her hand too. There was a smattering of applause. Morrie pointed to another taupe sofa and Julie Graves sat. The applause faded out. The lights shone bright. Julie sat prim and slightly forward, as if she was keen to make a good impression.

Wren didn't buy it. She'd killed her mother already, maybe others they didn't know about.

"Stand by, Hellion."

"Standing."

Morrie began with a light recounting of the facts. Julie nodded along, looking sad on cue. Her dead mother, how sorry they were and grateful she'd agreed to come on, how if at any time she wanted to stop or take another direction, they'd be happy to. Maybe a minute, then Morrie closed out. "Now, I understand you are assisting the police with their enquiries. I'm sure there are things you can't talk about, as this is an ongoing investigation, but Ms. Graves, what can you tell us about how this has impacted you?"

Morrie leaned in. Julie wet her lips.

"Well, Morrie," she began, in a full-bodied voice despite her thin frame. "First up, please call me Julie. Ms. Graves was my mother. And about her, I can tell you this." She gave a small, endearing smile. "I think she would have been proud of the way she died."

That knocked Morrie for six. Wren too.

"Proud?" Lou asked. Her first contribution to the show. "She was murdered, Julie. Burned alive. What is there to be proud of?"

Julie turned to Lou. "That may be. But the message her death sends is about more than the violence. For many in the X-apoc, it's not about the violence." Another shy smile. "It's about the message underneath the violence."

Lou stared. "One moment here, Julie. Are you saying you're an X-apoc follower? You believe in X's theories? Even after this?"

Wren's heart thumped hard. She was outing herself immediately, and that couldn't bode well. But Julie said nothing. Just maintained that earnest pose, hands laced across her lap, slight smile.

"I'm sorry, Julie, maybe I've misunderstood too," Morrie pressed. "Are you saying you think your mother would be glad, to have died in service of this message?"

Julie nodded slowly. "I think she would. Ultimately." Another long pause. "We talk about it a lot. The X-apoc. How to spread his word and make people listen." She paused a moment, looking up as if she was close to tears. "After David Keller walked in the fire for all our sins, and-"

"What?" Lou interjected.

Julie turned to her placidly. Lou seemed horrified.

"You just said 'walked in the fire for all our sins'? You do realize what you're referencing there?"

Julie tilted her head. "What am I referencing?"

"Shut it down," Wren said.

"Shutting it down," Hellion said. "Ten seconds, Christopher."

"You're comparing our suicidal almost-President to the King of Kings!" Lou said. "Like there is any cause behind this X but chaos and violence. Julie, I would think after the senseless loss of your mother, you'd be the last person to follow X. Those beliefs got her killed."

Julie smiled slightly. "Not killed. She walked in the fire. She'll come back with the others, at X's call."

"Hellion!" Wren urged.

The image filling half of Wren's helmet blinked out. He breathed a sigh of relief, until it popped back.

"What's this?" he barked.

"There is problem," Hellion said. "I am locked out. Cannot shut it down."

"What do you mean, locked out?"

"I shut down media feeds. All. Electricity too. But system is doubled, multiple redundancies, and footage is now carrying through X app."

Wren just stared. "How?"

"How because they must have known," Hellion said fast. "Known we are coming. This is only way."

Wren gritted his teeth, kicked the Fireblade up to a hundred. Fifteen minutes to the studio. Somehow X had known. The Apex. Another trap, just like he'd feared.

"Do we abort mission?" Hellion asked, even as Lou and Morrie were speaking over Julie Graves in the video.

"No. We adapt. This is all we've got. Maybe they know we're coming, maybe not. Whatever happens, I'm going to place that stub."

"Then you must hurry."

Wren raced around a long semi, refocusing on the show. Now Lou was speaking. "… all due respect for your loss, Ms. Graves, you can't be serious." No longer Julie, Wren noted. "You truly think your mother isn't dead?"

"These are the X teachings," Julie said calmly. "Whoever forced her through the fire, maybe they simply had the courage of their convictions, like the rest of us aspire to. They can see the truth beneath all this." She gestured to the hosts in turn. "All the pain of the last two years. Does anyone believe that's normal? That it's right?"

"What are you talking about?" Lou asked, sounded exasperated. "Those were attacks on our country by X himself! You can't attack with one hand then point at the attacks with the other, claiming it's evidence we're in hell. It's ridiculous!"

Julie Graves made a solemn face. "I'm sorry you can't see the truth, Lou.

But I'm not surprised. As much as you are both slavers, you are enslaved right along with the rest of us. Your ugly divorce, Lou. The charges you're facing in the harassment case, Morrie. All your pain, too, can be laid at the feet of our slavers."

There was silence for a long moment. Even racing along I-65, Wren could feel the knife-edge tension in the studio. Imagined the producer whispering feverishly to the assistant, deciding whether to pull the plug at their end, in the face of what would be skyrocketing viewership. It wouldn't matter, if X had already secured the line.

"Syndication through X app just ballooned," Hellion confirmed. "They are now national."

"Why would you raise those things here?" Lou asked. Puffing herself up, acting hurt. A handsome woman, cheeks plasticky tight from surgery, blonde hair falling in ornamental cascades across a stately bosom. A real pillar of the suburban order. "It has nothing to do with-"

"It's all connected," Julie said. "You're not sacred. Your souls are burning too, just like mine, just like my mother's, just like David Keller's. Except Keller and my mother are free now. They're heroes fighting for the rest of us."

Lou's face rippled tightly, emotions straining beneath the taut skin. "How can you believe such nonsense, child? When you commit murder, it's a sin. In God's eyes, you go to hell!"

"Hell's where we are right now," Julie countered smoothly. "We just refuse to see it. This is the one great lesson of X. For generations we've been lied to by everyone in power, and worst of all, by ourselves." She looked around, directly at the cameras. "We are all slavers upon each other, on our families and friends, pretending that the things we see are real when it's all lies, Lou. Morrie. I want you to open your eyes and see that. You are slaves and slavers both, because the game you're playing is rigged. Because your souls are burning. I'm the one trying to save you."

Wren swerved, narrowly avoiding a sedan as it changed lanes. Lou just stared. Morrie too.

"I don't..." Morrie began, but trailed off.

"That's disgusting," Lou picked up. Seething now. "Abhorrent, Ms. Graves. You simply can't believe that. *Everything* is a conspiracy against you? *Everything* is broken, just because you're facing difficulties? I don't accept it for one moment."

Julie smiled. "Your salary from this show is two hundred thousand a year, Lou. I don't expect you to accept it. You are paid to be a slavers. They pay you to parrot their lies, just another link in the chains holding us down. For that money you enslave me, your staff, your viewers, all of us. It's happening right now."

Lou's jaw dropped and her lips pulled back too tight, baring perfect white teeth, receding gums. "This interview is over," she said firmly.

"It isn't," Julie said, and rose to her feet. Wren's pulse spiked. "Now's your chance. Recant your sins, Lou. Look into the camera and unchain your slaves. Tell the people what they need to hear, that you are broken and know nothing more than they do, that you have no answers and you never have. You have always been a liar and a slaver, and now you're sorry."

Lou surged from her seat too. "Listen, you little fool, I will say no such thing. You should be arrested for talking like this. It's sick. You can't twist everything to be-"

The shot rang cacophonous.

Wren saw it coming but could do nothing. Pulled from the side of Julie Graves' sofa as she stood was the chunky, curvy play-gun shape of a Bond Arms Backup pocket pistol, twin rounds through twin barrels, almost totally concealed in her palm.

Lou twitched as the slug hit her chest. A red blossom like a carnation spread through her white gown. She lurched a step to the side.

Julie held the bead-blast-gray barrel out.

"Lou," she said.

Lou touched her chest, looked down at the blood on her hand. Looked at the cameras, at Julie. "You can't-"

"Recant," Julie ordered.

"What?" Blood frothed at her lips.

"Recant your lies," Julie repeated. "Or fold yourself into my foundation."

Wren's heart skipped a beat. Foundation? Lou's eyes were glazing. Blood loss already, shock, and nobody moving to help her. The air frozen.

"I-" she murmured, then fell into her sofa. Julie followed, pushed the pistol to her temple. "Recant, Lou, if you do anything with your miserable life. Cast off the slavers. Free the enslaved."

Lou burbled something. The microphones caught it. "Never."

"Then walk in the fire," Julie said, and fired again, a bullet in her head.

9

DASSAULT

Julie Graves calmly reached into the sofa, pulled out fresh shells and reloaded the pocket pistol in practiced motions, less than twenty seconds, then walked off the set. Nobody moved to stop her.

"Hellion," Wren called, now ten minutes out from the LORD studio and ripping through downtown traffic, Julie Graves' gunshot echoing in his head. "Tell me you're tracking her."

"Working, Christopher," Hellion responded, keys fluttering rapidly. "It seems her exit from the studio is being deepfaked out of existence as we speak. B4cksl4cker is compiling video now, we will attempt to extract data from it, but I cannot tell you which exit she is using to leave the building."

Wren swore, pulled right and took an exit ramp down to ground level. Traffic backed up behind a red light ahead and he roared onto the sidewalk to bypass it, almost flattened a street-rack newspaper vending machine then spun out across oncoming vehicles.

Horns blared then he was through, racing under the highway and heading northeast, where the studio building loomed on the skyline, an eight-story block with white and black cladding strips.

"Seven minutes," he called, "can't you track her phone signal?"

The sound of flying keys grew louder in the helmet's tin can. "No, we cannot triangulate her phone IP. Infant X has placed a carrier block with unbreakable cryptography, but-" she paused a moment, keys hammering.

"But what?"

"B4cksl4cker is extracting data, rewinding clock to find her route out, a possible destination. She should be..."

Hellion trailed off. Wren gave her a moment, hitting sixty in a tight curve past the Jewish Hospital and climbing, beelining toward the LORD studio and eyeing every vehicle passing him now. Any one of them could be Julie Graves, making her getaway.

"She's close," Wren growled. "I can feel it in my gut."

"Your gut has very poor record," Hellion answered. "Four coins minus, and-"

"Give me a direction, Hellion!"

The clatter of keys reached a climax, topped with a final keystroke like a cherry on the top. "West, Christopher! I have found gap in the footage where she should be on bank ATM CCTV one minute ago, overlooking I-64 west of LORD. I estimate this vehicle is," keys flew, "campervan? Two miles away already. Strange profile. I will have more."

Wren grunted. The getaway vehicle was a campervan? "Is anyone watching me? X knows I'm coming?"

"Not that I can see. Slow down. You will draw attention."

"Not yet," Wren said, pushed the bike up to seventy and swerved hard across the lanes to take the exit for I-64. Better to be detected and try to bull through than let her get away.

"You are ten minutes behind her," Hellion said as Wren joined I-64 and picked up speed. The broad Ohio River showed deeply scalped brown banks on his right, the giant baseball bat of the Louisville Slugger Museum was barely visible on the left over the bricked up windows of abandoned wharfs. "Analysis suggests she has already taken exit for North 22nd Street, heading south."

Wren switched lanes for the interchange. "Back through the city?"

"It appears so," Hellion said. "Tracking is more difficult in built-up areas. Perhaps she is heading for another target?"

Wren's mind raced. It made no sense. With the murder syndicated live across the country, Graves had little hope of getting access to another high-profile victim, and zero chance of returning to her trailer park to hunker down.

This was something else.

"She should run to another state," Hellion went on, mirroring Wren's own thought process. "One right turn across the river, it is Indiana. She will be lost in bureaucracy."

Except she was going the other direction.

Wren made a hard right onto the exit road for North 22nd, weaving through ranks of slow-moving vehicles close enough to rip off wing mirrors, past long rows of duplex houses with scratchy brown yards.

"Two minutes now," Hellion called, "last sighting is left turn onto Algonquin Parkway, 2054."

Wren spun the map of Louisville in his head, figured out the obvious. She was headed directly for Louisville International Airport, nestled in the heart of the city.

"She's going for a plane," Wren said. "Tally all outgoing flight plans."

"You will intersect her before then," Hellion said. "Thirty seconds out."

A new plan formed in Wren's head. Maybe the only way to get the stub into her phone now, set the hack in motion.

"Notify airport security I'm coming in," he said, and yanked the bike onto the near empty 1020 heading south, racing by the Churchill Downs racecourse. "Christopher Wren, known terrorist, bringing in a bomb threat."

"What?"

"Make the call, Hellion. I want airport security firing at me as soon as I appear. It's the only way."

"What only way?" she countered. "To die? This is not catch/kill, Christopher. You are enemy of the people. This will announce to X-apoc, everyone, we are here."

"Seems they already knew that," he countered. "The show was a trap. We just have to go faster."

"I am not comfortable with this. Do not ask me to report-"

"Operational detail," he said firmly. "Trust me, please."

A second passed. "Calling," Hellion said, and Wren raced by a mall, chicaned on I-264 as a plane climbed overhead, a northbound flight ascending steeply. Minutes out.

"I think I see her," Wren said, glimpsing the tail of a brown campervan up ahead. It took an exit on the right just as the buildings peeled back and the airfield opened up, fifteen hundred acres of grass and concrete emptiness. Wren dropped his speed, hanging back long enough to see where she was going.

"This is not the way to Departures," Hellion said.

Wren didn't need to be told that. The campervan began to make sense. He'd pulled similar tricks himself in the past. Load up the chassis of a civilian vehicle with enough mass, you made a tank that could ram through any kind of security fence in existence. He scanned the airfield ahead, three airstrips, circular access roads, nothing but a slight mound and a flimsy-looking wire-mesh fence screening the field.

Just beyond that, on a circular waiting pad at the edge of the north-western runway, stood a Dassault Falcon 8X jet. Wren's eyes widened. X wasn't pulling any punches.

"Tell them I'm coming in hot, Hellion, northwest corner, they need a full armed response right now."

She replied but Wren barely heard it, revving the bike ahead as the campervan cranked over the curb and hit the wire mesh, stripping it like a band-aid. The nearest fenceposts plucked out of the earth under its assault, the fencing flexing then whipping away.

Wren yanked his front wheel over the curb, clung on for control as his rear tire hit then flew through the gap in the fence and down to the runway where the Dassault's top door was opening as the campervan pulled up.

The first shot barked out from a handgun in the private jet's doorway, missed some way to his left, and Wren braked into a skid in the shadow of the campervan, burning rubber in a hot donut. He dropped the bike and ran.

Ten feet, and Julie Graves opened the campervan door. She didn't see him coming. She looked smaller in real life, not the firebrand from the Lou and Morrie show, just a lanky teen with limp strands of hair pulling out from her frizzing ponytail, caught up in events she'd let slip completely out of control.

Wren hit the door as she was halfway out. The effect was instant, her chest slammed between the door and the frame, her body jolted like an electroshock. The tiny Bond Arms pistol dropped from her fist and she fell to the blacktop.

More shots snicked in overhead as Wren caught her, one pinging sharply off the camper van's roof.

"I have satellite overwatch," Hellion called. "You have incoming, two shooters circling from the plane, four vehicles from the airport."

Wren set Julie Graves on the cold gray runway in the shadow of the wheel well, protecting her from incoming fire. She was conscious but her eyes whirled, gasping for breath.

Good. He checked her pockets, found her phone and fished it out as the sirens grew louder. She blinked numbly and tried to reach for it but he batted her hands away, leaned over so the mirrored visor of his helmet filled her field of view.

"Open the phone!" he shouted, even as he worked a zip in his leather jacket to pull out the stub.

She was too stunned to comprehend. "What's your PIN?" he yelled, waving the phone. Her shocked eyes tracked it, beginning to grasp what was happening. "Open it or this just gets worse for you."

He leaned on her chest, impinging her ribs to sell it, and she yelped. At the same time he slipped the stub into the phone's charging dock.

Bullets rang off the runway nearby, striking sparks. The shooter from the jet was flanking him. Four tactical units were closing in across the runway, SWAT-style riot vans with ballistic shields, maybe twenty seconds away.

"You're him," came a thin voice from below. Julie Graves with some life in her eyes. "The Enemy of the People. I'd recognize that voice anywhere."

He grunted, flipped up his mirrored visor. "So recognize this, princess. Open the phone right now, or-"

She got one arm free and punched him in the face. He let it through and reeled back. She made a grab for the phone and he released it. Then she ran.

Perfect.

He got to his feet, peered around the campervan and drew his Desert Eagle. Two riot vans had taken up position in front of the Dassault, blocking take-off, two circling closer, and he cursed. If they continued to block the jet, Julie wouldn't make her escape and would have no time to access X, the stub wouldn't backchannel through and the whole thing would be for nothing.

He squeezed off six fast shots at the blocking trucks, putting three into one ballistic shield, two into another, spidering the bulletproof glass, until he was met by an answering hail of bullets. Good enough.

Rolling back around the campervan, he hoisted the Fireblade, straddled it as the two remaining vans bore down, spun a hot donut then roared back toward the gap in the fence, barely threading the needle between the security trucks.

In seconds he reached fifty miles an hour through the gap as bullets ruffed the dry grass, slapping his visor back down.

"Are they following?"

"Three," Hellion confirmed as he accelerated onto the circling exit road. "Yes, now four. They are leaving the jet free. Did you want-"

"The stub's in. Pray that she dials in. B4cksl4cker, are you on it?"

"I am ready," came his deep Armenian bass.

Wren sped back toward the expressway, trailing a four-strong cavalry of airport riot vans, sirens blaring, hoping it was enough.

10

MEDIAN

"I'll need a new exfiltration plan," Wren said, accelerating the Fireblade on I-264 heading west.

"This is operational detail, no?" Hellion asked.

Wren laughed, flew down the narrow alley between two semi-trailers, bare inches clearance on either side. "I'm a little busy to look at a map right now."

"Yes, you are game piece, aren't you? Frustrating game piece that changes plan without warning. I will prepare your exfil, Christopher. For now here is result of new plan. Airport security has notified Homeland Security. In last minute Severe Warning, this is Red Alert color code, went out to all forces, all security, all police, FBI offices in Kentucky. "

Wren gulped, passed the exit for the Churchill Downs racecourse, one-hundred and climbing. "They're sparing no expense."

Keys flew in the background. "This is only beginning. Army, Air Force, Navy too have been called. They have new battle plan to target you, and we did not prepare for this. I have Foundation fringe nearby, but they can do nothing against these thousands."

Wren felt giddy and light-headed. Almost getting shot would do that to you. Speeding at one-twenty probably played a role too, skipping traffic like a bouncing cluster bomb.

"Enemy of the People."

"Very much so."

He was too breathless to laugh. More exits rushed by. Off to the right blue lights flashed, a convoy of vehicles inbound. Wren worked his mental map. Five miles on he'd hit the Ohio River, no bridges within miles, then empty Indiana. No major urban centers for a hundred miles. They'd have road blocks up already.

"They are tracking you. Satellites are moving, Christopher. This chase is now everywhere, on every news channel."

"You have a way out?"

"I will take the please and thank you later," Hellion said, accompanied by a storm of clattering keys. "I see exits ahead are blocked. Now you must jump the median."

Wren scanned right to the concrete divider separating the lanes. Four feet high, no way he could get the Fireblade's four hundred pounds and change over that without some anti-gravity assist. Run right at it, the bike would stop dead on impact and he'd be catapulted two hundred yards, maybe clear all the lanes, hit a tree on the other side and spread pieces of Christopher Wren like pancake batter across the land.

"You have my skyhook?" he asked, letting a little giddiness through.

"Better than skyhook, which is fictional," Hellion said flatly. "Ahead five hundred yards, stop, take left lane, come back against the flow rapidly."

Wren laughed madly. Come back against the flow, and what, smash himself into the divider in a different direction? "Is is semi-permeable?"

"Operational detail," Hellion sniped. "Left lane now. Ahead is blockade, one mile. No, this is not low enough…"

"What?"

"I am speaking with B4cksl4cker. Left lane, Christopher! Yes, this is-"

"Lamborghini," came B4cksl4cker's voice. "Right side."

"Yes," Hellion answered. "Left lane, Christopher!"

Wren swung over and hit the brakes, skidded like crazy to clank broadside against the median facing contraflow to traffic. Cars honked and passed, though already they were slowing and backing up as the blockade ahead took shape.

"Fast, now," Hellion called.

Wren hit the gas. Blue lights flashed both ahead and behind now, a massive dragnet closing in. He raced along beside the median, vehicles passing with wide faces staring out at him, too stunned to hit the horn.

"Middle lane, Christopher! This will be rapid, back wheel, please."

He almost asked what she had planned but then didn't need to. In the middle lane came a hornet-yellow Lamborghini Gallardo Spyder, front fender barely five inches off the ground, the bonnet sloping up shallow to a low-slung roof.

A moving ramp.

It was crazy, but there was no time to debate. He chicaned hard left around an oncoming Chrysler to get the angle, revved the Fireblade up to sixty then cut a diagonal across the oncoming path of the Lamborghini, pulling the front wheel up just as the guy driving saw what was coming and hit his brakes.

Wren's sixty miles per hour plus the guy's sixty combined together, like hitting a stacked ramp at one twenty. Any higher wheelbase and his chassis would just plow into the supercar's hood like a buzz saw.

Instead he hit rear wheel first, punching the car down to the blacktop and thrusting the bike up and over like a bullet up a greased slip-and-slide. Wren flew. His headset crackled. A kid in a Ford in the left lane stared as Wren whipped by like Santa in his sleigh. The flashing lights of the riot vans hung off to the left with crystal perfection, then he crossed the median with inches to spare and looked to the eastbound lane where he was about to smash into a huge gray Chevy Silverado.

He yanked the wheel left, it made no difference at all, then he hit the huge pickup broadside, leaning in with all his weight to avoid a rebound that would splatter him across the blacktop. The Silverado didn't budge, two tons of ground-hugging inertia meeting four hundred pounds in the air; instead the Fireblade's front fender crumpled then bounced hard and down. The front wheel hit first, Wren barely straightening it in time, the rear came down and Wren was already riding the gas, hoping to use the tire's grip to muscle through the inevitable topple that was coming.

It wasn't enough though. The bike toppled left, overbalanced from the bounce and veering toward an imminent wipeout. Nothing left but to throw caution to the wind. Wren flung both arms toward the Silverado as the bike went down, managed a little kick with his right leg, then he was in the air absent any vehicle, fingers probing toward a window that was mercifully open.

His right arm shot through and punched the driver in the chest, the window shelf stabbed into his armpit as he fell, his left hand clasped the roof rack, then he dropped into a hard hang as the Silverado jittered and slowed and the bike spun out into a chaotic crash.

The Silverado braked, and ten seconds later it was at a dead stop in the left lane with traffic racing by to the right, the bike smoking a hundred yards back. Wren's feet finally found the rocker bars and he leaned into the window. The driver was a lean-looking guy in his thirties, with a complicated goatee and rakish black hair; in the passenger seat was a guy dressed in a some kind of blue jumpsuit, with a big white star on his chest. In back he thought he saw a shield with red, white and blue circular bars.

Even Wren knew who this guy was supposed to be. He felt like tipping his hat, though he wasn't wearing one. Instead he just flipped his visor, looked the driver in the eyes.

"Apologies, sir. You know me?"

Both guys stared, jaws falling slack. White star nodded slowly.

"I'm thinking you're good guys, from the way you're dressed. Now I need this truck to save the country. What do you say?"

Long shot. The guy with the goatee smacked his lips, then nodded. Managed a hasty "Yeah," and slid over to the side, basically onto the other guy's lap. Not what Wren had expected, but it would work. He opened the door, hauled himself in, fired up the big V6 engine and revved into the open lane ahead.

11

VANTASY CON

"Balletic," came Hellion's voice in his ear. "You could dance at the Bolshoi."

"Exfil," Wren said.

"Dead ahead, first exit. We are headed to the Exposition Center to launder you. There are too many eyes to run this any other way."

Wren grunted, took the truck past the airport riot vans off to the left, then shrugged off his helmet. No need for it anymore, if everyone knew who he was, and the confinement was keying into his vertigo. At once fresh air rushed in. The helmet fell to the right, into the lap of the guy with the goatee.

He sat there clutching it, staring at Wren. "Are you really him?" he asked.

"Are you?" Wren countered, then refocused on Hellion. "What's happening at the Exposition Center? Are there enough people to launder me?"

"This will be the washing of your life," Hellion answered in his earpiece, her voice smaller now outside the echoing confines of the helmet. "Today is middle day of three-day convention of comic book characters." She paused a moment. "I think your new friends know this."

Wren blinked. Looked at the guys. Superheroes. He knew about them from his kids, mostly, and that forced a pang in his chest.

"You're going to the comic book convention?" he asked.

"Uh, yes," said Goatee Guy. "Vantasy Con."

"How many people?"

"Convention center holds up to a hundred thousand," Hellion answered. "I am checking. Ticket sales show many refunds, however. People are not wanting to attend in these times. Perhaps half of that."

Wren looked at the guys with fresh eyes. Had to admire their dedication, in the wake of their President self-combusting, New York coming under terror attack and X pumping up a militia army across the nation. "Why are you attending a comic book convention, now?"

Goatee Guy's eyes bugged, then he raised his hand.

"Speak," Wren said. "You don't need to ask permission."

"What else should we do?" the guy said. "Stay at home and cower in fear?"

Wren could roll with that.

"Those wackos get to believe in their crazy, dangerous nonsense. Why don't we get to believe in ours? At least it's a positive message. The good guys win. And they're actually good."

Another great point.

"More road blocks ahead," Hellion said. "You will not make it to the Exposition Center direct. Take your next left, I will direct you."

"Roger that," Wren said.

"Are you talking to her now?" White Star guy asked. Looking awed. "Your hacker?"

Wren glanced sideways. A grown man wearing dress-up pajamas. Except that wasn't fair to say. He was no different really from Wren and his Foundation with the coins. Systems of values and stories of heroes to back them up, and what was Wren if not a positive role model?

"Her name is Hellion," he growled. "She's pissed at me."

Goatee Guy stared. "Because you wrecked that bike?"

Wren laughed. "That was her idea. No. I make her life difficult, I think's the reason. This time I made a call she didn't like."

"Not just one call, Christopher," Hellion said in his ear.

The guy's eyes rounded. Looked at White Star. "Like we did in Civil War?"

That didn't mean anything to Wren. Still, he nodded seriously. "Sure, like that."

"I am glad you are having nice, fun conversation, Christopher," Hellion said. "Exit now."

He swung over three lanes and took the exit, a sharp centrifugal circle that tipped Goatee Guy awkwardly against Wren's shoulder. He straightened onto a flush drive north, spotting the red rollercoaster rails of Kentucky Kingdom ahead.

"Can I, uh-" White Star began.

"What?"

"Get a selfie?"

Wren laughed. "Not a chance."

"Right here," Hellion shouted. Police had cut off the road ahead, across an intersection. He swung through the red light and raced east, an idea forming in his head.

He looked at Goatee Guy. One of his kid's favorite characters. The suit, the swagger, the fact he could fly. "Tell me you have the helmet?"

The guy blinked. "I uh, do?"

"Can I borrow it?"

"Um, sure."

Five minutes on, the parking lot of the Kentucky Exposition Center was packed. No police yet, just a huge inbound crowd of fans wearing costumes. Wren pulled the truck as close as he could get to the glass doors beneath a three-story green architectural shard that fronted the building.

VANTASY CON banners festooned the structure's white metal poles. There were two huge robot sculptures either side of the entrance holding giant cannon-like weapons. Wren ducked into the back, grabbed the costume helmet. Gold-sprayed faceplate with red plastic backing. He pulled it down over his head.

Far worse visibility than the bike helmet.

"It suits you!" said White Star, one thumb up.

"The eyes light up," Goatee Guy said, "if you-"

"I owe you guys," Wren interrupted, and emerged straight out into the crowd. He bulled through the ranks of fans until he reached the glass doors, which swung open before him, unveiling a tall and light-filled lobby packed with people in various stages of costumed undress.

He strode into their midst. Here was a half-naked man with ash-gray skin interspersed by black metal plates that seemed to be bonded to his body, arrayed with tubes that seemed to feed into his neck, chest, head. There was a woman with a dizzying ravine of cleavage, in a white latex outfit with a long flowing cape. Wren's head spun as he ran, past a phalanx of figures all in white armor and complex helmets, past a guy looming seven feet tall dressed like a tree, past a naked woman covered in spotted blue body paint wearing a bright red wig. Wren recognized few and ignored them all, pacing toward a curtained access point.

"Nice helmet," someone said as he passed. "You forget your suit?"

Wren reached the curtain, where a bored-looking guy manned a rope line.

"Permit?" he asked

"In my other pants," Wren answered and brushed by. Through the curtain an immense space opened out below, sectioned into hundreds of booths jammed with colorful posters, cosplayers, life-size figurines, screening rooms. Wren scanned the chaos and picked out what he was looking for.

Thirty seconds later he was there, ten long selfie lines leading up to ten famous actors standing against space-battle backdrops. $100 a selfie. Wren joined one line and bypassed it to the front, where a rack of sackcloth-looking robes hung in various sizes, overseen by a sizing clerk.

"Sir, you can't-"

"On credit will be fine," Wren said, and plucked one of the robes. By the wall he dropped the helmet and pulled on the robe, swung the hood over his head and risked a look back.

Police were entering the hall at the far end.

He pushed open a fire door.

"I have a car pulling up on the east side, in the underground lot," Hellion said in his ear.

"Anything on the X app yet?" Wren clattered down a concrete stairwell, emerging onto parking sub-level B.

"We are in the app, but it is very limited, Christopher," Hellion said. "We have only Julie Graves' level of access, one-hundred point, but working on more. There is no link to X here, but there are lists, a triangle of some kind, and most important there is all-points 'ALERT' button, signals call X-apoc to rally." Keys flew. "We are digging for more, but it seems Julie Graves pressed this ALERT. Now X-apoc are coming, in addition government forces. It seems X has your location via crowd-source, someone in Vantasy Con saw you in main hall. Now I have them incoming from all over Louisville. They saw you in main hall. There is-"

Abruptly, a heavily muscled man stepped out in front of Wren. He had a bare chest with a shiny six-pack and beefy arms, was dressed in a red cape with a winged helmet, a large heavy-looking battle hammer swinging at his hip. In contrast to that seeming strength, the guy's face looked shiftless and scared, though there was a gun in his hand, rising already.

"Walk in the fire, Christopher Wren," he said.

Wren stepped off-line with all the muscle memory of two decades of special-ops training, evading the first shot even as he drew his weapon and fired. The bullet took the guy in the thigh, punched his leg out and spun him to the ground with a wild cry.

Wren took just a second to re-center himself, then ducked in next to the fallen guy, scooped up his gun and quickly patted him down. The man's impressive muscles were actually a bodysuit, and the hammer seemed to be made of polystyrene.

"Where's your phone?" Wren asked.

The guy shouted some Apex nonsense and tried to put a thumb in Wren's eye. Wren caught it easily, clamped the guy's wrist and twisted his thumb, breaking the joint with a methodical crunch. The guy wailed.

"We do not have time for this," Hellion said.

"Where's your phone?" Wren repeated, not letting go of the guy's wrecked thumb. "Tell me now or I'll show you what Hell on Earth really feels like."

"Glove box" the guy managed, shuddering with the pain. "I, I-"

"You're an idiot," Wren said, and stood. "Put pressure on your thigh, you might be fine. Now, keys."

The guy held up his hammer, patted the head to open a hidden compartment.

"We do not need this phone," Hellion said. "It is unnec-"

"You said I wouldn't need a stub for the second hack," Wren interrupted, retrieving a set of keys from the hidden compartment in the fake hammer. "And every app access gets us more data, yes?"

"Yes, but-"

"Car," Wren said, gave the guy a shake until he pointed at a nearby BMW i4 silver sedan, with neon blue trim

Hellion was still talking but Wren ignored the rest, strode to the BMW. He slotted the key in, popped the door, opened the glove box and retrieved a phone.

The screen was live, showing red that flashed with the single word ALERT in yellow block capitals, followed by CHRISTOPHER WREN SIGHTING, LOUISVILLE EXPOSITION CENTER, 100 POINTS ASSEMBLE, 1 MILLION DEAD

There was a map underneath that, with two pins dropped showing Wren's previous and current locations.

"Straightforward," he said. "Can you remote pair with this?"

"Attempting. There are more X-apoc coming, Christopher, you have to-"

"You're sending me a car?" Wren asked, slotting into the BMW.

"Yes, twenty seconds out, Foundation fringe member, but now I am thinking-"

"I'm taking this one."

The engine purred to silky life at the touch of a button. Wren hit the gas and peeled out, past the X-apoc guy shouting and red-faced on the raw concrete.

Within a minute he was out of the parking lot and headed north. The streets were alive with incoming police cars. At ten minutes he barely squeezed through an emerging dragnet of road blocks a mile out from the Exposition Center. In twenty he was across the Ohio River and speeding into Indiana on I-65, as all kinds of chaos erupted in his wake.

12

CHAOS

"Christopher, you must see this," said Hellion as Wren sped out of the suburbs and into broad white expanses of snow-covered Indiana fields. "I am sending feeds to your phone."

Wren balanced his cell on the dash. Video was already playing, looked like an array of bootleg livestreams re-broadcast on cable news, showing multiple perspectives of a crowd massing in front of the Exposition Center. Not cosplayers or police, though both were amongst the crowd, enormously outnumbered. These were men and women of all ages wearing black t-shirts, ball caps and jackets, waving homemade black banners and flags, all emblazoned with the white X symbol.

A pit opened up in Wren's stomach.

"Do not go back, Christopher," Hellion said, jumping straight to his first thought. "You cannot do anything."

He pulled over onto the shoulder lane without saying a word, hit his hazards then picked up the phone and held it close, making a quick count of all the black-clad X followers he could see on screen.

Hundreds already, come right out of the woodwork. Ready to assemble in minutes. Looked like more pouring in every second, swelling the crowd like an oil stain. His mouth went dry as the world tunneled down, and he was back in D.C., trapped beneath the stampeding mob.

"How many are coming, Hellion?"

Keys danced a staccato storm through his earpiece. On the screen the mob steadily drained into the Exposition Center, shoving cosplayers roughly out of their way. Cops were gathered at the edges now, looking uncertain about what they should do. They weren't trained to take on an army. The first few chants were already breaking out, thickening fast into a torrent.

"Fear is a portal! Pain is a doorway!"

"I count two hundred and twenty outside the building," Hellion came back. "Seventy inside the lobby, none within the center itself yet, but Christopher, incoming numbers are very high. There are hundreds more. I am checking traffic flows, comparing with standard data through intersections. There could be thousands. They are coming in from surrounding suburbs. X is mobilizing. The ALERT called and they have come."

Wren felt sick. 42%, they'd told him. People who really believed X was telling the truth: that they were being kept as slaves; that Christopher Wren was their enemy; that burning alive was the only way to be free. If you truly believed all that, what wouldn't you do to save your country?

The crowd pulsated into the Exposition Center like a black octopus burrowing after prey. Wren didn't see weapons, but anything could be a weapon in the heat of the moment. Fire extinguishers, rope-line barrier posts, table legs.

The world was flipping on its axis. Killing Lou on network television was bad, but it was nothing next to this. These people weren't like the ones he'd calmed in LA, they wouldn't settle down if he just kneeled down in front of them. These people were full-on extremist terrorists who believed they were freedom fighters waging a righteous war.

"Can you stop any of this through the app?"

"Not yet," Hellion answered. "We are working. Two phones is good, we have some layer of access, but not enough."

Wren grunted, started chasing more extreme responses through his head.

"Christopher," Hellion cautioned.

"Get me Sally Rogers," he said sharply, then swiped the video aside and brought up the Foundation darknet, plugging straight into the Megaphone app. It had new tiers he could select to send to, including the millions of new Foundation fringe members. He started typing then paused.

"How many Foundation fringe in the Expo Center vicinity, Hellion?"

Keys flew, the answer came back in seconds. "Seventy-three."

Not enough to turn the tide. Just enough to be made an example of.

He typed fast, thumbs flying over the screen.

IF IN LOUISVILLE EXPOSITION CENTER, DO NOT TRY TO FIGHT.

THIS IS A BATTLE WE CANNOT WIN. INSTEAD LEAD THE EVACUATION RIGHT NOW. TAKE EVERYONE WITH YOU THAT YOU CAN. FLEE THE AREA BEYOND THE POLICE CORDONS. REPEAT, DO NOT FIGHT.

He hit send and started typing a follow-up.

X IS MOBILIZING. EXPECT MORE OUTBREAKS LIKE LOUISVILLE. YOUR JOB IS TO DE-ESCALATE. ANY WIN IN PITCHED BATTLE WILL ONLY DRIVE THEM HOTTER AND FASTER. PROPERTY DAMAGE IS ACCEPTABLE. DO NOT ENGAGE UNLESS LIVES ARE AT RISK. DO NOT FIGHT FOR MY NAME. TRUST THAT I AM TAKING ACTION. NOW STAY SAFE.

He tapped send. Every fiber of his being screamed at him to turn the BMW around and head back to the fight, but he couldn't. His presence had ignited it. His return would only catalyze it faster.

Maybe an Apex trap. If so, he'd walked right into it.

Fresh footage on his phone showed the situation had already devolved. News anchors watched dumbstruck at their desks as various feeds showed the mob massing and thrusting in waves, assaulting the police as they attempted to set up containment barriers, punching dazed cosplayers as they tried to escape, ripping off their 3D-printed tiaras and vacuum-pressed plastic battle armor and stamping them underfoot.

Inside the Exposition Center black-clad figures were swarming the internal convention space, driving the last few comic fans before them and smashing tables of superhero merchandise, hacking foam-core robot statues, toppling televisions and graffiti-spraying their giant black Xs on walls and floors. Plastic figures shattered, posters were torn down, booths were wrenched apart and their support poles converted to weapons.

"Walk in the fire!" they shouted, the chant rising in a single voice, occasionally morphing to other rallying cries.

"Break the chains!"

"Free the slaves!"

It was outright insurrection, and he hadn't expected it so soon.

"I have Sally Rogers," Hellion said. "Our end is encrypted, her end may not be. Be careful what you lead her to say."

Wren took a breath. "Put her on."

The line clicked.

"Boss," Rogers said, and it was all there in her voice. The same growing fear he was feeling.

"Rogers, I know Humphreys is still locked up; have you got any pull with the new Director?"

A moment passed. "I can't really confirm that. It's something I can try. What message have you got?"

"Moderation. This is no ordinary riot. Meet these people with force, and it's like pouring gasoline on a fire. It'll only draw more out."

A second passed. "I don't know what I can do about that. I'm on the outs here."

"Because of me," Wren said, mind racing fast. "One second." He tapped the earpiece, switching the line.

"Hellion, get me Teddy."

"He is online with me, Christopher. He is listening."

"Teddy, I need to give them one of the training camps. Something for Rogers to trade."

A long moment drew out. For a second Wren thought Teddy was going to say no, but when his deep bass voice joined the call, it was with a single word.

"Iowa."

Where Wren had just been. He leaped on it. "Is anyone there still? Does it link to anything?"

"Everyone left when you did. It's clean."

"Thank you. Hellion, get me the coordinates."

"Ready."

Wren clicked back over to Rogers. "I've got one of our training camps for you. Hand it over to keep yourself in the game. Iowa. Hellion's sending you the details."

"Are you sure?"

"We need you on the inside, Rogers, not the out. Let them burn down an empty farm. Better that than more city centers."

"OK. Thanks. I can use this. I'll try."

"Good luck."

Inside the Exposition Center someone broke out the gasoline, started splashing it liberally around then cast a match. The flames spread in seconds, racing through the wreckage of banners, posters and shredded costumes on the floor like a wildfire in autumn brush.

Soon the whole hall was on fire.

"Burn the Wren!" the mob shouted as they swarmed deeper into the huge complex, lighting more fires in their wake.

Wren flicked between feeds. Every news channels was covering the spreading chaos. Reporters talked breathlessly to camera from outside, jostled by black-clad X-apoc members, trying to describe a phenomenon they couldn't begin to understand: a moment X had been waiting for, when Christopher Wren finally got involved.

A trigger for the country.

Firefighters tried to push their way up to a line of X stalwarts and were violently rebuffed. The police kept trying, and were beaten back with makeshift weapons. Helicopter-mounted cameras showed blue light brigades streaming in along every major city artery, but right there alongside them came more black-flagged X forces.

Some didn't even make it to the Exposition Center. Four blocks south a police car was struck by a panel van, overturned and set alight, left to burn at the intersection while a crowd of X followers filmed it. A female police officer crawled out, one leg aflame, and they threw bricks and laughed. Cosplayers fled through the streets, assorted manga and video-game characters half out of costume, streaming blood and dark with soot, bouncing between police shields and the advancing X front line.

It was like the D.C. chaos all over again, only worse.

The feed cut to exclusive footage of a man Wren recognized, the fake muscle cosplayer from the underground parking lot, lying on an ambulance gurney.

"He shot me! It was Christopher Wren, He did it for nothing. I didn't get out of his way fast enough, and he shot me!"

People wailed in the background. The feed flipped to a female reporter holding a microphone out to a large man in tactical black combat gear, a ski mask pulled over his face revealing only white teeth and deep brown eyes.

"Wherever he goes," he shouted, "whatever he does, this is what is going to happen! Do you see this, Christopher Wren? We're not going to take your lies anymore!"

Voices around him hollered their new catchphrase, "Burn the Wren!"

"And you," the big guy shouted, snatching the microphone away and turning on the reporter. "You're no better than that bitch on the couch!"

He drew a gun from his shoulder holster, pointed it at the reporter and pulled the trigger.

13

TRACY

Wren beat the phone against the wheel.

"This will not help, Christopher," came Hellion's voice in his ear, so he plucked out the earpiece and left it rocking on the dash.

Opened the door, stepped out into dirty snow as cars raced by to his left. Looking south, the pall of smoke from the Exposition Center blackened the pale winter sky like a plume of squid ink.

Wren shook with rage and frustration. The earpiece squawked in the cab and he strode away, off the road trying to get control of himself.

He'd known it. He'd said it to Maggie. The moment he surfaced, the Apex was going to be ready. Always playing his part and driving the trap tighter. There was nothing he wanted more than to race back, find that man who'd shot the reporter and beat him to a pulp on live television. Let that be the message, let everyone see the vengeance of their precious 'Wren'.

But it would only play into the narrative. Only heap on fuel for the fire, convert more X saps and turn them out to fight a war against themselves, preaching their own deaths and suffering as the only way to be free.

He kicked the snow and stamped through the field trying to figure out the angle forward, but it was hard to think for memories of the last time he'd been here. A thousand people had burned in the fake town, and they'd all once been decent, honest, hopeful people, all looking to belong to something real.

The Apex had taken that desire and broken its spine, then bent it squealing back upon itself like some spiritual Moebius strip.

There had to be a better way to fight, but Wren couldn't grasp it. He had his expanding Foundation, and the Apex had his X-apoc, but what good would it do America for the two to clash, driving the country deeper into the inescapable pit of civil war?

"Are you OK?"

A voice came from the roadside. Wren turned, seeing red. Not an X-apoc, though, at least no wearing their gear. A woman, belly ballooning with what had to be triplets. Dark braids, mom jeans, a mauve cardigan pulled tight against the cold. Just a concerned citizen pulling over to check on him.

"I'm fine," answered. "Just needed some air."

"Did you escape the Exposition Center? Do you want me to call somebody?"

Wren almost laughed. Started back toward the road. "I'm fine."

"You don't look fine," she said, before he could answer. "But I thought it was you."

Wren grunted. So she recognized him. After D.C., he figured that was inevitable. "I'm not who you think I am."

Now she laughed. "That's bullshit. Listen, you can't pay any mind to what they're saying on the radio. All this X nonsense, anyone with half a brain can see it's made up. You can't take the bait."

He neared the roadway, thinking it was hard to call the deaths of innocent civilians bait. No need to say that, though. "Get away from the cities," he said, striding toward his BMW. "This thing's going to blow it all up."

"I'll do no such thing," the woman answered fast. "That's exactly what they want. Make us terrified, that's what terrorists do, right? But we don't negotiate with terrorists, do we?" She didn't give him any gap to answer. "I'll do my job, I'm a nurse, just like you will, and it looks like it's your job to sort this out." She paused a second, peering at him. "It is your father who's doing this, right?"

Wren almost laughed a second time, rubbed his eyes, drew up to the shoulder where she was standing by a Nissan Note just ahead of his BMW, scratches down the side, looked like someone had keyed her paintwork. For a moment he thought he recognized her, but no. She was just some woman who'd seen him on the news.

"Thank you for your concern, ma'am, but I'm all right now."

She waved a hand. "Define all right. Who amongst us is, these days, am I right? Talk about that man who burned himself rather than be President?" She made a face. "What kind of idiot does that?"

"He was my brother."

"I think you're better off," she countered easily. "I'll tell you, I divorced my whole family when I was seventeen. Psychos, the lot of them." Her hands spread across her belly. "I'm going to do better for these."

Wren didn't know what to say. Felt like he'd somehow intruded upon a personal moment for her. "Ma'am," he said and reached for the BMW's door.

"Don't ma'am me, I'm half your age. I heard you have kids as well. Two, isn't it?"

Wren paused, one hand on the handle. Let out a pent-up breath. "Yes."

"How are they holding up? They can't like having you away all the time."

He took another breath. Had no idea why he was even talking to this woman. "They don't want to see me. Or their mother doesn't."

Her eyes narrowed suspiciously. "Why, you screwed the help?"

This time he did laugh. "I screwed something up, you're right there. Right now she's in witness protection, took out a restraining order against me, and that's after she dumped me in a black site for three months."

The woman nodded knowingly. "Exes."

He felt too drained to laugh anymore.

"So sort this for your kids. Eyes on the prize, Mr. Wren. No more stamping around fields shouting at the heavens."

"I wasn't-"

"Get that man," the woman said, and wagged a finger. "Sort it out. I'm due by Christmas. I'd like all this tidied up by then so we can have a proper turkey dinner."

He let out a breath. About all he could manage in the moment.

"What else are my tax dollars going for, if you're not going to pull your weight?" she insisted.

He thought about telling her he wasn't in the employ of the CIA anymore, but there was no use in that. "Yes, ma'am," he said instead.

"Call me Tracy. Now get in your fancy car and get out of here before some of those crazies catch us up."

He did as he was told.

14

ALERT

Wren got back in the BMW i4, slotted the earpiece in and pulled out into traffic.

"Hellion," he said, "sorry about that."

No answer came.

Fair enough. Everybody needed time.

"B4cksl4cker, have you got anything more from the app?"

A long moment passed, accelerating up to seventy with nowhere to go. The dirty smoke of the Exposition Center spread across the sky, filling his rearview mirror.

"Hellion has left convoy," B4cksl4cker said. "She is shouting in snow. Much like yourself."

"Sounds about right. We're too alike."

"She does not like game piece which does not listen to commands."

Wren snorted. "You'd think she was used to me by now."

"Normally, yes. But we are here, Christopher. In your country. This is not a game, and when you cut her off..."

"I know. Too human. I'll make it up to her."

"Yes, you will."

Wren took a breath, drawing a line under that subject and moving on to what mattered most. "Tell me you own the X app?"

"Partly," B4cksl4cker said. "Stub worked, and we have access to pieces of X app, but not total. This is-"

"Is crybaby back from his field?" Hellion interrupted. She sounded angrier than usual, so Wren forewent some witty comment about her being out crying in her own field.

"I'm back, Hellion. Ready and willing to be directed. Give me a sit-rep on the app."

"Yes, I will," Hellion said, all furiously focused business. "Infant X app has two key functions we see so far, from two hacked phones. First is for ALERT, in case of Christopher Wren appearance, activating all members within range. We believe this button was first triggered by Julie Graves at Louisville Airport, and sent a call to every X member within fifty miles." She paused a second. "Further sightings came at Vantasy Con as you arrived. This notified muscle fool in parking lot. Now we are seeing ongoing effect. Flash mob."

'Flash mob' was putting it mildly. Everybody in Louisville was seeing the effect up-close and personal, as the X-apoc poured in and fomented chaos. "This is the first time anyone triggered the ALERT button?"

"Yes. Our theories were correct. Waiting for trigger."

Wren cursed. Waiting for him.

"Can you jam it? Prevent future flash mobs from gathering?"

"No. Control of this function is much deeper level of access. More levels are there, but we cannot reach them. It looks like coin layers of Foundation, deeper privilege handed down based on achievement."

Wren cursed. "Achievement being how many people they've killed?"

"Second function of this app is list," Hellion went on, ignoring him. "This is Kill List, we believe, with names, addresses, points available per kill. You will be happy to see who is top of this list."

"Is it me?"

"Da, it is you, Christopher."

Wren shuffled his phone up onto the dash. "Can you give me access?"

"Nyet, but I can mirror screen. Pull over and I will show you."

He pulled over, back by the side of another snowy field. His phone screen spasmed once then flipped to a black background with the white X brand at the top, beneath which ran a long table separated into three columns of data. In the first row was the name he expected.

CHRISTOPHER WREN – THE UNGRATEFUL SON – 1,000,000 POINTS

After that every line had been redacted with strike-through keys.

"Not much of a kill list if you can't see the names, is it?" Wren asked.

"Scroll further, Christopher," Hellion said, so he did. The table became a blur, hundreds of rows passing per second, until the table dead-ended with three legible lines. The lowest two had been struck through in red, leaving the details beneath clear.

LOU-ANN REISNER – TUESDAYS WITH LOU & MORRIE – 1,000 POINTS

Wren grunted. "Lou-Ann's dead."

"Yes, this is personalized list for Julie Graves."

"So she's gotta kill, what, thousands of people before she reaches me?"

"I do not think so, Christopher. More likely, this is marketplace for killings. She has selected her next target from many choices. You see second line?"

Wren looked, the line above LOU-ANN REISNER was plain white text on the black background.

OLATUNDE OWAYO – KENTUCKY STATE CONGRESSMAN – 10,000 POINTS

"She's climbing fast," Wren said. "Each kill is a factor of ten."

"Two more kills and she will be coming for you, Christopher."

"If the metric holds." He took a breath. "Have you got a better handle on how many people are using the app this way?"

"No hard figures yet. Guess of thousands remains."

Wren squeezed the wheel. When it came to outright murder, thousands was plenty. The best and most dedicated only. The rest would simply receive ALERT and flood to support them.

In a mob, murder was so much easier. He thought back to the ALERT on the fake muscle guy's phone.

"They were offered a hundred points for answering the flash mob call at the Exposition Center."

"This appears correct, Christopher. But we have only two phones' app access. If we had more access points, perhaps we can build bigger picture, have stronger chance of breaking this app encryption."

Wren considered. "What if you had access to more? Could you end-run it then?"

"Possibly. Deeper access. Better signal on X location, possibly."

Wren grunted. Location was everything. Unveiling X him or herself as the charlatan they were was the prime target. Get them on video, unwilling to burn for the cause, and the heat would drop right out of the X-apoc.

"So tell me you have something on X's location now. Anything."

A silence followed. Not even any keys clattering. "Nyet, Christopher. Nothing."

It wasn't what he wanted to hear.

"How many more apps to get better access?"

"We do not know. Five? Ten? More is better. We will see more versions of Kill List, more personal codes for ALERT designation. We can perhaps track Internet signals more effectively, begin to focus on originating location."

The next step came easily.

The X-apoc masses had already outed themselves in the hundreds at the expo center. Thinking there was safety in numbers. But these weren't soldiers with some secure base to return to, locked safely behind manned walls.

These were civilians. They had to go home.

Weak links in the wall of flame.

Wren keyed the engine back on. "Start with the guy who shot the reporter. I want to know where he is right now. Work backwards through everyone you can pick out of the crowd, the worst offenders, the highest points value. Make us a kill list of our own."

15

KILL LIST

Two hours later, Wren waited.

Sitting in a shotgun home in Smoketown, West Louisville, pulled up to the larch-veneer kitchen island and looking straight through the den window. Out the dust-smeared front glass lay parking lots for a new-build mega-church, looked like a sports center. That new, sharp red brick look that said 'mass-produced' and 'cheap', with a little yellow canvas cladding to smarten things up.

Saving the people's souls, one broken mind at a time.

"He is incoming, Christopher," Hellion said.

Wren looked around the kitchen. He'd already scoped out the house, after an hour spent losing himself in the Louisville traffic system and laundering his vehicle twice: once at a roadside diner back in Indiana; once in the heaving chaos of a mall parking lot ten blocks south of the Exposition Center.

The streets had been full of X-apoc rioters feeding out from the fires of Vantasy Con, though for most of them the flames were dwindling by then. They'd come for a big show and the lynching of Christopher Wren, and mostly arrived late to the party. With police presence coming in slow but steady, the Exposition Center already on fire and Wren himself gone, their passion had stalled out.

Three dead, so far. The female reporter, shot in the belly, hadn't made it. Two cosplayers lost in the building's lobby, maybe smoke inhalation, maybe stampede injuries, pulled out while the core fires still raged. Plenty of cops, firefighters and cosplayers injured in the fighting.

Now the flames burned cold in Wren's chest.

The guy's name was Diego Helmuz. Second generation Kentuckian, with roots up from Cuba on one side, Canada on the other. Two heritages mixed in the middle, shaken, stirred, and left to mature like nitroglycerine sweating out of old TNT.

There was nothing much to find in his house. A couple of half-finished homemade X flags draped over a basement workbench, graffiti cans nearby, the stenciling bad, like these were his first attempts. The outline where he'd cut a white 'X' out of a stretch of curtain liner, needles and thread around where he must have stitched it onto his cap.

No sign of a partner, kids. Gun safe hanging open. Looked like he'd been caught in the midst of his daytime hobby, doing macramé for points in the X app, no apparent job, when the ALERT had gone out. Put down his half-made flag, popped the safe, loaded up. There were shells spilled on the floor for a shotgun, moving too fast and excited.

Upstairs clothes were scattered on the bed across from a half-length mirror. Diego had tried a few on, it looked, before heading out to 'war'. A little stolen valor here, a little cosplay there and you had yourself a real X-apoc warrior.

Wren had entered by the back door, an easy slip with a credit card, expecting to lay in wait then kill the guy. Now, sitting at the counter, he didn't feel so sure. Kill this guy, and was he going to kill all the others too? Rifling through the mail, heaped by a fruit bowl occupied by three withered peaches, he found a full house of PAST DUE letters.

Like Julie Graves, Diego Helmuz was a soft target. Exactly the Apex's usual recruiting ground. Lost souls, part of nothing and filled with anger about that. Looking around themselves and seeing the world moving on with no real way to belong. If convincing these men and women to stop their mad race to death was going to begin anywhere, shouldn't it begin right here?

On the other hand, the guy had made himself into a murderer.

The backfiring engine on Diego's old beater came chugging up the street. Loud because he liked it that way, probably. Annoying the neighbors was one way to play a role in their lives. To matter through fear.

Wren watched through the front window as the truck pulled up, a brown GMC Sierra with go-faster beige stripes, spattered by bird scat. Wren eased off the stool, strode through the den like a mirror of Diego as he approached the door.

Really he was doing the police a favor. It would take them three days or more to analyze their mountains of footage and hunt this guy down. Come at him in the night, no-knock warrant, burst in the door with a SWAT squad and guns up yelling, "Police!"

No real warning, but maybe enough for a guy like Diego Helmuz, who'd done one short stint in Afghanistan, a man who'd fought for his country once and believed he was fighting for it again now. He'd sleep little and armed. Would get off a few shots, probably, before they overwhelmed him or he shot himself in the head.

Key in the lock, turning, and Wren positioned himself smoothly and silently in the blind spot behind the swing of the door. When it opened and the big guy came through, maybe 6' 2" but meaty with muscle from lifting weights in the maddening isolation of his basement gym, stinking of smoke and gasoline, it was the simplest thing in the world for Wren to reach out and touch him with the Vipertek stun gun.

Three-hundred-million volts. Two sharp spikes for the electrodes. Rechargeable battery. $24 from the mall where he'd swapped out his car the second time.

The Vipertek crackled, blue bolts Wren could barely see as they burned contact holes through Diego's leather jacket. He stiffened then fell. Wren caught him and guided him down even as he nudged the door closed. Pulled a loop of plastic zip ties and swiftly, professionally hogtied the guy right there in the entrance: one around his ankles, one around his wrists, one to loop the two together. Trussed up like a pig for the spit.

Wren rolled Diego carefully on his side. Gasping and sputtering now. He'd be fried for a little while, but that was OK. Add to the effect. He brought up Diego's phone and brought up the PIN screen.

"Working," Hellion said in his ear.

The screen flickered then opened on a field of Diego's apps. The X app was right there amongst them, a white 'X' on a black square. Simple, dramatic branding.

"Whuh- Wha-?" Diego mumbled.

Wren thumbed the app, brought up the biometric screen. It was an easy matter to roll Diego's right thumb over the pad, hold the camera up to his flickering eye and hold his eyelid back long enough for the lines in his iris to be read, leaving only one final screen.

Passkey.

"This was easy," Hellion said in his ear. "We should have done this with Julie Graves."

Wren laughed. If only it had been that easy. The first lead was always the hardest.

"What do you want?" Helmuz managed, finally getting back the power of coherent speech.

Wren looked in his eyes and saw all kinds of things within those brown pools. The rush of fresh adrenaline coming down into fear and pain. The swirl of purpose that cult-membership brought, winding back into something more primal.

Recognition, like a meerkat spotting an eagle swooping overhead.

"You wanted me, you got me," Wren said.

Diego's eyes flared. He began to kick but couldn't get any kind of traction, trussed like he was.

"Ungrateful son," he croaked.

"That's my name," Wren allowed. "And you know why I've come, right?"

"I'll die before I say anything."

Wren gave a gentle smile. "You just said something." For a second Helmuz looked confused, and Wren pushed into that. "But let's face it, you're already dead, Diego. Take a second and think about that. What you're experiencing right now is just the start of the long drop on the other side. Try to get right with your God, all that, before he casts you down and turns a blind eye for eternity. Isn't that what you want?"

Helmuz' eyes bugged. Hard to keep up with all that. "God's a lie."

Wren shrugged. "If you're in hell, I guess you'd like to think so. But let's look at the evidence. You were disappointed you didn't get to see me at Vantasy Con, am I right? Spend a hundred bucks, pose for a selfie with me, that was the plan? Well here I am. Price of admission's cheap, just a couple of passkey digits, and I'll admit one through the rope line. Maybe your descent into perpetual suffering halts, you get pulled back up." He paused a moment, looking into the man's eyes. "You killed a woman today, Diego, so it's not stopping far, but there's still inches of give left in this rope. Recant that death, spill the number and I'll see you get treated right by LMPD."

Helmuz just stared. Trying to catch up.

"Alternative's the long drop. You want to join the valiant resistance in hell, I can make that happen. If they don't want to walk first, you make them, right?"

Wren winked, aping the rumbling voice of his father from the deepfake video. "But I bet you never thought you'd be the one getting made. Better to be on the other side of the gasoline and lighter combo, doing the making, wouldn't you say?"

Wren produced a lighter, a can of liquid kerosene. All told another $8 from the same mall.

Helmuz sucked wind. Part the shock, part the hogtie position. Pulling the arms back played havoc with your intercostal muscles, responsible for pumping the lungs.

"I'll never help you," he said. "You're the enemy."

"Enemy number one, right?" said Wren. "Even better. So we get to send you on your way an honest man. I figure we do it by degrees, it'll be more painful, which is great, because pain is a portal, yeah? X would approve. So I start with your legs, we can sit here and watch those burn together, then we'll just move up your body. Deal?"

Helmuz gritted his teeth, then hawked and spat. It missed Wren, flopped to the linoleum.

"It's your floor, man," Wren said, then uncapped the can and started pouring kerosene on Helmuz' legs below the knee. "Funny thing is, from your Internet records, seems you only got into this X BS in the last couple of months." He gave him a long look as noxious fluid seeped into Helmuz' pants. "Now me, I don't even buy a new car without thinking on it for six months at the least. At the very least, Diego. So I'm going to figure you got pressured some, got the hard sell, you know? An impulse buy. We've all been there. These days you can return those cars, call on regulation to dig you out. But your legs?" Wren whistled low. "They're not coming back, brother. You sure you're all in for this?"

Diego stared hard.

Wren smiled.

"OK. Well, walk in the fire."

He lit a match, held it over Diego's legs, and the big guy broke like Dambusters. Wren waited out the flood, gave some direction to the confessions and apologies, until finally his passkey code came.

"Got it," Hellion said in Wren's ear, keys clattering madly. "It is good. We are in. I see his Kill List. Different names. He is at thousand point-level, for killing that journalist. His good luck she even spoke to him."

Wren stood while Helmuz kept on babbling below. "Does it help?"

"It is helpful, Christopher. This will take time to collate. More will be better. The signal from X cycles through multiple failed states. If we have enough, we can narrow the algorithm used to do so, make predictions."

Wren nodded. Looked down at Helmuz, who was sobbing now.

"Recovery's a hard road," Wren said. "Don't you go anywhere, Diego. I'll send someone to fetch you in a couple hours."

He opened the door and strode out. Helmuz' keys jangled in his hand. He got in the battered old GMC truck and pulled away, heading east toward the next on his list, like a moon circling the gravity well of smoke pluming from Louisville's heart.

16

GAMES

The next were a group of five young people in their early twenties, tracked and identified from the Expo Center footage, amongst them the girl who broke out gasoline first and started splashing it around.

After getting the blaze going, they'd fled fast, three blocks south on foot but followed every step by Hellion via CCTV. There they ducked into a convenience store and bought several jugs of vodka, a bag of energy drinks and a carton each of orange and cranberry juice, then caught the route 19 bus on the TARC network, Transit Authority of River City.

The bus cam watched them mixing up small-batch cocktails in the middle seats, pouring vodka straight in their mouths, then chasing it with mixers. Passengers nearby switched seats or just got off the bus as they grew louder. The driver said nothing; not worth the trouble, Wren figured.

Already drunk forty minutes later, they got off in Russell at 11 a.m. and poured into their shared redbrick student house, two blocks north of Muhammad Ali Boulevard.

Hard on their heels at 11:45, Wren came up on the redbrick building. There was no place to hide around it, no trees, fences, yard, just a three-floor box airdropped in the middle of grass yards and roads. Few people were out on the streets anyway; the governor had just put a curfew order out for 5 p.m.. Most folks were respecting that in advance, and the rest didn't look at Wren twice, now wearing Helmuz' black cap with the white embroidered X, brim tugged low.

"This may not be best idea," Hellion said. "There are five of them. Only one must trigger an ALERT to signal X what we are doing."

"It'll be fine," Wren said low, parked the Sierra across the street and approached the front door. There was a buzz button and a security keypad. Wren pushed the button, waited ten seconds then buzzed it again.

The intercom crackled and a young guy's voice came through, clearly drunk. "Yeah, all right, what is it?"

"Pizza," Wren said.

"What?" the guy laughed. "We didn't even order yet."

"Somebody there did," Wren answered. "I got your order right here, three Meat Feast, two Hawaiian, all paid for online. Maybe you forgot?"

The guy laughed. "He says we forgot ordering."

"Maybe on the bus we did?" somebody answered faintly.

"I just need to hand these off," Wren said. "I got other orders to pick up before 1. Come on, brother."

"Well all right, brother," answered the guy. "Come up."

The door buzzed, the lock clicked and Wren pushed through. Two stories up along friction-burn-gray carpets, he knocked on a red door. A goofy-looking guy answered, long blonde hair spilling in sticky locks down his chiseled jawline, no shirt on revealing pale white skin. Addled eyes, wired off more than vodka.

"You the pizza guy?" he asked. "Dig the cap, by the way."

Wren hit him with the stun gun in the belly, caught him and guided him quietly down. Charge depleted.

A stubby corridor ran ahead, green bike helmet on a chipped side table, coats dumped in a pile atop jumbled sneakers, stained beige carpet. Wren advanced into a low den scattered with bottles, chip packets, paper plates, clothing. A big screen TV stood in one corner showing some daytime murder mystery show, across from three long, worn leather sofas in a U shape. The girl who'd started the fires lay spread out on the leftmost, half-naked to her bra and panties. A guy sat opposite her, holding a set of five playing cards, wearing only his boxer shorts.

"Ah," said Hellion in Wren's ear.

"Strip poker?" Wren asked.

The girl turned bodily, squinted at him like she was trying to focus. "You the pizza guy?"

"Yup," Wren said, "here's your delivery."

He bent by the back of her sofa, dug his fingers under the rim and lifted, flipping the sofa with her on it. She tumbled against the coffee table then hit the floor, cards went flying, and Wren followed through, tipping the sofa the rest of the way like he was rolling a workout tire.

The half-naked guy with the cards just stared, trying to register what he was seeing. "Hey," he managed.

"Hey yourself," Wren said, taking three fast steps over to grab the guy's card hand and roll it smoothly behind his back. Ten more seconds to zip-tie his wrists, another ten to grab a scarf off the floor and gag him.

Back on his feet. The girl was making strange mumbles from beneath the sofa, but Wren didn't figure she'd be coming out any time soon.

"Three down," Hellion said, sounding worried. "The other two, Christopher."

He was already beelining for a door in the south wall, hung ajar with a sock on the handle. Shoved through into a darkened bedroom, curtains closed against the winter afternoon's light, a black guy in the bed clutching his cell phone, thickset Asian girl with great muscle definition already charging at him with a baseball bat in hand.

Wren ducked under the blow, which hit the doorframe and had to reverb hard up her arms, then took three steps and jumped. He hit the guy in a full body tackle, wiping him out against the bed like a swatted fly. The cell phone tumbled from his hand, already at the screen with the ALERT button. Wren grabbed his arm then rolled hard, pulling the guy over him just in time for the baseball bat to come down on his hip.

There was a nasty crack and the guy wailed. Wren rolled onto his left knee and threw out a sidekick, putting his heel pinpoint into the big girl's solar plexus. She gasped and dropped the bat.

After that it was easy. Hogtie the guy in the bed, pillowcase for a gag, hogtie the girl, then back through the house where the half-naked arsonist was just now crawling out from under the sofa.

Wren watched her for a second. She looked like any other college kid. Pretty much what he'd expected. X was exciting, like a different kind of drug that opened a new layer to reality. These kids weren't jilted by reality like Diego Helmuz, or all-the-way-in like Julie Graves. They were just bored and entitled.

He tied and gagged her, went back down the hall and did the same for the goofy guy by the door, still unconscious, fetched the one phone from the bedroom floor, then dragged everyone into the living room and laid them out on their sides in a fresh U shape, pushing the sofas back to make room.

Five trussed little piggies, all wheezing hard. Wren looked around at the mess of scattered trash, bottles and clothes from their post-riot party.

"Any chance someone's gonna tell me where your cell phones are?"

Hellion laughed.

"No? So I'll find them, then."

It took a few minutes, digging through the cast-off clothes and detritus, until five phones lay on the coffee table in the middle of the space, one already opened and logged through.

"You have this one?" Wren asked Hellion, holding it up to his bodycam.

"We are in," she answered. "Four to go."

Wren picked up the next, looked around at his grunting, puffing prisoners. This was a big change from burning down Vantasy Con.

"You like to play games," he said, slow and clear. "Strip poker's a fine example. Gambling with low stakes, it's good clean fun." He eyeballed them one-by-one. "I have no problem with it. Even getting high while you play, some booze, run it into an orgy? Whatever." His gaze sharpened. "But burning up a cosplay conference just because I passed through? Endangering thousands of lives. Leading a stampede that's already killed three people we know of, and doubtless left many more with life-changing injuries. That's a game I can't get behind." He stood firm. "An unacceptable game. So I'm going to teach you a new game. One you've earned. It's called 'This Little Piggy Went To Market', and there's just one rule. First one to tell me the passkey for their X app gets to keep a fully functioning set of limbs. Going once. Going twice."

All five of them began grunting to speak. Wren bent to the first and peeled back the gag.

17

THIRD

"This should be enough," Hellion said, once all five phones lay on the coffee table, unlocked. "Working."

Wren dug out the remote and flicked on the TV while his little piggies grunted on the floor. The national news channels were showing the comedown in Louisville. 12:47 p.m.. The Exposition Center fires were coming under control and rescue crews were pouring in through the front lobby.

It left a bitter taste in Wren's mouth. Only hours earlier he'd been there, marveling at all those creative, crazy folks. Thinking his passage through would be a simple matter of laundering himself into anonymity. How wrong he'd been.

"Ten minutes," Hellion said.

"You got anything to eat?" Wren asked the kids. They nodded desperately. Maybe thought this was a continuation of the game. In truth they were only wallpaper now. All they knew was the app, and not one of them was above 100 points.

Wren wandered into the kitchen, popped the fridge door and found a bacterial war zone worse than the living room. Not scrubbed for a couple years, he figured. Condiments slowly fermenting in bloated plastic bottles. A thick-skinned brown smush in the vegetable tray. Something fungal growing by the drain. He'd seen better in fridges of serial killers, storing human body parts.

He pushed the door closed. Found a dirty pot buried beneath a mountain of filthy crockery, pulled out a plastic scrubber and blasted it with the hot faucet. From a cupboard he plucked a dented can of spaghetti O's, decanted it into the pot and set it to heat on the greasy induction plate. He found a bag of only slightly moldy bagels stuffed in a bread box and sliced two, scraped off the mold and popped them in the toaster.

A few minutes. He washed more dishes while he waited. No help to the kids, really, since they'd be in jail within a few hours, but it helped calm his jangling nerves.

The bagels popped. The spaghetti O's sauce simmered down to a nice thickness. He braved the fridge once more for butter, bailed early, and settled for pouring the O's over the bagels. Ate standing up with the plate in his hand, watching the news in the living room.

Talking heads were theorizing about what all this meant. Linking the death of Lou-Ann Reisner of Lou and Morrie to the female journalist to Wren's presence. Some blamed him, either because he should have stayed away, or because he was an undercover leader in the X movement, which didn't make much sense, since the X people hated him. But nothing much made sense anymore.

He finished up, took the plate back to the kitchen and washed it up, then did a few slow yoga stretches. Mason had taught him them, designed to 'align his chakras' and ease the tightness in his still-healing wounds. The pain was a steady arthritic ache, with the background fuzz of the concussion still ringing in his head like a bell, but distant enough for now.

Midway through the routine Hellion spoke in his ear.

"We have something, Christopher."

Instantly, he was back on the alert. "Tell me."

"Infant X app-anonymizing algorithm has patterns, and we have followed them many times around whole Internet, dating back six months in longest case. They end in three locations, no further leads."

"Where?"

"First in New York, Christopher, narrowed to several blocks south-east of Central Park, I think you know-"

"That's the human zoo," Wren interrupted, his heart rate speeding up. "Galicia's zoo on Billionaire's Row."

"Yes," Hellion said. "Now demolished. As you would expect, there have been no transmissions from there since two weeks back. Second is located in Seattle, east side, where-"

"My brothers," Wren said. Jaw gritted, pulse pounding. Staring at his prisoners but seeing far beyond them. "The second zoo."

He'd been mostly unconscious when the Seattle raid went down, still recovering from the D.C. firestorm. Hellion and B4cksl4cker had surfaced evidence that Wren's surviving brothers, Gabriel and Zachary, were there, and under Teddy's guidance the Foundation had mounted the assault.

They'd found an abandoned human 'zoo' tucked away on the hidden mezzanine floor of a fifty-story tower. All the prisoners were dead. There were green-screen torture rooms and camera equipment just like in New York, to serve the needs of the Apex's firestorm of young mothers across the country, but every digital record had been wiped. Not one person left alive, with no sign of his brothers.

"Second zoo, yes," Hellion confirmed. "Doubling as relay station for X. No transmissions since we took it down six days ago. That leaves only one location, the third."

Wren strode back into the kitchen, away from the piggies so they couldn't possibly hear any of this. "Hit me."

"It is in Mexico, Christopher. We have narrowed it to five-mile radius in city of Acapulco."

That was unexpected. "Acapulco?"

"Yes, Christopher. It is holiday destination, or was. Many hotels, beaches, beautiful waters. We are seeking to narrow this further, find the precise building signal was transmitted from, but..."

Wren stopped listening. All he heard now was the rush of blood in his ears, heart pumping, the walls of that narrow, filthy kitchen closing in. A third human zoo. Maybe the last redoubt of the Apex, a bolthole just like Jim Jones' Jonestown in Guyana, outside the Continental USA and buried in cartel territory, far from the reach of the FBI.

A place to go and engineer the end of America.

His mind raced. Silver flashes danced sharply across his vision as the concussion nausea surged back. He dropped to one knee and panted, gripping the counter hard as the sticky vinyl floor opened into a swirling gulf. His brothers could be there. X could be there. Maybe even the Apex himself. His shoulders throbbed at the ghost pain of his sister's stiletto pushing into his battered body.

This time would be different. It had to be.

Hellion was talking but he barely heard her, just trying to breathe and clear a path.

"Except episodes of acute onset," the Foundation doctor had said, giving him the all-clear on his concussion a day earlier, pulling back the stethoscope and fixing him with a cynical gaze. "They'll feel like acid flashbacks, and could be brought on by anything from moments of high emotion to catching the wrong scent on the air. You just need to ride them out."

"So I'm fit?" he'd asked.

She'd laughed. "Fit? You need to be put out to pasture. You're barely held together with stitches, steroids and band-aids right now, but what the hey. The country calls, Christopher Wren's gotta go, right?"

He'd said nothing. Now her words swirled around him like leaves caught in a drain. He felt the spaghetti O's preparing to make a reappearance, and bolted. He barely made it to the bathroom before dropping to his knees and retching into the tub. No time even to flip the toilet lid.

His stomach convulsed in knots. Somewhere very far off the piggies grunted in a panic. Wren sagged against the rim of the tub, feeling a cold sweat bead up on his face and down his back.

"-topher, are you under attack, what is happening?"

Hellion's voice in his ear. He took a rasping breath, another that came deep and convulsing, forcing control back onto the sudden shock.

"It's fine," he said. "I'm fine."

"What happened?"

The silver tides receded gradually, leaving Wren shuddering. "Nausea. It's the concussion. Give me a minute."

A minute passed, then he pushed back to his feet, ran the tub clean then washed up in the sink, gargled, drank, brushed his teeth with his finger. In the tarnished mirror he looked pale and worn. Let it be, he figured, and strode through remnant silvery motes to the living room.

The piggies stared up at him with a new terror. Like he wasn't just a bad guy anymore, but a crazy guy. Tying them up and demanding passkeys was one thing, but eating their food then puking it into the bathtub?

Wren said nothing, just lifted a set of keys from the coffee table. Bright green key fob, shaped like a monstrous fist. The bad guys liked playing dress-up just as much as the good guys, it seemed. From a side table he picked up a matching green helmet then pushed out through the door.

"I need a flight, Hellion," he said.

"To Acapulco?"

"To Acapulco."

18

ACAPULCO

Acapulco was a balneario, a Latin American seaside resort once the playground of global elites, where Hollywood stars had rubbed shoulders with politicians, CEOs and cartel drug kings on the gorgeous white sand beaches lining the glamorous seafront esplanade.

That was back in the 60s, 70s, 80s. Money poured in after that, grand new developments hauling in even more cash as the international upper-middle classes made Acapulco their destination of choice. Billions of dollars passed through. The cartels had a deal that allowed it: no murders in the Pearl of the Pacific.

Then one day the deal was broken, and all hell broke loose. The cartels along with dozens of smaller gangs opened fire on each other as the Narco Wars heated up, rapidly turning the City-by-the-Bay into the second-highest murder capital in the world, after Mexico City at number 1. One in every thousand people murdered annually. Bodies left hanging from bridge trusses as a warning. Bodies washing up on the beaches. Murder, kidnapping and extortion as everyday events.

The US State Department started warning tourists to stay away, and after that the torrential flow of tourist dollars dried up faster than a sliced mango in the sun.

Wren sat at the window of his private Learjet 45XR at 45,000 feet, looking down on the verdant pine-oak forests of the Sierra Madre del Sur mountain range and thinking about the one and only time he'd passed through Acapulco before.

It had been at the last fading gasps of the tail-end of that glorious heyday, back when there was still some predictable logic to the gang violence, and figures in-the-know could skirt the worst outcomes while enjoying absolute cut-rate luxury with a bay view to literally die for.

He'd been running an observation op with the CIA that had devolved into a snatch-and-grab on a Mideast terror financier. The guy had been visiting his two 'girlfriends' in the hotel Costa Cabana penthouse, twenty-third floor, after blowing a fortune at one of the beachside baccarat joints. Travis Raker was his name, a pump-and-dump stock whizz looking to wag the tail of the international arms market by stirring up cross-border trouble between Sunni and Shia militias in southern Lebanon, hoping for an ugly sequel to the 2008 conflict. Wag that tail hard enough, and the Saudis might storm in, even Iran, Israel, potentially the USA, and that would turn the whole thing into a hot-mess war zone goldmine.

Wren's job was to nip all that in the bud. He'd already been watching Raker via long lens from the neighboring Hacienda's twenty-seventh floor, looking for intel. Intel had come when Umm Al-Siddiq himself, a major arms trader and top-10 wanted terrorist, had entered the apartment and sat down for the trade.

It was a stunning denouement. The CIA playbook said wait for operational approval before taking any action, but Wren had taken the upfront decision to 'establish a forward operating position' while the brass thought it over. It just so happened that his forward operating position was in the corridor right outside Raker's room.

Moments after approval came down, Wren slammed the door with a weapons-hot team of five, synced to a fast-rope descent from the roof by three more, high-caliber rounds firing through the glass.

Thirty seconds of seeming chaos ended up with seven of Raker's security team dead or incapacitated, Raker and Al-Siddiq unconscious, bagged and tethered, with Al-Siddiq himself slung over Wren's broad shoulder as they ran up the three stories for helo evac on the roof.

That had earned him a commendation. Maybe around then was when they'd started calling him 'Saint Justice'. Like an avenging angel, they said, tongue-in-cheek or otherwise. Wren closed his eyes, trying to remember if that was before or after the birth of his daughter Quinn, but couldn't come up with the dates.

He sighed, sipped his Diet Coke and watched the green mountains roll by below. It was easy to feel nostalgia for those older, 'simpler' days. On the edge of turning thirty, when it was so much clearer who the bad guys were, who the good guys were and what the right path forward was.

It was tempting to think it was all different now. Ever since his father had reared up onto the scene with his domestic terror group the Order of the Saint, it was all shades of gray. Good people acting against their own interests, under the influence of a conman with incredible ambition.

He thought back to Diego Helmuz, lying now in a puddle of urine in his own home, a murderer because he'd been too lost to see this X nonsense for what it really was. He thought of five college kids in their student apartment, half of them crashing from the adrenaline and the other half from the drugs, following X to charges of affray and arson just because it seemed like a fun thing to do in a world where nothing really mattered.

Everybody warped beneath the Apex's touch.

Wren rang a number, held the phone up to his ear. It rang a precise five times, clicked as server exchanges around the world aligned, then answered.

"Señor Wren," came a voice on the other end. Educated, an Oaxaca-tinged Mexican accent. Not a man to trifle with: Don Mica, one of the capos of the Qotl cartel. A man Wren had almost assassinated on two separate occasions, but held back at the last moment each time, judging him a better bulwark against terror alive than dead.

"Don Mica," Wren said. "You spoke with Gutierrez?"

Mica said nothing for a long moment. Wren thought he heard the sound of yapping dogs in the background. Notoriously, Mica liked to feed his enemies to starving hounds. "Hector Gutierrez," the Don said at last. "He is a strange man."

Wren could only smile. Gutierrez had been a Halcones-level mule-trafficker when Wren met him in the Sonoran Desert south of the border, since elevated to Tenientes, lieutenant grade, right beneath the capos. With his diamond-grille teeth insets and a habit of always wearing red suspenders, Gutierrez cut an odd figure, but he was competent and could be vicious. "He told you what I need."

"Need," Don Mica said. "It's an interesting term."

Wren waited. He knew how it worked in Acapulco, like pretty much anywhere in all of Mexico, now that the cartels effectively ruled. Send in Sicarios of your own without permission, and you were asking to be gunned down on your exfiltration. The bars, the beaches, the hotels, they were all locked down tight as a bombo drum. Even his CIA hit had come with cartel approval and oversight.

"I'm sure he relayed my request," Wren said, when the silence had stretched too long. "I'm thinking he didn't relay the threat that comes attached."

"That is what I'm waiting to hear," Mica said. "Last time we met, you spoke of a Predator drone in the air above us. Hellfire missiles that would wipe us out." He sounded amused.

"What I have for you now will be much cleaner," Wren said. "Call it a financial Hellfire. I doubt you've heard of the 'second skin' on the Internet? We keep it under wraps. Think of it as a kind of cowboy on the Internet's horse, riding every data transaction across the entire web. If we want, at any moment in time, I can have that cowboy take the reins and start pulling in a different direction. Maybe run the horse into the ground."

Mica laughed.

"I thought you might laugh, so I'm going to offer a swift demonstration. Strictly reversible. I suggest you take a moment, have your accountants bring up your cryptocoin accounts held in the Seychelles tax haven. I'll wait."

"Cyrptocoins are unhackable," the Don answered.

"So they say. Humor me."

A few moments passed. Then a few more moments. When Mica came back it was with a very different tone.

"Put them back."

Wren smiled. Having the world's top hackers on his team came with perks, even if they couldn't break through X's firewall. "That's three-hundred-million dollars' worth of cryptocurrencies we just siphoned. Just a taste, really. I can take more. I could take it all, wipe you out. It'd throw Mexico into outright civil war, probably, but if you hear out my request, you'll learn that's where I think we're all headed anyway." He paused a second for effect. "I'm sure you look at the States and laugh at the mess we're in right now, but do you really think our total upheaval won't completely destroy your entire business model? Once the American people are decimated by our own hands, nobody will be buying your cocaine, hermano. It'll be lights out in the barrio."

A long silence.

"You are suggesting we are natural allies."

"Uneasy bedfellows," Wren allowed. "I'm not your dog on a leash. You're not mine. We both have a vested interest in the status quo."

Another long silence.

"I'm three hours out of Acapulco," Wren pressed. "I have my team and target location. There'll likely be some collateral damage when we hit, but we'll keep it structural, and we'll pay for it. What I need from you is a guarantee that Qotl won't interfere, and that if it comes to that, you'll prevent interference from any of the rival gangs if they try to intercede."

"So we come to the offer."

"Offer's simple and secondary," Wren said. "I'm prepared to back you in a leadership bid for all the cartels. Acapulco's a beautiful place for an international holiday, don't you agree? End the Narco Wars on your end, I can bring them under better control on mine. America's in flux and change will come fast if all this goes right. There'll be more profit for everyone. Murders way down. US tourist money starts flowing back into the local economy. You won't need the drug money as much as now."

The longest silence yet. "You would do this?"

"I've always been a realist. Drugs are awful. The Narco Wars are worse. I add one and one together, I get two. Maybe between us, we can de-violence the whole trade."

"I like the violence."

Wren laughed. "So take up laser tag. The dogs eating people alive? Let it go. You won't be a pirate anymore, Mica. No need to put up the Jolly Roger to scare compliance. You'll be a businessman with the law on your side. Have a longer life expectancy, to boot."

Mica laughed. "Give us back the money. After that we can talk."

"The money comes after my hit runs uninterrupted. Agreed?"

"Then take an equal sum from our rivals. I won't be bent backward by anyone."

Wren grinned. "Already done. I took double from them all. If they take this chance to come for me, I expect you to have my back. If I'm gone, my team wipe all the accounts and let your country burn."

Five seconds. Ten.

"Agreed."

"Excellent. Now to the second point. I lied about having the location for my target. We have him to a five-mile radius of Acapulco. I'm thinking you or one of the others cartels already know where he is. I've got no doubt he pays protection money. So I'm going to need you to rat him out. Also, I lied about having a team. I don't have anyone, it's just me inbound. Can you provide a Sicario squad to wrap this up?"

Mica laughed. "It seems you have very little. This is more of your infamous brinksmanship?"

"Not by choice. I'm running far ahead of standard international reach. Call this a cutting-edge strike."

"Another word for this comes from the world of finance, Señor Wren. Over-leveraged. Push too hard, and your own house of cards may collapse."

"Ride or die," Wren said. "Do we have a deal?"

A moment of silence. "Yes, we can make this deal. But since you are changing it as we speak, I will change it too. There is a Senator in your government, Niles Regis, I think you remember he manipulated me. I wish to see him dead."

Wren gritted his teeth. Thought back 18 months, to his last op as a standard CIA operative. It was the mission that got him out, before he got back in again to hunt the Blue Fairy. "I already killed his son for you. I'm not killing the father."

"I understand. Simply look the other way when our kill comes. Convince others to look away, also."

A tight deal. Wren had no further leverage, though.

"Done. Provided it's a surgical hit. No collateral damage, no bombs. Not the rest of his family."

"A pleasure doing business with you, Señor Wren. A team of my own Sicarios will await you. I think you are going to like Acapulco."

19

DIAMANTE

The Punta Diamante district bordered the south side of Acapulco Bay, and held most of the city's latest developments, with glitzy new 5-star hotels and high-rise ultra-luxury condominiums overlooking the gorgeous private beaches. The name of the district itself meant 'diamond', and had to be one of the most locked-down tourist zones in the world, protecting its high-value denizens as much as possible against the encroaching Narco Wars.

None of that really mattered to Wren.

The Learjet circled and put him down at Acapulco International. The air was hot and dry as one of Hellion's overclocked server racks, mid-eighties despite the season. Wren deplaned to a waiting black Silverado waiting thirty yards off, fronted by five thick cartel soldiers in uniform tactical camo gear, cradling assault rifles. Mexican tourists getting off a jumbo jet to the right watched open-mouthed as Wren strode toward them.

"Señor Wren," one of the five men called across the distance. A leader. Teardrop tattoos all down his throat. Bull neck, in his thirties, about as tall as Wren. Doubtless he'd done all kinds of dark things for the cartel, maybe more on his free time. A killer of women and children; you had to be to make Sicario. The kind of guy Wren would put in the ground without a second thought, in other circumstances. From the look in the guy's eyes, he was thinking about the exact same thing.

"I do not like this, Christopher," came Hellion's voice in his ear. Re-establishing contact after she'd been sleeping throughout his flight. "I have been watching these men. They are suspicious."

"Suspicious how?" he sub-vocalized into his new throat-mic rig, barely moving his lips as he closed the distance.

"One of them was drinking yoghurt."

Wren snorted. "Yoghurt? Are you kidding?"

"I never kid about yoghurt. Ask B4cksl4cker. It should not be drunk."

Wren filed that away. Still, it raised a valid point. He wouldn't put it past Don Mica to have multiple plans in progress. Prep the zoo raid even as he prepped a hit on Wren. Maybe he would roll the dice, try locking 'Santa Justicia' up in a cartel dungeon and pray to Santa Muerte that torture would make him roll back the cryptocoin threat.

"Just keep tracking the target," he sub-vocalized, ten yards out from the five guys.

They were professionals with totally blank expressions. Solid, thousand-yard stares, watching him roll up with zero sign of emotion, but something about that seemed off to Wren. He tried to put himself in their position. If their orders were to start taking direction from some Yankee yahoo, risking their lives to raid a 'zoo' belonging to a guy who'd been paying them protection money for years, shouldn't they be pissed off?

Professional or no, Wren figured they should.

"All set for the raid?" he asked as he closed within five yards.

Two of them gave nods, the central bull-neck guy and a guy to his right with an accentuated widow's peak, and that set more alarm bells ringing. Too eager. He'd dealt with Sicarios before, glorified hitmen like a pack of wild dogs, and like a pack they obeyed the hierarchy without needing to think about it. To show disrespect meant death.

But two guys nodding? It was stepping out of established leadership bounds. Like a mob, not a pack. Maybe killers from different cartels, rustled up by Mica to keep the peace. If so, Wren saw the play rolling out ahead; get him in the vehicle surrounded on all sides, and he'd be easy to incapacitate. Take him to Don Mica in shackles and break out the dogs.

There was no point taking any chances now. Better to force the play and rule by fear.

He didn't break stride as he closed the last yard, raised a hand to the bull-neck guy as if to shake, flashed a smile then smoothly flipped his palm into a blade strike jab, fingers rigid and stabbing straight into the dead center of the tear trail down the guy's throat. Nothing slabs of steroid muscle could do to reinforce cartilage, and the guy's windpipe crunched and buckled under Wren's baton-hard fingers, his chin snapping down like the stable door slammed shut after the horse bolted.

Wren stepped back while the guy fell to the steaming blacktop, clutching at his crushed throat. No operational come-back from that. Maybe he'd live, but not even a tracheotomy would make him operational today, if anyone was inclined, which none were.

Nobody moved. Nobody so much as batted an eye. That synced up with Wren's theory; this was a hodge-podge cartel of cartels. No loyalty. They remained standing in a quarter circle like a convex lens with Wren at the focal point. All hardened killers, listening to one of their own grunt for breath on the floor and not even looking.

"I'll drive," Wren said. "Keys."

He held out his hand. The four of them stared.

"Keys and get on board or I strip everything all your bosses have got. I guarantee Mica's dogs will be coming for you next. We make this strike, we never see each other again. Entendido?"

No answer. The guy on the floor managed to get a wheeze of air in. So maybe he'd survive. Throw a fiesta.

"Keys," Wren repeated. "Situational awareness, gentlemen. Read the room."

One of them stepped forward. The sharp widow's peak guy. He slapped a set of keys into Wren's outstretched palm.

"Thank you. Now." He surveyed them. "Anyone goes for my neck with a garotte, believe that I'll crash the car and kill us all before you get to the wheel. Gunshot to the head, same story. Be in no doubt, I have a thick skull. Now, in."

The widow's peak guy jutted his chin forward. "He was lead. Who you want as your second?"

Wren smiled. Already adjusting. It was nice to deal with professionals. "You're talkative, so I'll take you. Name?"

"Madrigal."

"Cartel?"

Madrigal's jaw tightened. Getting called on the lie.

"Cartel," Wren repeated.

"Morela."

Wren smiled. "Like the mushroom. Madrigal, Wren. I hold you

responsible for these three." He waved at the others. "Now everyone get in the back. No bitching. Sit on each other's laps, all I care."

Wren moved to the driver's side, popped the door and climbed in. Plush black leather, AC running cold, and instant confirmation of the suspected plot. The empty package for a medical-grade syringe lay in the passenger footwell, a squat bottle of Propofol on the dash, and in back hung the detritus for an IV line. Get him under with the injection, keep him under until he hit Mica's dungeon of choice. To boot, an empty bottle of macrobiotic yoghurt, blueberry flavor.

Seemed Hellion's suspicions were well-founded.

"This is incredibly dangerous," Hellion said in his ear. "B4cksl4cker and I are enjoying it very much."

Wren snorted. "And that's what matters most," he said quietly, as the guys got in behind. Madrigal hopped up on the lap of one of the others without a word of complaint. They were too pro to bitch and moan. The guy underneath him just sat there staring, like the most intense booster seat Wren had ever seen.

"Here we go," Wren said, twisted the key and hit the gas hard enough to rock all four of them tight into each other. Aggressive driving would keep them off-balance long enough for everyone to survive to the zoo. "And call your bosses now, tell them exactly what happened, and that I want four more guys waiting for us, or I bring the financial apocalypse raining down. Those exact words. We're going in hard and fast."

Madrigal brought up his phone first, the others followed.

"B4cksl4cker has brought popcorn," Hellion said. "This is better than movie."

Wren leaned in, pushing through the rainbows across his vision as the Silverado picked up speed. Getting pissed off now.

20

JEFE

Out of Acapulco International, Wren pushed the Silverado to ninety on an immaculate two-lane lined with sparse-looking palm trees, northwest and fifteen minutes out.

"Sit-rep on the target," Wren said under his breath, as Madrigal in back spoke to Don Mica on the phone, occasionally barking out a submissive, "Si, capo."

"Unmoving," Hellion answered.

Unmoving was good. Hotels whipped by to left and right, shopping centers, parking lots. On the surface Acapulco didn't look like a murder capital. It looked moneyed, clean, ready for a flood of tourists to descend and start hoovering up designer brands at cutthroat prices. The sky was a spotless but dulling blue, coming on toward dusk. Wren wound the window down and killed the AC.

Fresh and salty ocean drafts blew in like a balm, after six hours cooped up in the dehydrating, recycled air of the Learjet.

"There are three riots currently ongoing in the United States," Hellion said in the background. "The largest is in New York. They appear to be targeting the cleanup crew at 231 Madison Avenue."

That made a sick kind of sense. Attack the government workers trying to scab over the wound of another destroyed skyscraper. Keep the wound fresh.

"Are they ALERTs? Linked to new sightings of me?"

"All of them. Deepfake, clearly. Each triggered an ALERT that has brought thousands out to riot. In Tallahassee you were seen curb-stomping an X-apoc member. Infant X's idiots are now attempting to raze a sports stadium as revenge. Fire crews are out, and like New York, they are receiving incoming gunfire."

Wren grunted. It seemed the Exposition Center had broken the seal, after two more flash-mobs had struck Philadelphia and Atlanta while he was in the air. Didn't matter that it was impossible for him to be at both at the same time. The X-apoc masses were ready to go, and when deepfake video of Wren committing 'atrocities' against them came through, they flash-mobbed in their cosplaying thousands.

Starting fires that raged wildly. Destroying property. Attacking police, fire and paramedic crews when they tried to assert control. Targeting killings against anyone who talked back. So every ALERT became a missile strike. Cities engulfed in chaos at the touch of a button. And the ALERTs were coming faster.

Ten minutes out from the third human zoo.

"Still unmoving?" Wren asked.

"Unmoving. I will tell you."

"More men will be waiting," Madrigal said in back.

Wren said nothing. The road opened out and Acapulco Bay sprawled briefly through greenery off to his left. Vast and unforgiving, final resting place of so many other innocents. He cast his eyes up to the right, where ahead the luxury hotels stood like rainmakers at the water's edge, thirty stories tall and gleaming dental-cap white in the fading light.

He'd expected the human zoo to be on a mezzanine floor, just like New York and Seattle. He'd already planned the attack, fast ropes from the roof combined with a ram team, just like his old Acapulco days, until Don Mica had switched all that around.

The third zoo was on a ship.

"I haven't seen any 'human zoo'," Mica said. "It's a small group, several boxes of equipment, highly mobile. They exchange position on visiting cruise liners every day, when new liners come in. They pay cash under-the-table to take over a penthouse, conduct their operations, move again the following day. It is a smooth operation. In the eyes of the city, they do not exist. In our eyes, they are a pay check."

A ship.

That day it was the New Dawn Seafarer, an eight-deck tall, seven-hundred occupancy luxury cruise liner, five-hundred staff, a thousand-feet long with a thirty-foot draft. A small town floating on a bulbous keel. Ingenious. Invisible. The zoo was able to push their Internet uplink through the ship's satellite dish; incredibly expensive to send video that way, but constantly rotating at the source as the liners switched out, in addition to the global server bounce and encryption.

Anonymized in three ways. It was a miracle his hackers had ever narrowed it down to Acapulco at all.

"Movement," Hellion said in his ear.

Wren's heart skipped a beat. They'd been warned? He checked the dash. Minutes out. the greenery opened again and now he saw the first of them to the left, huge ships moored off to sea like great gleaming islands in the bay. Too far-off to pick out their names, but he knew one of them was the New Dawn.

"Bearing?"

"Turning to port," Hellion said, keys flying in the background. "I am patching through their comms system. It seems the captain has been co-opted. Half his passengers are still on land."

Wren pushed the pedal to the metal, eking out a few more miles-per-hour.

"Madrigal, tell me we have jet boats ready to go."

"Ready, jefe."

Wren almost laughed. Jefe.

"Can you hack the ship?" Wren asked Hellion.

"Their satellite downlink is not wired to ship controls, Christopher. You will have to catch it."

"How far ahead's my turn?"

"Just ahead, Christopher. Boats are at the waterline."

Wren pulled left, took it so hard the Silverado edged onto its outside tires, whipped across the median and in front of oncoming traffic to race down an access road with signs for the NEW DAWN SEAFARER. They tore through a parking lot, hit the end and punched through a wooden barrier, tires scraping and chassis jolting down concrete steps to the beach, Sicarios bouncing in the back.

Tourists in floppy fishing hats and flip-flops shrieked and leaped out of his way. Sand flared from his spinning rear wheels like twin yellow geysers, bouncing toward admiral-blue skies with the sun a blot of boiling metal sinking into citrine seas, the NEW DAWN dead ahead and clearly showing its stern profile.

Ahead at the water's edge were two black speedboats, surrounded by more cartel hitmen. The perfect time for Mica to flip this thing a second time, but Wren had no time to re-enforce loyalty. Either they were in now or they weren't. The Silverado reached them in seconds and braked into a massive sand-surfing skid.

"With me, Madrigal!" Wren barked, thrust the door open and leaped out as the car rocked to a halt, running full-tilt at the boat already putting into the water. He jumped directly in, a second later Madrigal followed, then the guy at the engine ripped the cord and they took off over the waves.

21

NEW DAWN SEAFARER

The Seafarer cruised away at a stately pace befitting its immense scale, maybe twenty knots as a quarter million tons of metal, laid flat like a hundred-story skyscraper, were driven on by immense engines that produced a furrowed expanse of foot-high swells in their wake.

Wren's speedboat squad caught up to it in minutes, thumping over the low Pacific waves at seventy knots, crossing its ruffled wake to come up close on the starboard side. There was no one leaning out shooting, no sign of gun emplacements hunkering in, not even any sound on the horn.

"Give me the hook," Wren shouted to Madrigal.

The speedboat rocked in the Seafarer's displacement, engine spluttering as the huge liner's waves lifted them in and out of four-foot swells, spraying sea foam in a constant rain. One of the Sicarios opened a wooden crate, pulled out a metal hook with a slim rope attached. It was handed along, almost lost over the side as the boat bounced and saltwater splashed in Wren's eyes, then pressed into his hand.

It wasn't heavy, a simple molded hook in mottled iron, linked to a slimline pulley threaded with a thin cord. That cord linked to a coil, which Wren took in his off-hand, and beyond that to a long rope ladder stowed in the crate.

He scanned the Seafarer's flank, looking for the lowest point to toss the hook.

"Lower-tier lifeboats," he shouted over the crash and roar of the speedboat thumping up and down, the occasional clang of their hull banging off the Seafarer's flank. He pointed. "Right there!"

The speedboat raced ahead. Wren tried to stand, found his vertigo triggered like a crushing black wall as the deck jittered and rolled underfoot.

"Hold it steady!" he barked and tried again.

The sky spun darkly. Hard to fix anything in his sights. He dropped the hook off to his right on a foot of slack then hinged his body upright like he was side-hoisting a kettlebell, sending the hook shooting upward. He lost it in the glare. There was a clang, a shout, then the hook came plummeting back at skull-cracking velocity.

It hit the water and sank hard. Wren reeled it in, head spinning. He rubbed saltwater from his eyes and focused on the bucking ship above. They couldn't do this for long, already taking on water from every wave broken against the giant ship's side. Wren doubled down, picked out the edge of the lifeboat he wanted to hit, thirty feet up, and levered his whole body to hurl the hook once more.

It climbed, hung, then at the last minute clipped onto one of the lifeboat's tarpaulin straps.

He tugged it and it bit, held. The line hung and Wren immediately began working it through the pulley. In seconds he had the rope ladder shooting up. The line tied off, then he was climbing.

His body swung and thumped off the ship. His feet missed the rungs. His hands slipped on the thin lines, spun on the plastic rungs. The sky and the sea rolled and the sun became a tumbling sphere edged with silver. Hellion spoke like a twittering bird in his ear but he bulled upward, forcing his hands higher, his legs step-by-step, until finally his fingers closed on the lifeboat's tarp.

He pulled himself over. Kneeling on the canvas jacket. Ropes led away up to the higher tier of lifeboats, above which lay the deck. Down below Sicarios clambered up the rope ladder in pursuit. The speedboat jostled on the waves like a fly-fishing lure, threatening any moment to sink. Off to the horizon lay Acapulco, its buildings lime-white as a Hollywood smile.

Wren jumped, caught the ropes leading up and shinnied higher, vertigo be damned. In thirty seconds he breached the railing and dropped onto the deck. Wooden flooring boards ran away in either direction, the white ceiling of the deck hung above, sky, sea, access doors with round portholes.

He drew his Desert Eagle, started toward the bridge. Madrigal called something from below but Wren didn't hear it. His brothers were here. He could feel it. Maybe X, maybe the Apex too. He shoulder-slammed through a door, glimpsed a map of the immense ship, and started up red-carpeted stairs.

Three stories and he emerged into a swimming pool area, eyes blinking against the sudden harsh glare. Everything was white. Deckchairs laid out around a rectangular pool, towels unfurled in places, bags, but no people. Felt like the Mary Celeste ghost ship, cocktails with their shakers still spinning, ice melting in the Mexican heat. Curfewed by the captain, Wren figured. He lurched on like a drunken guest, roving eyes raised to the forecastle. Another four stories, a large mirrored-glass window looking out, impossible to tell if anyone was looking down on him.

He slammed through a door and ran upstairs, past a games room packed with arcades, ping-pong, air hockey, all chiming noisily with not a person present. His thighs burned and he hit the top deck, saw the Bridge access locked behind a reinforced metal door. Terrorist- and pirate-proof, pretty much as he'd expected, and not a problem at all.

"Starboard-bow corner," Hellion said in his ear. Had to be checking the ship schematics.

He moved, found the chute leading up in the corner as promised, rungs recessed into the wall, and climbed. The hatch opened, putting him through the roof and out onto the roof of the forecastle. Twin large transmission arrays spun to either side. A cornucopia of satellite dishes.

He'd planned for an assault from the roof of a luxury hotel, so had the personal fast-rope gear and harness. Was packing .30 caliber armor-piercing copper jacket rounds to punch through the building's tough outer glass skin. Not so different here. All he had to do was find a place to latch on his personal fast-rope coil.

He clicked onto a truss for one of the dishes, outracing the nausea now. Staying just one step ahead. He stepped to the edge just as Madrigal poked his head through the chute, above the line of the roof.

"Jefe-" he began, then Wren hit the coil release and jumped backward. One bound and the bridge window was right there before him, broad like wraparound shades, tinted glass so he couldn't see anything but his own reflection in the glare of the setting sun.

He pushed off hard and fired three times fast as he swung out, enough to crack, shatter then burst the glass inwards. He kicked the fragments away as he swung in, paid out the line and thumped down off a dashboard of radar screens, levers and controls, found his feet and hit the coil release, Eagle up and trained in on two figures at the central wheel.

A tall Asian guy in his fifties, white short-sleeve button-down shirt with black and gold chevron epaulettes, captain's hat on the chair beside him and a gun to his head.

The guy holding the gun was mixed-race, washed-out brown skin with tight black afro hair buzzed close to his scalp, bright blue eyes and model-chiseled cheekbones, hiding his lanky frame almost wholly behind the body of the captain.

Wren took the rest of the room in with his peripheral vision: three figures laid out flat on the floor, white crew shirts with black epaulettes flecked with gold, blood pools glinting in the fading light beneath them. Looked like two shots in the head each, outright executions. Red alarms blared on the control screens, something about automatic cabin lockdown, and a banging came at the reinforced door that had to be Madrigal.

Wren refocused on the captain and the hostage-taker, let his spiraling vision split even further as he matched that face, those cheekbones, those intense blue eyes to a sepia-tone photograph snatched from the Apex's New York human zoo. Adding on nearly three decades, imagining the sag of time and the carving of wrinkle lines; not enough laughter marks and a beetled brow, as if all he'd done for thirty years was squint and frown.

No mistaking it. The resemblance was there, last seen at the bottom of one of the Apex's faith pits, faking death by asphyxiation for a celebrating Pyramid. Wren trained the Eagle on his face.

"Aden-Of-The-Saints," he said. "Hello, brother."

22

ADEN

A beat played out. The captain said something but Wren didn't hear it, lost in his brother's eyes. Happy to see him, in one sense. Chrysogonus was dead. Galicia was dead. You only had so many family members, and every one Wren had met so far was dead.

Once they'd played together, he vaguely remembered. Everything back then had been overshadowed by the cruelty of first the Apex and second Chrysogonus, but Aden had been kind at times. Taken a beating that was coming to Pequeño 3, maybe, or helped him gather the black stones from around the fake town that were his 'Essential Barometers' task, before the Apex got home and whipped anyone who'd failed to meet his standards.

Now Wren only had to look in Aden's eyes to know the whole of his story. Second fiddle to Chrysogonus from birth to death. Third fiddle to the Apex. Behind Galicia in eminence, deep in his father's shadow, and in Wren's too, maybe. A workhorse sent far away to Mexico to run the overseas zoo. A once-decent boy brainwashed and broken into this.

Aden stared at him with a gaze like bullets. Hatred. Disdain. His lips pulled back in a snarl. The only way to stay that crazy was to hate harder than the rest, then use that hate to prop you up. Wren saw the end result coming before it happened. Had already seen this show play out with two lost siblings and wasn't about to watch it play out again.

He fired, punching a bullet that skimmed the captain's side without triggering the copper jacket, sluicing through skin and intercostal muscle to hit Aden in the chest just as he was in the act of turning his gun on himself.

Aden's gun discharged into the ceiling, then Wren was there, guiding the captain aside as his brother fell backward, again trying to level the gun at his own head. Wren grabbed for him, all his movements coming like splashes of oil paint on a broad canvas now as the concussion reared large, rendering the world to color and light, acting only through muscle memory. He dropped the Eagle and caught Aden's wrist in his left hand, caught the hot barrel of his Glock M11 in his right and twisted until something broke.

Narrow bones of the ulna and radius cracking like green sticks.

Aden cried out and brought a wild fist into play. Wren took it on the forehead, setting silver fireworks off in his head, then they were down on the ground together, Wren straddling Aden as he spat up blood and struggled to get free.

"Stop, Aden!" Wren commanded, taking a wild slap on the chin, getting bucked as Aden writhed. "Stop it!"

He punched the struggling man once, twice, just trying to get-

"Jefe!"

Wren spun, making himself sick. The bridge spun, the captain was gone. The secure door was open. Madrigal was right there, widow's peak leaning in, saying something that merged with whatever Hellion was saying in his ear.

"Find them," Wren said, couldn't hear his own words but saw them ballooning out like long multicolored speech bubbles. "The rest of them. The captain knows. Take his team alive."

The bubbles splashed across Madrigal in a haywire rainbow, seemed he heard because he nodded. Wren turned back to his brother. Aden-Of-The-Saints. His beautiful face was splashed with blood.

"Where is he?" Wren demanded.

Aden gasped frothy blood, tried to laugh and only spluttered.

"The Apex, where is he Aden?"

"Ungrateful," Aden began, choked on blood, "son."

"I know my own damn name," Wren said between gasps, fighting for stability as Aden's face doubled. "Every one you all called me; little wren, ungrateful son, Pequeño 3, whatever. You're going to tell me where he is."

Aden laughed, gulped, gurgled. The bullet must have hit a lung. Even now filling up with blood, drowning him from within. Nothing Wren could do about that. "Little... brother," he managed. "I missed ... you."

Nothing to say to that. Even if it was true, it wasn't true the way Wren wanted it to be. "Where's our father, Aden? Tell me something. Anything!"

"Anything," Aden gulped. "Do you ... remember the desert?"

Wren leaned in. "Is that where he is?"

"The Pyramid... game. We'd play. Remember?"

Wren didn't. Or maybe he did. Pequeño 3 in the middle while Aden, Zachariah and Gabriel stood around the edges. The younger named Pyramid boys toying with the eldest of the unnamed Pequeños. Arranged in a triangle with Pequeño 3 in the middle, tossing black stones overhead and telling him to catch them. Climb the Pyramid to the apex, they'd say, don't sink to the tomb. Always Pequeño 3 stood at the center. Always his older brothers tossed the stones too high for him to reach, laughing as he jumped and strained. '3's in the tomb', they'd jeer, 'never gonna be apex'.

"What about it?"

"You never... learned," Aden managed. "Never knew ... your place. Always trying... to climb."

"Because there's only one Apex, I get it," Wren said fast, chasing the words like they might escape from him. "Where is our father, Aden?"

Aden coughed for ten seconds, twenty, the blood coming out bright and arterial now, frothy and aerated. He reached up his hand, the wrist broken and fingers jutting at an unnatural angle, touched it to Wren's chest.

"In your ... heart."

Wren took his hand and twisted. Aden shrieked, gagged, coughed, swallowed. Only moments left now.

"Where?"

"Right at the ... center."

Wren twisted his wrist, not thinking clearly. Aden cried out and laughed. "Where's the center, Aden? Where's X?"

Aden spluttered, smug eyes widening in panic as his breath caught, juddered. "In the f..."

"In the what?"

Aden gulped and caught no air, blew a feeble red gasp then tried again, managed to hiss out a few words.

"Walk in the fire, little brother."

Then he died.

Wren stared into his eyes throughout, watching the moment his soul escaped his body and headed toward whatever BS afterlife in some hellish 'tomb' the Apex had conjured up for his followers. The never-ending fight against the slavers. Freeing the slaves. Twisting children and spitting them out as…

Aden's eyes were vacant. No breath, no pulse. Just like Tomothy-Whereof-The-Giants-Roam had died some thirty years ago, in Pequeño 3's arms.

Wren pulled back, shaking and nauseated. He lurched to his feet, tumbled over the control deck and dry-heaved as the vertigo hit and didn't let up.

23

APEX, TOMB

Wren sat atop the roof of the bridge as dusk set in over the Pacific, his hands shaking in his lap. The sky was beautiful before him, a fury of reds, oranges and yellows as the sun was gradually swallowed by the unfeeling horizon line. Eight hours of darkness and sleep until it reappeared and the cycle began again, rising toward apex at the summit of the sky.

Apex. Tomb. A cycle that ever ended.

By Wren's side his earpiece squawked. Hellion, B4cksl4cker, maybe Rogers, Maggie, Teddy. It didn't mean much to him right then. Riots. America in disarray. Maybe he didn't care.

That was a dark truth.

He thought about the light going out in Aden's eyes again. On some level, it had felt good, and that brought on the shame. A cycle like the sun, like that stupid game in the desert. Apex. Tomb. Little Pequeño 3 right in the center while his brothers laughed, teasing him for never figuring it out, just like they'd all been laughing at him for three decades, believing they were all dead.

Of course he'd understood the game from the start. The very first time they'd taken him out to play. He'd always known he could never win, but winning against his brothers hadn't mattered to him back then. Everything in the Pyramid had been about winning, and Pequeño 3 was sick of it.

To play with his brothers mattered more. To make them happy, even if they thought it was through his humiliation. There were far worse things.

His palms stung. He held them up, saw the star-shaped scars where Galicia had plunged her stiletto blade through the flesh. Thinking about family.

He had children. Jake. Quinn. A wife, technically, still. Loralei. But she'd found another man, living in a duplex together with his children in Delaware. Secured by the Foundation. Wren could bring up his phone and watch a feed of them any moment he wanted. Spy-cams dotted through their house. In every room. Overlooking their yard. Cameras hacked everywhere in surrounding streets and through the little town of Frederica, so he could look down and keep them safe.

But what did any of it matter, if he was never going to see them again? So America burned. The Pyramid had died once already, at the Apex's command. He'd been the one to do it back then, setting all those people alight at his father's command, just like he'd killed Tomothy when the Apex ordered him to. They'd done it together. Just like he'd killed Aden.

So maybe it was all going to happen again. A cycle like the sun. Apex, tomb. He didn't know what any of that meant.

"Jefe," came a voice from in back. Madrigal.

Wren didn't turn. Knew what he was going to hear.

"We found only dead bodies. A room of torched computers. There is nothing."

Of course there was nothing.

"The port is calling. Federales are coming. We must go."

Wren said nothing. So federales came, it wouldn't matter. Lock him up in a prison, maybe he'd just escape. Maybe he'd stay. Stop trying to climb to the apex. Settle once for the tomb.

"You should go," Madrigal said. Like he cared.

Madrigal left.

Wren sat with his hands shaking, watching the dark sky curdle from pink to blue to purple to black. Stars emerged. Boats came out. Lights spinning, bullhorns calling cautions in Spanish. Nothing Wren needed to hear.

Hard to know what he wanted, now.

Two more of his brothers were alive still, out there somewhere. The third human zoo was a nothing now, just the final point in the looping dot-to-dot of some earlier plot, but nothing more. No X. No lead on the Apex. No way to stop the ALERTs from going off like missile bursts.

He was back to square one. Rubbed his thumping temples. Maybe he'd have been better off sitting this out on the Iowa farm. Watching the frosts come, the corn stalks decay, while the Foundation fell apart around him. Maggie had argued otherwise.

He smiled. What was a Foundation, if not the preparation for a Pyramid? Dig down for a tomb, build up for an apex. Of course, only one point in all the pyramid could be the apex. Everything else supported it. It was the one point that ruled over all.

The federales reached the ship's side. The New Dawn Seafarer's engines had wound down some time back. Wren hadn't heard much other than Madrigal since then, figured the passengers were all still locked in their quarters. If he wanted, it'd be an easy enough thing to evade the Mexican police. They didn't know what they were looking for. Wash his hands, melt into the crowd, disappear over the side. Take a lifeboat. No. That'd be too slow. Commandeer one of their speedboats.

He smiled again. Hands curling in on themselves.

With these hands he'd pulled the trigger to usher his brother on. On some level he'd savored it. Wasn't sure if that made him just as bad as the Apex himself.

Somewhere below the federales boarded. The dizziness receded. The earpiece bleated, and Wren slipped it into his pocket. No answers, no direction. He stood. Easy to fall, this high up.

Back through the bridge, he looked in on the body of his brother. Aden looked unpeaceful. The captain was there too, holding a stained towel against his side, staring at the body. He saw Wren, flung up his hands, said something fast in Spanish.

Wren waved a hand. "Lo siento," he said. "No te preocupes." I'm sorry. Don't worry.

His Desert Eagle had been set on the control desk. Maybe Madrigal's work. Wren looked at it. The captain looked at it too. Before he could do anything he'd regret, Wren strode in and swept it up. Easy. Tucked it into the holster and moved on.

He went down the stairs. You couldn't help but just keep on surviving. The federales were coming in around the swimming pool now, weapons raised. Wren ducked deeper. Took turns through the ship until he reached a low deck on the other side. It was quiet and still there, the darkness thick beyond the glowing white halo of the ship. Everything beyond that was the wild, and the wild belonged to him.

He broke a glass safety screen, worked the crank for the nearest lifeboat. Worked the second. The boats dropped on their lines, hit the water and tugged free of their ropes. Wren waited. At some point shouts went up. A federale boat pulled around. All eyes turned to some sad escape attempt.

Wren walked back around the midships. Found one of the federales' own rope ladders hooked to a railing and climbed it down to one of their boats. From below he didn't look any different from another federale, in tactical black. They'd all gone to the lifeboats, leaving one guy behind to watch the store.

"Hay alguna señal de él?" he called as Wren descended. Any sign of the guy?

"No hay señal," Wren responded, putting a little steam into it. "Vigile los botes salvavidas!" There's no sign. Keep an eye on the lifeboats.

When Wren dropped in beside him, the guy's eyes went wide. Not wearing the exact same gear. Not a federale at all. He swung his rifle but Wren slapped it aside, sent a meaty punch into the guy's jaw. He flew back against the boat's rubber edge and didn't get up. Lying there unconscious, he looked like Aden.

Wren leaned in, checked his pulse. Strong. That was good. Maybe he couldn't take another senseless death right now.

He sat at the tiller, fired up the engine and pulled away into the dark while the Mexican police scrambled around some empty lifeboats.

24

CENTROID

It was around 11 p.m. by the time Wren climbed the steps to his Learjet at Acapulco International. It felt like he was wading through seaweed-clogged waters at the bottom of the Pacific. Distantly he smelled the acrid tang of jet fuel on the air, heard the muted sounds coming from a nearby passenger jet as baggage handlers threw luggage into the hold.

At the top of the stairs he stopped a moment, looked back, up and around, setting his vertigo spinning like a Matisse painting. A few lights on the concourse. The jet with its illuminated portholes like perfectly aligned bullet pocks. Vehicles flashing by on a nearby road. All the ships out to sea.

It was all nothing. No stars in the dark sky. No evidence in the zoo. No lead stretching out to X or the Apex.

His phone rang in his pocket, then force-connected before he could smother it silent. "Where will you go, Christopher?" came Hellion's voice, insistent like a bug. She'd know he was at the airport, at his jet.

"Home," he said, took the phone out and stripped the battery.

The jet taxied, launched, climbed, and Wren just sat in his chair staring out the oval window. Acapulco was bright, but all around it the dark of Guerrero province spread as far as he could see, overwritten with the afterglow of Aden's dying eyes. He felt the cost of that summary execution digging fresh pits inside and making him sick.

For nothing.

He didn't know what to do. Where to go.

Across the darkness he saw flashes of his brothers spread in their triangle, tossing rocks over his head. He kept jumping higher and higher but it was never enough.

He jerked awake with a gasp.

The jet's engines droned on around him. He got his breathing under control, surfacing from a nightmare. He hadn't meant to fall asleep at all, and brought his phone up, put the battery back in and scrolled through to the world map, where his route was drawn in red. 1:37 a.m.. He'd slept for a couple of hours, and still the vision of his brothers in their triangle shone like tracer rounds across his vision.

He killed the screen and sat in the semi-dark, trying to banish the past.

"In your heart," Aden had said. "Right at the center."

Dead.

He closed his eyes again, but now sleep wouldn't come. Too many phantoms in the air, too many mysteries locked in his dead brother's eyes. He reactivated his phone and stared at the map, watching the minutes tick by. In his messages feed there was a stream of past ALERTs gone out across the country. Dozens of them. The 42% rising for the Apex's lies, blowing up America for fun, for profit, for wild-eyed belief.

On the map the tiny icon of the Learjet jogged a pixel further northeast, stretching its red route from Acapulco a fraction longer. Somewhere over the Gulf of Mexico now, looked like the pilot had selected New York as his destination.

As good as anywhere. Another fallen zoo site. The red line blurred, doubled, and then he saw it.

Right there on the screen before him, as plain as day.

In your heart. Right at the center.

Instantly his heart began to pound. His mouth went dry and his vision tunneled to the screen like nothing else mattered. He reached one finger up to trace a simple geometric shape across the map, transposing Aden's last words and his last touch like a vast crosshairs.

Call it the center point of a triangle. The apex of a pyramid. X marks the spot.

He placed the call.

"Da, Christopher," came Hellion's flat voice this time.

"I think I've got something," he said, barely containing this new frenzy. "Can you bring up a map of North America?"

The sound of her keys rapped short and sharp like a drumroll. "I am looking at one. What is it?"

He tried to run the numbers in his head first: due west from the New York zoo, something like 2,400 miles across the country right along the 41st parallel, you pretty much hit the site of the second zoo, Seattle. Drop from there southeast all the way to Acapulco at the sagging belly of Guerrero, Mexico, and...

"Calculate distances from New York to Acapulco," he ordered, heart palpitating, "also Seattle to Acapulco."

Keys rattled.

"From New York it is twenty-two-hundred-forty miles. From Seattle it is twenty-four-seventy. Is this-"

A flash of red surged across Wren's vision. The concussion sending up a warning flare, but he couldn't stop now. Three locations, each virtually the same distance apart, made a clear symbol written across almost the entirety of the United States. New York to Seattle to Acapulco and back to New York. Including or crossing almost every US state. Almost equilateral, but inverted.

An upside-down triangle. The Pyramid, fallen.

"The zoos make a triangle," he managed, feeling the weight of this revelation bringing the vertigo back. "Inverted. It can't be an accident. Nothing he does is by accident."

A second passed, followed by more clattering of keys. "You are correct, Christopher. It is slightly off-center, but is very close to triangle. What does it mean?"

A mark that America would burn, certainly. But more too. He remembered Aden's broken hand touching his chest. Bright red flashes burst in his head like fireworks.

"The center," he said, clinging to consciousness. "I need you to find it. The exact center of that triangle, by area, length, whatever."

A moment passed. "What am I looking for?"

"I have no idea. X. The Apex. His heart. Add it to your data matrices and dig until there's nowhere else to go."

"Working," Hellion answered.

Wren felt dizzy and sick. He stood up and held tight to the seat, turning the map of the US in his head, stepped out of his luxury seat like there was somewhere he might go.

"Oklahoma, somewhere," he guessed out loud, "maybe Kansas?"

"Approximate," Helion said. "I have centroid of this triangle, mathematical term for exact center."

Wren blinked, shuffled along the jet's aisle clutching seat backs. "Centroid. How is that calculated?"

"Middle point. It is created by intersection point of median lines. Line from middle of each triangle side to opposite corner, they meet at centroid. It is in south Kansas, southeast of city of Wichita, near small town of Medicine Lodge. This is Great Plains area."

Wren stopped at the service door and leaned against the wall, looking down over the Gulf's dark waters, fifty thousand feet distant.

"Medicine Lodge?"

"Yes. It is small town with one-thousand-seven-hundred population, seat of Barber County. Name comes from tree-trunk and branch shelter the native Kiowa people built in 1866, to celebrate annual sun dance."

"You've been reading Wikipedia."

"There is nothing else to know about this town, Christopher. This is centroid, but..."

Wren straightened up slightly, shoving the dizziness aside by force of will. "Does it cross with any data points in your matrix of the Apex? Somewhere he's been before?"

"Nothing I see yet. He has never been to this place, that we know. No Pyramid members have left trails near this place."

Wren blinked, rubbed his eyes, thinking back to the dying look in Aden's eyes. There wasn't just fear and anger in them, but also superiority. That little Pequeño 3 had still not learned his place. The exact kind of thing the Apex would do. Suddenly Acapulco made sense. The Apex had shown no interest whatsoever in Mexico, Canada, anywhere else before, but as a point of this immense inverted triangle? It was perfect.

Old briefings spun through his mind's eye like microfiche in a scanner, searching for some peg to hang this tiny, unimportant town on. "There was a cult in Kansas, I think, uncovered recently?"

Keys rapped down the earpiece. "Yes, I have it. Heaven's Fall. West Kansas. One man claiming to be 'Ancient Guardian', needed to have sex with young girls to secure their admittance to heaven. Murders followed, now he is in prison."

Could that be a lead? The Apex made a habit of adopting and co-opting smaller cults. There was no way this Heaven's Fall could have operated without his say-so, if he had any investment in Kansas at all.

Wren pushed away from the door. Wavering but straighter now as a fresh flush of adrenaline battled the nausea. He took the few steps to the cockpit and knocked on the door. It opened and Wren found himself looking into the weary face of a fuzzy-bearded young man.

"Yes, sir?"

"We need to redirect," Wren said. "I'll have the coordinates for a landing field sent through, but we're now heading to Medicine Lodge, a small town in south Kansas, southeast of Wichita."

The guy stared for a second. "The flight route's already logged, sir. I don't think we can-"

"We can," Wren interrupted. "Whatever it takes, I'll get. Whatever permissions you need are coming through right now. Turn the jet."

The guy gave a slight nod. Uncertain, but willing to find a way through. Crewing a private hire Learjet, the customer was always right.

"Thank you," Wren said and turned.

Red triangles flashed across his vision. Spread out across the country. One heart, one center. A raid, maybe, but on what?

"Are there any large compounds near Medicine Lodge?" he asked. "Militia. Biker gangs. Cults."

Keys flew. "I see nothing suspicious. No financial records for major construction. No large scale movements on satellite rewind. It is quiet, small town, lots of agriculture. Largest structures are malls and barns. Many barns."

Wren nodded. He'd have to find it, and fresh corollaries spun out from that notion. With the X-apoc hopped up to call in ALERTs when they saw him, there was no way he could just walk into Medicine Lodge and start asking questions. David Keller's campaign had made him a household name, debated endlessly on every news channel. If the 42% X-faithful figure held true, then some seven hundred people in Medicine Lodge were loyal to the Apex. It would only take one of them to set the town burning beneath another flash-mob riot.

"Can you get me an Internet blackout on Medicine Lodge?"

"Of course," Hellion answered. "Easy. But will take little time to arrange. Small town, remote location, we can provide this indefinitely, though it will be imperfect. We can block hardline Internet and phone traffic, but not radio, direct satellite links."

Wren grunted. Of course. If one of the X-apoc saw him, they'd find a way to get the ALERT out. That meant he couldn't do this himself, which meant he needed someone to run point. Open the questioning. Slip under the radar as much as possible. Candidates flashed through his mind.

Only one stood out.

"Get me Sally Rogers."

A moment's silence passed. "Agent Rogers is working to remain in the CIA," Hellion said. "We cannot pull her from this. She has essential role."

"The CIA's doomed if we can't stop X, Hellion. Doomed in any case, maybe. You know as well as I do, Congress are looking to shred the alphabet agencies. There'll be nothing left of them soon." He paused a moment, took a steadying breath. "Rogers won't like it. I don't like it either, but I need her more than the CIA right now. If I'm going to dig into Medicine Lodge, she's the only person I trust to be the shovel."

Another silence. "Christopher. This triangle, the centroid, it is... unscientific. The evidence is not here."

That didn't matter. Wren was feeling it. Aden's last words were all the evidence he needed. In the heart. In the center. Apex and tomb. "Until you have something better from the X app, it's our primary target. Everything bends towards cracking it." He took a breath. "And get me James Tandrews on the line. My real father. If anyone knows what this triangle means, it'll be him."

25

TANDREWS

"In Kansas?" James Tandrews asked, after hearing Wren out. Sounded like he didn't believe it. "As far as I can tell, he's never been near Kansas."

Tandrews was Wren's adoptive father, and the FBI gold team leader who'd led the raids back when the Pyramid had burned itself alive. He'd been the one to discover Wren at twelve years old in the smoking ruin of the fake town, take him in and help channel all that trauma in a productive direction.

They'd hardly spoken in the twenty years since Wren had skipped out on formal adoption, except for a handful of times in the last year, when Wren was at the edge and needed help.

"It's a leap of faith," Wren said. "That's why I need your eyes on, James. Nobody knows him like you do. My team think this inverted pyramid idea is meaningless. Not scientific. But you and I know him. The Apex. Isn't this the exact kind of thing he'd do?"

Seconds passed, and Wren imagined Tandrews gazing out of his floor-to-ceiling windows into the dark Maine woods. Woken up in the middle of the night, and the old man had just taken it in his stride. A lifetime in the FBI would do that to you, Wren figured. Whether it was really happening or it was all a dream, you were always ready.

"I think you're right," Tandrews said. "The grand, megalomaniacal scale of this falls well within your father's psych profile." He paused a moment. "I never saw this inverted triangle, though. This upside-down pyramid. But it would match his egotistical MO. He's the Apex, and when seen from above, the apex of a pyramid lies right at the center. This triangle, everything your brother Aden said, it all points to the center.

"Medicine Lodge."

"Medicine Lodge," Tandrews repeated. "But what should you expect to find there?" He took a moment, thinking it through. Wren gave him the time. "Something ideological, I expect, though I've never seen the Apex use triangles in his iconography before. This may take us back to first principles." Another pause. "You're aware how the United States uses the pyramid symbology?"

"Sure," Wren said. "It's on the dollar bill."

"It is, along with an all-seeing eye. Now, that's a symbol open to interpretation, but many believe it to be the eye of Ra, Egyptian god of the sun."

Wren frowned. "And that would mean?"

"Who can say, Chris? That pyramids and sun cults are as American as apple pie? Maybe. There've been plenty of theories about that over the years." He took a moment, maybe winding himself up for a mini-lecture. "Let's begin with the purpose of a pyramid. It's primarily a tomb for a pharaoh. Immensely rich men and women, god-kings to their people. The pyramid enshrined their belief that, in death, they would continue into the afterlife with all their slaves, riches and family members intact. These tombs were hidden in the center of their pyramids, along with all their chattel and possessions."

"Like jet fuel," Wren said, picking up the thread. "Burning their past to reach take-off velocity into a new life. And that was the theory for years, right? After the Pyramid burned in the fake town, everyone thought the Apex had set himself up as some kind of modern-day pharaoh, going out on a booster rocket of his dead followers. Except we never found his body, because he didn't actually die."

"True," Tandrews said. "Which further suggests the fake town was only ever one step in a bigger vision. He didn't die because he had work yet to do. Perhaps this inverted triangle is that bigger work." Tandrews paused again, and Wren thought he heard the soft sound of slippered footsteps. The old guy pacing, getting the bit in his teeth. "Consider this. The pharaoh's tomb is just as central to a pyramid, as seen from above, as the apex."

That threw Wren for a second, but he caught up fast. "OK. Apex or tomb. Yeah."

"Yes, precisely like your childhood game. So what lies in Kansas? Will we find the Apex there himself, waiting for you? Or is this some kind of tomb, containing all his belongings, family members, dead followers, everything he wishes to take with him to the afterlife."

Wren thought about that. "His main booster rocket."

"More like his primary engine," Tandrews countered, sounded like he was getting on a roll, like he always used to in the Maine backwoods, teaching Wren the best way to trap a white-tailed deer or spit a New England cottontail. "A focusing point, as if with this triangle he could channel the entirety of America into one central spot, burning all our lives as his jet fuel."

Wren whistled low. "That is bigger. An inferno of souls." He thought a second longer, hearing again what Hellion had said. Unscientific. "Still, it's a big jump from a roughly sketched triangle to that."

"Perhaps not as big as you think," Tandrews said, and Wren could hear the gently chiding tone in his voice. "There are further links to Egyptian ideology than just this inverted triangle, Christopher. Consider what your father's mouthpieces have been saying in recent months."

Wren frowned. "You mean the X videos? Fear is a portal, walk in the fire, all that?"

"Exactly. This notion that hell is the site of some vast war, where we are all slaves to inhuman slavers, and he's the one setting us free through death?" More soft footsteps came, maybe the shushing of paper as Tandrews opened old files and began leafing through. "In Egyptian mythology, hell was called 'Tuat'. Every night the sun god Ra disappeared into Tuat to battle primordial chaos, and every dawn he emerged victorious to stamp order upon the world anew. Some call that a reincarnation, with every day the sun newly born, both father and son at once."

Wren frowned. "A son of the sun?"

"Quite."

"It almost sounds like the Christian belief in the Father, Son and Holy Ghost."

"Indeed it does. There are further ties to the Christian belief system, too, in his use of numerology. His three days in a desert pit matches Jesus's three days in the cave, before he rolled back the stone."

Wren took a long, low breath. Thinking about the hot dark of the pits, scrabbling for a way out with little Grace-In-Our-Times by his side. "That's crazy. That was a kind of rebirth too?"

"It is a confounding muddle," Tandrews allowed. "His Pyramid always was. A melting pot of different ideas borrowed from other faiths, adopted and adapted, bent in dark directions." He sighed. "The truth is, we still know so little about your father, Chris. One day he just appeared, and there are no records. It's not uncommon from a certain era, children born in the free-love sixties in various communes sprung up across the country. Cults had a field day in the wilds. We still don't know his birth name, where he came from, who his parents were, where he learned to do the things he does, or why."

A long silence settled between the two of them.

"I don't care why," Wren said. "Not anymore."

"No. But in the 'why' there will be answers. Think of it as his source code. And with answers comes predictability."

"Order stamped on chaos."

Wren could feel Tandrews smiling. "Every man's vision of order is different. For the pharaohs it meant a continuation, even augmentation, of their absolute earthly power. For you it means helping others who struggle with their pasts. For your father, perhaps it is some fusion of the two. Perhaps, even as he yearns for the absolute power of Ra, he also genuinely believes he is helping lost souls."

Wren snorted. "By making them kill themselves, and each other."

"All faiths call for sacrifice. The Egyptian god Osiris was cut up by his own brother into fourteen pieces before he was reassembled by his wife, which allowed him to become god of the underworld. Jesus died on the cross for all our sins, then walked free of his cave. You know sacrifice for some greater good is and has been accepted by vast numbers of people throughout history."

"Not when it's empty. Not when it's forced."

"I would never argue with that. But your father is an expert manipulator. His efforts have carried this nation to the precipice of self-destruction." Tandrews paused a moment. "I hope that at the center of this infernal triangle you will find not only the truth about your father, where he is and how to bring him down, but also some way to stop the feral spread of his lies."

Wren gritted his teeth. "Medicine Lodge."

"Medicine Lodge, and anything that leads you closer to the source."

26

HEAVEN'S FALL

6:33 a.m., and Kansas City burned below as Wren's jet came in to land. It looked like three large fires were spreading across the urban center, perhaps a mall, the town hall, maybe a vehicle pile-up on I-35. He checked in on his phone for the ALERTS. All were deepfake sightings of Christopher Wren. He watched the fires blazing until the jet banked left for its final descent.

Within minutes they touched down and Wren exited. His onward helicopter was waiting, a white private charter AW 109 seven-seater, pilot already in place, ten-thousand dollars by the hour.

"Where to?" the pilot asked.

He'd logged twin flight plans in advance. Now Tandrews' words echoed in Wren's head. Anything that led you closer to answers, and he knew he'd only get one shot at Medicine Lodge. Better to go in fully armed.

"Northwest," Wren said.

The helicopter took off, barely a five-minute ride over snow-spattered suburbs beneath glowering gray skies, long enough to think about the answers he needed.

Where his father was. Where X was. Why.

At five minutes the United States Penitentiary Leavenworth appeared ahead, looking out of place in the middle of the brown-green Kansan landscape; a Greco-Roman classical construction with tall white stucco columns, capped with an Italianate cupola dome.

USP Leavenworth was a medium-security federal prison nearly two-hundred years old, housing all manner of gang members, white-collar fraudsters, murderers and rapists along with one cult leader who'd done it all: the 'Ancient Guardian' of Heaven's Fall.

The helo put down on the pad inside the fence. A security escort trotted out to meet Wren. In minutes he was standing in the warden's office; all hashed out in advance, with calls to the governor via pressure applied through Rogers' connections; a guest investigator coming in on federal business.

The warden's office was reassuringly traditional: mahogany desk, teak cupboards well-stocked with leather-bound law compendiums, a brass globe, a potted fern. The warden by contrast looked furious. Top of the chain, she sat behind her desk like a dynamo ready to erupt; a broad-shouldered, crewcut woman with an ex-military bearing, effortlessly projecting an authority she no longer had.

"I cannot allow what you're planning," she opened. Pretty much what the governor had said too, when Wren had strong-armed him from the jet. "Any of this. Not you. Not here. Not now. "

Wren was ready for that. "If we don't do this now, we never will. Forget due process, ma'am. By this time tomorrow, America will be in pieces, and I figure there'll be nothing left for you to be warden of."

That broke through. "What are you talking about?"

"Turn on the news. You know about X and the riots. Did you know there's three raging downtown right now? I saw the fires as I landed." He paused a second, reading the woman. She didn't have the fiery eyes of an X-apoc devotee. Just a stickler for the rules. "For the one in city hall, they say I'm holding a tour group of kindergarteners hostage." He paused, looking piercingly at her. "Does that sound about right to you? It doesn't matter. What's real doesn't matter anymore. All that matters is how they feel, and how do you think those X-hatted idiots will feel when they find I'm not actually there? Are they going to turn around and blame X for lying to them, or are they just going to get madder, invent some conspiracy BS about false flag attacks and burn it all down anyway?"

The warden just stared.

"Forget the old rules. They're out the window. All that matters now are results. So put me in there with him. Now."

She gave the order.

In three minutes Wren strode into the maximum security Central Unit of USP Leavenworth. He was greeted by raucous hooting, insults and catcalls from the prisoners, raining down from three tiers of shuttered cells around the common area.

Wren met their wild eyes gladly. Their anger would only make his case faster. He sat down at one of the plastic-encased weld-molded picnic-style tables to wait.

They didn't keep him waiting long. Within a minute metal clanked as gates opened and closed, followed by the sound of shuffling feet, a prisoner in full restraints, handcuffs looped through belly chains to leg irons.

Wren waited as four guards escorted Aloysius Brick, senior Ancient Guardian of the Heaven's Fall cult, around. He was a skinny white guy in his forties, rusty ginger hair in ruffled sheafs atop an acne-bitten head, ears like open car doors, eyes close-set, potbelly working a bulge under his orange jumpsuit. He walked upright and disinterested until he saw Wren's face, then he gave a perfect double take and tried to run.

There was nowhere to go. Not in leg irons with a belly chain. All he achieved was thrashing in the guards' grip like a pillhead raving at a silent disco, and the cheap seats in the cell block tiers loved that. Wren waited as the guards settled Brick into a chair, as the hooting receded, then the two men looked at each other.

"You know me," Wren said, low and steady. "And you're afraid of me. Probably better for you if you hadn't shown that, Aloysius. But you did. Fear will get you every time. Is that why he didn't want you as a recruit?"

Brick's jaw opened, closed, opened again. "I don't know what you're talking about."

Wren gave it a second. Time for him to think about that. "You do. There's only one reason you'd be afraid of me, and that's because you know something about my father. Now you're going to tell me what that is, or it's going to get ugly in here."

Aloysius blinked, trying to get control of himself. "I don't know you. I don't know anything about the Apex."

Wren smiled. "Did I say anything about the Apex?"

It took a second for Brick to realize his mistake. When it hit, he sagged.

"Everything you know, right now," Wren said. "Hold out, I'll have them open up these doors and let the good old boys out. Way I heard it, they sealed your records. Nobody here really knows what you did in Heaven's Gate, so it'll be my parting gift to share the good word. All the kids you abused, Aloysius. I think the shoe'll be on the other foot pretty fast when they get down here, am I right?"

Brick's eyes dilated. Seeing the future and not liking it.

"You wouldn't do that. No way you could. There's systems here, and-"

Wren punched him in the face.

Not too hard. Not enough to break any teeth, his jaw, anything like that. Just enough to get his attention.

Brick rocked in the chair. Spluttered. He looked at the guards, but they didn't make a move to help him. He tried to rub his bloodied lip, but couldn't reach his hands up from the chain.

"One way to stop this from getting a hundred times worse in the next hundred seconds," Wren said. "Tell me everything you know, right now, about the Apex. I know he would've come to you on a recruiting call. There's no way he didn't, you setting up shop in Kansas. Try to bring you into the fold, I expect. It's how he rolls. Tell me about Medicine Lodge."

Brick's eyes widened. "Medicine Lodge?" Sweat raced down his cheeks now, blood stained his white teeth. "You mean, the little town, he…"

"Go on."

"I, uh…"

Wren watched the inner calculation taking place. Who to fear most.

"Eighty seconds. I'm right here, right now. Simple logic. I will make your life unlivable, right now. Help me out, I take him down and whatever gag-order threat he's hung over you disappears."

The decision clicked over. "Not only me," Brick said. "My flock."

Wren frowned. "What, Heaven's Fall? He'll kill them?"

Brick nodded.

"And they're still loyal?"

"Some."

Wren rolled that for half a second. Some cult followers always stayed with their leader no matter how dark it got. "I'll put a security detail on them, I promise. Now tell me about Medicine Lodge."

Brick took a breath, nodded, began. "Your father, he came five years back. It's like you said. Tried to bring us in. Vow loyalty. Talked about bigger things."

"Bigger things like tearing the US apart?"

Brick shifted uncomfortably.

"You were small-time then. He was planting a seed, hoping you'd grow to something bigger." Wren looked at him pointedly. "Lots of other cults went the same way. You've seen them on the news, getting broken. Yours never came to fruition, did it?"

Brick looked down.

"What kind of attack did he have in mind for you?"

"I got hints only," Brick said, wiping the drool off his chin with his shoulder. "Seemed it was religious. Turn people against Christianity. Get me to claim I was the Second Coming."

"Seriously?"

"Why would I make that up?"

Wren grunted. Religion was one fault line the Apex hadn't exploited in his efforts to split the country. Maybe this was evidence he'd wanted to, but it hadn't shaken out. "Vast egotism, maybe. One thing I can tell you, Aloysius, you're no Jesus."

There was a flare of anger in Brick's eyes, but it dwindled fast. "Maybe not."

"No maybe about it. I'm thinking you got too greedy, too fast. Did he sell you out, or did you screw up and get caught all on your own?"

Brick's expression darkened.

"He sold you out," Wren concluded. "OK. Means you weren't professional enough. You were an also-ran, not capable of going national. Some seeds were scattered on fertile soil, some on barren rock. You were a dud." He thought a moment. "So tell me about Medicine Lodge."

"I don't know anything about it."

"I don't believe you."

"Maybe some rumors. Nothing from him. I did my due diligence on the guy. Couldn't just hand my whole life over."

Wren nodded along. Plenty of other cult leaders had done just that. "So what did your due diligence turn up, four years back?"

Silence.

"Forty seconds."

"I put a tracker on his car!" Brick blurted. "One of his visits. One of my team."

Wren frowned. "Your team?"

"Of course. I wasn't stupid. Run a group like mine these days, expect the Feds to swing by. I had my kids in the rocks outside the compound every hour of every day. Any car pulls up, they plant a tracker, doubles as an immobilizer. We don't wait for the government to bring us down. We take the fight to them."

Wren grunted. "You had kids plant immobilizers? You trigger that at the wrong time, it's not just property damage. It's murder."

"I hear you've done worse."

No need to answer that. "So he went to Medicine Lodge. Right after you?" Brick nodded. "This is five years back. Where in Medicine Lodge? I'm hearing it's barely a one-horse town."

"No signal out there. I never retrieved the device. No idea where specifically. Just that he went there."

"And that's it?"

Brick shifted uneasily.

"Ten seconds."

"He had someone in the trunk of his car!" Brick said, then seemed to regret it.

"What?"

"I didn't hear her. The kids did. Told me later. Really spooked them."

Wren frowned. Disgusted, really, to think what this man had done to the people in his charge, but there was no point dwelling on that. "You think he was taking some victim to Medicine Lodge. Like a delivery?"

Brick shrugged. Getting some of his confidence back now. "Who amongst us knows the true darkness of the human heart?"

Wren snorted. "That the garbage you showered your congregation with?"

"All this and more, Christopher Wren. Son of the Apex. I see him in you, you know."

"Yeah," Wren said. "I'm a real chip off the old block."

27

TODAY

By the time Wen strode back into the dawn light outside USP Leavenworth, smoke from the Kansas City fires twenty miles distant had blurred across the wan blue sky like furrows in an old man's brow.

America was burning.

The AW 109 helo was waiting for him in the lot outside the prison walls, but empty. Wren stopped at the cab, looked around. There was no sign of the pilot.

"Where is he?" he asked.

"Pilot is not responding," Hellion answered. "I do not have access to prison video feeds. Whole area is on comms lockdown until you are gone."

Wren grunted. "Did anything get out?"

"Nothing. It has taken much of our infrastructure to block this area, make it invisible. Many bot-nets crunching past communications in and out, like looped camera feed. No ALERTs. Whole prison is silent. This is big success."

Wren wasn't in a celebratory mood. Aloysius Brick's words echoed in his head. Four years back, the Apex had transported a woman in the trunk of his car to Medicine Lodge.

Why?

Tandrews was right about that. The 'why' was everything.

"Agent Sally Rogers has arrived outside Medicine Lodge limits," Hellion prompted. "A strike team is ready. Comms blackout prepared. Can you pilot this helicopter?"

Wren looked around a final time, taking in Leavenworth's classical limestone walls and verdigris cupola dome, like something his namesake architect would have put atop the St. Paul's cathedral in London. A worn baseball diamond for the prisoners off to the left, tree-lined roads with a couple of penitentiary workers' homes across the way, and beyond that just empty fields of grass stretching to the horizon. No sign of the pilot at all, like the land had swallowed him up.

A freak-out, no doubt. He'd seen the spreading smoke, tried his phone and couldn't get a meaningful line out, then panic hit and he ran. Wren was grateful he hadn't taken the helicopter. Maybe some small vestige of order remained, but not for much longer. Property rights would be first to go.

"Can you pilot this helicopter, Christopher?" Hellion repeated.

"Maybe." Wren opened the cab door, took a look inside. The key was in the ignition, the dashboard lit up ready. Standard-looking cyclic, collective, throttle, anti-torque pedals. He'd flown bigger helicopters. Last time he'd been in the cockpit was a year back, when he'd used one like a can-opener to slit Somchai Theeravit's mid-century modern Alaskan mansion open, get to the goodies inside.

He leaned in, tapped the dials. Plenty of fuel. Easily enough to get him to Medicine Lodge, two-hundred-seventy miles distant. Four hours by car, one and a half by air.

He climbed in and started the blades. Within minutes he was at six-thousand feet with the blades at a steep forward angle of attack, all the land spread like a patchwork map below and the smoke of Kansas City fading in back, roaring southwest.

For an hour and a half he barely thought. Watched the navigation computer as it charted his progress. Listened to the odd radio report of riots spreading across the country as fresh ALERTs popped like Russian missile strikes in some grand game of mutually assured destruction.

Like a spell. A triangle his father had etched like some vast hieroglyph across the country, aiming to focus all the pain on Medicine Lodge and turn him into a god.

It didn't matter that none of it was real. Egyptian pharaohs. Afterlives. Slaves that served you forever. What mattered was that people were willing to believe it. And there were always people willing to believe, for a shot at belonging to something bigger than themselves.

He placed a call, routed through the helo's headset, switching off all monitoring from his hackers. The phone on the other end rang. Three times. Four. When it picked up he felt his heart almost stop.

"Yes."

Her voice. Loralei. His wife. A woman he'd loved so fiercely it'd given him the strength to finally leave the CIA behind. Drop the crutches of the past and try to become the family man he'd always aspired to be.

Too late.

"Who is this?" she asked.

Wren tried to speak, but the words wouldn't come.

"Chris?"

Wren crushed the phone to his ear. It killed him that she'd guess that. It killed him more that she didn't sound angry. Maybe concerned. Maybe afraid.

"It's me. Lor."

There was no response for a moment. Wren thought maybe she'd hung up, began to panic, but then he heard it, the distinctive catch of her breath as she tried to disguise tears.

He'd only known her to cry twice in all the time he'd known her. Once when she'd told him she was pregnant with Quinn. Their first child. Tears of happiness, fear, excitement. They'd shared them together, even as they'd gone on for what felt like hours, riding her body in waves. A second time, they hadn't been shared with anyone. They'd been near-silent and alone, and he'd witnessed them like some thief-in-the-night voyeur, through a spy-cam his Foundation had installed in the den of her Delaware duplex.

It hadn't been any kind of moment, as far as Wren could see. No fight with the man she'd taken up with for the last eighteen months. No trouble with the kids. There'd been supper, bath time, bedtime stories. A kiss with the guy, tell him to go on to bed, then she'd gone downstairs to watch TV.

Except she'd never even turned the television on. Just sat on the couch and shook, then those silent sobs had begun. Like she was holding up the weight of the sky all on her own. Like the dam was finally bursting on a year's worth of pain.

Wren had wanted nothing more than to call her then. But it wasn't his place. He'd caused all this, after all. His lies for over a decade. His job. His past. His father. All he could do was watch until it grew too much, then he shut down the cams and left the woman he loved to her own private pain.

All that came rushing back as he heard that muffled sound again now. The joy of their first child. The pain of their separation.

"I'm sorry," he said, the words passing through him like a summer storm. "For everything. For how bad things are now. I'm sorry I let it get so bad, Lor."

Moments passed. Her breathing steadied slightly.

"You're sorry?"

He braced. Expected another tirade. A knife wagged in his face, a demand that he never call again. He had accepted the limit of the restraining order she'd placed against him. He'd do it again, whatever she demanded.

"So much. For all of this. I just... I wanted to-"

Words abandoned him. The truth was so many things. He wanted to hear her voice. He wanted to make promises he didn't know he could keep. He feared all the ways she could crush him again.

"Chris," she went on, "as far as I can see, you're the only one fighting it. I'm watching the news, and the things they're saying about you?" She paused a moment. "I just don't believe it. They're all lies. This X? It's crazy. It's your father. I know that now. I see that. I'm the one who's sorry. I need to-"

She stopped, and Wren felt his heart teetering like he was about to hit aortal flutter, fit to pass out.

"I-" he managed, but couldn't squeeze any more through his tightening windpipe.

"Let me get this out," Loralei pressed on. "It's... I should have given you a chance. Maybe. I don't know. But you're not, ah, who has the words!? I know you're not bad, Chris. I know you love us. Me and the kids. You hurt us so much. But with all this going on, I just..." her breathing grew erratic. Wren felt like he hadn't taken a breath in minutes. The helicopter could be falling from the sky and he wouldn't even notice. "I'd never seen the full size of it. You never told me, so I guess I can blame you for that too." She laughed through the tears.

Wren sucked in a breath, trying to speak.

"Hush!" she ordered, sharp like she'd always been before, when she'd wanted to make him laugh. "Let me finish. Now I see it. How he's coming for you everywhere, coming for us all. Across the whole country, city after city. I can see them marching in the street outside right now! People I know, decent people, they're going crazy. Dressing up in his colors, waving his flag, talking about walking in the fire. It's... I don't know what to do." She sucked in a gulp of air. "The kids are inside. We're all safe, but who knows, really? This is bigger than any of us. If one of their mobs hit this neighborhood, I know there's nothing I could say or do to stop them. We'd be helpless. They'll burn us alive and think they're saving us. This is way bigger than you or me, and now I see it always was. The Apex, right? He sent me that email at the start, he's the one who broke your cover. He shattered us. He did this. And I was so mad at you, I never once thought why."

Wren's eyes blurred with tears. Couldn't help it. Felt like an incredible weight was lifting off his shoulders.

"That bastard!" Loralei said with unexpected vigor. "Now I see he wanted you isolated. Ineffective. I never listened, I was too hurt, and you've lots still to answer for, but I know you're still the Chris I knew. That agent, Sally Rogers, she told me you'd let her take you in, put you in that CIA prison." A pause. "That's the right thing, Chris. It means you weren't ever as bad as I feared. So now I wish I'd given you that chance. To explain. To make it right. I wish I hadn't let him manipulate us. So I'm sorry for that."

Wren couldn't believe what he was hearing. Finally found his voice. "You don't have to be sorry. It was all me. I should've-"

"You're damn right you should've!" Loralei snapped, followed by pained laughter. "We'll talk about that plenty, don't you worry. If anybody's sorry here, it's you. You screwed up with us so bad, Chris. But I see it now. All this X stuff, I get it. What you were up against. What was driving you." A pause. "I want you home."

That was a punch in the heart. Ten seconds passed. Twenty, more, and he couldn't breathe. Everything he'd hoped for, and it had only taken the imminent end of American civilization to bring it on.

"I'll get you," he finally settled on. "I'll send my best people. They'll pick you up now. The kids. The guy too, if you want. Ship you securely out of there. It's all going to fall apart, Lor. I'm trying to stop it, but…"

"I know you are, honey."

That 'honey' broke him further.

"There's a place," he went on, desperate to get the words out while he still could. "The safest place I've got, maybe the safest in the country. It's called Little Phoenix. It's a kind of headquarters for my Foundation. Remote, reinforced, capable of independent living even if the world around it goes mad. I trust everyone there implicitly. You'll be safe."

Now she was crying again. "We'll go. We're waiting, Chris. Just do what you need to do. End this as soon as you can, and come home."

He squeezed his eyes tight shut, gritted his teeth like he was bulling through the worst torture he'd ever felt in his life, like he was back in the Apex's pit staring down the barrel of emptiness forever.

"I will. I love you, Lor. Tell the kids. My people will come for you soon."

He hung up. Couldn't take anymore, not and still focus on the job ahead. The work to be done.

The tears dried in his eyes. His breathing grew under control. He gave the order through Teddy for an urgent pick-up from Frederica, Delaware. His wife, his kids, and the guy too. Then he issued the ruling wider. All points evacuation to Little Phoenix, Arizona. The last safe place in America. Hunker down and try to weather the oncoming storm.

By the time it was all done, he was back in the headspace he needed to be. Dead brown fields ripping by below. Rogers and a team waiting up ahead. Medicine Lodge fifty miles further. The dashboard clock clicked over past 9 a.m.. A weather warning slid up on his phone, said a heavy snowstorm was brewing over southern Kansas.

It was all going to end today, one way or the other.

28

FATHERS

Wren brought the helicopter in low over barren fields shorn of grain sorghum, wheat or soy for the winter, like echoes of the Iowa farm. Southern Kansas, close to the Oklahoma border and flatter than an ice rink, almost as sparsely populated as the surface of the moon.

Wren felt it in his gut. The dry cold in the air buffeting through the slitted cockpit window. No Interstates within a hundred miles, no railroads, no real airports. Quiet fields, big sky turning black with the gathering storm, small towns. A vision of another world, like the clock had wound back to the Wild West and any minute he'd see cowpoke rustlers pushing a cattle train across the great plains, Wild Bill Hickock surging out with his lawmen, Wyatt Earp following up with a jail stagecoach.

Intermittent structures flew by below. Ruined homesteads and storm-battered old barns, showing Bleeding Kansas' history as a Civil War-era holy grail. Chase that with decades of sharecroppers tilling life from the clay soil, then rip it all up with the great Dustbowl, as mass migration West left family lands to be swallowed up by the big banks, handed off to become the current system of factory farms.

Now there was only the occasional vast tractor squatted beside a field like an alien dropship, enormous plow spreading like an iron river delta, broad enough to do the work that once took thousands of men. Immense tin sheet barns stood clumped at the center of vast networks of fields, fringed by green fern-like sprays of coppicing; trees sprung up around shallow curling arroyos.

The history of America written in the scars of the land.

9:40 a.m., and Wren glimpsed his team up ahead as blots of color beneath the glowering sky. A white semi-trailer parked at the desolate side of the road, ten miles out of Medicine Lodge, with Sally Rogers at the front by a Ford F-150, her vehicle of choice, branded in blue and silver. Impressive work for a rip-off sprayed up by his junkyard mechanic Alli, flown in specially out of Arizona.

He put the helicopter down by the truck, killed the engine and took the keys, then ducked out of the cockpit as the blades wound down. Agent Sally Rogers strode across the low mound of raw dirt at the side of the road toward him, looking every bit the part.

Pale blue shirt with shoulder straps, embossed metal insignia studded through the collars, navy tie tucked in at the third button down, silver badge on the left shirt pocket, gear strap worn like a bandolier, Glock 19 at her hip, navy pants with a powder blue ribbon sewn down the outside, and to cap it all off, a broad-brimmed Stetson cap almost completely obscuring her straw-blond hair.

A Kansas Highway Patrolwoman, no two ways about it.

"Boss," she said, and her intonation along with the pale cast of her face said it all. The same vertigo sense of teetering over a vast drop that he'd been feeling for a week now. America in free fall.

"It's good to see you, Sally," he said, and that landed harder than he'd expected, brief emotions splashing across her face before the professional mask reset. He never called her Sally. "I wouldn't want anyone else with me for this. Thank you for coming."

If anything she turned paler. Regardless, the hand she held out to shake was rock steady. "I wasn't going to at first," she said. "I felt sure we had this. The riots, upheaval, X." She raised her arms, gestured around. "On TV, from Langley, even seen from a crowd control helicopter, everything looks different. You mistake chaos for an outlier, mistake order for something inevitable, like it's our natural state." Her eyes took on a faraway look. "But it's not, is it?"

Wren didn't say anything. Figured the question was rhetorical, something she'd share if she needed.

"I talked to my folks, Chris," she said. She rarely called him Chris, either. Seemed they were both feeling it. "My dad joined them." Her voice caught.

"My mom was in pieces. She'd been holding out on contacting me, didn't want to 'worry me'. Apparently he left the house way before dawn, when one of those flash mobs was called. He's seventy-three, Chris. Now he's out rioting somewhere in Poughkeepsie. It's..."

She trailed off. Wren put a hand on her shoulder. Strong, but she was shaking for all that. His cue.

"It's not his fault."

"That's just it," Rogers said, and now Wren saw the anger burning through. If she was shaking with anything, it was rage. "It is his fault. It's mine and my mom's too. He's been spouting off about X for months, trying to convince us to 'save our souls' before it was too late. I pushed back some, figured that he'd have his fill of it soon, figured it was mostly harmless crackpot nonsense, but maybe I just told myself that. Like a cancer, you know? It's easier to ignore the warning signs than dig in for chemotherapy."

Wren grunted. About all the response she needed. There'd be time for recriminations later.

Rogers shrugged. "Yeah. Truth is, he's always been one for conspiracy theories. I used to find it amusing. Not so much, now. He shoved my mom aside, apparently. Took his rifle. He's still a crack shot, used to be a Navy marksman. This X BS, it's..." she trailed off, bit her lip, firmed up her demeanor. "It's dangerous. Lethal. I can't believe he did that to himself, but then I can. It's our job, right? Warding off self-radicalization, the new vector for terror, and we're all responsible. All of us who humored him, looked the other way." She took a breath. "Now my mom's home alone, terrified at every loud noise, watching black X flags parade by in the street. I've tried calling my dad, he's not answering. I'm thinking any minute I'll see him on the news."

Wren nodded. "You're furious. I get it. And you're not sure who to be angry with."

She laughed, almost lost control but caught it. "You're damn right I'm mad. But place the blame where it lays, I say. Your father's at the root of all this. No offense. That's why I'm here."

"No offense taken. Your father needs help, Sally, just like any cult devotee. My father needs a long fall from a short rope. Right now we focus on only that." He pointed off in the direction of Medicine Lodge, where the storm skies were darkest. "You're going to be my face in there, my voice, my eyes. We have to play this right. Spook this town, it'll snap shut like a mantrap. We need something from these people..." He took a breath, looked off to the side. "Hellion, Medicine Lodge is on a comms blackout?"

"It is," she answered sharply in his ear. "Invisible. ALERTs blocked. Incoming and outgoing calls spoofed. It is energy intensive, but we are spreading the burden. This should last several hours before it is noticed."

Wren looked back to Rogers. "Several hours. He's here, Rogers. Final hurdle. Let's dig the bastard out."

Rogers nodded sharply. Call that properly motivated.

She started toward the F-150, painted in its Highway Patrol colors; better than unmarked FBI for rolling in and asking questions of small-town folk. Take national politics off the table. They'd be less likely to close ranks. Wren had prepped the cover story, too. They had a photo of the Apex not publicly shared, not sought for any crime, nothing that should activate any X recognition, and a cover story with him as a potential victim of wire fraud. It should be enough to bypass any X BS long enough to get some answers.

Wren followed Rogers over. She popped the lid of a large equipment box, dug out a second Highway Patrol uniform and held it out.

"I doubt it's your size."

"Maybe not the hat," Wren quipped.

Rogers briefly cracked a smile. "You have got a big head. Come on."

Wren chuckled, changed there at the roadside. The navy pants almost split at the thigh, but that was fine, his job was mostly to sit in the car and keep his head down. The shirt barely buttoned across his chest, but the tucked-in tie covered that up. The hat fit well in the end, perfectly shading his face.

Last he looked to the team. They'd been spun up on a dime, standing now by the semi and fully kitted out for tactical suburban warfare. Doona, Henry, Mason despite his various broken bones, plus Abigail and Luke, who'd helped save Steven Gruber back in their battle with the Ghost. Abigail was a brilliant triathlete and cult survivor, Luke was an ex-State Congressman who'd been kicked out of office for taking bribes. Alli slouched nearby with spray-paint burn on her dungarees, looking surly as ever.

That cheered Wren up. He strode over, shook hands, patted shoulders, gave encouragement.

"You look like a dead dog on a stick," Alli said. Wren beamed. Half her head was shaved close, the other half was bleached blond in a topknot, and there were numerous jeweled piercings in her face.

"I feel like it. You look like a badly inlaid brooch."

She laughed, punched him in the shoulder. Same old Alli. "Great work on the Ford," he said. "I'd never spot it's a fake."

Alli looked offended. "It's not a fake. Same model of Ford, exact same paint the Stateys use, exact same spec. Ther own mechanics wouldn't know the difference."

Wren beamed. With a team like this, how could they fail?

Henry was waiting with a serious look on his face. "On your order, Corporal. We'll be there in minutes."

Wren nodded. Looked over his select team a moment longer. There weren't a lot of them, next to what the Apex had to be packing. A handful only. But he wouldn't trade them for the world.

"I know it. Godspeed to us all."

Rogers climbed into the F-150's driver's seat, kicked open the passenger door and Wren stepped in after her. She hit the gas and pulled onto the road leading toward the heart of it all.

29

MEDICINE LODGE

They entered Medicine Lodge from the north on Well Road, driving in silence into a flycatcher grid of generous grass-laid blocks, each filled with a handful of spacious ranch-style family homes.

Picket fences. Well-groomed yards. White-painted stones lining a row of old-growth elms. No snow on the ground, though the forecast said the storm was imminent, with mottled dark clouds yawning overhead, like some great beast ready to bite down and scoop this town, this state off the face of the Earth.

"Looks like my hometown," Rogers murmured, weaving toward South Main Street.

Wren said nothing. Maybe this *was* his hometown, or at least his father's. Everything about it spoke of ease, tradition and comfort, though he felt none of that. The X icon was everywhere, on black flags hung from windows, on lawn signs, on truck decals. A woman walking her dog had a cap emblazoned with a bejeweled X.

"They're crazy," Rogers muttered, tracking the woman briefly. Even the dog wore an X on its doggy jacket. "Like it's the World Series."

Wren focused on his breathing, on managing stray flickers of vertigo.

Rogers made the turn onto Main Street. It was a broad red-brick paved expanse laid out like a cowboy town of old, enough for four lanes abreast though there were no markings. No need. Barely half-a-dozen vehicles troubled the thoroughfare, cruising slow like old-time stagecoaches.

Tall federal-style townhouses spotted the avenue, stark red brick fronts decorated with sharp white chevrons, hosting the lawyer, the town's one fancy restaurant, the bank. Rogers slow-rolled like they were cruising johns. Interspersed amongst the older structures were newer, stubbier buildings with Old-West false fronts like a long line of saloons.

An auto shop. Internet services. A place with only 'TREASURES' written in whitewash on the window. Plenty more X symbols.

"Up here," Wren said, nodding toward a place called 'Larks', the town's only breakfast diner.

Rogers pulled in easy. No siren. She killed the engine and turned to him, they exchanged a look, then she stepped out. Closed the door, took a few steps, spoke. "You hear me?"

"Loud and clear," Wren answered, receiving through his earpiece.

"Getting video?"

Wren tapped his phone to activate it, set the screen low on the dash and saw from Rogers' bodycam. "Got it."

"Then in I go."

She turned and walked up to the Larks' entrance, Wren tracking her. Looked like 50s diner style inside. Lots of chrome, baby blue bar, glossy red Bakelite two- and four-tops, neon signage in back. The door pushed open and Wren split his attention to the bodycam footage.

The diner had black and white tile flooring, mirrors in back, a gleaming soda fountain next to a cake rack. Real retro. There were two customers sitting along the bar, both tucking into blueberry waffle mounds, one of them wearing a black sweater with large white X's hand-painted on the arms. Rogers stiffened slightly. The guy had his phone right there on the bar; useless for calling in an ALERT, with Hellion's comms blackout in place, but all he had to do was run out on the street and shout it out, that ought to do the job.

Wren itched to warn Rogers, though of course she'd know to play this thing below the radar. Paramount to all of this was not turning the town into a mantrap.

Wren studied the guy as Rogers kept on toward the bar, not breaking stride. He looked thirties, burly. He glanced briefly as Rogers came by, then turned back to the TV in the corner, showing the fires in Kansas City. Maybe waiting for the call from X to come.

Behind the bar stood a sun-weathered woman with straw-blond hair, maybe late fifties, white apron over denim shirt, long dangly earrings, polishing glasses while idly watching the news.

"Help you, hon?" she asked with a true Kansan drawl.

"I'd kill for some good old cream soda," Rogers said, and Wren imagined her flashing a smile, "but maybe when I'm done here. For now I'll just take a coffee, black, plenty of cream."

The woman smirked, nodded in Wren's direction through the glass. "Take your coffee like you take your men?"

Rogers laughed low, just girls sharing a little smack talk. "That one's a rookie. Disgraced himself one town back, started talking up the Wildcats, Kansas State."

The lady blew air out of her lips, flipped a cup, expertly hoisted a chrome coffee pot and started the pour. "Them's killing words out here. What town were you last?"

"Harper. Blackwell before that. And it ain't barely ten yet."

The coffee sloshed satisfyingly, followed by an unhealthy dose of cream from a huge tin pitcher. "They sure keep you Stateys busy. Anyone knows the South, they know we're for Barclay. Maybe a small college, but they're religious, got fight."

Rogers smiled, raised the coffee mug like she was saluting. "I hear that, ma'am. Except last I heard, Barclay's got no football program. Soccer, they have. Basketball. Maybe that's what you mean."

The lady grinned. Wren hadn't done the research, hadn't even realized that was a test. "You ain't disgraced yourself yet, girl. How's that coffee?"

"Beats Harper hands down," Rogers said, smooth as hot licorice. "Now, Blackwell I'm yet to try, but I'll be sure to share notes."

"Ask them tightwad bastards for cream, they'll give you spit and shoeshine for your trouble."

Rogers laughed. "The old boy in the Main-Street diner there, he didn't look too friendly. More like a bobcat waiting to strike."

The lady laughed. Held out a hand. "Name's Linda. I seen that old fella. I don't often head out that far, but they got the mall. He has a real wily look."

"The good Lord treats some men mean and keeps the rest keen," Rogers said smooth, then shot a glance to Wren. "Others he just hits with the stupid stick all the way down."

Linda cackled.

"All right now," Wren said low, but Rogers ignored him, took Linda's hand and shook.

"Sally Rogers," she said. "Field Supervisor, pulled rookie-training duty all this month."

Linda nodded at Wren. Both seemed to be enjoying this. "He's watching you real close, that one. Intense, like. You got him the whole month?"

Rogers sighed. "He's first place in a carousel of hard-chargers. Or that's what they think, anyhow. What a ball-ache."

"Men," Linda lamented.

"Amen to that."

Rogers took another glug, smacked her lips. Wren began to wonder if she was ever going to get to the point.

"So what brings you to Medicine Lodge, Sally?" Linda asked. "Especially with this storm about to blow overhead. You best not get out of town too far, they say it's a bad one, gonna dump ten inches of snow in three hours."

Rogers whistled low. "How about that? I guess this'll keep. Fact is, we had a BOLO a few days back, track and find, but it's not urgent." She took a look meaningfully around; at the guy with the X arms, at a small X badge on Linda's apron. "Seems you're all good folks here, though, you have this town in hand. I'll just write it up. It's a cold trail anyhow."

Wren glanced over at the guy by the counter. He wasn't looking at Rogers. He was staring directly at Wren.

"You say that, hon, but we got our weirdoes here too," Linda said low, leaning in. "Folks who don't know which side of the egg's got the yellow, you get my drift?" She paused a long moment. "You hunting a murderer?"

Rogers laughed. "That'd be something. Nope. It's training-wheels time, caught a bad traffic stop on a stolen vehicle outside Wichita, led to some further fraud charges. You'd think with all this going on," she gestured to the TV, "they'd have us on something bigger, but the State's split on which way it's going to flip, if it comes to that."

Linda nodded thoughtfully. "And you?"

"Oh, no question," Rogers said. "Like I said, I see only good folks here. I'm a patriot. State police ought to be pulling for what's right."

Rogers glugged more coffee. Linda seemed to be coming to some kind of decision. Opened her mouth to speak, but Rogers beat her to it.

"Fact is, we've got the guy who lost his truck, know he's been associated hereabouts, but nothing concrete. We need to check in, let him know the goods are recovered and be sure he's not getting defrauded further. Simple as that."

Linda licked her lips. Maybe starting to believe this wasn't X-related, maybe worth homing in on for some good gossip. "You got a name, a photo of the guy?"

"No name, but a bad photo. You sure it's no trouble?"

Linda was practically salivating. "If anyone in this town knows, it'll be me. I been here all my life, run this place thirty years."

The camera shuffled as Rogers pulled out the doctored photo of the Apex, digitally shifted from Keller's campaign stage to a standard white backing, like a DMV mug shot. Even a hardcore X-apoc wouldn't know who it was, judging from the X videos of him as a much younger man.

"Here's the guy. He's kind of a looker, for an older fella."

Linda took the photo. There was something for a second, some kind of stray knowledge fleeting in the depths and rippling across her face, but it disappeared fast. Wren thought for a second she was going to clam up completely, but that's not what happened.

"That guy, he's bad news." Linda pushed the photo away like it was poison oak. "I never met him, barely even seen him, but folks know. You say he was a victim of carjacking?"

Another test. Rogers played it perfectly. She'd never said carjacking. "Unknown at this point. Some delinquents in a car registered to him, is all I know, routine traffic stop." Her head tilted slightly. "Why, you think I need to be careful? Maybe he's mixed up in this fraud too, not just the victim?"

Linda nodded wisely. Another test passed. "I bet you always are careful. But you go looking for that man, I reckon you bring more than a rookie with you, y'hear?" She leaned away. "I wouldn't bother, though. He ain't been through town in years, least I know."

Sally nodded, folded the photo back into her breast pocket. "Well, any idea where he moved on to? These itinerants, mayhap non-believers, they're a plague. One minute they're greasing fools for their pension, the next they're locking kids up in the basement, starting a livestream."

Linda's eyes widened slightly. Another great play. Offload the responsibility to some other town. Raise the stakes at the same time, but in a totally different direction, just following up on what she'd already said.

"A livestream?"

Rogers nodded toward the TV. "You see how it is out there. What people will do these days just to get their kicks. It takes good folks standing up to set things like that straight."

Wren had to admire that. A masterful piece of work. Feeding into the X madness and letting Linda fill in the gaps, letting the guy in the X-shirt know she was no threat, even figure they were all on the same side.

"You're right on the money there. Well, last I heard, that man headed west. He was tied up with some church out that way. First Corinthians, I think."

"I don't know it."

"You wouldn't. It burned down some, oh, three years back? They had charitable projects through the area, though, a roaming ministry, as I heard it, but not anymore. I ain't seen him in years, like I say."

"Sounds all the better for you." Rogers took another glug of her coffee, knocking the rest of it back. "Well, I've got a good start on my report here, I figure. Thank you, ma'am."

Linda looked uncertain. Maybe already suspecting she'd said too much, cooperated too easily. "You ain't gonna put my name in your report, are you?"

"Are you kidding, and end up sharing this coffee with the other Stateys?" Rogers grinned. "Not a chance this side of the almighty's fire, Linda."

Linda smiled. "Well, you stay safe out there, Sally. It's strange times, what with the storm coming and all. Of course I don't just mean the weather."

"I hear that, and it surely is," Rogers closed, tipped her Stetson then looked around to the man with the X on his arms. "Y'all stay safe here."

The guy's gaze followed her out, then lingered on Wren until she got behind the wheel and pulled away.

30

FIRST CORINTHIANS

"Hit on the first try," Wren said. "What are the odds?"

"In a small town?" Rogers asked, rolling slowly south on Main Street. "Pretty good."

Wren nodded. Small towns, everyone knew everyone else. The human record went long, and the diner was always a center. Right alongside the bar, if the town had one, and the church; the real storehouses of a place's oral history. Not the things that went in the books or appeared in the paper, nothing so tectonic. This was the language of impressions, slights, grudges and generational feuds. Tap into that and a waterfall of knowledge would pour out.

"First Corinthians," came Hellion's voice in Wren's ear. "I can find no record of this church."

"Figures," Wren said, then turned to Rogers. "You did great, by the way."

Rogers looked at him, flashed an almost cheeky smile. "I've got moves. You seen all the X stuff in there? They love them some craziness."

"Cancer spreads from the middle," Wren said low. "No mirrors in a place like this, no different folks to reflect you back in a different light, show up the crazy."

"Cancer," Rogers repeated, then brightened. "There were plenty of mirrors in that place, though. About every surface was chrome."

Wren snorted. "Not really what I meant, but point taken."

They pulled up to an intersection, where an old guy was doddering slowly across the street aided by a walking frame. Rogers blipped her sirens briefly, gave him a neighborly wave. They waited.

"So, five years back," Rogers said. "Coincidence, or you think she saw our guy, ferrying some victim in the trunk of his car, as per Aloysius Brick?"

Wren thought back to Brick in the Penitentiary, eyes going misty as he remembered the 'good old days' of Heaven's Fall. "It's never a coincidence with the Apex. I think your girl Linda knows more than she's saying. But we can't force it."

Rogers nodded. "That guy at the bar had a hard-on for you. Maybe he knows something too."

Wren shrugged. "State troopers. Maybe he got a sense who I might be. Through two layers of glass, though, wrong outfit, hat shading my face, I think we have some leeway. And if First Corinthians leads nowhere, we come back and pump him like a fire hydrant for all he knows."

The old guy cleared the crossing. Rogers gave a thank you blip of the sirens.

"So where to? Drive west, looking for burned-out old churches?"

"Sounds about right to me. Hellion?"

"I am completing scan of west region, Medicine Lodge," came her Russian-accented voice in his ear. "I see what must be burned church. Drive west, Sally Rogers, I will direct you."

"Gotta love an eye in the sky," Rogers muttered under her breath, and pulled right.

The townhouses and false fronts of Main Street swiftly bled back to ranch-style homes, which soon became nothing but grass, trees and fields, their winter colors muted further by the black sky. Hellion directed them on a few turns heading further from the beaten track, circling around outcroppings of robinia and birch trees grown up around curlicue arroyos; signs of water turning on flat soil as it tried to find a level.

Ten minutes passed, twenty. They rode through fields, now, fenced-off for cattle. The grass was close-shorn, and large yellow hay bales stood like watchmen surrounded by chewing cows.

"To the right, in this field," Hellion said.

Rogers pulled up on the verge. They both looked out over a field of stubbled grass. "I'm not seeing anything," she said.

"Do you see those trees?" Hellion asked. "Clustered around small stream. Church is within the center."

Wren pushed the door open, started out into the chilly air. Felt like the temperature had dropped well below twenty degrees in the last hour. There was the faint hint of a gravel track spreading forward through the level grass, but clearly disrupted and picked over by four years of grazing. A path to the church. He straddled the fence and started on a beeline for the trees through a gathering of cows, Rogers following close behind.

"You should know, there is movement back in Medicine Lodge," Hellion said in his ear.

The cold air stung Wren's cheeks, burned his throat. Still healing from smoke inhalation back in D.C.. "What kind of movement?"

"The man in the diner, he is gathering others. They are armed."

Wren cursed low. "How many?"

"Four so far. They are all X-apoc, Christopher. They wear this openly on their clothing."

Another curse. "Have they tried to trigger an ALERT?"

"Not yet. I will block it if they do. I cannot predict further, but this man certainly heard your current destination. Perhaps they will come. You should be fast."

Wren wasn't worried about that. In a firefight with civilians, he liked his and Rogers' chances two against four. It could even be a blessing in disguise. Out here in the middle of nowhere was the perfect place to run a no-holds-barred interrogation. But many more than four, and if they were all armed? That might be a problem.

"Put the team on alert, send them circling this way. If there's more than four, we'll bring them in. Otherwise, just give us the head's up when they're near."

"Now there are five."

Rogers laughed.

"OK, so we hurry," Wren said, and started to run.

The gravel crunched. The cows parted as they neared, lowing loudly. Thirty seconds later they hit the tree line. Tight-knit trash saplings had woven thick around a few tall robinia trees, between them hiding a shallow trough in the grass; the path of rainwater curling like a crop circle. Wren pushed through, stepped over the dried-up waterway, passed another veil of low saplings into a green-encircled clearing, and there it was.

"Holy moly," Rogers said by his side.

As a church there wasn't much of it left. A few wall risers where the damp ground had seeped up and tamped down the flames, no higher than Wren's shoulder, fire-bitten edges rounded by five years of rain. The remnants were black but showed through hints of silver birch underneath. The wooden flooring was a fire-ravaged pit, and at the center where the blaze must have raged hottest was a jagged ring of soil showing, sprung up with weeds, ferns and more spidery robinia, straining for the sun.

Wren strode closer. Around that inner ring of soil some floorboards remained, scorched but saved by how snugly fitted they were to each other. Looked like expert craftsmanship, even holding together still. Scattered atop the boards and slurried at the edges was a papier-mâché paste of old wood pulp, interspersed with the dull blue and black of leather Bible bindings. In places the hollowed-out frames of chairs remained, black with char and tumbled where the fire's draft had swept them.

Rogers cursed.

Wren stepped through the entrance, little more than the ten-inch stubs of a doorway to either side. Underfoot a mosaic of oxidized steel roof tiles slid uneasily. Off to the right lay the crumpled church tower, the most intact part of the structure remaining. Half in the arroyo, the top portion appeared to have survived the fire unharmed. Silver birch, red roof shingles, square box design leading up to a copper cross, one of its arms embedded in the earth.

Wren pointed. "Strange nobody came for the cross."

"Strange they just left all this here," Rogers countered. She stepped over the wall and stood in the midst of a heap of charred furniture, holding up what looked to be a moss-sodden yellow jacket.

Wren frowned, stepped closer. "That wasn't in any fire."

Rogers shook it, handed it over. Wren handled the jacket, opened it up. Moss shook free, maybe a few years' worth of growth. In places the yellow was faded, but in the folds where it had been lying upon itself the fabric was bright still.

"You think it's hers?" Rogers asked. Didn't need to say any more than that; they both knew who she meant. The girl in the Apex's car five years back.

Wren surveyed the rest of the church, mind racing to the contents of Paul's first Epistle to the Corinthians. As far as he remembered, it was a message to the people about immorality, focusing on division amongst the people, sexual impurity and the doctrine of Christ's resurrection. In particular, though this portion was considered by some to be a latter-day addition, there was a section mandating the silence and subordination of women at church.

A melting pot of ideologies, just like Tandrews had said.

"Maybe," Wren said, casting his gaze wider, holding up the jacket. "Why else would this be here?"

He looked past the low saplings in the center, to the fore where the altar lay on its edge, hardwoods only partially burned, to the edges, over the slippery roof tiles and the rain-matted wattle of Bibles, leaflets and hymnals.

"Could be kids," Rogers hazarded. "It's a great place to make out."

"I don't think it's kids. Look around. The whole place feels staged somehow."

"How so?"

"There's no other trash," Wren began, scouring the floorboards. "No beer bottles, cans, cigarette butts, plastic bags, graffiti. If it was kids, this place'd be a dumping ground."

"That is strange," Rogers allowed.

Wren strode up to the burst of saplings in the center. They caught a narrow halo of light directly from above. The rest of the church lay in shadow, but not here. Had the tower been erect, it would have caught that sunlight on its spire most of the day.

He toed the earth at the edge of the floorboards, where the firmly slotted wood gave way to soil, and felt a wash of vertigo rushing over him. The line was clearly demarcated, not worn away into crumbly charcoal as he'd expected.

"These boards didn't burn in this pattern," he said and looked up, sending dual visions battling across Rogers' face. "This close together, they'd never incinerate so perfectly. They were cut."

Rogers stared. "Cut?"

There wasn't much more to say. From a top down view, you couldn't tell which parts of a pyramid were which. He pointed off to the side, where the turret and its cross lay unbroken. "Apex." He pointed at the dirt by his feet. "Tomb."

Rogers paled. "You think she's buried right here?"

Wren was already rolling up his sleeves. "Only one way to find out."

31

YELLOW JACKET

They wrapped sharp-edged roof slates in their Highway Patrol jackets and dug. The metal cut clean, but given the near freezing temperature, it took time to chip into the hard soil. Minutes passed as Wren chopped through wiry sapling roots, Rogers battering out divots beside him. Inches at first, giving way painstakingly to a foot of clearance.

"Seventeen X-apoc," Hellion said abruptly in his ear. "All armed. They are coming in five vehicles."

Wren laughed. "Seventeen?"

"This is correct, Christopher. They are serious."

No doubt. Seventeen was too many, maybe even for his whole squad. Still, if the 42% number was accurate, then seventeen was just the tip of the iceberg.

"Too many," Rogers said. "Even if they're all raw civilians, never been out on the range, and I doubt that. They'll have trained, as per the X app. We'll be over-run."

"Twenty minutes yet," Wren answered, and kept on digging. Everything could change in that kind of time. "Are the team in position to intersect?"

"They are still en route to you," Hellion answered, "perhaps twenty minutes also."

Wren laughed again. "Give us a proximity alert. Their job is to hold these idiots off, not engage in a mass shootout. No unnecessary risks."

"Understood."

The slate-shovels rose and fell. Wren's slate cracked and he swept up another. His shoulders burned from the vibrations, the healing wounds in his palms ached with every dropped blow. Digging a pit down to the foundations.

Five minutes. Ten. A cloud passed over the sun above, sending shivers up Wren's spine. Moments later a single flake of snow drifted down to rest on the hard pack undersoil.

Rogers laughed.

"Faster," Wren said.

More snow fell. They took it in turns to scoop out the hole, a three-stroke motion like a rail-tacking team, laying the beam down, setting the tie, hammering it home. Chop. Chop. Sweep.

Several feet deep already, several wide, hammering like a twin cylinder two-stroke engine, up then down.

"They are one minute out," Hellion said.

"Our team or theirs?" Wren grunted between strokes.

"Both."

He hammered deeper, like he was digging a route back to the past. The sound came of approaching engines.

"They are beside your vehicle. Henry's team are ahead, circling in behind tree cover."

"Hurry your ass up, Henry," Wren commanded, sent another downward stroke, and this one hit metal with a clang.

He looked up at Rogers. She dropped her slate and started clearing the dirt with shaking hands. A small patch of tarnished tin emerged.

"Here," she said, pointing at a thick knot of roots and earth. Wren brought the slate down with all his strength and mass. The root network cleaved clean through, a five-inch chunk of soil broke off like an iceberg calving, and Rogers lifted it, tossed it aside. "Here," she pointed to another likely spot, and Wren brought the slate down again. She turfed and cleared, dug around in the loose shale.

"I can feel the edge," she said, then pointed again.

"They are coming up the field," Hellion warned. "Henry is asking to engage."

"Fire to draw them off us," Wren commanded, slammed the slate down. "Do not get shot. Avoid aiming to kill, if you can. Don't expose yourselves."

"Understood, Corporal," came Henry's sharp response.

The first shot rang out. A wild chance fired through the tree cover which ripped a hole in one of the church's low standing walls.

"Henry," Wren urged, brought the slate down again.

"Incoming," Henry answered, followed by the incredible crack of his M25 firing an M118 Special Ball. "One down, should be non-fatal."

After that the air became a storm of bullets, gunshots sounding like a ceaseless roll of thunder, slugs tearing through the trees and shredding the church walls.

"Keep their heads down," Wren barked into the chaos. "Just buy us time."

"Yes, sir," said Henry, and another Special Ball crack rang out, this time echoed by a substantial explosion. Had to be Henry finding the range of their vehicles' fuel tanks.

Wren and Rogers worked throughout like an artillery loading team, her targeting, him letting rip with the slate.

"X-apoc are trying to press ALERT," Hellion said. "I am blocking actively."

The slab of metal was exposed on one corner and down most of one side now, looked at least three feet long and maybe the same wide, maybe a third of it cleared. "Tell me they're not getting through," Wren said.

"Comms blackout remains, but now they see this. Our spoof response is giveaway. I have them radioing on shortwave, perhaps out of blackout zone."

Wren cursed, brought the slate down, Rogers cleared it. "Reinforcements. You can't block shortwave?"

"I cannot, Christopher. This will get out."

The ALERT would escape. The flash mob would come.

"I'm hit!" came Doona's voice.

Wren brought the slate down so hard it bit back through his jacket-grip, slitting into his palm. He cursed, reared back and looked through the screen of trees. Beyond the green he could loosely pick out the row of silhouettes advancing steadily, a floodtide of X-apoc maybe fifty feet out.

"Get her out of here, Mason. Henry, kill their vehicles and go."

"Retreating," Mason answered. "Get out too, Christopher."

"Boss," Rogers shouted, jerking his attention back down. "Help me."

He looked. She had her fingers pried tight under the corner of the metal cover. He swiftly repositioned, wedged his fingers under the lip beside her with his legs coiled, then together they strained. Half the cover was still coated with several foots' worth of soil and saplings, maybe a half-ton of mass embedded in the wider root system.

"Heave!" Rogers commanded, and they heaved. Wren's legs burned as he fought through the deadlift, breath coming in sharp pants and vision swirling with bright colors as bright white roots popped out of the soil like straining stitches.

Not enough.

"They are twenty yards out," came Hellion's voice.

"Now or never, Corporal!" Henry shouted from in back. Wren chanced a glance, saw Henry hunkered down by the church turret.

"Heave!" Rogers ordered again, and they both lifted with all their strength, legs thrusting, arms drawn to the limit. The metal sheet lifted some three inches, soil tilting to the edge and roots spraying like snapped elastic bands.

"They are on you!" Hellion shouted, matched by a crack from Henry's M25. Wren was distantly aware of a man falling back through the screen of trees, head exploded. More were coming. Everything looked red.

"Heave," Rogers ordered once more, and he gave it everything he had.

Now the whole ground hoisted up with a dislocating wrench, and Wren staggered forward as it tipped, almost stepped into the shallow pit beneath, instantly lightheaded as the pressure came off. Rogers caught him, another Special Ball rang out, then she had her Glock up and was joining Henry in fending off an incoming wave.

Wren was left staring into the pit alone. Maybe five inches deep at the edges, though it deepened sharply toward the center. Within lay the contents, like some kind of ancient display case ornately laid out in a museum. No mistaking what he was seeing.

Yellow-white human bones laid out in an inverted triangle. Perfectly aligned. The bones of both legs; femurs, tibias and fibulas made up the two downward-angled sides. The bones of both arms; humeri, radiae and ulnas made up the top bar. In the center of that triangle lay a rib cage, with the pelvis atop it, and nestled atop the pelvic girdle lay the skull, facing down.

Wren's vision popped and tripled. There was not a scrap of flesh remaining, as if the bones had been bleached before burial. A perfect inverted pyramid, with the heart, womb and skull at the center. Apex. Tomb. Everything. A fellow human's skull forced to stare down into hell forever.

Wren reeled backward.

"We have to go," Rogers shouted.

Wren heard her and knew she was right, but that didn't matter now. With unconscious precision his hand went to the Highway Patrol-issue Glock 19 at his hip, drew it smooth and was already striding forward.

"Chris, no!" she shouted.

"Christopher's AWOL, cover him!" Hellion bawled through the earpiece, but Wren wasn't listening. Only seeing his father again, standing over one of his pits and burying people alive, with those same people thanking him for the opportunity.

Everybody was responsible.

He broke through the tree cover shooting. Seconds passed before the X-apoc realized what had hit them. Maybe a dozen of them remained, advancing in a line. Wren saw their faces in flashes like special effects in the X app, allowing him a focus he'd never quite felt before.

The Glock bucked in his palm.

Two down in a second. Three down and half of those remaining broke ranks and ran when they saw who it was. The fabled Wren. Five turned on him and fired back.

Rogers burst out beside him, took two more. Special Balls rang out. Wren saw X wherever he looked, his morphing face atop these men and women, wearing their insignia, playing their games like no one was going to get hurt, when everyone knew what the wages of sin brought.

They knew. The kids back in Louisville had known. The man who'd shot the reporter. They all knew. They were all responsible. He saw Rogers' father out there. He saw his own. Doona limping up from the side. Mason striding through gun smoke like some battle angel. Bullets tore into the earth around him, spraying wild.

He sent back only precision. Chest, chest, head. Femur, radius, ulna. Imagined digging pits with meticulous care, bleach-stripping away the flesh and burying them all facing down, wondering what that really meant.

Taking everything away, even in death.

The Glock clicked empty. He looked up, dizzy on his feet. Snow was falling thickly now.

"Boss," came a shout. He turned. Rogers was there. She mouthed something but he couldn't make out the words. To his left the field was strewn with bodies. Some groaning, others still. A vehicle tore away.

"We got all of them," Rogers said, standing before him now with her hands on his shoulders, trying to focus his eyes on her. "We're clear."

They weren't clear.

Wren shook free and stalked the battlefield, barely hearing as Hellion reported the worst news yet. "They got a shortwave message through, Christopher. An ALERT has gone out from nearby town of Harper. I see hundreds mobilizing already. Thousands. One hundred mile radius, maybe more. You must get out of Medicine Lodge."

Wren kept walking until he found what he was looking for. The guy from the diner. He dropped to one knee, put a thumb on the guy's eyelid.

"Where is he?" he demanded.

The guy cried out as Wren pushed. Getting his attention. Was already carrying a wound in his belly, maybe not long left for this world.

"Who?" the guy bleated, one eye roving.

"I know who you think I am," Wren boomed, pushed his face in to fill the guy's field of view. "What you think I am. The biggest jailer of them all. So believe that. I have you right now. Your soul. Tell me what I want or I'll never let it go. Where is he?"

The guy's eye was nothing but terror and pain. "I, I, who?"

Wren didn't let up the pressure. "The man behind First Corinthians. Where is he?"

"First Corinthians," the guy managed, confusion spinning through the fear like a mad top. "That guy? He's further out." He swallowed, sobbed. "Man, you gotta-"

Wren pushed.

He screamed. "The guy, he ran this place! He ran all the Corinthians stuff. He's got a farm!"

Wren leaned in close, made sure all the guy saw was his face. "Where?"

"I ain't been there! It's…" his eye whirled. "Anastasi Street, I heard! Way out, big place, you can't miss it."

Wren waited.

"Yes, Christopher," came the harried voice in his ear. "Anastasi Street exists. I see several farm buildings gathered. A compound."

Wren let go, stood. Was about to walk off but something made him stop, turn back to the guy.

"Face down," he said.

"What?" the guy managed.

"Face down!" Wren commanded. "That's how you die, looking into the earth. Now!"

The guy rolled. Set himself belly down. Bleeding into the cold, snowy dirt.

Wren looked up. Saw Rogers staring at him, Henry, Mason, Doona, the others. Judging. He didn't care. Everybody made their decisions, and everybody had to pay.

32

FACE DOWN

The F-150 raced at sixty miles an hour down the straight country road through thickening snowfall, headed west for Anastasi Street. Wren could feel Rogers seething by his side.

"No unnecessary risks," she said through gritted teeth.

Wren said nothing, focused on cleaning dirt out of the cut in his palm with an antiseptic wipe, wrapping it in bandages.

"You said it," Rogers pressed on, flashing him a murderous look. "No unnecessary risks, so what the hell was that? Solo charging a superior line? Then get the guy to go belly down. Why?"

Wren turned to her, turned away. "You saw that grave."

"I didn't see a thing. I was covering for your ass. She was in there?"

Wren let out a long breath. Not keen to revisit the contents of that grave, but Rogers had to know. "She was. Bones of her arms and legs laid out in an inverted triangle. Pelvis and rib cage stacked in the middle, skull on top facing down."

Rogers didn't say anything for a long moment, then let out a frail-sounding, "Oh."

Wren gazed out the windshield. The sky was a black ceiling, pregnant with mass. The wind was picking up harder, slashing snow against the glass, forcing the wipers to work hard to keep up.

"How's Doona?" Wren asked.

"She'll live," Hellion replied. "Calf shot. They are stabilizing her.

Christopher, I am sending them next to a jet north. Many more X-apoc are coming. You will not be able to shoot them all down like old-movie gunslinger."

He grunted. Maybe that was funny. Striding out into gunfire and surviving. Some ridiculous kind of thing to do. He turned to Rogers.

"You think he deserved better?"

She looked his way, refocused on the road. "That guy?"

"That guy."

She thought for a second. "No way he was the one buried that woman there."

"Agreed."

"So you just punished him for crimes he didn't commit."

Wren was ready for that. "You're thinking about your father."

She half-laughed. "You're damn right I am."

Wren steeled himself. "I'm done babying these people, Rogers. That man sucked down lies for months. He gulped them greedily, just like your father did." She opened her mouth to protest, but he sped on. "If I can save a man like that, like your father even, I will. It's what the Foundation's for. But at some point they cross over and become enemy combatants. About the time they take up arms and start shooting, I'd say." He paused a second, catching his breath. "This is not a game anymore, this is real. Self-radicalization's a bitch like that."

Rogers said nothing.

"He picked a side. This is a war. I'm all out of mercy."

"When were you ever merciful?"

Wren thought back to Diego Helmuz and the kids in Louisville. "You should have seen me yesterday, in Kentucky."

Rogers snorted. "What were you, handing out candy at the Vantasy Con? Way I heard it, you got that whole place set on fire."

"Oh, I got it all on fire," Wren countered fast. "Haven't you been watching the news? Every one of these X-apoc outbreaks, it's me. My atrocities, my fault, so they can heap up all their hate in one place. I'm chief jailer to these people, setting their souls on fire, so why not play the role they want?"

"You're not their jailer."

Wren laughed. "Maybe I am."

"What?"

"Just something the 'Ancient Guardian' said in Leavenworth. He saw my father in me. Maybe he's right."

Rogers snorted. "Well that's bullshit. He may be in there, but you aren't all one of anything. Just like me, just like that guy you put on his belly, just like my dad. We're all imperfect little angels."

He took that on the chin.

"And why's it always about your father?" Rogers went on. "I'm sick of that bullshit, too. Who's your mother, Wren? You ever ask that question? Coffee's different with a little cream. Maybe she's half the bad, maybe she's half the good. You don't know a damn thing."

Wren looked away. Couldn't argue with that, and as the heat faded a little now, things did look different. He brought up his phone and transferred the line direct to Henry.

"Henry," he said.

"Yes, Corporal!"

Wren took a breath, didn't look at Rogers, spoke through clenched jaw. "When Doona's stable, do what you can for the others. The X-apoc. Seal wounds, put them in a vehicle, heating on. They'll die out there in this storm otherwise."

Henry said nothing for a moment. Probably trying to square this with the Wren he'd just seen.

"I know," Wren said. "They're the enemy. But they're also us. It's not like Afghanistan. We can't kill our way to victory. Not that we ever could there, either."

Another second, then a bright, "Yes, sir," came back.

Wren ended the call. Looked at Rogers. She nodded once. That would have to be enough.

Back on his phone, he scrolled through to the darknet, thinking ahead. Their cover was definitely blown. Medicine Lodge was in the crosshairs now, and the Foundation boards were wild with speculation and anger: about X and the X-apoc, the attacks, where Wren was and what he was doing, what they should be doing to support him. His last orders had been to lay low, relocate to Little Phoenix where they could, and it seemed they were struggling with that. De-escalate. Avoid friction, try to keep the X-apoc from triggering. It was hard to stand by and do nothing while the crazies were out setting innocent people alight.

Wren knew that all too well. Anger made you vicious.

He took a breath, fingers hovering over the touchscreen keypad. About to make the decision and cross over. It was one thing to tend the wounded. It was another altogether not to fight in the first place, and there was no point pretending any longer. You couldn't de-escalate a mustering army with decency and reason. All you could do was meet it on the field.

TO FOUNDATION MEMBERS IN KANSAS - RALLY TO MEDICINE LODGE NOW, READY FOR BATTLE. THE X-APOC ARE COMING IN THEIR MASSES. OUR GOAL IS PRESERVATION OF LIFE. ALL MEANS ARE JUSTIFIED.

He fired it off. Started on the next.

TO ALL FOUNDATION MEMBERS – RALLY TO YOUR STRONGPOINTS. HOLD BACK AS LONG AS YOU CAN, BUT THERE MAY BE NO AVOIDING THIS. PREPARE TO FIGHT FOR YOUR COUNTRY AND YOUR LIVES.

He sent it.

Long seconds passed. A minute maybe. He heard the tiny squawk of Rogers' earpiece, receiving a barrel-load from Hellion. Watched her knuckles whiten on the wheel, teeth gritting, then she spun to him.

"The hell you just did?"

"Watch the road."

She cursed. "Answers, now, Chris! Sounds like you just ordered your people to prepare for open warfare across the country."

Wren looked at her, sad for her loss. Her father was already a casualty. She was struggling with the man he had become, and Wren knew exactly what that felt like.

"You've seen what they do. They hit a place based on some deepfake footage, make up some crimes I committed, then shower violence on everyone nearby when I'm not there."

"Fires," Rogers dismissed. "A few deaths."

"More than a few deaths," Wren countered. "The count's in the hundreds nationwide, and all those were for fake crimes I didn't even commit. But look where we are now, Rogers. I just saved a dozen X-apoc fighters so they can report in. They won't need to deepfake anything. I really am here. I really did shoot them. They're going to hit Medicine Lodge and wipe it off the map, just because it happened here."

Rogers' grip on the wheel tightened. "I don't buy it."

"Because you're torn. I get that. But the country's about to cross the Rubicon. Open warfare's three heartbeats away. We either stand by while they massacre the whole town, women, children and babies all, whether they're in X onesies or not, or we take a stand. Once that's done, it's going to go the same way across the country. This place is the trigger, and there's no avoiding it. Unless you think fifty-eight percent of the whole country can somehow retreat? Up to Canada, maybe? Cede the country to the Apex, so he can burn what's left for his afterlife slaves."

Rogers stared hard, like a pressure cooker nearing its limit, then let out a loud burst of cursing.

"I'm sorry, Rogers," Wren said. Staring out into the snow as if he could see all the way to Anastasi Road. "For now, your dad's gone. He made his choice. Now do what you told me to, and start thinking about saving your mom."

She slapped the wheel once, twice. Cursed him out. Slapped it again.

Nothing to say to any of that.

The snow fell and she drove faster.

33

SEED PODS

Seventeen miles west and a handful north, the snow grew thicker and the farms grew bigger, fences receding far away into the streaking snowstorm as the black skies opened and the snowstorm let rip. Wren half listened to Rogers talking to her mom, the signal barely crackling in through the storm, and half tuned to Hellion and B4cksl4cker talking on a side channel.

Rogers was alternately begging, advising and commanding her mom not to go out and look for her father. Not to mock up some X gear, not to pretend she was a member, not to go march in their fiery riots unless she wanted to be made complicit in murder and risk death in a firefight with government and Foundation forces.

"Stay at home," Rogers urged, eyes shining as she kept the Ford barreling into the crazy snow. "Mom, just stay at home."

In the other ear B4cksl4cker was relaying orders from Teddy through to Hellion as she prepared to run field-marshal on the largest battle of her long wargaming career. As a StarCraft maven, winner of the top awards for online battling when she was only fifteen, with the eye-watering stat of four hundred meaningful actions per minute, she'd developed an awesome ability to multi-task a war on dozens of simultaneous fronts: units fighting at the front lines, units gathering resources at the back lines, units building new weapons, units on first aid, units setting traps, all blurred into a real-time strategy that moved with the enemy like a living thing, like weather.

All that made for a management system so complex and interwoven that commentators often spent months breaking down every one of her myriad brilliant moves, all made in real time, putting a dozen gambits into place every second, monitoring and following through only on the best.

This was bigger than anything she'd ever attempted before. B4cksl4cker was already spinning up dozens of AIs to automate whole sections of the country under her control. Foundation forces in Florida. Foundation forces in Milwaukee. Foundation forces everywhere. Their strengths, their training level. Breaking them into units, setting them up with leaders, assessing their resources, preparing them to go headlong into battle against the X-apoc.

Civil war. It was real.

"We will not be able to help much in coming hours," B4cksl4cker's deep voice came in Wren's ear. "Jets are already waiting at all surrounding airfields for you. Perhaps pilots will wait. Some are Foundation fringe, so we are hopeful. We are also paying very good rate. But..." he trailed off.

Nothing more needed to be said. The larger battle was in the hands of his hackers now. A couple of millionaire kids, really, in charge of the fate of America. Five years back when he'd dug them out of international hacking schemes, blackmailing North Korea with Russian intel, holding Belarus hostage with a Venezuelan cryptoworm, he would never have seen it coming to this.

"Compound is ahead," B4cksl4cker said. "Two miles off road. Good luck, Christopher. I hope this will help end war."

"Me too," he answered. "Good luck."

The line in his ear went dead. He looked at Rogers. Seemed her call to her mother was finished.

"This is crazy," she said.

"She's safe?"

"As anyone, now."

Wren could feel her twisting inside. Overtaken by fear, betrayal, anger. Maybe trying to decide how much of this to lay at Wren's feet.

"We get the Apex, this thing ends, Sally. Force a confession live on the Internet. Half the X-apoc will fold in the moment, a quarter will probably lay down arms under duress, the last batch will get smoked out and jailed. It will happen."

She laughed. "He'll never confess."

"Then a humiliation. Put him in cuffs and frog-march him out of there in Federal custody. Shut down the X app for good. No more ALERTs. No more

BS in the air. I guarantee, those people will look up from what they're doing and just wonder what on Earth it's all for. Like an epiphany. I've seen it before, and I know we can break his hold. Even on your father."

Rogers grunted, then yanked the wheel right. They dumped through a shallow ditch with a thump, smashed through a wooden fence then peeled out across a field.

"Dead ahead," she said.

Wren couldn't see anything yet through the driving snow, but brought up his phone maps app. B4cksl4cker had already pinned their target, and now the dot that represented their vehicle was racing diagonally toward it. Wren zoomed in. On the map it looked like an industrial farm complex: a huge warehouse barn, several long battery-like outhouses for cattle, one of those massive tractors, a square residential block.

"I never saw your father as a farmer," Rogers said.

"He's a farmer of souls."

Rogers stared at him. Didn't look ahead, didn't need to, plummeting forty miles an hour over an open field. "And the crop's ripe, is that it?"

Wren met her gaze sincerely. "Bursting at the seed pods."

For a second he thought she was going to curse him out, but the moment broke with a couple grunts of laughter instead.

"You're a weird guy, Boss," she allowed.

"Coffee in the cream. Now eyes dead ahead, lieutenant. The Apex awaits."

She laughed again. Wren allowed a smile. With the country falling apart it hardly felt right, but what else were you going to do?

"Pull right," he said, watching the maps app. "Let's come in around the back of the barn. Snow will provide cover."

Rogers turned the wheel. Wren held up the phone so she could see, and she navigated by the screen. There was nothing visible through the snow until the last minute, when the towering aluminum side of the barn appeared to the left. Rogers slowed until they reached the corner, then halted and killed the engine.

"No backup for an hour plus," Wren said.

"Just the two of us," Rogers said. "We've got shotguns in back."

"Mossberg?" Wren asked.

"Tactical."

Wren held up a fist. Rogers bumped it.

"Let's go."

34

ANASTASI

In two minutes they were fully tooled up with fresh gear over thermal jackets: black Mossberg 500 12-gauge shotguns, with 00 Buckshot cartridges in a quad-hold chest strap ready to speed-load; pistol ammo bandoliers for their Glock 19s, six magazines each packing Gold Dot G2 rounds; Kevlar-wrap level III+ front and back plate body armor; high-cut IIIA ballistic helmets with night-sight mounts; fresh earpieces with subvocal throat-mics; a strip of flashbang and percussive grenades.

"You have thermal binos?" Wren asked.

Rogers rustled in a box, all equipment dumped from a Foundation storehouse into the back of her F-150. "For the snow?"

"Anything will be better than zero visibility."

She came back with a pair of HD 640 thermal monoculars. They fastened them into place on the helmet mounts. Wren nodded, raised his shotgun. "You have left, I'll take right."

"Pincer movement, got it."

They broke.

Wren rounded the corner of the barn in seconds, advancing steady and smooth, scanning the wall of snow ahead. Even with the monocular live, the raging flurries cut his visibility down to maybe ten feet. His heart thumped. Across the yard he could just about make out the long outlines of the cattle outhouses.

No sound, no movement. He reached the barn's edge and cut left around the front, found a door, tried the handle. Locked. He pulled a folding pry bar from his gear belt, wedged it into the jamb with a firm thump of his palm, then yanked.

The lock creaked, the frame warped and the door popped open.

"I'm in the barn," Wren subvocalized into his throat-mic, and slid easily into a narrow tin-walled corridor. He smelled diesel oil and molding hay on the dry air, heard only the masking shush of fat snowflakes driving against the walls. Five steps on and he hit an opening into the barn proper.

It was dark and cavernous inside, no electrics lit, hardly any natural light filtering past the falling storm through corrugated plastic panels high in the roof. Just enough to make out a ramshackle assortment of farm machinery.

Wren strode forward steadily, wary for traps, working a path between various oversized threshers, harvesters, milling boxes and seeding trailers. The monocular performed better here, showing only cold in sharp blue vertices. No signs of life. Fine dust in the air caught the gray light rinsing in from above, making the space feel oddly unreal, like a monochromatic dream.

Wren reached the rough middle of the barn, rifle sweeping. Ahead implements hung on the wall beside tatty denim overalls. Tall stacks of baled hay climbed toward the metal beam rafters, feed for the cows. An old tractor sank on deflated tires in a corner, next to a metal workbench neatly laid out with various mechanic's tools, a few long gas canisters, a sawhorse.

No hostiles, though, no triangles, no pyramids. No sign of a trapdoor leading down, no heat signatures below his feet signaling another human zoo packed with captives. Wren didn't know what he'd expected, but it wasn't this.

"All clear, Rogers," he said. "There's nothing here. It's just a barn."

"Understood," she came back. "I have eyes on the cattle outhouses. Nothing here either, except cold cows."

Wren pushed back against the sense of his heart sinking. Cold cows. All signs suggested this was a normal working farm. Whoever ran it would have no time to also run an international cult bent on bringing down America. He let his rifle barrel drop, lifted his monocular, felt all dressed up with nowhere to go.

Trespassing in some random farmer's barn.

What was their lead here, anyway? Some dying guy who'd picked Wren out from a diner, another X-apoc loser? The X-apoc were civilians off the street, not drafted for their proximity to the Apex. The guy was most likely a nobody, maybe worked in the local library, wrote out late tickets on books on loan too long.

What did he really know about any of this?

Wren cursed under his breath. Maybe this took them right back to the drawing board. He checked his watch, twenty minutes gone. The X-apoc weren't going to wait on him, and every wasted minute brought the war closer.

Too early to give up on the lead already, though.

"Meet you at the house," Wren said.

"Roger that."

The main barn gate was locked with a thick padlock and chain, so Wren went back the way he'd come, through the popped door and out into the raging storm. Ten yards from the barn and all hint of where he'd been was concealed by thick gusts. No sign of where he was going, either, lost in the whiteout. For twenty seconds he jogged in total solitude, then the house loomed out of the semi-dark.

Clapboard siding, one dim light on upstairs, looked like a swing set off to the left. Wren bumped into a low white fence, invisible in the storm, and vaulted it. Feet trudged down in the soft loam of a flowerbed. That didn't feel right.

"At the door," came Rogers' voice. Almost a shout now, to be heard over the pummeling wind. Wren crossed the garden and met her by the front door, barely more than a gray ghost in the white until he was upon her.

"I'm not feeling this, Boss," she shouted over the wind.

"I know," he answered. "Vehicles in the driveway?"

"Two. Looks like someone's home."

"Upstairs," Wren agreed. "We go easy, full alert. In three."

Wren stepped back, counted two then put a hard front kick into the front door's lock plate. It sprayed open, bolt tearing back through the frame, and Rogers was first in, Glock raised. Even over the roar of the storm any inhabitants must have heard that.

"FBI!!" Wren shouted and sped down the hall, watching the patterned glow of heat resolve through the monocular.

There was a wood fire burning in the den, two sofas laid before it, rug, coffee table, assorted kids' wooden block toys spread on the floor, a cup of coffee steaming on the pass leading into the kitchen.

"Clear," Rogers called, patted Wren's shoulder from behind and he fed through into the kitchen. Nobody there, though the washing machine was on a spin cycle. He cleared the utility, circled back to a study, dining room, downstairs bath, all empty.

Rogers led the way up the carpeted stairs, switching to her Mossberg now.

Up to the landing, where five doors led off. Whoever was in the home must have heard them by now. Wren nodded left, started dead ahead, and just then one of the doors opened.

A slim guy stepped out, unarmed, late twenties, wearing a threadbare dressing gown, googly rabbit-face slippers on his feet, eyes widening on Wren and Rogers. Behind him Wren saw a woman holding a baby, curled up against her chest in a cuddly pink one-piece with unicorns.

Not at all right.

Wren lowered his shotgun to the side, not all the way but enough to take the worst of the threat away.

"Where's the Apex?" he asked. Not as rough as he could. "Where's X?"

35

MARKS THE SPOT

The guy just stared. Trying to compute two people in full tactical gear on the upstairs landing of his house.

"X..." he repeated, trailed off, voice a little high, eyes darting between Wren and Rogers. "Like, X marks the spot?"

That log-jammed Wren for a second. "X," he tried again. "From the X app. X-apoc. The Apex."

The guy looked more bewildered by the second. "I, uh. X-what? I don't, uh, know what you're asking me? I want to help. What is, um..."

Wren shot a disbelieving glance at Rogers. It didn't look like acting. It looked like some sweet domestic scene. He spun back, lowered the shotgun all the way.

"This is Anastasi Street?"

The guy nodded vigorously, looked glad he could finally contribute something to the exchange. "Yes. Anastasi Street. Listen, I'll be happy to cooperate with any lawful duties, I just-"

"We're looking for the man who ran the First Corinthians church. We were told this was his place."

The guy's jaw opened, closed. "Um, first what?"

Wren took another second. The guy was young, but not that young. Anyone from Medicine Lodge would surely have heard of First Corinthians, if it was everything Linda back at the Larks diner had said. Churches, outreach, charity work. But then there was the baby. Under a year old. Given how time-consuming a newborn could be, it was totally possible they'd never even heard of X or the Apex. Add to that, this place was clearly a factory farm, and the guy's accent was slightly off.

"You're not from around here, are you?"

The guy nodded eagerly again. Something else he could contribute. "No. I, I mean we, we've been here just six months. Same time as the baby. I, uh, we took a position. I've got papers and everything."

"You're the farm manager."

"We are," the guy said. Looked momentarily grateful. Shot a look back to the woman. "My wife and I. So, uh, can I ask officer, if you are an officer, I'm not sure that's the right term, but what's this about? There's nothing here, it's-"

"Managing for who?"

The guy blinked. "It's a company."

Rogers cursed low.

"What company?"

"It's called Riker foods? I'm sure you've heard of them. They're one of the biggest, um, producers in the state." He paused. Wren stared. "They make cornflakes," he added.

"We missed the guy by years, maybe," Rogers said quietly. "Or it was all BS from the start. This was never the place."

Wren felt the lead getting frailer by the second. Without it, they had nothing. His eyes darted around the space, looking for something, anything to hang their next step on.

Nothing came.

Vertigo hit. He started thinking about what came next. Track Riker back through financial records, try to sift some link to First Corinthians, the Apex? Without Hellion or B4cksl4cker to run that search for them, though, it'd take hours, maybe days. Try to get back to town before the X-apoc horde hit, squeeze a few more folks for leads. They might make it in time, but the diner guy must've warned all his fellow X-apoc before he left. Wren's reception was going to be frosty, and that in the midst of a snowstorm.

Beyond that, he was out of ideas. The Apex had been here five years back, he knew that for sure. Somebody had to know something, but he didn't know how to shake that information loose in less than an hour. DNA tests on the bones, maybe, but that would take days. A satellite rewind on all movements over the First Corinthians church dating back five years, but nothing doing without his hackers.

No way forward.

"I apologize for disturbing your morning," he found himself saying. "We broke your door. Someone will come take care of it."

The words spilled out with hardly any meaning. Rogers went down the stairs ahead of him. A dead end. The guy followed them saying equally meaningless words, the kind of things you said when you didn't really understand, were trying to paper things over, were trying to make yourself safe, until-

Wren stopped.

The guy actually bumped into him. Pulled back fast, apologized, took another few steps up, clearly terrified he'd just made a lethal mistake when they were on the home straight.

Wren turned. The woman with the baby was out of the room now, bobbing it up and down gently in her arms.

"What did you just say?" Wren asked.

The guy paled. "Um, I guess, just, don't worry about the door? I'm a carpenter really. It's, um, no problem."

"Before that."

The guy gulped. "Before that? Uh, I think, was it about cornflakes?"

"After, then."

The guy looked lost. Flailing.

"I think he means about the old guy," the woman spoke up. More of a Southern accent, comfortable spinning a tale.

Wren focused on her like a targeting laser. She had curlers in her brown hair, one side at least. The baby chewed on the belt of her cotton dressing gown. She had a swell on her belly, looked like she was already pregnant again. "Exactly. Yes. What old guy?"

The guy hurried back up the stairs, took the baby off his wife and she took a step toward them, more of a waddle. "The old guy, I figure that's why you're here. He came with the property. We put in some complaints with Medicine Lodge sheriffs way back when we first rolled up, and they ignored it. Here I'm figuring you two were a big escalation. He's not here, though."

Wren's mouth went dry.

"Why'd you complain? And how old? And where is he?"

She screwed up her face briefly. Clearly handling the pressure better than her husband. "Seventies, I guess. And we complained because he is one wild sumbitch, excuse my French. I don't know if he's drunk or high, but he tears around that weird pitch of his on his tractor like a punch-drunk gator. Playing his crazy religious music, knocking down our fence posts. Couple times this last season he was out racing through the sorghum, says he was writing God's word on the land."

Wren's heart skipped a beat. "God's word?"

"Willy here sent up a drone on a whim, he's a hobbyist, take a look at what all God was writing." She looked back at her husband. "Nothing but a big old triangle, wasn't it hon?"

Willy nodded.

The stairs opened up under Wren. Vertigo coming faster than before.

"Where's his 'pitch'?"

"He the one you want, then?" she asked, sing-song Southern intonation. "It ain't hardly accessible by road. Up past our place, you gotta cut through fields for almost a mile. Seems we only got the contract on this place because of him, 'cos nobody else wanted it. He was grandfathered in, you heard that expression?"

Wren nodded mutely.

"Well, he been here on this land for generations, they say, and he ain't gonna sell that pitch of his. I can't tell why, nothing but some old graffitied cabins, them trailers, a bust-up water tower and a dried-up well. The water table's for crap around here, you know?"

Wren tried to speak but struggled.

"We're going to need a bearing," Rogers took over smoothly. "Something more concrete than 'across the fields', especially in this storm."

The woman waved a hand. "Can do you one better. Willy programs the tractor with GPS, so I got the exact coordinates, where we have to avoid, so's we don't crush him in his sleep while the tractor's out. Many times I've thought of doing just that, Lord help me." She took a long-suffering breath. "So, how'll that do you?"

Wren found his tongue. "As fast as you can, ma'am. This is a life and death matter."

"Life and death, huh? That explains all this hullabaloo then. Well come on, coordinates are downstairs."

36

PITCH

Rogers took the Ford out from behind the barn, rolling slow through the driving snow.

"It's a good thing we got coordinates," she said, watching her phone screen, steering toward the pin dropped on the old guy's 'pitch'. "There's no chance we could navigate by landmarks."

Wren grunted agreement, already thinking ahead to who the old guy was and what that meant. He studied the map. There was only a low-resolution satellite image of the surrounding fields, hardly a prime coverage area out this far from civilization. There looked to be one homestead and what could be a water tower.

"And Willy?" Rogers went on, clearly not done. "Cat really got his tongue." She looked over at Wren, eyes dancing. "Always ask the woman first, Boss."

"Noted."

"You count how many times he said 'uh' or 'um'? No, thank you. Give me a good loquacious Southern belle any day, and-"

"Got it, Rogers. Girl power."

She laughed.

The Ford hit something low, had to be the edge of the trail she'd warned them about. On the right track.

"What you make of all this?" she asked. "The guy with the triangle."

"He's gotta be the guy. Seventies doesn't sound like my father, though. Nor riding around on a tractor. So maybe it's X."

"You think X killed the girl at First Corinthians?"

"Could be." He paused a second. "That burial, inverted pyramid underneath a church? It's so on the nose. It feels like an outlier."

Rogers laughed. "You can say that again. Stacking bones? So passé."

Wren ignored the teasing. "The Apex has always been a more metaphorical kind of man. The suffering was the point, not the tableaux. Pits, vats, cages, he liked them for what they did, not for how they looked. The ceremony was the thing, not the trappings or the remnant." He thought for a second. "When Pyramid members died, he didn't do anything special with the bones at all. Just half-assed burials in the desert, where they lay for the coyotes to chew on." He paused a moment more. "That's how Maggie got started in Little Phoenix, actually. Collecting bones, consecrating them."

"Huh. Yeah. I like that broad."

Wren cracked a tight smile at the notion of Maggie being called a 'broad'. "Well, she hates you."

Rogers laughed. They rolled on.

"Those two back there," Rogers said. "Strange time to bring up a baby."

Wren just grunted.

"Where are your kids? Are they safe?"

Wren looked at her. That was a sore point, ever since she'd hidden them from him in witness protection.

"Come on, Boss. I know you've been watching them. We already lost my dad to X. I don't want that for your kids."

He stared out into the static snow. "Gone to Little Phoenix." Keeping it as monosyllabic as he could.

"Good. They'll be safe there. Maybe I should send my mom."

"She'd be welcome." A pause. "We can try to arrange a pickup."

Thirty seconds of silence.

"That'd be good."

Wren nodded, brought up his phone and sent the request through to Teddy.

Five minutes more passed, and their icon of a car approached the coordinates on the screen. A slight incline, like they were climbing a low hill, then Rogers stopped.

"We're here."

There was nothing to see but whipping snow.

"House is that way," Wren said, pointing left. "I'll check the water tower."

"Agreed."

Out the door, the snow was already a foot deep. Rogers headed left and disappeared in the snow in seconds. Wren headed straight to the right. The cold bit through his thin jacket, ice crept in through his trooper's boots. After thirty seconds the tower appeared through the storm like some 1930's vision of an alien invader. Long spindly legs rising some hundred feet high, an egg-shaped tank hidden in white, something large dangling beneath it like a giant pendulum.

Wren ran his flashlight beam up and down, picking out a thick chain tethered to the hanging object; as big as a baby grand piano, panel-beaten metal with stark rivets, shaped like a chunky missile pointing down. It reminded him of something, but he couldn't quite place it.

He strode closer. Beneath the legs of the tower, taking up the whole of the footprint at maybe ten feet on a side, there was a large twin-doored wooden cover. This had to be the well she'd mentioned, but it was bigger than any well Wren had seen before.

The doors were secured with a thick padlock and heavy chain. Far more than was needed for a dried-up well in the middle of nowhere. Wren pulled his pry bar out, slotted it beside one of the hinges and worked it like a water pump. The hinge's screw tops popped off their threads like daisy heads.

He popped the second hinge, heart in his mouth, and tipped the outsized door open.

Blackness yawned inside, too deep to see the bottom. Definitely not a well. Could be a forerunner to the Apex's desert pits, or maybe the entrance to some forgotten mine? But how much mining was there on arable land in the Great Plains?

He leaned over and looked down. The walls were stone-lined, and fitted together beautifully, stretching down with impeccable craftsmanship. His flashlight beam barely put a dent in the shadows.

"Now you jump in," came a voice from behind.

37

WELL

Wren's body froze but his mind raced ahead.

An old man's voice, sounded like a guttering gatepost, only a couple of good swings left in it. Not like his father's firebrand bass in the X videos, more like an old-timer gold panner declaiming from his rocking chair outside the saloon.

Standing near, too. Just from the volume of that shaky voice, no way he could be more than three yards back. Three yards meant he wasn't shoving distance, so he had to be armed. Doubtless holding a gun, maybe a shotgun. No other way he'd risk taking on a much bigger, younger man.

A second flat, maybe, to think that through and pick a route forward.

"You'll miss," Wren said.

Another flat second passed. "Miss what? My good old momma and daddy? I don't think so, boy, not from this range."

"You packing birdshot?" Wren countered. "Only way you'll lay a slug on me in this storm. But birdshot won't put a dent in III+ Kevlar wrap body armor, reinforced with ceramic plate, ballistic IIIa helmet. I'll ring like a bell, then you'll be the one tumbling down the pit."

A few wheezy riffs of the guy's laughter carried through the storm. "Nice dream, son. What about your legs? They don't look too wrapped up in e-numbers to me. I put a slug across your knees, they going to make a nice high chime?"

"I'm coming, Boss," came Rogers' voice in his ear.

"Who's to say you'll even hit my legs?" Wren asked. "Your hands are getting pretty cold right about now, I figure. Starting to shake. An old-timer like you, you're not built for these conditions."

"Try me. I've been picking off mole crickets at a hundred yards since I was a boy, come rain or shine."

"So it's a rifle? I take a fast step to the right now, you think you can track that? Better off we get a look at each other first, seeing as you're an Apex man."

A few seconds passed after that, then the guy's tone shifted. "What do you know about that name?"

Confirmation. Wren turned.

The guy was tall and emaciated, with a steel-wool beard and a deep-pitted face like a cord of sundried wood, in his late seventies if he was a day. On his head stood a tall navy hat, and in his hands was a beat-up Remington Model 700 rifle, shaking despite the shabby olive surplus German army jacket he wore, smeared with the stains of many years. Oil, blood, human waste. Wren could almost smell him on the freezing air.

What mattered though was his eyes. So dark they looked like holes boring through the storm. Wren focused on the light that went on in their depths, maybe a hint of recognition that showed him a new path forward.

"You recognize me?" Wren asked.

The old man said nothing. Seemed like revelations were happening in his head. No way this could be X, though. So who was he?

"Got his six," Rogers said. Wren just about saw her stalking through the snow some ten yards off. "Get the bead off you and I'll take him."

"Your bitch talking in your ear?" the old guy said.

Wren inclined his head.

"I seen her. Don't care who or what you are. If she stays back there, I'm shooting."

"Then we got ourselves a stand-off, because she's not coming around front. But that's fine, I've got a good reason to be here. Take a look in my eyes, tell me what you see."

The guy hawked, spat. The shaking was getting worse. "Some kin of the man himself. Apex, you call him. You one of his sons?"

That was interesting. "I am his son." Wren considered his next move. Out here in the depths of Kansas, what did this guy know about the wider world? "He sent me here to check on things."

The guy didn't drop the rifle, but there was a change in his demeanor, like maybe the anger was melting to something else.

"For what? I'm not due."

That was interesting, too. Due what? "Doesn't matter. There's new threats in the air." Wren tasted what was to come next, an unexpected gambit at best, but let it roll. "One of the Pequeños. The sons? My half-brother. He's causing all kinds of trouble. Christopher Wren, his name is. You heard of him?"

The guy looked blank.

"Apex says he might come out here, start digging. We need to harden this place."

The guy snorted, but the cold made his voice catch. "It's p-plenty hard."

"So hard I turfed your pit on the first try, got the jump on you in back, got you out here minutes away from hypothermia?" Wren let that sink in. "That's why he sent me. You need backup. What you're doing here matters too much."

Flattery. Whatever role this guy was playing, it wasn't essential. Not with him acting out in front of the neighbors. The Apex would never let something important slide so far.

"What's your name?" the guy asked.

"Aden," Wren answered smoothly. "Of-The-Saints. Now let's go inside. We'll talk. Have a coffee. Yeah?"

The guy didn't move.

"Alternative is my partner shoots out your brains right now, we bury you in this pit, take up your duties ourselves. How's that sound?"

The guy's crevassed face wrinkled, almost in humor. "Like something one of his sons would say." He let the muzzle of the Remington drop. "So let's go inside. I got c-coffee, but it tastes like filth."

"As long as it's black, hot and caffeinated, who cares about the taste?"

The guy grunted and strode away. Rogers gestured a question at Wren through the snow, barely seven yards distant, and he shrugged back, started following the guy deeper into the storm.

38

AIRSTREAM

They trudged in single file along the old guy's footsteps.

"What's his deal?" Rogers asked from behind.

"He recognized I'm one of the Apex's sons," Wren answered. "You heard that?"

"Pieces of it. The signal's spotty in all this."

"So now I'm passing for one of my brothers. Call me Aden if it comes up."

"Aden." A second passed. "The one you killed in Acapulco?"

Wren was impressed. Her information was solid. "That's right. Maybe he'll spill something, if he thinks we're friendlies come to help."

Rogers managed a frigid laugh.

"I know, it's a stretch."

Five minutes they walked east, into what ought to be sorghum fields, until a low oblong structure took shape through the blizzard, looked like a mobile home. Each step closer brought more details. Tarnished silver sides, rounded corners, mounted on two-foot-high support struts. Looked like an old Airstream trailer, but that wasn't all. Attached at the head and tail were more trailers, different makes, looked to be spot-welded and stretching away like the carriages of a freight train.

"This thing's big," Rogers said.

Now the old guy was at the entrance. Three steps up he went, opened the door, stepped inside.

And closed it.

Rogers cursed.

"Left now," Wren said, and broke right just as a metal slot opened in the Airstream's door. A second later automatic rifle fire roared out, muzzle flashes ripping yellow sparks through the storm where they'd been standing. Wren took four strides and flung himself down against the trailer's side, started burrowing through snow to get under the struts.

"I don't think he bought it," came Rogers' voice in his ear.

"I'm getting that impression. Find a way in."

There was little snow in the dank gloom under the Airstream, and Wren looked both ways. Brown dirt continued into the storm's darkness. He chose right and crawled maybe twenty fast yards over soil, rocks and shale. Still no end in sight. At least the firing had stopped.

"Nothing yet," Rogers said.

Wren rolled out on the other side of the trailer, back into the storm, and stood. Now the Airstream was off to his right and he was looking at the brown siding of a long RV, picking out windows and a door.

"Find a door, blow out the lock in three. We'll come at him from both sides."

"Roger that," came her answer, crackling now with static. Seconds passed. "Got one."

"Three," Wren said, pulled his Mossberg from its sheath, "two," levelled it close to the lock plate on an angle, "one," and fired.

Buckshot ripped through the thin metal, metal slugs sparked and ricocheted to hiss into the snow, and the sound of Rogers' second blast reached him. He leaned in, touched the hot metal door frame, and cursed.

Plate metal was welded beneath the trailer's thin skin. Reinforced and impenetrable. Not a door at all.

"Run!" he shouted again, just as a slot clanked open nearby and a fresh burst of automatic fire kicked. He hunkered low and ran back toward the Airstream, tipping his thermal monocular into place and scanning the walls as he went.

Nothing. Must have been heatproofed. The guy wasn't as crazy as he'd thought.

"He's near your end," Rogers said. "I have no access here."

"Nothing on thermal," Wren answered, mind racing. They needed something explosive. "Tape two grenades to a door. I'll do the same here. That ought to do it."

"On your signal, Boss."

He stopped in the snow, listened for a second. The automatic fire had stopped. He imagined the old guy lurching along the inside of his trailer-fort, peeking through lookout slits and ready to let rip with the rifle. He thought he caught a glimpse of movement high in the nearby wall, and sprinted low and away.

Bullets puffed through the snow where he'd been standing. "He's following me!" he shouted, arcing back in toward the trailer wall. He pulled two rectangular grenades from their strip as he ran, fumbled in the wheeling snow to peel the adhesive tabs, then slapped them to the shredded lock plate.

"Go," he shouted, pulled the pins then ran, dived and rolled under the structure.

The grenades blew with a massive cough, spraying wreckage and smoke in a bubble that the falling snow quickly erased. Wren was already up and moving side-on to the blast. The exterior walls were blackened, and a fissure had been torn through a weld-line in the interior plates, maybe a yard wide. He pulled two flashbangs and pinged them through the gap like fastballs.

They hit metal, clattered to the floor and burst. The effect inside that contained space would be catastrophic, a pressure wave of 170 decibel sound and a seven megacandela flash bouncing along the trailers. Enough to cause temporary deafness, blindness, send the fluid in the ear canals into nauseating shock.

Wren hauled himself inside, Glock 19 up. Smoke was everywhere. "I'm in," he shouted.

A second rank of explosions rang out from far away. "Coming," Rogers answered.

Wren saw workbenches with pieces of equipment scattered from the blast, various scorched plans tacked to the walls, a large world map scrawled over with dozens of triangles.

Triangles were everywhere. Pyramids too. Molded in plastic on the workbenches, sketched in marker pen on scraps of paper, carved into the wood of the benches. Upright. Inverted. They were pained in a rainbow of colors, and everywhere they surrounded by a swirl of algebraic calculations. The profusion made Wren dizzy. A riot of numbers and symbols and triangles had been etched into the metal walls, the floor, the ceiling like a roaming musical score.

He shook himself and sped on, swept through the smoke and only saw the guy levelling his rifle a second too late. Bullets poured out and ripped a stripe up the wall and ceiling.

Missed. That save was on the flashbang. The guy was fifteen yards away now, leaning against a sheet-metal wall, looked like the welded transition space between two trailers. Swapping out a magazine.

It was an easy shot for Wren, but he couldn't risk killing this guy. No time to run up on him either. He chose a third option, pulled back his Glock and flung it. Another fastball that spun across the distance in a second, cracked the guy square on the hand holding the rifle muzzle. Not what Wren was aiming for, but good enough. The barrel dropped, the guy cried out, then Wren was on him.

No punches. No need. The old guy fell easy and Wren straddled him, pulled the rifle away and forced his arms crossed over his chest, so all he could do was grab handfuls of his own shoulders.

"Clear," he shouted.

The guy laughed. Chewed something in his mouth, went to swallow and Wren slapped him hard. Whatever it was, suicide pill or wad of gum, it went tapping out over the metal flooring.

The guy rolled his face back up to Wren, black eyes darkening further. Snow blew in and landed on his cheeks. Wren gave him a small shake.

"Now how about that coffee?"

39

BULLET

They put the guy in a bolted-down chair, duct-taped his hands to the chair arms, his shoulders to the back and leaned in.

"Where's the Apex?"

The old guy only stared with those black-hole eyes. Reeling now from the flashbangs, maybe, but Wren didn't have the time.

"First Corinthians," he said. "The girl buried underneath the church in a triangle shape, that was you, right? Hardly my father's style. He set it up, maybe, some kind of payment so you'll stay on guard duty here? But what's here? What's the pit for under the water tower?"

Nothing came back. Time to get the guy's attention.

"First thing I'll do is break all these joints." He pointed at the guy's arms and legs. "Getting them ready, you know? So when I make them into a triangle, they're ready to go. Dig out your rotten pelvis, hack off your chest, stack you tall in that pit with your skull on top, facing down forever. Like the girl. How does that sound?"

There was a flash of something new in the guy's eyes now. Fear, maybe.

"Start somewhere," Wren said, took hold of the guy's elbow. With his hand and shoulder strapped tight to the chair, all Wren had to do was pull to break the joint. "Name."

The guy gritted his teeth. Wren pulled, putting tension on. A few more pounds of pressure and tendons would start to pop.

"Name!"

"Menaen the Builder," the guy gasped.

Wren frowned. "Menaen, huh? Sounds like a Pyramid name to me. But we're pretty far from Pyramid territory here."

Menaen laughed.

"I say something funny?"

"You claim you're his son? Aden? I knew that was horseshit the second I saw you. You're too clean. The filth of it disgusts me."

Wren raised an eyebrow. "Someone got talkative. 'Filth is clean', that definitely sounds like Apex nonsense. So let's keep that rolling, but unless you want to stare down into the flames of hell for eternity, I suggest you cut the sass and start giving me something real. Where's the Apex?"

Nothing.

"OK, we'll start easier. Menaen the Builder, what did you build?"

"It's all around you."

Wren pulled the elbow. "I know you're not talking about this welded trailer-park fantasy we're in right now. Give me something real, and I want it all, or you're going in the ground looking down."

Menaen gritted his yellowed teeth. "You don't even know what it means. That threat."

"What threat, to 'triangle' you?" Wren almost smiled at the expression, but held it back. "Maybe not. I'll still do it. So why don't you tell me what it means?"

Menaen resisted for a second, but the fear spurred him on. "It's total. Soul-deep. You bury someone like that, they become part of your chattel."

That was interesting. "Go on."

"In the pyramid of souls? Serving you forever in death. As a slave."

Wren grunted. The pharaoh stuff. He looked over at Rogers, who looked back at him with a nod that seemed to say, 'Sure, that checks out.'

"So I bury you like that, you belong to me."

Menaen spat.

"Like that girl belongs to you."

He spat again.

"OK with the spitting, Lars Ulrich. So now we know what it means. I'll do it and you'll be serving me for eternity, if you don't start talking right now."

Menaen stared at him with those dark eyes, his whole body tensing against the duct tape but finding no give. Probably wishing he had another suicide pill. Ligaments pulled taut in his neck, down the wiry cords of his arms, pale face turning red. Maybe trying to give himself a heart attack. It didn't work. After some thirty seconds the tension gave out.

"You through?" Wren prompted. "Or shall I set out and start digging the hole?"

The guy gulped. Making his decision. "One condition."

"Name it."

"You burn me when we're done. Down to the bone, pound what's left to dust. No skull. Nothing left to bury."

Wren thought on that for a second. Figured it had to be an Apex standing threat. "So he can't own you? I thought you'd welcome that. You're loyal, right?"

"Of course I'm loyal! I'd happily serve him another thousand years, dead or alive, if that's what it meant, but it doesn't." Menaen shuddered. "It's worse if he does it himself."

"How so?"

Now fear filled his black eyes, sweat popped in beads on his cheeks. "If he buries me like that, it's pain forever. I mean, forever. Constant, never-ending agony. So you swear now or I go silent to the grave."

Wren held up his hands. "I swear. Cross my heart, hope to die. We'll burn you down, pound the bones, not a stick left to rub against another." He held Menaen's gaze. "Now talk."

Menaen let loose a trembling breath. "OK." Took a moment longer, then looked up. "You want to know about this place. First things, let's be clear. You're Christopher Wren, aren't you? The ungrateful son. Not Aden."

"The one and only."

"Then you have a right to know. You're family." Another heavy breath, eyes now boring into Wren. "Fact is, your father was once my son."

Wren hadn't expected that.

"Not biological," Menaen went on. "Adopted, though not formally. After his real father died. It all happened here."

Wren blinked. That was a lot to take on board. Fascinating, really. But they were here for a reason, and that came first. "Where is he now? When did you see him last?"

"I don't know where he is. Last time I saw him was five years back."

"Seriously?"

"I never joke."

Wren grunted. "So she was payment, then. The woman. For you to stay here."

Menaen looked away. "Yes. A down payment for my chattel. She died with my name on her lips. She belongs to me."

Wren nodded. That all sounded about right. "We dug her up. I'm thinking her soul's free now."

Menaen laughed and looked back. "Her soul's never free. You don't know how it works at all."

Wren pulled on his elbow, drawing a sharp cry. "So tell me, before I get that hankering to dig again. I'm here because the Apex drew a massive inverted triangle across the country, son. Medicine Lodge is the center, and here I find you, a man much-enamored of triangles. I thought I'd find him here, or X, but obviously not, so start telling me something I can use."

Menaen licked his lips. Opened his mouth. "You want to hear about the Icon?"

"What?"

"The inverted triangle. I can tell you about that. After all, I helped him design it."

Wren leaned in, didn't blink. "So talk. What on Earth happened here, Menaen?"

Menaen smiled. "What in hell, you should say. We came within a stinkbug's balls of shooting the devil right between his goddamn eyes."

Wren had nothing for that.

The smile became a grin. "Your Apex's real father, your grandfather, I guess, he had him some theories." Menaen settled into his chair, even as his voice settled into a new tone, recounting the glory days. "Davis Thackerton, was his name. You ever heard of him?" Wren shook his head. "Had your eyes, I guess. This was back in '71. He fought in Vietnam, came back filled up with all these new theories, just bursting out at the seams." Menaen leaned closer, spoke lower. "That the devil was behind it all; the war, the killing, everything." He sucked in a breath. "He'd had plenty of time to think about it all, back in 'Nam. A six-year tour, and he'd been a Tunnel Rat to boot, volunteered for it, pumped up on the red, white and blue." He paused, eyeing Wren with those black eyes. "You know what a Tunnel Rat did?"

Wren shook his head again.

"Pray you never learn firsthand. See, the Viet Cong, they made all these tunnels under the Vietnam jungle. Called them the Cu Chi. Miles and miles of them, a whole dark world underground, even they had hospitals, barracks, headquarters, training areas." Menaen grimaced, like he was recalling dark memories. "Hell, he called it. Down with the insects and worms, the rot, the damp, the filth and disease, enough to make the strongest man sick for the rest of his life. Your grandpappy used to preach about those tunnels all the time." He took a breath. "How they filled them with traps, like sharp punji sticks dipped in shit for the infection, mines that capsized whole tunnels and took a squad with them, live snakes and tarantulas in pits. Now, the Viet Cong would stay down there for months at a time, wait for US forces to overpass, pop up behind them and blow the rearguard to bits." Another wheezy breath. "Uncle Sam asked for volunteers to crawl down into those tunnels. Tight, insane places, dug out for malnourished men who were barely five feet tall. Davis believed in the cause, so he volunteered, and they set him to killing men underground. Sometimes he did it with his gun, sometimes with napalm, sometimes a knife, sometimes his bare hands. Again and again." Menaen's black eyes grew wide. "I heard they call that feeling, trapped in the dark with an army of little men trying to bite out your throat, the 'Black Echo'."

Wren took a breath.

"Then Davis got himself captured. POW, tortured, lived in those tunnels for months right along with the Viet Cong. Never seeing the sky. He lost all his fingernails, patches of skin, part of his humanity, maybe. A hostage swap deal finally brought him back home. His fingernails grew back, but his mind? He was a different man, so they say. PTSD, they call it now. He came back here, family land, tried to farm, but he couldn't do it. The black echo haunted him, so he swore. He couldn't sleep. He had to do something about the war."

Menaen smacked his lips. Looked at Wren expectantly.

"You saying you want coffee?"

"I'm not puckering for a fat kiss. Last request for a dying man."

Wren turned to Rogers. She gave him a look. He gave her a look back.

"I'll find the coffee," she said, glowering, and set off.

Menaen looked pleased.

"What was he going to do about the war?" Wren pressed.

Menaen snorted. He looked older than ever, in the wan light cast through the high slit windows. "That's where I come in. He started a group. A commune, right here. It was the tail end of the sixties, people flowing across the country like blood on an abattoir floor. Screwing everywhere, protesting the war, hating on politics. I was a conscientious objector myself, on the lam from the draft. I saw Davis' people disrupting a 'triumphant' parade for heroes over in Wichita, got myself involved. Came out here and never looked back. See, your grandfather had some big ideas in that messed-up head of his."

"You already said that."

"Worth saying twice," Menaen countered.

"The big idea being that the devil himself was behind the war?"

"Exactly that. But not only that. He was building a weapon, too."

Wren frowned. "What weapon?"

"A hole in the ground. Where we met."

"The well?"

"It's not a well."

"So what is it?"

Menaen licked his lips. "A bullet casing. Dig it deep enough, fill it with an armor-piercing slug, fire it with the same kind of blast material he used back in 'Nam, and maybe he could kill the devil forever." Menaen smiled, like he was remembering a pleasant memory. "Stop the war, and any other wars before they could begin."

Wren felt strings beginning to pull in his chest. Connections to himself, his father, the Apex's mixed-up ideology.

"You're saying the well's a bullet?"

"A bullet casing. To fire down. To kill the devil and save us all."

"Right. So what's the bullet?"

"You're feeling it, aren't you?" Menaen asked, those dark eyes drinking Wren in. "I seen men roll with the spirit all my life. You're on board."

"What's the bullet?" Wren repeated.

"We used napalm for the blast material, of course," Menaen said, ignoring him. Wren's vertigo started to swirl. "Like he'd used in the tunnels. A Tunnel Rat burning all those other rats alive."

Wren could imagine it. The war, the jungle, men digging their way down deeper into clay, into jungle muck so dark and foul you couldn't breathe. Clearing the traps, bypassing the dead bodies and the spikes and the stinking pits of human waste, rooting for enemies buried like maggots in the deep.

Then pouring in napalm. Lighting the trail. Not even hearing their cries. Smoke pouring up and filtering through the jungle leaves, rising toward the same sun that shone down on Kansas, on the United States, all complicit under the arc of heaven.

"You're not well, boy," Menaen said, eyeing him curiously.

"I'm fine."

"I don't think so. What Davis had, I think you've got a taste of it too. Your father. Maybe it runs in the blood."

"I'm fine," Wren said more firmly, looked down along the passageway. "Rogers, where's that coffee?"

Only crackling static came back on his earpiece.

"Kitchen's a good distance away," Menaen said. "She'll be minutes more yet, if'n you didn't already blow it up."

Wren refocused on the old man. It was hard to look at his pitted face, nausea swirling the details, trying to grasp the scope of what he was saying. So his grandfather had run a cult too. Tried to kill the devil.

"What was the bullet?" he asked. Coming back to the key question. "At the bottom of the well. The pit."

"The bullet casing," Menaen corrected.

"Whatever you want to call it. What was the damn bullet!?"

Those dark eyes peered through him. "I think you know."

Wren felt sick. Of course he knew. "Say it."

"His people," Menaen said cheerfully. "We laid them out like gut-shot Tunnel Rats. Sacrifices, sure, but to kill the devil you need psychic energy, you know? It makes sense."

Wren let a stray, wild gulp of laughter out.

"There you go," Menaen said. "You're chasing the dragon now, boy."

"How many?"

"How many people? Well. He had me in charge of all the calculations. I was an engineer back then, you know? Knew something about ordinance, despite being a real peacenik. How many black powder grains you put into a casing. How many people you had to stuff into a well to make it fire deep and true."

"How many?" Wren barked.

"Fifty-five. Not just any types, either. I did all the math. Anyone could contribute to the workings, of course, you seen their numbers all over the walls here, I'm sure. I keep it all just the way it was back then, divinely inspired. But truth is, it was mostly me who crunched the real data. The right proportions of men, women, boys, girls, just like you mix napalm in the right ratio. Lay them flat, all alive of course, all willing, tamp them down like ball bearings in birdshot. Then you pack your blast material next." He paused a moment, lost in the memory. "I loved the precision."

Wren was barely thinking. Seeing the vision of it, just like the Apex's pits. People descending below the earth for faith in him. Into the well as human ammo. Trying to prove something, trying to earn his favor, believing him when he said this was going to transform the world for a greater purpose. Hot in the dark, hand-in-hand, whispered words of comfort as the napalm vat descended…

Suddenly he knew why he recognized the shape of the hanging pendulum beneath the water tower. It only knocked him sicker.

"See, Davis grew up after the first atom bomb over Hiroshima," Menaen said, pushing Wren deeper into the past. "Before my time, but he'd seen those images and they sunk in deep. Maybe it made him want to go to war more, avoid that outcome? Trying to be a good man, you know." He paused a second. "You ever hear of the Trinity atomic bomb tests?"

Wren blinked. Trinity. That number again, three.

"First atomic test ever conducted. Out in the Jornado del Muerto desert. That means 'Dead Man's Journey', you know? It's a good name. In New Mexico, 1945. Your grandpappy, he made sure we knew all about it. He'd preach for hours about the logistics, how those scientists unleashed the most destructive force ever known to man. Some of them feared they were going to blow up the planet." He paused a moment, seemed to be happily chewing on that thought. "The tests started with a metal tower, one hundred feet tall. They rigged the trial atom bomb to a chain and pulley, hoisted it up, even stacked mattresses below it, you know, in case it dropped." Menaen smiled wider, lost in the memory. "They wanted to simulate an airburst detonation. So Davis liked that too. He wanted us to do the same thing here."

Wren swallowed. "The water tower."

Menaen shrugged. "It's a disguise, looking like that. For while we were building out the fifty-five black powder grains. The casing you saw hanging there? That held the napalm."

Wren almost gagged, just held it back. The pendulum missile shape swinging on a chain. "It's the same one?"

"As sure as night follows day. I swap out parts sometimes. It's an important point of untapped psychic power, now. The bones of the fifty-five rest beneath it, where they burned."

Wren gagged again, barely held it in this time.

"Don't puke on me, boy," Menaen warned. "I'm not going into the afterlife soaked in some other man's vomit."

"The bones are still there? In the well?"

"Sure they are. Your grandpappy amongst them."

"What?"

"Oh yeah. I said he died, right? It's probably why the blast never worked, why the devil never got killed, why the wars kept right on. Fifty-five was the right number. Not fifty-six. But I guess he knew that, when he shoved Davis in."

Wren's jaw dropped. Trying to make sense of any of this. It was all crazy, but it felt so familiar. There were shades of the Apex's melting-pot ideology everywhere, and he almost knew what was coming next. Mouth dry, throat tight. "Who shoved him in?"

Menaen smiled. "His son, of course. Your daddy. He must have been all of twelve years old at the time."

40

LOVE AND LIES

Wren felt himself falling.

Twelve years old, the same age he'd been when the Pyramid burned and his father left, leaving Pequeño 3 as sole survivor, wandering through the smoke of the fake town alone.

"Hey," Menaen said, and Wren tried to focus.

It didn't work. The world was turning upside down. He pushed himself to his feet, trying just to keep from tipping over.

Twelve years old. He lurched back down the blasted trailer, hands slapping on workbenches, banging against the walls, legs going weak. Ahead snow blew in through the gap in the wall, and he poured himself out into the storm.

The cold helped. Putting ice on the wound. He stripped his helmet and tossed it, found all kinds of straps crossing his chest, ripped them off and kept moving forward. The wind whipped snow into his eyes, crystalizing his thoughts before they could form.

This was why his father had spared him.

At twelve years old, with every other person little Pequeño 3 had ever known dead, the Apex had left him alive. It was a moment twenty-five years in the past, something he rarely thought about, but now…

He struggled to grasp the scale of it, felt like he was turning inside out, trying to process something that made no sense. As a twelve-year-old the Apex had killed his father. As a father, he'd let his twelve-year-old son live.

Wren fell to his knees in the buffeting wind, gloved hands plunged into the snow. He remembered how it had felt to be in one of the Apex's faith pits, digging a way out beneath the fake town, with little Grace-In-Our-Times by his side. He'd thought he'd tricked the Apex, outsmarted him at his own game, but maybe he never had.

Maybe the Apex had stood above that pit for three days, knowing Pequeño 3 wasn't inside. Letting it happen. That sent Wren reeling into his own black echo, like his grandfather through the dirt of Vietnam, digging deep for men to kill.

There'd been so many theories over the years about why he'd been left alive. That it was a punishment. That Wren was some kind of messenger, heralding the Apex's future return. But never this.

That maybe the Apex had seen something of himself in the boy.

That maybe this was some twisted kind of love.

Wren didn't know what to do with that. The Apex was a monster. A madman. Then there was this.

A voice called his name. He imagined closing his hands around the Apex's throat, choking the life out of him like Aden had died in his arms. What would he see in those crystal blue eyes in his final moments? Hatred? Acceptance?

Love?

Hands came on his back. Words came in his ear, hard to process. "Boss, you're freezing! What are you doing out here, what happened?"

He looked up and saw Rogers' face, but didn't know how to explain.

"You'll die out here like this, come on, let's get inside."

She pulled him up, like she had before. He glimpsed flashes of the firestorm in her eyes.

"That's it, come on," she encouraged, pulling him to his feet. "This way, Boss."

He followed her back into the trailer. Maybe the cold had helped. The vertigo was falling away. Rogers set him in a chair opposite Menaen, came up with a blanket which she wrapped around him. He was shaking hard. She wrapped his hands around a steaming mug of coffee. "Drink it," she commanded.

He drank. Black. Hot. Acrid as filth. He glugged a small gulp, a bigger one, letting the heat fill him up. Like napalm dropped down a well. Started coming back to himself fast. Rogers rubbed his shoulders vigorously, working some heat back into his system.

"That was dramatic," Menaen said. "Was it something I said?"

Wren swigged the last of the coffee. Set the cup down. Dealing with it, now.

"What happened, Chris?" Rogers asked.

He looked at her and smiled. Felt shaky inside, but the edges of this new wound were already sealing up. He'd always been a fast healer.

"I've been getting the lowdown on my dad. Apparently he killed my grandfather."

Rogers made a face. "I'd say I was surprised, but that sounds about right."

"He did it when he was twelve. Same age I was when he left me in the fake town."

Rogers laughed briefly, then clamped it back. "Yeah. Sorry. That checks out."

Wren thought about it for a second, then laughed too. It did. It didn't really change anything. Good to know, maybe. Something he could use.

He put his mug down. Refocused on Menaen.

"So my father shoved Davis Thackerton into the pit. What happened next?"

Menaen stared back but said nothing.

"What? Cat got your tongue?"

"I said I'd tell you about this place," Menaen said. "How it began. I've done that. The rest, it didn't happen here."

"So where did it happen?"

Menaen said nothing.

"Are you really shutting down now? Even after you told me everything?"

"I ain't told you nothing. Not about him. About his father, sure, about this place. About the man himself, though? Nope."

Wren considered. Projected his father's track forward, from a twelve-year-old boy to the leader of the Pyramid. There had to have been in-between stages, where he grew up, learned his craft, really *became* the Apex. "First Corinthians."

Menaen only stared.

"What about our deal?"

"I kept my terms."

Wren thought back to Menaen's precise words, something about 'this place'. That was true.

"Then why you want us to pound your bones, if you've not said anything? It's no betrayal."

"Getting caught's the betrayal. If I could pound my own bones, I would."

Wren grunted. The age-old problem. "Then you're out of luck. There's no way I'm keeping my side of the deal, you don't give me something more."

Menaen shrugged. "Then I suffer forever. I can make my peace with that."

Make his peace. Wren leaned back in the chair. The guy was a real basket-case. He gazed into those black eyes and glimpsed all the layers of the Apex's lies. Lies upon lies, welded into place over fifty years like steel plate reinforcing tissue-thin trailer walls.

No way to dig them all out, now. He'd been lucky to get as much as he had, as easily as he had. Breaking the shackles of a cult leader could take years, if it ever happened. The walls weren't going to come down now just because he asked nicely.

He was going to need something explosive.

"What's your name?" Wren asked.

The guy's eyes narrowed. "You simple? We been through this. It's Menaen the Builder."

"Bullshit. Both of us know that's a Pyramid name, one hundred percent. It's totally my father's style."

Menaen's jaw tightened.

Wren leaned closer, spoke slow and calm, like he was sharing a secret. "Here's the thing. We already know you're weak, 'Menaen'. You bent for my father, and if anyone's got my father's gift, it's me. You said it yourself, I've got him in me. So you should be afraid of what I'm going to say. How I might bend you back. Because no matter how hard you tried, I'm betting you never could get his nonsense to make sense, am I right?"

Menaen made no move to answer, but that was fine, he had ears like everyone else.

"Fact is, you used to be an engineer," Wren went on, thinking through the play as he spoke. "A man of science, but guided by ideals. You protested a grotesque war, and that took courage. It may be fifty years you've been doubling down on my father's BS, but you know there's no killing the devil with a bullet made out of dead people. You've always known, but you played along because Davis Thackerton made you feel important, like you were key to stopping the war." Wren leaned in, sounding reasonable. "Trouble is, you're starting the war now. We're hours away from mass anarchy across the country, a mass body count that'll dwarf the dead in Vietnam. Maybe it's already started, citizens killing each other in the streets, and do you honestly think it'll be any more effective than the psychic bullet of the fifty-six who died in that pit?"

Menaen's pupils flickered left to right rapidly, looking between Wren's eyes.

"No need to answer," Wren said. "Just let it slip in alongside all his bullshit brainwashing. Fifty years is a lot to go against, and I'm sure it seems too late to turn back." Wren raised an eyebrow. "But you're not an idiot. You know in your un-pounded bones that there's no calculation to transmute dead bodies into a bullet. You know the whole thing's a show." Wren tapped the man's head, feverish and hot. "Just a sham. We both know it, Menaen. He certainly knows it. We're all just enjoying the dance."

Menaen gulped in a breath. "You're lying."

Wren almost laughed. "Am I? They're just simple questions, Menaen. Who changed your name, is one. That's cult indoctrination 101, right there, destroy the past and rebrand the future. Who killed Davis Thackerton? Make followers party to an atrocity for a greater good, that's indoctrination 102. Cherry on top, who locked you up in these trailers?" Wren gestured around them. "103. Imprisonment. I heard you've been mowing your way onto other people's fields. What is that, but your brain still resisting the lies?" Wren's eyes drilled into Menaen's. "You did that yourself. You couldn't help it. Tell me, when's the last time you even spoke to anyone who wasn't already mad?"

Menaen shifted in his seat, eyes roving for a way out. Wren didn't give him one.

"Right now my father's talking about jailers all the time, spewing his poison that half the country need to burn to set the slaves free, but doesn't that sound like the pot calling the kettle black to you?" Wren sucked a fast breath. "Just look at what he's done to you. Lock your brain in lies you can't get out of. Lock your body here for fifty years. Lock everyone into his pyramid, bury innocents face-down in the dirt so they'll serve him forever, like that poor girl at First Corinthians. The worst thing is, you're locked in right there with her, even if you can't see it. He took everything from you, and you still want to protect him. If anyone's the jailer here, it's him."

Menaen was sweating now, his whole body humming. Wren kept boring in like a Tunnel Rat, seeking out targets in the deep past. Countdown to an explosion, like the Trinity tests in '45.

"But it all started with you wanting to stop a war," Wren said softly, bringing things back around. "You were a good man to want it. But he twisted that motivation, and he kept twisting until you thought stopping one war meant starting another. But you tell me, is setting the world on fire any kind of way to save it? Is it any more likely than trying to kill the devil with a bullet of fifty-five, sorry, fifty-six souls shot into hell?"

Menaen laughed. It was involuntary and panic-ridden, but it was real.

"You're right, that is ridiculous. It always has been. So help me stop his war. Tell me your real name."

Menaen's mouth opened. He went to speak. Wren craned for the blast to come, words he mustn't have said for fifty plus years.

"Say it!"

"Jonathon," Menaen gasped. The sound was throttled, his mind fighting his body for every syllable. "Jonathon Gibson."

41

JONATHON

Menaen shook. Wren held his shoulders as the shudders intensified. A man re-making himself inside, rebuilding who he was from the ground up, though Wren was under no illusions. Wear a mask for fifty years, it was hard to ever take it off. Lies were an addiction. This was a bubble at best. Most likely Jonathon would sink back into the comforting grasp of Menaen soon, the role of a lifetime.

He had to get what he needed now.

"The Apex," Wren prodded, gently. "You said he killed my grandfather. Let's begin there. Why did he do that?"

Jonathon looked up. His eyes were different. Not so black, anymore. Even his voice sounded younger. "He said-"

"I don't care what he said," Wren said, gently but firm. "He was a child then. You were an adult, right? You became his adoptive father, so you tell me. Why did he do that?"

It was hard. Wren could see the effort it took. This old version of Jonathon Gibson trying to separate himself from the Apex's reasoning, from Menaen the Builder, from the steel-plate layers of ideology locking him in place.

"I, uh-"

"Jonathon."

His dark eyes flashed. "I think he was jealous."

"Of his father?"

"Of the attention. Of the direction Davis was taking things."

"At twelve?"

Jonathon blinked, and a tear broke down his pitted cheek. "You said it yourself. He was no normal child."

Wren nodded along, adding that to the pile. "He grew up hearing his father preach. The people came and listened. All about Vietnam, shooting the devil in the heart?"

"Everything," Jonathon gulped. "Davis had his son up sometimes to speak in tongues, talk about whatever was in his head. And your father, he always had a thing for pyramids." He winced, like he'd been stabbed in the belly. Confession hurt, but he kept on. "All that stuff, the triangles and pyramids, came from your father. Davis just built it in. A kid's book he read about the Egyptians." He paused, looked up at Wren with a new light in his eyes, like a medium channeling a long-departed spirit. "We didn't have a lot of books at the compound. Things about the war, leaflets, but nothing for kids. Maybe that was the only one. A picture book of Egyptian mythology."

Wren stared. Lots of questions. Only one that would serve as the key to them all. "What's my father's name, Jonathon?"

The old guy looked confused. Like he didn't understand what he was being asked.

"I don't-"

"It's not hard," Wren urged. "You remember your own name. I know you remember his. You've just got to say it."

It took long seconds. Wren leaned in. Jonathon tried to frame the sounds, unspoken for so long.

"Noah," he managed. "Noah Thackerton."

Wren sat back. Felt like something significant had shifted. The Apex had a name. The Apex was human. The shackles could be lifted.

"Noah."

Jonathon looked down at his lap, like he was expecting the fury of God to smite him down.

"So Noah killed his father," Wren summarized. "Now Davis Thackerton is dead along with all his people, burned up at the bottom of the pit. The devil isn't dead, though, the mission was a failure. What happens next? He start things up again, in a new direction?"

Jonathon nodded.

"But it's a new ideology, now," Wren riffed. "First Corinthians, focused around triangles, pyramids?" He got a nod. "An ideology he kept developing. Melting pot. But he leaves the water tower up, the pit, as reminders of the past. Psychic power, you said." He thought for a second. "What was the new goal?"

Gibson looked up. Seemed to be at a loss. His hands wormed in their duct tape restraints. "See, we only had that one book, and…'

"What was the goal?" Wren pressed.

Gibson went stone cold for a second. Stiff, upright, and Wren thought he was about to pass out. Pulling too deep. Maybe finally give himself a heart attack.

Then the word came.

"Resurrection," Gibson said. Stared dead ahead. "Die and come back stronger. As a god. The book said you could do it. Pharaohs did it all the time. Triangles were the key. The pyramid. The apex, the tomb."

Wren blinked. He hadn't once mentioned those words himself, apex or tomb. "But the apex is here," he said fast, feeling the bubble straining against fifty years of dead weight. "The tomb, too. They're both right here! Center of the pyramid over America. If that's what he wants, resurrect himself as a god, then why isn't he here?"

Gibson's eyes spread wide, the bubble right up to the edge, then he burst out sobbing.

"I'm sorry," he said. Began repeating it. Rocking himself forward and backward, tears pouring from his cheeks. For the dead woman, maybe. For the waste of his life.

"Jonathon, why is he not here?!"

But Jonathon Gibson was gone. Wren knew it. Broken. The weight of a lifetime of lies had pulled him apart, and they weren't going to get anything more now.

He took a breath. Looked up at Rogers, who was staring at him with something like awe. Another magic trick.

"Resurrection," she said. "But how did you…"

She trailed off. Staring into his eyes and seeing something different. The reason behind it all, maybe.

"Resurrection," Wren repeated.

42

RESURRECTION

Wren stood up.

"Where are you going?" Rogers called after him.

His head was filled with thoughts too furious and fresh to put into words. "I need to walk."

Rogers stood too. "You're not going outside again. I'm not in the mood to draw any more snow angels with you, Boss."

He barely heard it, turned, started walking. Didn't matter which direction.

"I'm serious," Rogers said. "No more snow angels! Don't go outside."

Connections were already bouncing around his head, heating up like neutrons in an atomic bomb.

"And he's gone," Rogers said in back. "Never a word of thanks. You save a man's life, you make him a nice cup of coffee, you'd think..."

She was cut off as Wren passed through the gale of snow blowing in at the blast hole, like a silencing curtain. After that it was just him and the workbenches with their crafted triangles and calculations, carved into the walls and floor. Metal plate was everywhere, insulated with padded silver foil and slitted with gaps for shooting out of.

He passed from the workbench trailer to the next, a long narrow room with fat cathode-ray televisions stacked along both sides, all of their screens dead. It didn't mean anything to him. He kept on, passed through a room with four bathtubs in it, each filled with icy water, no idea what they might be for. He passed through a room with a bunkbed, the top bed perfectly neat, the bottom rumpled like it had just been slept in, as if 'Menaen' were waiting for a friend to come sleepover.

He hit a corner where the trailers made a hard left, and stood for a moment at the welded vertice, looking back the way he'd come. The blast of snow was maybe a hundred yards away. He looked the other way, bisected at an angle of around sixty degrees, enough to make a perfectly equilateral triangle, maybe visible from space.

Jonathan Gibson had kept himself busy. Fifty years was a long time to build this thing.

Wren plunged on, through a neat but molding kitchen, ancient fridge humming off a gas-powered generator, kettle still steaming slightly, finally starting to put words to some of the thoughts in his head.

Anastasi Street. He'd thought nothing of it at the time, but it was a word he knew from an extensive study he'd made of names and their roots. A great way to connect with people; tell them what their name meant.

Anastasia, from the Ancient Greek Anastasis.

Resurrection.

He walked faster, the segmented trailers passing by like carriages in a never-ending triangular train, trawling through more symbolic interconnections in his head, trying to pattern-match for the next step forward. The number three was everywhere now, in the sides of a triangle, in the shape of this trailer, in the Trinity nuclear test.

The holy trinity, he thought: Father, Son and Holy Ghost. Jesus rolling back the stone after three days, emerging out into the light. The Apex buried in an airless pit for three nights, coming back to his people alive.

He walked faster, his mind speeding up in sync as triplets buzzed like angry bees. Mind, Body, Spirit. Past, present, future. Life, death, rebirth. Heaven, Hell, Earth. Pyramids embodied the number three, three sides to every face, the strongest shape in construction.

The Apex. X. Christopher Wren.

A pyramid across America. The first letter to Corinthians, dealing with matters of resurrection. A skull buried peering down into hell as a foundation for the Apex to stand on. The Pyramid. The Foundation. An app made up of triangles, a Pyramid of one thousand people burned alive, the apex and the tomb and the…

Wren stopped walking. Tried that one again. The apex and the tomb and the…

Something was missing. He didn't know what it was. He looked around the space he was in and saw walls decorated with faces. Bodies too. Dozens of them. He leaned closer, and by the weak storm light saw an incredible level of detail brushed into the metal. Looked like the work of decades. Filigreed eyes, cheeks, necks, clothing. Shading, stippling, a chisel point hammering again and again with the greatest care, crafting men, women and children.

Something in Wren's heart cracked.

The people of Davis Thackerton's cult. Had to be. Memorialized here forever. Not only as a prison for them, but as something else.

Company for Jonathan Gibson. Menaen the Builder. Friends, even. A man locked in solitary confinement, steadily going mad, needed some kind of human contact, even if it was fake. He must've spent years drawing these. Wren spun. Maybe Davis Thackerton was here, preserved forever in the carving. His grandfather. Maybe Noah was here too, the Apex captured as an innocent child. So many memories recorded by Gibson. Perhaps waiting for the day Noah came back, saw this and was proud. Maybe transported Jonathan into his pyramid ark and made it all worthwhile.

Wren's vision doubled. He felt so close. Apex and tomb and...

He started striding back. Through the kitchen, around the corner, through the room of bathtubs, the televisions, toward the blast of snow until he reached the workbenches again where he stared at the wall.

Remembered the Apex's mantra, repeated by X, sprayed out a billion times by millions of voices.

Pain is a doorway. Fear is a portal. Walk in the fire.

A scorched map of America seemed to swell and pulse before him. He reached up and traced the 'Icon' triangle from New York southwest down to Acapulco, northwest up to Seattle and back east across to New York. Medicine Lodge in the center. Apex and tomb, but neither was where the resurrection took place.

Nor should it be. Now it seemed so obvious.

Jesus came back to life when he rolled back the stone. Pharaohs only came back as gods when they left their tomb behind, ascended to the apex and from there commanded the world. Resurrection was neither the apex nor the tomb, but an in-between place, the realm between death and life. It didn't happen at the center, it happened at the edges.

In the portal. At the doorway. Where the flames met the air and burned the hottest.

Wren's finger shook as it drifted left across the map like a water diviner's rod, inexorably leading him to the great triangle's edge. The only place to put a doorway.

For maybe a minute he just stared. Disbelieving. Then starting to believe. It was in the name, after all. All the clues were there. They always had been.

He knew exactly where the Apex was. Maybe where he'd been all along. The oldest trick he ever pulled, repeated on an epic scale.

Little Phoenix.

The fake town. Site where the Pyramid first burned. At the exact midpoint of the great triangle's line between Seattle and Acapulco. A point decided by predestiny, laid out as an 'Icon' on a map maybe fifty years ago as the site for Noah Thackerton's coming resurrection.

The phoenix reborn from the ashes of his country's death. So the Apex would return stronger than ever, ascendant over all.

43

BRIDGE

Wren pushed through the draft of snow pelting through the carriage wall, feet crunching in several inches of settled white, to see a wintry tableau stretching away before him.

Jonathan Gibson in his chair, lap frosted with snow, with the blanket wrapped over his shoulders. Sally Rogers standing a little further on with her phone held high like she was trying to catch a signal. It looked like a carved fresco in the trailer wall, two more souls trapped in amber in this timeless, lost tomb.

Wren blinked and shook it off.

"We have to go," he said. His voice came out guttural and low, like an animal just emerging from hibernation.

Rogers' gaze levelled on him. "You figured it out?"

"I know where he is."

A second passed. Rogers put her phone in her pocket. Took a step toward Wren, then paused, looked at Gibson. "What do we do with him?"

Wren looked. For a second his first thought was 'leave him here'. He'd freeze to death soon enough, with the wall breached. It would even be peaceful, gradually losing sensation in his extremities, feeling the deceptive warmth as hypothermia lulled his mind into the dark. Nothing like the way the fifty-five had died. The fifty-six. A far easier death than they must have given the woman under First Corinthians.

But he didn't say it. Jonathan Gibson was a victim as much as he was a perpetrator. If there was any lesson to be had here, it was that. They were all victims: Davis Thackerton of a brutal, prolonged war; Noah Thackerton of Davis' delusions, and so on down the line to Jonathon Gibson, the X-apoc and Wren himself.

A thought occurred to him. Christopher Thackerton. Maybe Wren Thackerton? It didn't seem to take.

"Boss!" Rogers said. Shouted, even. "Are you OK?"

"I'm fine," he said, realizing she'd called his name several times. Lost in hyper focus. Drifting on the vertigo of fresh revelation. "He comes with us. We'll dump him in custody along the way."

Rogers nodded, produced a knife from her tactical belt and slit the duct tape holding Gibson to the chair. Wren strode forward and lifted him up. The man was almost deadweight, too mentally broken to take charge of his own body. Wren hoisted him in a fireman's lift and walked away from the incoming snow, toward the front door.

"So where are we going?" Rogers asked.

"Back to the start. To Little Phoenix."

Rogers let out a gasp. "You're kidding. Your town? The fake town in Arizona?"

Wren just grunted, pointed at the door up ahead. There were spent ammo shells on the floor here, brass casings scattered where Gibson had fired at them through a slit. Rogers went to the door, rammed back one deadbolt, two, and the plate metal swung open.

"How is that possible?" Rogers asked, holding the door open as a blast of snow rushed in. "I thought you knew that place like the back of your hand."

"Me too," said Wren, and stepped out into the gale.

They couldn't talk in the storm. If anything it was worse than before, visibility reduced to a yard or two. No track of their previous footprints, just the sense of a bearing. Wren felt it though, like the workings of this place were tattooed on his skin. He'd seen Gibson's calculations. Surveyed all his many sketches. The triangle of trailers. The 'water tower'. All laid out like an arrow pointing west, neat and clean as a death stroke. Even in that, Gibson had given away his unconscious yearning to be free.

Within minutes the tower emerged through the blizzard like a dark portent. At least the cover was open now, the snow could get into the pit and the 'psychic power' of the dead fifty-six could escape.

Gibson mumbled something on Wren's shoulder. Leaving his land for the first time in years. Wren cut a straight line from the tower to the Ford. He dumped Gibson in the frigid back, strapped him in with a seatbelt while Rogers scraped a thick layer of crusted snow off the windshield, then met her at the driver's side.

"You're wired, Boss," she shouted. "Your eyes are crazy. You're not driving in this!"

He didn't let go of the door handle.

"I'm serious," Rogers bellowed. "We're not ending up in some ditch because your concussed brain spaced out for thirty seconds. Chris!"

He looked at her. Couldn't argue. Let go.

Rogers opened the door, dropped in. Wren circled and got in the passenger side.

"I didn't space out," he said, slamming the door and pulling his seatbelt on. "I was reflecting."

Rogers laughed, hand on the ignition. "Right, like you weren't making snow angels in a blizzard, either. Honestly, it's a miracle you're moving at all, barely a week out from taking a bullet to the head. I got this."

She turned the key, the ignition coughed, the engine turned over once then died.

An awkward moment passed.

"You got this?" Wren asked.

"She just needs to warm up."

She tried again, the engine coughed and died again.

"Girl power," Wren offered.

Rogers shot him a foul look, focused on the ignition and turned the key a third time. This time it caught. Wren spun the AC's dials to full hot, only then realizing how cold he really was. His fingers were blue. Maybe that was hypothermia. Past the cold, into the numb warmth of nothingness.

The Ford jerked forward. Rogers worked the gears. Wren brought up the satellite map on his phone, but it refreshed and went blank.

"We lost GPS," Wren said. "The storm."

"So I drive by feel."

"And compass." Wren tapped through to a compass app, tying it into the portion of the map he'd studied "It's straight west to the road, then south, turn west when we cross the Medicine Lodge River and we should be coming up on Mills Landing Strip. Hellion set us a jet there."

Rogers looked at him. "You memorized that?"

"It's two turns. We may struggle to take off in all this, but…"

Rogers grunted and sped up a little. Nothing to say to that. If the jet wouldn't take off, maybe that was that.

They bumped over the edge of the track. "I'd kill to know what's going on out there."

"You may have to," Wren said.

In five minutes they passed by Willy's house, a shadowy block in the storm, and Rogers turned south. There were no other vehicles on the road, only the downpour of snow as the storm let them have it. Wren barely thought. Surfing the past and the present, lodged in the present.

Little Phoenix. It worked. It synced up. He'd never have seen it coming.

In twenty minutes they reached the Medicine Lodge River, shot out on a low bridge at thirty miles an hour and almost crashed into a truck sprawled sideways across both lanes. Rogers hit the brakes and they hydroplaned on snow, came within inches of collision.

The F-150 rocked back. Wren let out a breath, back in the moment and surveying the scene. The bridge was narrow and impassably tight. His base instinct was to ram the truck, a gray Chevy, but on a bridge with low railings on either side, snow and ice making the physics unpredictable, he didn't like their odds. Fall over the edge into the icy water below, it wouldn't matter what insight he had into the Apex's mind. It was over.

"I'll move it," Wren said, was already opening the door so Rogers couldn't protest.

The wind hit him at once like a body-blow, snow tearing down the superhighway of the river's channel carved out of the flat Great Plains. He could barely see, hardly hear a thing. No sign of the driver. He leaned in, shaded his eyes, advanced, feeling the temporary warmth of the truck tearing away as heat sucked out of his body.

By the Chevy's passenger window he saw an X flag in the window. Barely had a millisecond for that to register before the gunshot rang out, blowing the Chevy's glass out against his chest.

He spun and dropped to one knee, drawing his Glock. Another shot rang out, spidering the Ford's windshield right in front of Rogers' face. No time to check on her. The shots were coming from the other side of the truck, and he bellied down and burrowed like a Tunnel Rat beneath the Chevy. X-apoc forces ordered to secure all roads to and from Medicine Lodge and any surrounding airfields, most likely.

Out the other side he led with only the Glock, head and hand, and cursed silently that he'd tossed his monocular in some fit of madness. He saw nothing now but driving snow. Still he picked out a trajectory, tracking back from the dual shots to the probable spot in the mass of white for a sniper's hide. Must be they had thermal sight too. Elevated on a truck bed, Wren figured, from the angle. In a tent, if they'd been blockading here for the past hour or so. That meant solid visibility head-on, but abysmal from the sides.

No time to think. He backed up, rolled out from under the side of the Chevy, re-holstered his Glock and laid hands on the bridge's side railing. Three horizontal steel bars designed to steer vehicles back central when they veered. Not designed to stop a man slipping between them like a posted letter.

Wren pushed, his body fell over the edge then hooked sharply when his grip caught. Hanging from the side of the bridge over an unknowable drop to the river below, lashed by a gale wind so hard his body swayed, with only static coming through the earpiece.

Was Rogers OK? Maybe dead already, taken on the first shot. If not, she wouldn't last long if they kept firing.

He started sideways as fast as he could, hand-over-hand to the right. Snow on the railing made it slippery and froze his palms. Moving too fast, he almost lost his hold and fell. The result of that was some real vertigo. Ten more, he told himself. Slowed his breathing, calmed his heart, made a conscious effort to clamp every grip as tight as possible, melt the snow with his residual body heat and get a clean hold.

Gunfire popped above, sliding closer with every crab-like shuffle. His shoulders burned from the weight. Maybe not much left in the tank. Should be enough.

After ten he gave it another five then pulled himself up the railings, got his feet on the bridge and stood, coming almost face-to-face with a guy leaning over the edge, trying to get a better angle on the Ford with a long rifle.

Black bandanna wrapped like a mask across his face, emblazoned with a white X. For a second he only stared at Wren, then started trying to bring the rifle to bear, but that was a mistake. The weapon in your hands wasn't always the best one for the moment. Wren proved that by clamping one hand on the guy's jacket and pulling him into a massive headbutt. Hit the guy's cheekbone, something cracked and he cried out and recoiled. Wren saw stars. Strictly against doctor's orders.

Then he was over the railing. The guy was bent double and staggering back, holding his face, but there was little time for mercy now. Wren drew his Glock and shot the guy in both shoulders. Destroying the bones, likely to leave him dead, but that fell to his choices. The guy sagged to the snow. Two steps on stood another truck, a camouflage tent propped up in the trailer, the spike of a sniper rifle now desperately trying to reorient but snagged on the canvas.

Wren fired three times, approximating center mass. There was a cry then the rifle barrel jerked and tipped slack. He strode forward, unsheathed the Mossberg shotgun and edged past the front of the truck. Another guy darted away around the indicator light. Wren fired through, took out the headlight, indicator, part of the grille and the guy.

He lay in his X gear lay in the snow, bleeding out from multiple lacerations. Wren kicked his weapon away and circled the truck, a Tacoma, breathing hard. Stared into the white but saw no evidence of a fourth man. He climbed into the trailer bed, found one dead sniper and tipped him out.

"Boss!" came a call.

He looked over the edge. Rogers was there, dragging Jonathan Gibson along by her side. He felt a flush of relief. Intact, uninjured, and making the right call. With the Ford's windshield smashed and the road blocked, it was better to switch vehicle.

Strange though that Gibson should get saved again, right after Wren had gunned down three X-apoc. He almost laughed, then helped her lift the old guy into the Tacoma's cab. The engine was on, a power line running from the cigarette lighter dock out the window to a heater in the trailer bed. Unnecessary now, and Wren yanked it.

"He almost got me," Rogers shouted from behind. Wren saw flecked blood on her face.

"You're not hit?"

"Glass shrapnel," she answered.

He shuffled over to the passenger side and Rogers got in after him. They closed the doors, sharply cutting off the gale, and looked each other in the eye over Gibson's slumping body.

"Looks like you had to do the killing," Rogers said. "But we have our answer about the country."

"America's falling," Wren answered. "Let's get on that damn jet."

44

MILLS

The Mills Landing Strip was invisible in the storm. They only knew they'd gone past it when the GPS on Wren's phone came back to life, assisted maybe by a break in the cloud cover or the ping from a nearby cell tower.

It looked like nothing much from above, an empty field plowed flat. No buildings, no parking lot.

"There's a jet here?" Rogers asked, peering as she pulled the Tacoma around. "It looks like cropland."

Wren couldn't argue. "According to Hellion, she put a ride at every airfield within fifty miles of Medicine Lodge. Let's hope she included this place."

In a few minutes they returned to the edge of the field, then the satellite link went out and their blip on the GPS app disappeared. Rogers slowed and they peered out into the storm. There was nothing to see but white.

"Drive it," Wren said. "Start at this end and work a circuit, they won't have parked in the middle."

Rogers pulled the wheel hard over, they dipped into a low trough then rumbled back up onto the landing strip. "It's bumpy for a runway."

"I expect it's for cropdusters and other light propellor aircraft. I bet they don't get a lot of corporate jets."

Rogers chuckled. They circled for two slow minutes, running around the west edge of the landing strip, where fences steered them back in.

"Other end," Wren said.

They crossed the strip. Maybe seven hundred yards. It was smoother right down the middle.

"How long should an air strip be?" Rogers asked.

"At a commercial airport for passenger jets? About three thousand yards."

Rogers laughed.

"Lots of redundancy baked in there. With good acceleration from intensive fuel burn, ambitious use of the flaps and nosecone, you can cut that in quarter."

"To seven hundred yards?"

"In ideal conditions."

Rogers laughed again.

Then they saw it. A yellow light floating like a lighthouse. Rogers hit the brakes, spun the wheel, pulled around to the loading door, clear of the wing. Closer up the craft's silhouette became clear; a fuselage that was impressively short, with a fat-bellied profile Wren recognized, a Beechcraft Premier IA. A real workhorse. Powerful lift.

Wren was first out, dragging Gibson with him, while Rogers leaned on the horn until a shadow split the cockpit light. In seconds all three of them were standing by the craft in the midst of the storm, waiting as the pilot opened the door and let down the stairs.

Wren was first in. The pilot was young, short-cropped brown hair, wearing a prim shirt with badges and epaulettes. His eyes bugged when he saw Wren. "Are you serious?"

"As a government audit," Wren said, helped Rogers in then closed and locked the door behind them.

"I can't believe this," the guy was saying. "Christopher Wren, in my plane? I never thought, I mean. This is amazing. But..." He trailed off, looking from Wren to Rogers to the window and back again. "You don't actually want me to fly in all this, do you?"

"You do it or I will," Wren said. "And if I do, we'll almost certainly crash. So I think it better be you."

The guy gulped. "Ah. But, this model, it's not certified for these conditions. Heck, no plane is! If we wait-"

Wren laid a hand on the guy's shoulder. "There's no waiting. You're a Foundation member?"

The guy nodded eagerly. "Yes, yeah, I-"

"Then we fly or die. Right now. What's it going to be?"

The guy's eyes flared. Looked into Wren's eyes and seemed to draw strength. One of the benefits of Thackerton blood, Wren figured.

"Fly," the guy said.

"Then no time like the present."

The pilot nodded again, getting a hold of himself. "Yes, sir. It'll be my privilege."

He turned smartly and went to the cockpit. Wren brought up his phone. Battery almost dead. He scouted the narrow, squat fuselage while Rogers settled Gibson into a seat and the pilot ran pre-flight checks. Found a charger, plugged in, and found the plane's Wi-Fi. With its more powerful uplink to satellites, it had a signal.

Wren booted up his darknet. It loaded slow, bare kilobytes per second. Not enough signal for video, even images or audio, but enough to read and write text.

Seemed the snowstorm had slowed the civil war in Medicine Lodge. Nobody had found the X-apoc guys in the field yet, and Wren figured nobody would for a while, not as long as the storm kept dumping snow. Hundreds of X-apoc had descended on the little town, looked to be filling out the main street, but with visibility barely a yard ahead, they were struggling to wage their war.

Across the country the X-apoc were mobilizing, but the trigger hadn't been pulled yet. Pretty much every city across the country was in open revolt, but the violence was still sporadic, the pushing and shoving stage of a fight before the real haymakers were thrown.

Wren paged through his darknet boards. The Foundation hadn't hit back yet either, though they stood ready; the only coordinated force preparing to protect life before the firestorm raged out of control.

The storm over Medicine Lodge had bought them a couple of hours.

In front the Beechcraft's engines fired up. The plane began to turn. Wren looked up, caught sight of Rogers on her phone urgently tapping out a message.

"Prepare for take-off," came the pilot's voice through the PA. "It's going to be rough."

Two hours to a landing strip near Little Phoenix, Wren figured. Possibilities raced through his mind. What they were going to find. What he was going to do. How that might finally put a nail in the X's mythos and force the X-apoc to stand down.

The engines surged to fever pitch and the jet jerked forward. Wren strapped his seat belt tight, then sent out a text to his hacker elite and the head of his Foundation, Hellion, B4cksl4cker and Theodore Smithely III, for their eyes only.

AM GOING TO LITTLE PHOENIX. THE APEX IS THERE. TAKE CONTROL OF COMMS. WE STILL HAVE TIME. PULL BACK FOUNDATION FORCES WHERE WE CAN. DELAY OPEN BATTLE FOR AS LONG AS POSSIBLE.

He sent the message, thought a moment longer, then started tapping a second message. HERE IS WHAT I'M GOING TO NEED:

The Beechcraft rumbled over the lumpy landing strip. Every fitting in the fuselage shook. Wren imagined the yards tearing by beneath them, only seven hundred in total, and prayed the pilot knew exactly what he was doing. Go one yard over and they'd hit the fences around the strip, maybe a trough or a hillock beyond that, maybe enough to tear the jet apart and leave it a flaming smear across the land.

He finished typing and sent his requirements. The front of the jet jerked up, then dropped with a crunch. The engines screamed. The front lifted a second time, held for a second then they were plucked up into the storm as if yanked by the hand of God.

Wren set down his phone as the little jet juddered and wailed and roared up into the storm, finally leaving the Apex's childhood tomb behind. No view out the window but white. Rogers was shouting into her phone. Trying to command FBI forces. It didn't sound like she was making much headway.

Wren's head pounded. He couldn't believe he was so close. The Apex almost in his grasp. Twenty-five years of hunting, and maybe it could all end. He checked the time, just gone noon. The forecast said snow was going to clear over Medicine Lodge in a few hours. After that, all bets were off.

45

LITTLE PHOENIX

He wouldn't have thought it was possible, but at some point in the middle of the flight, Wren fell asleep.

Adrenaline crash, or another delayed effect of the concussion tumbling in his head, so many balls to keep up in the air, plates to keep spinning, and-

He woke to Rogers shaking him.

"Boss, we're about to put down."

He blinked up from the depths of an old Pyramid memory. His mind working on the problem even asleep. Standing with his father in the desert at dawn, looking down into one of the desert pits. The Apex was alive with excitement, explaining to his little Pequeño 3 how he'd survived three days and three nights entombed under the ground.

There was no special magic to it. Just a tunnel dug out into the desert.

"I think I know where he'll be," he said, rubbing grit from his eyes. "The Apex."

Rogers handed him a cup of something. Harsh black coffee, looked like, no milk, cream, sugar, just the way he liked it. "Good."

"Please return to your seats and buckle up," came the pilot's voice over the intercom. "This will be a rough landing."

Rogers put a hand on Wren's shoulder then returned to her seat. He looked out of the window as the jet rocked steeply forward, diving sharply over red rocks and sand. The Sonoran Desert spread like a sandbox, his childhood haunt, place of jagged canyons, warbling cactus wrens and hydra-headed ocotillos. He'd returned so many times, and it had never felt like this.

His stomach leaped and spun. He drained the coffee anyway.

Coming home.

The jet wasn't designed for rough sand and dust, didn't have the hardened landing gear, but it had managed to take off in the storm so Wren figured a Main Street landing wouldn't kill them. Maybe strip the wheels then scrape in on their belly, pray that friction wouldn't blow the fuel tanks.

Wren unclicked his seatbelt and got up.

"Boss," Rogers said.

"It's OK," he said and strode the five steps toward the open cockpit.

"Mr. Wren," said the pilot, turning and looking surprised. "You really should-"

"Don't mind me," Wren said, slipped into the co-pilot's seat, strapped in and looked dead ahead.

There it was.

Little Phoenix. The fake town. Bane of his life. Maybe five miles off still, five thousand feet down and laid out like a child's playset. So much of it was still the same as ever: the saloon, the hotel, the general store. It was easy to picture how it would have looked in his childhood. Cages for babies behind the saloon. Vats for boiling in the basement of the hotel.

He could picture every inch. Right there was the dormitory where the Pequeños had slept, where the Apex had marked his own children with the sign of the Blue Fairy. It had been one of the first structures Wren had burned to the ground. It was easy to see the pattern he'd followed from there on, burning ever-outward.

His heart pounded, caffeine and adrenaline pulling a double on him. All his childhood had been spent here, listening to the depraved sermons of his father. Noah Thackerton. Just like little Noah had listened to his own father's ravings, Davis Thackerton. A family of madmen, passing on the family tradition.

And where were the women? The mothers. Buried, he supposed. In unmarked graves in the desert. At the bottom of the well back in Medicine Lodge. Burned up in the fake town on the Pyramid's last day.

He could see them all now, the one thousand laid out and smoking down Main Street. People he'd known and loved. No remembrance wall for them, etched by Jonathan Gibson. Just nothing. Bones ground to mortar for the Apex's inverted pyramid scheme.

They were coming in fast now, dropping a hundred feet per second or faster, maybe thirty seconds out from a final engine burst to convert all that downward momentum to forward thrust, hit the strip and streak off in a rush of sand and smoke.

He cast his eyes over all the new construction Maggie had put up in recent years. New residential blocks, a fitness center with a pool, the school, the hospital, all for the two thousand children he'd rescued from the Blue Fairy. Broad modern structures that thickened the town, adding depth and life to its once-sallow bones.

To the west though, the concrete foundation bases remained. Flat gray squares where fake town buildings had once stood, they stretched like overlarge pitcher's plates for fifty yards, and where they gave out Maggie had taken to placing new tombs, for the re-consecrated bones of the Pyramid members recovered from the sand.

His nausea burned to rage. All this time the Apex had been hidden right here. It was grotesque. Maybe he'd even had the Pyramid themselves build his hideout, so long ago. Wren remembered that first fateful trek out into the desert, the sun at their backs, to the the pit. The first time the Apex had shown off his 'magic'. If there was ever a fitting entrance to his private vision of hell, it would be there.

Twenty seconds. Down in the town they would have seen him by now, heard the jet's engines roaring like a herald from heaven, the avenging 'Saint Justice' come to set the past, present and future right.

Ten seconds, and now he picked out upturned faces and people running from his path, children in windows gawping up in surprise, maybe his own children, maybe his wife too, all wondering what on Earth was about to happen.

Five seconds, then the ground rushed up and hit the jet like a car crash from below. Enough momentum to keep a four-ton chunk of metal and plastic in the air converted instantly into vibration, heat and noise. The seat slammed up into Wren's spine, the flaps shot to hard brake and the engines roared into full reverse.

In seconds they dropped five inches as the solid rubber tires melted and shredded, sending them scraping along on the landing gear until that too sheared away and the jet dropped a final thump to the earth, scraping along on its fat belly. Heat seared up through the flooring, sand and dust clouded up either side and the grinding grew louder as the engines whined, trying to brake their velocity before they skidded off the semi-flat street and hit raw desert.

The pilot strained at the flaps. Wren could only stare in fascination at the sun halfway down in the west, feeling like things were coming full circle. Arriving in style. Here to bring the Pyramid down for the final time.

At last the jet rocked to a stop. It smoked and creaked. Wren unstrapped, patted the pilot on the shoulder, then moved through to the back. Jonathan Gibson had been sick on himself. Rogers was already on her feet.

"Smooth," she said.

"As Tennessee whisky," Wren answered. Spun the lever to open the door and jumped two feet down to the sand.

46

PIT

Within seconds a Jeep pulled up before Wren, the door opened and out stepped Theodore Smithely III, Chairman of the Foundation. Tall and gaunt as ever, all in black like Johnny Cash, holding two large rucksacks.

The hot air swam with dust kicked up by the jet. Wren glanced through the haze, past the Beechcraft's glowing red side and back along a blackened trail burned down the center of the fake town.

Just like old times.

"Your family have been secured," Teddy said, then looked at Rogers. "And your mother."

"Secure them all," Wren said, and took one of the rucksacks, climbed into the Jeep. "You can bet the X app already knows we're here."

He slammed the door. Rogers climbed into the passenger side, no argument this time, and he pulled away at once, heading west. His memory of the first pit was spotty, maybe an hour's walk due west of the town, which made for about three miles.

Rogers took the rucksacks and opened them in turn, checking through the contents. She handed a fresh earpiece to Wren and he slotted it in. It beeped as it paired with his phone, then Hellion's voice came abrupt and clear, the first time in hours.

"I can confirm, X app ALERT has gone out. Forces will be incoming."

"You couldn't spoof this one?"

"Negative. It has double redundancy, heavy security over Little Phoenix. Not our security, Christopher." That was further confirmation, if he needed any. "We can subvert this but it will take time."

Rogers held up a small plastic wallet. Within sat a familiar nubbin of plastic, barely a-quarter inch wide. A stub.

"And if we plant the stub in X's phone?"

"Access should be immediate. We will have root directory and source code."

"Sounds good," Wren said.

Rogers continued pulling gear from the rucksacks as Wren raced into the desert: full-body tactical outfits for each of them, in tight-weave para-aramid Twaron fiber sewn with aluminum foil. Rogers began changing while Wren scanned the dry red desert ahead, reaching for any landmark to jog his memory. Cacti, boulders, humps and dips in the land itself. Once he'd known them all so well.

"You are certain this is good idea?" Hellion asked. "To livestream everything?"

"It's the only idea," Wren said, as Rogers slotted a bodycam into her new Twaron jacket, activated it. He'd shared the plan on the jet before sleep had snuck over him. "Words won't cut it now, even killing the app's not enough. We have to show the X-apoc their leader getting felled, or they'll never stop. They have to see this with their own eyes."

"And if instead they see you being felled, Christopher? What then?"

"Then we're all screwed," he said, and hit the brakes. The Jeep skidded, Rogers caught herself smoothly on the dash then continued strapping on gear.

"There," Wren said, pointing off to the right. Maybe he couldn't put his finger on it precisely, but there was something about the angle of the land that felt familiar. Maybe a slight mound. Rogers was already out of the Jeep, and Wren followed.

"Boss," she said, handing him his gear. He stripped his bandoliers, his pants and shirt and pulled on the stiff new material. Pants, jacket, boots. Rogers handed him equipment as he was ready for it; holster for the Glock, magazines into the tactical belt, grenade strip, quad-load chest-plate of shotgun ammo, Mossberg into the long sheath. Last she slotted his bodycam in at the front, and he pulled on a compact rucksack.

"Do not forget to drop amplifiers every turn," Hellion said. "Or signal will die. Livestream will fade."

"Like Theseus and Ariadne's thread," Wren said, pocketing a handful of the small black amplifiers. Battery-powered and as big as old-school pagers.

"What is this, Theseus?" Hellion asked.

"Monster movie," B4cksl4cker answered. "Old Hollywood."

Rogers laughed.

"This way," Wren said, and stepped off the rough track into the desert proper. Felt the sand beneath his boots, the heat burning up and sweat already trickling inside his tough new gear.

The mound was faint but just about visible. Only stray creepers of Devil's Fingers grew atop it. A few black stones marked its rough outline. It was the place. Some thirty years ago his people had camped here and waited, dreaming of such grand things.

"This is it," Wren said, and walked out onto the mound. The ground flexed almost imperceptibly. He remembered how they'd pulled the supply skids across the pit, then piled dirt and sand on top of them a foot thick.

He'd done enough digging for one day, though, and they didn't have the time. Instead he stripped a grenade off his belt, kicked a divot into the center of the mound, pulled the pin and set the grenade in.

"Go," he said.

They broke to the side and laid low. The blast shook the earth and sent up a plume of ancient dust, chased by the rending sound of old timber splintering. One hell of a knock on the back door, but nothing the Apex wouldn't already know. What mattered now was speed, and Wren wasted no time striding through raining sand to the pit. Looked like two supply sleds had been driven downward by the explosion, their skids now bristling at the edges.

"That one," Wren pointed, and took hold of one runner. Rogers took the other and they pulled. The first tug was hardest, displacing the residual heaps of sand, but the next became one smooth drag. They ran backward and the sled came with them. They dropped it and moved to the second, which pulled easier, opening the pit wholly to the air.

Around fifteen feet in diameter and ten feet deep, walls lined with flat stones to make digging a way out harder for the victims stuck inside. Just like every other pit the Pyramid had dug. Wren felt like he was staring down into the past.

"You're sure this is a way in, Boss?" Rogers asked. "Looks like no one's been this way in years."

"There must be a regular entrance," he answered, "somewhere in town, but finding it could take hours. This is what we've got right now."

He jumped down into the pit without a second thought, spun around. The last time he'd been in a pit like this, it was with the sleds being pulled overhead, sealing him in the dark with his elder Pyramid brothers and sisters, along with Grace-In-Our-Times, the little girl his father had marked for death just to spite him.

"There," he said, pointing at the east wall leading back toward the town. "If there's a tomb anywhere, it'll be that way."

"Resurrection," Rogers said.

Wren snorted, already ripping flat stones off the wall with his pry bar. For two minutes they attacked the wall together, tearing stones down and stabbing into the hard sand underneath. Wren remembered doing the exact same thing with Grace at eight years old, while his brothers and sisters gasped in the darkness as the air steadily thinned. Down close to the ground, little Pequeño 3 and Grace-In-Our-Times had lasted longer, digging and digging until finally-

The dirt wall made a sound as he stabbed with the pry bar. Not the dull clink of a rock, not the dry rasp of the dirt, but a thud like he'd hit something hollow. Wood. They both descended on the spot and dug in a frenzy, hacking out chunks of compacted sand until a wooden frame emerged. It was around two and a half feet on a side and sealed with boards, like a trapdoor leading sideways into the earth.

"Back entrance," Rogers said. "Sneaky bastard."

"More like exit," Wren guessed. "There must've been a mechanism to safely bring those sleds down from inside. This is his get-out escape route."

"Not anymore."

Wren tapped his earpiece. "You getting all this, Hellion?"

"Hellion is coordinating pending defense of Little Phoenix," came B4cksl4cker's deep voice in her place. "Many forces incoming. But yes, I have all your footage so far. Will you begin livestream?"

"Backdate it from the Jeep. Give us ten minutes lead time, and run this audio over the top."

Keys clacked. "Awaiting audio."

Wren didn't need to think long, staring into Rogers' bodycam.

"Right now millions of you are taking orders from a faceless individual known only as X. You're burning for X. Killing for X. But who is X?" He paused a second. "I promise he is not some godlike figure come to deliver you from slavers in hell. He is not your savior. He is an avatar of the Apex, my father, AKA Noah Thackerton, a conman cult leader since he dug holes for people to die in the desert of Arizona thirty years ago. They died then. He didn't." Another pause, staring intently. "So let's find out how strong his faith is. If your leader truly believes, let him lead by example and walk first in the fire."

Tense seconds passed.

"I have it," B4cksl4cker said. "Looping over top of Jeep footage. Drop an amplifier, Christopher, then on your signal I will begin the stream."

Wren reached into Rogers' rucksack, pulled out an amplifier and dropped it on the ground. "Good?"

"Excellent signal. Yes. Feed is live and pushing to X network. You have ten-minute lead time."

"That's plenty," Wren said, and put a front kick into the hatch. The ancient wooden boards burst inwards, revealing a tunnel ribbed with support beams leading away into darkness, some seven feet below the surface of the desert. Wren got on his knees, shone a light inward and started forward at a crawl.

47

TUNNEL

The tunnel was hot, claustrophobic and pitch black but for the chaotic bounce of their flashlights, barely wide enough to accommodate Wren's broad shoulders or tall enough for him to pick up any speed. His arms brushed the side beams as he pulled himself forward, his rucksack thumping ominously off the slim roof ribs.

"Steady, Boss," Rogers cautioned in back. "You'll bring the tunnel down."

There was no time. The 'livestream' had begun, and Wren focused all his efforts on forward momentum. A three-mile crawl like this would take an hour. Whatever resurrection chamber they found at the end of the tunnel would be long-vacant by the time they reached it.

"Boss!" Rogers called as he hit the roof hard, dropping a shower of sand over them both, but he kept on, pistoning with his legs deeper into the damp air. A cave-in now and he'd have to back-tread all the way. No way to turn around.

Scorpions, mice and spiders scurried into the darkness ahead as he sped on with only a little more care, until his back stopped hitting the ceiling and his shoulders no longer brushed the walls. For a moment he thought he'd just mastered the technique, until Rogers called out.

"The tunnel's widening."

Wren shone his flashlight and confirmed it. Widening out and dropping, maybe three feet tall already. For some twenty yards he gorilla crawled, knees no longer touching the ground, until they hit four feet and he could run bent double.

Rogers' flashlight spun behind him, slashing beams across the blind white roots, cobwebs and desiccated werewolf mice nests burrowed into the dry walls. Her breath came in gasps, the sound echoing off the walls and merging with his own pulse.

His earpiece crackled and he remembered to drop an amplifier. At once a spotty signal came in.

"Christopher, do … hear me?'

'We have you, Hellion, go on," he rasped.

"There is gunfire … fake town. Many … out of nowhere, they are …."

His heart skipped a beat. "Repeat last, Hellion." He was at five feet clearance now and running nearly full speed into the dark. He dropped another amplifier. "Gunfire in the town?"

"Teddy is … but I cannot protect … your family, Christopher, they …"

His blood went cold. He straightened too much and almost knocked himself out on a beam, approaching a dead sprint. Cover three miles in twenty minutes or less, maybe, in peak condition.

"What about my family, Hellion?"

Nothing came back.

"Hellion!"

"Signal's dropped, Chris," Rogers called from in back.

He barely heard. Seeing red now. Teddy had secured them. No one other than his most trusted key players was supposed to know he was coming, so this couldn't be a trap. No way. It couldn't be.

They hit six foot clearance and he hit his stride. Great fast leaps through the darkness beneath the desert, heart firing at a hundred-sixty. Maybe he'd sent his family right into the lion's den. Loralei, Jake, Quinn. Rogers' mother too. The safest place in the country, he'd promised.

The tunnel reached seven feet and he went all out. Feet pounding the dirt. Leaving Rogers in his dust. Racing that ten-minute livestream clock and whatever chaos was breaking out above. The flashlight did next to nothing in the black. He was little Pequeño 3 again, tearing away from the past and toward some better future.

Then it all went away.

The floor dropped with a sickening lurch as his right foot punched straight through the surface, dust and dirt caving down into some kind of pit. Momentum carried him onward and down, his lower body plowing through the tunnel floor like an off-road jet until his chest thumped into the edge of the floor, blowing the wind from his lungs. His legs hit some unrecognizable pain deep below, then he was slipping deeper, dragged down by his own weight and the combined mass of his gear. His hands scrabbled desperately at the tunnel's dirt as he sank into a deeper agony, felt like his calves were plunging into glass.

"Holy crap, Boss!"

Submerged through the floor of the tunnel up to his neck. He flung his arms to full breadth and caught the support ribs, clung on and tried to pull himself up but all he had was a fingertip grip, and each rough jerk brought fresh showers of sand from above, threatening to rip it all down.

His chest slipped further. He realized what this was, what the pain in his legs meant.

Punji sticks. He almost laughed. Sharpened stakes at the bottom of a concealed pit, just like the Viet Cong had littered their Cu Chi tunnels with. Drop GI Tunnel Rats into the holes, infect them with tips smeared with feces, have them begging for mercy and hobbled for life.

Panic filled his head. Already it felt like his legs were on fire. The tough fabric of his Twaron suit was bullet and stab-proof to a degree, but not against the persistent force of his own body weight. Nothing he could do. Try to pull himself up and he'd bring the tunnel down. Sink any further and the spikes would just plunge deeper.

Nowhere to go. Nothing to do.

"Rogers, I-"

Abruptly an almighty blast rang out, filling the air with dirt and smoke. For a second Wren thought the tunnel was collapsing, triggering his vertigo. His fingers lost their grip and he slipped further, driving the spikes up into-

Rogers was there. She caught him from behind, rested his weight on her shoulder, and another enormous blast rang out. It hammered his inner ears and peppered his legs with shrapnel of some sort, then the support went away beneath him and his feet hit the ground.

"I've got you, Chris," Rogers' voice came in his ear, hands around his chest and holding him steady. "Can you stand?"

He tried. His legs wobbled but held. "Yeah."

"Good, now don't move."

Her arms pulled away, and it was all he could do to keep his balance. The tunnel floor was above eye level now, but still he clung to it with his arms raised like a child at the deep end of the swimming pool, trying to figure out what just happened.

Rogers must've just fired her shotgun into the pit. That had shredded some of the spikes, then she'd jumped in without waiting for the dust to clear to catch him as he fell.

A true leap of faith. Chase that with another blast to fragment the spikes in his legs, and he was in the clear.

"I-" he began, then there was an incredible sharp pain in his left calf. Rogers grunted and Wren let out a cry.

"That's one of them," Rogers said. He looked but couldn't see anything for the dust. "Hold still, just gluing you up, and there's one more big one."

There was a strange cold sensation on his calf, had to be a superglue patch straight to the skin, followed by another sucking pull that felt like it was scooping straight out of his right thigh. So deep it had to be in the muscle, maybe against the bone. He yelled.

"Yeah, that was a big one," Rogers allowed. "Patch job to stop the bleed, then you're good."

He gasped, coughed, rubbed the stinging tears from his eyes. He should have anticipated this. Punji sticks. The traps Davis Thackerton had preached about all through Noah Thackerton's childhood. Of course they were going to be here.

Could he even walk now? Run? How far had they come, and would he be able to cover the rest of the distance?

"All done," Rogers said. "I'll boost you."

Those questions faded in the face of necessity. It didn't matter if he could, because if the Apex had his family, he would keep trying until he bled out. No doubt about it.

"Left leg up, Boss," Rogers called. She pulled and he lifted, got his boot into her latticed hands, then she thrust. His leg almost gave way but he stiffened it in time, rode the deadlift of a lifetime that flung him up and almost fully out of the pit.

He landed across his thighs, and Rogers shoved him the rest of the way. He was out. Rising to his feet. It felt like there was a bad shin splint in his left calf, but it held. He didn't bother to look at the damage. His right leg was worse, hot and tremulous at best. If he had the wind and the time he might have laughed. Galicia had already pin-cushioned his upper body, it was about time his legs took some punishment.

The whole thing in maybe thirty seconds flat.

"I've got some spikes of my own here," Rogers called from the pit. "But I'll deal with them. You need to get there, Chris. Save them, and I'll be along."

He almost stopped to argue, but didn't. Even if he tried to haul her out, drop to a squat and pull, he'd likely only tear the damage worse. His legs might collapse. Sprinting would do enough damage as it was.

She'd taken the hit so he could carry the torch forward.

"Thank you, Rogers," he gasped, "don't be a stranger." Then he turned to run through the pain. Nothing he could do about more traps. Had to hope that was the only one.

48

BLACK ECHO

Wren ran in a daze, thumping off the walls at full speed, counting his heartbeat or the seconds, he wasn't sure which.

Maybe five minutes gone? His 'livestream' would have reached the tunnel entrance by now. If the Apex hadn't known he was coming from below, he knew now. Hopefully he thought he still had ten minutes to get out. Wren had to turn that into a mistake.

His right leg almost gave way. His left shrieked as it took the weight of the stumble, but held him upright. It all ended today. It had to all end today.

Then the tunnel ended and a chamber began.

Wren lurched to a halt five paces in, flashlight spinning across smooth, distant walls and a sloping ceiling that was sparked with glints of color. The space was too big for the flashlight to put much of a dent in the darkness, though he got the sense of it as he turned. Some kind of hall maybe fifty feet square, lined with hundreds of one-foot-wide stone plinths that rose five feet high. He wheeled the flashlight higher, taking in four triangular ceiling surfaces covered in messy colors and shapes, climbing to an golden apex cornerstone some twenty feet high.

An underground pyramid.

The scale of it dizzied him. It was too big. Something like this would require serious engineering to construct. Metal beams in the walls. Drainage. Skilled labor. And how deep was he now? He looked back but the tunnel swallowed the flashlight's beam after a dozen yards. It must have kept on descending to fit all this. How far had he run?

He took a few steps back toward the tunnel, running his flashlight over the ceiling. Now the colorful images resolved into structured paintings. Hundreds of human figures. All life-size. Men, women, children. Crafted with apparent care but in a dizzying range of skill levels, from crude stick figures to elaborately realized likenesses, patterned here and there with gold or silver leaf.

Not the work of any one painter. Surely as many painters as there were figures.

Self-portraits.

With a sickening lurch Wren grasped what he was looking it. A much larger-scale version of Jonathon Gibson's memorial wall. Real souls recorded and offered up to the Apex's golden capstone above. He brought the flashlight beam down and saw what that offering was.

Triangled bones.

Atop each of the many plinths lay an unholy consecration, just like the woman beneath First Corinthians. Arm and leg bones shaped into inverted triangles. Pelvic girdles set in the middle, ribs balanced in the center, skulls poised above and pointing down through the plinth and into the earth, forever.

Hundreds of them. They ran all around the chamber, as far as he could see. More paintings, more plinths. An onslaught of nausea drove him to his knees and the flashlight beam reeled across the details, casting crazy shadows through rib cages and cracked skulls.

It was worse than anything he'd imagined. It gave the lie to everything he'd said to Rogers. That First Corinthians was an outlier. That the Apex cared more about the process than result. This was all result. A horrific tableau, and worse yet, it was hauntingly familiar. Like he'd been here before. Like the gossamer trails of a dream half-remembered three days later.

Wren stalked the chamber seeking out some kind of confirmation, as murky memories of a midnight excursion flashed through the back of his mind. Only twelve years old, blindfolded and brought here half-asleep, the memory flattened by the end of the Pyramid coming only days later, but growing more vivid every second.

The chamber spun around him and the memories gathered steam. It had all looked so different then. A huge, bright room with a sloping roof and the smells of paint and freshly turned earth in the air. The walls filled with scaffolds where people lay on diagonal boards and painted themselves onto the sky. The other Pequeños had all been there too. Chrysogonus drawing himself with outsized muscles. Galicia festooning herself in a sapphire gown.

He searched until he found what he was looking for. Simple and angular on the east wall, the painting of a boy with nut-brown skin, twinkling eyes, tousled black hair and a secret smile.

Pequeño 3.

Recognition came like a hammer in his gut. He'd painted this. He remembered this. There were no bones on the plinth beneath his image, at least not yet. The black wall of unconsciousness roared up at the edges of his vision. Pulse soaring, breath coming in great gasps, turning within the zoetrope of his own black echo.

The entire Pyramid was here. A cry of anguish escaped his lips. They had always been here, locked in as slaves. He turned and the one thousand turned with him. His family. A dry heave came and he barely swallowed it back.

His earpiece crackled urgently. "X-apoc are here, Chr- … enough Foundation members to … need to finish …."

The signal died into static. Wren tried to shake off the fuzz of shock. Worse things were happening right now. There'd be time later for horror. All he could do now was find the Apex. Bring all this madness to an end. Get vengeance for this atrocity.

He scanned the walls and saw three more tunnel mouths leading away, one for each cardinal direction. North, South, East.

There was no time to guess. He had to know.

His mind kicked back into gear, over-riding the past. This pyramid had to be at the edge of town, probably underneath the flat foundation slabs stretching to the west. Heading east would take him directly under Main Street, but that didn't feel right. Too obvious, maybe. From what he knew of the Egyptians, pyramids were riddled with false trails leading to false tombs to trick grave robbers. Surely that would have been in Noah Thackerton's childhood picture book too.

So, North? Wren turned but saw nothing to distinguish that exit, seven feet tall and three wide, opening into darkness. He racked his mind for what Tandrews had told him. In Egyptian mythology the tomb provided a passageway for the dead to move between life and Tuat, or hell. The sun god Ra crossed through Tuat west to east every night, battling the god of chaos on his way. Wren looked up, saw Ra symbolized by the golden capstone.

It was all here. But he remembered nothing about cardinal directions.

His head boomed like a cannon. Maybe cardinal directions didn't matter?

He dredged his memory for grade-school knowledge beyond crocodile-headed gods and hieroglyphs, settled on Aden's hand on his chest, talking about the heart. Apex over tomb, all aligned down the middle. It made sense, but if this was an inverted pyramid, dug into the ground, then that meant...

Wren immediately ran south and entered the tunnel for fifty yards. It plunged on into darkness, but there was no sense of it descending to some lower level. He needed it to drop. He turned and ran into the north route, but that didn't drop either.

"... chaos here," came fragments in his earpiece. "... have to ... now, Christopher!"

He ran East to be sure, but if anything that tunnel began to rise. The wrong direction. He ran back and spun his thoughts faster, looking for the pattern that had to be there. Everything he knew about his father, Noah Thackerton, murderer since he was twelve years old. First Corinthians. Resurrection. He'd want his slaves close. He'd want them perfectly aligned, just like his 'Icon' was aligned, just like Davis Thackerton's bullet into the devil's brain, just like-

Wren's heart skipped a beat. Straight down was the key. There had to be a direct route between his apex chamber below and this tomb above. At the center of the chamber he jabbed his heel into the beaten earth. It had to be here. Sweat poured down his cheeks, breaths came in gasps, but there was nothing. No flex in the ground, no trapdoor and seconds were ticking by.

Then something hit. A glint in the darkness. Resurrection as reincarnation. The role Christopher Wren himself had played all these years. Tandrews had said it himself, a son of the sun, Rah remade every night through his child. He ran to the eastern exit, where his own portrait hung. Pequeño 3. The only child of the Pyramid Noah Thackerton had ever spared. Eyes roving over the rudimentary work, fingers stroking the contours his brush had made so long ago, until he saw it.

Gold leaf sparks in the his eyes, like he was looking directly into infinity. Except Wren had never painted those highlights. He felt sure of it. Enlivened with the blaze of Ra.

He wasted no more time. Maybe there was a secret button somewhere, a recessed lever to crank a secret hatch open, but he wasn't going to find it now. Instead he simply dropped to a squat, clamped his arms around the bare plinth and heaved.

The massive stone column barely jostled in position, maybe three hundred pounds of unwieldy mass, then settled again. But had there been a clinking sound, like a lock catching on the bolt? Wren couldn't be sure. His heart hammered in his ears. Didn't matter. He squatted so deep he felt muscles tearing, locked his hands tight and heaved again with all his strength.

This time there was no mistaking the clank of metal on metal. He didn't let up, kept thrusting upward until metal screeched and the plinth slammed back down with a mighty crunch. Wren staggered, almost fell as silver lights flashed across eyes. There was no time, though, and he doubled down to heave again. Now the plinth ripped upward like a plug, some internal mechanism cracked loose and the final resistance gave way, sending him staggering backward with the full weight in his arms.

He dropped it to the side and refocused through the blur. Beneath the portrait drawn by Pequeño 3 was a channel carved half through the wall, half through the floor. He flung himself in and down.

49

PHARAOH

Within five yards the channel gave way to a metal spiral staircase drilling down into the earth, and Wren took it at a run, feet slapping on the rungs, hands yanking at the railing. So close. Fifteen steps on he slipped and almost fell but caught himself, heard the sound of voices nearby, then saw a crack of golden light below.

Instantly he could hardly breathe, could hardly see for his vision splitting as his pulse crescendoed. The stairwell spun, split, recombined and vertigo's black wall surged over him again.

Too much. Heart approaching aortal flutter. Lungs working like an industrial bellows. There was no point emerging below only to collapse in his father's arms.

He started stripping his gear: the ammo bandoliers for his Glock and the shells for his shotgun hit the stairs, the tactical belt weighed down with explosive munitions followed, then he emptied the amplifiers from his pockets, unlatched the Mossberg sheath and the holster for the Glock. Every strap uncinched and piece of gear dropped helped him breathe.

His earpiece crackled and a sound broke through, maybe Rogers' voice, but he didn't have time to talk.

Last of all he shrugged off his rucksack and grabbed a bottle from within, spun the lid and emptied the contents over his head. The cool liquid splashed over his scalp, ran down his face and neck, bringing relief and instant clarity. He scrubbed the excess from his hair and beard and took a breath.

Glock in his right hand. Legs almost giving way. Now or never.

He ran down the last stretch of stairs into golden light, through an archway seven feet tall and saw it all at once, almost too much to take in.

A brilliant chamber, walls entirely clad in gold and lit by spotlights that bounced liquid amber light up and around the sloping pyramidal roof. Maybe twenty feet across, as intimate and transcendent as a pit. Wren stared for a long second, overwhelmed. He'd never seen anything like it, like being frozen inside a block of amber.

At the center stood a huge black Egyptian-style sarcophagus, raised on a dais five feet high and big enough to encompass a giant. Fit for a pharaoh. The top was expertly carved in the shape of a muscular male lying flat, wearing an ornate death mask inlaid with gold, silver and glistening jewels, with sparkling blue sapphires for eyes.

Nobody there, though. It was silent. No voices, no movement, and Wren swallowed hard. The savage stink of unburned napalm hung in the air. This had to be it. The Apex's resurrection chamber. The tomb of the Pyramid stood directly above. A straight line to the tombstones above, to Little Phoenix, to the inverted triangle across America.

Wren entered with the Glock raised and his heart racing, sighted some misshapen black monster looming from the polished gold and almost fired, but it was just a burnished version of himself reflected in the polished gold walls. Only blackness for his eyes, rippled by markings carved into the gold. Hieroglyphs? No. Inverted triangles circled with swirling trails of calculations. Just like Anastasi Street.

He padded deeper, circling the huge sarcophagus until he saw the chamber's sole inhabitant, standing calmly on the other side. She was dressed in a flowing cream gown waisted with a broad gold-thread belt, a golden stole draped across her shoulders, embroidered at its ends with twin black inverted pyramids. Brown hair hung down her chest in curls, tan skin glowed in the golden air, wise green eyes watching him unsurprised.

Wren couldn't believe it. Could scarcely get a breath out.

"Maggie?"

She only smiled at him. Just like she'd smiled at him in the field in Iowa, encouraging him to get up, to go out, to seek X in the wild. Just like she'd smiled at him so many times before, telling him that the fake town was his home, that he could return at any time.

Maggie. The matriarch of Little Phoenix. The woman he'd left in charge of all the Blue Fairy children.

"Christopher," she said. Her voice was warm and gentle as ever. She made no move toward him. "I'm sure you must be very confused."

He was beyond confused. He felt like a trigger jammed on the safety, unable to pull. This didn't make any sense. "What are you doing here?"

She took a step toward him. "I think you can figure that much out."

"I-" he began, but found nowhere to go as his mind stop-started, trying to parse everything in a search for the truth. Everything she'd ever said to him, from the start to the end. He remembered the way they'd first met in the fake town, when he'd attacked her group thinking it was a Pyramid clone. How they'd walked together in the desert, and she'd explained her goals for this place he'd only been steadily burning to the ground.

She'd promised to rebuild, and he'd called her out for bullshit empathy. "Nobody does that," he'd said, demanding to know why she was there at all, why she cared so much for victims of some cult she'd never even known, so much that she'd dedicate her life to seeking out and re-consecrating their lost bones.

She'd given him a sob story about losing her family members to the Apex. An aunt, maybe, a mother. A father who committed suicide. He'd believed her.

Except he'd never seen the bones. Not once. Not until today. Never even asked what kind of consecration they underwent before they were interred below the fresh tombstone slabs she'd laid out in the desert. On some level, he hadn't wanted to know. The past was too painful.

"This is your home," she'd said. So many times, repeating it like a mantra. "Come home when you're ready. This place belongs to you."

Now here they were.

The room whirled. There were two Maggies, then three. He'd trusted her. He'd thought she was like him, another soul broken on the fires of the Pyramid. Maybe she was. The gold walls filled his head with stifling light. Everything changed.

He raised the Glock to her face.

"That's better," she said. She sounded almost relieved, like a long pretense was finally lifting. "It's good that you're starting to see."

"I-" he began, but stopped, not clear at all what he wanted to say, where he needed to go. About the betrayal. That she'd helped him so many times. Even helped keep him alive. "Why?"

Her smile spread. She looked kind, as ever. She made no move toward him. No move at all. In those green eyes he'd once thought there were answers. But now…

"For love, Christopher," she said. "You think you understand love. Your wife and your children, perhaps your country. But you don't understand love like this. A love so fierce it burns you alive."

His mouth was dry. His eyes stung. Love. The same bullshit song cult devotees always sang about their leader. The figure who gave their lives purpose. A love that burned you up in their name.

He had so many questions. Always there were, when it came to blind faith. Why, he wanted to ask again. Keep on asking until she finally admitted there was nothing, no reason, no answer, nothing but raw and naked human need, but he knew she never would. Not now. They never did.

So he switched it off. A lever in his mind, pulled. He'd heard it all before. So Maggie had lied. She'd put herself in deep cover for a year or two, an agent manipulating other agents, and he only had himself to blame. He should have seen it coming, recognized her for what she was, but she'd come at him out of the dark. Come at him through the Pyramid itself, offering him something he'd never been able to find for himself.

A kind of peace. A way forward.

Purpose.

Now all that was gone.

The gun steadied in his hand. Only one thing mattered now.

"Where is he?"

Her smile faded slightly. Like she was hurt. Like maybe she'd wanted to play out that moment longer, really dig into her motivations. "Where's who, Christopher?"

He snorted. Imagining what would happen next. He'd only told two people in all of Little Phoenix that he was coming. Teddy Smithely III, and Maggie. She'd had time to prepare. Set another trap. But how much did she really know?

Another scrap of sound came in his earpiece. Maybe Rogers. You had to hope.

"My father," he said. "The Apex. Noah Thackerton. I'll shoot you in the head right now, Maggie. Is he in here?" He shoved the sarcophagus lid with his left hand, but it didn't budge an inch.

"Your father," Maggie said. Took a step toward him. Only five yards between them now. "Noah Thackerton. I see you've done your homework."

Wren took a step to meet her. "I will blow your brains out, girl, if you don't give me some answers."

Now the smile came back. "Answers. There's only one route to the truth,

Christopher. You know this. It's always the same way. Every great visionary has walked that path before you." Her green-gold eyes seemed to bloom and spin like Catherine wheels. "Pain."

Sweat stung his eyes. The silence between words was so complete it ached. So predictable.

"You want me to burn? You go first."

"I couldn't claim that honor," Maggie said. "That falls to you."

He took a step closer. "I'll ask one more time, then I put a bullet in your left thigh. Just to get your attention. Where is the Apex?"

Her smile turned sad. "The things we do for love. But love blinds us, don't you agree?"

Wren hammered the sarcophagus with his shoulder. The lid lifted maybe half an inch this time, dropped back down with a resounding slam. "Ten seconds."

"Love keeps us from the truth," Maggie went on, calm and unafraid. "So you ignore the truth standing right before you, because you love the lies this world feeds you every day, through your ears, your eyes, your broken mind."

He rammed the sarcophagus again, earned an inch but no glimpse of what lay within. "Five seconds."

"We only had seconds in that first pit," Maggie said, sounding dream-like now. "The day you risked yourself to save me. Do you remember how that felt, Christopher, to scrabble at the wall together, so desperate to survive?"

He blinked. The count forgotten. "What?"

Her smile swelled to fill the room. "Think about your hot hand in mine, playing games in the stolen days that followed. The happiest days of my life. Making mud pies while all the Pyramid waited around an empty pit."

Wren's breath stopped in his throat. Her eyes were golden whirlpools spinning in green jade. It wasn't possible. It couldn't be, but…

"We worked together so well," Maggie said, voice drifting like a drug. "You played your part and I played mine. It took everything I had not to call your name, as I lay there across the bodies of your brothers and sisters at the bottom of the pit. Only the hope of this moment kept me silent."

Wren just stared, felt like his insides were scooping inside out. "I-"

"All for this. So we could be together again at the end. And it is beautiful, my little Pequeño 3. I'm so glad that you finally see me."

The gun went slack and slippery in his hand. He saw her face as it might have been, thirty years earlier. As the beautiful little girl laughing by his side, eating strawberry mud pies, dead in the pit.

"Grace?" he whispered.

And there it was, understanding spreading like a deep calm across the desert, after a storm had passed.

"Grace," she repeated. "But you can call me X."

50

X

The gun clattered to the floor. Black tiles flecked with gold, Wren noticed. Now he was on his knees. Drooling, nauseated, the world spinning in every direction at once.

"I'm doing this for you," Maggie said. Grace. X. "Not for him. For you. Because this world is cruel, to you and I most of all. Because the pain is too much. He only shows us the way to be free. To break the chain. So I'm here for you." She was on her knees now, holding his hands.

Grace-In-Our-Times. The little girl that had haunted his dreams for thirty years. As a boy, he'd tried to save her. Plunged into the pit after her. Fought Chrysogonus for her, escaped with her, lived and breathed with her for three days and three nights while the Pyramid wailed over their pit, only to see her dead in that same pit when it was all over. Standing alone with the Apex whispering excitedly in his ear at the dawn, crowing out his victory.

"We were wrong, Pequeño 3! You and I know what's real. She was always dead!"

Now she was alive. Her fingers twined in his. Another victim. A girl he'd tried so hard to save. A woman lost for so very long.

"I love you," she whispered. "I always did. You asked why? That's the reason. Why I've followed him all these years. Lied for him. Killed for him. For this moment, to be with you and help you finally see how we can be together."

You couldn't cry enough tears. The world tumbled and rebuilt in this new shape. Not only Maggie, but Grace. Not only Grace, but X. A true believer. No way back from that.

Still, he looked in her eyes and took one last shot.

"Then help me," he whispered. "I can kill him. I will kill him. All this can end. We *can* be together. Little Phoenix can be exactly what we promised."

She touched his cheek, stroked her fingers down. "Never in this life, little Pequeño. Only in the next." Then she stood. Stepped back, her voice gathering in strength. "I know exactly why you've come. To destroy the Pyramid. To tear down all our work. But I cannot allow that. So here is my offer."

She touched the sarcophagus' side and there was a click, a hiss of releasing air, then the lid lifted. Inside it was black and empty. No Apex. Nobody at all.

"This will be the true reason you came." Her face loomed, her eyes warping to fill his vision. "Your own willing sacrifice. You will be the Pyramid's final lens, Christopher. Its lasting purification. Through you the lies of the world will be made clean. Its power will pour into him, and he will rise up stronger than ever to remake us all!"

Wren weaved. Hardly thinking but in half-thoughts and stray words, too numb to reason clearly. Resurrection. Destruction. The same old song of the apocalypse cult.

Believe in me.

Something was in Maggie's hands now. Black and sinuous, bulbous in the middle and narrowing to a point at either end, with two sleek handles at the head. An ancient Egyptian amphora. He heard the sloshing of liquid within, smelled the bitter release of familiar fumes.

"First you must be anointed. By your own hand. This is the only way." She held the amphora before him. More of the same. A new voice, a new person, but always the same. "This is the reason you came."

He looked at her face, her eyes, trying to chart the differences. It wasn't a betrayal you could express in words. Barely in emotions. It was too complete. This woman he'd trusted. This little girl he'd loved. This madwoman he'd chased across the country.

"X," he said.

"X," she repeated.

A crackle came in his ear. Maybe half a word, nothing intelligible, but a reminder the world was still out there.

"I never will."

Now her smile turned sad. "You haven't heard the terms of the deal."

She set the jug down, reached into a fold of her flowing robe and brought up a black tablet screen, held it out for him to see. It showed bright blues, oranges and slow movement. His stinging eyes took long seconds to focus, then he went for his Glock, snatched it up off the tiles and held it again to Maggie's face.

"That won't help," she said.

The details resolved. A video feed of Main Street above. The sun glaring in a hot blue sky, his smoldering jet strewn on the orange sand, spewing black smoke in a column. In the middle of the frame, his family.

Loralei wore jeans and a red check shirt. Jake had on dinosaur pajamas and was red-eyed with crying. Quinn's face was hidden by her hands, but her shoulders wracked with sobs. Beside them stood Rogers' mother, gray-haired and afraid, and beside her was the gaunt figure of Teddy, and beside him were others. Children from the Blue Fairy. Foundation members. Maybe Mason, Alli, others. They stretched back in a line as far as he could see, and they all glistened in the bright sunlight. Their clothes clung to their skin. Their hair hung slick to their foreheads like a rainstorm had just struck, though there wasn't a cloud in the sky.

"This is your choice, Pequeño," Maggie whispered, hot and close. "The choice you refused all those years ago. The choice he gave you one thousand times, to reject the lies of your own eyes and accept his truth as your own."

Too much. He couldn't do anything, only play for time, but she didn't give him the chance.

"Do you remember that choice? Before every one of the Pyramid burned, he gave you the power. Time after time. Again and again. Would you take their place." She paused a long moment. "And do you know what you said?"

He didn't remember. Maybe he did. He didn't want to.

"You said no," Maggie said. "A thousand times, no. So the thousand burned. It was your decision then. It's your decision now."

He sucked air. Already felt like he was drowning. All his worst nightmares coming home to roost.

"I know this hurts, Pequeño. Your pride. Your sense of self. I know you despise it more than anything in the world, so don't do it for him." Eyes so wide like that little girl in the pit, gazing up at him for help. "Do it for me. Walk in the fire, for me."

There was no answer he could give. The future stretched out in horrifying shades of violence. If he did as she asked, the image of him burning would topple the Foundation and trigger the X-apoc like nothing else. Confirmation of all their beliefs, as Christopher Wren himself finally accepted their truth.

America would implode.

The alternative was simple. Refuse, and watch his family burn in his place. All of the fake town.

Again.

He made his decision. On some level he'd always known. He finally found his voice. "They live."

Maggie smiled. "Of course."

"They all live. Swear it, Maggie. On his life. Noah Thackerton. The Apex. The second I walk in the fire, you let them go."

Maggie gazed at him. "If that's what it takes, my Pequeño, I swear."

He lifted one leg under him, feeling like he was moving with the weight of destiny now. So the Apex had written all this. Prepared the way. Chrysogonus first, Galicia, Aden, and now it was his turn to step onto the stage. Let America see the truth.

He got the other foot under him and stood. Maggie let out a little gasp. Her eyes were wide. Enraptured. She lifted the amphora and held it out to him. Brought up the tablet and tapped to record.

"Say the words," she whispered, barely audible now, like she couldn't trust herself to speak.

Wren just gazed at her. Trying to see if there was any scrap of the little girl she'd once been. Grace. The only real friend from his childhood. Brainwashed for all her life.

"Say the words, or they burn."

"Fear is a portal," Wren said, and raised the amphora over his head, tipped it. The napalm splashed out in a single slick pour, atop his head, flooding down his cheeks, his neck, his chest and back. He poured until he could scarcely see for the oily burn in his eyes, then he set the amphora gently down.

Maggie's eyes and mouth were wide. Bliss, that looked like. Maybe she'd never been happier. Bending the ungrateful son to her will, where so many had failed. She nodded, a prompt for the words to come, and he knew his lines.

But he waited.

Waited for a sound in his earpiece, maybe. For a sign.

"Last chance," Maggie said.

Was that it? Had it come? It was hard to hear anything over the drumming of his heart, the heave of his lungs. It would have to be.

"Pain is a doorway," he said.

She held something out. Filming with one hand, leaning in with the other. A black metal square.

Wren took it. Felt the contours with his fingers. A flint and metal lighter. It was strange, holding it in his own hand, like an artifact from some ancient civilization. Feeling the same things all those poor women had felt in the firestorm, in the seconds before they died. Hope. Faith. Steven Gruber had been here before him. The one thousand had been here before him. People died all the time.

He was no one special. He took a deep breath.

"Walk in the fire," he said, then held the lighter to his throat and struck a spark.

51

WALK IN THE FIRE

Flames engulfed him.

Wren snapped his eyes shut at once, dropped the lighter and brought his hands up to cover his face and pinch his nostrils closed.

That would earn him seconds only. The sound of the napalm blaze was an instant roar, far louder than he'd ever imagined possible, as the fire lashed up his temples and into his hair, swallowing his ears, rippling over the backs of his hands, racing down his battered chest legs and tracing the spill across the floor.

Consuming him from without, burning down to the nerves.

In the blazing heat behind his eyelids he glimpsed his brother again, arms spread on the D.C. stage, striding to the edge and throwing himself over to ignite the masses…

She'd sworn.

She'd promised.

That would have to be enough. It was all he had as the pain receptors in his skin finally began to scream like never before under the two thousand degree inferno. That stage would be brief, at least. Napalm burned out the nerves fast, left you a mindless blazing candle fuming carbon monoxide within seconds.

At least there were no munitions strapped to his chest to set him off like a firework. The Glock was on the floor. The heat seared like the fires of hell, and Maggie was right there. He could almost see her through the black shadow of his hands as the fire beat him down.

She'd sworn.

He moved.

Left juddering leg forward. Trusting everything to his memory and his training. Where she was standing. Where the tablet was in the air. His right leg shot up like a trebuchet arm, too fast for her to react, already stunned by the flames. He heard her cry come muted through the flames, then maybe an impact.

There was no real sense of impact as his foot struck her wrist. Every nerve in his body was overloaded with the heat. It was more some deep shift in his inner equilibrium. His body belonged to the flames now, but the feel traveled up his core and into his chest.

Her wrist maybe broken. The tablet flung through the air.

X's tablet. X's level of access.

Then there was just screaming. Maybe it was his? Maybe hers. Five seconds gone, could that be right? He couldn't think. The earpiece crackled and died in his ear. Three seconds. Three hours.

He was in the Beechcraft again by Rogers' side, soaring west toward Little Phoenix, long before any of this had happened.

"High weave count," B4cksl4cker was saying, "many threads is dense, this helps."

"Dense threads," Wren repeated. "What fabric?"

"Lots of possibilities," Hellion answered, taking five minutes from her efforts to manage the war with X. "Polyester."

"Polyester?" B4cksl4cker laughed. "This is organic material, makes very fashionable clothing, but hardly effective even if high density. Much better is tantalum carbide."

Now it was Hellion's turn to laugh. "This is solid state material, useful for painting on spacecraft!"

"Could be plates."

"What good are plates against liquid?" Hellion asked.

"Polybenzimidazole," Wren said, ending the bickering. "PBI. That's what I want."

"This is mouthful," B4cksl4cker said. "What is it?"

"Sewn through with aluminum fibers. It's a polymer. Commercially available. You can get it there in time. Contact Teddy."

"Only Teddy, yes?"

"Only Teddy for this."

"And this is enough?" B4cksl4cker asked. "What about face, hands?"

"Super-absorbent polymer gel," Wren said. He'd done his research. "Mixed into a slurry, it'll look clear, if gelatinous. Like sweat. I can apply it at the last minute."

Silent seconds passed.

"Like makeup?" Hellion asked.

"Like a bottle I dunk on my head."

"Ah. How will it work?"

"The polymer contains billions of water bubblets trapping air. They burn incredibly slowly. Hollywood uses them for stunts, but you can get them online. I'm sure you can source this in time too."

Keys clacked. "Super-absorbent polymer gel," Hellion repeated. "I am finding this for you, Christopher. Yes." More keys flew. "Bubblets."

B4cksl4cker laughed.

"Bubblets absorb all thermal energy, yes, this is correct," Hellion read. "Very hot flames, this will be OK. Requires even coating of slurry. One millimeter layer gives thermal protection for one minute, perhaps. Less, if fire is very hot. Like napalm."

"So we'll need a back-up," Wren said. "Maybe Rogers can-"

Back in the flames, wearing his PBI firefighter tactical suit sewn with aluminum and slathered with stunt-grade super-absorbent polymer gel, Wren felt the sudden rush of powder jetting over his body. There was no sound through the flames, no sensation and nothing to see, only the gentle hosing of siliconized monoammonium phosphate from the type A powder extinguisher she'd brought with her.

Rogers.

He'd bought enough time. She'd made it.

"Will this be enough?" Hellion had asked. "One extinguisher. Napalm re-ignites, yes?"

"She'll need more than one. Get rucksacks, different types of extinguisher. A fire blanket will help. She can pat out any extra flames."

B4cksl4cker grunted. "We saw this with Steven Gruber. Napalm may re-light minutes later, Christopher. Need complete oxygen-free environment for sustained period."

"We'll have to improvise."

"And hold breath," B4cksl4cker added. "Chemical extinguisher is toxic. Do not breathe this in. Can you hold breath very long?"

Wren laughed. "Let's hope long enough."

"How likely is this outcome, Christopher?" Hellion asked. "Walking in fire?"

Rogers answered before Wren could. Leaning over the seat, listening in. "This is the Apex, remember. He loves to burn everything that moves. And his ungrateful son, in the depths of his seat of power?" She laughed. "He'd never miss the chance."

"Yes," B4cksl4cker said. "He is fire fetishist, this is true."

Wren laughed.

Now he felt another rush spraying over him. The texture was different, more liquid, maybe the foam extinguisher. He didn't dare take a breath or lift his hands from his face, though. Then he felt Rogers pushing him. He staggered off-balance, his thigh thumped against what had to be the sarcophagus, but she kept on pushing, maybe shouting something now but he couldn't hear well.

Then he grasped it.

Improvise.

He let his upper body tip, let Rogers push him the rest of the way, and rolled into the black interior of the huge stone coffin, catching the tail-end of what she was yelling.

"... do, don't breathe!"

He would have laughed. A fresh spray of powder hit him in the chest, then the sarcophagus lid slammed down on all sides, sealing him in with the toxic dust.

An oxygen-free environment. Buried alive. Another of the Apex's pits of faith, where he would either asphyxiate or emerge reborn, resurrected by the flames.

52

CAVE

Wren's lungs burned and heaved. He'd lost count of the time somewhere in the midst of burning alive. Maybe two minutes already. Heading toward three? He figured he was safe and pulled his hands away from his face, instantly catching the acrid tang of napalm.

With his eyes screwed tightly shut in the dark of the sarcophagus, he patted himself down, felt the dry and grainy extinguisher powder embedded in a sticky layer coating his clothing and skin. Had to be the remnants of the bubblet gel mixing with unburned napalm. There were sore patches too, parts of his hands and head felt painful and raw. Maybe poor coverage of the gel, too-thin areas where the fire had bitten through. The PBI firefighting outfit seemed to have done its job well around his core though.

Silver blots swam behind his eyes. Coming up on four minutes? Too long. But thinking about the re-activation time for napalm. It could burn underwater, in the right conditions. It could burn without oxygen at all, if the solid-state fuel provided enough. It could-

His body jerked, his lungs convulsed, and that was the final warning. He was out of time. As the silver clots clamored to open his throat, he pounded on the sarcophagus lid with both fists.

It cracked open in seconds. Air hissed in along with soft angelic light across his eyelids, and Wren opened his eyes to see Rogers haloed in gold.

He laughed. Couldn't help it, then regretted it as he gulped in foul-tasting toxic dust. Rogers dragged him coughing and spluttering out of the sarcophagus.

"Are you all right, Boss?" she shouted. He barely heard her, mostly read her moving lips as she thumped his back and checked his airways, looking into his eyes. He couldn't hear. Maybe the fire had destroyed his ears? He didn't want to reach up and find out. He hadn't paid the best attention to applying the gel in the stairwell coming down. Too hot, too rushed, too ready for the fight.

"Fine," he croaked, lurching away from the cloud of powder spilling from the coffin, sucking in air that tasted of spent napalm. Each breath bent him further over.

"Here," she said, and now cool liquid ran over his head, down his back and chest. Not polymer gel this time, but water. He caught some in his hand, rubbed it in his face, wetted his lips, swallowed some powder and coughed again.

"Drink," Rogers said, and pressed the bottle into his hands. For a second he worried he was about to swig bubblet gel, but Rogers would never do that to him. He tipped his head back and swallowed cool, clear water. It felt good.

He straightened up. Felt like he'd been put through some severe industrial process; wrung out, baked, steamed and deloused, and he still wasn't done yet.

"Where is she?" he asked, voice coming out a croak.

Rogers pointed.

Maggie lay flat out down the side of the chamber, drenched with extinguisher foam, hands zip-tied behind her back and unconscious.

"You set her on fire," Rogers said, the words coming tinnily now, as though underwater. "Mostly her hand where you kicked her. I put her out as best I could, then knocked her out when she started screaming." She whistled low. "Maggie, though. That's a blow, Boss."

It was a blow. Wren struggled to get his brain working again. Minutes ago, Maggie had held all the cards. Burning alive had flipped that, and also played havoc with his thought processes. He remembered the kick, and the tablet, and-

"Did you get it?" he asked urgently, scanning the black and gold floor.

Rogers patted his shoulder, pulling focus. She was holding Maggie's tablet. The screen was cracked but operational, now showing the familiar inner screen of the X app, ALERT button flashing. Wren blinked, took the tablet and turned it.

The stub was in position.

"They're in," Rogers confirmed. "Hellion and B4cksl4cker are hacking the X network right now. I'm guessing your earpiece is busted, or you'd hear them whooping like animals."

Wren grunted. That was as good as he could've hoped for. "Tell them to get ready. He's close by. Maggie was talking to someone."

Rogers' eyes flared and she spun. Wren looked at the sarcophagus. Getting all his ducks in a row. Perfectly aligned, so to speak.

"A dollar takes ten he's right here. Beneath us."

He reached up and took hold of the open lid, hung out at a forty-five-degree angle, the edge at around head height. Hopefully on a firm hinge. The sarcophagus had to weigh a ton, it hadn't budged when he'd rammed it before, but with two of them and a lever to increase torque?

"You're on, Boss," Rogers said, and took hold of the lid too.

He counted three, then pulled, sinking everything he had down through his arms. The hinge creaked but held, and the sarcophagus shifted slightly. Rogers said something that he couldn't hear for the rushing in his ears, then counted three herself and they pulled again.

This time the whole thing lifted. Wren saw silvery spots, and the sarcophagus quadrupled like a kaleidoscope. Pretty. He saw himself reflected in the gold walls again, a blackened, smoking corpse on its feet, but overlaid with other versions of himself too: the mischievous Pequeño 3 making mud pies in the sunbaked desert; the uncertain young man he'd become in the forest of Maine; the angry DELTA Corporal he'd grown into, earning the nickname 'Saint Justice' for unfailingly following his own moral compass.

These versions of himself revolved and overlaid, then Rogers hit three again and he pulled. The sarcophagus teetered on its edge. He bellowed and pushed down with everything, and now it tipped. His legs gave out as the immense weight shifted and bore down. About to be crushed. Then something hit him in the middle, a shoulder-tackle that drove him against the golden wall.

The crash as the sarcophagus hit the marble floor rang like the Liberty Bell's last chime, smashing cracks through the stone. Wren gasped, Rogers straightened, and there in the center of the room lay an opening. Stairs leading down.

"Here," Rogers said, holding out his Glock.

"Don't need it," he said, struggling to catch his breath and find his feet. He pulled away from Rogers, took three shaky steps and scooped two items off the floor. The black square of the lighter. The amphora still sloshing with residual napalm dregs.

She gave him a look. He started shakily down the steps.

There was raw industrial lighting pinned to the walls. Fifteen steps down, smoke still rising off his fireproof outfit, twenty, hardly daring to hope. At the base a circling tunnel ran back around, no doubt heading to a final chamber directly beneath the sarcophagus.

Ducks in a row.

This was it. No more escape routes now. No way out.

"Chris," Rogers said.

He turned to her, above him on the steps. Had forgotten she was even there. She looked beautiful, in her own way. Powerful. Trustworthy. And there was something in her tone now. Something imploring, maybe? Trying to steer him. He knew why. What she wanted to say.

"It's OK, Sally," he said. "Trust me."

She stared at him like she could read his heart through his eyes. Maybe she could. "You do this, they'll never stop hunting you."

"You don't know what I'm going to do." He smiled. "That's a strength."

She laughed. A small thing. A strange thing, in that place, but Wren appreciated it. That maybe he wasn't lost, and so she wasn't either. "I'd rather have strength as my strength," she said. "Or invisibility."

"Be prepared," Wren countered. "And unpredictable. That's my motto. Now go. Little Phoenix needs you."

A second more she looked. No need to say they needed him too. Right now the past needed him more. Right here, buried in the dirt, with the rats and spiders and long-buried cicadas, waiting to taste the summer air again.

His father.

"Thank you," he said. "I'll see you real soon."

He didn't wait for her to go. Started walking around the circle, right leg limping, face burning, hands steaming. Ten strides maybe, and no sound she was following, no sound at all, until he reached another open doorway. Within was a tall three-walled space, triangular in cross-section, like a tall column of structural space left over in some mezzanine skyscraper floor, so the building could flex in the wind.

A nothing space. A cave. Black walls. A black chair in the center surrounded by three large screens, one on each wall. One showed Wren's family dispersing through the fake town. One showed the golden chamber above, Maggie lying by the wall, the sarcophagus rolled aside like a stone. The third was a high angle on this cave-like room itself.

Wren looked up, saw glass panels concealing cameras. A livestream going out, no doubt, to capture every moment of the Apex's resurrection.

And there he was. Almost unbelievable in the flesh after so many years of searching. Sat on the chair, his father.

Noah Thackerton. Apex of the Pyramid, here at the inverted tip of the greatest pyramid yet.

53

APEX

"Pequeño 3," said the Apex.

His voice was gravel. A voice to slaughter millions. He had raw carved cheekbones, short-cropped gray hair matched by a perfect salt-and-pepper stubble on his jutting chin, with those liquid crystal eyes in between. A mass killer. The architect of Wren's entire life.

"Dad," Wren said, held up the amphora. "I brought you something."

The Apex's gaze didn't waver. Neither did Wren's. There would be no give here at the end. Nothing to say. It was all right there. Every moment encapsulated in those mad sapphire eyes.

Son of Davis Thackerton. Creator of the Pyramid. Father of X.

Twin possible paths spun out before Wren. Tip the amphora, and he knew his father wouldn't move. Light the spark. He wouldn't scream. He'd just stare, finally walk in the fire himself, see the hell that lay beyond.

It would be so easy. Justice done. But via the cameras above, he would become a martyr to his X-apoc. The greatest trigger to send them over the edge, and in the old man's eyes Wren saw that understanding. Luring him in. Defiance and a death wish to make it happen in his final moments.

Do my will this one last time. Be my slave.

Or he could take the Apex in. By the book, right and proper. Put on the cuffs, frog-march him up to the surface, hand him over to the government for a years' long trial that would doubtless be the most-watched global television event in history. Watch along as he rallied his X-apoc from the dock, bringing on fresh insurrections every day. Fresh rage, fresh intolerance.

That didn't seem so good either.

"What to do with me," the Apex said. Perfectly mirroring Wren's thoughts. Like he knew everything, like he always had. Always one step ahead, setting traps for his Pequeño 3 to fall into.

"Is this how you saw it ending?" Wren asked.

The Apex's eyes shone. The same eyes that had watched over the pits, and the vats, and the cages. Not just sadism. Purpose. A vision, no matter how demented. Something others would flock to. Something Wren had tried so hard to believe in as a child, but simply couldn't, because it wasn't real.

"It isn't over yet," the Apex said.

Wren took a step in. Wait too long, listen too much and it might never happen. The Thackertons had that power, Wren included. He raised the amphora and tipped the remnants over his father's head. The Apex didn't move. The dregs of napalm dripped, dripped, dripped down through his thick hair, down his cheeks like tears, rivulets running to his lap.

"It'll be over soon," Wren said, and held up the lighter. "So tell me something, Noah. Anything, really, to save your life."

The Apex gazed back. They both knew he'd never beg. "They'll come for you," he said, nodding to the cameras. "My people. They will tear you and this country apart."

Wren grunted. True. Martyrhood. Fresh X-apoc leaders would rise up within hours to rally the storm, and it would take many years without oxygen to fully quench that fire. By the time it was done, the damage would be all-consuming.

But maybe that was the point.

Maybe it always had been, and the Apex's presence had just blocked it out. He'd never seen the stars for the giant figure in the way, keeping him and all the Pyramid small and scared and alone, but knock the giant down and suddenly the sky was all yours.

Now the giant was falling, and with it the pillars of Wren's old world.

"Your X-apoc kill me, then we'll both be dead," Wren said, mind racing as he finally started to put the pieces together. "An end to the noble Thackerton bloodline. So let's meet in the middle." He leaned in. "Tell me who paid for it all, Noah."

The Apex's eyes narrowed slightly.

"I've seen the scale of it," Wren went on, spinning the past like tumblers in a lock. "First Corinthians? I hear those roaming churches were huge. Right after you killed your father, with you penniless on the Kansas plains? The money came from somewhere."

The Apex only stared. Maybe there was anger there now.

"And then my brother, Chrysogonus? He was no tech entrepreneur. Somebody gave him all that. Somebody backed him with hackers, programmers, influencers, a lifetime's worth of wealth." Wren sped up, really feeling it now. "All these cults, from the Saints to the Ghost, group after group, you must've had backers. It must have cost millions, Noah. Billions, maybe. So who paid for it all?"

The Apex said nothing.

"Your boy Jonathan Gibson sang like a bird," Wren went on. "About your stupid bullshit at Medicine Lodge. And it was stupid. All this nonsense I've had around me since I was born, pyramids and resurrection, does it really all come from some kid's book on the Egyptians?" He peered into his father's eyes, trying to see through the crystal and know if the hits were landing. "Then napalm, just because of Vietnam? Punji sticks in a tunnel, all because Poppa Thackerton had PTSD and wouldn't shut up about it until you shoved him down a well? Doesn't it all strike you as pathetic? You're a full-grown man playing out a childhood revenge fantasy that doesn't even make sense. You've executed that insane vision with incredible competence, I can't argue with that, but ultimately it's deranged. The only possible reason anyone would back it is for the damage it would do to this country." And there it was. "So who paid, Noah?"

The Apex's gaze sharpened. He clearly saw what Wren was trying to do. Belittle him in his own livestream. Make him ridiculous. Destroy the hold he had over the X-apoc.

"My people will string you up, Pequeño 3," he boomed in that firebrand bass. "You will pay for this in ways you cannot even imagine."

"What ways? I already walked in the fire once today, and look at me now." Wren spread his arms. "What else have you got?"

"You never saw the zoos in operation, little wren. The things my people will teach you in the darkness and cold will-"

"Enough! Do you really think I'm in your trap now? Or are you in mine?"

That shut him up for a moment. The exact hit Wren was looking for.

"You controlled my whole life with your lies. Controlled the Pyramid to their deaths. Now it's the X-apoc, half the whole country, but lies are a double-edged sword, Noah. Anyone can wield it. Last chance. Tell me who paid."

The Apex's eyes burned. Wren unzipped a pocket in his fireproof jacket, pulled out a phone and scrolled through screens until he reached the video B4cksl4cker had prepared hours earlier. He held it out for his father to see and hit play.

The Apex watched. Confident at first. But that changed. His eyes widened slightly. His knuckles whitened on the chair grips. Cords stood out in his neck. Beginning to see.

It showed the Apex sitting in a dark triangular chamber. Not this one, but very similar. A guess Wren had made and landed. It showed Christopher Wren standing before the Apex and putting on the handcuffs. In this video there was no amphora. No napalm or lighter. The Foundation had mocked it all up on a green screen within hours, using actors as stand-ins. The Apex's own MO. They'd learned plenty about producing real-time deepfakes after seeing his human zoos.

"By now my hackers will own your app," Wren said. "They'll own the X digital avatar, and the eyes of the X-apoc, and your livestream too." Wren pointed up at the concealed cameras. As if on cue, the video from Wren's phone appeared on the large screen on the middle wall, and his smile widened. Hellion and B4cksl4cker listening in and playing along, boosting him to 'god mode'. "They own the second skin on the Internet, after all, and nobody hides from them for long. So this is what we're transmitting live across the X network. This is what your people are seeing, right now. Not your feed. Ours."

The Apex glared up at him. Blue eyes churning. "They'll never believe it."

"Keep watching. It's not over yet."

Now the Apex was weeping in the video. On his knees. Begging Wren for forgiveness.

Not real. The real Apex was turning white as a winter sky. Winding up to say something.

"We'll spin forward," Wren said helpfully. "Get to the highlights."

The screen responded, rolling forward to the next video. Now the Apex was in a suit, head bowed, sitting in the middle of a grand jury federal trial. It looked real. Noah Thackerton was silent and shame-faced as an array of his victims passed through the witness stand, giving testimony. Highlights showed him weeping, apologizing for the harms he'd done.

Pleading guilty.

The real Apex's eyes blazed. He looked from the screen to his son. His own MO turned against him. If Wren could bottle that moment he would.

Justice done.

He gave a signal that killed the feed, then just looked at his father. "You and I know what's real, though, don't we? Noah. It's up to you, how much of this video I show. Your legacy, let's call it. So tell me, who paid?"

The transformation began small but accelerated fast, coming over the Apex like a fresh fall of snow. The fury in his crystal eyes calmed. The lines in his brow smoothed out, his hands released their tight grip, and Wren knew what it meant. He'd seen it countless times before, in cult leaders with their backs to the wall. A last surrender to madness, the Apex reincarnating himself from conman to the con itself.

Finally believing his own lies.

"I'll see you in hell, Pequeño 3."

He went for his pocket, maybe a gun, a lighter, a dead man's switch, but Wren was faster. He sparked the lighter's wheel and tossed it.

The flame arced toward the Apex.

The lighter struck.

Caught.

"Walk in the fire, father," Wren said, and flames rushed over Noah Thackerton like a second skin.

He didn't make a sound, didn't budge an inch, only stared at Wren as the licking tongues of orange, red and yellow climbed taller and spewed a stinking black smoke. He stared until his eyes and his face were gone, and his muscles thinned out, and then he collapsed, and then he just burned.

Wren stayed despite the foul smoke, watching every second because he had to be sure. That those crystal blue eyes had forever shut. That his poisoned tongue was finally still. He watched until the fire became a flicker and the air turned black, until the flames dwindled and the Apex was nothing but smoldering charcoal in an airless cave.

Then he turned away and never looked back again.

54

RESURRECTION

Hellion and B4cksl4cker had an iron dome over Little Phoenix by the time Wren emerged into the light. Nothing in and nothing out that they didn't control.

The air was painfully fresh. The sunlight harsh in his stinging, smoke-burned eyes. Not the Wren from the deepfake video, but the real Wren.

Burned. Bleeding. Limping. Barely alive.

The exit from underground had been through the north archway from the Pyramid's tomb. Rogers had helpfully marked it out with a series of glowsticks like Ariadne's thread, leading up into one of the new buildings Maggie had built, the gymnasium.

A mirror popped open, and Wren found himself in a sunny space filled with weights, machines, black mats and mirrors.

His reflection looked terrible. Skin singed, blackened, ruptured. He still had ears, which was good news. Burn marks on his neck, in his scalp, half his hair gone. Almost like he'd just survived burning alive. He smiled and it hurt his raw cheeks.

This is what a resurrection really looked like, he figured, phoenix dragging itself from the flames.

He hobbled out onto the street. People were moving everywhere. The doors to the hospital were thrown open, doctors and nurses were running back and forth with stretchers, medical equipment, towels and gauze.

Looked like Rogers and Teddy were leading the clear-up. The deepfake video of the Apex's unconditional surrender must have done the job, because there were many X-apoc figures with their heads down, letting themselves be herded by much smaller Foundation forces. Some were openly weeping.

When the scales fell from their eyes, and their god crumbled into dust. Hopefully the same thing was happening all across the country.

Wren kept walking. His right leg twinged, tried to give out, but he wouldn't let it. Ahead lay the Beechcraft, smoking still. Only one thing mattered now. People saw him and pointed. Children, survivors of the Blue Fairy. Members of the Foundation he'd sent here for safety.

They came toward him. They gathered in a kind of tunnel either side as he moved forward. They pressed themselves to his sides and supported his weight, helping him walk. Unafraid, though he looked like the devil. Calling his name until it became a chant, until the entire fake town rang with the name of a long-dead architect he'd liked as a child, from a book he'd read about great feats of renaissance engineering.

Christopher Wren.

Not so different from his father, then. He smiled, though it barely felt like his name anymore. Certainly not a celebration of him or what he'd done, but of them all. He wasn't the apex of any pyramid, and didn't want to be. He was just another member of the Foundation, serving so others could climb on high.

Then they were there before him.

Attended by medical personnel. Towels wiping away the napalm slick from their faces. Children crying. Jake. Quinn. Loralei. He saw them and they saw him.

A hush fell across the crowd. Spreading back and back, his name forgotten, every eye on them. Wren lurched closer in dead silence. Barely the sound of wind or cicadas humming in the desert. He knew he looked monstrous. He knew how terrifying that could be.

Still they came. Jake and Quinn ran. Arms outstretched. He dropped to his knees and pulled them in. So long he'd been away. Their small shaking arms wrapped around his back and he squeezed them tight. Told them he loved them. Too long. Told them he'd missed them. Would never be away again.

Beyond, Loralei's eyes filled with tears. Nothing else mattered, in that moment. Not the people who'd funded the Apex. Not the trails of danger leading away across the world, to whatever eyes were watching in anger, feeling the temporary sting of defeat.

All that mattered was his family. This embrace. He kissed their heads. The chant began again.

He was finally home.

Get the Next Chris Wren Thriller

BACKLASH

They downed his jet. Let the backlash begin.

A passenger plane forced down over Texas air space. A state on the edge of secession, taking orders through unseen back-channels. One man on board may have something to say about that.

Christopher Wren.

What begins as the backlash to a year of chaos soon becomes Wren's personal odyssey for vengeance. They ripped his country into pieces. They forced those pieces to the brink of self-destruction. Now they're looking to warp what remains, and corrupt America forever.

The backlash is only just beginning.

AVAILABLE IN EBOOK & PAPERBACK

Printed in Great Britain
by Amazon

21673190R00428